A Brocade Army

AMALINA DALCA
· EPISODE 4 ·

C.L. HOLMES

BAD HOUND PRESS

TSBWPGYOHWTZAS
LWDBHPOS, TZMPZ
SHTNEKSTNDL. A.P.

Episode 4

Dedicated to Dickens, Clavell, and Sparks,
masters of character, place, and time

A Brocade Army
Amalina Dalca, Episode 4
© 2022 C.L. Holmes

Previously published as:
Amalina and the Brocade Army
Episode 4 in The Count at Play & Slaughter series
© 2022 C.L. Holmes

Bad Hound Press
A Division of Giant Dog Books
www.giantdogbooks.com
All rights reserved.

ISBN-13: 978-1-949043-46-4

Cover, design and layouts by Dominic Wilde

A Brocade Army

Prologue

Revision by Knife

When Amalina Dalca opened the door to her apartment suite, well pleased and clutching a pretty jewelry box from the local market, she had not expected to find, hovering at waist height in the middle of the outer room, revealed by the narrow slash of light from the hallway, a long, pale, haunted face. But before she could react—to gasp, or fall back from this startling apparition—her eyes adjusted to the darkness inside, and she saw the face belonged to a man down on his hands and knees. And Genadie, with a greasy, grizzled smirk, was above him, out of the light, straddling the man like he was riding a large dog, his right hand gripping the man's forehead, his knife stuck below the man's jaw.

Now she gasped.

"Genadie!"

Genadie said nothing, but he inched his blade across the man's throat—pressing, not slicing yet—as he studied Amalina's reaction.

"What are you doing? My god!"

"You know this man, Ms. Dalca," said Genadie, not so much a question.

"No."

Genadie frowned.

Amalina panted, her eyes wide in shock, unbelieving; terrified she was about to watch Genadie kill someone right in front of her.

But then, as she tried to absorb and assess the situation, she realized she'd denied him too fast. She'd had only a glimpse of the man before blurting her answer. So it was a lie. This lie, her lie—*the easy lie*—it had been sprung in the moment. A reflex.

But her lies would not work if they could be spotted so easily—especially by the little rat.

"You need to have a closer look, Ms. Dalca," Genadie's voice rasped, sounding its accusation. With a cruel jerk he pulled back the man's head. The oversized wig on it crunched and tumbled to the side. "His name's Guwerte. Eh? Is he familiar to you?"

Now that she looked at the man, there *was* something familiar about his face: narrow, with a long curving nose, like a slender sausage, heading down toward, but just avoiding, a miniature slot of a mouth. His blue eyes were large and as round as saucers, with eyelashes forming wet prickly points around them, as they gazed at her in empty horror. His pale skin was shiny even in the low light and dripped with fear sweat. His clothes were dark and tight-fitting, cut sharply in an eastern fashion, out of place here in Paris. But an expensive suit, with a couple gay, colorful touches—some ribbons and flowers—placed here and there. He was an artist, or an afficianado of the arts. Wealthy or tangental to it. There was something familiar about him, yes. But she didn't yet recognize him until he spoke in his distinct, shivering, keening voice.

"*Princess*," he said, sounding helplessly sarcastic even when terrified. "Lady Princess Tepsji. *Please*."

"He knows you, Ms. Dalca," said Genadie, his scratchy voice carrying both disappointment and condemnation. "He knows everything about us. And how is *that*, Ms. Dalca?"

"Please, Princess—or is it Countess? Please Noble Lady, gentle lady," the man warbled pathetically. "Get him off me."

"Let him alone, Genadie. I can't imagine what he's told you—"

"You know what must be done now, Ms. Dalca," said Genadie. His knife sawed a little. "Oh, this is all you could expect. The rules were simple enough. I can't believe, after all this time—"

"Please, I didn't know," cried the man. "I didn't know or I wouldn't have—"

"What do you mean you didn't know?" growled Genadie. "Now I have two liars on my hands? You know *everything*, don't you? Don't you?"

"I don't have to know! I will never speak of it again. I promise. Noble Lady, please!"

"He approached me as familiar as if we were dear friends," explained Genadie to Amalina, scornful. "And asked me if it were true that my ladyship wasn't really just a baker's daughter, who'd been kidnapped to a castle by some fearsome monster who pretends to be a count of royal blood; become his slave in a plot to steal away the princesses of the west for his pleasure. This is what he asked me, Ms. Dalca. Asked if it were all true."

Amalina gulped. This did look suspicious. "I don't know how he could ..."

"A misunderstanding—" the knife drew blood, cutting the man short. He whimpered and cried.

"No I can't imagine when you told him, Ms. Dalca. Or why you would do such a thing. And when everything was going so well, wasn't it? What could you have been thinking? All our Holmaster's carefully laid plans, all these years of perfecting your languages, your delivery, your deportment, and you might now have brought it all down. And for what? What did you hope to gain?"

"I ... I really don't remember telling anyone, Genadie," said Amalina, to which he snarled brutishly in objection. "It must have been in our first trip, when I was still upset about it all; in a weak moment. I didn't know what I was doing. It could only have been then."

"Yes, yes," said the man, breathless, desperate. "Some years ago. In Zweigelbahn ..."

"At the inn!" declared Genadie. "Yes, I remember that stop!"

"And if my accusations ... my confession ... was a mistake—which it was—" assured Amalina, in a placating voice, "if this man promises not to say anything more of what I told him to anyone else ... you won't say anything more about it, will you, sir?"

"N-no. I promise. Of course. All is well, Noble Lady; *Genadie.*"

"If only it *could* be taken back," said Genadie. He shook the man's head violently between his thighs, his belt buckle scratching at the man's skull. "Tell her what you told me!"

"But of course," said the man, sheepishly. "Uh, but you must mean that—"

"It's what I mean, all right! He told his friends all about it, Ms. Dalca. This supposed *truth* of yours. And one of them has written a book. A book!"

"Oh," said Amalina. "You mean ... it's published?"

"I ... I can't say. I don't know," whimpered the man. "But I assure you, you needn't worry, Good Lady, Genadie, sir. It wasn't—there weren't any names, of course. And it's not like he believed me. No, listen: he thought it was a fanciful story I had made up. *Too* fanciful. 'Not credible in the least,' he said. And he didn't really like my version, as he calls it, either. He said it wasn't very interesting, as he saw it: A baker's daughter kidnapped by a ghoul-of-some-kind from her home, and then sent forth from his mountain keep to kidnap princesses?"

"Oh, aye?" said Genadie doubtfully, though it was not clear to what aspect of the story he was objecting or countering.

"Better told if she were the baker's *only* daughter," said the man. This brought the knife hard against his throat. Because, unbeknownst to Guwerte, that was the reality of it. "What! Listen, it is all different! It is the father in the story who is at fault. He takes a valuable trinket from an empty castle where he took refuge in a storm, intending to give this beautiful trinket to his daughter as a gift. But the castle is the lair of a hideous monster, who catches the merchant stealing his most valuable possession and threatens to kill him. He will only grant the merchant his life if he gives up his daughter to him in return. The merchant does so, and his daughter is forced to live with this beast for the rest of her life ... in the castle. It all takes place inside the castle, you see. There's no plot to lure western princesses to him. Better for the story that there are just two players, to keep it simple. And in it there are the ultimate questions of love, marriage, and family ... You see? It is all different."

"It is all different from *what*?" challenged Genadie.

"Wh-wh-wha-wha-what?" the man stammered, his eyes rolling to the back of his head, trying to read his assailant; to understand.

"Different from *your* story, sir," Amalina prompted helpfully to the man. "The one you yourself *made up* about the baker's daughter."

"Oh, yes," he cried. His adam's apple bounced up and down as he gulped air, before he began to titter uncontrollably, even as his eyes poured down tears. "Yes, yes, *I see*. Yes, the story—*my* story—which I made up. Of course. Yes, I—you are very correct. The both of you. You see."

Genadie's grip didn't loosen, but tightened. "I only see someone who knows too much."

"What do I know? Just a story. Just a story. And my friend's version is so much better. Why should I bother mentioning mine ever again? Nobody would believe it, and they would like his so much more."

"I can't see anyone liking either one," Genadie's voice scratched. "Better call him off. Tell him not to publish. Try a different hobby."

"Yes, of course. If that's what you think is best. Of course, that is what I'll do. Please, sir. I will forget everything."

Genadie removed the knife.

"But is that how the story ends?" said Amalina, trying to keep the worry out of her voice. "In the book? She lives out the rest of her life with him? with the beast?"

"What is that, Princess?" He was still whimpering and weeping, his powdered face sagged into the floorboards. "Oh, no, I think not. Something about ... Yes, her lover comes to rescue her or something. But when the monster is near death—I suppose because the lover stabs or shoots him— she pities this horrible beast from all the time she's spent with him, and declares her love for him. Suddenly he recovers, and is turned into a handsome prince. He'd been cursed, you see, years ago, by some errant witch, and only if a maiden might fall in love with him would he be returned to his glory and all his wealth and kingdom recovered. There's a happy marriage and all that. As I said. You see."

"He thinks *that* is more believable?" she objected.

The man gathered up his puffy wig and set it on his head like it was a hat. "It's a love story, Princess. Never mind."

• • •

"I can't believe you did that," Amalina scolded Genadie once the man was out of the room. She hadn't realized she'd been squeezing her jewelry box into pieces the whole time until her hand relaxed and the wood creaked back into place. "Were you really going to kill him?"

"You aren't out of danger yet, Ms. Dalca; what you did."

She appraised Genadie now. He was nervously gobbling millet from the small bag he had on his hip. He had looked so huge, so powerful standing over the poor man. Now he'd returned to his small, bent figure, with the nervous ticks and gestures. And recently she'd noticed the small vertical wrinkles growing around his lips, folding inward, making him look as if he were beginning to whither and shrink. Not so much a threat anymore. More like someone to feel sorry for. But still.

"You would have killed this man?"

"Guwerte. Guwerte Merts. That's his name. And I'll be keeping a close eye on him from here on out, I promise you. As much as I'm going to keep an eye on you. Lying to me? I should never liked to see the day. Not you, Ms. Dalca. A liar?"

"But *would* you have killed him. Really?" she said, to get him off the subject.

"I will destroy whatever threatens Master's plans."

"So you say," scoffed Amalina. "But why do you care what *he* wants, Genadie? Why even bother? Ridiculous to be willing to murder someone for him; after what he did to your entire fam—?"

"*That* is a story I wish you'd stop mentioning," he grumbled, pieces of millet clinging to his jiggling lips. As he scooped the little grains to his face, his crooked, broken fingers lost the bits through their awkward gaps, sprinkling seeds everywhere on his mouth, chin, and shirt. "I would always kill for our Master. And I have."

"I can't believe it."

Something sunk low in her stomach. Genadie had killed someone? She hoped it was an empty boast. But he was such a toady to the Count sometimes. Look how willing he'd been just a moment ago. And he *had* helped kill the Strange Man, it's true. But that one—the Strange Man—hadn't been human. So that one didn't count, did it? Not to her mind.

"How awful," she said with a frown. "I'm turning into a casual liar, a change we both don't care for, and you're becoming a breezy, stone-hearted killer? I don't think I can take it. Look what the monster's done to us."

"Believe me, you will kill for him, too, Ms. Dalca," he said, confidently.

"What!"

"Mark my words."

"Never."

"Don't think you're too good for it."

"Never."

"Well ..."

"There's no 'well' about it. I should never hope to."

"Mark my words."

"In all honesty, Genadie," she sighed, "would you really rather stand by someone who would do what he did to your wife, your children, and her family? and who has tried to kill you, too? He's almost done it twice—*really almost killed you, Genadie!*—since I've known you! Would you really carry out all *his* ugly deeds, do whatever he wants of you, when you are in a land this far outside his control? Would you? Would you? … *really?*"

Genadie weighed the words with nervous glances, eyes darting warily one side to the other, as if looking for the very man in question. But then, finding himself free to answer, a new light appeared on his face. He said, "Well, when you put it that way, Ms. Dalca …"

Part One
New Loves

1

A Return to Form

Attila Bronk had never felt so low in his life. He was more sunk down than the night, a number of months ago, when he'd gone to confront the creature he'd been out to destroy for nearly three years, only to discover another such creature had joined the first. He'd watched these two monsters, inflated to biblical size, try to murder each other on the Kyrgil mountaintops, and instead of doing so they'd gone on to stomp apart a castle under their feet, toss peaks around like playtoys, and then tear down a mountain so that it collapsed on the village below. Whatever Attila's intention that night, he had arrived in time to witness this incredible destruction and understand that he was not only not up to the task of destroying such a creature, but he never would be.

In the weeks after, when the Cardinal of Netz took him in, comforted him, and gave him insight into the creature's truer weaknesses, Attila had revived his hopes. There was still a way to bring his adversary, this 'Count Tepsji', this inhuman force, to justice. There were weapons that could be fashioned. Attila had launched immediately into the project to bring the creature down and labored earnestly for months.

But now Attila approached the large, white tumbledown house, shoulders slumped, his feet dragging with defeat. And though his face betrayed nothing—his eyelids were set at half-mast, his lips untroubled and, if anything, he looked bored—he was, however, feeling at his lowest ebb. He wanted to turn around and leave. But, he reminded himself rather automatically, he was a man of duty.

Only … how can I make this right?

"Mr. Bronk?"

Attila nodded to the woman in the doorway. She must have seen him walking up the path. She had long, stringy blond hair hanging out from under her cap. She did not look as hostile as he had expected, though there were signs of a hard year since he'd last seen her. Her pale blue eyes were steely.

He bowed to her. "Mrs. Vogoneyevic. And where are your children?"

"Where would you expect? Down by the river, looking for more saviours to come floating along. I've orders for them: if they find any, sink 'em."

Attila nodded once, slowly, in polite acknowledgement of her shot at him.

She smiled vaguely. "For what else could he want but to call away their mother and have her killed, too? Now, what are you doing here, Mr. Bronk?"

"I'm here, Mrs. Vogoneyevic—"

"How can I be Mrs. Vogoneyevic," she interrupted, "if I don't have a husband anymore? Or has it been so long, you don't recall what happened? I haven't a last name anymore. And less one so fancy. Call me Gug."

"I am here to deliver to you my final report."

"Well you can give it to me in the barn," she said, coming out of the doorway and brushing past Attila, headed for the large barn twenty yards away. She was dressed in a simple, dirty, threadbare white dress. Work clothes. "Have my chores, as always. What does 'final report' mean? Can never tell by the looks of you what you're saying, but you don't make it sound good."

"I felt it my responsibility to let you know how things stand," said Attila as he followed her. "The outcome of my mission."

"I take it the monster is still running around, while Hak is still dead as that stump." She pointed back at the tree stump where her husband Hak would chop apart wood and chickens.

"I promise you I have done my best," said Attila.

"Say my name," said Gug. "Say: 'Gug, I promise you I have done my best.'"

"Gug, I promise you I have done my best."

"There," she said, swinging open the large door. "Makes you sound human. And like you mean it."

"You know I've always acted in earnest. I swear to you I have tried everything in my power."

"So you stood back up that army of yours—?"

"Hak's army—"

"You don't be interrupting me, Mr. Bronk."

"No."

"Never interrupt me again."

"Certainly not."

"So now," said Gug, "you stood *that* army back up? and threw yourself and them boys right at that enemy you were always going on about?"

"I tried."

"I didn't tell you to go try, did I, Mr. Bronk? I told you to go do it. To honor my husband."

"But the men who were once willing to fight to the death under the greatness of Sir Hak Vogoneyevic now refuse the honor, ma'am. Even when promised success—guaranteed success—they deny their duty and renege at the oaths they swore to him."

"Who can blame them? They probably don't like your looks no better than me," she said.

"It *can* be done," he mumbled, a glumness marring his implacable mask. And there was an actual note of emotion in his voice. Frustration. "They just won't listen. And without a force there is nothing one man can do …"

"Yeah, that's all right, Mr. Bronk," said Gug. "You tried your best. That's all I asked of you."

"I really did try."

"I know." She sounded sympathetic. She grabbed a pitchfork and stabbed at a drift of hay against a stall's door. "So what are you going to do now?"

"Well, as I said," he said gravely, "It is my final report."

"Yeah, I got *that*. I mean, what are you going to do now that you aren't going to do what you promised ol' Hak's family you were going to?"

"I can do nothing along that line without support," he said once more, defensive and self-justified.

"Didn't intend to make it sound mean, Mr. Bronk. That's not what I meant." She stopped stabbing randomly at the hay and turned to him. "Remember how you were layed out in here? Shot full of holes? Soaked through, freezing cold, half drowned?"

"You and your family saved my life."

"The kids saved your life. I just mended you. Then Hak listened to all your stories of glory … Well, never mind that, Mr. Bronk. It always comes out mean, but that isn't my intent. Just telling you my memories. That's pretty much all I have now. Memories of what was. Of ol' dumb Hak. He should have stayed away from you like I told him. Was his fault more than yours. Though I warned you, too. But that's okay, never mind. Good ol', dumb ol' Hak."

She was smiling as if fondly recalling a favorite childhood pet. She didn't sound mean at all, if that was what she was worried about. Her cheerfulness was perhaps making Attila feel worse.

"You've received your payments on time?" he asked.

"I get them. Thank you."

"They will continue. In perpetuity."

"That means a while longer, I take it."

He eyed the inside of the barn, looked back at the house. It wasn't much compensation she was getting, but she could afford to leave this forgotten corner of Ardeel. She could raise her and Hak's children in a town and even pay for their education. Perhaps hire a servant or two. Definitely buy more decent clothes. He calculated the level of insult if he said something of the like to her.

"So, Attila," she said in a softer voice. "I'll call you that now. I think I deserve it. Don't you?"

"As you like, Gug."

"You never did answer my question of what you are going to do. Now that you aren't in the monster killing business, and you've been run out of the government, and nobody in this country seems to like you much. What *are* you going to do?"

"I haven't thought it through yet."

"I find that hard to believe. You think, and think, and think. That's all you're good for is thinking, Attila Bronk. You have to have already had this next part all thought out, I imagine."

When he didn't answer, but stared with his dull gaze, she leaned the pitchfork against a wall and stepped close to him.

"Or are you good for something else?" she asked, her voice becoming husky. "Are you good company?"

Attila felt like it would be a slight to her if he stepped back. But when he didn't move, or say anything again, she stepped closer still. She began to remove her dress.

"Mrs. Vogone—"

"Ah! That's *Gug*. From now on, Attila, you will call me Gug. And you are going to treat me with respect. And kindness. And love."

"I don't believe this is proper."

Her face, the top of her chest, and her arms were darkly tanned. Where her clothes had covered her body she was a pure milky white. The body of a perfectly sculpted marble woman, firm and voluptuous. Entrancing and smooth, except at the center, where her legs met.

"This is proper, Attila," she said, touching his shoulder. "This is right."

"Not in God's eyes."

"Well, it's all right by mine," said Gug. "You took Hak from us. From me. And I needed him. And all the little coins you send me isn't going to fill that hole I feel."

"I don't think I'm the one for you ... for that," said Attila, softly. He stepped back but she followed. She was fitting herself to him. Wrapping her leg around his. She took his hand firmly, commandingly, and slid it around her hip.

"It's not for you to think, Attila. Not anymore. It's my turn to tell you how to make things better."

Attila took a wider step back and pushed her arms away. "No, this cannot—"

"You're going to touch me, Attila. And you are going to give me the family I was *supposed* to have."

"No—"

"I could have let you die, Attila Bronk. I could have thrown you back in the river. I could have told those soldiers who were chasing after you—all the way back in the beginning—told them just where they could find you, and they would have killed you. And I would still have my Hak today. But I didn't tell."

"And I am grateful for that, Gug."

"Is gettin' killed by them better than loving me, Attila? Show me your love, Attila. Give me what you took away!"

. . .

Attila was a mile down the road when he stopped running. He could hear the river on the right and he wondered if Hak's children might be nearby. He listened for their voices. He looked back to make sure Gug wasn't there.

His analytical mind had been running a secondary track during the whole incident. When she went for the pitchfork, Attila had calculated her ability to stab him with it. And how best he could dodge the deadly tines, or redirect them in a way that wouldn't hurt her. He had noted the smell of the hay in the barn, and how different it smelled in this season as compared to when he was laying in it, fresh out of the river, with his limbs numb and unresponsive, his insides feeling raw, and with his pursuer's lead balls still burning inside him. He had wondered if, by being convinced he might die at the time, at that long ago moment, it had affected the hay's smell or the memory of it. He had calculated how fast he could run, fully clothed, compared to a naked Gug, who looked much more athletic than he. Could he get away, or would she catch him? And could she really force him to do things he did not want to do?

In another mile, his mind fell off those diverting pieces of thought. The excitement had distracted him. He began to analyze the exchange itself. Because logically it did not sit right. Why would Gug turn on him like that? He had never presented himself as a potential mate for her. It's not as if trapping him into a physical relationship would gain her economically; not more than what he was already providing, which was promised in perpetuity. So *why?*

"Aren't you human?" she had screamed after him, as he'd sped away from the barn. "Tell me you don't need love too!"

But that was beside the point, decided Attila. Whether he needed love was immaterial. *Gug* had had love. With Hak Vogoneyevic. They had been united in marriage and before God's eyes, hadn't they? She had had the love of a man and would always possess the love of heaven. She'd borne his love in their children. She could want for nothing more.

This was the line of Attila's thinking, his cool reasoning.

Clever, he thought to himself and almost smiled, as he began to reinterpret the incident. His lids weighed down heavier with such self satisfaction that they almost closed. *She didn't want you like that, the way she was pretending. She loved Hak. Gug may be an earthly woman, it is true. But she isn't a sinner and lustful. No. She is righteous and always does what is proper even if it should offend her.* **Pay attention,** *man. She was trying to provoke you. She wanted to drive you away in shame! Think on it clearly: before the insult, she first reminded you of how she once saved you. And how you'd sworn to fulfill Hak's mission against the Count after he died. Think on that and it all becomes clear, doesn't it?*

"Attila Bronk?" growled a heavy voice.

Attila looked up suddenly, surprised that he'd been caught off guard. Gug had so thoroughly perplexed him, he'd lost sight of his surroundings.

Now there were four men sitting on a fallen log in a clearing, with their horses chewing in the grasses behind them. The men were wearing the banner of the new Ardeel government over their light metal breastplates. One pushed back the helmet on his head to get a better look at Attila, and Attila thought the man just might be one of the ones who had been chasing him so very long ago; when they'd shot him and he'd gone over the falls ... and he'd ended up in Hak's barn.

Could it be possible these were the same men?

They were getting to their feet in a hurry and picking up their weapons.

It seemed to Attila like he was in some kind of fantastic dream.

As he spun and ran into the woods, his brain had already calculated that, with them on horseback, the road would be useless as an escape route. That the trees would block the horses if he picked his route well enough. And worst come to worst, if they were closing in on him and he was likely to be captured, he could pitch himself right back into the fast running river. It might not be as cold as before.

2

The Surprise

Here, there, and all around, Amalina asked her newest acquaintances: "What comes to mind when I say the word 'bed'?"

"Sleep," answered young Lady Chretien.

"Comfortable," said young Lady Arriene.

"Escape," said young Lady Sadie, which was an interesting answer. *Escape.* Now, what could that mean when paired to the word bed?

"Sin," concluded young Lady Orreste.

Uh, oh, Amalina remarked to herself without so much as batting an eye at her friend. *Sin? Mark* that *one off the list. I know what the Count likes.*

Then, her work settled for the day, Amalina went in search of her own bed.

With a somewhat lazy, yet pleasing electric trickle down her body, Amalina hoped Lieutenant Ivanti Ion Vokent would be there. But she knew she couldn't count on it. The life of an adjutant to a famed general, when armies seemed to be constantly in motion, seeking each other out, killing each other, making peace, pinning medals, moving again, made for an irregular life.

At first his absences meant frustration and annoyance. She wanted every minute she could with the handsome lieutenant, his arms around her, her hand running over his strong limbs, his beautiful, almost luminescent hazel eyes staring gently, warmly, affectionately, acceptingly, upon her; her fingers combing through his luxurious lion's mane of dark brown hair. But after a while she'd learned to accept his constant journeying. It gave her space to think, to enjoy her new life on her own. It allowed an anticipation to build for his return that was both painful during his loss and satisfying when concluded.

She knew she couldn't be ungrateful or greedy about their circumstances. It was incredible that she was with him at all, this young man she had loved from the time when she had really been too young to be thinking of such things. He had ignored her, and then left her village to find his fortune in the world. They should never have met again. But life had a way of making things happen—perhaps the Count had said as much to her. Or she'd read it somewhere. But Amalina and her secret love had found each other again, and not in their hometown of Korr. It was on the other side of the world, in a crowd in Paris. They should never have seen each other again, but here she ran right into him, and he took her into his arms. And they both looked into each other's eyes and knew they were meant to be.

And so when you are meant to be—as life had as much as announced for Amalina and Ivanti with trumpets and church bells—you had to allow life to have its way when it wanted, certain that what is just, and what is meant to be, will turn out in the end. Ivanti—Ion, when she was being familiar— would not be roaming the battlefields forever. And Amalina was still too young to wed someone, really. And she had a new world she was still discovering. She could not, and *should* not, be ungrateful, or greedy.

But Amalina knew that if he wasn't in her apartment, or waiting outside in the street, standing handsomely by the riverbank, tossing pebbles and flower petals into the current to pass the time til she arrived, she would feel a small pull of disappointment. Because she would be missing his company, and all she had left in Paris besides Ivanti, the only other people who knew her fully and she could confide in, was Genadie and Aklan. Those two were no substitutes for what she really wanted. Aklan, the young boy, was much like a tomcat, the way he disappeared and caroused as he liked, looking for adventure; returning to a comfortable spot only to get some rest. As for Genadie, after the frightening incident with that poor man, Guwerte Merts, with Genadie running his knife across his throat and some heated conversations following, he hadn't been around much to bother Amalina. Not in a while. Oddly, this then made the boy, Aklan, seem more reliable.

"Have you seen the lieutenant?" she asked Aklan, who she found sleeping at the foot of the stairs to her building.

"Here?" said Aklan, smacking his lips, scratching his bushy blonde hair, and batting his blueberry eyes dreamily.

"Yes. Is he here?"

"The lieutenant, you say?" said Aklan, awake now. "I'm afraid you'll be disappointed, Pretty Princess."

. . .

Lieutenant Ivanti Ion Vokent dismounted from his horse, feeling the dragging hands of the day tugging down on his limbs. His uniform felt ten times as heavy and as constraining as it ever had. He was exhausted from riding from his master, General Volante, at headquarters, to the drills taking place over sloppy fields some miles away; battalions were shifting, making them nearly impossible to locate. And then he'd had to wait until the old general dismissed him, late in the evening, assuming his handsome adjutant was going to crawl into the side tent to get some sleep. The lieutenant raced away on the fastest mount he had.

Paris was a close enough ride to be back by morning, if one had it in him. Young Vokent had it in him: the memories of a soft, warm, perfumed body danced inside him, providing an almost superhuman energy. The energy spread through his body eagerly, tossing aside the small aches and heaviness, as he climbed the stairs and pulled the key from his pocket. He knew she would be waiting for him. She always was.

Here came the thought of her body against his. The solidness of her shape, her curves; the sureness of her movement as it sought to match him, to have him enter. He knocked twice on the door, with a spicy rap of his knuckles, before he inserted the key.

The lights were out. She hadn't waited up. Or she'd been waiting too long and assumed he wouldn't come.

"Gamina," he whispered. "Wake up darling, I'm here. Get your clothes off, we haven't much time. And I do need some rest, it's been a hard day."

He sat on the small sofa and tried to pull off one boot while at the same time opening his belt buckle. His eyes were pointed to the doorway to her bedroom. Something flickered. A weak, warm light. A small lamp had been lit.

"Good girl. Come out and help me with these dirty boots. We haven't time to waste." But then: "Oh, my! Dear God! Dear God!"

What came out of the room was not Gamina Renee, with her generous breasts and sensuous hips, and light trail of hair leading down from her belly button, but someone else: Amalina Dalca!

The shock was too much and he clutched at his chest.

Amalina looked old. Wizened. Even ugly by the incredible shift from what Ivanti knew her to be to how she appeared now in the candlelight, staring miserably from the doorway.

Her voice croaked, "You cheater—"

But he was already rushing away from her, on his way down the stairs. His horse, surprised to find his rider so soon returned, whinnied loudly in protest and then, sensing the danger, carried him back to camp at full speed.

When Ivanti had fled from Amalina in that apartment, she had looked like something prematurely aged. When he returned to her later, as he knew he must, his old world morals kicking him in the gut to do what was right, her youth had done its work and she looked younger than ever and he felt bad for having turned away in the first place. He apologized to her, almost with some tears of his own.

· · ·

"What are you apologizing for?" said Amalina, somewhat defiantly, though she was surprised he'd returned to her; and found herself also surprised to be glad for it.

"For everything, I suppose," said Ivanti, disconsolate but holding his head up and trying to look her straight in the eye. "What can I say? But that was a dirty trick you played, Amalina."

"Don't try to turn this around on me. I couldn't have played a trick on you if you hadn't first …" She couldn't bring herself to say what he'd done.

"Well, I didn't mean it that way. But how did you know about this apartment, and about Gamina Renee?"

"Is *that* what we're going to talk about, Ion? Really?" While Amalina looked as young as ever—*too* young, perhaps—by the sureness in her voice they both felt suddenly as if they could be two village elders; or rather, a very old married couple. They were suddenly speaking as adults when they knew within themselves they were too young to suddenly be doing so. They paused here. "Why did you come back, Ion?"

"Because …" He didn't finish, but he gestured helplessly at her. His eyebrows then raised high and met, pleadingly. "I only asked about how you knew … because I … Well, I'm very sorry, Amalina."

"It wasn't hard to find out what you were up to," she said. "You are the most handsome lieutenant this side of the Rhine. Everyone talks about you. Where you go. Who you are meeting for lunch, or at night. Even when it's ones like *her*. Like your precious Gamina."

"I *am* sorry."

"And there *have* been a lot," added Amalina. "A *lot* more than her. That's common knowledge. You do get around."

"Not that many." He cleared his throat. "I'm trying to apologize to you, Amalina." He started forward, as if he might reach out to touch her, to reassure her. But something kept him at a distance.

"I thought you loved me, Ion."

"Now I have never said—"

Amalina burst into tears. Just like a little girl. She curled into a ball and fell to the side. Then she suddenly sprang up from the sofa and wiped her eyes, shaking her head to rid herself of the sadness and self pity. To clear herself. "Okay. All right. What did you say to me then? Remember? You said we would be married, didn't you? You said we would escape together."

He said "yes," and "well, yes," to it all. But in the end he scratched his head and made a face that only brought more tears to Amalina's eyes.

"Then what did you mean?" she asked. "Why are you sleeping with all these other women? Tell me what I'm to make of it."

"I meant it when I said it, Amalina," he said, his deep voice becoming soft and rich with kindness and sympathy. "Of course I did. But then ... But then I just thought it was unfair."

Amalina wanted to run away. She stepped closer to him.

"It's going to sound stupid to you, I know. It is stupid. I'm stupid, Amalina." It looked like he might cry. His miraculously colored eyes welled up with tears.

"No, you aren't. You aren't sorry ... Well, maybe you are. Go on."

He gestured helplessly again. "Think of it, Amalina. I'd left Korr. It was a big step for me. What did I know of the world? What could *we* know of it, you understand? And suddenly I wasn't the son of a farmer anymore. I was moving up very well in the regiment. Making a good name for myself. A great name, if I'm honest. I was climbing the ranks and being courted by generals. Me, a boy from nowhere, just a backward farmer's son who never had any hope for anything else."

Ivanti laughed a small laugh and shrugged. Then he dared to reach his hand for hers. She moved hers closer so he could find it.

"I really do care for you, Amalina. You were always so good and sweet. That's all I remembered of you. Your father is a great man, an honest man. Your family was one of the best in the village. But, you know, here I was out in the world. You've seen it now, Ama; you know what I mean. There is so much to do and to see. So many people. So many interesting things. And I had even started to get ideas of my own, you know. From what the general would tell me; the promise of my future. The attention from ladies and their families I could never have hoped or dreamed to have met. It was almost like a fairytale."

"Go on," said Amalina, sensing this is where his dewy confession would turn bad, but she did not withdraw her hand. She did deaden it, though.

"So it felt unfair to me," he continued, noting her hand's weight, gesturing with it in his gentle, warm palm. He leaned forward, trying to impress his message into her with a look, apologize with a cock of his head, and a smile of pity—a pitifully beautiful smile of pity—for her or him. "Here I'd gotten all this way. Then, in the blink of an eye, and no matter how far I'd come in the world, I was sent right back where I started. I was with you: a girl from Korr. Someone I could have expected if I'd just kept to the farm, piling hay bales and cutting pigs; a boring arrangement by the matchmaker or that meddlesome Sadra."

Amalina almost laughed, even as the tears came out. It was funny to hear Sadra's name so incongruously spoken in an apartment in Paris. She wondered if Sadra, the nosy minister's wife back in Korr, felt her ears twitch.

"You know what I'm saying?" Ivanti said hopefully.

"Go on."

He didn't know where to go on to. He faltered. He picked up a trail: "When we met, Ama, it felt like it was something magical. As if we were something meant to be. As much as I love this world, here I was given someone who I was familiar with. Who understood what it was like growing up trapped in Korr, in the Ardeel. Who shares the same values. We could talk; talk in the old language. Enjoy ourselves freely. And how amazing it was to see you dressed like a princess, looking so different and beautiful. That you were accepted as a true lady of title. That you have so much money. It is as if I somehow sprang from Korr as a military man, and you sprang up just behind me as royalty ... But you know what I'm saying, don't you? You must."

"Go on."

"You keep telling me to go on," he said. "What do you want me to say? You want me to hurt you? That isn't too fair of you, either. But let me say it, anyway, Amalina. But understand, I never wanted to hurt you. I didn't tell you about Gamina Renee. About any of them. And if I had my way, you never would have known about them.

"Look, you sweet little girl, what can I say?" he went on, as her look told him to come out with it, whatever it was. "As happy as I was to have met you again, there was something in me that was angry about it. Not at first. But as I thought about it. Because it felt like you weren't some part of destiny any more, but a trap. Korr had come to reclaim me through you. As I said, I'd gotten so far away from there, and I was happy for it; I would miss it, but I could never be there again and be happy. And now Korr has thrown the rope around my ankles and is dragging me back. Does that make any sense?"

"But you returned to Korr on your own," said Amalina. "Cristine told me you came back looking for me. You wouldn't have done that if you didn't care."

"Of course, Amalina. That's what I'm trying to tell you: I cared. No question. And also I had to see for myself. Crazy as it all was, I didn't know if I'd just imagined meeting you in some wild dream. I had to go and find you, see if you weren't still in the bakery, if you really hadn't somehow become a lady of title ... which you never once explained."

The last part was spoken slower, and heavier. *Which you never once explained.* Like an accusation.

"What does that mean?"

"I'd never heard the royal name Tepsji," he said. "And you didn't tell me about—about *him* until we met here again ... Look, I never knew about any of him, or it. I was too young when I was taken into the army. Father had never told me about this ... well, I still don't fully understand: this monster of the mountains, and agreements and compacts signed with him. There were superstitions, but I was never shown the history, or this contract you've told me about. It would have been very hard to believe it before, when I was younger, and it has been made more difficult after what I've now seen of the world. And still, I can only believe in it because you've told me, and there could be no other explanation to … I know who you are, Amalina Dalca. I grew up with knowing your family, your father, and you. And suddenly you are transformed into a right and regular Lady, with a footman and servants, and a carriage, and fancy dresses, and gold coins and great apartments all through Europe. It would be impossible otherwise, if your story wasn't true. So I must believe what you've told me. Even about this … this nobleman."

Amalina nodded shyly. It was an embarrassing subject of course. Her elevation to the status of a royal lady, playing the part of a niece to a great old Count from Ardeel; and the shameful secret behind it all: Amalina was now in the service of a bloodthirsty creature and furthering his agenda out in the real world.

"Well, it's all fine for you, isn't it?" said Ivanti, resentful. "You got what you wanted, didn't you? You became some fairytale princess, and you got the boy you always wanted, didn't you? Oh, don't pretend you never had eyes for me. I saw it. I know it. And now you worked your witchy little magic and here I am, all yours."

"That's not—"

"I don't care what it's not. Because that is what it *is*. You got everything you wanted, including me. And what did I get? I got a rope around the ankles, pulling me back to the mountains. Setting me against the will of some timeless thing that I should never wish to have known. Well, that's just unfair, isn't it? Tell me that isn't unfair." He had tears in his eyes again, and now they were spilling in self-pity.

"But we already agreed, didn't we?" said Amalina. "We're going to escape. From him, from everything."

"Yeah, that's great," growled Ivanti. "Maybe you aren't a real Countess, or Lady of Court, or whatever it is. Maybe it's easy for you to leave that sort of life because it wasn't yours, really. But I made my own way, I *am* a lieutenant. And I *have* a great future. And so where am I supposed to escape to? What happens to all that I've done and what I still want to do? Where does that go when I desert and we escape from it all?"

"So go have your women, if it makes you feel better," said Amalina. "If that's all you really care about."

"Look me in the eye, you stupid little girl, and tell me it's fair."

3

The Portrait

If the matter was considered from Ivanti's perspective, he was right. Admitting the fact, though, did nothing to lessen Amalina's unhappiness. The parade of women the dashing lieutenant had bedded had been a means to empower himself, perhaps a way to provide some escape from an unfortunate fate, or even a sly way to get Amalina herself to end their relationship without him having to bear the burden of actually revealing his bitter truth: that Amalina was a trap to haul him out of the west and to cheat him of his good fortune.

But still, at the end of it all, the women were also a fact. It was a betrayal. And an especially harsh one since the handsome young man had been such a comfort to Amalina, such a relief after several years of fear and oppression by Count Tepsji. She now felt like a seablown gull robbed of anywhere to land just when she thought she'd found a patch of solid earth among the waves. Cruelly, her life-long love had turned out to be a trick of the air, a mirage.

Maybe she'd known the heartbreak was coming and it was no coincidence that for so many months Amalina had been reduced to tears over every lovely and joyful thing to happen to her, or pleasant attraction she encountered. Whether because she didn't believe it was truly hers, or because she was certain it would be taken away at any moment by some soul-sucking creature more than a thousand miles away, she wasn't sure. But hadn't she already been secretly anticipating the loss of her contentment, which she'd been gathering during this happy time with Ion?

. . .

"It was stupid for me to have ever believed … " Amalina muttered angrily to herself, on the edge of another tremendous tearfilled cry. She could feel it coming. " … and I let myself …"

"Believe what, Pretty Princess?" said Aklan, lazily coming awake. He was attuned to her moods and sensed something had happened.

They were in her suite's sitting room. She was half-dressed and pouting at the floor. Aklan had been sleeping on the silk-bolstered couch next to her.

"Oh, it's nothing, I suppose," sniffled Amalina, now forlorn and irritated with a witness to her private suffering. "Nothing at all. All my fault, really. It was never anything to begin with …"

But still, the tears came.

"My, that's a lot," said Aklan. "You keep carrying on and you could be the mouth of a new river. What's got you blubbering now, Pretty Princess?"

"Why do you call me that?" snapped Amalina, sounding too much like an imperious lady of the court; one taking unnecessary offense at the least provocation. She wiped her nose and skewered him with a look.

"Because you are pretty and you are a princess," said Aklan, matter-of-fact, but looking surprised at her outburst.

"That's a lie."

"No, it's not."

"Yes, it is. Take it back."

"What are you talking about, Pretty Princess? Are you sad or mad? What's going on here?"

"You know what I *really* am," she protested. "*Who* I really am. Just a fake—"

"A fake, Pretty Princess? But you're real, real as can be!"

Amalina huffed and folded her arms, hoping the tears would go away and leave her with her anger. At least the anger would make her feel stronger.

Aklan petted her arm once, quickly, as if she might bite his hand off if she caught him, and continued: "Here now, look: *I* am a prince, aren't I?"

"Used to be. Until you decided to become an adventurer. And really you've just become my servant, haven't you? And so what?"

"Oh, but that's my point right there," smiled Aklan, nudging his body closer to her. "I used to be a prince. Yes! Well, maybe I still am, if I were back in my home country. But, as you said, I'm nothing more than an adventurer now—or a servant, if you like. That's how I spend my days. So there you go. You may have been a baker once, but you spend your days as a royal lady now. And so you really *are* one then, aren't you? You are—so it is, Pretty Princess—if you can tell me I'm just a servant."

"'Pretty Princess' sounded cute when you were a little boy," answered Amalina. "But you're growing and it's beginning to sound impudent."

He thought about it for a moment and then looked ashamed. There was the beginnings of something serious and mannish in his look. He was still young, with a bushy scrub of hair on his head, but the straight ridge of his nose was lengthening now, his eyebrows thicker, his cheeks gaining definition, and his lips taking on a masculine, tart curl. One could imagine what handsome man he would become in several years.

"So what would you like me to call you then?" he asked cautiously.

"You need to grow up. You figure it out," she said, still in an unregulated fury.

Then, after a controlled breath, Amalina apologized and confessed the whole story of what had happened with her lieutenant, letting her upset flush out of her tumbling heart.

"If I had died before learning what he was up to," said Amalina at the end of it, "I would have died content with the world ... I wish I *had* died rather than to know."

"All this over that soldier?" said Aklan, astounded. "It's not like he's even a general, he's a lieutenant."

"What does that matter?"

"Generals lead armies, the lower officers only move their general's slop buckets around. But anyway, all lieutenants are known scoundrels, aren't they? So then he's nothing to be worked up about. Just get over him, eh?"

"Thank you for trying to cheer me up, Aklan," said Amalina, wiping her nose again. Feeling the anger subsiding, if the dribble of tears weren't yet exhausted. "But it's not that easy."

"Sure it is. I saw my sister do it plenty of times."

"Ion meant something more to me, perhaps," said Amalina, "than they did to her."

"If you're really this hurt, and hurt over an ape who would turn you into a rain cloud," smirked Aklan, "why don't you do something about it, eh?"

"Like what?"

"Get some revenge. Make him wish he'd never done it."

"I can't imagine how."

"Sure you can. Reveal him for the heartless rake he is. Spread the word until his honor is put in front of a firing squad, and then the army gives him the boot."

"Everyone already knows what a romancer he is, don't they? Everyone except me. If I say anything more about it, I'd only be adding my name to his list. It could only enhance his reputation, and then the line to his shiny boots would grow."

"Stick a knife in his liver, then. That'll serve him."

"You little brute! I don't want him dead. And I certainly don't want to be tried for murder. They'll have me in front of a *real* firing squad."

"I'll do it for you if you're scared, Pretty Princess. I could get away with it."

"I said I don't want him dead."

"You don't? Are you sure? There's no saying he'd die, necessarily. But he'd feel it."

"I just wish I didn't have to feel it. If I could be over it."

"Revenge, then, eh?" She saw the heat in Aklan's eyes, the excitement, he was working himself into another playful romp. "That's the best way.

Put your mind at ease faster than a seven course meal and a cask of wine. Revenge. You have to show him what he is. We just need to figure a way to serve it to him where you can't be caught."

"You amazing boy," sighed Amalina. She shook her head. "Why couldn't you just have been a dog or a cat?"

"What for?" he asked, slightly confused, and watched as she massaged her eyes and temples in frustration. "How would that help—hold, are you being mean to me again? You mean so you can throw me in the river and be rid of me?"

"Not be rid of you. So I could feed you and pet you and look at you, but I wouldn't have to listen to your nonsense."

"Can't say it's nonsense until you've tried it."

"But if I hadn't listened to you—If you hadn't told me about that apartment, I wouldn't have *known* in the first place."

"Wait, you're blaming me, Princess?"

"No. But If you hadn't opened your mouth when you shouldn't have—"

"Shouldn't have—!"

"—to this very day I would be as happy as ever. I wouldn't want myself to've died."

Aklan's head turned red to his straw-blond hairline and he balled his fists. "Then you *are* blaming me. That's why you're mad at me, 'cause you're blaming me! I don't like how you're upset for what he did, he turns you into another French fountain, and you're taking it out on me with a lash. Can't say I like it one bit. *That's* nonsense."

Amalina apologized to Aklan again, realizing he was right and she was being cruel to the wrong target, but now he was smoldering. "I didn't mean to insult you. I—"

"Isn't fair, is what I say."

"No it wasn't, it's true. Unkind of me, Aklan. I hope you can forgive me."

He turned away from her, but then spun right back with a smile: "Of course, Pretty Princess. You're just mad, and you wouldn't *ever* mean it, would you?"

Amalina almost laughed, he wasn't too much different than a dog, anyway. Ready to bounce back to her heel.

But then Amalina, just as readily, was right back in her thoughts of Ion and sighed, "But what's to be done about it now ...? It's over ... It's over ... I was such a fool ..."

Aklan got a curious expression, and then he slapped the floor hard and ran out of the room with a cry: "Don't worry, and *don't blame yourself*, Pretty Princess!"

When Amalina went to check, he'd fled the apartment entirely. Whatever he was up to, she felt more alone with him gone.

"I'm such a fool," she said again, just before she heard a squawk, and a heart-skipping crash into the window.

On the pane of glass was a spot of blood with a couple small grey feathers stuck to it.

Outside lay a pigeon with a twisted neck, blank eyes, and a greasy feathered body so drawn and sickly looking, it seemed to have been flying for days without food or relief. The thick glass of the window had put it out of its misery. Tied to its grey leg was a tiny, rolled paper note.

Amalina scooted the body with her foot until it reached the gutter. Then, after a thought, she continued moving it down and into the fast flowing river. It floated away like a toy boat, the note along with it.

That night, Aklan did not return.

Amalina felt she couldn't handle losing two dear friends in so short of a time. In her loneliness, and though she knew the city was too large to search for Aklan on her own, she would give it a try.

• • •

Amalina liked to stroll, and Paris was a city built for movement of all kind. It was constantly in motion, even under moonlight. The river and the breezes and the people flowed and circulated throughout; coming into and passing on. Amalina had imagined the city as a great magnet, pulling all the loose pieces across the continent (she being one of them), but rotating and agitating, too, to send them around, never letting them rest. Usually it was to her pleasure. But then there were times like the present, which felt restless and put upon. She was happy enough, even in her sadness and loneliness, to accept it either way. She liked the motion. *This city*, she felt, *is my true home*.

As she took the steps into the darker quarter of Mal Grave, she recalled Lady Princess Isabeau DePense telling her a bit of this magical city's history, as Isabeau was wont to do. And this history lesson Isabeau willingly gave, even after all that had happened to her in Ardeel; after visiting Amalina there—or, that is, visiting Katarina Tepsji and her uncle, the Count—and escaping the destruction of the Kyrgil Castle and the mountain it sat on, and the rumors of monsters bigger than giants who had laid waste to the whole city sitting at the mountain's feet. Most of the other Ladies who had fled the scene after that calamitous event had kept a comfortable distance from the dark little eastern young woman when she'd returned to their lands—forcing Amalina to redouble her efforts to enter the ranks of high society and acquire fresh new friends. Isabeau, with her penchant for *needing to know*, sought Amalina on her return, asking all kinds of questions, and then answering them with her own guesses, and larding that with other extraneous knowledge, like a bird reinforcing a nest with globs of mud. At some point Amalina was allowed to answer her questions. And Isabeau, as a reward, had told her Paris' history.

Paris had been founded by a race born to movement, so Isabeau had explained. They worked the waterways of France for commerce and enlightenment; like fairies without feet, always on the wing. And Amalina supposed that is why she felt an attachment to this place, more so than her hometown of Korr, or her home country of Ardeel. This was a land populated with and haunted by the spirits of people who were adventurers and movers. So unlike those of Korr and Ardeel: locked up and unmoving for centuries, for generations. The stagnation of her hometown felt impossible to Amalina. She could never return to it. Living there for the rest of her life would be like trying to live in a coffin. She could relate to Ivanti's reluctance and resentment of it.

Genadie enjoyed a small, shabby, greasy-windowed restaurant in the Mal Grave district. As Amalina came to it, she saw his small, crooked body, dressed in his regular worn outfit, and not the silky vestments of a countess' bodyman. He was leaving the restaurant arm and arm with a taller man who wore a dramatically large and swooping cloak. The two had their heads turned slightly to each other, as if in close conversation even as they moved.

Genadie's associate had a powdery face. The powder, an indicator of possible nobility, filled in the crow's feet and the other deep lines—the effect of this overall flatness bringing out the sharpness in his eyes. But even as she fell in at a discreet distance behind them, by the looks of his cloak, on closer inspection, caked with dirt, and patched over with a matching fabric seemingly by his own rough, inexpert hand, she feared they would be headed into a darker, more dangerous section of the city than they already were. The streets became impossibly crooked, darker, and narrow to the point where the two had to walk single-file, and Amalina let them put on more distance so if she tripped over something they would be less likely to be alerted; though their loudly mumbled conversation probably would have covered any sounds. But this questionable route turned out to be a conduit which emptied into a section of the city renowned for old money. The facades of the buildings were colorful and gilded with gold. The place seemed to glow of ancient wealth.

The two made their way around the side of a grand looking building and stopped at its side door where they rang the bell. The bell was answered by a silk-suited servant. He looked Genadie and the man over gravely, and with the sniffily stiff, grudging acceptance of a person receiving a contraband parcel as a favor to someone they cared for and could not refuse, he motioned them inside. Amalina felt the impulse to plunge inside just as the door closed. But she was not invisible, and the little magical item that could do the trick, a small bone the Strange Man had given her, was in her pocket but not coming out. There wasn't enough time, nor did she feel it was necessary. The bone was reserved for emergencies only. So she'd promised herself, anyway. She didn't know how long its powers would last, the Strange Man was long dead. But she did want to get into the house and find out what they were up to. Also, she didn't want to stand out in the street all night.

She rang the small bell at the door. It took longer this time for the door to open. It opened a crack, with a harder eye peering out than what had met Genadie and his friend.

"I'm sorry to bother you," said Amalina. "But I'm with *them*. With the gentlemen who just entered here."

"Who?"

"My name is—" but then she didn't want to answer that. And then she realized that wasn't what he was asking. "The two men who just came in through the door just now."

"If you are *with* them, then you can tell me who they are. Or are you just another little harlot, hired by Giacomo, eh? To dig up some dirt?" The door wavered. The servant's hand on the door wanted to shut it hard, but part of him needed to know if she wasn't telling the truth.

"Genadie. I'm Genadie's, uh, servant."

"And just who is Genadie?"

As the door shut, Amalina called into the parting: "Just tell him it's urgent!" Then she shouted through the closed door, "I don't want to bring *others* here!"

There was a pause, then the door opened wider this time. The silked-up servant stared down at her suspiciously.

"The *gendarme*, the police," she said.

"That's an old trick," said the man. "You think it'll work here again?"

Amalina reached into her pocket. She felt the small, dry bone resting in the lining, but what she brought out instead was a gold coin. "No trick. This should get me inside and to my master, shouldn't it?"

The servant tested the coin with his teeth. Then he looked surprised and doubly wary. Then he brought her into the house. Just to be careful, he guided her with his vise-like hand on her shoulder.

She was delivered to an octagonal room that was set up with plush, dark purple velvet drapes which looped down from ceiling to floor in a circular fashion. There were several candlestands, but only candles enough to bring the room up to a soft focus. At the room's center was a long, wide, soft red couch, with a gargantuan man, decorated in a gorgeous gold suit with medals, lying and spread out on it the way a fat, lazy cat wearing medals would. In the reclining position, his stomach rose almost as high as his head. His wig looked handsome but barely attached to his wide, fat head. There was a large bowl of fruit just before him, and he was eating a pear, the juice slathering the side of his mouth and rolling down the several mounds of jowl and chin; the juice left trails in his face powder. He was lost in this effort of eating and didn't notice his servant and Amalina enter.

Genadie and his associate didn't notice their entrance, either. They were absorbed in a canvas on an easel pointed at the man and were making remarks.

The servant stood without announcing Amalina, and more drew a line with his eyes to the centerpiece: his gargantuan master. He also cut a strange, conspiratorial look towards Amalina, and at first she didn't understand what it meant. Then, after coming to the conclusion that the fat man was a bit of an embarrassment to the servant, she realized he had allowed her to get a good look at him to get her money's worth.

The fat man was remarkable. Like a giant white slug in a costume. After having encountered the creature that was her own master, the Count, and several other similar entities, Amalina easily wondered if this man might be another superhuman beast of some kind. He did not look natural.

"Reinier," said the fat man, tossing the pear's gnawed core into the silver basin with a twang, "who is it you have there? Esmerelda?"

"Genadie's servant," said Reinier with an unkind smile. "She's come for him just now."

"And who the blasted hell is Genadie?" demanded the fat man with greedy, piggish eyes. "Why should he have all the fun? Bring her in and let me get a better look at her. Dando, dando, get more candles in here. You want me to go blind?"

A new servant, Dando, began a scramble to light candles.

"It'll ruin the esthetic," said Genadie's chum blandly. "Genadie?"

Genadie lost his surprise very quickly. He was used to Amalina's strange stunts and sudden appearances by now. His shoulders slumped perceptibly and he came to her side.

"I suppose this is Genadie," said the fat man behind him. "Bring her in!"

"Of course, Grandiere." The servant, Reinier, gently pushed Amalina into the room. There was a different air within: warm and close, and stinking of something old, perhaps rotting. She kept her face neutral only because she'd had years of practice holding her expression as solid as a mask.

The Grandiere's recessed, buried eyes glinted within his soft pudge and shifted in an analytical way. "Ah, a servant girl. Never mind the candles, Dando, you're too slow."

His great head turned and he was done with the sudden drama, his eyes became vacant. As if the brief exchange was all he was worth, and now he needed to recharge.

Genadie took her arm and was about to lead her out of the room, but his friend made a quick noise and pointed at something at his knee. Genadie scurried over, Amalina trailed unsurely behind him. The ugly smell was enough for her to make for the door, but her curiosity was always her unconscious guide and kept her in place, watching.

As Genadie's friend rooted through a small trunk of paints, Amalina looked at the large canvas on the easel. In the picture, the Grandiere stood tall; stocky but full of life. A light coming from out of nowhere seemed to surround his frame like a crackling energy. His eyes were not piggish, but were large brilliant orbs, commanding the viewer's attention, while his wry, charming smile completed the seduction. One could identify the man in the painting as the inhuman blob collapsed on the sofa very easily, and so Genadie's friend was a fantastic liar with his skills, a professional flatterer. Amalina also noted that he'd omitted from the work the overflowing chamber pot tucked undecorously underneath the sofa.

Genadie took what he was given from the trunk. His painter friend lifted an eyebrow at Amalina, gave her his own appraising look, and nodded. Then the two were sent out.

• • •

"Never leaves that room," said Genadie when they were back out in the street. "That's why Louis-Strange paints him there instead of in his studio. Do you know who the Grandiere is?"

"No."

"Never heard of him?"

"No."

"Well, doesn't that say something, then? The Grandiere is perhaps the oldest man in Paris."

"Doesn't look *that* old," said Amalina. "Old is not what I'd say at all."

"He believes the fatter he keeps himself, the less his skin winkles. But he also has expensive salves to keep it all up. He is ninety-one. And never mind that, he is also perhaps the richest man in Paris. Because he descends by blood from one of the oldest families in the city. One of the founding families. So old, so wealthy, so influential."

"And so fat," said Amalina.

"Let's call him 'tremendous', as Louis-Strange's painting does. *The Tremendous Grandiere*. And despite all he is and has, in a city of a million people, he is unknown. Perhaps even hidden from the king. Makes you think."

"About what, Genadie?"

"About the meaninglessness of it all. Does he look happy to you?"

"I couldn't really tell."

"No," said Genadie, sadly. "One can't tell."

"What's that your friend gave you, eh?"

"Why don't you tell me why you followed me, Ms. Dalca? Why did you show up here? and not as Lady Tepsji, either?"

"No. I asked you first."

Instead of arguing, as Genadie might have done in an earlier time, he reached into his pocket and pulled out a handful of canvas squares. On them were images of some of Amalina's friends; the Ladies of Paris.

Amalina's mouth dropped open, "What?"

At her reaction, Genadie pocketed them again, protectively.

"I thought you made those yourself, Genadie. You have your friend do the portraits?"

"How could I make them?" asked Genadie, hiding away his crooked fingers—the product of his own master's cruelty. He shrugged. "These hands aren't fit for the finer things anymore. As Master wills it. I just hire out the best of them, wherever we go. But don't tell Master. He thinks I haven't lost my touch, despite the damage. Doesn't notice the differences in the styles."

"I thought the Count knows everything."

Genadie shrugged again. "He *pretends* that I still make them anyway, which is nice of him. I was a skilled artist, once. But no bother. I still get to dabble. And I've met very many interesting and talented people this way. It's been a rich education and I should be grateful for it."

"You'd thank him for the dirty little hole in the ground he planted you in," said Amalina. "For all the worms and minerals you'd get to study."

Genadie scratched out a guilty laugh. "And now it's your turn to tell me why you've caught up to me. After all this time? Had me convinced you were really going to try to live here forever."

Oddly, when he said that, the image of the Grandiere popped into Amalina's head. She imagined herself, or even Ivanti, as bloated and stuck in place.

"Maybe not *here*, forever," said Amalina, a bit sourly. "No. Just not back *there*, at the castle. Not while there's a whole world for us to explore. There's no need to step foot in those mountains ever again." At this moment she didn't even feel bad saying such a thing about her old home. "Don't you see? He can't get to us out here if—"

"You've read Master's letters?" he interrupted.

Amalina was uncertain what he meant.

Genadie pulled a couple small notes from his other moldy pocket. Not for her to read, just for her to see.

"This is the third I've gotten, Ms. Dalca. He's getting frustrated, it's pretty clear. If we don't return soon, I'll have to buy a whole pigeon coop to store the poor things."

"How does he know where to send them? How do the birds find us?"

"You've gotten them too, then," he said. "I thought as much. It's time we go back, I think."

"But I'm still working on two of the princesses who've just come to Paris. Their parents have accepted my offer to visit with them."

Genadie patted his pocket of miniature portraits. "We've enough, Ms. Dalca. More than ever before. It's enough, and it's been too long. Ms. Dalca, I listened to you, let you convince me time and time again. And I allowed things to get out of hand. I'm afraid to admit that I, too, was beginning to feel comfortable here—"

"Then why not?" she enthused, grabbing his thin arm excitedly. "We don't have to stay here in Paris. Of course we don't. And he doesn't have to know we've gotten his messages. We move on and find another place. I've so many friends now who are to the west and the south and the north."

Anywhere but back to Ardeel, she thought. This modern world was changing and shuttering its doors to the old one; to the past. In the western kingdoms there were far fewer who believed in monstrous creatures than in her country; there just weren't enough supernatural horrors to support a fear of them in a reasonable population. It was an evolution leading away from such things. A change perhaps as quick and definite, and similar, to how the Count had once complained to her he was physically stiffening, losing substance, and coming apart; that there was nothing left for him to *learn*. Here in the west—and in the future!—was where Amalina wanted to be. She wanted to be free. All the way free. And freedom was wherever he wasn't. But of course, here, in Paris, there was a certain lieutenant. So not just *anywhere but back to Ardeel*, but perhaps *somewhere else than Paris*, too. Somewhere altogether new might be better.

"I see." Genadie now gave her a theatrically appraising look, almost in imitation of what the Grandiere and Louis-Strange had done. "That's why you came for me after all this time. You want to leave. What's happened?"

She didn't answer.

"It's not that you're bored," he decided, looking shrewdly at her. "It's either the Master's messages have found you and frightened you, or ... or what?"

But she couldn't say what. Not exactly. There's no way Genadie should know the whole truth about the young lieutenant.

"Something has turned you against the city, Ms. Dalca. All the more reason we should be leaving; leaving to return to where we belong."

She now felt the fabric of his sleeve, its greasiness waxy in the night air. Still she held on.

"We belong wherever we feel we belong," she said.

"If you're pointing to all points on the compass and saying we should go, then you haven't found such a place, have you? And in life, it's not a matter of feeling of belonging, it's more a matter of *knowing* where we belong. And by what's stuffing my pockets, I know where. Or rather, know *who* we belong *to*. And it is to *him* we should go."

"Wouldn't you like to stay, Genadie? Really? Here in the west there is hot chocolate."

"I can buy as much as I want to take with me." He licked his lips with that thought, "Should I?"

"And you seem to have many friends here. More than back home. You've no one there at all."

"At home, there is my most important friend of all." He was speaking of Count Tepsji, of course. But he wasn't transported into a rhapsodic state by mentioning him as he usually would be.

"He's no friend."

"Oh yes, I can't say 'friend'. I dare not presume so much."

"I mean, he's not *your* friend," said Amalina, pouncing. "You know it. It's not that you are unworthy. He is just your master. That is all."

"He needs me."

"No he doesn't."

Genadie laughed to himself and looked to some scene in his head. "Oh yes he does. He's said as much."

"He said he needs you? when he doesn't need anyone else in this world?"

"Oh, yes. Once when he was trying to figure out why he can't speak to bees, or control them, you know. And he likes to study things, and he'd brought a whole hive in just to figure out the mystery. Well, he burst the hive somehow and they swarmed him, and he just ... Well, you had to've seen it. He was flailing his arms around, looked confused. Didn't know which way to turn, they were all over him and around him, he had no control. And he called out. And he didn't call out to Old Torga, who was there at the time. Or to Young Clever Brabas who might've still been there, I can't remember. No, when he called out, he shouted quite clearly, 'Help me, Genadie. I need you!'"

"Did he?"

"Helpless, really. It was a sight. I never would have believed."

"And you saved him? Why would you—?"

"Oh, I really couldn't do anything for him. What do I know about bees? I just tried to brush the little miscreants off him. Eventually they settled down and he took care of them. Killed them all ... you know Master ... But it was nice of him to say he needed me. And let me see him look helpless like that. That was very kind of him. Made him seem human."

"A shame he didn't die."

"Ms. Dalca ..." he said, dismayed.

"He's not your friend," she said firmly. "And bees or not, he doesn't need you. And right now, without him we are totally free. We can go anywhere. Do you know much about England? that land across the English sea? Or the New World colonies? over the ocean? I've been hearing all about them, and they both sound so interesting."

"No. I don't really know."

"Or ... Or why not uh, um, uhhh ...?" here she thought for what might deliver a coup-de-gras to the vacillating wretch. "Haven't you ever wanted to track down your son? To reunite with him? To see what he's become?"

"Oh, no, Ms. Dalca. Never. Never that."

"What! Of course that, Genadie. You could do anything if you wanted. Your only living child? How long ago was it? He could have a wife by now, and you might have many grandchildren."

"No, no," he repeated, looking rather sad. "No, no, no, no, no. No good. No good."

"What's that?"

He said sheepishly under his breath, as if to keep the thought from her but he couldn't help but say it, "If I did, Master might not like that at all."

"Oh, what do you care! We're rid of him!"

Amalina tightened her grasp on his arm, hoping to see him wince. Then she threw his arm away. Then she hated herself because doing so was a sadistic urge straight from their master. Or was it? She didn't know herself anymore.

"Do not forget who you are and how you are here, Ms. Dalca. Don't grow complacent because you don't see him, when it is *his* money providing your lifestyle. There are obligations."

"Oh, quit playing his little saint."

"It will have to be soon, Ms. Dalca," he said. "We leave."

Amalina didn't pout as she might have done before. She lowered her chin to her chest, her lips straight and tight, and held back the coming tears.

"Oh, yes," rasped Genadie, cruelly. "Tomorrow, I think. Have your wardrobe readied. I will bring the carriage around in the morning."

But it had been an unusual tone he used. She looked at him. He had an odd smile on his face.

"What is it?" she asked him.

"Well ..." he winked his beady eye at her. "I suppose ... Maybe just a little while longer, eh? What do you think? I don't see why not. You have your wardrobe readied in the morning, and you can tell me wherever you'd like to go."

"Really, Genadie?"

"He doesn't *really* need me, if I must admit. And he can have only so many pigeons to send."

"How long? Or do you mean forever?"

Genadie turned his head away from her quickly, his mouth wriggled nervously. *Maybe shouldn't push him too hard*, she thought. *Just bit by bit*.

"I can't tell if you're being serious."

"You'll just have to trust me, Ms. Dalca."

"I will. But we can't leave Paris just yet, though," she told him.

"Another seasonal ball or something? You've been to enough of those already. Missing one won't be the worst thing for you."

"The reason I came to find you was I needed your help," she told him. "Aklan's gone missing."

"Who? Oh, the boy?" He made a brief and vigorous shake of his head. "I don't see how that is a bother at all. Makes it all the more easy for us, doesn't it? I'll just hire some heavies to bring down your trunks. You can prepare your wardrobe yourself."

"We can't leave without him."

"That stray won't miss us," he pronounced with his chin high in the air. "And assured, I won't him. *We* definitely don't *need* him."

"He is a little more important than a stray, Genadie. Um, no, not a stray in the least. I never did tell you exactly *who* he is, did I? Well, I'll tell you who he really is. Then you have to help me find him, because we need to. He told me not to blame myself as he ran off, and I can't imagine what I'd blame myself for, but he also told me not to worry, and I'm getting worried. I think he's up to something. He'd said something about revenge."

"Oh, Ms.Dalca. What have you done now?"

"Me?"

4

Weapons of War

"It's that dog-breathed rat of yours," said Lady Celine, after one of her servants whispered in her ear. "He's scratching at the door and insists you come at once."

Amalina wanted to picture Aklan there at the door, but the little boy didn't fit the description. Genadie then. The little rat being insistent didn't sound too promising. Amalina felt a pit in her stomach. Bad news about Aklan?

"You won't go to him, of course," said Lady Celine, with a peculiar remonstrating look: one eye wide, the other half closed. Something more fitting on an older face. Amalina could see already how she would look in another twenty years. *Strike this one off the list*, went an automatic thought. The Count wasn't too particular about absolute beauty; an easy attitude was just about everything before it. Celine did not have ease. And Amalina, if she ever returned to the high castle, would prefer not to be scolded through the Count's eyes, the way Celine would cause him to with *hers*.

"I'm afraid I must," insisted Amalina. "He was on an errand for me—"

"Well I suppose this errand is very important then. Better you mind your servant's bark. Yes, better that you attend to him. That you go immediately. Bark, bark, and off you go, little Lady Tepsji."

"Not to offend you."

"No offense taken, of course," she said as Amalina made for the door, opened by Celine's rouged footman. "I only freed my morning to study with you, instead of accepting the invite of Princess Dankwasser. Abuse my time how you like. I suppose that is the custom in good old rustic Ardeel?"

"No, sorry, it's just that I—it *was* an important errand. It should only be a minute."

"Take all the time you like," snarled Celine. Then she added with a modified tone, as if being kind, "You've become a very popular draw recently, Katarina. But it takes effort to *remain* popular."

. . .

Where Celine was red with agitation, Genadie was white with anxiety. His crooked hands shook after he stopped wringing them.

"Searched everywhere," said Genadie in his scratchy voice. "But you know better where he spends his time when he runs off. I made a search as best I could and that was that."

"What's the matter, Genadie?"

He held up his small meandering finger. "The one place I failed to search was the carriage. Then I remembered I would find him in there from time to time. So I looked."

"He was in the carriage?"

"He'd *been* there all right," said Genadie, darkly. "This could be very bad, Ms. Dalca."

"He wasn't there?"

"No. And something was missing. When I searched the carriage I looked everywhere, high and low, over and under. Because you know how he can hide when he wants."

Amalina nodded, trying to hurry him on. It wasn't like Genadie to keep her in suspense, but it showed how much he'd been thrown by whatever the boy's surprise was.

"Well, I noticed the interior bench box had been pried into. And the lockbox inside had its lock broken. And not neatly, as if to try to hide the fact. He didn't care if he was discovered."

"It was Aklan?"

"Must have been. Whoever it was went directly for that box and in a hurry. The only ones who knew it was there was he, you, and I."

"He took our money?"

"Worse. The money was untouched."

"Then what …?"

"There was only one other thing, Ms. Dalca. Don't you remember? I took it away from him and put it in there for safekeeping."

"The—?"

"The bomb."

One of the little hand-bombs that Commander Kralov and his men had used in their attempt to kill Count Tepsji. During one of his many runs through the castle, the boy had discovered one that had gotten away. He'd kept it hidden and didn't reveal it until the third week of their journey into the western kingdoms, when he'd grown bored and wanted to show off to the Pretty Princess. He'd even lit the fuse during his presentation, confident he could tug the sparkling end out just in time before it blew them all into the sky.

"I should have gotten rid of it," groaned Genadie. "Why did you insist I keep it, eh?"

"I thought it might come in handy," said Amalina, feeling foolish. She'd seen the devastation one of those bombs could do, remembered the bloody carnage. It wasn't a toy to be kept around. But still, one never knew when one would need …

"Let me see," she said, not wanting to panic yet.

• • •

The secret bench box inside the carriage had been pried. The lockbox sitting inside it had obviously been damaged by the repeated stabbings of something sharp to its lock. It could have been the work of an untrained thief, but then, why would they leave its haul of gold? The gold was there, or at least most of it, the coins would have to be counted to see if any had been taken. But, Genadie was right, the hand bomb wasn't there. And the last time she'd seen it, it had been resting half-buried in the gold.

With a sound of worry she dug her hands deep into the small, clinking treasure.

"There's no need," said Genadie, "I already searched."

But her hands hit something solid near the bottom. She shifted and stirred the coins. Then she started bringing things up.

There was a wood mallet, several stakes—both wood and metal, with sharp points—and a long, curved dagger that was crusted with a reddish-brown patina.

"What is this?" asked Amalina, as she pulled them out.

"Well, those are … Well, those are …" stammered Genadie, unsurely.

"They're yours?"

"Oh, yes, Ms. Dalca. Those are indeed mine."

"Well, what are they?"

"You don't recognize them?"

"No. Why should I?"

"Well, those are what I used to … Well, used to … Well, Ms. Dalca, you know …"

She couldn't at first guess, but the way he was fidgeting and frowning and staring at the items, as if they might leap up and stab him, she suddenly had a suspicion. "You used these on the Strange Man. To kill him."

Genadie nodded, looking guiltily at the compartment floor, his lips pursed. But he couldn't help glancing at the pieces every other moment.

"What was it, erm—?" Suddenly distracted, staring at the brown stain of blood on the blade, she had wanted to ask him what it was like to do it. How it felt to deliver the mortal blow to such a powerful creature as the Strange Man and the Count were. But she couldn't ask him something so dark, so personally disturbing. No, she couldn't ask him that. The more natural question was: "I mean … What are they doing here?"

"I really don't know, Ms. Dalca," shrugged Genadie, looking embarrassed. "I had meant to destroy them after what happened. Burn them. Melt them down. To have such weapons … It isn't right. But then … I didn't do what I'd meant to. I *couldn't* destroy them. I meant to do it at some point, certainly. Master wanted me to, of course. But I forgot them, I suppose. After a while."

"No, Genadie," said Amalina, feeling seized by a hot thought. "That's not why you have them in there. Have them still."

"No?" he looked at her with questioning eyes, as if he hoped she would tell him the reason he'd kept them instead of throwing them away.

"You have them *just in case*."

His eyes dropped again, and it seemed he would never look up. "It would be a foolish thing for me to think … even if I did. It would be impossible to try something like that again, to kill, to assassinate—no, not ever. And we'll never have to."

"*Shouldn't* have to, but—"

"I don't know what I was thinking, Ms. Dalca. I just forgot them in the box, that's all. I will destroy them now. Throw them in a burning barrel."

"No," said Amalina.

"No?"

"You're going to keep them right there. Just in case. You never know, Genadie. You know what I mean?"

"Know what?"

She held up a metal stake between them.

"You'd do it to him if you had to," she said. "You've done it once already, and you know you can free yourself. Free everyone—if you did it again."

"Oh, I don't know. I cannot think …"

"Of course you can think. And you have. You said it was easy. You said it was fun."

"That was the imposter I … *did* it to."

"But after what the Count *did* to your family, Genadie. After what he did to your wife, Mala, you *must* want to—"

"I trusted you to never talk about that again, Ms. Dalca. I should never have told you …"

"When *can* we talk about them? Why not now? These weapons tell me you want to be free. Some part of you wants to and knows it. It's true."

"I don't ever want to talk about what happened to them ever again."

"All right. But you can't pretend anymore that you don't want your liberty. These are the proof. Admit it, Genadie."

Genadie said nothing, but his lips wriggled and his eye twitched terribly. With a nervous shake, he ran his crooked fingers through his greasy hair.

"You are clever, Ms. Dalca. But you are not honest."

"Not honest?" she protested.

"You hide yourself and your motives. Oh, those motives may be good and honorable most times, but you mistrust too much and you couch what you ask for, wheedle and manipulate to get to your ends. It makes it difficult for anyone to think you as a true friend. Your problem is you are too afraid to ask for what you want, but scurry around with your words, dodging with them."

Amalina couldn't believe he was saying this, of all people, the constant bootlicker to the Count!

"One day," declared Genadie with an almost insufferable moral superiority, "you will stand up straight and declare what you want without resorting to the old prop 'cleverness'."

"I want my father and my cousin to be safe and not have their lives under constant threat. That's what I want."

"And ..."

"I want *us* to be free. I want us *all* to be free. To do what we want, to live wherever—"

"You want *yourself* to be free."

"Okay, and so what?"

"Well," he said. "You'll admit that very thing to the right person one day. But naught can be done about it by me. So you needn't push me to it."

"But *we* could do something about it," she said, holding up the weapons. "That's what I'm telling you. Both of us. Not just you. We can both do it for ourselves. I wasn't asking you to do it just for me."

Genadie nodded at her without agreeing. His eyes were blinking faster now, still transfixed by the weapons. But he wasn't saying 'no'.

"Keep them, Genadie," she said. "If it comes to it, I'll do it, too. I'll help you. We'll help each other, eh? We'll free ourselves from him. We'll stay here in the west, and if he comes this way—"

"He won't come this way."

"But if he does, and he threatens one of us, the other will do it. Yes?"

Genadie stared into her eyes now, and even with the cascade of twitches and blinks she saw the yearning in them, the *want*. He so *wished* it could be true.

"Genadie—"

"Now you are willing to kill, Ms. Dalca? Eh? Now you are a killer?"

Amalina swallowed a lump in her throat.

"No," he said, with some finality. "What do you hope to gain here, Ms. Dalca? It's all fantasy. Someday we must go back."

"No," she said. "You want it too, just as bad as I do, I see it in you, please—"

"What were we looking for?" asked Genadie, sounding testy now, trying to get off the subject. "It was the *bomb*, Ms. Dalca, and not these."

"Oh, right."

Amalina poked her hands throughout the bench box, then around and behind the locker.

"It isn't here," said Amalina. "The bomb is really gone."

"As I said. He has it now, Ms. Dalca. And what could he possibly intend to do with it, do you imagine? What's this thing about revenge?"

• • •

The disappearance of the bomb might have been just a sign Aklan had run off for good, taking it with him. But Amalina knew it wasn't. If he'd taken the bomb, no matter how carefree the boy was, he would have made away with at least some of the money. Which, after counting, he hadn't.

By the way Genadie snapped the whip and drove the horses, he believed the worst, too.

"I don't believe it," growled Genadie. "We should be driving out of France now as fast as we can. Let the stupid child have what he wants, let him blow up whomever he likes, as long as we aren't there to take the blame for it."

"But you know we can't just let him—"

"It's why we're *not* leaving! It's why we're risking our whole mission, Ms. Dalca. Oh, when Master hears of this, he will rip the child to pieces, royal hide or not, for how he might have ruined His plans. 'Prince' Aklan? Prince *nothing*!"

"You'll not say anything to the Count about Aklan," warned Amalina, dismayed they were talking as if they were not going to be staying on in the west after all. As if they *were* going back. But just in case: "You aren't supposed to know who Aklan is, don't forget."

"Doesn't stop me from telling Master what the boy did, whoever he is. Prince or not."

"But you won't tell. You mustn't say anything. I still count Princess Lisbet Spaarvierlet as my good friend, and so her brother, Aklan—well, the Prince's well-being, anyway—is my responsibility ... until I can restore him to his family. Or get that little monkey to restore himself."

Genadie was quiet as they rode on, releasing small hums and remonstrating coughs and troubled growls at various times in response to a conversation he was having in his head. His eye had stopped twitching, but it wasn't because he was no longer agitated. Rather his body had slowed, become weighed down, even his simpler movements thickened by private turmoil; his face was as heavy and inexpressive as a wooden mannequin. His eyes pointed unmoving into the distance. Then, after awhile:

"For you, Ms. Dalca, I will betray my confidence with the Master ... But then we're even, don't you think?" said Genadie. But she knew he was too fond of her to ever consider them even. It was the same way that she cared for him. They could always count on the other for a favor; pretty much; to a point. "But we'll be lucky if we catch him. I can only say nothing as long as we manage to do it. What could that soldier friend of yours have said or done to have provoked the little boy?"

"I don't know," said Amalina, cautiously beginning the dance of evasion. "They didn't get along. You never met him, Genadie, I don't think. But he's from Korr. He's strong headed, and a little gruff, in a peasant's way, because of it. And now he's a lieutenant. Got a little pride in him, then. He might have said anything that would upset a little prince whom he mistook for a simple child."

Genadie shook his head.

"Well you did too, Genadie," said Amalina. "You've cursed and threatened Aklan many times, haven't you? Because you didn't know."

"But he didn't send a bomb my way for it, did he?"

"Maybe he felt more threatened by a man of rank."

"Threatened about what?"

Of course Amalina could never tell Genadie she and her 'friend' Lt. Vokent were lovers—*had* been lovers. That would shock him right off his seat; he might hide Amalina away for good. And to think the boy had gone into the full mode of a chivalrous knight, and went to blow Vokent to pieces to defend her honor. Best to find another explanation.

"Aklan's a real prince," said Amalina. "Who can say what goes through his head? But there's the encampment! It must be! Look at their uniforms! Let's just hope we've gotten here in time."

"Hyah! Nk! Nk! Move, you beasts! We haven't a second to spare!"

Amalina hoped, presently, that the exotic appeal of a young Ardeelian noble lady would help locate a lieutenant inside an army camp faster than a fanciful but determined little boy with a bomb.

5

The Littlest Assassin

General Volante stared at Amalina in an inscrutable way, and occasionally threw bits of his stare at Genadie behind her. A princess in full make-up and dress with manservant was an uncommon sight within his headquarters, much less his camp. His dull grey eyes, one partially covered by a small cataract, blinked once, heavily, and no more. His only motion was to tickle and pull at his long pepper-grey whiskers that bristled over his high collar. He was slouched in a low-backed chair, with one boot resting on a simple leather stool short enough to serve as a make-shift ottoman.

"Seems to be our lieutenant's day," observed the general less than jovially. It was the same withering upset heard in Lady Celine when Genadie came to call. Amalina felt the French air growing colder by the minute. "You wouldn't be that which has kept my best man up every night, young lady? The face that launched a cherished lieutenant from my tents?"

"I'm not sure what you mean, good general. I don't know."

"Do not think this army, *my* army, is governed by batting eyes and open bodices; no matter how the younger generation may feel about it." Then he blasted out two motto words, for her instruction: "*Martial rigor!*"

"Yes ... I mean, no, General, of course not. It was just—"

"We've met."

"Have we?"

They hadn't. Amalina had avoided him at many turns during the court balls. They'd clasped hands once in a waltz, but she got off the floor before he looked at her too closely.

"Yes, we have. You're that ... that eastern lady. From over the mountains. Around where the lieutenant's from."

"You know me?"

"I know everything that needs to be known, young woman. It's how I stay in business and keep my forces running at their best. Now what was your name again? Step closer and let me have a look." She did as he commanded. He seemed to strain his catracted eye at her. "You heard me? about how my army is governed? Lace and perfume hold as much sway in my camp as a done-up polecat."

She nodded. "Yes."

His expression softened. "Can't see why I shouldn't grant my staff lieutenant this favor, though, after the service he has rendered me this morning. A remarkable lad, and deserving of a moment for a beauty such as you. And so you may see him, my dear. Bear in mind, he rides in a quarter hour!"

"Yes, of course, General," said Amalina, curtsying bashfully, feeling the sweat thicken on her back. She didn't want to see the dashing and remarkable lieutenant at all. But she must. Amalina trembled and straightened her hair. "Where do I go?"

"You stay here. It is bad enough you made it to my tent. Like a daffodil sprung up through a crack in my horse's hoof. Seems like this whole army is losing its way. Any city is a false star drawing off discipline. Mind you, little lady, this is my philosophy: to field an army is a matter of strict martial rigor; if you don't shape your men, they will shape you; and so you must break the will of the strongest and most obstinate man into a fine powder, and reform it into a concrete respect for your command. Fail to do so, and when the time comes you've nothing but a handful of friends at your back. Oh, there will be examples made for today's lapse, I can tell you." The general harrumphed this last point as he struggled out of his chair and bowed shallowly from the hip. Then he left the tent, growling under his breath, "Odd day, all over." Then, to a soldier standing guard, "Make sure they don't wander out anywhere. Nothing more dangerous than a woman in camp. She could get herself killed and then I'm in for it."

The soldier gave Amalina a look of ravenous appreciation. Afterward, he turned only partially, to half face into the wide tent, so he could continue to sample her with his glances.

It wasn't long before they heard the general's voice again, as he came up outside the tent: " … hope I've taught you something about what life really is, my son," he barked warmly. "You don't mind if I call you that, do you? 'My son'?"

"No, sir," said a voice familiar to Amalina. She felt her heart quicken.

"I would like to compliment myself that our marches have scrubbed that filthy backwoods mud off your boots, and you are a true, sharp-eyed, pike-and-musket man now."

"Yes, sir."

"I should never have to worry about a skirt sweeping you from this camp."

"Sir?"

"I express my confidence that I should never find my son dragged from my side—from my service—having become entangled in the threads of some lady's lower-stockings?"

"On no account sir! I would never give up this service! Not for my life, and especially not for a silly woman! No, sir! Believe me, sir! Believe me!"

"I believe you. You've sworn to it, I've heard it! Splendid, splendid." The General's voice became martially efficient without losing its warmth: "Don't forget you ride in a quarter hour."

"Yes, sir. Of course, sir."

"Now go see your surprise, Lieutenant."

"Oh, yes, sir."

• • •

The young and handsome Lieutenant Ivanti Ion Vokent, wearing his riding cloak and boots and with a large leather satchel, entered the tent. He stopped abruptly when he saw her. He didn't smile. "Amalina."

Genadie made a noise of disapproval when he noticed the lieutenant called her by her real name. She told Genadie with a look, *you already* know *he knows who I am.*

"I'll speak with the lieutenant alone," she told Genadie. When he seemed to forget the part he was playing, she added, "Shut the tent on your way out, Genadie. See to the horses and carriage."

The soldier posted outside didn't care for the plan—of the tent being shut against him—but the lieutenant nodded firmly in agreement at the order, and the leather flap closed after Genadie exited.

"So what are you doing here?" said Ivanti, when they were alone. The sounds of the camp seemed to amplify inside. She wondered if their voices would carry out.

"Believe me, I would rather have cut out my eyes than see you again," she whispered in their native tongue.

"Yes, here come the dramatics one can expect from an immature girl," he said with an impatient sigh, his eyes closed. "I haven't the time, so—"

"I came to see you anyway," she carried on, straightening her back to present a strong front, "because—"

"To see if I was still alive."

"No. To warn you, about … about …" she paused at his look. "But … then … ?"

He shook his head. "It didn't work. Sorry to say."

"So he came here?"

"I caught your little assassin. I can't understand it, Amalina. Drama's one thing. But to go this far? I didn't think you had this kind of jealousy in you. So very hot blooded."

"I didn't send him. I came here because Aklan disappeared and I was afraid … but what did he do? Where is he?"

"There's something attractive in a *hot-blooded* woman," said Ivanti in a low voice, repeating the words with emphasis. Only it was a warning tone, and almost inaudible over the noise outside. "But you were always a good little girl. Innocent. That is what made me feel for you. Your sweetness. To think that these clothes and titles could change you this much—"

"No, Ion. Listen—"

"I could have died, you know. This isn't a game. Would you really have me dead just because I have a healthy ambition for my own life? What would Sadra say about *that*?"

"I'm telling you, I didn't send him. And who's changed, really? Me? What would Sadra—no, what would your father say—about how you're spreading yourself …?" Amalina huffed now: "… like a grease over the world."

"Like a grease?"

"Like a filthy grease. And what would your mother and your sister think if they found out about all the women you have seduced—including me, from your own village?"

"I didn't seduce you, Ama. *We* fell in love. And I still love you." He made a quick gesture with his hand as if to redirect something. "But I'm not doing anything that a thousand other soldiers don't do on the march. And it isn't seduction, either. It is finding comfort where one can."

"That's very cold to say. And ignorant. Just because all the other soldiers are doing it, doesn't mean you have to. It makes you common and it breaks my heart."

"Well, it shouldn't. And if you can't be wise enough to understand what I'm saying, that isn't my fault. It's clear you still need time to grow up and learn the ways of the world. But now I have to ride, so let's just say our farewells and have done with our foolish little go around, *little* princess."

Amalina wasn't finished yet, she still saw in her man something to be recovered: "If thousands of soldiers decided to throw themselves off a bridge, would you follow?"

"I go to war with them, which is as good a substitute. When you're in the army, girl, you learn to follow orders and you move as one." He paused to regroup and then renew his counter-assault, which he did without relent: "I have a duty here, Ama, like no other, and offered *nowhere else* in the world; and I shan't lose that duty—be robbed of it—by getting netted from my rightful waters like a common carp, caught in the frillies and corset strings of a woman, no matter who she might be. To think otherwise, is the height of girlish vanity."

"It appears that General Volante really did break you down," said Amalina with contempt, "and shaped you into something very fine. Very fine, all right. I can't believe, such a cold thing—"

"I've no more time to explain to you how the world works. For what it's worth, I did love you." Nodding briskly, he added, "Good bye, Amalina."

"Where's Aklan?" said Amalina, leaping in his way.

"On his way to an assassin's reward," said Ivanti, with a firm tone of regret as he began readying himself. "It's out of my hands. I'm very sorry. Even if he was intent to finish me, he is too young for such a fate."

"But where? Where is he?"

"It's too late. Best you leave camp directly. Show an association to him now and you will be answering some severe questions from General Volante, never mind your rank."

"He's just a child. You mean—"

"If you're old enough to come after a man with a pistol, you're old enough to swing from a rope."

"Rope? My god. Where is he, Ion? Tell me."

"I won't have you risking your neck, Ama. Go home. Don't make the same mistake he did. This army and this general are nothing to play with." He straightened coldly, as if to deliver the final blow: "Now, and for the last time: *I love you!*" His eyes bulged comically by a wrong choice of words. Then he added quickly with a smirk of annoyance, "… um, I mean, *good bye!*"

Lieutenant Vokent threw on his cap, cutting her from his sight, and pushed out of the tent with a determined stride, muttering ruefully a needless parting shot, "I doubt we'll see each other again."

• • •

"Sorry to bother you, General," said Amalina.

"What? You're still here?" General Volante didn't look displeased, and almost as if it were part of some humorous joke. "The lieutenant should be gone by now. He didn't find you?"

"Oh, yes, I spoke with him, General. Thank you very much, General."

"You're satisfied then?" He laughed almost with humor, his cataracted eye winking at her. "Must envy youth. But let's not make this a regular occurrence, hnh? A camp isn't a place for a lady of any kind, much less one of your tender age and beauty." He stiffened. "Now, can't find your way out? Due west. Any more trouble, just ask for directions. If I had the time I would give you a tour, since you are already here. But I am very busy as you couldn't probably imagine, with all your knitting and riding and reading lessons. A man's business is very regulated and demanding: Cannon; then the Reading of Afternoon Orders. Nothing you'd enjoy; but my business all the same. And I wouldn't ask for anything more."

"But a moment," said Amalina, bowing and clutching her hands to attact his attention. "If I can ask something more of you. I heard about the boy who tried to kill Lieutenant Vokent. I was very aggrieved to hear about it, and I wished to speak to him before any punishment is dealt. To comfort him and pray forgiveness for his soul." Amalina delivered this with a delicate voice, filled with the innocence she imagined the general would have expected. At the end of her delivery she swallowed hard and determined she would never use that sickening voice again. Rather be strong and forward than silly and simpering.

Maybe her fight with Ion was still chafing.

The general laughed again, now with a condescending delight. "Tried to kill the lieutenant? Well, I'm afraid you misheard it. Or did the lieutenant embellish the story for your pleasure? Well, no need, no need. The boy came for me."

"For you!"

"He won't yet say who set him after me, but of course I have many enemies; pusillanimous foes who would stoop to sending a child to do the work where many men have personally failed."

"Are you sure he was after *you*?"

"Never mind what that remarkable lad, Vokent, might have said. The boy came at me with the pistol. Before I could move, the lieutenant threw himself between the two of us and disarmed the brat. A good man, my lieutenant; *your* man. Such great eyes, and reflexes like lightning. Ah, to envy youth. But that is how it was. It was very dangerous for him, to be sure. And very brave. No need to massage the story so that he was the intended target. I mean, what assassin would seek to kill a secretary when the general stands before him?"

"Let me go to the child, sir. For his youth, no matter how misguided; to give him prayer and support before his punishment."

"We have our own chaplain. There's no need to worry yourself that way."

"It's nothing, General. Just something I would offer anyone condemned for offences they might not have designed for themselves, but were prompted to by bad sorts of actors and circumstance."

The general stood there shaking his head, his grey skin growing red underneath the peppered whiskers. He closed his eyes. His patience had quickly reached its limit. Amalina started to back away.

"If he isn't already dead, you'll find him on the east side of camp. Near the woods and the firing range. Due east." He chopped his hand in that direction. "Tell the men there I've granted you five minutes of religious observance. And if you can find out who set him after me, I would be obliged." He sighed. "No more than five minutes, though. I have afternoon orders and a particularly rousing speech to deliver to the men. So be quick about it."

'If he isn't already dead'?
This is all my fault, she thought. *What have I done to that poor boy?*

. . .

As a regimental camp, it wasn't large by the standard of continental armies. But Amalina felt every inch of it as she made her way towards the firing range and the eastern woods. The camp was a construction of unending rows of small white canvas tents held up by rods of wood and string. Rifles, pikes, powder horns, canteens and various handmade signs hung out on the front of them, while small smoky fires were spaced intermittently. She pressed and pushed past groups of soldiers already in full field dress standing in the narrow space between the tents; rough-looking men who laughed quietly, or childlike men who stared at her, interrupted from whatever their conversations were, ashamed enough to drop a subject when they noticed her. They smelled of cologne, gun powder, sweat, and mud, along with a note of grease and burnt chicken or rabbit, or boiled cabbage. Some of them offered to help her, with greedy inflections in their voices or suggestive remarks.

A cannon fired, drowning out their words, and startled Amalina. Other cannon joined in. The blasts reminded her of the slaughter of Commander Kralov and his men, or rather the prelude to it, when they entered with their booming explosives; and also the battle between the Count and the Strange Man, who had taken after each other with cannons and other things that blew up; and then the entire mountainside collapsed under the weight of their battle. *That* had been the loudest sound she'd ever heard in her life. She thought she might have died then when she heard it. She thought she'd never recover her hearing from it.

All these memories could not sweep aside the guilt and sorrow threatening to bring out her tears. The soldiers took the obvious welling in her eyes, which she tried to hide, as fear of the booming cannons—failing to note she did not flinch under their shocking sound as much as they did—and that amused them, causing them to pat a mate on the shoulder and point her out. But it was not fear of sudden loud noises that had her ready to crack. It was the anxiety that she would find Aklan already dead. Or just about to die, only catching sight of him at the last moment; and he her, to give her a look of accusation. Just the way Commander Kralov and his men had done when they were executed. She had not yet been able to shake that guilt-laden vision of their stares. Accusing her.

It was all her fault, she thought. If she'd only sent Aklan home to his family, if she hadn't gotten involved with Ivanti Ion Vokent, if she hadn't told Aklan what Ion had done, none of this would be happening, and the boy about to suffer a similar fate—all her fault—as Commander Kralov. Amalina thought she might contain the tears if she could just get to Aklan in time, to save him somehow; or ask for his forgiveness anyway. And as she left the last rank of tents and saw the open field, it all became a green blur as the water built in her eyes to overflowing.

All her fault. All her fault.

And she knew she felt all the worse because this was the first adult decision she had ever made: her relationship with Ivanti. Her whole life prior to this seemed to have been lived in a processional fashion; with no choices, just being there to observe. How many times, when given the smallest opportunity to decide on something—something inconsequential to that stiff tapestry promenading by—would she consider her father and what he would advise her, or what he would have done himself; or, failing that, what Sadra, the minister's wife (Amalina's substitute mother), would have told her to do. But since coming to Paris she hadn't bowed to that convention of imaginary advisors. There had been no examples to follow in the courses she took. So now, having been given her freedom and taking it as if it were long deserved, she had failed; failed in what felt to be historic proportions. It had all been done hastily, irrationally, perversely. Decisions made from between the legs. Embarrassing. If only she had not given herself over to emotion but had proceeded carefully and logically—restrained and constricted ...

But then she wouldn't have been free, would she? It would have been just like falling back—as she always had—on her advisors. And the whole point was that she had been—finally—free.

This is what freedom had wrought. What *she* had wrought. She had destroyed that which she most loved and cherished: her love for Vokent; ruined any admiration he had for her; and sent an innocent little boy—a prince, of all things—to the firing squad, or the hangman, that is. As soon as she'd squandered the precious freedom she'd been given, it had been stripped away. And now life was proceeding processionally once more, with her as the sad observer.

She recovered when she began to stumble across the grass. She wouldn't become a spectacle for the watching, leering, cackling soldiers.

Where was Aklan?

6

Amalina to the Rescue

"**P**retty Princess," mumbled Aklan, beaming up at her through puffy, blackened eyes. Purple welts were all over his naked torso; some already darkening and discoloring and would become nasty black-and-green blobs shortly—if his life wasn't snapped out sooner at the end of a noose. A rough rope secured his hands behind his back, and he was leaning forward from exhaustion, his chin almost on his knees but for needing to look up. He blinked and squinted at her as if trying to stare into the sun, but he was happy to see her. "What are you doing here?"

Amalina stood over him, hands on hips inside the crudely fashioned pen. She wasn't familiar with military life, but to her eyes the enclosure looked like something they would use for livestock in Korr. Wood poles as high as her head, with sharpened points on top, were stuck in the ground intermittently, forming a large rectangle. At the moment there was only Amalina and Aklan in the far corner, and a man reeking of alcohol curled up on the ground near the entrance.

"What are *you* doing here?" hissed Amalina, trying to stay quiet despite her anger. "What were you *thinking*?"

"Don't be mad at me."

"Why shouldn't I? What you did … I did not ask you to do it. Not in the least."

"Oh, I know. Never said ya did, did I? I was just going to give him a real treat, that lieutenant of yours. Have a little fun with him."

"Fun!" exclaimed Amalina with disbelief. She wanted to pinch him hard, but she leaned forward to appear to anyone outside like she was praying. "Look where you are now! You're going to be hanged."

"And by our allies," he said shamefully. "That's an awful turn."

"You're going to die," she said to impress on him the fact. He seemed as dense as the Count in this regard. Or was he in some kind of shock and he didn't really understand?

"Don't blame yourself, Pretty Princess. Honestly, it was all my fault. Don't blame yourself."

"I'm trying not to, but—Ion didn't mean *that* much to me, idiot. It's not worth murdering him over my mistakes, much less getting yourself killed."

"I didn't try to kill him."

"You tried to kill the *general?*" she gaped, incredulous.

"Not anyone." It seemed he wanted to yell in protest, but he could only manage to lift his head again and look in her in the eye to prove it.

"Then how are you here?"

He gave a little laugh. "Well, it was a mistake."

"What did you intend with the bomb if you weren't trying to kill him?"

"What bomb?"

"The one Genadie locked away. The one you took on your way over here."

"Oh, that? I didn't bring it here. Why would you think—?"

Amalina told him they'd found it missing from the carriage's secret treasure box.

"Ah, now ... I took my bomb back a long time ago. Wasn't that old crumb's right to nab from me, the way I see it."

"So you didn't bring it here to kill the lieutenant?"

"No, I hid it in your room. Then I was afraid you might find it and yell at me, or you might accidentally set it off. So then I just put it back in the carriage. I stuffed it in the armrest cushion. The one on my side; so nobody would ever find it, but I could still get to it if I needed." Explaining all this seemed to revive Aklan's spirits. He was grinning in amusement despite his fattened lip. "That's all there is to that. Who said anything about a bomb, anyway? They caught me with a pistol."

Ion *had* said pistol, hadn't he?

"And what were you planning to do with that?"

"Steal it. It was the lieutenant's. I snuck into the camp and found his tent. I thought I'd tell him off, but he wasn't there. So then I thought I'd play with him a little. I spilled some ink around; loaded some into his scabbard. Then I saw his pistol and thought he might catch some trouble if they thought he'd lost it. But a rockhead saw me coming out of his tent. They all tried to catch me when I ran. Almost did. But I started dodging through the tents." He laughed, then spit, then laughed. Then he groaned. "Ran right into the general's tent. And there was your lieutenant, too. I shouldn't have stopped, but I was straight shocked. And the men after me were on my heels, just outside. I had nowhere to go. That's when your lieutenant knocked his pistol from me—and it's been knockings for wee Aklan ever since. I wasn't trying to kill anyone, I promise you."

"Why didn't you tell them you were just stealing?"

"Stealing will get you hung as fast. But that silly general thinks I was after him and there's no way to get him to let go of that. He likes that story best."

"And why didn't you just tell them you are Prince Aklan Spaarvierlet?"

He laughed. "You think they would believe me, Pretty Princess? And the way the general is about it, if he did believe me, he'd still say a prince was after him and then they'd be marching to war against my father."

"That's ridiculous."

Aklan shrugged a weary shrug.

"You aren't going to tell them? You aren't even going to try?"

"You aren't here to rescue me?" he asked with childish innocence that didn't quite match his maturing looks. He was young, but not *that* young.

"Well," said Amalina, thinking, "I could vouch to the general who you are …"

"He wouldn't believe you, and there would be a lot of explaining …"

And, thought Amalina, *the Count, even back in Ardeel, would hear of any explanations spoken in France that included him and Prince Aklan Spaarvierlet. Then there would need to be some* real *explanations. To* Him.

She frowned. "You can't tell me that you're just going to let this happen to you."

"I've never been shot before," he said. "That should be interesting."

"They're going to hang you."

"Oh, right. Well, I've had an interesting life."

"You're too young to die," said Amalina, growing more upset by the second.

"Nobody is too young to die," said Aklan, speaking the response that was already mournfully tolling in her head.

"Well, I won't have it. I can't. This is all my fault."

"No, it isn't."

"I should have sent you home the first chance I had."

"I wouldn't let you."

"Stop arguing with me."

"I've almost died so many times, Pretty Princess. If I slip out of this one, it won't be the closest. If I don't, then that's the way it was supposed to be."

"You *still* think you're getting out of this, don't you?"

He pulled weakly at the ropes. "Maybe not. Please forgive me. You will, won't you?"

"Of course. I can't believe you have to ask. There's nothing to forgive, really. But you don't deserve to die for a mistake."

"It would feel silly," he admitted with a shrug.

The boy could not have looked more pathetic at that moment.

"I have an idea," said Amalina. "It's very stupid, I think. But we have to try."

"Yeah?"

"I'm going to go to the general and beg for him to release you into my custody."

"That *is* stupid … you think it'll work?"

"I'll say you've confessed, you were just trying to steal the pistol. You didn't mean him any harm."

"I still don't think he'll believe you."

"And that *I* believe you have taken stock of your life, and that you are willing to turn to good works. And I will see that you are entered into a monastery that my uncle is the abbot of."

"A monastery! You aren't really going to do that, are you?"

"I'm a baker's daughter and I have no uncle who's an abbot."

"Oh right."

"But I would toss you in a monastery, or a jail, if I could. And really, I should get you back to your family and home."

"I don't think your plan is going to work, sorry to say."

"That's just the first part," said Amalina. "If it works, it works. The second part is trickier." Amalina took the small bone from her side pocket. She pretended to be praying fervently over him and showed it to him. Then she dropped it onto the ground by his side. "Remember that?"

Aklan stared at it warily.

"It makes you invisible," she said.

"I remember. The gypsy witchcraft."

"Just clamp the bone between your teeth. They won't be able to see you."

"They'll see the ropes and my pants."

She looked back at his guards through spaces in the pickets. They'd moved ten yards away and were discussing something. Bored or embarrassed by the spectacle of the young lady and the doomed boy. They didn't suspect.

She quickly loosened the knots on the rope around his wrists. Then she stood up.

"First get rid of the ropes. Then get rid of the pants. But you have to wait until I tell the guards I'm going to the general to beg for your life. Then I'll go. It won't be long, I think, but you will have to wait a little more after that. Just stay in this spot. When the time comes for it, get out of the ropes and pants, put the bone between your teeth and fly this coop and into the woods. You'll meet us at the Duexieme Bridge. You know where that is, right? Stay out of sight. But take the bone out of your mouth when you see us approaching the bridge. Can't have Genadie knowing about it."

"Is it going to work?"

"It should. We won't need to try it anyway if I can convince the general to let you go." She took a breath. "But if I can't, then things get harder. Still, I think it should work."

She then told him what was going to happen and his signal to act. And then cautioned him to be very careful he didn't get killed.

"Sounds like it'll be fun."

"But you'll be praying that the general lets you go so we don't have to do it."

"Of course." It didn't sound like he meant it.

"Because the other way is much more dangerous," she cautioned. "And with the general's suspicious mind, your escaping won't look good for me either. I can only hope enough time will have passed after I leave, and that I'm just a girl, to make him come up with other reasons than it was I who freed you. Who knows what will happen, really. Better I didn't have to do it, though, you understand?"

"Of course," he said again.

And yet, as she left—and with a glance to make sure the drunk in the pen was still unconscious—Amalina wasn't sure just which outcome Aklan would pray for.

. . .

Nearly twenty minutes later, Amalina had Genadie ready the carriage for a run. Her disappointment and frustration at General Volante's condescension, and his denial to release the little assassin, slipped into worry as she made her way along the lightly wooded, south-eastern edge of camp. She wished she could use the bone herself, but that was for Aklan. Genadie's old cloak would have to do for camouflage. With the thick clothes bulked around her and the hat's wide brim pulled down, she was sure she wouldn't be assumed a woman. But perhaps not being seen as a woman was more dangerous, if anyone got curious and she was spotted; she could be taken as another spy within the woods, and they might fire on her. Still though, better to disguise herself as much as she could.

There were no sentries in the woods and no guards around the holding pen's side closest to the forest. It seemed like an oversight on the general's part. Amalina could see through the slats where Aklan still lay, and then, further along, his minders, who had wandered farther off and had pulled into their circle two more men.

Their attention was drawn down field. The cannons had stopped, their blue smoke thinned to a light haze. Most of the regiment had been formed into squared ranks, tall pikes in some sections, rifles casually slapped over shoulders in others. She could see General Volante's small, round, whiskered head before their columns, and hear his words in a garbled way, blowing through them. His voice came in waves, and he seemed to come up on the tips of his toes when he was making a louder point. But his rising and falling did not match the delayed rush of his words. It looked almost comical with the mis-timing. But all the world was silent for him. Even the birds and noisy forest animals seemed to have gone quiet, ceding the stage to the mighty general. His address to the regiment was the focus of every living creature. For the moment.

Amalina gave a little prayer, hoping that nobody would be hurt. That she wouldn't be spotted—and that what she was about to do would be enough of a distraction for the boy to get into the woods and away. And then what? It would be on to the coast, at speed, buy passage for three across the sea … then who knows where, as far away from General Volante—and Ivanti Vokent, of course—as possible; and most importantly, out of the Count's reach, forever.

She lit the bomb and threw it hard.

7

Lover's End

"**S**o she wants to end it—*this way*? Well, there's more pretty girls in the world than just her. But feather and claw, *feather and claw*."

"What's the matter?" said the tall man.

"Oh, nothing, I suppose," the shorter man grumbled. But his high voice made his grumble sound more like a woman's sigh. Then he chortled to himself. "It will mean I dispatch a note to the castle tomorrow."

The tall man shifted awkardly, shyly, but he smiled a vicious smile. "*I wouldn't mind doing the required work.*"

"Oh, yes, I see that. And I appreciate that about you. You're a good one to have around. Someday, maybe … maybe you *might* be cut in on it. But for now it is status quo. Bringing the letters to me was the right thing, and that is more than I could have asked. So you have my gratitude. It could have been very bad if she'd been able to post her letters of accusation, and rumor, and lies, and word had gotten out. But to behave like this, doesn't the poor girl know how these things turn out?"

The tall man chugged out a laugh, but his eyes looked disappointed, he'd be missing out.

"But feather and claw, it's the last of the birds, isn't it?" said the shorter man, now explaining himself. "Then I'll have to go out to the castle and bring them back, reset the whole process. Can't say I look forward to that trip. The cart shakes so much, it hurts." He thought to himself, *if only she could feel the pain, her forcing me to do this.*

"I can go," said the tall man, wiping his wide mouth with his hairy wrist. "I know the way."

"Patience, patience, my friend," said the short man. "Maybe next time. I'll take you with and show you how it's done, and I won't have to bother with it ever again. But for now, this is my duty, isn't it? Everyone has their part to play in this sad affair … and to which this naughty girl has driven us: She misbehaves; you let me know; I catch her before she can act; and I duly deliver the messages. Even the Count does his part after that—does what he's told—doesn't he?"

The tall man ducked his head in a deep and quick nod. "Oh, yes. Yes."

"So just listen to me and you'll get your reward soon enough, and have patience … better patience than that bad girl had, enh?"

"Oh, yes. Yes."

The tall man thanked him and left the room. As he did so, he dragged his foot behind so that it gave him a forward pitch, as if working against a heavy wind. Watching him, the other chuckled to himself.

Well, no matter the lame leg and rather unsavory air, thought he. *He's definitely useful. Who am I to complain about beauty?*

"Now," he said aloud to himself, "As for that girl."

That evening he attached a message to the carrier pigeon and, as predicted, it was the last in the flight. He would have to go to the castle and reclaim the birds. A long and painful journey for him. And all the while a powerful creature will be about his business, carrying out orders he must obey. And when the man returned, the pretty, naughty, bad, selfish, and impatient girl will have been dealt with and no longer be his problem. But there would be another. There always was.

Maybe the next would be that one he'd seen up at the castle, the rude one. The Count's niece, did she say? She was pretty enough. Katarina?

Oh, ho! That *would be dangerous. No, no, off limits. Off limits, even to one such as AXP.*

Anyway, he hadn't seen her in a while. Maybe the Count had already done something with her. Word was she was a troublemaker. Well, it wasn't his business, so never mind. But it would be nice to see her again, if only to see her. Maybe something else. One never knew what could happen in this world …

As he pulled his large, heavy body onto the creaky cart, with all the empty pigeon coops stacked high in back, he broke into a song that would help soothe his nerves and quicken the miles ahead:

"One white leg, fat and fancy. One white arm, that is my doll. One breast, two breast, plump and pert. All apart … then into the dirt!"

He snickered loudly to himself.

Part Two
Intro to Chaos

8

Old Ghosts

I

"Tell me about the western princesses and the ladies of title," purred the Count in his deep basso voice. He was reclined on the divan, wrapped in a silk housecoat, his eyes aimed at his private study's ceiling as if to picture up there in the shadows what Amalina was to recount.

This scene, Amalina noted, was laid out exactly as it was last year.

And almost identical to the year before that.

Amalina, just out of the carriage, who was tired and half slouched, wanted to scream in frustration. She couldn't believe she was here again. Again!

There were differences, of course. The Count's study had been redecorated, with a large trunk next to the desk; and where the secret passage to the treasury and message center used to be concealed by a massive cabinet, before Commander Kralov and his commandos blew it up, there now stood a gold-framed floor-to-ceiling portrait of the Count dressed in ancient courtly attire, surrounded in its ink-black darkness by flaming wreckage and a fallen mountain, with a strange leer under his long mustachio. In the portrait, the Count's clean right hand was raised from a golden washbasin filled with bloody water. His left foot rested on a large broken chunk of white marble with an image of Ardeel chiseled into it. His left hand held aloft a long-necked sack that looked like it held a large cannonball inside it, but for the tell-tale crimson stain at the bottom of it, which dripped blood. Over this bag, his apparent prize, was written out in ghostly white letters: *Cavete: Omnes Ottomani, et omnes amici perfidi Soldani, et omnes exteros homines, et imitatores, et homines me breviores*: "Beware: All Ottomans, and friends of the treacherous Sultan, and all foreign born men, and imitators, and men who are shorter than me." The enigmatic curl at the end of the Count's lips was a subtle, smug smile at his conquest of the Strange Man.

But the portrait, the trunk, and a rearrangement of furniture were physical changes, and could only be expected after a passage of time.

Different than before, but deeper, and more important: The Count himself was flicking his large brown eyes at Amalina; almost helplessly so.

She felt guilty avoiding his looks; and guiltier still over what she had become while she'd been away: the independent woman, the heartbroken lover. And heavier than the guilt, she felt embarrassment that he seemed to not have a clue that something significant had changed in her.

Her distracting concerns were definite differences to this annual ritual.

But, to be fair, as much as Amalina had changed, the Count had changed too. Of course he had. And he had done so most dramatically just before her latest departure—right in front of her unbelieving eyes. In fact, that is what had spurred her to flee his castle at the time, and had remained a silent force causing her to dread any return and to scramble for ways to escape his influence. His change—his astonishing transformation—he had declared openly and frankly to her during a lengthy confession, in which he told her he planned to take several wives from those western noble ladies who were visiting his court—a total of nine wives being the rightful and perfect number for a man so immortal as he. He would bestow, upon these lucky women he'd chosen, the gift of his immortality (or supermortality ... *whatever* he was).

But also, as his confession had continued, he had admitted to Amalina that she, while in his service, had grown on him; to the point he'd learned to trust and rely on her. And so he expressed in that moment, with an insistent excitement, his most triumphant joy in life at having first discovered her that one fateful night, she hanging out her window, and not only that he had had the good sense not to tear her to pieces, but had ultimately brought her to his castle and into his employ. And then, most amazingly, before her eyes—just before she fled the castle as fast as she could—he thanked God for bringing her to him. The most irreligious man she had ever known, hostile to any form of spiritualism, had said his thanks to God in his heavens and announced he would make Amalina his ninth wife; to cap off the other happy marriages.

In this new, amorous Count, Amalina faced a desperate and unwanted desire backed by inordinate, inhuman power. As docile as he appeared before her now, she trembled inwardly at having, during her extended trip, forgotten his passion, and that she had gradually lost the very real need to escape him. She loathed that she'd been so stupid, and reckless, and distracted by her love of Ivanti that she had not taken the opportunity to *quit for good* the Count. Instead she had, in the confusion after the break-up and the necessary flight from Paris after the bombing of General Volante's camp, barely one step ahead of the pursuing crown agents, returned to him! Now there was no guarantee she would ever again have a chance to escape. She could only hope he had forgotten his interest in her.

Yes, she hoped and prayed in her exhaustion, *as scattered as he is, and fickle, he might have forgotten everything.* Or he might have even soured on her; or taken a stronger infatuation in someone else. *Who? Is there anyone else still here?* With his eyes darting at her, she feared he would declare, in his voice which rumbled as deep and low as a quake, with words that dripped with his ardor, "I'm so glad you've returned to me."

"Ah, you are tired, Ms. Dalca?" said the Count, instead. She looked at him. "That is to say, little mouse … Yes, I remember now. You've just returned home and you are tired, certainly. And probably hungry, aren't you? I'm not unaware of these things anymore. And the way it has become with us, there's no need for haste. We can be thoughtful and meticulous in your long delayed report to me. But it is good to have a full belly and a good rest before these exhaustive debriefs, no?" With a snap of fabric he sat up, a clever smile on his face. "I will have you dine immediately. We can discuss these other, incredibly important matters later."

Genadie, who stood next to Amalina waiting for her to give a name so he could present a small portrait, straightened up, his eyes lifting in surprise, his hand coming out of the leather case it was dipped into. "Not now, Master?"

"See to yourself," the Count instructed Genadie, his eyes on Amalina alone.

• • •

In the old days, hundreds of years ago, the castle's formal dining hall also functioned as its great audience chamber; or perhaps the other way around. Depending on the occasion, it was outfitted with tables and benches and strewn with rushes, or otherwise a throne and pews and swept clean. It was a room neglected these many years but for simple services, such as the reception and acceptance into the castle of the great General Marosh and his small army, who'd come to provide protection for the Count. For Amalina's stay, the Count's guests dined exclusively, and instead, in the castle's massive entrance area, *l'entrée grande*; or later, more frequently, food was served in the comfort of one or another lady's chambers and apartments. But today, the great audience chamber looked set up for a feast as in the days of old, the long tables awaiting servants, guests, and their meal. The giant wood and iron wheel of the chandelier, which hung high above the floor, blazed with tri-wicked candles as thick as an arm. The pleasant smell of a roast game and some pies scented the air. And still, no meal could be seen. Amalina looked around curiously, as the Count led her further in. He did not stop in the hall but took her through a door she hadn't noticed before.

They entered a side chamber. Perhaps it had once been a waiting room, or a room of preparation for the castle's noble lord before he made his entrance into this great hall, headed to the throne. Now it was repurposed into a smaller, intimate dining room. A short, oblong table at its center was set with a tasteful number of plates, cups and utensils, all aglow from several candlestands in the corners. The food Amalina had smelled was already set out on platters. Anka, the old head maid, and Pils, the castle's man servant, looked tired but happy to see Amalina after her long absence. Anka bowed and smiled, washed Amalina's hands in a bowl, and whispered as she dabbed them with a towel, "So glad to have you back, milady." Pils bowed and smiled and brought her to her chair and whispered, "Me too, milady."

Dinner with the Count. An intimately lit, delectable feast with gleaming tableware. Just the way Amalina had imagined a private dinner with a king, so many years ago, when she'd first been brought—when, by deceit, she had first been *abducted*—to this castle. Several difficult years had gone by before this imagined experience finally came true, she thought testily. But, she noted as well, this was a strange and ungrateful thought to have.

The Count skulked around the table, appraising the settings and the food, not coming down to land anywhere. Pils at first followed after his master and then gave up when told to leave. "Mouse knows how to feed herself," he said. Pils and Anka exited.

"I'm to dine alone?" asked Amalina, feeling uncomfortable sitting by herself before the gorgeous layout.

"I'm with you."

"But it doesn't look like you're planning to stay. Or are you serving me yourself, sir?"

The Count gave Amalina an indulgent smile but sat down promptly at the head of the table.

"I also wondered," continued Amalina, "whether anyone *else* would be joining us?"

Was there any other guest still here at the high castle? She hadn't seen any signs of it when she and Genadie rode the carriage into the courtyard. But she and Genadie had been rushed straight from there to the Count's chamber. No chance to rest or peek around. Yet when they'd left the castle so long ago, Princess Margeta had threatened to be a stubborn hold out, even when the other women had begun to leave in fear for their lives after what had happened at the Kyrgil Castle. Could Margeta have stayed on this long? It would seem improbable. And what about Pia?

"It's only us, nobody else; and it is all for you, you *are* the hungry one," explained the Count. "You see how I remembered, Ms. Dalca—ah, er, *my little mouse*? You are worthless for our debriefs when you've just returned and you haven't eaten. So now I provide for your needs."

"You had this ready to go the whole time? Even when we met in the study? Instead of coming here first?" Maybe she *was* tired: she'd said it aloud instead of just criticizing his eccentricities within the safety of her private thoughts. Amalina noted the slight withdrawal of humor in his face. But it fell back in place almost immediately, accompanied by a strange warmness in his regard. She couldn't be too sure, though, that it wasn't a trick of the soft light.

"It wasn't a ruse on my part, if that's what you mean," he purred magnanimously. "I knew your hunger was a possibility of course, but I couldn't be sure it would be a matter I need contend with until I saw you; when I could establish your ... let us call it, *attitude* ... for certain. I should think you'd know by now I plan for every possibility and eventuality. And you'd appreciate it."

Amalina nodded. There was something in the overall selection of the food before her, with its strong wafting notes of citrus—noticed now, up close—that cut through, and reigned over, the deeper, heartier bite of the traditional mountain spices, paprika and anise, and included at least one platter, near the Count's elbow, bearing the telltale glistening gold crown of pasta, that suggested the meal's origin. She didn't even need to taste the wine to make a guess.

"Did Princess Margeta's servants prepare this?" asked Amalina.

"She ordered her staff take over the kitchens after General Marosh's cooks left our service," said the Count.

Amalina smirked. General Marosh, his army, and all his people had been killed in the Count's battle with the Strange Man at Kyrgil. They had not 'left' of their own accord. They were all beheaded, gutted, rended or crushed beneath the old castle and the rubble of its mountain. Even Marosh's underling and replacement, Vezel Umalasju, had sacrificed himself. Marosh's people were *gone*. The Count did not seem to notice her reaction. Well, anyway, that seemed to confirm Margeta was in the castle. But for this long? Had he changed her by now, given her his 'gift'? Had he *married* her? And *was* Pia here? Had she *survived*?

"How could I argue against Margeta's kind gesture?" said the Count, running his hand over his swooped back head of thick black hair. The darkness of his hair made his pale skin look as white as snow. Something gentle, delicate. "You would prefer a cook more familiar with Ardeelian cuisine, my little mouse? or would it be French, now?"

Instead of waiting for an answer, he continued on, as was his way, with this well-pleased, sighing, self-involved observation: "Cuisine is not a subject I care much about, one way or another, no matter how I try, little mouse. I remember it from the old days, of course, but too long on my own I suppose. Nothing here looks appetizing. As it is, I will be leaving tonight to satisfy my own needs, you understand; something you have about as much sympathy for as I have for these common meals for common people." The Count sniffed, but then smiled cleverly and warmly. "And now that I've told you I will be leaving for tonight, you might feel it is important for you to rush through this little feast, perhaps forgo a good rest, so you can tell me all what you learned on your *extended* mission—your *greatly* extended mission—before I go; the good girl that you are, the loyal and helpful girl that you are. But there is no hurry. Tomorrow is as cream as it is today. Do you feel the change coming? Trust you and I will eventually begin what will become the flowering of my Palace of Pleasures. Just eat now, and be satisfied."

Amalina nodded ... and almost gasped at herself when she, quite automatically, brought her hands together to say a prayer over his table. She broke her hands apart awkwardly, noted the flare in his large, dark eyes, and she nonchalantly pulled a platter of pheasant to her and forked some pieces onto her plate and began to eat.

"I doubt I'll be able to finish it all," she said. "Maybe Genadie would like some."

"Have his tastes refined during your prolonged travels? No, I am sure he must still be accustomed to eating at the side door. Or perhaps ... well, *did* something change in France?"

Because he seemed to be hinting at something, Amalina stuffed her mouth in order not to answer.

"I *was* surprised at how long you were away, little mouse. It seemed you would never return to me. And with no responses to my messages. I began to think you'd met with an unfortunate accident." He tugged at his mustache, a mild sneer growing under it. He carried on in his usual circular, self-referential way—*I, me, I, me, I, me*; something she hadn't missed, and she remembered it now disagreeably: "I would think that could be the only explanation why I could be ignored and you had forgotten me so."

"You were never forgotten, sir," said Amalina.

This perked the Count immediately. He sat higher in his chair, and stared at her hungrily over the fat tan hump of roasted goose.

"As I was going to tell you, sir, it was a much busier outing. We met with so many more families than before. Word is starting to get around about us."

"*Us.*"

"You, by way of me, sir. I'm the one they meet."

"I won't bother why you never replied to my letters, which your words, I believe, while good to hear, still does not adequately explain the reason to *me.*" *I, me, I, me, I, me ...*

Amalina nodded vaguely, which was good enough for her, anyway. She took another forkful. But then, remembering the opulent dinners and the company of her sweet, new, lively friends in the west, she felt resentment and disagreement form a knot in her stomach. She could have been dining with friends right now; in a nice restaurant, or a palatial estate with a score of guests and teams of well-trained servants waiting on them. But she was here again in the high castle, and away from all that. It felt like a theft from her life.

"Is there something you want to tell me, Amalina?"

She could have held back. She would have. But something, the knot in her stomach perhaps, moved suddenly. She blurted with a ringing note of annoyance, "Sir … Sir, why can't I just *stay* there? … stay there and simply *send* the ladies and princesses to you?"

The Count looked startled by her sudden shift in tone.

"Well, doesn't it just seem it would be more efficient, sir? I could write down my reports, and send them back to you along with Genadie's portraits. It would accomplish what you want all the same, wouldn't it? But I could continue the work without having to interrupt it and leave. It would save so many wasted weeks traveling here and there. I could work on your behalf year round, even in winter, in summer, whenever."

"But, Ms. Dalca," he said patiently, "you must be here to receive my guests. That is the plan: they begin their journey believing they are to spend time with you, not me. That was *our* plan, no? It will hardly work if you are never here."

Amalina flagged her eyebrows up and down as if to acknowledge the truth of it, while feeling the helplessness of it all. The Count had once complained that he was trapped in Ardeel, as if it were a cage; held in by the impossibility of getting past the mountains to reach the rest of the continent. That was the reason she was sent out, to lure the rest of the world in to him. But she felt that she was caged too. By the Count's plans, and by his threats.

The Count was only held in Ardeel out of his own fear for his safety. If he could trust traveling in the daylit world by carriage, and stay in lodging less fragile than a thick-stoned fortress—if he would risk his life to escape his situation—he might break free the mountainous borders of this country. And, Amalina supposed wearily, she was in the same circumstance: while not in the exact situation as the Count, fear bound her here; bound her to the mission and to this creature.

She ate in the silence.

"Hm. Is there something else you wish to say to me?"

"About the trip, sir?"

"Anything you like. Whatever comes to mind that you might think I should know. Or to ask me. It doesn't have to be about *there*. It could be about *here*. And not just this castle, or Netz. *Anywhere*. Your father, your village." He didn't quite say it like a threat, but the odd tone and pointed look made his words more than empty conversation. She took it as a veiled reminder of his usual menace against her family in Korr, should she not obey him. *Yes, yes*, she thought irritably, with a touch of enervated boredom, *he will destroy them if I do not do as he commands. Of course.* "Or anything at all that I might need to know—about anywhere, *here*, or *your village*—you might like me to know."

"You'd know more about local events than I, at this point," she said snippily. She realized she must be completely exhausted and out of her mind to be talking this way.

The Count smiled politely, and curiously, taking up the burden of her attitude with patience. And something else. "I know *everything*. About anywhere, *here*, or *your village*. But you already know that about me, don't you. But you've nothing to say to me about any of it?"

There was a sudden knot again, in her throat this time. She couldn't swallow. What was he talking about? What was he implying? What could be more important to him than learning about the young, royal women she'd met on her trip? The conversation was centering uncomfortably, not only on Amalina, but on Amalina ... here *in Ardeel?* What could have happened here? What could have gone wrong?

"Of course I know you know *everything*," she said, nonchalant. "You never let me forget because you're always reminding me. So if I'm leaving something out, or forgetting something, maybe you can give me a hint. If you want me to talk about it."

He sat silently at the end of the table, staring meaningfully but not elaborating.

They were in each other's company for two hours by the time Amalina marched to bed. Never once did they speak of Lady Pia Lampeda.

II

"Pretty Princess, you'll never guess who's still here," said Aklan, full of energy and joining Amalina on her exhausted walk to her bedroom. He was looking serious, but excited, a dog returned home. His body had already healed during their travels, the lumps and bruises gone in a week, and only a discoloration in the white next to his left blueberry eye remained as a reminder of the damage he'd suffered.

Amalina turned her head from him and stared at the wall.

"Pretty Princess," said Aklan. "Hey, are you ignoring me?"

She walked a little faster.

"What's the matter? You're *never* going to talk to me again? Really? We're back in the castle now and I have something important to tell you. Don't you want to hear the news?"

"You shouldn't be here," she huffed.

"Of course I should. I'm your servant, aren't I?"

"I don't know *what* you are."

"What's that supposed to mean, Pretty Princess?"

She looked down at him and said, "… other than a pest."

"Aw, what's the matter now? What? What?"

"As if you couldn't guess," she muttered.

"What?" he asked, looking honestly mystified. "What, Pretty Princess? Almost getting myself killed for you?"

"That's getting close."

"You're still upset about that stupid lieutenant?"

"As if!"

"Then what?"

Amalina tried to muster up a very hard look to skewer him. Because, after she had set off the hand bomb in the regimental camp, and then drove her carriage to the Deuxieme Bridge to rendezvous with Aklan, he had never showed. She'd sent Genadie back to the camp to determine what had happened, fearing the little boy had somehow been caught, or perhaps killed in the blast, or executed. But it wasn't so; he *had* escaped.

General Volante determined immediately the boy's associates had made a try, once again, on the general's life—with the bomb Amalina had thrown—while others had broke the boy out in the ensuing confusion.

Amalina and Genadie had waited until the next morning, parked by the bridge, waiting for Aklan to show himself. Had he gotten lost in the woods? Had he been wounded? Or hurt himself? Amalina knew by experience how awkward it was moving invisibly for the first time, he could have tripped on any random log, fallen into a hole, or broken a leg. She and Genadie searched the woods for him, calling his name even at the risk of running into a patrol of infantry doing the same thing. They found nothing.

It wasn't until the third evening, when Amalina had packed to leave, ignoring another urgent demand from General Volante for questioning about an incident at his camp, when Aklan appeared and he made his sobbing confession.

Given the gift of invisibity, the boy couldn't help but run wild in the countryside and then into Paris, getting up to who knows what; he wouldn't say. Just that he was very sorry, that he knew he should have followed Amalina's plan, and begged her to remember that he was young and used to getting his way—having once been a prince and then become a free-wheeling vagabond.

But he also confessed, and sorrier still, he'd broken Amalina's magic bone.

"I don't know how I let Genadie convince me to take you back," said Amalina, presently.

"You're still sore about that bone?" he said in a whisper, reading her. "Still?"

"I am still mad," she said. "How can I ever forget?"

"I thought you must have by now."

"How can I *ever*?"

"Really, Pretty Princess? But what does that one thing have to do with *now*? We're back in the castle! Please, I've been trying to be helpful all this time. And I am trying to fix it, you know. I promise you I will find a way. When will you forgive me? You care more about that stupid little bone than me?"

"If that stupid little bone hadn't broken," snapped Amalina, "would I have ever seen you again?"

• • •

As Amalina reached the door to her own suite of rooms, feeling half-asleep even as she lifted her hand for the door handle, she was interrupted by a hurried movement to her right. She spun, instantly alert. A swarthy little woman with a supplicating look bowed at her several times, holding out a wrinkled hand to assure Amalina she shouldn't be frightened, and begged forgiveness for the interruption. She was dressed in the somber black dress which Princess Margeta attired her staff and herself with. She was one of Margeta's maids. She wore a little cap with a thin black veil that draped down along the left side of her face. She continued to bow and began to emit a stuttery welcome in Italian.

"S-s-sorry, Countess Tepsji. My lady heard of your arrival and has been waiting for you, in order to greet you after your long absence. She-she-she wished to speak to you, you see, before you should retire for bed. If that is not too much trouble for you, Countess?"

"Call me Katarina," said Amalina, with a sigh not meant for the old woman. She was very ready for bed by now.

"Oh-oh-oh, no, I *shouldn't*, Countess."

"My uncle is the Count. Leave him the titles. I'm just Katarina in this house."

"Well-well-well, to my Princess Margeta, you see, you are *Princess Katarina Tepsji*, or *the Countess*, in deference to your uncle. And so it should be for me, you see." What was left unsaid was that it should be that way for the old woman—unless she wanted to be *punished* by her mistress.

Amalina nodded and followed the maid. Her name, Amalina remembered as she watched the hunched, teeter-tottering gait from behind, was Bardina.

They went to Princess Margeta's suite. It had been rearranged and redecorated so thoroughly that it looked as if someone else's castle had been secreted inside the Count's. It had all the vibrantly colored but mournful articles (paintings, tapestries, rugs) of Margeta's severe Roman Catholic tastes. There was a crucifix attached to each wall, sometimes two. Amalina could not imagine the Count entering such a religious hideout. And perhaps the point of it all, besides reminding the pious princess of her Italian home, was to repel him. Or challenge him.

Margeta wore a long, tight-fitting black dress with a large headdress. Its lace was lost in the darkness of the fabric. She sat in a tall-backed chair as if it were a throne, and she accepted Amalina into the room as if this were a formal audience. Amalina held back from shaking her head at the pomp. The memory of Lady Princess Margeta and the depth of her scheming and ambitious nature came back in all its ridiculousness and danger.

But she wasn't wearing a marriage band. She hadn't secured the Count's hand.

"Oh, Princess Katarina," intoned Margeta with false cheer. "It is good to see you've returned to your uncle's company and in good health. He was very worried about you, little girl. And I can't say I wasn't concerned for you on my own part."

Amalina bowed deferentially, as she imagined Margeta would have wanted it. "Princess Margeta. I'm glad to see you're still here after all this time. Though I'm surprised you've stayed on here at the castle for so long. But you are looking well … and in your element, I think."

Margeta raised her pointy chin in order to look down her long, straight, Roman nose at Amalina. Her smile was coarse. "I'm well pleased to see you again, too. Of course I said prayers for you every day, hoping for your safe-keeping and return." She put her hands together on her little crucifix, hung on a beaded necklace around her neck, and closed her eyes, muttering a thankful prayer. "Heaven's will. Heaven's will."

"You didn't seem to care for uncle's high castle, Princess Margeta," said Amalina. "Or much for uncle's views on sanctity and the church. You *are* happy here? He hasn't been keeping you unnecessarily? I'm sure your family misses you—"

"It is God's will I stay."

"Oh?"

"Not just to see you safely home again, though that is a blessing in itself. Of course I am here for Princess Pia." Margeta cleared her throat and repeated: "*Princess Pia.*"

• • •

So Margeta knew Princess Pia Lampeda had not died in the catastrophe at Kyrgil mountain.

When had Margeta finally learned the truth? How much did she know of the circumstances? But Amalina didn't want to ask. It was generally thought that Pia had died during the collapse of the mountain—attributed to a strange volcanic eruption, but really the result of the Count and the Strange Man's battle, which had stretched the two monsters to the limits of their power, and illuminated brightly to any living witness just how much otherworldly power these creatures possessed, as they tore up the castle and mountain in order to strike at each other and deliver a mortal blow. But Pia had not been lost there in the wanton destruction, as so many others had. She had simply been drained of her blood and replenished with the Count's own, a procedure that, once endured, would empower her and transform her into the same kind of entity he was. The rite had taken place prior to the battle, and she had been secretly relocated to the Count's high castle in Netz. There she would take whatever time she needed, under his protection, to recover from the process or not.

Amalina had left the country long before Pia's change resolved itself; before Pia had come out of her seeming enchanted sleep, or died as the rite's victim, as poor Robine Beaujeulle had. At the time, Amalina could not wait to get away—away from the Count, Ardeel and everything in it—and not least because she didn't want to be around if and when Pia did wake. She didn't want to face the altered princess who had once been her friend.

Pia might even have died while Amalina was away, for the lack of any information in the Count's letters, and so that had become Amalina's easy belief for so long.

At the mention of Pia's name, Amalina's heart skipped. But still, she did not want to meet her. She did not want to know.

• • •

Since Margeta knew of Pia, she had at least been told that Pia had survived the mountain's collapse. But for all Amalina knew, by now Pia was wedded to the Count as his first immortal wife. Yet by the way Margeta, who had sworn to take the Count as her husband before any other rival (being unaware of his true nature and his unholy power), was now sitting so imperiously in her high chair—

Had the Count performed the rite on Margeta? Had he given her his curse—his gift?

"Are you all right, Princess Katarina?"

"What?" muttered Amalina, her eyes looking around, wondering what had happened.

"You were stammering idiotically. Perhaps you *are* too tired for a polite chat."

"Yes, I think—"

"But I was telling you that I remained here for Princess Lampeda. To keep her company in her time of need. The company of a fellow countryman, you see. And one who could see to her proper maintenance by prayer."

"Oh, yes, that was nice of you."

"You haven't seen her since you arrived."

"I went straight to my uncle; as it is done, usually—"

"I see. Which explains not calling on me."

"A rest after the long journey is understandable, but my uncle always insists I speak to him first—"

"And you had a meal."

"Yes. It was so very good, too, Princess Margeta. It was nice of you to lend uncle some cooks—"

"Though you're probably the first Lady here, besides myself, to make proper use of them." Margeta said this meaningfully, and crossed herself slowly.

"What do you mean ...?"

Her voice tightened. "Not many people in this castle eat. Eat *properly*. Certainly not your uncle. And neither Princess Pia."

"Oh," said Amalina. Margeta was getting at something, but not in a direct way. Was it more a probing conversation? Amalina warily ventured away from it. "The dinner was very good, though."

"Do you not want to speak of Princess Lampeda? You seem to be avoiding the subject. While she and I were—are—fellow countrymen, you two were very close. Much closer than she and I."

"Oh, yes." But Margeta's was an understatement of her and Pia's poor relations: after exhausting all other methods of sabotage, misdirection, threats, and lies to keep Pia Lampeda—her assumed rival to the Count's affections—away from him, Margeta had sent an assassin after Pia. It was the Count who had saved Pia's life—before taking her mortal life and transforming it; elevating it. "You didn't seem very fond of her, Margeta, so I thought you wouldn't want to talk about—"

Margeta cleared her throat meaningfully again.

"You didn't seem very fond of her, *Princess* Margeta," Amalina corrected herself. "So I thought I would let the subject pass. But if you wish—"

"She *was* your close friend, after all, Princess Katarina."

"However, your staying here to offer companionship to her was very thoughtful, Princess Margeta."

"And yet *you*, her close friend, ran away immediately."

"Well, I hope it didn't seem like that. It was just that so much had happened at the time and I—"

"—As if you intended to abandon her," she accused.

"But that's not true at all," said Amalina. "It was all so very traumatic what had happened at the mountain. And everyone else, all my guests left but you, didn't they? And uncle was becoming a grouch because of all his injuries and he—he practically sent me away." She switched tack, trying not to sound defensive: "You see, Margeta, he insists I travel when I can. To see the world is very important, he says. He *wanted* me to leave. I couldn't really help it."

"I stayed to mend your uncle," said Margeta. "And I prayed for him and his soul, of course. And when Pia was found—rescued, whatever—I did the same for her. And have remained here ever since."

"And as I said, that was very kind of you. Very thoughtful."

"You still have nothing to say about her," Margeta observed with a shrewd look.

"I—what … What should I—?"

"You're beginning to sound like my annoying old Bardina. I hope I don't have that effect on people. But let's move onto other subjects, if you find it so difficult to discuss your old friend, Princess Pia Lampeda."

"I—I don't understand what—"

"I haven't seen the princess, you know," persisted Margeta, despite her offer to move on. "Never once. Your uncle has been very protective of her. I can speak to her sometimes, through a door. And I have written letters, to which she responds through your uncle or one of the servants. She is slowly regaining her strength, I'm assured. Because I can't see her, I can't attest to her full condition. But I know she is getting better, day by day."

"Well, that's good," said Amalina, feeling like she *was* acting idiotically now. But she still couldn't tell what Margeta was driving at. It was as if the Count and Margeta had determined, upon her arrival, to be as mysterious and as impossible as they could to fluster her and drive her mad. Maybe Aklan *had* had some important information for her. Maybe she should have listened to him.

"Soon she'll be as strong as your uncle," said Margeta. She nodded, and gave a small, pinch-lipped smile. "It must be so. The way he, your uncle, survived that eruption, and the destruction of the mountain. And so did she."

"We *all* survived it," Amalina reminded her, trying to derail Margeta's dangerous train of thought. She *must* know more about Pia then; about her transformation. Or she suspects it. *She's trying to get information out of me.*

"It was a bit of a miracle," Amalina went on positively, with a put-on naïvete. "Though uncle wouldn't like me talking about it that way, as a miracle. You should appreciate that—"

"Your uncle left this castle for business this evening, just after your dinner," said Margeta flatly. "We can speak as directly as we want."

"You've something more direct to say than you already have?"

"You didn't expect to find me here, did you? You thought he would have scared me off, or I would have grown impatient and bored, and left of my own accord. But I did tell you my family's wishes, and you know my resolve to be attached to your uncle. I'm more stubborn than a mule. I could give Job a run for his money."

Amalina nodded, allowing Margeta's confession to flow uninterrupted.

"I confess to you, Princess Katarina, that there were moments I was uncertain. Where I had my doubts. Where my desires and my fears would have me seek a different fate. But let me tell you, little girl, I have eyes, and I have a mind to think; and I have a will that won't break."

Amalina nodded again. She saw Margeta's servants frozen in their spots, looking upon their mistress in an almost religious awe.

"I've spoken to Princess Pia Lampeda," said Margeta. "I've spoken to her and I've reasoned. And I've considered and I've reconsidered, and then I reconsidered again. No one will tell me the full truth—not ever—and yet still: I know what has taken place in this castle, little girl. What has happened and what is happening to Pia, you understand. And there is no way I'm leaving here. Not when I know just what is being served here on the plate."

• • • •

Amalina should have known the nightmare waiting for her in the high castle. But after her many delightful, if mundane, adventures in the west, as well as the making of new, enchanting friends, her romance with Ion, the plotting of her escape from Ardeel and the Count, and the irrational notion that, being so far away from her old troubles, all her dreams could come true, she'd managed to forget. With a light jolt of her limbs and an increased temperature in her body, which grew as if someone were stoking a fire under her bed, the nightmare came for her in her sleep, just as it always did once inside the castle.

The nightmare:

A blue sky over a field of barley. Or was it rye? Bees buzzed and zagged above the shifting rows of tall yellow grain, and a song filled the air. It was a song sung by a young girl, Lucinda Skeldar, who she had once seen slaughtered by the Count; in fact, the first time she had seen him was when Amalina had watched Lucinda die in his horrible grasp. At the time, the doomed girl had been the same age as Amalina was now. And now her voice sang out within the barley, and her head bobbed in the distance up above the tan crowns, staring at Amalina, only to fall back down. Lucinda was skipping high and coming straight at Amalina.

Only Lucinda wasn't really singing, was she? It was an annoying song, one Amalina didn't like. And though it was Lucinda's voice that sang it, Lucinda was rather saying something else. She was talking to Amalina.

Lucinda was demanding something.

"Kill him, Amalina Dalca!" said Lucinda Skeldar. "Kill the man who killed me! Exact vengeance for me, Amalina! Do it so that I can finally sleep! Take pity on my soul and kill him! It has been too long. He yet lives. Kill him, Amalina. Kill him!"

Lucinda was within five rows of reaching Amalina. Her head went down once more, and with her head's monotonous up-and-down motion, a knot cinched in Amalina's stomach when Lucinda's head did not pop right back up. Amalina waited for it. And she waited. The pain in her gut grew along with the unbearable heat as she anticipated the head. And as she waited, she was sure the head would certainly not emerge, but up would fly the stump of Lucinda Skeldar's neck, blood gouting in all directions. Amalina waited. She waited.

. . .

Amalina shot up off the mattress, her limbs wrestling with the sheets. When she landed, she panted and tried to calm herself. She was no longer in a field of barley. Lucinda wasn't there. She was simply on her bed again, in the dark. "Oh right," Amalina mumbled to herself, as she pulled the sheets back on, feeling the sweat all over her skin. *Oh yes,* she thought, *I'm back. And so: the nightmare.*

After a small moment of relief, Amalina shouted and spun off the bed.

Someone had crawled into bed with her.

Someone had reached out and touched her with a cold, searching hand.

But it wasn't Lucinda Skeldar, newly emerged from Amalina's dreams.

It wasn't Aklan, either.

It was someone large and—

"Why don't you want to talk about me?" sighed Pia Lampeda, with a pretty, lonely pout.

"Pia?" gasped Amalina.

"I just wanted to see you …"

There was a black blur, and suddenly Pia was gone.

. . .

Given the perspective distance of many years later, it could be argued—and Amalina would do so on occasion—that a direct line could be drawn from Amalina's return to the castle, with all its chaos and confusion, to the worst disturbance yet in the Palace of Pleasure's short history ...

It is the World that is Mad

It wasn't long after Attila Bronk was placed in the small Tsobl jail cell that the country's new high constable, his five personal guard escort, and the new governor of Ardeel—formerly the high constable—crowded into it. Attila Bronk sat in the cell's damp, dank corner, feeling the cold seep into him. He glanced up at his visitors with a look of complete boredom.

"You'll change that look soon enough," said the new high constable with a laugh.

"Well Attila, we've finally caught you," said the governor. As he spoke, the fat under his chin wobbled beneath his rubbery smile. "And you deserve everything you will get for your unending traitorous and seditious behavior."

"I am a man of the utmost loyalty to this country, Governor."

"You've defied this very government repeatedly and sown chaos among its people. Hardly a loyal man's occupation."

"You're done for, Bronk," sneered the high constable.

"I suppose I should be flattered by this attention," murmured Attila. "I expected after my arrest to be ignored, left to rot down here and never see a human face again."

"Not when you have continually embarrassed the high constable, the sheriff, and the Permanent Council's forces during your flight from the law," explained the governor, adding a greasy chortle. "Three or so months at large now, since you were spotted in the outerlands. Made fools out of them with escape after escape until we finally tracked you down to General Umalasju's abandoned property. Your base of operations, I suppose? That was a wily, if cynical, dodge, Attila. But, you see, the people were starting to sympathize, and root against us. Unnacceptable. So now it requires a direct, public response by this government, to right the Law's humiliating failures. But let me tell you why *I* will be happy to be rid of you, former Low Constable Bronk. I am bored of having to put out these fabulous fires of superstitious nonsense you set wherever you land. Every visitor to Sobelburg now has some new story of monsters, unholy creatures, and divine cataclysms. And some of your fantastic drivel has begun to escape Ardeel and reach the king."

"It was General Marosh's estate," said Attila.

"What's that?" snapped the high constable as if the governor had just been insulted.

"I was hiding in General *Marosh*'s estate," explained Attila. "Er, former estate. Since Marosh had abandoned it."

"Oh, well," said the governor, not really seeing the point. "I heard it was Umalasju's place."

"Who is Umalasju?"

"What?" said the governor.

"I've never heard of a General Umalasju," said Attila. "And I am quite familiar with this country's many military leaders."

"General Vezel Umalasju," explained the governor.

"He doesn't know what he's talking about," said the high constable to the governor. "It was Umalasju's estate. That is the report."

"There is no Vezel Umalasju," countered Attila. "And I know very well it was Marosh's mansion, since I was nearly executed there some years ago by the general himself; coincidentally, when I was being pursued by this office, even back then. Governor, you know who I am talking about. Old Sir Zsolt Marosh."

"Yes, I remember old Zsolt."

"He made off with his army and the government's munitions and artillery to help—"

"*Vezel*," the high constable shot in. "Vezel Umalasju." He pointed toward Attila for the Governor's benefit, as he continued on, making his voice sound official, "We apprehended this man, Attila Bronk, on Vezel's property, after receiving reports that he had been sneaking on and off said property. I think the people of that region should know whose—"

"There is not, and has never been, a field commander named Vezel—"

"And Marosh *I* am unfamiliar with," the high constable interrupted. "One of the ancient family names, I think? But ..."

"Interesting," said Attila, folding his hands together in contemplation. "Marosh occupied the interest of this very government not long ago, as I was saying, as he took his men and his cannons and went to assist the Count—"

"You see," interrupted the governor. "It is this kind of pointless argument which has me convinced you have lost your mind; and which I will be happily rid of come dawn."

Come dawn.

The governor nodded to the high constable who then made a signal to the guards. The guards charged forward with heavy irons and chains. It was a painful procedure, even with Attila presenting his hands and offering no resistance. The irons were clamped loosely around his thin wrists and ankles, and the chains sank him back down to the floor. He noted the chains had also been run through an iron ring in the wall.

"That should see you behave," said the governor. "And at last I will finally be finished with you, Attila."

"You're going to kill me?"

"Execute, yes. If only I could do so, personally."

"Tomorrow?"

"At dawn. Yes."

"You could have just had them slit my throat and thrown my body into the underbrush and not bothered with all this."

"But I already told you: a public display is needed. A popular criminal who disappears or is assassinated becomes a legend. A proper public execution, done under the strict auspices of the law, sets an example."

"For what crime am I to be executed? Will there be no trial? And what is so proper about that?"

"How many times have we tried you in your absence, former Low Constable Attila Bronk?" smirked the governer. "I'm sure you must have read about it in one of the releases, or heard about it, anyway. You are very well informed and seem to know everything else. Now, I don't wish to gloat, but I will say there is some satisfaction when I counsel you to pray for yourself. And may God have mercy on your soul."

The governor and the rest swept out of the cell, closing and locking the heavy door behind them.

• • •

So tomorrow morning, come dawn, I will be executed? thought Attila, weighing the chains on his wrist and judging the strength of the iron ring's mounting. *How many times have I faced this moment? But this seems to be the final one. No getting out of it.*

He watched the rectangular patch of light on the floor change shape and climb the wall as he thought of the nursemaid who had named him in his crib, and who had instilled in him her sense of righteousness as he grew. Should he curse her now because this is where her gift of strict morality to the young boy landed him? Had this been her purpose after all? Did she know it would send him on a senseless quest that would end in his ruin?

As the light in the cell faded, he saw his own faults had caused his capture. Why had he felt so confident he wouldn't be noticed on Marosh's estate? Hadn't the old groundskeeper had it in for him? Maybe the old man had stuck around after all and informed the authorities.

You have behaved nobly and with immaculate honor, the former low constable comforted himself. *You can only thank nursie for your proper instruction. It is the world that is mad.*

• • •

Some time around midnight the cell door was unlocked. Two hooded figures entered like monks. But Attila's senses were keen in the darkness, he recognized the scent of one man and the prodigious bulk of the other.

"Governor," said Attila to the fat one. "Is it time already? And you've brought the Cardinal to receive my confession?"

"God no," said the governor, pulling back the edge of his cowl so his face showed. His rubbery lips were no longer smiling. "You will have no confession in the King's Lands or received by the King's Men."

The Cardinal made a noise in his mouth.

"No offense to you, Cardinal," said the governor. "But Attila is from the west. Or his family was. A direct political excommunication by the King holds a more terrible weight to him than a Papal church's."

"My parents arrived in this country after the invasion," said Attila. "Whether I am from there or here is debatable. Sometimes I think, by my actions, I am the only true man of Ardeel."

"Insufferable as always," said the governor. He turned to the Cardinal, his jowls shaking. "Let's get this over with so that he can be out of my sight."

Attila looked to the Cardinal, who still hadn't removed his hood. But his hands were out and the various telltale rings were there and they carried the scent of the St. Grigori church. His hands held out a key toward Attila, as if presenting it to him for inspection. Presumably, it was to Attila's irons.

Attila studied it, and then studied the scowl inside the gloom of the hood.

"Look at you two," the governor chided them in the momentary silence. "I'm about to grant one of you your life, and one of you your wish to save the other, and there isn't one smile between you."

"Simple people smile stupidly," said the Cardinal. "Men of learning and intelligence smile only out of uncontrolled wickedness or spite." The Cardinal smiled briefly at his own witty sentiment; the governor did not. "Otherwise one keeps one's reserve—and one's mouth shut."

"A smile can also be used to show gratitude," said the governer unhappily, "*if* it must be *used*, instead of simply *enjoyed*. Ah, you two are of a piece and deserve each other."

"He should be made to understand the conditions," said the Cardinal.

"That's next," said the governor. "Understand this, former constable, I am granting you a reprieve from your sentence. It seems you have allies in high enough places. Some of whom I wish to keep happy for everyone's peace." He gave a pointed look within his soft features. "You see how it can be done, Attila? Instead of sowing chaos it is better to straighten the fabric."

"A mixed metaphor," said Attila. "But I think I understand you, yes."

"The Cardinal claims you were on a mission for him. Is that so?"

"Whether it was uttered from the Cardinal's mouth, it was—and is—a mission by the laws of heaven."

The Cardinal's fingers clapped together and pulled the key back from sight.

"You see," spat the governor, his rolls jiggling, "it is this kind of thinking I want avoided from now on, former Low Constable. I will have a lot of questions to be answering to my high constable, to the Permanent Council, and perhaps to the king himself if this does not turn out as well as we all hope. I need to know you won't complicate my life further by such arrogant and fanciful proclamations: *Missions from Heaven.*"

"I gave you specific information," said the Cardinal to Attila, as if reminding him or giving instruction, but also almost sounding wounded. "I gave you shelter and access to all you might need to fulfill your mission against our common enemy."

"You are ridding this land of a miscreant," whispered the governor to Attila, as if he were afraid someone—that *particular* someone—could hear them through the thick walls. "A troublemaker perhaps worse than yourself, who sows his own kind of chaos among the citizens of this backward land, by breeding and spreading unreasonable and unscientific thought."

"Among his other crimes," said Attila flatly. "But no one will stand against him with me anymore, even out of moral duty. And I do need an army, and so I *do* need righteous men for—"

"You can't have them from me," said the governor. "Not men of this government, anyway. Not sure what the Cardinal is capable of, but that is between you and him. For now, I just need to know that you will devote yourself to this cause, as it is, but no longer agitate the common folk with it."

"I can only do my best."

"You are determined to have your head removed in two hours time," he growled. "I can leave this chamber right now and it will be done. Not even the Cardinal can save you then. Former Low Constable, this is your only chance to save yourself."

To save this land, corrected Attila. Though he was sensible enough to say nothing and just nod.

"Yes," said the governor with a smirk. "I think you're getting it. You will use whatever means to bring this enemy of ours, this peace-disturber down, with the blessing of the Cardinal here. But you will do so within a framework of a rational explanation. This cannot be declared publicly as a fight against the forces of darkness, against an eastern superstition. That will not sit right with our king."

"Why do we care about what the king thinks?" asked Attila.

"Can we name our grand opponent in this game a 'witch'?" suggested the Cardinal.

"He is not a witch," said Attila.

"And that is too supernatural," said the governor. "I understand to suspect witches among us is reasonable. But such beings inflame the passions of the mob. Name one witch, and the people will find a hundred more within a week. And then we have a blood bath. And they begin to see monsters in every closet, and under every bridge. After what has happened in these mountains, with cities being crushed and the like, this populace needs to be brought back to reason and logic. It needs a return to order. The king must believe Germania is influencing the natives, and not the other way around."

"Can we call him a 'heretic'?" suggested the Cardinal.

"Count Tepsji," said Attila, pausing to let everyone know the name had been officially spoken aloud, "is not a heretic, either."

"That's not the point," said the Cardinal, exasperation seeping into his voice.

"And heresy implies religion," said the governor, tacking onto Attila's objection. "And religion is perhaps too sensitive a topic, as well, Cardinal?"

The Cardinal withdrew further into his robes.

"Well, he isn't a heretic," said Attila. "So there's no argument about it."

"Attila," said the governor, trying to sound patient. "The Cardinal assures me you have a way to conclude this problem of this ... this *man-you-have-named*. To an absolute end. Is that so?"

"Yes."

"Good. If you can do that, I will rehabilitate your good name in the community. And I will even consider going so far as to reinstate your position as low constable. But if you wish to see tomorrow's breakfast, you have to give me a rational and reasonable excuse for your mission; and for the prosecution, the persecution, and the execution of a noble citizen of Ardeel. One that does not involve even the hint of superstition or flummery; one that is down to earth and which I can credibly present to the people and to the king. Do you have such a reason?"

• • •

"You're very clever," said the Cardinal as he and Attila slipped away from the Tsobl jail, taking a back street. "I never would have thought of such a thing. With that mind of yours, I'm glad you're on my side."

Attila never knew how to take a compliment, so he just held onto his trembling left hand. He'd just escaped the executioner. Attila supposed he should be grateful to the Cardinal for having saved his life, besides paying him a compliment. He tried to formulate something in return that would please his savior.

"But bear in mind," the Cardinal said now, in a lower, more ominous voice, interrupting that thought. "I was the one who put the pressure on the governor in the first place. If it wasn't for me, you'd be dead." He cleared his throat and added, almost helplessly, with a faint smile, "You owe me."

· · ·

"I have been adding to my understanding of the creature," Attila informed the Cardinal a little later, as Tsobl and its jail disappeared behind them, and he relaxed into the carriage compartment's soft cushions. "When you told me your church's little secret, I theorized there may be other such secrets scattered throughout the mountains. I got hold of other towns' secret histories. You know, it's true that each of these books has its own insight into the character of Tepsji, and possible weaknesses that can be exploited."

"So that was why you were traveling in the south," surmised the Cardinal. "Research. Instead of working to capitalize on the useful information with which I'd already supplied you."

"More information is always better than less."

"I know you enjoy finding lines of evidence and information to exploit, but we only have so much time. We don't live forever."

"And I still need a force," said Attila. "I was also recruiting. Or was trying to."

"It must be a blessing, or a sign of some kind, that I found you in time," said the Cardinal, blandly. "I didn't know you had been captured, but I was riding south to see if I could find you."

"Oh, yes? Your travel wasn't just to stir the Ardeelian folk against the new Germanian churches?" said Attila, which drew a look from the Cardinal. He saw how the Cardinal was stroking his well-manicured beard in agitation. He noticed a couple grays in there. "Never mind. But we can both do two things at once. And sometimes more. Why did you want to find me, Cardinal?"

"You like *information*," he said, his words dripping with sarcasm. "Well, I have something quite perfect for you, that will help forward what you hope to achieve in your mission."

The Cardinal eyed Attila after he spoke, hopelessly looking for a degree of interest, of suspense, in the other.

"Go on," said Attila without expression.

"What better way to get the information you need against our common enemy, but to have a spy placed within his castle?"

"A spy inside the high castle? The one outside of Netz?"

The Cardinal nodded.

"That's very good news indeed," said Attila, dully. "Who is it?"

"You."

Attila stared. "How am I in the high castle?"

"Not yet. There is a Lady, perhaps even more than one, from the western kingdoms now residing there who is attached to our faith and requested one of our priests to conduct services. It is a service I have provided briefly, but one liked to be made permanent. A personal chapel within the castle has been created for such a purpose. I must attend to the St. Grigori, so I am tasked to appoint someone to see to their religious conduct. It can be anyone. It will be you."

"I think not," said Attila, shaking his head slightly. "I am not a priest."

"You don't have to be one, just pretend to be. Most do anyway. I will write the sermons. You deliver them. And then glean whatever insights you might like at your leisure. Whatever insights you might desire ... and in the company of a beautiful Lady or two."

"Ill advised. Marosh spent many hours with Count Tepsji, and Marosh knew about me; he almost killed me when we met. We can't know how much the Count has been informed about who I am, what I am about, and my purpose against him, you see? No, my presence in that castle won't be required until all is properly prepared. Prior to that time, it becomes a hazard to the whole scheme. Send someone else."

"Who?"

"Your lackey, the one who assists you in poisoning innocents: Rosczy. He's expendable."

"Father Rosczy is already there," admitted the Cardinal. "But your keen eyes would be preferable. I think you'd agree. You've something better to do, Bronk?"

"First of all: keep myself alive."

10

The Chaos, Part 1 (of 7):
The Invasion of Epris

Somewhere in the swirling chaos of the months following Amalina's return to the castle, Lady Princess Erin Epris—of France's Bourgogne region Eprises—had leaned in close to Amalina and absolutely demanded to know: "What do you *want*? I mean really, *really* want. I mean that is, what do *you* want for your *life*?"

Lady Erin Epris had thrown this at Amalina with a high, quavering tone of frustration. As if it were ridiculous for Amalina to think that she *could* want something for her life; had the right to insist and expect anything at all. Not that Amalina had said any such notion. Very few people at that time felt they had any claim to self-determination—it boiled down to certain men of power, and certain well-endowed species of animals, such as the complacent bear, the proud lion, the unstoppable elephant. And as the daughter of a baker, and later tangled up in the service of Count Tepsji, Amalina fit neatly into those who could not, and shouldn't ever, expect to breath that rare air of liberty.

But as a small irony, it was Lady Epris' question, that very question, delivered in extreme exasperation upon noticing in her friend, Katarina Tepsji, a disappointment at some thwarted expectation—as if any little disappointment over something *so minor* was not only selfish, and undeserving, it was contemptable in a Lady of High Station—that reawoke in Amalina the spark that she had experienced during her time in Paris: the idea that maybe she *could* have a say in things; that there was a chance she *might* be able to determine the course of her life.

Oh how she was hating herself for coming back to the castle. Brutalizing herself for returning to the Count, for chickening out on a chance at true freedom and happiness. Oh, what had she done? What could she do about it now?

"What do you *want*, Katarina?" asked Lady Princess Epris; so very to-the-point, but on some other subject.

Amalina could only stare with a guilty smile at this proper young woman of Bourgogne, and dare not speak what was parading in her mind.

. . .

When Amalina had been rested and ready, all those months ago upon her return, she had finally delivered to the Count her report on her western travels; with Genadie providing small, hand-drawn portraits as back-up evidence to a noble lady's physical charms. The annual process of luring young, titled women to the castle, the ones from Amalina's findings who the Count assessed to be the most suitable, desirable, and corruptible, began anew.

And in time the young Ladies of Title—like Lady Princess Erin Epris— began to arrive at the high castle. First one letter of acceptance to Katarina's invitation, and then another, and then another. Then a guest shows up at the gate, and then another, and then another; the appearances of notes and guests increasing and overlapping, and then, like the build up of drops preceding a rain, the deluge. The full festivities commenced.

There was no explanation for the success at convincing families to send their daughters to the castle of an unknown, inauspicious count of a far eastern country, other than what was experienced in a gold rush, on a different continent, some centuries later. Rumors were circulating in the royal courts about strange happenings to the east, and of an enigmatic aristocrat, a bachelor, who was wealthy beyond bounds. The way these rumors spread, and from multiple sources, it whirled their combined heads. And nobody wanted to be caught flat-footed when a vein of new riches had been identified and was yet unclaimed.

With each recounting of Count Tepsji's history in these foreign courts, the particulars became more fantastic. But any denial of them, made by reasonable people trying to convince the true believers otherwise—as they would say, "someone who knows the *real* story; and who knows *better*"— only confirmed that the full truth must be that much *more* incredible for the way these killjoys were desperately trying to cover it up.

With the rumors accepted, the convenient excuse for dispatching a daughter to the Count was the pleasantness and charm of that count's niece, Katarina Tepsji, who had stolen their daughter's heart. Their daughter now pleaded to visit Katarina as soon as possible, regardless of the time of year, circumstances of war, or danger in the crossing. It was an urgency unheard of, and was seemingly contagious to their parents, their circles of family, and any eager, softer-headed acquaintances.

The 'eastern stir' became popular enough that one shrewd entrepreneur and former adventurer, Gaddis Humphrey, had set up a profitable business of mercenaries escorting these young women safely from their hopeful homes into what was once known in the old language as *ultrasylvanum*, the "land behind the forest", or the "land inside the mountains"; an *otherland* nobody in the right mind would visit. To pump up his business, the shrewd

Gaddis Humphrey, with the aid of his connected and influential wife, Titra Salo-Humphrey, of the delicate waist and exquisite porcelain hands, also spread the dream of wealth among the minor nobility; inadvertently aiding in the success of Amalina's mission and contributing to the later influx of young Ladies of Title to the castle.

Some would arrive and turn right back around at the sight of the budding crowd. But more of their number inserted themselves into the roiling chaos with a renewed enthusiasm after boring weeks on the road.

Each new Lady was unique in her own way. And as was his way, the Count flitted through the visitors; after they were, of course, subjected to the mandatory quarantine in Netz village, where they and their people were relieved of anything that might offend his acute senses; and where Amalina would introduce them to his homemade medicine, disguised as honey-flavored candies, to neutralize the wilder nature of their bodies. Until:

. . .

"No need anymore," the Count told a surprised Amalina one day, when she asked after the candies for resupply, her stock having run out weeks ago. With an almost resigned shrug, but capped over with a game smile for her benefit, he carried on evenly: "I've quite given up on the whole thing. There are so many people in my castle now it is like a miniature city, no? With so many willful women—both the noble ladies and their maids—even if I could keep up with the required amount, it would prove impossible to enforce my preference that they eat it. You know how women are with their *willfulness*. Well … Anyway, when it was just you and Genadie alone here, the air was crisp and clean, my senses were heightened. Now every stench has a sibling, lost in the din of rose water, sweat, offal and common sewage. I'll just have to make do; and so you and they are now relieved from my candies."

"Oh, that's actually too bad, sir," said Amalina. "I kind of preferred them."

"Did you?"

"I never enjoyed the pain and the blood."

"I'll do you the favor then," he burbled merrily to Amalina, "if I have time. But understand, there are several ways to relieve a woman of the nuisance of menstruation, and they are thus: death; my candies; or, you know, my special *gift* that I can bestow. Perhaps you see the advantage in that last method, my gift, to at least *one* of the others, little one, if you think about it."

She didn't.

"Then tell me, just what *do* you want?" asked Lady Princess Erin Epris, presently.

Yes, thought Amalina, *what* do *I want?*

11

The Chaos, Part 2:
Halma's Curse and the Count's In-Yang

With the 'eastern stir'-mania in full swing in the west, and the many enablers acting as a conveyor belt, the Count's high castle had been transformed from an empty hulk to something like a popular university, or a wild, secular nunnery; the empty chambers crowded with raised and singing voices, twirling, supple arms; long, thickly piled hair; ballooning silk dresses walled off by brocade torsos of every size, and the air between filled in by competing perfumes. (Which made Amalina wonder again just how the Count *was* handling it all, considering he *had* resorted to poisoning his female guests with his homemade concoction of chemicals just to prevent their bodies from defiling his air with the *natural* stench of menstrual blood …)

The atmosphere in the castle had become electric.

Later, when Amalina tried to recall all the different Ladies of Title, these young noblewomen, in this time of the high castle's awakening, it was difficult to do so without the entire picture falling apart and mixing wildly; the many faces and the many experiences. She blamed Halma Inovala for the worst of the confusion.

Lady Inovala had asked Amalina to taste a small substance she'd smuggled into the castle which turned out to be a powerful intoxicant, that had then caused Amalina to lurch about, her heart beating wildly, and worry she was about to die, or lose her mind; or that she might stay this way forever, unable to focus, while understanding things in incredibly vivid detail but only to be distracted by another detail; like a magpie darting about a heap of treasure, each piece a bright shard of a broken glass to which it could not define the edges, the individual facets dovetailing incoherently into one solid, kaleidoscopic work …

· · ·

And so, like that experience, Amalina's memory of the past months were a confused synesthesia of the personality and the sensory. Much like when Lady Aria Ecci, who had been the first princess to flee the Count's court after the other year's disaster at Kyrgil Mountain, had told Amalina years before that, when Amalina was first introduced to her in Venice, that the sea was made of mountain water. She had explained how the rivers cascade down from the mountains in uncontrolled torrents, only to smooth out and join with the ocean. A pretty, calming idea to Amalina that had caused her to run and drink a handful of the Mediterranean—because a mountain river was so cold and delicious, of course—only to find herself choking on the sea's too-warm salt water.

"What an education you must have had," chided Aria Ecci at the time, with an amused smile. "A mountain education. I'm glad we could get you out of there."

And Amalina was still sick with the taste of salt when Princess Ecci later showed her the small octopus stuck to a stick. She was told the creature with the eerily intelligent eyes could change color at will. And with its stretching, grasping, seeking, undulating skin, which seemed to also choose its own texture, she was reminded later of the way the Count and the Strange Man had the ability to change their shape and color to mimic almost anything, and even alter their size to that of a mountain. So now when she thought of the Count, because she so associated his being with that of the shivering, slimy creature from the sea, she also experienced the unpleasant taste of salt water.

The Count was, through this association, a great inland manifestation of that octopus; haunted in his manly form with the earthy smell of roots and herbs and rodenty fur (though she tasted the salt water keenly on top of that anyway). And she saw in him the octopus' smooth and deliberate movement and ever shifting shape, so that he was more unpredictable than ever. And her revulsion at his inhuman nature did not go unnoticed by Count Tepsji, who asked her: "Why don't you touch me anymore, Ms. Dalca?"

• • •

"Why don't you touch me anymore, Ms. Dalca?"

"I touch you," answered Amalina, feeling uncomfortable, trying not to squirm.

"You haven't since you've returned. Not once. I noticed."

"I don't think so. There's nothing different."

"You were always a touchy person."

"I'm not touchy."

"Genadie, hasn't Ms. Dalca been a frequent and unhindered toucher?"

"Oh, yes, Master."

Amalina sneered discreetly at Genadie.

"And how often have I touched you?" she asked him.

"Touch me," said the Count, in an off hand, amused tone. "Come here and touch me."

"Why?"

"Please don't be upset with her, Master."

"Quiet. I'm not upset. Why would I be? Here, my little mouse, come by my side and touch me. Touch me, won't you, as you did once before?"

"But why? There isn't a reason."

"I just want to know things haven't changed too much between us."

"Well, nothing's changed, sir."

"Come touch me."

Amalina cleared her throat and looked uncomfortable.

"It isn't because you think these aren't my real clothes, is it? I know that 'man-who-will-not-be-named-any-longer'—" he was speaking of the Strange Man "—*certain persons*, let's say, bragged how, since he could transform himself into anything, he made great use of the ability; becoming anyone he liked, and even fashioned clothes out of his own flesh."

She blushed.

"I think that worry has caused a reluctance to come near me. Yes? An aversion to my being?"

"Oh, no, Master," said Genadie. "She wouldn't think such things of you."

"Let her answer for herself. But, understand, my little mouse, I would never resort to tricks like that pitiful dwarf did. However, I thought we had agreed to forget about him. Forget *all* about him."

Amalina stepped over to the Count, and with a gulp, laid her hand on his shirt-sleeved forearm in a reassuring way. The sleeve felt like rough and real cotton thread.

"I'm not much of a child anymore," she explained, in order to convince him that she wasn't disgusted by the thought of touching him. "I no longer seek reassurance, or cling to people like babies do. Do you understand?"

"Well, that's a pity," said the Count. But then he began to rhapsodize to Amalina in that quiet moment, with her hand petrifying on his arm. "Do you remember how wonderfully peaceful this castle was when it was just you and I living here?"

"Genadie was here, too," said Amalina. She also remembered the backbreaking labor of the many chores falling to them, and the solitude that nearly drove her mad.

"But I suppose by that look," said the Count, "that you would have grown a little lonely without company. Which is why this selection, this vast menagerie of ladies, is here, is it not?"

Is it? Amalina wondered. *Aren't they here for you—?*

"However, it pleases me that you were thinking after me and my comfort, Ms. Dalca."

Was I?

"But, let me call you Amalina," he breathed amorously. "Yes. *Yesss*. Let me call you familiarly, Amalina, my dear. I assure you I have been thinking of nobody else but you for the longest time; since you've been away. Not one of them is like you, or can distinguish herself enough to compare to you ..."

. . .

But even worse, this amorousness grew unbridled as the time went on. When the Count would find times to steal away to her, or she accidentally stumbled onto him in a private moment, and he would breath huskily at her.

"There is a belief in the Orient, my little mouse; far off in the land of the Khans." He added the last part needlessly, which told Amalina he was winding up for a long explanation. "Their philosophy is represented by a circle—*Taijitu*—the summation of life—with one half of this divine disc white and one half black. And these sides push into each other because each contains the opposite of the other. Light/dark, good/evil. *In-Yang*. Are you paying attention? Each tries to conquer the other, to fill the other. They never will, they never can. But where they meet, this struggle powers one against the other. And so you take my meaning. As I have just said, you are my opposite. Do you know how?"

"Because I'm a young woman and you're an old man?" she guessed. But she thought: *Or because I am good and you are evil?*

As if reading her mind, he said with a self-forgiving slant and an encouraging tone: "I am the world's incarnation of power, though some may deem it, quite uncharitably, as 'evil'. I am power and what comes with it. And you, you are the perfect representation of purity and innocence. I am certain of it now, Amalina. It must be true. As I originated from kings and queens and their will to slaughter, and have ascended from that unbroken line to the peak of all that might mean, into a race unto my own, you descend through a line of uninterrupted innocence, from the beginning of our— your—race; unsullied by spilled blood from the time of Eden. A *blood innocent*. Ours is a pairing beyond contrast, the meeting of the mightiest of the two poles of existence. The Lion and the Lamb."

Amalina worried her jaw was hanging open. She ground her teeth to keep it shut.

"A perfect union. Yes. *Yesssssss*. It can only be. It was meant to be. Why else would I have caught you hanging out of your window that night, just at that very moment? And not only did I not kill you, but I found a use for you. Many uses. Because you are so wonderfully capable, Amalina. Oh, how I adore you."

"But if you change me ... " she said. "You know, you don't need to change me though, to have all that."

"It won't be a change of your spirit," he enthused. "Just your body. To a thing of permanence. But you're afraid, that is all. It is natural. Would I have been afraid of the change if I had been made aware of it beforehand and been given a choice? Yes. But I would have regretted every day after, if I *hadn't* transformed to what I am now, I swear to you. Nothing will change in you, but your impermanence."

"Uh, well, sir, that isn't exactly why I came in here, just now ..."

• • •

"What *do* you want?" asked Lady Princess Erin Epris.

I want to get away from Him, thought Amalina.

12

The Chaos, Part 3:
Sock Personalities: Inovala, Hachter-Friecke and La Nevers

While the kaleidoscope effect on Amalina's memory of her noble guests, which was the result of Lady Halma Inovala's stunt of drugging her unawares, had momentarily reminded Amalina of Lady Aria Ecci, Halma Inovala was more personally like the mad, life clutching Lady Gillette Arronde, from the other year, who'd dared everything, tried everything, and gone to bed with General Zsolt Marosh. But Marosh was dead and Lady Arronde was back home suffering shame at having blown her chance with Count Tepsji. And now Inovala was here to provide her service as the provacateur.

Just as Lady Jean Hachter-Friecke was, it seemed, in her uncomfortable shyness and timidity, now here to replace Lady Ragonde la Basca, who had been as much of a suspicious, lonely soul, but who was now dead, of course; the first royal guest to die in the castle for having figured out there was something wrong, something supernaturally wrong with their host, and had tried to escape to spread the truth to the outer world.

Lady Jean Hachter-Friecke was not as quick as Lady la Basca to pick up on the danger, a delay which spared her life. But once inside the castle, she had distinguished herself and her peculiarity of shyness by deferring all her respect to her maid, Gemna, who maneuvered her charge around the room like a frustrated mother duck trying to thrust her duckling out of the nest. And after a while, Hachter-Friecke began to transfer that neediness to Amalina, who her Gemna encouraged to do so.

"Well, I love her, I suppose," Lady Hachter-Friecke had said fondly of her Gemna, in a retiring voice, her chin disappearing into her chest; while the Lady herself seemed to disappear into the sofa cushions. "Because of my father, you see. When he gets angry he pulls at his temples, and swears at me, and I would think, 'Oh, no, what have I done now?' But Gemna would just tell me, without my saying what I was thinking, but as if she were reading my mind, 'You should not bother yourself about his tempers, milady Jean. No, not at all. But only say to yourself, when he acts a tyrant, not what fault *you* have, but instead: *Well, what's the matter with* him?' That won her to me, and why I won't do without little old Gemna, ever. You, Katarina, I think, seem to be about as fearless around your uncle as she is my father."

Hachter-Friecke hadn't been so ridiculously shy at home, but a clever, talented sort, or she would never have been considered for an invitation. But then, at the time, she had been in her element and her father not in sight.

At some point, Amalina came to realize that some things in life you can only appreciate by their repetition. The way so many of these new ladies fit directly into the dresses of the ones who'd come before, Amalina no longer resented the strange changes in her friends' personalities when they happened; like in Lady Jean Hachter-Friecke's case. Where Amalina had first thought the alteration in a Lady's character when they came to the castle was a strange phenomenon, it seemed now more a natural event. The ladies on their own and in their own home environment acted one way. But once they entered the cauldron of the castle, and were put into a race against the others, each one had to differentiate herself; and just as a single ray of light sent through a prism breaks down into specific and defined striations of color, so must the ladies find their color to make themselves known—or they will become indistinguishable, or buckle.

Though the Count had told Amalina he wanted in his wives a blonde, a brunette, a red head, a moor, a woman of olive skin, a lady of cinnamon, a lady of sunglower, a plain one, a pretty one, a fair one, a freckled one, one that was scentless and one that was tangy, a tall one, a short one, a petite and a plump one, what he would receive at his castle was in personality: the bold and the timid, the pious and the profane, the learned and the ignorant, a brave one, a smart one, a brash one, an innocent one, a loyal one, a treacherous one, and more and more and everything in between. His guests vied for the persona they most preferred, but ultimately chose the one most suited to them in the spectrum. Yet all those roles were of a type.

· · ·

Lady Greta La Nevers, the frisky Nordic girl who was a true princess, daughter to a crowned king (a king who had run out of money, it seemed), with her muscular frame and blond locks, was physically opposite to the slim and sable-haired Lady Aria Ecci, but by the way she gave excited encouragement to Aklan running naked—and with bold shouts—through one of their parties, she was an exact match to Ecci's dark and devout carnality.

"Aklan get some clothes on!" shouted Amalina.

"Oh, he isn't hurting anyone," tittered Greta with a mischievous grin. "Look at your little cherub now!"

The ladies had taken to calling Aklan a cherub, or 'Katarina's angel'. He took no offense by it because it meant they found him pretty, after all, and it allowed him to hover around these beauties in the corners of any interesting scene. But now he'd gone mad!

Amalina seized the 'cherub' roughly and wrestled him into a side room as the ladies were throwing pillows and bread rolls at him.

He spit something into his palm and held the little broken pieces of the magic bone out for her to see.

"I put the bone back together and I thought I'd got it working," he said.

"Well it's not!" hissed Amalina. "And you think you'd come in here and pester us if you had? You're ridiculous!"

"You're still mad at me, Pretty Princess?"

"I am still mad," she said. "How can I ever forget what you did? Haven't I told you that enough already? Its magic is gone, it's broken to nothing, and you're responsible. Just throw that useless thing away before it makes me madder."

"Please, we've been through quite a lot, Pretty Princess, haven't we? And I *am* trying to fix it. When will you forgive me?"

Amalina dragged Aklan out out of the room to stifled and embarrassed laughs.

Greta saw him off with pinches at his bottom and thighs and a lingering look, just as Aria Ecci would have.

At Amalina's discovery of these character archetypes, which the castle mob imposed on the individual, she idly wondered what the chemical result would have been if Aria Ecci had never left the castle but Greta La Nevers had arrived. Which one would have been shoved off the branch belonging to the shocking sensualist, and what alternate stocking-personality would the other have, by necessity, slipped into?

There could only ever be one name to a given role.

• • •

But what role did Amalina have? She obviously wasn't herself. Or was she? She thought dizzily: *or am I something even further different that what I already wasn't?*

Dizzy indeed.

It was perplexing, but Amalina decided she played the part of the outside-insider. The one who belonged to the Count and the high castle and who had to be both clung to by the ladies to curry favor with the uncle, and to be suspicious of and to resent if he wasn't paying enough attention to them; as if she were in charge of the whole proceedings and such things.

"What do you want?" asked Lady Epris.

I want to become the person I am meant to be! thought Amalina. *To no longer be stuck in an artificial role!*

The Chaos, Part 4:
The Knowledge and Adventure of de Roye

Lady Genevieve de Roye took the place of Lady Isabeau DePense as the resident know-it-all. But this frizzy-haired version, with the owl eyes, was much better informed than the previous model. In Paris she had introduced Amalina to poetry, and even some translations of an English genius who she claimed was the greatest playwright. "French, well, all the romance languages," de Roye had opined, "are melodic in their way and beautiful and pleasant to listen to. English, by contrast, is a wonder *to experience*." De Roye's insight and excitable erudition was infectious instead of annoying, and she had managed to sell to Amalina the romance of learning the English language into the idea of emigrating to that mysterious island of lovers and warriors, which owned the most masculine, hairy, hardy folk, and to take to the stage there as an actress—until Amalina recalled the fate of Katrina Flauna, the extraordinary actress whose real-life role Amalina had been fitted into after the Count had killed her for her treachery. *Well then, maybe not that*, thought Amalina.

Lady Genevieve de Roye had arrived at the castle championing the greater romantic notion of England (despite her French ancestry, perhaps because she was a wildly curious intellectual traveler, or perhaps secretly an anti-Catholic Huguenot sympathizer!), and celebrating that brash island country's new exploits on the American continent, spurred by a friend de Roye had made from its colonies. While she seemed mostly to talk about shipping off to the wilderness of this new world some day, the Americas, her vivid descriptions and detail of any land beyond the shores of this continent only caused Amalina further hunger for the new, and a yearning to devour.

"What do you want?" said Lady Erin Epris.

I want to learn everything there is to learn in the world! I want to read everything ever written and know everything there is ever to be known! I want to explore!

The Chaos, Part 5:
Power Queen: Brignol

This longing for freedom was only exascerbated further by tales from another Anglophile, Lady Anne Brignol, who was as proud as Lady Margeta la Brichese was when she'd first arrived, and who regaled Amalina with tales of the mighty Elizabeth, Queen of England, her hero; a formidable woman who had taken the reins of power and ruled like no monarch before her—even besting King Arthur.

Lady Anne Brignol declared at one point: "As I wish to do it—and I will, because it is in my blood, my family's circumstances be damned—the world can be mine and will be mine. I know I am meant to do something incredible. You can be a champion, too, Katarina, you know. You can do something incredible and change the world. Differently and in your own way. I see it in you."

"What do you see?"

"You've got survivor kind of energy." Lady Brignol pronounced this with admiration and enthusiasm, so that it felt like a pep talk. "It's remarkable! When every one of us is about to keel over in exhaustion, you can just suck yourself up, square your hips and move on as if you've just woken up."

Instead of being pepped by this flattery, Amalina grew self-conscious and assumed her observed 'remarkable energy' might be because she had grown up with a baker's taxing schedule, of early morning-to-evening labors. But that had been long ago, and even if it were true, she couldn't admit to anything like that to her Lady friend. "What are you talking about?"

"You see, even now, you just did it. It's like you have someone else inside you. Two spirits' worth of energy. Oh, the one you show us is very nice and pleasant and functions very well. But when the need arises, you slap that one away somewhere inside you, done with it. A new, hard look comes into your eyes, and suddenly you are completely no-nonsense, with the unflagging movement of a waterwheel."

"That's not true," said Amalina trying to sound dismissive, terrified how this young woman could peer right through her and see something she'd never noticed, or considered, in herself.

"I wouldn't have said it if it wasn't true," said Anne Brignol without offense.

"Well, I don't see it that way."

"But it's not yours to see. *I'm* telling *you*. Don't worry, I'm not saying it to hurt you. That kind of thing will get you places. Understand that you are very different, and I like that. We're both rather different than the rest, if you think about it. I'm very tall, you know. But I also mean in other ways. Internally. We different women here need to stick together, you know. The others are so common, and unremarkable in a way, if you think about that, too. The superior ones, like you, me, and of course your uncle, need to keep close, so that we don't lose ourselves and can make our marks in the world. Of course, I could never lose my long legs. I might still be growing! But you understand what I mean."

The dominating giantess was a keen observer from her height. Always spotting little details with her eagle eyes, and announcing her findings from the roof of her watchtower, immune to return fire. A foil to Genevieve de Roye and that know-it-all Lady's opinions on everything under the sun.

"Who do you like best?" was a common refrain when Anne got Amalina alone. "I didn't really like the de Roye today. Her personality is a bit punishing when she's allowed to talk too long. Maybe she's trying to cover a deficiency with her bluster. Not like Inovala, who is a bit of clutz and mindless, and will probably get herself killed by innocently walking into danger. At least she doesn't try too hard, and because of that she's *interesting*. But that de Roye! Oh, but *we* should stick together against her, shouldn't we?"

Amalina was already in love with the story of Lady Anne Brignol's Elizabeth Tudor, Queen of England, who warred against the Emperor of Spain and sunk his Armada with her fleets, but Lady Anne Brignol was a battering ram of personality, trying to live it out, which was also impressive.

"What do you want?" said Erin Epris.

I want to be as assertive and fearless as a true Queen in the world, a free spirit taking only what I want, brushing aside all enemies without losing a hair from my cap! thought Amalina.

15

The Chaos, Part 6:
Hot Love: Montraine

Lady Claire Montraine was like Lady Spaarvierlet, with her ethereal beauty and swept by romance. By how delicate her features were, she impressed upon everyone just how exquisite she wanted her lover to be. She spoke of which parts should be shaped like a chisel, and which like a rock.

The Count appeared to oblige, in his oily, unctuous, accommodating way, subtly shifting his body to more reflect her ideal. To the point Amalina sensed he was somehow coming apart with the constant push and pull of his many visitors. Even some ladies giggled and remarked that he seemed to be losing his definition when he stood before a looking glass. Amalina imagined he was being boiled apart in this tumultuous vat of women.

But Lady Montraine's description of her imaginary lover was not unlike the features of Lt. Ivanti Ion Vokent. And Montraine's verbalized fantasies of her nights together with this man were so captivating Amalina could not help forgive the man she had abandoned thousands of miles away.

• • • •

In the middle of these passionate longings, Amalina was thrown from her heights of reverie by the sight of the rickety cart in the courtyard, and the squat man with the large black hat as he hooked another birdcage onto it. Amalina now recalled another of the castle's hidden horrors: the ugly little wrinkled green man behind the Count's murder service. The one who owns the greasy pigeons and on whose cart she'd tried to escape once while he drove off, unaware she was invisible and sitting on the cart's gate. She saw him now, remembered him and shivered. She could still hear his high, shrill, mocking voice singing as he drove the cart, confident he was alone and no one would hear: *'One white leg, fat and fancy, one fat arm, that is my doll, one breast, two breast, plump and pert. All apart … then into the dirt …'*

He was here and it was all still happening, this murder service, with his ugly little messages printed in unsettling, coded block letters, written on squares and rectangles of rough pigskin and goatskin, with hairs still attached, which the Count lovingly preserved in that book with the giant metal letters on the cover: AXP. How many of those messages bore the drawn likenesses of poor young women, like Lucinda Skeldar, who were marked for death by the Count, at the say-so of this AXP monster, and the Count obeyed?

To be thinking of Ion, and then be confronted by this disgusting fiend, it was too much. And when she saw the ugly green man notice her, she fled into the main building. But it was as if, now that he saw her, he decided to pursue her. Like she was a fox who'd broken cover but ran into the local, most familiar game reserve. He entered *l'entrée grande* with a nasty grin cut into his face, and a strange, backward tilted strut, that showed a confidence like no other, as if he owned the place even more so than the Count. And as Amalina bolted up the stairs to get away from him, she heard him whistling that awful tune. It followed her, stalking her.

She ducked into an empty room and waited for him to pass by, but then thought she had only to get to her room on the other side of the castle and she would be safe. Or at least Aklan, or one of the guards, could be called to protect her.

When she darted from the room, and shot around a corner at full speed, he was there at the end of the next, marching right towards her, grin still in place.

"Niece to the Count, if I am not mistaken," he said in his high, womanly voice. His head was not turned directly at her, but he stared at her from the corner of the evil slits of his eyes. "Fantastic to see you again, milady."

He dropped to his knee in front of her, head bowed and large hat swiped off his greasy head, in a grandiose display of respect, or romantic chivalry. Out of reflex she put her hand in his as she would have in any royal court. But she gasped at having done so so automatically. And as he darted his head forward to kiss it, his long nose brushing the side of her hand and his dry lips pressing to her wrist, his black glove squeezed tight to her fingers. She pulled her hand, but it stayed caught in his.

"Ohhh," he sighed, apparently staring at her wrist as he held it. "Never tasted a hand so sweet. And look at that arm. So warm, and nothing like your uncle's. So alive ..."

"What are you doing here?" said Amalina.

"Come to fetch my pigeons, milady. You remember me, don't you? We've met before."

"I mean inside the castle."

"Came to find some relief before I left, milady. A long road home."

"However, I meant upstairs. Why are you up *here*? These are the ladies' quarters."

"My pardon," said the ugly green man. She saw his wrinkles, all the lines networking his face, flex unnaturally as he gave her a smile, still regarding her from the corner of his eye. "But I must have gotten turned around. Glad to have seen you again."

"Can you release my hand?" she asked.

His grip tightened on her fingers. They began to hurt.

"Do you want me to, milady? Just ask it of me."

"Let go and leave me alone."

"But that's no way to ask a gentleman for anything, and no way to speak to me."

"I'll speak to you as I like," snarled Amalina. "I'm the count's niece, and the mistress of this castle."

"Oh ho," said the man, still smiling. He stood now, but his head was below her height. It didn't seem to bother him. He grinned wider. "So I know, so I know. The count's flesh-and-blood niece. And so be it. A girl with a temper doesn't turn me off."

"You need to get away from me and leave me alone. My uncle won't like what you're doing; bothering me."

The ugly man tottered his head back and forth, but squeezed her hand harder. "I don't think he has much say, when it comes to true love, enh?"

His high-pitched laugh made her cry out. She began pulling her arm, and slapping his hand, and kicking at his shins. This caused him to laugh more, but it didn't free her.

"Please, *ma jolie*. Do not resist cupid's arrow."

"Love? Are you insane? You know what he could do to you if I just ask! Let go of me!"

"You don't know who I am, milady, or you wouldn't speak to me this way. Is it my face that throws you off? But it is only nature—"

"I know exactly who you are," growled Amalina. "And you are evil, through-and-through. Don't think you can pretend. I know what you get up to with my uncle and all those poor girls. Let go—!"

The black glove opened and Amalina fell backward and sprawled out onto the floor.

"What did you say, girl?" he wasn't smiling. He held up a warning, black-gloved finger. "I won't put up with any slander. Ignorant slander."

"'One white leg, fat and fancy …'" said Amalina, glaring at him.

"I don't know what you're talking about. Are you playing a game with me?"

"AXP?"

"Feather and claw!" He slammed his long-brimmed hat down on his head, then glared out from under it. "You'll shut that mouth of yours. You've no idea what you are saying, and it won't come to any good if you think it will. Where have you heard such things, such nonsense? It doesn't bear repeating."

"I know more than you think." Then she repeated: "*A-X-P.*"

His hands clutched themselves as if they were wrestling before his wide body. It sounded like he was laughing or choking deep in his throat.

"Don't you play with me, girl ..." he cautioned with deadly firmness, "you're playing with fire."

"Go now, take your birds," commanded Amalina. "If you don't leave me alone, if I ever see you again, I'll see to it you're punished, and punished good."

"Look at those eyes," said the man, backing away, but smiling again. "If you were Medusa I would be stone. But you aren't. And I wonder, will those eyes see what is coming? Keep that mouth of yours shut ... *mon amour.*"

And Amalina would keep her mouth shut about his visit, and try to put it out of her head along with all the other horrible unspoken secrets of this Palace of Pleasures: the slaughters that have taken place, the Count's bloody proclivities, the murder service, the wretched undying woman still trapped on a spinning wheel below the dungeons of the castle, and her guilt in any of it where it applied. But the ugly man's hold on her hand, her inability to fend off him and his bulk, as if he were an erect pool of tar in boots and hat, replayed in her mind. And she imagined herself punching him and scratching at his wrinkled face; and she would scream for help, but Aklan and Pils and Anka could do nothing to free her from him, and the Count would stand there and laugh.

But because the fond memories of Lt. Ivanti Ion Vokent lingered in the air, and perhaps a forgotten corner in Amalina's head recalled Guwerte's friend's story of the lover come to rescue the woman from the beast, in her mind Ion was the only one who could strike the ugly green man down and save her. She replayed this image repeatedly, the ugly green man breaking apart as if made of pottery under Ion's blows, and fell more and more in love with him. Amalina was more enraptured with Lt. Vokent than Lady Claire Montraine could ever be with her imaginary prince.

"What do you want?" asked Lady Epris.

I want my lover, Ion—Lt. Ivanti Ion Vokent—*to return to me!* thought Amalina. *To rescue me from this foresaken castle!*

16

The Chaos, Part 7:
Pattipo and the True Meaning of a Friend

Lady Elisavet Pattipo was much like Lady Robine Beaujeulle; who was also dead, of course, the first guest to die in the Count's quest to fashion a woman into an eternal companion. The Count's failed first attempt …

Lady Pattipo resembled Robine in how wrapped up she was in Amalina. Pattipo wore a cameo necklace with Amalina's likeness on it, and presented upon her arrival a pearl box stuffed with Amalina's letters—all but a few of them, though unknown to her, actually forged by the Count. Because Amalina could not produce the same collection of Elisavet Pattipo's personal letters, or the matching cameo necklace with Elisavet's image on it which she had sent, the fragile dear was wracked in tears for a little while.

At the time, Amalina had run to ask the Count if he had preserved the cameo or any of Lady Pattipo's correspondence, as he did, meticulously so, with all his own personal posts. But he had lost Elisavet's somewhere. He promised to dig them out. He then remembered that Amalina had received some private letters while she was away and delivered those to her immediately from a side drawer in his desk.

Amalina had hoped they were from her father. But they were from her old friend Cristine, addressed 'to Ms. Dalca, formerly of Korr, at the High Castle of Netz, via Katarina Tepsji,' as Amalina had instructed her to do before leaving Ardeel on her latest mission; though Cristine had added after a dash and in brackets at the bottom: '—[Countess?]'.

"I am crying and tearing my room apart," Cristine wrote. "I am not able to meet you in Paris as I'd thought. I don't know if you heard about the eruption in Kyrgil and what happened in the mountains. But after that, Papa said it isn't safe and won't let me out of his sight. No travel. Was the eruption the danger you warned me about? It sounds horrible but it didn't reach us. Didn't even feel a shake. All it did was lock me down here in Korr!"

There were maybe fifty letters. Amalina opened them one by one and read. Cristine shared her excitement about how she'd grown taller. Gave the gory details of fights with Bossy Bessa, the wicked captain of the gang of bad girls who were eternally picking on her, the pretty little rich girl. Then in another letter came the announcement of Bossy Bessa's disappearance— which was entirely expected, as the bad girls of Korr often became victims of the Count, explained away by the townspeople as an attack by wolves. Considering how Cristine would flog the memory of previous girls who had victimized her, even while their mangled bodies were still warm, she dispatched Bessa's vanishing—her presumed death—a little dispassionately. But maybe, like Amalina, Cristine was getting older and maturing. Now that she was much taller than before she was handling the rest of the gang, and bragged about giving them a taste of their own medicine.

Then her friend moved on to sunnier things. She recalled their childhood relationship, and how she missed Amalina. She was so lonely sometimes, she couldn't wait until they met again. And she asked, and then implored as time went on, if Amalina could not reply to her letters, to get herself away to Korr sometimes; or whether Cristine might come to the castle to visit her.

Her friendship and longing was touching, but it made Amalina feel slightly ashamed. She had not thought of Cristine in a while, and instead of thrilling to the voice of her old best friend, Amalina began to feel that awful, guilty throb she did not care to think about: the emotional distance from her home and homeland.

· · ·

This feeling had been so intense, she remembered, when she and Genadie were returning to Ardeel this time. Amalina had asked him to take the highway that led through Korr, thinking she would stop and visit her father (and maybe Cristine). But as they passed through the village, it was a late hour of the night. Seeing the village all shuttered up, Amalina didn't recognize it as her home. Not even a little.

Home to Amalina was now city streets lined with shops open late, and with people of all kinds wandering in each other's arms, talking, laughing, singing, kissing sometimes. The colors, the pageantry, the cheer, the teeming life.

This awful feeling of remove must have been what Ivanti had felt on his first return to Korr, after so long away from it. It looked shrunken and miserable and old and sunk within its own parochial, uninteresting preoccupations, bound by pointless customs, bothered by superstitions that clung on only here within the mountains (this included the Count, of course). It, and they, seemed so trivial and divorced from *real* life.

These sad thoughts of alienation wrapped around to envelope her own father, her cousin, Jenna, her best friend, Cristine, and the many people she used to consider as her extended family. Feeling as ashamed as it should make her, Korr was no longer her home. That night, as Amalina passed through her old hometown, she knew it as a cold fact: the quaint little village was now someone else's dog.

To soothe this miserable feeling, Amalina told herself that it wasn't the place that mattered but the people in it. Certainly she still loved her father and Cristine. They could be set down anywhere in the world, it was the bond of affection that held them close. So it had been with her love for Ion, shifted all the way to Paris.

And she remembered: it was only her continuing service to the Count that kept her family, the people who truly mattered to her, safe from his wrath. She was keeping them alive! That was what she was doing in this castle, by playing this silly role. It was her duty and responsibility, and it was an honor to make such a sacrifice. This warmer feeling of solidarity and rightness extended even to Pia Lampeda, who Amalina had seen only once since returning, on the very night she'd arrived at the castle, and never again; and who Amalina still had not bothered to send a note to in the time afterward, as Margeta boasted she herself had.

"What do you want?" asked Lady Erin Epris.

I want to be strong and do my proper duty as a good daughter, friend, and a righteous and responsible person in this world!

17

The End of Chaos

No new arrival could replace Princess Margeta la Brichese as she was now; who, to make room for others, had elevated herself above mere extreme personal pride and sat as a rock of the Holy Roman Empire within the castle and refused to budge. From her high ground she launched her missiles of scorn and poured her judgement down like buckets of boiling oil on the morally questionable, if only to brush them back from her territory.

With Amalina, Margeta was forced to be civil, and used their interactions to point out everyone's failings besides her own. More often though, she would ask after Pia Lampeda, but in strange ways. "Has she eaten yet, do you know?" "I think I should be very hungry if I were her by now." "Do you *know* if she is well? Have you spoken to her? " "Find out if she has eaten."

How was *Pia faring these days?* Amalina shied away from asking the Count. She feared what he might tell her, and she was still trying to avoid him and his sentimental looks. No, the only clue to Pia's health came from Lady Lampeda's bitter rival, Margeta.

"Well? has she eaten yet?" asked Margeta with a sneer, on some day. "You *do* care about her, don't you, Princess Tepsji? Have you heard nothing? Have you asked after her not at all? Are you hiding from her?"

"No," said Amalina. "It's just there are so many here …"

"It hasn't always been that way," scowled Margeta, pulling at her prayer beads so that they clacked loudly. "And there is always time for something you *want* to do, if you really want to do it. But the same could be said of Princess Lampeda. Why doesn't she send you a note? Or one to me? What is she hiding? *Why* is she hiding?"

"I don't think she's hiding," said Amalina, feeling immediately defensive for Pia. She had briefly visited Amalina on her first night back, after all. Though she had gone to ground afterward.

"If you have any care for your friend, Princess Katarina, you will join me in the chapel for prayers tonight on her behalf."

…

At Margeta's request, the Count had permitted a small church to be contructed in an unused room inside the castle. Though stripped of most of its religious implements, it was as serious a place of worship as Margeta's personal living quarters. And no matter what faith or denomination a lady held, Orthodox to heretical, Margeta would get them all in there for services, or make them feel hellbound for having missed. Some would wait until the Catholic service, led by the local Cardinal's acolyte, Father Rosczy, was over before quietly having their own Protestant one. Some would choose either service, whichever one their better friend was attending, and pray in their own way. Amazingly, even the Count attended a few sessions, but it didn't seem it was for Margeta's benefit.

"You did this to endear yourself to me, sir?" asked Amalina on a hunch.

"I am seeing to the comfort of my more permanent guests," he said, his lids lowered heavily over his over-size brown eyes. "If you like it, suit yourself."

"Or are you trying to convert yourself back to the religion in which you once believed?"

"Every once in a while I go a little mad," he admitted. "But then I think, why would I bind myself to the arbitrary will and prejudice of my prey? Though, I suppose some of you are no longer prey. Or no longer will be such. But those human interests of theirs deserve renewed respect, however immaterial or fleeting in the long run. It will be interesting for me to see, later, how you view such things as these religious services." Then he repeated, with extra meaning: "*In the long run.*"

"Genadie, we should find a way to leave," she told her old friend, overcome with loathing for the Count again, and worrying that she might not survive much longer.

. . .

"Genadie, listen," she insisted, "I'm serious. We really need to leave."

The grizzled rat scowled and waved a hand at her, then checked the air to see if the Count was hanging off the walls or the ceiling to spy on them. He had been growing so fearful—what, in the modern day, would be called rampant paranoia—because he knew well the creatures' ability to transform into anything, mimic any living person, so that he now feared that anyone in the castle, even one of the Ladies, even Amalina herself, might be the Count testing him and his loyalty. This made him shy away from roaming the castle halls and keep to his little hovel in back.

"Don't worry about him, he's gone again," said Amalina. She was referring to how the Count had recently been disappearing for long stretches without warning. "Worry about yourself, eh? Did you feel the quake the other day? Didn't it feel like what happened at Kyrgil? When the mountain broke? Why, this mountain might collapse at any minute!"

"Olympus never falls from the sky," said Genadie.

"Why are you still going on like that? You're acting like he's your god again and this is Olympus, when you know he isn't and this castle isn't."

"We *are* here all over again, aren't we?" he said, sounding defeated. "We *are* here. All over again."

"But you know he isn't Zeus anymore. I mean, you killed one of their kind yourself, didn't you?"

"Master killed him. I just set the fire to put the smoke into the castle."

"You cut his head off."

"We aren't to talk of such things."

"I'm just saying that you know he's no god. And if you don't like being here anymore—well, you know how I feel about it. Wouldn't you like to be back in France? In Paris? You could visit your artist friends every day for the rest of your life, and drink hot chocolate by the barrel. Now think about *that*. We should find ourselves a way to escape—"

Genadie waved his hand more violently this time, putting an end to the conversation. Which left her alone. Or it left Amalina to the women, anyway.

. . .

They, the women, *had* begun to all look the same in the midnight gloom of the hallways, Amalina thought. How a stack of hair sat—or reached the ceiling, or billowed out toward the walls, or was shaded—or the size and the height of a certain pair of breasts, the wideness or slenderness to the hips, the angle of the posture, the elegantly gliding gait or childish mincing step, were sometimes the key to differentiation. Anne Brignol had the long legs, which was easy enough. More often, though, it was too close to tell. Just how many names and faces could Amalina possibly know and make friends with? She began to feel the storehouse in her head was only so large and the memories of some were starting to hang out the window because of the crush inside. But maybe it was because of how tired she was beginning to feel. The exhaustion.

Part of Amalina's exhaustion was due to the continued nightly visits of Lucinda Skeldar demanding Amalina kill those responsible for her death. And more so: Amalina was experiencing the fullest effect of the chaos' tumbling Kaleidoscope effect, and realizing it for what it was, and that even if the Count didn't somehow cajole her into doing as he pleased, consenting to be transformed, she might lose her mind. The real-life shapes were shifting through each other and her memories, even in her waking mind. So that Amalina would be looking at her friends' smiling faces in the courtyard, and see over their shoulders Commander Kralov, just where he'd been a couple years earlier, with his scowling, level look of accusation at her as he and his men were being burned to death. Or over there, there were the poor soldiers of Marosh's army, of the following year, having their faces scarred with acid—*"My dear, Katty, what's wrong? What's come over you? Do you need to sit down?"* Amalina patted away her friends' hands and denied her suffering to them; denied her suffering to the ladies who did not know what she saw, who wouldn't want to know, and wouldn't understand if she told them. She was all alone here with the ghosts of the past. Pils and Anka were the only ones who had watched as General Marosh's men were maimed, and perhaps Genadie had seen what had happened to Kralov, perhaps not. If he hadn't, it was her memory alone then. The loneliness was draining. Amalina was confused and being driven to the peaks of madness by this cracked kaleidoscope of women and experience; perhaps more than the Count was, who seemed to be disappearing with more frequency (as the mountain's shaking increased), between bouts of assuring them the castle wasn't falling down, declaring the Palace of Pleasures was only nearer to its grand flowering, and he dissolving to oily fractions in his Ladies' many open arms.

But mostly Amalina's exhaustion came from how often she agonized about having returned to the castle itself. She wished to have never returned, that she had slipped the crown agents guarding the piers and made off on a boat, or stayed on in Paris after Ivanti's betrayal. But that was backward looking, and to keep moving she could only project forward her wants and desires for herself. So then: go back to Paris? or head off to England? or chance a voyage to the new continent? But how? *No … stay and improve yourself. No … stay and toe the line, and keep the Count happy so your loved ones will be safe. No … grow strong and destroy the Count and claim your rights as a woman of true power!*

Amalina was subjected to convolutions of thought, so much like the last time she went stir crazy in this castle: when she had been all alone, with only Genadie and the Count (and, of course, with the wailing woman strapped to the wheel in the cellar, don't forget *her*) as companions, and nearly thrown herself out a window. Now this 'Palace of Pleasures' was stuffed full, and she was older and wiser, but miserable all the same. And still she knew she had to do something to help herself before a leap out a window looked tempting again.

She *was* at that point again, she realized. The same point every year, though experienced at different times, in different seasons: Amalina had to decide what to do with herself. Only it was more crucial now, because she was older and the drive inside was stronger, and she knew she had very little time before she would no longer have the freedom to make choices anymore. While it was in her hands, she had to make up her mind.

But what was right? There were so many options, and she didn't want to let herself down by choosing the wrong path. She had messed up so badly in Paris. If only she could know. If only there were some way to get some guidance.

"What do you want?" Lady Erin Epris had asked.

Amalina resolved to make a decision next morning, after a good night's sleep. But before that, in the solitude of Margeta's new chapel, she got down on her knees and pleaded for strength. *I don't know what I want, or what I am doing here! Where should I go? What should I do? Who should I be?*

If nothing else: please, give me a sign!

PART THREE
ESCAPE

18

The Escape Hatch

The high castle's bell rang at the front gate. The guards along the wall had spotted a new arrival on the highway, someone who might require a formal reception. Everyone in the castle quickly pictured in their minds a covered carriage, perhaps several, perhaps attached with Gaddis Humphrey's armed escort. The sound of the bell had been frequent enough so that it demanded no more than a light increase of activity by the castle's support staff, arranging themselves and certain particulars to shore up the presentation of a fully functioning household—perfected after so many trials and errors. The clang and peal echoing down the stone halls no longer inspired excitement among the Ladies or their retinue.

"Now who could *that* be?" huffed Lady Genevieve de Roye, in her native French tongue and resentfully, as if not only upset that her language lesson was being interrupted on purpose, but that the intruders were bothering her in her own home.

"Kitty," said Lady Halma Inovala in a mock-chiding tone that really wasn't mock-chiding at all, "How many of us *did* you invite?"

Lady Jean Hachter-Freicke somehow made a commotion in her chair just by turning her head brusquely at Inovala's question. She watched Amalina in the following silence, awaiting a satisfactory answer from their host, until she herself began to grow a light sweat and felt compelled, having attracted everyone's attention, to add to the moment: "Katarina was afraid nobody would come, I think?" she said, apologetically. "And so she was quite profligate, and over-generous, in her invitations. Doesn't it seem so? Don't you agree? No?—*Gemna*, where are you?"

Amalina smirked and let Hachter-Freicke's conjecture pass, but studied the other ladies in the room for their reactions; to see if they agreed, or had some hidden judgements against her. By this point, Amalina also felt the bell more as an irritation. The only difference between her and her guests was that she felt bad about feeling annoyed. The bell *should* remind Amalina how popular she'd made herself, even if these friends were collected more out of a mission for the Count than personal interest in her.

Only Margeta, who wore her lemony scowl, seemed pleased by yet another addition to their group. From a nearby couch—as she was always nearby, forming a disapproving cloud beside whatever common action was being taken—she crowed with delight, "It's about time someone—some decent soul who is a true *Popist*—came to keep me company ..."

In her pious lament, Margeta was neglecting to include her servants with her, who were as devout as she (or were forced to be). Neglected, as well, the curious assembly of Wanger, Regio, and Balbo, three old and brilliant engineers and architects, who had been brought to the high castle to consult with the Count on the building's ancient and unsteady structure, and who agreed to provide limited tutoring to the noble ladies who were interested in a lesson or two about the art of construction. These three old, serious-minded men were also fervent enough in their religion to converse with Margeta about the opinions of the greatest man in Rome, and do so quite often.

But Margeta carried on: "The Catholic Church commands half the known world, and you would expect *some* of my Italian sisters and French cousins would respect our Pope. With our arriving new guest, the odds move in my favor. But still I shall pray for delivery."

"Nobody's keeping you here, *Princess Margeta*," said Greta La Nevers with a hot little laugh that caused the others to join in despite themselves. "And we're going to need to start making room if this keeps up. To think of it, *Princess Margeta*, if you were back home you could kiss the Pope's stinky feet every morning, noon, and night. Knit a little sweater with the hair on your lip and his big toe."

Margeta speared Greta with a cold look, and grew a half-hidden smile that only Amalina understood: *Once upon a time I brought an assassin here to whittle down my rivals*, Margeta was thinking. *I can do it again.*

"I'd better go," said Amalina, setting down her hand of cards.

"But we've only just begun!" protested Halma Inovala, who had been losing every hand to this point. "Your people can see to it."

But Greta had already scooped up the cards and merged them into the deck and begun shuffling. "She's won enough, I think. Run along, Katarina, dear."

Amalina didn't need to be given permission twice.

• • •

The castle felt like it had a bustle to it, with both the Count's and the Ladies' servants exchanging places regularly, as it was, and everyone's odd tasks getting them circulating. In the years before, Georg's family and General Marosh's people had stuffed the castle in their own way. But the air had never burst with such a vibrancy of life and purposefulness. The combined threads of so many interests and efforts by a range of personalities so enthusiastically pursued were barely contained within its walls.

And someone new was coming to join in; Amalina wearily went out to meet them, pausing with worn patience for servants to curtsy and back out of her way. *There will now be more of them*, she thought with a sigh. *How could this many people really fall for my false and ridiculous lines? Who would want to come* here *when they were already back* there, *back in the* heart of civilization? Amalina shook her head.

Oh, to be able to trade places, she thought. *I would never have come to Ardeel.*

Why would anyone choose to come here? she wondered again as she made her way to the gate, forgetting she had worked and practiced for weeks and months to get them to do so. Forgetting, as well, her prayer just the night before for some kind of sign—a sign for what she should do with her life.

She knew she should be grateful whichever princess had come, however brief and shallow the friendship was. But knowing that when a noble lady was removed from her native element, and assembled unnaturally within the Count's high castle, with the unspoken goal of matching herself with the Count (and his money), Amalina did not look forward to the change in her friend's character from what she had known in her home circle; how much harder, or stranger ... how very different or disappointing she would become. And with this apprehension, where before Amalina would have begged for any of these noble ladies' company and approval, it was now easier for Amalina to disassociate herself, feel they were unwanted strangers; wish she was away from them all.

Here comes another.

• • •

Joining the watchman on the wall, Amalina peered down the slope of the mountain to see where the procession was and guess who might have now come to visit. Even though Amalina was in charge of writing the invitations, the Count handled all their follow-up correspondence. And it wasn't his will to tell her who'd responded when, or who might be coming, unless she asked. The Count preferred to leave it as—what he thought it would be—'a *pleasant surprise*' for her.

Just reaching the bottom of the mountain approach was a black carriage and four riders on black chargers. They stopped before the highway's incline, the riders dismounting to let the horses graze. This she saw blurrily through the spy glass that the watchman had handed her.

"What do you think that's about?" she asked the watchman.

"She's getting changed out," said Balbo, at Amalina's side, startling her. "Shaking off all the dust from the road to make herself presentable, and resting their horses before the climb."

This was Balbo, of the Wanger, Regio and Balbo contingent of foreign engineers and architects. He smiled kindly at Amali, but with a bright look of anticipation.

"Oh! What are you doing here on the wall, Mr. Balbo?" she said curiously. "I haven't seen you in a long while, and wouldn't have expected ..."

"Just come up for air," he said, nonchalant, still smiling. Balbo was older than the others, bearded and white haired; with tufts sticking out the side that he was perpetually slicking back with a palm he wetted with his tongue, as if nobody could see him doing so. He did this now.

"Up from *where*?" asked Aklan.

"Eh?" Balbo turned to the boy. "Up from the castle, of course."

"Best not to get too interested in the Ladies, sir," advised Aklan, to the preening old man. "The last fellow to try, he left the castle with his head in his hands. Literally."

Balbo patted his grey whiskers contemplatively, and nodded. But he suddenly looked suspicious as he turned guilt-red and his eyes bugged. He tried to keep his composure. "Well, as I said, I just came up for air. Nothing more than that."

He nodded a "good day" to them all, and with hands on his waistline wandered away, with just one last hungry glance back down the mountain.

"Going to be trouble if he doesn't watch it," said Aklan.

Amalina glared at the boy. "How many times have I told you not to do that?"

"There's nothing to get mad about," said Aklan, sounding frustrated. "I was just asking him the question you were afraid to ask yourself."

"I didn't ask you to do that, though, did I?" Amalina tried to raise anger in her voice, the anger that was supposed to be there. After so many months of doing so, it was difficult to keep it up. Even Aklan didn't look like he believed her.

"Oh, come on, Pretty Princess, how could you be mad at me about *that*? I wasn't meaning to bother you, you know. Just trying to help. You don't want Balbo getting himself killed, do you? You can't *still* be mad at me, not by now."

"I should be," she said. And reminded herself that she definitely *should* still be mad at him, as she did on every occasion Aklan tried to talk to her. After all, he'd cost her something very important, something beyond that magic bone he'd broken, and besides Paris, after his little stunt: After everything, he'd cost her her freedom. And he had done it for no good reason other than he was a selfish little, spoiled little child.

"Look," said Aklan, pointing over the side, "She has changed into her good dress. Now she's back on her way."

"Do you recognize the carriage?" said Amalina, putting her flagging anger aside. "Who is it, do you think? Did you see her?"

"No."

"Then how do you know she was changing into a better dress?"

"It's what they all do. Just as sure as she'll be greeted on her entry with a fine wine, and one of Lady La Brichese's excellent cheeses, eh?"

At Aklan's prediction, the watchman seemed to nod in agreement. It had all become rote. The arrival was a predictable bore.

"I can't imagine who she is," said Aklan, with a lick of his lips. "She must be pretty poor, though. She didn't pay for Mr. Humphrey's escort, they don't have his flags, and that carriage is rather dull and tiny. Couldn't fit very many."

• • •

"Good day to you," called the man riding the lead escorting black courser. He waved to the castle watchman. "This is the castle of Count Tepsji?"

While the watchman answered in the affirmative, a ragged, grey, withered face with a cascade of grey curls on either side of it scowled at him through the carriage window.

The man on the courser said, "Very good. We are dispatched from the government of Germania, on important business with your master. My master is Judge Wolcraft, and I am the sheriff of Esterbregen, and here is the writ from our governor," he held the piece of paper aloft. "If we might enter and speak to the Count, we shall leave within an hour."

The watchman looked to the sky. "He might not be ready to meet you before sundown. He is a busy man. But let me announce you, sirs. If I might have your orders."

A basket was lowered and the governor's writ hoisted back up.

"I'll take it to him," said Amalina, feeling a strange stirring inside her chest. This carriage no longer felt boring, it felt dangerous. There was something to it she could not—

"I think not," said the watchman, keeping a firm grip on the paper. He had dark circles under his eyes and a mean spirit. Who knows where the Count had gotten him? He didn't sound like he meant to be offensive, but any question she might have had for him was answered in his proud, self-important tone, "It's *my* trust, little mouse."

Little mouse?

This man had obviously learned who she was. That is, who she really was. Was he a friend of Pils and Anka's, perhaps? Had one of the two told him Amalina was not nobility at all to the Count's people, and to be treated as menial unless another noble lady or one of their servants was around to serve as a witness? Since only Aklan was there, the watchman decided to press the point: he and Amalina were equals, if she weren't something less. Who knew just how *much* he knew about her circumstances, though. Maybe only that she wasn't really the Count's true relation, one with a stupid nickname.

Amalina followed behind the watchman anyway as he sped off, sensing there was something important at work here. Or maybe she'd grown so bored and frustrated with her imprisonment in the castle, the novelty was good enough to work her nerves in a positive way.

. . .

"Who is it?" said the Count in his study. He looked as if he'd just woken from a troubled sleep, which he probably had.

"Germans, Great Master," said the watchman.

"But which one?" snapped the Count, sounding greedy. "I wasn't expecting anyone for at least a month, maybe not until next year with winter so close."

"Here, Lord of Everything," said the watchman, holding out the writ. "Their introduction, High King. It's not a lady at all, Great Overlord."

The Count muttered, with a look of annoyance, "A bit overbearing, Radu."

"What is that, Your High Eminence?"

"I said your delivery is a bit much, Radu."

"Yes, your Lordship. Um, my name is Durok, sir."

"Durok?" said the Count looking tired and puzzled at being further annoyed by this man. "I've known you since you were a little boy, Radu. Always a splendid and loyal soldier, we have shared many drinks against the invaders."

"Radu was my great-grandfather, sir. Then came Michael, my grandfather. Then was Boro, my father. I am Durok, Great All Seeing All Knowing Emperor of Time and—"

The Count pointed the watchman out.

"Next time send a page," he told Durok, who was now backing toward the door, bowing to his knees. "Keep to the wall, like a good soldier. Someday you will be sergeant. Or maybe captain."

As the watchman was still closing the door, the Count sighed: "And so you see the trouble, mouse. Always the trouble with having servants. As soon as they know too much about you, the power they might gain from you, so begins the struggle against each other: trying to be seen by me first, trying to pry at my vanity and gain my affections, trying to be noticed for their importance, trying to claim something from me for which they can ask the ultimate price. But *you* have never given me such trouble."

"No, sir," said Amalina, inwardly cringing at the heat in his voice. The only trouble she wanted to give him was to get away from him. She hoped she hadn't said that aloud, or that he could read her thoughts in her eyes. He was staring into her eyes too deeply.

"You, my little mouse, would never ask me for anything like that."

Only to let me leave, she thought. "No, sir. But, uh, the visitors, sir?"

The Count nodded, then flicked open the paper. He motioned Amalina closer. As he read the letter, his eyebrow arched sharply. Then he began to laugh his low, basso laugh. "No, it's not one of our ladies after all, Ms. Dalca." He laughed louder. She hadn't seen him this amused in a long time. "It appears someone has come to take you away from me."

19

The Accidental Rescuer

The current defense force for the high castle—men whom the Count hired to replace the fallen army of General Zsolt Marosh; Durok being one—appeared to be cutthroats, mercenaries, and dullards. And they numbered only a dozen. No match for an invasion force, of course, but when had that ever concerned the Count? He'd been satisfied with just Amalina and Genadie as his company for years and saw fit to his own protection. But he knew appearances mattered, and so in order to ease the noble ladies and their people, and to do it at the cheapest price, he had gotten just enough bodies into armor and under helmets to pace around the castle with polished weapons in their hands.

Amalina had cautioned the Count that twelve men, no matter how well-trained, would obviously be insufficient. And these men were the least trained by the looks of it. But, as it went, the Ladies were too polite to question such a matter publicly—it being below them and outside their realm—and left it to the servants to gripe and voice their worry; a worry which would not carry past their own cautious circles within their Lady's chambers. So the Count, who prided himself on "thinking of everything", had savvily predicted this politely-civil, or cowardly-muted, reaction from his guests, and his cynical calculation, that hiring a dozen low-lifes would be enough to keep him from hearing any complaint—and save him money, besides—had paid off.

But what would happen if a contingent of Germanian lawmen entered his castle?

• • •

With the entrance of the stiff-backed sheriff of Esterbregen and his accompaniment of three deputies, the castle guard were not, by finger count, outnumbered. But by the volley of curious looks between the two groups—sizing each other up—with smug confidence the sheriff and his men understood that they outclassed the castle guard in every way. The guard looked like the dregs of humanity that these men-of-law regularly scraped out of beer halls and rolled into stockades *en masse* without suffering a scratch.

Amalina would have laughed from her vantage point along the wall, but she didn't want to attract their attention. Judge Wolcraft looked a frightening force at their center, scowling about in every direction as if searching for someone to yell at. Two more men emerged from the black carriage. They were younger and wore official looking robes. One of them struck Amalina as familiar somehow, though she couldn't place him. Neither one was—as she'd strangely hoped, and then hoped against—her former love, Ivanti. *He* had not come to rescue Amalina. It was both a let down and a relief.

Once this curious, solemn group entered the main building, Amalina came down and then, as the Count had instructed her, followed them to the audience chamber.

Along the way she nabbed Aklan. "A couple of them have stayed with the carriage and horses. Go mingle. See if you can't find out something useful, eh?"

"Are you wearing Anka's dress?" said Aklan, before running off.

Amalina chased after the new guests. Anka's large dress, smelling of old apples and smoke, hung loosely and heavily, so she had to hold up the skirt at the sides to not trip. The puffy hat's brown veil looped down in front of her face like some harem dancer's. She was ignored by the visitors as any menial servant would be, especially an ungraceful one. So went the Count's plan.

The Count himself was already sitting on his thronal chair within the great hall and nodded cordially as the men from Germania entered. He twisted one end of his mustache, which he had grown out to some length.

"Thank you for accepting us into your home, Count Tepsji," said Judge Wolcraft, his voice high, nasal, and warbling with age, or with barely contained outrage, or with a little of both. As Wolcraft's head trembled, his grey locks shivered like leaves troubled by a mild, shifting wind.

"Of course," answered the Count generously, his deep voice filling the room and vibrating everyone's innards, pausing Wolcraft's own quiver for a moment by startling him. "I wouldn't flout a request by a visitor as important as yourself, Judge Wolcraft, or your governor; though, it seems your jurisdiction ends somewhere outside Ardeel."

Wolcraft's lips fell at the corners, but he nodded. Then he continued as if the last part had not been spoken. "What brings us to your door is the matter of a young woman who has traveled through our country, and also within France. And, so it has been heard, other countries of this continent. She has presented herself as someone from a noble family, variously a lady, a princess, or a countess; there seems to be some confusion there." He took a breath before enunciating dramatically: "But her name: *Katarina Tepsji!*" He looked to the sheriff, the deputies, then back at the Count. "The niece of *Count* Tespji! *Do* you have a niece, Count Tepsji, by the name of Katarina?"

The Count stared down at the old man, stroking his mustache, an amused smile on the corner of his lips.

"I am direct," said Judge Wolcraft without a note of apology, "because we've been traveling for some time, and there is a matter of urgency to my mission, which was entrusted to me by my governor; and because I am an old man who can never tell when I shall draw my last breath." This got a mischevious grin from the Count. "And so I mean no offense when I ask, as I say I do, *directly*." Then he repeated his question, "Sir, have you a niece, Katarina Tepsji?"

"I have a very large family, Judge Wolcraft," answered the Count, with a labored tone of being patient despite his wishes. "I believe I have more than several nieces by that name. And I would imagine that they get around as they will. Their business is their own and not mine."

"This one appears to be operating—or claims to do so—at your behest. Making a name for herself in certain circles and inviting them to your home here in Netz of Ardeel."

"Is that what she does?" said the Count with a small laugh. "I wondered how my recent visitors had come to learn of my little getaway spot. *Katarina.* Yes. *Yessss.* I believe I know the little rascal you are referring to."

"Countess Katarina Tepsji?"

"*I* am a Count," he answered, but did not elaborate.

"Or *Princess* Tepsji?"

"But it is unclear to me what would cause a government—a whole government—to take notice of her, whatever she calls herself, and to send an envoy—"

"I am not an envoy, Count Tepsji," said Wolcraft.

"There seemed to be something in the letter," said the Count. "But it was unclear what she has done to justify what amounts to an invasion of Ardeelian sovereignty. A matter, in my humor, I am willing to overlook."

"Ardeelian sovereignty is another matter," said Judge Wolcraft with a flick of his shaking, withered hand. The hand was grey, with long, yellowed fingernails. "Something to be dealt with between your governor—situated in *Sobelburg*, eh?—and the King of Germania. This idea of sovereignty was a matter I thought settled by the acquisition. But it is no matter here at this moment, I think." Then he growled loudly, "We are smaller components here, dealing with larger things—*grossere Dinge!*"

"I was saying, Judge Wolcraft, that his letter was unclear. Perhaps you can clarify for me the full offense and your purpose ..."

"I am to meet with her, this Lady Katarina Tepsji. To see her. To identify her—"

"Identify her."

"As you have said, Count Tepsji, and I will allow: you have an extensive family. Perhaps you don't know all of them well enough. I do not wish to trouble your brow, but maybe you don't know some of them as much as you should —*so tief*—as you should. Have you heard the name Hedvikina Von Schiederhausen, or of the Esterbregen Von Schiederhausens?"

The Count shook his head slowly, but an excited glow appeared in his eyes.

"A prominent duke by the name Von Schiederhausen, in Germania—he and his extended relations—conspired and committed the highest form of treason against our King, our state, and our people, and brought upon his whole family the sentence of death. This would include his daughter, Hedvikina. It was believed by many she escaped to the east. Perhaps into these mountains."

"And you believe I have mistaken this woman for my niece? My blood relation?"

"That would be *quite* impossible," said Judge Wolcraft, as if the Count were ridiculous and wasted his limited time for introducing such a thought. "*Ziemlich unmouglich*," he repeated in his harsh German tongue. "This was a time ago. She would be older than *you* by now, perhaps. To be *realistisch—wirklichkeitsnah*—she settled here after escaping justice. Then she became entangled with a native of Ardeel; perhaps one of your family members. That union consequently produced a child. And that child has proven as foolish as all criminals are, and she has dared to show her face to the very same families whom her ancestors, those traitors, would have executed or murdered. You can imagine the fright."

"It is a fantastic assertion, Judge Wolcraft. If that were so."

"This Katarina Tepsji has been witnessed in the courts, and bears a striking resemblance—*eine aufflende Ahnlichkeit*—" he shouted, his curls flopping "—to Hedwikina Von Schiederhausen!"

"You tend to repeat yourself," observed the Count drily, yet coldly.

"When I am caught in a frenzy of emotion," grinned Judge Wolcraft, spittle on his lips. "Even this old man can be driven to it. Let me tell you. It has brought men to tears to find her in their homes. This Katarina Tepsji. This Von Schiederhausen doppelganger."

"I don't see tears in *your* eyes, Judge Wolcraft."

"I have outlived tears, Count Tepsji. Perhaps if you are as unfortunate as I, to live to my great age, you will know what I mean. I am only capable of the farthest end of human nature: *des Zorns*."

"Wrath," the Count interpreted. "I think, perhaps, after a while, one can even grow tired of that, Judge Wolcraft. Well, I can't speak for the girl, I am afraid. I am not as curious as some are about lineage. But I doubt it's true. Could it be a mere coincidence of features, I wonder, that moistened the eyes of some German aristocrats, and kindled their misplaced lust for revenge, I believe?"

It became obvious they weren't used to the Count's curlicuing, self-referential way of speech—*I, me, I, me, I, me*—but the latter part of his statement was taken as a possible insult.

"A mere coincidence of features?" Wolcraft rocked back on his heels and then forward, his teeth clamped together in a fury. "So it shall be determined. For there are other features that also bear a coincidence with this girl. The activities she has recently been engaged in, in the vicinity of Paris, France, smacks of the Duke and his lot. This girl has been involved in bombings and attempts at assassinations."

Count Tepjsi's eyebrows shot up.

"Anti-state undertakings that expose the heart of the criminal, the draw to anarchy which inexorably flows within the Van Schiederhausen bloodstream. It is the very mark of their breed—*kennzeichen!* But where her ancestors failed, she almost succeeded in murdering one of the French King's favorite generals. Threatening the terms of peace between our two great powers."

Amalina cleared her dry throat very quietly.

"I wonder if there is some proof to this outrageous claim, Judge Wolcraft? I can hardly believe."

Wolcraft thrust a hand into the air. In his open palm, he held two pieces of gold.

"Proof?" shouted Wolcraft. "Proof and—again—coincidence of features. Here, look at this, look at this!"

Wolcraft handed the shiny pieces to one of his assistants, who brought them to the Count. The Count leaned over to study them. He picked them up and took them into his hand. As this was carried out, Wolcraft carried on.

"If you look closely there, these medallions pieced together bear the profile of a man with features like your own. I would propose, it is your own portait. On your very own coin?"

"You're mistaken, Judge," the Count chortled. "Have you not seen, or taken the trouble to inspect its markings? This is the face of the great Voivod of Ardeel, of hundreds of years past. Not me at all; I can tell you with great confidence. I trust you believe me, too, that I don't seem so ancient. I begin to suspect, Judge Wolcraft, many people look alike to you." The Count delivered this in a good mood, as if sparring with a failing challenger at a chessboard. "However, I still don't see how this relates to—"

"It is no matter," interrupted Judge Wolcraft. "A coincidence, then. But, as established by your own words, a coin from this realm, once known as Ardeel, now a Germanian territory. And as this criminal young woman evaded the French authorities, she attempted her escape, to book passage across the English sea, by bribing incorruptible agents using these pieces of gold coin."

The Count's smile faltered. He glanced directly at Amalina, almost drawing everyone else's eyes to her. Her heart pounded. She couldn't imagine what he was thinking.

"That doesn't sound like *my* niece," said the Count. "Across the sea? Who knows what persons might lay their hands on these old coins, or what they might do with them? There is nothing conclusive here, Wolcraft. To England, do you mean? Why would she think to do such a thing?" He paused, almost dramatically, and glanced at Amalina again.

"However, if you do not accept these pieces of gold as yours, given to your niece for her travels, you will not mind my reclaiming the evidence?" Wolcraft observed the Count for any hint of reluctance.

"Be my guest."

The assistant picked up the fragments of gold coin the Count casually cast to the floor.

"We are of the same mind, Count Tepsji," said Wolcraft, with undeterred confidence. He tapped his forehead, which shook his locks. "Why would she attempt to cross a sea? *Ja.* As I said to my governor: why would she not return to the fold, instead of running to some strange country with no guarantee of safety? And so I am here, to find her out; this Van Schiederhausen."

The Count nodded, tapping the armrest absently with his fingers, his eyes occupied with deeper thoughts.

"Wrath, Judge Wolcraft. You were speaking of wrath." The Count's sudden smile wasn't a happy one. "Do you wish to turn this wrath upon my niece?"

"I wish to see her. To speak to her. To identify her positively. If it warrants, we shall speak to her parents, who you can direct us to, so this confusion can be sorted and matters brought to a satisfactory conclusion."

"The conclusion ... if my Katarina *is* one of these Schiederhausens, Judge Wolcraft: you will take her from me, from here, into your custody? And then?"

"I cannot speak for what will happen to her, but you must understand that if nothing else, her family, her mother—"

"Is dead."

Judge Wolcraft spun in place as if caught in a whirlwind. It looked unsettling, his balancing on the tip of his toe, for one as old as he was, with his curls bouncing like so many springs hanging off his head. At this point, Amalina noticed one of the Judge's other assistants, the one who looked familiar, had his eyes on Amalina and not on the action in the room. She had let her veil slip too far. He was staring at her face.

"Dead by more than a few years, I promise you," explained the Count. "Does that settle the account, Judge Wolcraft?"

"I come before you in pursuit of the truth, and satisfaction for my liege lord and the peoples of Germania, whose souls have not rested with this terrible outstanding debt of the Von Schiederhausen. A debt that needs payment. Collection. *Befriedigung*!"

"Tell me, Judge, I am curious on these foreign matters: A debt for what happened in the drawingrooms of your Landsmen, for their upset and tears? Or, might I venture a guess, and pardon the cynicism. Is it *also* for what you claim happened in France? Might you not prevent a feud and settle their King—a French King—by delivering up the would-be assassin; to placate them by displaying the wrath which you have carried out upon your fellow countryman, whoever you've dug up for this dirty business, for *their* benefit as well as to content your own royal houses?"

Judge Wolcraft looked like he might choke on the implication. "The former," he said with a withering look. "But I'm only here for the truth. Nothing less. Now, at last, Count Tepsji, let us come to it: might I see and speak to this young girl, your niece?"

"She isn't here." The Count gave two tugs to his mustache. "But I believe you are in luck, Judge Wolcraft, and you will get your chance nonetheless. She is coming this day. Why don't you and your men settle in for the night? If I am correct, she will be here by this evening."

· · ·

The Judge's assistant nodded at Amalina. His eyes were a little too wide open, his brow and upper lip set a little too low; as if he were putting on a brave face, but deeply afraid for his life. He gave her a signal with his hands which she did not understand.

Amalina accompanied the visitors out to show them where they would stay, leaving the Count alone in the great hall whether he wanted it that way or not, glad to get away from him and whatever suspicions he might now have of her. She tried to keep her face hidden from the delegation. Judge Wolcraft didn't want to be shown anywhere, but remained polite as much as he could permit himself, and sat on a bench in *l'entrée grande*.

His familiar-looking assistant broke off from the group and asked after the privies. Amalina and he walked a long way down the corridor before he spoke. When he did, they both stopped and turned to each other, each knowing it was to be a whispered, secret conversation.

"So it is true," said the man, his face losing some of the sternness, fear taking full hold of his eyes. "This *is* where you are."

Amalina didn't fully understand. Was he one of Judge Wolcraft's witnesses against her—against Hedvikina Von Schiederhausen? Or against the mad political assassin from France? But his familiarity, his almost conspiratorial tone suggested something else. She said nothing, but waited.

"Of course you don't recognize me," he said. "You likely never noticed me. But you have been in touch with a close associate of mine, Guwerte Merts. My name is Crutio. We saw you when you came to the inn. Just outside Zweigelbahn. It was some years ago, of course. Well, you've grown a bit, but I recognize you, even in your disguise."

"You're the friend of Guwerte—from Antwerp?" Amalina pictured Genadie sliding the knife across his friend's throat, his friend's sweating face pleading. The man, Guwerte Merts, terrified for his life, promising he would forget everything and not tell a soul.

"I had to see for myself," said Crutio. "I thought the story couldn't be true. But here you are ... the pretty little maid to the mad Count; and when not traveling, she is no longer the princess but a prisoner, a slave, in his castle. I can't believe my eyes."

Amalina didn't know what to say to him. She could deny it, of course. But ... "Why did you come?" she whispered. "And to bring all of them with you?"

"I didn't *bring* them. Guwerte and I weren't the only *hoehere leute* to notice you, girl. The Judge speaks the truth: he is warranted in pursuit of Von Schiederhausen's suspected granddaughter, and daughter if he can get her. It's just that I am placed in the right circles, and I heard them speaking of this Katarina Tepsji—"

"But ... so they don't know everything about me or—"

"I've never said a word. And Guwerte swore me to secrecy after what happened to him in France. But when I told him of this delegation, and the obvious possible connection, though he warned me against joining on, I had to see for myself. He cautioned me that if I would not heed him, then to just observe; to see the truth out. But always to be careful. I, on my part, wagered if the story were indeed true, which I could not allow myself to believe— never in the world—I would rescue you. But it *is* true. It is true. *It is true!*"

He kept saying it, and it looked like he was descending into some kind of shock, as if he couldn't break free and was being sucked down into madness.

"But you shouldn't have come," she told him. "Your friend swore he wouldn't tell anyone. This is very dangerous."

"Even so, now that I am here there is a matter of honor I must satisfy."

"A matter of honor?"

"Of course. I am here, so are you. You begged for help in that Zweigelbahn inn. Now you don't want to leave here, to escape? We have the perfect excuse. It looks like your Count would be willing to accede to the judge and the governor's authority. Declare yourself the child of the infamous duke's daughter, admit you are Schiederhausen's blood, and we can take you with us."

Amalina's mind grabbed the plot even before he'd finished: "And would you help my father escape, too? His life is in danger if the Count should learn what's happened." She felt her heart pump hard with sudden fear. She lowered her voice to the barest it could go, the sound of her mouth making more noise than her words. "My God, keep quiet. He can hear everything."

The man shook. "So impossible to believe. But could it *all* be true? His power ...?"

"My father," she mouthed, "will you?"

He nodded quickly.

"You have the authority? Judge Wolcraft won't object?"

"I am his assistant for this journey, but I outrank him by birth. He will listen. Or he will accept my money."

"And my cousin, Jenna?"

He nodded again. "Just them? How many more?"

"Maybe my father's wife? If he insists."

"Your mother? But if she's still alive—"

"She died. He remarried."

"She died?" now he looked surprised. "Then ... your real mother ... was she Von Schiederhausen?"

"If it will get me out of here," said Amalina.

Looking at Crutio, she couldn't help think of what a dangerous thing he had done coming to the high castle; and then she thought of the other such daring men—Erik Kosche and Piotr—who'd had their young lives ended so cruelly after making the same mistake. This man, Crutio, was a little older than them, and not as handsome, but he had the same air of bewildered innocence. His eyes carried the exact charge of mortal fear and upset of having wandered into a greater challenge than what he'd counted on.

Back in that tavern, so many years ago, Crutio and Guwerte should have believed her story.

20

The Calm before the Storm

"**A**malina," Genadie beckoned her, his eye twitching, his lips trembling, which was never a good sign. She followed him out of the main building and up into the bird loft. There were several greasy-feathered pigeons pecking at bowls of seeds on the loft's long counter. And the furry ceiling shifted with disagreeable chittering as the cool air that swirled in stirred the hundreds of bats hanging from the rafters.

"What is it, Genadie?"

"Did you recognize who is in this German detail?" Genadie whispered hoarsely. "Did you see him?" When his voice was too low, the scratchiness reigned, so she pretended she didn't understand what he'd said; because, if Genadie had recognized the man from the inn, there might be trouble. Better to not have heard, better, instead, to put him off.

Genadie repeated his question several times, never any louder for fear his Master might overhear, but getting increasingly agitated. He exaggerated the shapes of the words with his quivering mouth.

"What?" she said, finally. "The … *him* … in … *who*?"

"You saw him, then," rasped Genadie, and wagged a crooked finger at her. "Or you wouldn't be acting this way. I warned you about your being too clever, Ms. Dalca." Then he wiped his mouth and returned to his anxious ticks. "Ohhhh, but Olympus … Olympus, what could he want! This couldn't be a coincidence. Oh, no. That associate of Guwerte's? There will be pandemonium; that is all he could be good for. And what will that mean for us?"

"Do you mean that one of the men here now, with Judge Wolcraft, was at that inn with Guwerte?"

"I couldn't mean anything else, Ms. Dalca, could I? And here I threatened and warned that rascal Guwerte away—"

"How do you know they were friends?"

"They sat next to each other at the same table."

"You remember?" Amalina had always figured Genadie had trouble seeing out of his beady, rat-like eyes. Apparently, his eyes were as faultless as his memory, once he was worked up.

"There is no coincidence at all. First the one comes to us in France. Now this one dares to enter Master's home. It couldn't be for anything less than treachery. Pure treachery. But I dare not tell Master, or the whole story must come out. Oh, Ms. Dalca, you're good at these slippery matters, what can we do? It's all my fault. I should have been clearer to Mr. Guwerte Merts. Maybe I should have been more violent—"

"No."

"Why couldn't I make the fool understand how dangerous it is to risk your life against Master; that it is better to leave *Him* well alone; to stay as far away as you can rather than to push your luck?"

"But isn't that what I've always been telling *you*?"

"I'm not talking about *us*. We're supposed to be here. *They* had no reason to come, to bother our Master. *They* should have kept themselves *to* themselves. And now I've failed. Failed to warn them properly and we have a situation that will only be worse for us all. Oh, Olympus! I'm not sure my little body can take much more. No. Oh, it should never have come to this."

"But it isn't your fault, Genadie. I'm telling you." She leaned in. "I've already spoken to him."

"*You*?" He looked as if she'd just performed a magic trick.

"Just now."

"Well now, so you were being smart with me, Ms. Dalca." He sulked and blubbered. "And so?"

Amalina explained the gist of what Crutio had told her, more or less, but omitting her hope for a rescue. "You see, this delegation was coming for me anyway. Because I look like Hedvikina. He just tagged along to see for himself."

"But ... if I had only been more *convincing* ..." but Genadie's blubbering began to weaken.

"How could you have been? You almost killed the man," said Amalina. "There's nothing to worry about, let it be. Go hide in your hovel so he doesn't see you and so you don't give anything away to the Count. And don't worry about what happened in France, deny it all. They're here about the duke's relations, the Von Schiederhausens, and that's all. When they're satisfied that I—or, that is, Katarina—isn't Hedvikina, they will leave. He'll go with them. He won't say anything to give us away."

"I'll breathe once he is out the gate. Oh, yes. I should have been more convincing to that Guwerte Merts. More forceful."

. . .

Amalina went to the courtyard to call Aklan off mingling with the drivers and to tell him the good news. But the boy was hurrying along, leading a horse toward the gate, wearing his cloak with a bundle on a belt. His face was flushed around his blueberry eyes, and his bushy blonde hair was standing on end.

"What's the matter?"

"I'm leaving!" At Amalina's look of astonishment, he explained: "My family … There is a rebellion. They've been deposed! Deposed!" He repeated the words in his own language as if to get a better handle on it.

She should have been relieved to hear the boy finally talking about returning home; returning to a family who was probably still distraught at his loss after so many years. But she didn't like the way he was snarling and shaking like a desperate animal.

"I don't think you should leave just yet. Have a rest and—"

"There's no time! I have to leave now! Don't you understand? They've been *deposed*!"

"But what does that matter now, Aklan? You're here not there. You said you never wanted to go back."

"If they have been deposed then I am no longer a prince! I must go back and help them. Papa has to retake the throne. They must be saved and the Spaarvierlets returned to power."

"As long as they are safe, they should be happy to see you," she said somewhat encouragingly, though the shock of him about to leave her began to feel unsettling. Suddenly she didn't *want* him to go.

He handed her the broken magic bone. "Good bye, Pretty Princess."

"But are you sure?"

"I will help Papa win back his crown so that I can return here to serve you with my head held high as ever."

"Held high? What difference does it make being a prince if you're acting as a servant? Doesn't that still make you a *servant*, and nothing to be proud of? Didn't you tell me—?"

"Doesn't matter what I do, servant or chamberpot scrubber, when I know I'm not really one but a prince in disguise!"

He patted her hand and closed it around the broken bone. He stood on his toes, kissed her on both cheeks, and then left the castle.

Balbo, who appeared to be scrounging for flowers along the edge of the forest, waved Aklan good bye; before realizing it was Aklan and not a princess as he'd hoped. His ardor died quickly.

Just like that, thought Amalina of the young boy disappearing down the road, *he's gone. Gone forever. It's so simple.*

Her feeling of loss was cut in half by her amazement that it could be done so easily, then quartered by the thought that she would be doing the same thing in a couple of hours. If all went as planned.

. . .

But sometimes life doesn't go as planned. Sometimes there are moments when, everything seeming most clear or easy, suddenly becomes complicated. Sometimes it seems to happen for no reason other than it would be entertaining to an omnipotent observer, possibly a capricious one, who was free to dip a finger into the still waters to create ripples.

Anka came to Amalina and announced that Balbo was looking for her.

"What does he want?"

Anka shrugged. "He's at the gate with flowers in his hand. Perhaps he plans to propose to you, milady. I caution you against the match—unless it can get you out of here."

"Should I change clothes?"

"I wouldn't bother."

Amalina, still dressed in Anka's borrowed uniform, dodged the other Ladies and returned to the place where she'd just seen Aklan disappear. Balbo was standing there with the flowers bunched in his hands, his face flushed pink-red under the light white tufts on his head. He slicked one side down when he saw Amalina.

"Well, Lady Tepsji, I almost didn't recognize you in such understated vestments. But then, you know the purpose already?"

"I don't know what you're talking about, Mr. Balbo," said Amalina. "Anka said you wanted to speak to me?"

"Oh, well," said Balbo, looking confused. He raised his hand and indicated the treeline. "If you will come this way."

"What is it? I really don't have time for picking flowers. This was unexpected and ill-timed, Mr. Balbo."

"But this has nothing to do with me or flowers," said Balbo, taking hold of the bunch with both hands again, as if he was strangling a small animal. "It has only to do with you, and I am just an intermediary. But if you will come this way, just a little, you will see."

Amalina followed reluctantly, eyeing the treeline for what he might have in mind for her.

"Now," he said in a low voice, "as I was gathering this bouquet, I spied something quite unusual, quite unexpected, Lady Tepsji. There was a spy lurking just inside the forest."

"A spy?"

He smiled down at Amalina. "So it seemed. But she is very young for a spy. And too pretty, perhaps. But she was observing the castle, and when I approached her she said she wanted to speak to someone named Amalina."

"Amalina?" said Amalina, raising her eyebrow. "And why do you bother *me* with this?"

"I told her I didn't know anyone in the castle by such a name. She then asked to speak to the young Lady Katarina Tepsji. This name I knew. She swore me to secrecy, but that I should bring her out of the castle so that she would speak to her and no one else. She is there."

Balbo pointed to the dark shape that stood from behind a tree, just inside the forest.

Amalina's heart leapt. It was impossible. There stood Cristine.

"Ah," said Amalina, as if this were expected. "I see. Thank you for your service and discretion, Mr. Balbo. Do the guards know? Were you observed with this one?"

"They were focused on the German delegation," he said. He looked back at the castle, where Durok was peering at them from the top of the wall. "That is, until you came out, Lady Tepsji. We are now being watched."

"That's fine. We're having a conversation about the miracle of these beautiful, late blooming dianthuses and roses."

He shook the bouquet. "It is a bit of a miracle, isn't it? So very late in the season."

"Those things tend to happen here; at uncle's Palace of Pleasures. You may return to the castle, Mr. Balbo. And please mention nothing of this to the others. Including Uncle, if you don't mind. This is a private affair."

"A private service for you, Lady Tepsji? A pleasure, to be sure." He bowed and headed back to the castle. Amalina wondered if he wouldn't immediately blab to the Count. But then again, the Count was busy and probably would not entertain the architect with any conversation.

Amalina turned back round, entered the forest and shifted the veil from her face.

"Amalina!"

"Cristine."

• • •

Amalina and Cristine didn't immediately hug, but stared at each other, not knowing how to procede. Like two stray animals who've met in a forest dell.

"What are you doing here?" asked Amalina, not sure how the words sounded as they came out.

"I asked for Lady Tepsji," said Cristine, sounding apologetic. "He said he didn't know anyone by your name."

"Well, I'm here. What *are* you doing here?"

Cristine's cold blue eyes looked Amalina up and down. "Are you mad at me?"

"Mad at you? I can't believe you're here! Of all things! And of all the times!" Then, seeing the blue eyes blinking, reddening, and growing soft with tears, Amalina changed her tone. She stepped closer. "Well, of course

I'm happy to see you. That you are here. But you shouldn't be. It was very dangerous to come."

"Well, it's just that I was … I mean … you're here, after all … and I was lonely …"

"How did you even get here? It couldn't be on foot. You didn't *walk* all this way?"

"Practically," she half grinned a sharp grin. "I had a horse. But he wouldn't climb the mountain. He bucked and bucked. I tried to walk him up but when we got halfway, he broke and ran."

Should have gone with him, thought Amalina. "At least one of you knows the danger. I wish you had taken the hint and gone back."

"I was already halfway up," said Cristine. "Go back where? All the way back to town?"

"Well, what are we going to to do now?" said Amalina. "I can't take you inside."

"What! Why not?"

"Because it can't be done. The Count controls everything and everyone in the castle. All the comings and goings."

"But you work for the Tepji's. Couldn't you just say I came to visit you?"

Amalina's already overworked mind couldn't handle the thought. Bring Cristine in? And then what? Pretend she is a friend of someone named Amalina, who everyone knows does not live in the castle? a name they have never heard of? Or pretend Cristine is a friend of the Katarina Tepsji herself? And by doing so, reveal to her friend that she really was living there as Lady Tepsji, all the time; living as some Count's niece, a blood relative to royalty; as an imposter?

"No," said Amalina firmly. "You have to go back. Maybe I can get you another horse from inside, but—"

"You can't mean it! I came all this way!"

"I can't help that! You should have told me you wanted to come, and I would have warned you away. What you did is crazy. Do your father and mother know you came here?"

"What difference does that make?"

"How silly, stupid, and dangerous," fumed Amalina. "So dangerous. Wildly dangerous."

"Not *that* dangerous," objected Cristine. "I'm here, aren't I? Now are you going to let me in, or are you really going to send me away? All the way back down the mountain? I'll be walking until sunrise. Walking at night."

That was dangerous, too. It was bad enough she was hiding in a forest crawling with bears and wolves, which were fattening themselves for winter.

And so what? She would have to bring Cristine inside after all? And just when there was the promise—no, not a promise, but the faintest hope … yet still a hope—that Amalina might be rescued? taken from this castle this very day in Judge Wolcraft's custody, never to return? Cristine's arrival could complicate things, or ruin it all; she could reveal Amalina as a simple baker's daughter, and so then no relation to a criminal, Judge Wolcraft's quarry, the Germanian duke. That would spoil everything.

But Cristine's wrinkle sparked a thought in Amalina, and she grabbed at it with what hope she could.

"As it turns out, I'm leaving," she told Cristine, whose mouth fell open in surprise. "Not very long from now, either. So you wait here outside the castle. I don't know how long it will take, but if nothing else, by evening I will be on my way, and I will stop to take you with, or else find some way to sneak you inside."

At the mention of the possibility of entering the castle, Cristine's eyes lit up. "You can't sneak me in now?"

"They're watching. Just stay here. I'll send someone I trust to keep you safe until the time comes. All right? If it gets too late, and the sun begins to set, go to those tall rushes over there, close to the road. Before long there will be a carriage, I will be inside it. Step out into the road, make yourself known."

The promise of adventure seemed to perk Cristine up but also annoy her. Here was a castle, within sight, just outside the forest, which she would rather get into and roam around in than remain put. But she nodded.

Amalina went to Cristine and hugged her tight. She was not the little bony girl she'd last held in her arms so many years ago. "I *am* glad to see you. Please, just be patient."

Amalina made sure to pluck a few roses and smell them and poke at them for Durok's benefit on her return to the castle. After all, she'd just been out there in the woods admiring the flowers Balbo had pointed her to. Nothing more.

"Pils," said Amalina when she found him hauling firewood in the main building. "Never mind that. I don't know if Anka told you, but I have a visitor. That is, an old friend of mine from Korr. Nobody else knows yet, and I want to keep it that way. You're going to go be her company until I can deal with her later, okay? Her name's Cristine. Go to her in the forest and start gathering flowers. Bring a lantern because it might be late before I can join you. Take a rifle, too, eh? In case of wolves. Meet her and protect her. Can you do that for me?"

Pils left as a willing agent in Amalina's scheme, as he didn't see the harm in it—except the wolf part; and not to forget the bears. Anyway, anything to step outside the castle, he felt. And for a brief moment, Amalina reflected how the often helpful-on-the-spot Aklan had now been replaced by a very convenient Cristine. If the negotiation with the Germanian delegation went as planned, when the carriage exited the castle they would be halted on the road just outside by a young woman, who would be able to verify to Judge Wolcraft and the sheriff, once they were safely down the road, that Amalina was not a relative of Tepsji at all, nor the relative of Duke Von Schiederhausen, and so not someone to be tried, executed, *or* returned—but to be saved, at last, from her imprisonment. To be free.

• • •

That evening, with a renewed spirit, the Count announced to Wolcraft and the delegation they would be dining with Katarina, the very subject of Judge Wolcraft's investigation. At first the Judge objected, but the Count reminded him he had little choice but to accept the invitation. And he went on, adding more particulars:

"Wolcraft, you and your men will conduct yourselves in a manner suitable to the operation of—as you called it—my home. This castle, I will have you know if you were indeed unaware, is known around western society as the Palace of Pleasures—soon to be in its flower—and it will remain that way despite your presence. You've entered it on business, and I am granting you the liberty to pursue your purpose. But only to a point. My niece, my Katarina, is a sensitive girl. You may ask your questions, but not in the fashion and mode you spoke to me earlier. We will sit down to a pleasurable meal together, and you, in the artifice of a conversation, will draw the information you need from her."

"I really don't see the point of it. I am a direct man."

"You can be direct as you like, only under my conditions: with gentility and a smile, and on a term of friendship. She will think you are my guests. She will suspect nothing and answer all you have to ask. But she should not know at any point she is under any threat."

The Judge's wrinkles deepened between his eyes as he scowled. "First I had to put up with your delay, which I find suspect; now this. It would seem I am putting on a show for your entertainment; that you arranged for events to play out this way. You should know, Count, I haven't lived this long to become someone's puppet and player—*eine puppen!*"

"I have found that wrath is not a lasting emotion," observed the Count, "it is held onto; willfully. I think in the end, curiosity, forgiveness, and a sense of wonder are what prevails."

"What are we talking about?" said the Judge, bewildered, as if he'd missed a part of the conversation. "I've lost my place, I'm afraid."

"Our dinner will be a fine little feast, Judge Wolcraft. You may ask your questions, but you will not disturb the placidity of her nature or my sanctum. I trust you understand and will not violate my rules."

The judge shot an incensed look of outrage to his sheriff; a look requesting him to come off his seat and clap irons on the Count. The sheriff shrugged furtively. The shrug said: what harm would it be for the judge to restrain himself during the questioning? The sheriff and his men were confident that at any point, if they needed to, they could disarm the handful of soldiers in the castle, and then have their way. The shrug went on to say: *Please this eccentric Ardeelian noble as long as he likes, as it won't cost you or the delegation's dignity; we won't be humbling ourselves by obeying the Count's rules, but only humoring him into a deeper, weakened state of complacence. I have this under control.*

. . .

"You must help me," the Count told Amalina in the hallway, after explaining the situation with the delegation and the coming dinner—

"What the Judge said, sir," interrupted Amalina, feeling sweaty and guilty and that he could see right through her, "about what happened in France, in Paris, it isn't—"

"Never mind that," he said impatiently, his fun delayed. "You're here, you returned to me. And you would never hurt a fly, would you?"

"No, sir."

"No. *Noooo*," he agreed. "Of course not. My little mouse, my little innocent, my Lamb, a raving political murderer? Some rogue player in France got hold of our coins and was trying to throw their pursuers off the scent. It's only logical that political nefarious-sorts would prefer, for their purposes, to acquire and utilize a currency of the highest value which they can secret in their pockets. Could happen to anyone. It would only caution, Ms. Dalca, for more care on how you put our coins into circulation. Didn't I advise you to exchange them for the local currency at a bank?"

"Yes, sir."

"Oh, I understand it all: these Germanian scoundrels are simply trying to purchase their French rival's affections with a body, one that they will also abuse to shore up their tearful political class at home. Or they think they will, at any rate. Don't worry about it, I have their game figured out. And for Wolcraft's part, he dares claim to my face you are a Von Schiederhausen because his vision is impaired either by ambition, or his hatred for the Von Schiederhausen. Can't say you don't look like her, though, now can we? I chose you very well. Ho, ho." Amalina looked confused. "But never mind. Now listen:"

He explained the coming dinner with the excitement of a prankster at work, and what Amalina's more direct role would be with the delegation: the performance.

"Why all these theatrics, sir?" she asked him when he was done, amazed at his minuteness of thought. Not realizing she was repeating what the old judge had said, but feeling it was true, she continued, "Did you ... did you arrange this for some reason? It seems you must have."

The Count grinned without comment.

21

A Sufficient Enough Force

By the time Attila arrived in Korr there were only a few hours left before sunset, when this small, western bordertown would close for the night. Attila reserved a room at the Rock Cup Inn, a somewhat non-descript building that had been purposed into a boarding house and pub. It wasn't expensive and it looked popular with out-of-town travelers, and so was a suitable place to store himself incognito until he had gathered what information he needed before revealing himself to the general population.

He knew to be cautious in his movements, but the Cardinal's pessimism and concern about Korr's potential danger had him on edge.

• • •

"Where are you going?" the Cardinal had asked Attila as he was packing for the trip. He scoffed when Attila told him. "Korr? Why there?"

"It's time. I've worked over the data. Most of the secret histories I've read specifically reference a handful of foundational towns, and Korr is one of them. And of all those several foundational towns that are still standing, I've seen their accounts but for that one. So logically—"

"I can't imagine what you think you will find there."

"Neither can I, that's why I am going. Maybe I will discover as much a beneficient surprise there as was present in your church. Maybe one even better."

"We've nothing so spectacular as a cathedral there," said the Cardinal, testily. "Our church in Korr is modest and it doesn't enjoy as much popularity as it should. You can't hope for something 'better'."

"I see." Attila looked levelly at the Cardinal. "You're afraid I'm going to get out of your sight."

"Not quite. But how am I to react? You've been locked away in your room here all these months, I'd thought you'd become a monk. Now all of sudden, this? No, no. I'm worried what trouble you might get into and I won't be able to help. There are disagreeable elements in Korr. It is a border town, but it has remained small and backward."

"Backward? Even under the sway of the encroaching modern western churches?"

"I will have Rosczy continue to gather what intelligence he can from the castle while you are away," sniffed the Cardinal. "Though you understand how much I am losing by your continued refusal to go there yourself. Well, never mind. You find what you will in that backwater and return here as soon as you can. You assured the governor you have a solution worked out for our enemy. You assured me this as well. Is that true, or has something changed?"

"Yes, I'm quite positive even now," he said dully. "It will take some doing, but yes."

"Yet you insist on going to Korr?"

"Precaution. And that is where I shall begin to assemble my army."

The Cardinal's eyes widened and his lips tightened.

"I *need* an army," said Attila. "A small one, but a sufficient enough force to pull off my plan. Korr is close enough to Netz to be practical without drawing the Count's attention. And far enough away from the governor to avoid any friction by my recruiting efforts."

"Very well," the Cardinal allowed. "As a precaution, you will tell me your plan in full detail before you go."

"A good, solid plan stays in the head of its commander," said Attila, looking as if he were falling asleep, "lest the plan get out and be ruined. In Netz, so closely placed to and associated with Tepsji, what would happen if he were to take you and torture you and force you to talk? Everything would have been for nothing."

"And what if you get yourself killed in Korr?"

"You would not be any worse off than before we met," said Attila. "Which wasn't a bad position for you at all, if I recall."

"See my bishop in Korr, Attila. At least. His name is Perdu and he is very much mine. He will be of help against the unclean hordes there."

"I'll take the coach from here to Korr," said Attila in a breezy voice, and moving as if he were about to leave that instant. "But as you are overall responsible for this mission, could you stake me some money?"

The Cardinal made a face.

"I know, Cardinal. I owe you."

"Do not forget that."

• • •

Attila wore a large brown cloak, not too different from a monk's habit, and below the hood he wore a long brimmed hat in order to shield his face. In this get-up he wandered through Korr from street to street, seeming at random but in a circling fashion so that he would have seen most of the place and understood its rambling grid. He noted several churches of various faiths and denominations, as well as a plain but pretty temple. Attila found and then wandered into the Catholic church, the one that belonged to the Cardinal, to appraise the man he might be working with: Bishop Perdu.

Attila did not plan to identify himself to anyone, he would simply observe what he could. But on entering he found he was the only one inside. A quarter of the benches, toward the back of the service hall, were draped over with a tattered and stained canvas cover. That and the rest of the pews seemed to have a layer of undisturbed dust on them. Because of the dust, Attila looked to the rafters to see if the ceiling was crumbling. It wasn't. The church seemed to have fallen into disuse.

"Is someone there?" said a heavy voice. "Well, yes! There is! Bless you, bless you, my lost sheep. Come in, eh? Come in and let me greet you, my wandering child."

A man with a squat, pyramidal head and a matching body waddled toward Attila, his arms outstretched. He had large but deep-socketed eyes layered over with fat eyelids, and an undulating, oversized mouth that was smiling with all the teeth, which were black and grey. This priest, presumably Bishop Perdu, was the opposite of the Cardinal, beaming over with friendliness and openness. An almost obnoxious desperation for human contact pervaded his look. Attila took a wary step back, letting the man know he did not want to be embraced or to be known too familiarly.

"Did you just arrive?" asked the man. "The carriage come through? Well, where are you from then, my weary traveler?" He then said, in the respective tongues: "*Germania? Amsterdam?*"

Attila shook his head and motioned with his hand. But the priest kept smiling wider and wider, and waving him closer to accept his embrace. He asked the same questions in a number of other languages, trying to peer deeper into the darkness under the bill of Attila's hat.

What makes you think I am a traveler from somewhere outside of this country? Attila wanted to ask. But for Attila's purposes, and to put the priest in his place and to inform him of his own nativity to this country, he said quickly in a deep Ardeelian accent: "Don't know how you got past the Cardinal with that familiar attitude, Bishop. I heard him preach in Tsobl, and he said 'Simple people smile stupidly; men of learning and intelligence smile only out of uncontrolled wickedness, or spite. Otherwise one keeps one's mouth shut.'"

The priest's smile deflated into an aggrieved scowl. But there showed a slow flicker in his eyes—maybe he was deciding whether Attila was one of the Cardinal's agents come to test him—and then he hefted himself proudly, as if in counter-attack, and declared, "You tell the Cardinal when you see him that a stern, dark, mysterious church does not sell as well as he thinks. That Lutherite minister smiles like a damned soft-headed idiot and has gathered almost all our old sheep into his pen. I'm trying my best, eh? Is it wrong to be proud of one's church? You go ask him that!"

• • •

Later, Attila was back in the Rock Cup Inn, taking measured drinks and gauging what he'd learned after his short tour; and, as well, observing the people who shared the eating area with him.

Despite the Cardinal's misgivings about Korr and its people, the Rock Cup's patrons weren't any harder than what he'd find in taverns along the outskirts of Tsobl. Had the Cardinal forgotten Attila was once part of the country's constabulary, readily familiar with dens of the lowest repute? If the Cardinal had consulted with the governor deeper than he had, he might have learned how Attila was no stranger to the rougher side of living, and had even been jailed for drunken misbehavior, which had required three officers pull him off the rope in the Tsobl bell tower.

That little trick of 'drunken' misbehavior was how Attila had first gained access to the high constable's copy of the Secret History of Tsobl, which was hidden in a safe just outside the jail cell. All he'd needed to do was pretend to be intoxicated to the point of being locked up for the night. When the constable had left him alone in the cell, Attila went and got it; with a set of picks and the studied skill of thieves he'd arrested.

The secret histories were usually kept by either the mayor or the highest ranked officer of law in a town, so it would probably be in the deputy sheriff's office here in Korr. Attila glanced down at the cup of wine he was holding and calculated whether he could pull the same stunt he had in Tsobl. Here he was a stranger and without a title; there would be no reason for his potential marks to show him any respect if he started trouble.

But still, the drunk trick would be an efficient way to get into the deputy sheriff's office. If, instead, he just identified himself to the deputy and asked to see the book, it could lead to more problems. And who knew if the deputy was part of the Count's extensive network of informants? And even if he wasn't, he might blather to someone who was.

Well, there's no relying on the Cardinal's man, Bishop Perdu, he thought coolly to himself. Too lightweight and inconsequential. And maybe too simple to keep secrets. What Attila needed here was an ally who could match him in cunning and fervor for the mission. Otherwise it was going to be all up to him.

Attila took a long drink from his cup, upping the end for anyone to see if they were looking. If he were going to try this ruse again—of getting thrown into the town jail where he could scout for the book—he would need to begin making some noises so the others here would think he was capable of becoming an obnoxious drunk. Preferably the someone who noticed him would be local and would have influence with the deputy sheriff.

In the Rock Cup's social space were the inn keeper, his wife, six men divided into two groups who were all obviously highway travelers, and as well: two coachmen, a carter, a couple of miners judging by their dress, and a shadowed couple in the corner. About an hour after the bell had rung, and they were all sealed into the inn for the night, a handful of men from the town gave a jovial coded knock at the door and were let in for drinks. These were older men from Korr, unconcerned enough with superstition to fear for their lives by having some nighttime comeraderie. They pulled out a tatty deck of cards and began gossiping immediately, including into their tight circle the inn keeper and his wife.

If Attila wanted to properly angle himself into the deputy sheriff's custody, *they* would be the ones he would need to show himself off to. He eavesdropped and looked for an opening.

. . .

One of the coachmen who sat closer to the locals' table than Attila had also been listening in on the conversation there, and called out from his chair. "You speak of Kyrgil, enh? Do you *know* what happened in Kyrgil?"

"Volcano," said one of the locals. "Saw the smoke from here. What a terrible tragedy."

"More an earthquake I think," said another who was dealing cards. "Felt the ground shake."

"Volcano did the shaking," said the first one.

"Earthquake, had to be. Where was the lava?"

"I don't know about no lava. But what about the smoke? You saw it yourself."

"Earthquake brought up the volcano then."

"Well," said the coachman, "while you two decide what did it, let me tell you that you're both dead wrong. I know it isn't one's place to spread rumors, but the truth is the truth and it is important everyone should know it if they're going to be acting like they know it, and jawing on and all around to their neighbors about it."

Attila sat up and studied the coachman. He was old and wiry and by his features was a native-born Ardeelian.

Before the town gamblers allowed the coachman to say anything more, they invited him to the table for a drink and asked him for his name and where he was from. It seemed a custom to run through all of one's particulars, establish the line of work and lineage, before being allowed to talk about anything else.

As the coachman's story went: though he was now trying his luck at driving the highway route to Korr, for years he had worked the Tsobl route to Kyrgil; until the incredible event which had swept Kyrgil away. By this point, the conversation seemed to attract the room's attention, even the couple tucked away in the corner. Their hats turned in the coachman's direction.

"So you were there when it happened?" asked the dealer.

"Good thing I wasn't," croaked the coachman, with a trembling grimace. "But I was there by next day. I've never seen anything like it, but I can tell you it was no volcano and no earthquake. I helped search for survivors. And as you know, there weren't any in the town. It was crushed."

Some of the men scoffed, but Attila scooted his chair from his own table so he could listen better.

"Crushed?" asked the man with the cards.

"Crushed and burned and crushed again."

"So what was it, then?"

"Some of you are too young to believe," warbled the coachman, sitting back and relishing the attention. "But you older gentlemen will know what's true. I spoke to one of the folk from the nearby farms, and he saw the whole thing from beginning to the end."

Again, Attila scooted his chair closer, loudly this time, and they all looked in his direction. Attila nodded for the coachman to continue, while pretending to take a deep drink.

"A dragon. A balaur dragon." He paused as the older men inhaled deeply in surprise. "An earth one, I suppose, as it must have burst up out of a mountain cavern. And it must have been angry having slept so long. For a century at least. When was the last time we've seen one of them?"

"A dragon?" said Attila, sounding offended but looking perfectly bored.

"What's that? Who's there?"

"You said your witness saw a dragon?"

"Come closer," the dealer ordered Attila, and narrowed an eye at him. "Join us in a drink."

"A balaur dragon," said the coachman, nodding sagely. "There used to be a good many of them. Terrible creatures. Could smash a mountain in a minute, could burn down a city in an hour. Breath of fire."

"Your witness told you this?"

"You don't believe, young man? Well, you're too young—"

"I may be young, but I can tell you exactly what happened in Kyrgil. Because I saw it with my own eyes. And it wasn't a dragon."

Now the chairs in the room turned in Attila's direction. Even the couple in the shadowy corner leaned out of their booth to look at him.

"You were *in* Kyrgil?"

"I was camped in the mountains when it happened."

"Why would you be camping in—?"

"Why don't you come over here and tell us who you are?" said the dealer once more, pointing to an opening next to the old coachmen. "Eh?"

"I was surveying for the Tsobl—I mean, the *Permanent Council of Sobelburg*." Attila squared his shoulders and tried to appear at least a little more official than he looked, projecting authority, as he'd learned to do when training Sir Hak Vogoneyevic's army.

"Well if that's the case," challenged the coachman. "Why don't you tell us what you seen?"

"I saw a comet pass over the town from the direction of the castle atop the mountain. And it wasn't long before a mist spread through the valley from where it struck the ground. It spread almost like a living cloud—"

"Balaur breath."

"It was a spell," said Attila in a loud but monotone voice. "An ancient spell cast by someone who knew how to use it. And he used it to cloak himself from the sun. So that he might make his way back to the Kyrgil castle above the city, and return to the man who had cast him down from it."

"You're sure it wasn't a dragon?"

"I heard the screams," said Attila. "Even from the mountain vantage I listened as the people of Kyrgil tried to resist him, but fell. The mist wound through the valley, over the farms and past the bridge, destroying it in its wake so that no one in the city might leave, and then it struck at the city itself. At every move came the blast of guns and the cries of the men and women. Then when Kyrgil had fallen, it rose to the castle and plucked it and the whole mountain down upon the city."

"A water dragon has been known to cloak itself in mist, and air dragons in clouds," the coachman insisted. "And they are often controlled by sorcerors. Isn't that what you saw, sir?"

"I saw a creature, but it was not a dragon. Instead, it was one familiar to you. Who you all know. With whom you are all complicit." Attila's hint of accusation brought some frowns, he glanced nonchalantly at the bottom of his cup. Then he stared into their eyes, directly, one by one. Challenging them.

"What are you saying, sir?" said the dealer. "What *is* your name, eh? Whose people are you?"

"My name doesn't matter. What matters is that a danger which *we* have permitted for centuries to exist, a creature who we have allowed to thrive without check, has proven himself a menace once more. Do not deny it! It is written out in the infernal agreement signed by your ancestors, and even the good men of this city!"

This started a commotion. The innkeeper ordered his wife out of the room, tasking her to get more bottles of wine from their cellar. She appeared eager to leave.

"You'd better speak your mind fast," warned the inn keeper.

"You've heard it," said Attila, confidently. "No need to veil this truth from your wife, or from outsiders any longer. For the threat manifests even now, though no violation on our part to that infernal contract has occurred. The time of punishment has come."

The innkeeper eyed the foreigners in the room. He gave them a placating smile and nodded his head at the fool talking. But his eyes were heated and he returned his full attention to Attila.

"If you don't believe me, let's call for the mayor. Let us call for the deputy sheriff. Let us bring forth the Secret History of Korr and its attached contract." Attila gave them each a look of accusation again, even the two in the back corner who were now standing. One of these men was tall and thin, the other short and dark. The way they stood marked them as something different from the regular Korrites. They weren't frightened by him or what he had to say, they were *interested*. Maybe they had access to the book. Maybe they would be able to get him to it. Attila continued: "Let us read from it, as I have before in other places. Let us study its lesson. Because in it we know what is coming and what must be done."

"You've had too much to drink," said the innkeeper.

"Six cities began the contract," said Attila, as he placed his cup down firmly on the table. "What were their names? Well, we no longer know them all. Two have been struck off the list, as they themselves were struck out of these mountains, never to have existed. What did they do to offend the creature? How did they violate the contract so that he would remove their protection? We will never know, just as we will never remember the names of those cities, or the names of their people. But we do know the names of the cities which remain: Tsobl, Korr, Netz, and Kyrgil." Attila lifted his finger dramatically, though his eyelids were at a dull half-mast. "Kyrgil ... *Kyrgil* ... Do you understand? Kyrgil has suffered the fate as those before it. Why? We shall never know. But how, and by whom, it can no longer be denied."

The room had descended to rapt silence. There was only the crackle and snap of the fire in the fireplace and their breathing.

"Has the name of Kyrgil now been burned out of the book, as those of the other towns and villages have? There is only one way to find out. Let us bring forth the book, bring forth the contract, and refresh ourselves with its words and its warnings." Attila was impressing himself with the quick route he had found to the book. Much faster than he'd expected. He could already feel it in his hands.

"To what purpose?" came a hoarse whisper.

Attila couldn't tell who had asked. He didn't bother. He swept his eyes over the room to include everyone, just as he had with the countless other groups of men when recruiting for Sir Hak.

"He is striking now," said Attila, "because he is afraid! He is afraid of us. Because that contract is an ancient thing and we have multiplied in number. And we have grown in strength. Our progress and technology have made us equal to his power. And now he has begun to strike in order to preserve himself. To protect himself before we wake to what we can do to him. Men of Korr, listen to me. Let us find and read that book. And let us understand that at this moment, if we work together, if we harness our strength, we too, as the people and the blood of Ardeel, have the ability to strike a name out of that shameful document, that embarrassing history, with our own hands: His!"

The men's faces were either wide-eyed or hardened. Except the two in the back, who were now looking *very* interested. The short, dark one was grinning. All Attila could see was the man's teeth.

"Brave men," said Attila, sensing he'd struck them wrong. "Yes, we can wipe *him* out from our history. If we only try."

"You should leave," said the tall one in the back.

The innkeeper nodded. "I think you should go. Before my wife returns, sir."

"I offer you the promise to free yourselves from bondage," said Attila.

"You said you were working for the Sobelburg Council?" asked the coachman.

"Or, I should say, it was a private interest," said Attila. The atmosphere in the room was charged, but against him. "A private concern, but in order for that party to file a report to the council."

"You sound Ardeelian," said the coachman. "But you look like one of *them*."

"I assure you we are one, sir. I am Ardeelian more than most Ardeelians. And I am willing to fight."

"And now it is time for you to leave before you cause any more trouble," said the innkeeper.

"If you will only listen to me."

"You were there in Kyrgil. Maybe you said the same thing to them, enh?" said the coachman. "You brought the trouble down on *them*."

"No, I—"

"If you don't leave now," said the innkeeper, "Me and my friends will show you out."

"But it's after sundown. Where will I go?"

"Set up camp," said the innkeeper. "Plenty of mountains around. Just not here."

Almost as a single body, the group seized Attila. He saw his route to Korr's Secret History slipping away. As he protested, and tried to convince them to listen, he was called "Troublemaker!" "Upstart!" and, most hurtful, "*Liar!*"

He was tossed onto the cobblestones where he landed painfully.

As the door closed, the coachman's voice echoed: "You heard him. The cloud of a sorcerer? It was a balour dragon summoned. Believe and never doubt it ..."

When Attila turned toward the inn, he was grabbed at both arms and dragged roughly and hastily away. Attila tried to kick his feet on the ground to right himself. The two on either side of Attila kept him off balance. They overpowered him and he wasn't released until he was rolled out into an alley.

The tall man and the short man stood over him; the couple from the corner booth. Somehow the light was better in the alley, the street lamp was shining more directly on them. The tall man looked seedy, but the short man was bizarre. His color was abnormal, with a greenish skin that was incredibly wrinkled and seemed to be crisscrossed with deep, green-lined patterns. His nose was long and sharp and it pointed at Attila like the tip of a small sword.

"Trying to sprout trouble here, scum?" said the tall one, as he snagged up Attila, and spun him, and wrapped him in his arms. He was as strong as a horse and Attila could only comply. He pressed a blade to Attila's throat when he was done. "You've got it."

"Where do you come from, enh?" said the short one with a high, womanish voice. He slashed his finger in the air and the tall man pressed the knife harder. The short man was in command, apparently. "What's your name?"

Attila stared, looking bored. He wondered if the knife at his throat was already drawing blood.

"He's on his own," surmised the tall one, an eagerness to be unleashed in his voice.

"Yes, I think so," agreed the ugly, little wrinkled man.

"Good thing we were there tonight, huh? Told you somebody strange wandered in. Somebody needed watching."

"*Feather and claw*. Finish him."

Without hesitation, the knife sliced across Attila's throat.

22

Was!

At the appointed hour, the entire Germanian delegation was removed from *l'entrée grande* to the small private dining room just off the great hall. The Count was already there, seated, wearing a broad, enigmatic smile; which was hard to see, as the room was barely lit with just one candlestand. Judge Wolcraft objected, growling it was too dark. Instantly, more candles were brought in to accommodate the judge's old eyes, and his dinner guests remained unsuspecting that there was a purpose to the whole set-up. The Count secretly signaled to Pils, the secondary side door was opened. Lady Princess Pia Lampeda entered.

"And who is this?" said Judge Wolcraft as Anka washed the princess' hands at the sideboard. Pia then shuffled around the table, all of them standing politely in their places for her to be seated.

Lady Pia Lampeda was deathly white. Her head hung forward from shyness, with long red hair that cascaded clumsily around the slope of her cheeks to land on her chest. When she stopped beside her chair, her dark green eyes held on each man for a lingering moment. Then, as she bowed to them, she said, "I am—"

"You don't recognize her, of course," interrupted the Count, to Wolcraft, almost as a challenge.

"No," said Wolcraft. "Should we? Excuse me, madam, are you the young lady, the countess? Is your name Katarina?"

Pia shook her head and said with a weak voice, "No, my name is—"

"This is a fine noble lady from Italy," the Count interrupted again, with a courteous smile, and a nod to Pia that everything was all right. "She is of the Roman Lampeda line. Are you familiar with the name, Judge Wolcraft? Please sit down, my dear."

"No," barked Judge Wolcraft, shaking his locks. "No, I haven't had the pleasure. I warned you, Count Tepsji, I am a direct man. I hope this isn't a game you intend to put us through; a parade of pretty faces and guesses at who they might be. This kind of test is unwarranted."

"Lady Lampeda is my niece's dearest friend. They always dine together. Don't you, pretty one? Well, not recently, of course. Katarina's travels have gotten in the way. But tonight, they will share the table again after so long apart. Doesn't that make you happy, Lady Lampeda?" Pia nodded with a weary but genuine smile. She pulled back a ribbon of red hair that had fallen in front of her eyes. Her green eyes immediately jumped to the men across the table. If the men noticed, her gaze fixed directly below their chins. "And Lady Lampeda is very punctual. Unlike my rascal, the little mouse. I mean, of course, Ama—that is, *Katarina*. Pils, where has my niece gotten to? Have Anka bring her to my table immediately."

After a minute, Amalina entered wearing a flowing dress and layers of makeup, her hair combed and shaped into something proper and princessy. She had been waiting just outside the door on the great hall side for a signal, but breathed heavily as if she'd just rushed down from her room. As orchestrated, she gave her apologies while Anka washed her hands. Being expertly self-trained to govern her body so as not to give away too much, she only glanced once to the Judge's assistant, Crutio, on the way to her chair, to mark his spot so to not look there again; and didn't miss a beat when she saw Pia for the first time in months on the other side of the table.

Her composed delivery was marred only when she did a double-take at Pils. *So who's with Cristine? She's out in the forest on her own?* Pils flashed an apology with his eyes. He had to return to the castle for this. Amalina was shaken, Cristine *was* now all alone in the forest.

But she had to be careful. Amalina well understood that the outcome of this dinner could decide her fate: whether she was leaving the country for good, or staying here, perhaps forever. She had to concentrate only on the moment at hand, nothing else. She put on the perfect, polite smile.

The Count clucked over Amalina, how pretty she was, considering the late hour and that she had been traveling all day. He exclaimed how Pia had so looked forward to their reunion at the dinner table. Pia gained the courage to glance up from her lap, and smiled warmly, almost pleadingly, at Amalina. In the candlelight, Amalina remarked to herself how unwell her friend's color was. So much worse than when she'd appeared in her bed so many months ago.

"You will introduce us of course, Count," said Judge Wolcraft, not sounding like it was a request. "Katarina Tepsji, I presume? I would recognize you anywhere—*irgendwo*."

Amalina bowed. "Have we met, sir?"

"This is Judge Wolcraft, my little mouse," said the Count, "and these are his associates, come all the way from Germania."

"Germania?" said Amalina, seating herself under the Judge's uncomfortable glare. She said in High Deutsche: "*So far away. A very beautiful country.*" Returning to her own language: "But, sir, you say you recognize me? I don't remember—"

"Your pronunciation is excellent," said Wolcraft, suddenly pleasant. But still there was a storm in his eyes. "We were never formally introduced, my dear. I saw you at certain functions, in certain houses. I noticed you. *Bemerkt.* You were noticed by *many* people in our land."

"Well, thank you, sir."

"Your mother is from Germania, of course," said Wolcraft.

"I-I don't … Why do you say that?"

"Well, it is obvious. The eye, the strong cheekbone. There is something quite distinct—*ganz anders … zehr Deutlich!*—in the structure of a Saxon face."

"I hope everyone is hungry," said the Count. "I know I am. Please, let's not stand on ceremony, I don't abide religious custom. Let us have service and eat."

"This is hardly the point," growled the Judge, as Pils and Anka, looking ashen, began to robotically deliver platters of food to the table. "You insisted on this meal as the format, sir. The food is quite unnecessary for my p—"

"You don't have to eat if you don't want. But Katarina has just returned from travel, which makes her quite hungry. And I see to the satisfaction of all my guests in my *Palace of Pleasures*. I believe I said as much to you, Judge Wolcraft. Please allow them the satisfaction."

"As I was saying, my dear young lady," chimed the Judge to Amalina, after a deliberately slow, deep bow of his head to the Count. "You caught most certainly the attention of many families in my country. And France, I think. You've traveled there recently? To Paris?"

"And Venice. And Rome. And—"

"Yes, an extensive traveler you are. *Zehr gut!* But if you would allow me my questions."

"Yes, sir."

"Now, more importantly, your uncle is a very busy man, and despite your closeness he could not furnish us with the information of your precise lineage. I conclude it is Saxon, or a strain from within Germania. This is easy enough to ascertain … Though, I'm afraid I have heard your mother has passed on?"

Amalina nodded, her lips dropped from a smile to a glum limp line. This answer caused a stir in the Judge; at first excited, then angered. "Recently," he tried.

She shook her head. "Some years ago. When I was very, very young, sir."

He laughed condescendingly. "You are very, very young now. How much younger could you have been? But that means you did not know your mother?"

She shook her head.

"You knew her name, though?"

"Mama."

"I mean her Christian name? Or, more telling, her family name? No? Your father never told you of your beloved mother's history?"

She shook her head and started to feel resentful. She resisted the temptation to look at Crutio, who she assumed was giving her subtle little nods. This was all for her benefit, she had to remind herself. For her benefit, that is, if it turned out well. *Allow the old man his way.*

But the old man wanted Hedvikina dead. So for Amalina it was as delicate as dancing with a sword-point pressed to her heart.

"Your father must have told you once or twice, young lady. Think about it. Did he ever mention the name Hedvikina? Or, Von Schiederhausen?"

"Hedvikina …?"

"Or perhaps more familiarly, Hedwigga? Or lovingly, Heddy?"

"Heddy? Hedwigga Von Schiederhausen?" said Amalina. But the silly thing was, she did recognize the name now: Hedwigga Von Schiederhausen, the daughter of a duke from Germania. How could she have forgotten? She was the one Amalina had pretended to be once upon a time—so long ago at this point—in a macabre masquerade. Hedwigga was the one who'd married the grave attendant, Neku Jonker. She had died and the Count had had Amalina pose as her to lure Neku out of the graveyard so he could be killed, and take back the body of his own wife: this was the Count and Amalina's first adventure together. Yes, Amalina recalled, almost falling into a trance, he had dressed her up in a funeral dress and aged her a little with make-up, and given her lines to recite, actions to perform, and she had led Neku Jonker—*"Heddy? Meine Heddy?"* the grave attendant had drawled stupidly— out past the cemetery gates and to his doom. And everyone at the table saw the confusion and revelation on Amalina's face.

"Are you all right, Katty?" asked Pia, sliding a hand tentatively along the table toward her.

The Count laughed in amusement. He wasn't eating but pulling at his mustache, and looking triumphant for some reason.

"Yes, Von Schiederhausen," said the Judge. "Hedwikina Von Schiederhausen. She came to these mountains some years ago. Long enough ago, I should say, that she could have married someone and bore many children. And it would not be unlike her to marry someone of a good rank within your country. She was a beautiful woman, and she had strong tastes for luxury and power. Von Schiederhausen, girl."

"The name sounds familiar."

"Ja, ja!" said the Judge. "Ja, *naturlich*. This only makes sense."

"You aren't feeling hungry, my dear Pia?" inquired the Count. She shook her head and looked as if what sat on her plate offended her. She glanced to her lap, to the Count, to Amalina, and then to the men across the table.

"So you do think your mother might have been Hedwikina, girl? Or was she Heddy to you? Can you bring us to your father so that we might enquire of him?"

"Yes, we should ask my father." Amalina kept her eyes off the Count while agreeing with the old judge. Her heart was already beating hard and he must know it. He probably knew there was something happening before him, some betrayal on her part, if a light one. Nothing he couldn't wipe out in an instant if it offended him too much. "But I really don't know. I don't think—I'm not sure—my grandmother, or was it—"

"Grandmother? *So?* If not your mother, why not? They breed as quick and plentiful as rabbits. But it was your mother, no?"

"No, I was just saying ... it couldn't be ..." she hesitated again.

"Tell them everything, little mouse," said Count Tepsji. "You can admit to whatever you know. I believe you are kind and truthful, and I don't think it becomes you to try to hide what is real."

She raised her brow at the Count. Did he really want her to tell the truth? But wouldn't that upset his ploy of her being his own true blood-related niece? What did he want her to say? She shook her head to let him know she didn't understand.

"Don't look at him, girl," shouted Judge Wolcraft. "Look at me, and tell me what is."

"He wants to know if you are Hedvikina's daughter," said the Count helpfully, "because if you are a relation to Duke Von Schiederhausen, he wishes to take you with him. He wants to remove you from me, this castle, and Ardeel and return you to Germania. *If*, that is, your mother was a Von Schiederhausen."

"You are trying to signal her," the Judge howled at the Count, his locks shaking, white flecks forming on his grey lips. "What game are you playing here? I warned you."

"I told her she can say whatever she believes is the truth. *Whatever she likes*," he said meaningfully. "Never mind *my* will."

"Well, let's have it, young lady. You know. You *want* to tell me. *Sag mir!*"

Amalina looked from the Judge to the Count and back, and then back again, uncertain. Something was happening here that she didn't yet understand.

"It matters not, little mouse," said the Count. "Say whatever you want. They won't be leaving with you as their prisoner." He turned to Princess Lampeda, and leaned toward her, "You see, my little Pia, this Judge Wolcraft, these men, they want to take our girl away from us. To bring her back to their lands so that she can be executed. That is why they are here. Their purpose."

Pia's head snapped up. Her eyes twitched. She bit her lower lip.

"Oh, yes," said the Count. "They are quite convinced they have their girl. Germania won't be able to rest until they have her back and she is quite dead and her lifeless body paraded through their streets, perhaps with the kind judge at the head of the procession. Then it's on to Versailles, is it? Yes, it's true, Pia. How's it to be, Wolcraft? Hanging? Beheading? Burning at the stake? Exposure? All these and more?"

"Why are you saying this, Count Tepsji?" Wolcraft scooted out of his chair. "You are trying to scare them unnecessarily."

"Only the truth," said the Count.

Pia said, as if in a fog, "But Katty is really—"

"I doesn't matter who she is," said the Count mirthfully. "Her blood *is* from their land, at least in part. Isn't that true, mouse? All of Germania will recognize her face, isn't *that* true, Judge Wolcraft? And if I don't let them take her from us, they will remove her by force. That is why they came here in number and with arms."

"What are you up to, Count Tepsji?" protested Wolcraft. "*Was?*"

"So they cannot leave," the Count told Pia. "They must not. Should I prevent them from taking her today, they will be back with more writs and larger forces. And why would we want that trouble for our dearest friend? They want to kill her. *Kill* her, Pia. We have no other choice. We must kill them. Kill *them!*"

Remarkably, the sheriff remained in his chair. His deputies shoved back their chairs and stood, half-bowed, looking alarmed and slightly confused. Nobody was charging into the room with weapons drawn. The servants had left minutes ago. It was only the Count and two young women in the room with them. It shouldn't feel like a threat.

Crutio stared at the Count and began to gulp uncontrollably, his face whiter than the Count's or Pia's skin. The pupils on his wide eyes were pinpricks of terror. He, at least, understood what was coming.

Pia shook her head.

"You must, Pia," the Count encouraged, his canine teeth elongating to give her an example. "They must die. Otherwise, they will have little mouse executed. They *want* to kill her. There is no reason to hesitate. Now is your chance, with no reason to hold back. Please, my little, Pia, please. It has been too long."

"*Was?*" The Judge pushed back fully from the table and pulled out a small pistol. "What game is this now?"

With a black blur, the judge's pistol arm, the forearm, broke in half, tearing from elbow down to the wrist. Blood flew from the gory rend in the black sleeve. But the Count had already pulled the limb toward Pia's face, dragging Wolcraft's body over the platters of fowl and bowls of stewed vegetables. Blood spread across the table.

"Drink, Pia," he said over the judge's unbelieving wheezes, whe old man's eyes vacant in shock: *Was? ... Was? ... Was?* "You need to. It is the only way. You *knew* this, dear. There is no reason to hold back. You are not one of them. You are *changed. This* is what *we* are!"

Pia jumped out of her chair and pressed her back against the wall. She looked to Amalina, ashamed and embarrassed and angry at herself. She began to cry.

The sheriff and his men were shouting now. One tried for the door, but the Count was there and broke his back. Released, the judge fell to the table, panting and screaming, trying to stem the flow of blood with his other hand. Crutio had fallen under the table and was gagging. The second young assistant was trying to hide behind the broken line of deputies.

Amalina didn't know what to do, so she continued to sit there, her hands balled up in front of her mouth, wanting to scream. She stared into Pia's pathetic eyes.

With a yell, Pia leapt over the table—she looked like a deer vaulting a low fence—and sunk her teeth into the sheriff's throat. Inexpertly, but in the manner Amalina had first seen the Count kill someone, Pia bit through the flesh of the man's neck and sucked down onto the geysering wound.

"Yes! *Yessssss!* Yes, my Pia, yes!"

Two of the deputies pointed their pistols at the princess. They were so close to the action the sheriff's blood spurted onto them. Before they could charge or pull the trigger, the Count had their arms broken at right angles. He was moving slower than he was capable, perhaps because he was not yet recovered to his full power, or perhaps by way of demonstration for Pia, who was not his equal in speed. He kept things at a quickened but visible pace, as he broke the men into docile shapes, and he held their whimpering bodies; waiting, watching Pia. The last deputy stood without movement, either shocked into dumbness or realizing it would not help.

Pia yelped. She'd taken her mouth away from the sheriff's neck, and gave off the most lamented cry Amalina had ever heard. It was as if she were dying. Her eyes were closed and her head held back, and for a moment Amalina thought Pia would cough all the blood back up. But she cried again and shook her head and took up the next man, folding his limbs as if he were nothing but a doll, and tore into the vein she wanted.

"Yes, Pia, yes. It is what you want! You are helping your dear friend Katja and you are helping yourself. You see how silly you were not to listen to me! You will feel stronger, you will feel better, you will *love your life with me!*" The Count glanced to Amalina and gave a meaningful look. "With *us!*"

Pia swung her head to look at Amalina too, her eyes filled with shame, but the brutal hunger fell into place on top of that, and she lost the look of recognition. Of anything but hunger; the blank eyes of a starved wolf. A wolf targeting her prey. Pia launched off the deputy at an incredible speed, directed at Amalina.

A fast black blur shot between.

• • •

Four men were on the floor, necks and wrists crudely torn, with Pia weeping silently next to them, wiping their blood from her mouth. The Count had torn apart the others, avoiding the taste of male blood, which he had once said he did not care for. Judge Wolcraft lay across the table, his upper-half hanging over the side. The Count had saved him for last, though the old man was pretty much dead by the time the melee was over.

The Count put his arms around Pia, patted her back, and hummed soothingly to her. Then: "Ms. Dalca, remove that man from under the table."

Amalina, her limbs trembling, overcame paralysis and lifted herself numbly from the chair and took herself around the table. She felt the blood drying on her skin, tightening and pulling on her hair. The front of her dress was stiff with it. She took Crutio's hand and guided him into the open. He began to gulp sickeningly again. His head was bowed down, he would only stare at his feet.

"*Nein, nein, nein,*" he was muttering between gulps.

"Can you hear me?" asked the Count.

The assistant nodded, and gobbled, "*Ja ja ja.*"

"*Gut.* You will return to your *Land* and you will tell them the girl was not related to Von Schiederhausen. The truth is, you understand, that she is *not*. So you will not be lying. And you will tell them that your party met with an accident in the mountains. A terrible accident. You alone survived. You like the sound of that, don't you? That you survived the terrible accident?"

The man nodded, his tongue flickering eagerly on his dry lips.

"And you will forget this ever happened. You are lucky to be alive. Try me again, and you won't find fortune smiling on you so happily. Now go."

Amalina led Crutio out, one steady hand on his shoulder, one arm around his waist. Along the way, he giggled to himself madly and mumbled, "It is true, isn't it? And I wondered why we were all invited to the table. I wondered." He shook his finger in front of himself. "I knew there was something wrong. I *knew* it."

He had lost his mind. Who knew if he'd ever get back to Germania, she thought. On her way out the door, she heard the Count's consoling voice— felt the basso vibrations in her chest: "It's alright, Pia. It will be much more satisfying next time. I promise."

"I'm sorry," Crutio mumbled to Amalina as he limped through the great hall, both of them leaving a trail of red marks on the floor. He leaned close to the wall, as if it might provide protection, or would catch him if he collapsed. He giggled with his rising madness. "I'm sorry. I'm sorry. I'm sorry it wasn't meant to be, your rescue."

"No, it's all right," said Amalina. She felt numb. As if nothing were real and so her lost chance to escape didn't matter—it had never been more than a phantasm anyway.

At least Aklan, thought Amalina, had found a way out.

"Amalina," groaned a heavy voice from behind her. She turned. She and Crutio both.

Crawling from the doorway were the Count and Pia. The Count was above the princess, one arm wrapped around her at the shoulders. Pia was staring in that blank-eyed, ravenous way again. Thick strings of blood and spittle ran from her lower lip, looking like strands of her red hair caught in her teeth. Amalina almost cried out, thinking Pia had turned on her once more.

"Bring him back," the Count was saying, almost apologetically, but with a proud, yet somewhat abashed grin. A grin with elongated teeth. His skin had grown black in many places, where fur was threatening to press out, looking part the wolf. "It isn't over, I'm afraid, Amalina. No, I think it isn't over quite yet."

Crutio didn't run, but dug his fingers so hard into Amalina's arm she moaned and thought they would tear through her skin. He moaned with her, falling backwards, "Nein, nein, nein, nein. Nein, nein, nein. Nein, nein, nein … !"

"But you said he was free," said Amalina, while her body, seeming on its own, cleared out of their way.

23

The Cleanup

Amalina's hoped-for escape was ended with the death of Judge Wolcraft and the Germanian delegation. That fact was naturally lost in the horror of what happened in the small dining room, and in the conversion of Pia Lampeda from a gentle, docile lady of some refinement into a crazed, blindly ravenous monster. Especially that. So shocking was Pia's change that it consumed Amalina's mind to the point it seemed to recreate now, in a more immediate way, that hallucinatory, kaleidoscopic effect that had diced her memory of the preceding months. Every conversation immediately after this unnatural event, the image of a blood-drenched Pia Lampeda dominated. Along with it came the feeling of the deep loss of her friend, and the question of how so terrifying an alteration could have happened. Set on top of that was the desire to get away from her, and this place, so that she never had to witness something as soul shattering again.

But as Amalina had learned through the years, there was a simple trick to survival within the castle. Another part of her, a hardier piece within, put on that old iron mask of inscrutability Sadra had given her, which passed for normalcy, and dealt with whatever was before her as if this were any other ordinary day; setting aside the guilt she felt in Crutio's death, as if she had betrayed him in the final moment—just as she had betrayed Kralov, and she could feel his cold look of accusation even now—to push her along, to get her past it, to get her through to whatever was waiting on the other side.

And then there was a hidden facet in that kaleidoscope, a buried but parallel track of thought unknown even to herself, which carried on in the background. The part of Amalina that could not believe she had lost out on her freedom—*not when it had been so close.* And that part did as it always did in any adverse situation, and sought for a solution so that she could turn things back around. So that she would not lose this day, but regain the path out of this lousy castle that she had been promised.

The three competing parts in Amalina's mind had her stumbling about, the late evening inside the castle feeling like an unreal fog rolling about her. She entered one conversation after another, all of them detached and perhaps a dream; her iron mask prevented anyone's perceiving that she was on the verge of breaking apart, all while she strived valiantly to come back together whole. Amalina's 'survivor energy' which Anne Brignol had described was in effect, leading her through the odious cleanup.

• • •

The first person Amalina noticed outside her head, and the churning thoughts within it, was Genadie, who was looking into the small dining room, standing cautiously at its threshold, the blood slowly leaking out of the room and making islands of his brown leather boots. His troubled expression matched Amalina's mood. His face sagged, and one eye twitched and blinked nervously, indicating perhaps a greater despair than her own. Or was it disappointment there? His lower lip twitched and a tear dropped down his cheek, which he wiped away quickly, mumbling: *"Oh, Master … the little body is growing ever more tired. It can't take much more, I fear. Oh, Master, Master, Master …Master … Master … Master …"*

"It really is awful, Genadie. Isn't it?" It was a devastating scene of death, of course, Amalina thought emptily. She was at least aware, in this brief clearing in the fog, her nerves felt ragged, her body tense.

" … Master wouldn't want you to be here," he answered her, as if that was what he had intended to say all along.

"What are you talking about? Look at me; my dress. I was here for all of it. He *invited* me. I was sitting right there at the table when it happened. I was *wanted* here."

*He wanted me to see Pia's chang*e, she thought morosely.

"Of course, Ms. Dalca," said Genadie, wiping his face then shaking his shoulders to put some energy into them. "But not for this. This part is my job. You've done enough. Wash yourself, go to bed."

"But you'll need help," said Amalina, feeling the tremble deep within her, the dull shock that was working slowly through her system; unaware of the bifurcations and trifurcation in her mind, throbbing already. She was sitting on the floor of the great hall, trying to push the blood off her skin; marveling at what had happened. And she knew there was no way to wash the blood off so thoroughly so she would forget it, but she also knew, as a rising bubble of awareness emerged for a second, that she wasn't going to bed tonight with this nightmare unsettled. She needed to escape the horror of what she'd just experienced—as if there were still a way—and maybe this *was* the way, no matter how grotesque: to wallow in it, and accept it and become a part of it. "I'm about as filthy as I can get." she continued. "Pils and Anka will be screening off the guests for us. And *He* doesn't want the castle guard to know what's happened."

"Why not?"

"You're questioning him?"

The old Genadie would have dropped to the floor, pounding the grey stones with his fists, kicking them, denying any accusation that he would ever doubt his beloved Zeus, his infallible Master. Now he just gave a tremor of surprise at her question, like a cold breeze had gone up his back, then he slouched into disappointment all over again—though it wasn't clear if it was a disappointment at himself, or a renewed disappointment in his Master.

Amalina said, almost cruelly: "I suppose it's going to have to be the same old thing then."

His voice scratched as he nodded, "Their carriage and horses mustn't be in the courtyard when the house wakes, to have the guests wonder where the judge and his men have disappeared to without their transport."

Amalina recited the old narrative: "Yes, of course: they left while everyone was asleep." It was the same old excuse when one lady or another (and her entire entourage she'd arrived with) had to be disposed of quickly, and required that no further questions were asked. At least when it had happened before it was up to Georg's people or General Marosh's forces to do the dirty work. But they were all gone now. Despite the crowd within the castle these days, it was really back to Genadie and Amalina alone to serve the Count where it really mattered. It is *just* like the old days, but worse. Seeing the upset so clearly on Genadie's face, Amalina's voice lashed out and then strengthened with bitterness, projecting her feelings into him, "It's *his* fault. We should leave it all to *him* to clean up; to do it all *himself.*"

Genadie gave an angry sounding cough. "No. Genadie's to be trusted. More than the servants or the brutes in armor."

Suddenly Anka was in the hall. Without effort, she held a replacement dress for Amalina and a big basin of water to wipe away the blood and the gore. But the old woman was stricken by the sight she should have been expecting. She cleaned and dressed Amalina, with a vision of Pia tearing flesh and meat with her sharp teeth clouding over the process. "Poor princess, what happened to the dear? What happened to her?" asked Anka, her eyes squeezing tight, not wanting a real answer.

"It doesn't have to be this way," said Amalina sourly, more to Genadie, who seemed as paralyzed as she was. "It never has to be. He never had to kill anyone in his life, and now he brings Pia into it? I told him before, and I've told him a hundred times. If he needs blood to keep himself going, he could use the animals. Or he could draw it off a person who is near death. Or off of the condemned. Or not take so much that they die."

Ganadie coughed, then growled. His eyes pointed unmovingly into the mess. "And yet here we are. As he wills it. There is only to do and to serve. And with the night almost half over, I suppose all there's to do is we bring the carriage back to my shed and break it down." He gestured lamely into the room. "Same for them."

"What about the horses?" asked Amalina.

"Set them free."

"They might wander back. We have to get rid of them permanently. If someone notices them …"

"Render them, too, then."

"Kill them, you mean."

Genadie winced.

"How's about we stop keep killing as a solution," she admonished. "Let's not destroy anymore. Eh? If we keep doing that, we'll get as bad as *him*. Eh? Eh? We don't ever *want* to be like him."

Genadie grunted miserably at her statement, admitting the truth in it. "Well, what then?"

Amalina's cool side was thinking: suggest riding the horses down to Netz, where they could sell them on the market. And from there …

"Get me ten or twenty yards of oil cloth, if you please, Ms. Dalca," said Genadie in the silence. "You'll find it in the storehouse above the barn, under the straw. Just leave me alone for this part. I wish to be alone. Oh, and get out of those pretty clothes that you've just put on if you're going to help. This isn't the job for a good lady."

"This isn't the job for a good *anybody*," Amalina said as she left him, but sensed more than knew that a clever idea was forming in the air above her head, one that might solve their problems. When she changed clothes in her bedroom—back into something better suited for helping in the ghastly job ahead than a formal, immaculate Ladies' dress—as she cooled down some more, and with the grotesque horror of the hour fading then waxing, waxing then fading, she suddenly remembered her friend was still outside in the dark.

Oh, Cristine!

She peeked out the window for her. *Was* she still out in the forest? Out there all alone? *What of the wolves!* If only she could send Pils or someone out there to bring her in.

But then, remembering Cristine, and the need to get her away from the castle, the hidden third part of her mind made an appearance again, and the idea of selling the horses down in Netz improved. She could pick Cristine out of the forest and take her along. But why stop there? Oh, yes, the plan was taking hold and improving by the minute. It came together, as a beautiful whole, as she hurried downstairs, and she knew it would work. It must! She just needed to convince the one person that mattered most of all: she needed to convince the Count.

That's when Pia Lampeda found Amalina there in the hallway, cornered her, mouth dripping hungrily—still famished—and leapt.

. . .

Margeta came next through the fog. Margeta? Amalina shook her head to clear it.

Amalina had reached the entrance hall, Pia's attack had been imaginary.

Margeta was seated at a table, her eyes fixed on the antechamber door that led to the Count's private study; her fingers spit prayer beads rapidfire and she was murmuring prayers. Margeta sat up when she noticed Amalina and understood the direction she was headed.

And Amalina recognized there was something hot there behind her gaze.

"Princess Katarina," the dour princess said, with a strangely sing-song lilt. "And where are you going? To visit your uncle? Strange clothes you are wearing, *Princess*. Your dress, I don't think I've ever seen you wear something so lowly."

"But, really, it shouldn't surprise you too much, should it?" said Amalina, still walking, feeling wobbly, straightening her old Ardeelian clothes. Then, under Margeta's scrutiny, she patted her her face defensively, feeling for missed spots of blood. Had she removed it all? The stuff never seemed to come off completely. But, yes, they must have gotten everything. Anka had been satisfied and run off to help Pils keep people—like Margeta—safely out of her way. But Margeta had found Amalina anyway.

Where had Margeta come from to be right here? she wondered.

Where am I now? she wondered again, woozy.

Get through this. Never mind her.

"You *are* a bit too humble at times, of course. But *so* humble?" Margeta called after her, frowning and twitching her head; throwing off the matter and the awkward silence. "Come. Stop. Talk to me, Princess. Give me some time. I've heard Princess Lampeda has finally emerged from hiding. Have you seen her?"

"What?" said Amalina.

"Have you seen Princess Lampeda tonight, Princess Katarina?" asked Margeta, more forcefully. "Is she improved do you know? How is she?"

"What? What is that?" asked Amalina, stalling, trying to get out of the room before she had to answer anything.

"Has she finally eaten, Princess?" Margeta's mouth trembled, the tight lines deepened. "Did she *eat*?"

Margeta's eyes fixed onto Amalina's now; communicating a truth; telling her she knew. Knew something more than she should. Margeta's look stopped Amalina mid stride, but she didn't answer. She could barely remember where she was, her mind whirled:

Eaten what? thought Amalina, dazedly. *What was acceptable to say to another Lady about Pia Lampeda? What was permitted by the Count to admit—to reveal?*

Amalina could never tell anyone what she'd seen. Those eyes. That mouth.

Those teeth.

"Well, Princess Katarina," said Margeta presently, sounding contented by the non-answer; sounding haughty. "It's been so very long for her. I thought tonight she would finally have found herself. Perhaps not. I can't believe Princess Lampeda could be so hesitant when your uncle has favored her. If she doesn't pull through, she will never leave the nest. That couldn't be what your uncle wanted. I don't know what he could have thought by— well, why he thought he could trust *that* one. I've proven my strength time and time again." Her voice lowered, so did her eyelids. She looked deadly. "I would not hesitate. Not if given the choice. She *pretended* to make the choice. But if she cannot see it all the way through, then she denies it even now. She shouldn't have wasted his time." Then Margeta repeated, for some meaning Amalina didn't know, "I don't know what your uncle was thinking with that one. I'm sure you know, Princess Katarina, that I would never be the disappointment Princess Lampeda has proven herself to be. Why did he do it?"

Her imperiousness did not sit well on Amalina's agitated nerves. "She ate," Amalina stated icily, hoping to put an end to it and move on. She started to turn.

"Oh, did she?" said the now *unpleased* princess. Her frown dug into her jawline. "Well. Very well. She's wised up, finally. We'll see if it takes, if she improves. Or if she will regress to her natural weaknesses."

Amalina stared back at Margeta but tried not to give away too much, just in case. But she was curious: "Princess Margeta, did Pia tell you what is happening to her? or uncle—?"

"Both," she smirked. "The months were long. We were alone. One had to give, then the other. And you must know he has made his intentions known to me. His interest."

"For you to follow after Pia?"

Amalina could imagine Margeta chewing her way through a Germanian delegation easily, and she did so right then. But Pia Lampeda's face popped back into place within the daydream. A ravenous face, with burning green eyes, turning toward her, as ever.

"I wouldn't put it that way, Princess Katarina," said Margeta, waking her up. "That is unkind. *After?* I think he's made an error in his selection and we must live with that, one way or another. However, I would not *follow* anyone."

"It wouldn't bother you?" said Amalina, tentatively, still not knowing if it were true that Margeta knew all, but: "It wouldn't offend you to accept … um … accept what Pia has now?"

"Offend?"

"Your sensibility? Your faith?"

"Princess Katarina, that is not the question. And what I don't understand is why you have remained … well … It's not as if *you* are so devout that you couldn't agree to any offer." She made another throwing away gesture. "I suppose you think by holding back it means you are displaying some kind of moral strength."

"But your *faith*, Princess Margeta. Given the choice he is offering you, I can't believe you are still here. He intends to take many wives and—"

"As did the founders of our very religion," she answered dismissively. "How can I question your uncle and not, in turn, question the plentiful marriages of the prophets themselves? The Son did not overrule them. Therefore, I will not question."

Amalina thought: *Margeta doesn't know what she's talking about. She hasn't seen …*

"But what uncle promises to anyone who joins with him," said Amalina, even more insistent, "it should be the highest offense to you. What will happen to you. What you will change into. What you will become. It is so *opposite.*"

Margeta swallowed hard, but her deadly expression didn't change. "The transfiguration … well … well … With the truth of what your uncle offers us, doesn't it modify the universe, Princess Katarina? You must see it that way. The holy promise deals with what exists outside this realm. So what does it signify then if you remain always *within* the world?" She smirked, though it didn't look much different than one of her frowns, or a smug smile. And somehow her left hand continued to shift the beads of her rosary. "I am still here, of course. I told you that very thing before you left for France: I am intent to win, to have, or to take what I came for. And when I do, should you go away again, I will not only be be here the next time you return, I will be here *forever.*" Her lips twitched into a nasty grin, which took on a different meaning for a new thought—and for this grin alone, Amalina swore she never wanted to see Margeta's face again—but then: "No, wait … I see now. How blind of me. The only reason you haven't chosen to take this route to eternity, Princess Katarina, is not because you have some superior morality, if there could be such a thing, it is because you haven't been offered it. My apology."

Amalina never *ever* wanted to see Margeta's face again.

• • •

Annoyed and flummoxed by Margeta—*I was offered the very same gift, Margeta! And yes, why* did *he do that to Pia first if you're so great?*—so that she wanted to get away from her as fast as she could and return to her more urgent business of getting away *altogether*—from the Count, from the castle, from the disappointment and tragedy of Pia, from the incessant scheming—get away from it all, and *for all time*, Amalina did not consider why the door to the Count's study was slightly open, but entered with a purposeful step, only to be stopped short just inside by an unusual sight.

The Count, his face cleaned and his clothes changed, sat on his divan, back straight up, feet touching the floor. He stared contemplatively into a mirror—a large, footed looking-glass Amalina had never seen before. No, he wasn't contemplating his reflection. He was transfixed by it. So distracted was he, that it seemed even with his heightened senses he hadn't noticed her enter. It was not unlike the time she had used the magical little totem of invisibility, and she had moved through this private study undetected by the Count while he went about his private business. As she watched him now, he scooted the mirror with his foot to adjust its angle. Over the preceding hour he'd lost his mustache. But that wasn't what appeared to be holding his attention. When he tilted his head, and his large eyes narrowed intently, Amalina noticed the Count's image in the mirror, almost as a trick of the light and the glass, was somehow softer and gave the impression that, at this angle, one could see through his skin as if it were a light gauze, and could view clearly what was in the room behind him. He pressed and probed his diaphanous cheek with his fingers. A torch, which was behind him in the mirror, made an upside down nose on his face. It looked ridiculous. The Count muttered moodily, "This is getting worse."

"Hello, sir?" said Amalina, to let him know she'd come in.

"Ms. Dalca?" The Count pushed away the mirror and turned. "You have finished with the clean-up *already*?"

"Almost, but—"

"Then what do you want, Ms. Dalca? You've much to do, and only so much time."

"But it's a little complicated, sir; what needs to be done. I think I have an idea—"

"Yes, I am certain no-doubt you have a clever idea. But it can wait until after removing the material so disquieting to our other, more innocent guests. And we can also settle our Lady Lampeda by telling her that we have taken care of, to its conclusion, this unfortunate necessity."

"Yes, sir. And it has to do with that, sir ..." said Amalina, glancing around the room, nervously, suddenly realizing there might be someone else who was as potentially dangerous, or more so, in the room. Someone ready to attack. "But, um ... where is Pia, sir?"

"Naturally after such a trying episode Lady Lampeda is resting in her chambers."

"Oh, yes, of course. But, um ..." But still Amalina couldn't shake the image of Pia looking at her as if she were something meaningless to devour, still felt the horrible hunger in her friend's eyes, directed at her; someone who had once been her close friend, ready to kill her. It was inhuman; unsettling. The unthinking, vicious hunger. Like a monster's. And so ... so *not* Pia. Not Pia in the least. "Uh, sir, about Pia, may I ask, is she really all right? Has she recovered herself?"

The Count purred positively, maybe mistaking her purpose: "Assuredly, Pia is doing well. As you witnessed for yourself: she has finally passed the first test of survival. She can feed now; is willing to! At last ..."

"Yes, well ... " said Amalina. "But she never would have been willing to do that before ... when she was *really* herself."

"Of course she would be willing," said the Count with a bouncy air of victory. "Always has been. We *all* feed."

"Not like that. She never would have eaten blood; like a raving cannibal."

"There's nothing cannibalistic about it—"

"Like a wolf, then. Because it isn't in her nature to do such a thing. That ..." *that carnage?* She saw flashes of torn flesh and flowing blood, the blanking eyes. "And to innocent human life? That isn't Pia, sir. So you can't say she hasn't been altered."

"You have changed," he'd said to Pia in the moment. Amalina remembered this clearly. *"This is what we are!"*

"Ah, I see," said the Count presently. "But naturally she has altered. As a babe moves from milk to meat, she has accepted a new hunger. That is all."

This statement made Amalina gag. She kept it to herself well enough. The room seemed again to be whirling; whirling around both her and the Count's giant, depthless eyes, following a current out of her control. Circling back. "And still—"

"What does your look mean, little mouse? You abhor the hunger which comes naturally to a higher power?"

"It's just that I'm not sure how all this works, sir."

The Count's eyebrow lifted. "How what works?"

"This process of her changing. And—"

"You of all people, Ms. Dalca—um, that is, my *little mouse*. You should understand how it *all* works. Besides myself, no one else has been more intimately involved."

"Maybe I don't mean the *process* itself, sir ... no. Maybe what's confusing me is this master-apprentice thing between you and her, and how far she will become—become you."

"Our process will strengthen her. She will transform into something greater than herself. But she will retain herself. She doesn't *become* me."

"No? But—"

"I didn't cut out half her brain and replace it with my own." He smiled the smile of someone not wanting to frighten, but it had the contrary effect. "But is *that* what you are afraid of then, little mouse? That's what this is all about? That I will take away *your* will, when the time comes?"

It was the first time in months that he'd fully and explicitly revived the subject of turning Amalina into a creature. In *keeping* her. Maybe it was her fault for bringing up Pia, but it was so opposite of the conversation she wanted to be having. And so soon after what she'd just witnessed. *What she would become!* She wanted to escape. But now, by the sound of it, he was trying to make love to her:

"I won't change one part of you, Amalina," his voice purred in the way she'd seen him use on the other Ladies. He leaned forward, his large eyes growing warm. It seemed genuine, but ... "Not one iota will be lost, little mouse. Only more gained. And how could I want it any other way? You *must* understand my complete sincerity from what I've said before: you are a quick young woman; a gentle young woman; someone with such deep innocence and purity. The complete opposite of me."

"Sir, I don't know what to say, but—"

He didn't need her to say anything. He was still talking: "The Taijitu. The In-Yang. Yes, the Lion and the Lamb. The brute and the blood innocent ..."

"But it's about—"

"Your fear."

"No."

"Yes, it is. I see it in you. You *are* afraid. When you shouldn't be, but you are. Admit it to me, and free yourself of it. Unburden yourself, Amalina."

"I *am* afraid," she blurted, wishing he'd just stop. What a ridiculous thing to deny when she had just been covered in blood. "Of course I am! Who wouldn't be? None of this is what Pia wanted, or what Pia asked for, is it? And you want me to accept ... ? But how can I when I don't even understand ... anything? Not what's happening. Not what it means. And not even you. I never understand *you*. Why did you do that to Pia?"

She felt like she was on the verge of crying. All the horror of earlier, and the feeling of the loss of her friend—and indeed the fear—began to take hold. And at the same time there was something that struck her, what Margeta had asked before she came into the room. There was a sticking point there. This informed what she would say next. "Sir, you must tell me ... Why *did* you transform Pia? when you and she are nothing alike?"

"It should be obvious."

"Because she is nothing like you, which means she's just like me?" she asked hopefully. "She's *also* your In-Yang? Well, if you you have one opposite to yourself already, why do you need me, too?"

"No, she isn't the opposite I require; not the way you are. She's nothing like you at all. She's from royal blood, and that kind are all murderers at heart."

"Then really: why her, sir? You loved Aria Ecci when she was here. And you enjoy Margeta la Brichese, her ruthlessness, for some reason. But then you went and performed the rite on Pia. On dear, nice Pia Lampeda! I don't get it!"

"But I already said, it should be obvious—"

"But it isn't! Was it to upset me? To anger me?" He was watching Amalina with so impenetrable a look now, it was like he was holding back just for the enjoyment of watching her flail. To thrill at her guesses. She continued, feeling a fury grow as she went: "Or maybe it was to punish Margeta, because she had tried to kill Pia? And so you set her on top of Margeta as some kind of joke?"

The Count smiled obscurely. No that wasn't it. But she was getting somewhere. There was *some* reason.

"I thought you liked Pia, little mouse," he offered. "Pia worships you. Very much so. I thought it would make you happy to have her with you, as you have me."

Amalina shook her head. That wasn't it either, he was lying to her still. He was just feeding on her emotions and confusion. She tried to read the twisting thoughts behind his smiling eyes. There was some truth within their words, whether it was from what Amalina had said, or what he had said, but … But there was more. Always more.

"Oh, I get it," groaned Amalina, suddenly quite sure of herself. "Now I understand. You performed the rite on Pia because you *did* prefer Aria. Even Margeta you favored more. Princess Lampeda you didn't care one thing about; just like Robine. It never made any sense why you tried the rite on Robine first, when she was so definitely not to your liking. I thought it was because she was the most weak and willing. But now I remember: you are a bit of a scientist. You would not risk putting a woman you *wanted* through the rite, until you'd tried it out first and succeeded on someone who didn't matter at all. Robine, Pia, they were your experiments. Pia just got lucky and it worked."

"No luck in the least," said the Count. "I'd already perfected the rite, you clever little mouse. With Robine, well, what can be said …? With Robine it was really your fault, now isn't that so? The poor girl might still be alive if you hadn't been so clumsy." He saw Amalina's face turn red, and he eased back and spoke on gently. "Even if you can't admit it, dear little mouse …

But with Miss Lampeda, I was confident it would work. I was very confident or I would have chosen someone else for another trial run ... If you want me to admit to something, that is it: Pia Lampeda was—*is*—my gift to you."

• • •

He lied there too, thought Amalina when, for the second time in an hour, she was headed for the small dining room, now dragging a rolled up piece of oilcloth. At least she was feeling sharper-headed. *Pia isn't some kind of gift to me. Well, maybe she is. But she's also meant to be a trap. Our friendship to keep me here in the castle; and quiet; and with him. As if,* she sneered at the thought, *had he trapped me here, somehow I could possibly, willingly, truly, give my heart over to him!*

She laughed cynically to herself as she readied for what horrors might still be left to see in the cleanup, but also preparing herself to give Genadie the good news. The very good news.

"We're getting out of here tonight!"

But she found Genadie in a worse state than before.

Genadie was weeping into his hands outside the dining room. He stopped when he noticed her. He shrugged. Then he leaned toward her and, in a low voice, whispered confidentially: "This one *was* my fault, Ms. Dalca. It *wasn't* the Master's doing, this delegation coming, but my mistake, my oversight!"

By way of further explanation, he pointed into the room and at the first body on the floor. The long table had been shoved aside and all the men, in whatever state they could be cleaned up and reassembled, were lying next to each other in a row. Added to the collection were the delegation's two drivers, who the Count had presumably taken care of in the courtyard and brought here. But the closest man to Genadie was Crutio, Guwerte's friend, Pia's final victim for the night.

"It *was* him," hissed Genadie, almost falling into a sob again. "I knew it! It should never have come to this, but I—"

"You're still blubbering about that? *I'm* the one who spoke up at that inn, Genadie." He looked at her, suddenly concerned at just what she'd said— admitted to—aloud. "Don't worry, we can say anything we like. After all the excitement, *your* master needed to go out and hunt tonight, and so he has. None of this blood was good for him, I guess. And so, anyway—listen to me, we haven't much time now, eh?"

Genadie nodded but immediately returned to looking miserable. So did Amalina, the Count had gone out to hunt ... with Cristine out in the forest. Her friend was hiding just outside the castle, and with the Count in the mood for a quick snack! There was no time for Genadie's sudden guilty conscience.

"Stop that," she scolded Genadie, trying to shake the terrible thought of Cristine being wrung out by the Count and to move things along. She patted Genadie's back, but he only gained a darker look. Amalina continued: "I've got news for you. But, take heart, Genadie, *I* was the one who spoke up at the inn, eh? But that was years ago, and I mean, how was I supposed to know what would happen? What they would go and do, and what they did ... and ..." Amalina smiled weakly. " ... and you almost killed Guwerte. What more could you have done? If you'd gone and killed him, *that* murder would have been your fault. Not this man here." Amalina swallowed hard on another thought: Crutio was *her* fault, by how she so easily parted from him. If only she had stood her ground between Pia and him, then maybe—

Amalina heard again Crutio's desperation and his death: Crutio whimpering, Crutio screaming, Crutio quiet again. She had *given* the poor man to Pia, hadn't she? Given him to the vicious animal and her trainer.

Amalina threw away the thought and continued on to her point of pardoning Genadie. Move along, move along: "Either way, one man would have been dead. But why are we racing to blame ourselves? Ridiculous. There's only one person at fault here and that is ... *you know who.*"

Strangely, even as Amalina paused in her words to allow Genadie to make the expected scornful denial, the cry of blasphemy against his god, he didn't. His head sank an inch between his shoulder blades and his expression soured by the same amount. This mess, and the feeling that it was his fault, must be reminding him of the horrific scene of his wife and her extended family and people, in that lonely clearing, the Count standing over their bodies.

Good.

"All right, let's get to it," she said, rolling out the cloth at the feet of the bodies in the room. "No time. And you know I'm right. You *know* it," she pressed him, because she had to soften him, to get him ready for what was to come. Because she needed him. She tugged at one of the driver's legs, to shift him onto the cloth. "You know it's true, don't you? You see it now."

"He's always been nice to me."

"Oh? And how is that, Genadie? How's he been nice to you?"

"I'm still alive."

The answer made him seem pathetic. But not entirely lost. He still appreciated life. She refused to lose hope now. Not when she was so close. Instead, feeling an up-welling of anger, or spite, or optimistic giddiness—a combining of all her inner tracks, as they merged; it was an energy, anyway—she pushed: "Not good enough, my friend! Not at all! I know you've had enough of this. Otherwise you'd be helping me instead of just sitting there in tears." He scooted himself up onto his feet, looking ashamed for leaving her to the work. "Look around you ... This is it, isn't it? You've had it ... You don't think your 'little body can take this anymore,' right? ... and it *shouldn't* ... and it—and you—don't *have* to." He looked at her questioningly. "Listen, Genadie. Didn't you hear what I said? We're getting out of here. Forever. Tonight."

"What's that?"

"What are we to do with all these bodies, eh?"

"Get rid of them."

"I spoke to the Count and his plan is we dispose of them proper and take them out of the castle. Carriage and everything, right down to the horses."

"Yes?"

"So that not a shred of them can be found here by sun-up and have the ladies asking questions."

"No. Of course."

"So that's what we do, eh?" She squeezed his bony shoulder. "Only, we pretend we are going to lose them somewhere ... but then we keep on going. Just keep on riding until we're back in France. Never have to deal with something like this again. Do you understand? Escape."

"Oh, Amalina." His disappointment was bottomless in its delivery. She felt it in her gut. Her giddiness was hard struck.

"Or Germania, or Italy, or wherever you want," she said. "Let's do it. Let's escape. While we can. This is our one last chance."

Genadie thought and thought. His fingers added little bloody checkmarks to his stubbled chin as each thought bobbed his body, and his eyes squinted harder, and he began to lean.

Very cautiously, as the barest scratchy whisper, like a leaf blown across the floor by a mild breeze, and with eyes rounding now to Amalina as if pleading to her: "Escape ...? Really? But he would never let us get *too* far away—*that* far away—not so far from the castle ... that it would allow us to slip away from him ..."

"Oh, he would though." Then she added the words that were crucial: "Never too far, no. You're right. But far *enough*? Yes."

"Dawn is in so many hours. By then, we'd be to the woods, maybe. Or to the river."

"But that's not very far at all. I'm saying *much* farther than that."

He looked at her dubiously. She couldn't believe it was true either. Just the day before she was at odds on what she should do with herself, begging for a sign. And now fate had delivered its clearest message. She was leaving the castle and the Count for good. Yes, if while alive, the prosecutors from Germania (and Crutio) couldn't get her out of the castle—never mind the country—they would achieve it in their death. They were the perfect excuse to hurry to the border. And then, being at the border, if she and Genadie were to scurry over into the western kingdoms and continue on, it was something the Count could seethe over until he burned to dust, but he could do nothing about. The horror of Pia was finally dissipating and they were back on track. They were leaving Margeta's game, and Pia, and that whole new horror, and slipping the Count's trap. They were leaving it all. Finally. Forever.

Hold on Cristine, I'm coming.

"He wouldn't agree to it," said Genadie, his features atremble with hope and doubt.

"This is what we're arguing about, Genadie?" She smiled brightly. "He's already said yes. We're going."

24

The Getaway

Amalina and Genadie were seated on the delegation's carriage facing the gate, waiting for the doors to be opened. Genadie looked back nervously, down along the side of the carriage into its main compartment. Even leaning all the way out, the bodies inside, the judge and his men, couldn't be seen. Small black curtains were drawn over the windows. In front of the carriage the delegation's six horses, of varying breed and size, were reined up and it looked awkward and ridiculous on such a small carriage—but it would work.

"How did you get him to agree?" whispered Genadie, more in wonder now than suspicion or doubt. "It is *your* plan? Master agreed to it, really?"

"Did you pack anything?" she asked, pointing to some splotches of blood on his chin he still needed to rub off. "I have as much as I could get under this coat."

He patted the large box next to him. "Something to eat and drink should we get hungry. And maybe a little more. But tell me how."

"I just laid out the facts," said Amalina, as they waited. She spoke quickly, as if it would hurry Durok along to the bolt in the door. "He thought we would take all of this, and them, to the old farmhouse—remember, the farm Kralov and his men used?—disassemble this carriage, set it inside what's left of the barn, and burn it some more. Bury the bodies there, too. Then be back before dawn."

Genadie grimaced at how nonchalantly she'd said it. He blinked at her and swallowed, in a way that made her feel bloodthirsty; or jaded beyond all measure. It seemed they had *both* done worse before. Who knows where all the bodies had gone? It felt blasphemous, thinking about it.

"Well we don't have to do that anyway, right? I just explained how his plan wouldn't work. Because if this delegation never returns to Germania, someone from over there will be sent to find them, and to ask what became of them and also to enquire after me—I mean, about Hedvikina Von Schiederhausen. It would be better they think the matter is resolved. All of it: that the delegation died and will not return to them; that Judge Wolcraft already came here to the castle, found what he needed—which is that Katarina is not the missing niece—and they were on their way home. This can only be done convincingly if their bodies and the wreckage are found at the bottom of a great precipice, and the tragedy reported to their countrymen. In Wolcraft's papers will be notes exonerating Lady Tepsji."

"But that can still be done right here, in these mountains of Netz," said Genadie.

"That's what he said."

. . .

What the Count had said was, with a growing agitation, his eye secretly seeking his faint image in the mirror, "All this can still be done within range, Ms. Dalca. The object is for you and Genadie to be back before sunrise. To meet our guests without them wondering if something has gone wrong in this castle; comfortable that the delegation has left of their own accord. If you and Genadie go missing at the same time that they left here, there will be questions and suspicions. It cannot not be helped."

"But the discovery has to happen on a highway *outside* of Ardeel," said Amalina. "Not too far, but over the border so that the Germainian government won't suspect blackguards or agents within this country in the accident; should the thought arise, that is. It would be a foreign matter after that, far away from you."

"Yes. *Yessss*," the Count had said, still looking saggy-eyed and tired, but impressed. "You have a keen mind for these kind of intrigues. I can see an advantage in it. But as for you ... no. I will assign some of the men to do this instead—"

"No."

"Why do you always contradict me, little mouse?"

"We've such a small staff here in the castle, anyone missing will be noticed. My going away on a whim, it won't be inconsistent with how I am, you see. You'll find some reason in any case. And the ladies will probably be relieved, because they can have you to themselves while I'm away. They won't look for a reason why I might have gone, but concentrate on their own concerns; so much so they won't even *care* why I left."

"Yes, I do see ..." he murmured.

"And besides, who else would you trust to get everything done properly? Durok? *Pils*?"

"As always, Ms Dalca, have it your way," he had said impatiently, turning with a *humph* from his mirror. He went to his desk to begin forging Judge Wolcraft's papers of assessment, and Amalina's—Katarina's—exoneration. "As it is, there is very little time left and I need to eat. Go do it. Go and have your way. I suppose this is just some excuse to visit with your father. You're making off to Korr, don't deny. I know it. Oh, you don't have to say it, though, I know all your excuses." At this, Amalina could not help but look guilty. But he was too busy writing, expertly copying Wolcraft's script, to notice. "Well, why not? It has been a long time for you two, hasn't it?" He paused to look high along the wall and run the great plume of his pen along his lips, a thought amusing him. "Or … now that I think of it, rather you should *not* go to Korr at all. Perhaps up through the Borgo Pass would be the better route for *all* of us. I think it would be quicker, as it prevents any chance for delays; no distractions for you. Yes, that would be more acceptable to me." *I, me, I, me, I, me.* But now the Count turned to face her fully, some strange meaning burning in his eyes, though his lips were smiling almost gently. "Well, I will leave it up to you, Amalina. Just know that I will miss you. And that I *prefer* you ride the Borgo Pass. And don't take long. It's late into autumn and I don't want to have to fish you and Genadie out of a snowbank half frozen to death as I did before."

This memory seemed to please him and his smile became even more benevolent, though he stole a glance at the mirror, as if to reassure himself he *was* still there.

. . .

"So we're on our way," said Amalina to Genadie, atop the carriage. Willing the door to open. "But why are you looking like that?"

Genadie said nothing and continued to stare forward with an odd, dead expression.

Durok, the only member of the house guard who was trusted to see to their departure, the only sentry who was awake at this hour, finally got the bar off and opened both doors wide. He waved them through. They clattered forward and the delegation's carriage passed outside the high walls.

"Olympus," Genadie mumbled at last, when they were out and they could hear the doors closing behind them. He panted in a shallow way, as if he'd been discreetly holding his breath the whole time. "Olympus …" He looked impatient and threw glances back at the castle, to see just how far away they'd gotten. Not more than a few yards. Still too close. But he couldn't contain whatever was on his mind. He whispered into her ear: "Can we do it? Can we really?"

"It's up to us," she said, squeezing his thin but iron-hard arm encouragingly. She looked around for signs of Cristine in the forest, or in the high weeds along the road. She didn't know how she would explain the girl's sudden appearance and asking for a ride, but was confident a good reason would present itself. As long as Cristine hadn't been eaten in the mean time, that's all that mattered. "We're in control now, Genadie. We've just to get there."

"Oh, there's a thought, Ms. Dalca."

"And we will." As they trotted slowly away, Amalina couldn't help but say: "We're getting out of here."

"Yes, Ms. Dalca."

"We're *really* getting out of here."

"Yes, Ms. Dalca."

"It hardly feels true. Like something will stop us—*must* stop us. But it can't!"

"Yes, Ms. Dalca."

"We're free," she whispered. She was thinking: *Anything can happen now.* An image formed before her eyes, of Amalina and Ivanti Vokent dancing close to each other in a dark room, an image that was so palpable she sucked in a breath and could taste him. Yes, she hadn't given up on Ion yet! And he was waiting out there—somewhere—for her, if she wanted. All she had to do was grab Cristine, return her home, and then they were gone. "Free to do anything we like."

"Yes, Ms. Dalca."

"Why are you looking like that now?"

"Have to get as far away as we can," he said quickly. "Very far away. So if somebody comes after us—well he *might* send someone after us if he doesn't do it himself, or if he can't reach us—"

"Who?" But Amalina knew the Count had minions everywhere willing to do his bidding, willing to do whatever he asked. To follow. To apprehend …

For some reason she now recalled the ugly little wrinkled green man behind the Count's murder service. He lived in Korr, and they would be under his watch when they passed through. She felt her hand caught in his black glove.

But that was later. This was now.

Genadie was still talking quickly, excitedly: "We need to get so far away they can't reach us in time. So far away, before he knows …"

"Maybe we'll catch up to Aklan," she cheered him on after swallowing a nervous lump. "Nobody says we have to ever *stop*—"

At that moment, in the distance, Amalina heard a muted yelp and saw a small shadow duck fast to the right, off the angled castle approach. She sat up, tracking where it might have gone; a grey-black shape too large for a wolf, too small for the Count. Cristine! But why didn't she come onto the road? As Amalina turned on the bench, half-standing, following the shadow's likely path, wondering maybe it wasn't just a phantom of the mind brought on by talk of someone chasing after them, she was caught short and let out a cry.

Behind them: Pia Lampeda stood at the outer gate of the castle. The gate was shut and she was a slender white candle against its dark wood. She had stripped down—or been stripped down—to her lower vestments—but still there was blood. Dark blobby stains dotted the white linen, her breasts, her neck, her chin. Her eyes glowed eerily. Her mouth was set straight, making her look serious, or hungry.

25

Sisters in Blood

"**N**o," whispered Amalina hotly under her breath.

Genadie had already stopped the carriage. He was now looking back over the roof.

This couldn't be happening. Why was Pia there? What did she want? What *could* she want?

"Isn't that—?" croaked Genadie.

"Wait here," ordered Amalina.

"But, Ms. Dalca …"

Amalina dropped down from the riding bench and went to Pia at a quick march. She didn't know why she felt the urge to. To put space between the carriage and them, it seemed. So Genadie wouldn't hear what they had to say? Or maybe it was only to keep Pia from rushing at them, to surprise her by stepping forward herself to challenge her, instead of being challenged. Amalina wanted at least to show that she wasn't afraid. A lie, but it was important to convince her that that particular lie was true. She saw the raw power remaining in Pia's eyes and still hadn't fully shaken the image of Pia coming for her across the room. This was a reverse of that confrontation, then. *I am coming for* you.

Or maybe it was for Amalina to place herself between the princess and Cristine, who was still out here somewhere; if the Count, or Pia, hadn't already found the poor girl … *She* hadn't eaten Cristine, had she?

Pia smiled cautiously as Amalina arrived. "Dear Katty."

"What are you doing out here, Pia?" asked Amalina. "It's freezing."

"Is it? I don't really feel it right now. Maybe later. I'm still … well …"

"Hungry?"

"Burning," said Pia, dropping her eyes. She pulled a long red lock of hair and looped it behind her ear. Then she wiped the back of her hand across her mouth.

"Are you all right?" asked Amalina.

"I haven't felt better in such a long time."

Amalina almost asked, *so it was worth it, then?* but that would prolong the conversation. Instead she said, almost as a suggestion: "I thought you were inside, in bed, resting."

"Why not come out?" said Pia dreamily. "*He* has flown the castle for the night. I felt restless. I heard you leaving. Well, I heard someone leaving. I *sensed* it might be you. Your smell—your, uh, vibration."

"Vibration?"

"Difficult to explain." She smiled shyly. "It's all so strange, Katty. But it's like I can feel everything, smell everything, see everything. And more." She shook her head. "Maybe I can't explain it."

"*'Merging with the world,'*" said Amalina, quoting from the Strange Man's diary, who had described the sensation when he'd become such a creature.

"Something like that," agreed Pia, smiling wider, her green eyes warming. She reached a hand to Amalina, but it came up too fast. She dropped it back just as quickly as if afraid of the speed; or worried she'd frighten Amalina by it. "May I touch you?"

"If you like."

"Do you want me to, Katty? Do you miss me?"

"Of course." Amalina hoped she'd had enough experience with the Count to regulate her breath, her body, to keep her heart from speeding. From giving away the truth. Still, her body shivered and trembled. She covered the shake by looking back to Genadie, to see if he was watching. His head was politely turned back round. She blew a visible cloud of breath into the cold evening air. That way—toward Genadie; forward—was escape. But she had to turn from it. She scanned the distance for Cristine. Nothing. "Go ahead," said Amalina. She lifted her own hand, limply and lamely, and handed it over to Pia. Pia took the offered limb. The princess's skin felt as hot as a red coal.

"I'm so glad we can see each other again," said Pia, almost melting into Amalina's hand. "It's what I looked forward to all these months. You'd gone away to Italy before I'd ... before I *woke up*, I suppose it is. And I asked for you, and he told me you'd already left me ... on your trip ... Well, I don't really blame you ... you didn't know when I would wake up. Or if I ever would."

"Sorry I left you like that; alone, with him. Well, and with Margeta, too ..."

Pia gave a sad little laugh. "I can't say they made up for it."

"I imagine not. And I have been keeping to myself since my return."

"Oh, and honestly I've been hiding away, too. Silly now. I was afraid of ... but I don't know what I was afraid of ... Tonight couldn't have been worse than what I'd imagined ... You know ... What happened ... Tonight ... What happened ..." Pia wiped her mouth again.

A silence fell between them. Amalina didn't know what to do with it. Her eyebrows danced around and she ground her jaw, wishing she could take back her hand and leave. Escape—her future—stood just a number of yards away. *C'mon, let's go.* She looked back at the carriage again. And still no Cristine.

"I," Pia began, then stopped, her own drama playing out in her head. Her hand tightened on Amalina's. "Well, Katty, I was going to kill you. You know I never would have. Never would have thought I would do something like that. But I lost myself. I needed to—I needed the blood, but I didn't know how much I needed it. And once I started ... Everything was different. I couldn't even see, Katty. I could only sense. Not sense who was there, but that what I needed was there. And I couldn't stop."

Amalina nodded, a blush on her cheek. "That's how it looked."

"I beg you to forgive me. To understand. It's all so unusual and new. I didn't know."

"It's all right. *He* should have known."

"Well, he did, didn't he? He was there to stop me. To guide me. To bring me around to right. Well, 'right' is the wrong word. So I wouldn't harm someone I care for. Deeply care for. But of course what I did, it wasn't exactly wrong, either, was it? I saved you from them. They wanted to take you away. To execute you. It wasn't all bad."

"It was very scary. For me."

Pia smiled softly: "You know, it scared me too ... how much I wanted to do it. And that I *could* do it. And so easily." She released then squeezed Amalina's arm tenderly now. *Just let me go*, thought Amalina. "But I haven't changed. Not at all. I hope you don't think I'd turn into somebody else because of all this. I have control, I do. It will never happen again, I promise."

By what she said, had the Count put her up to this apology? Or had she been close enough to their conversation in the private study that she'd heard? In any case, this was an attempt to smooth things, to prevent or persuade her from leaving. That couldn't happen. She assured Pia it wasn't as she thought.

"Why are you leaving?" asked Pia. "It's not because I frightened you?"

"We have to get rid of the carriage and the horses. And the, uh, um ..." The *bodies*, of course. Pia's lips turned down. She stared heavily at the carriage.

"Nothing alive in there," Pia said of the carriage, with not quite embarrassment or shame. "So many of them ... men. They've become a part of me in a way. But it's frightening to think about. And it doesn't really feel like it's true. I feel no attachment to what happened, even if it is. But let's not talk about that anymore."

You're the one who brought it up, Amalina thought impatiently. A thought from the darker part of her mind. She shifted to pull away. "I should be back soon enough. I will."

"You can't send your man along to do it by himself?" Pia squeezed Amalina's hand, pulling it back into her. She was definitely trying to keep her here.

"He doesn't know the whole plan, and he definitely needs my help. And we're the only ones who can do it, you see. That's why the Count tasked us both. For me to go, too."

"Well," she said, her eyes lowering, "If *he* decided it was for you two to do—"

"Oh, yes, oh, yes," said Amalina, too eagerly; but she couldn't help herself. She had the opportunity and the excuse to get away. Now it felt like Pia was a giant snake trying to pull her back into her coils. But … there was an opening in the loops. *Aklan found a way out, so why not me?* Amalina carried on: "Oh, yes, he *was* insistent. Very much so. And he probably thought you wouldn't miss me, you seemed so weak after … well …"

After you killed all those men.

Pia nodded shyly, and said: "He doesn't know how strong I've become, though, I think. He thinks I'm still little Pia. But I leapt right up on top of the castle tonight. Did you see? And I jumped all the way down to the ground right here. And I felt almost nothing. Like leaping up a stair and then down. You can't imagine how wonderful it is, Katty."

"No, I can't," she said with a tone she hoped carried the notion that she wouldn't want to know, not first hand. *Did Cristine see this leap?* Amalina wondered, trying not to glance away into the grasses. That would be hard to explain.

"You know, Katty," said Pia hopefully, with several more soothing, pulling squeezes, "if he were to give *you* the rite, he probably wouldn't expect you to do some of these things you do; getting rid of carriages and horses and the rest. You wouldn't be a servant anymore, you know. Never again."

Amalina nodded her head, rushing it along. "Oh, I know."

"It's something to consider, Katty, isn't it? Wouldn't it make you more … Well, *more Katty*? Wouldn't it? And not stay the little Amalina?"

"I don't really mind—"

"Oh, no, Katty, you shouldn't," said Pia quickly, afraid she'd given offense. "There's nothing to be ashamed of in who you are. Or were. But I can't tell you how much more wonderful it is—Wait!"

Pia's eyes rounded in that animal way she'd had in the dining room. The famished, tunnel-visioned wolf eyes stared into the darkness beyond Amalina. Her ears seemed to prick up high along the side of her head. Amalina's skin crawled and she tried to take her arm away.

"Oh, no, it isn't you, Katty," said Pia. "There is someone out there. I thought it was an animal. The whole world is moving with creatures great and small and I thought—Well, they're starting to move again, and it is someone. *Someone.*"

Cristine.

"No, it's probably nothing," said Amalina.

Pia called into the darkness, "Ay, out there! Come! Come to us! There is nothing to fear, but make yourself known or we will summon a patrol! No, don't run away! But come. *Come!*"

The last word thrummed in Amalina's chest. Nothing like what the Count could do (or the Strange Man had done), but it was stronger than a drum, and something no human could attempt. The train of six horses on the carriage whinnied and shifted and Genadie held onto his hat as he begged them to steady themselves. A dog barked in the distance.

"Probably just a dog."

"I said come to us," warned Pia sternly, "or I will come to you." And after a short wait, she softened and lifted her hand toward the darkness. "Now, that's a good little thing. Keep walking. Come to us so we might see who you are that would give us such a scare. Who are you?"

Someone had stood from the grass. They walked slowly, almost limping into the light of the carriage lanterns; it was the shadow Amalina had seen slipping off the road. And now, as the torch light shone bright on the small figure, Amalina was relieved. Cristine was alive.

But Amalina could only act just as she had earlier in the day; as if she could not believe her eyes. That this sudden appearance was impossible. "Cristine?"

• • •

Cristine stood there in a heavy cloak. At first her posture appeared hunched and beaten and exhausted. But, as if realizing what she must look like, she pulled her shoulders back into the proper bearing of a good young lady. All the while, her face never changed, it was set into something friendly, supplicating, and disarming; but there was a nervous, almost feral quickness to it.

"Who are you?" asked Pia, not acknowledging the name Amalina had just called.

Cristine pinned Princess Lampeda with her sharp blue eyes, a return question in them, then cut them to Amalina for a moment before slashing them back to Pia again. Her smile lengthened on one side, into a strange, challenging grin. She pointed to Amalina. "I am *her* friend."

"Oh, yes?" said Pia, with the officious voice of a discomforted princess whose patience was being pressed by a servant. "And just who do you think *she* is, young lady? Do you know her name?"

"It's all right, Pia," said Amalina in a cheery voice to remove the tension, while motioning to Cristine discreetly with her free hand, signaling she should bow. "We know each other very well and are very good friends. This is Cristine."

"From Ardeel, I think." Pia looked to Amalina for confirmation. "So she's a friend of *Amalina's*?"

Amalina and Cristine nodded at the same time and in the same way, almost mirror images, though physically they could not be more opposite: Cristine with her sharp face, icy crystal-blue eyes and blond hair; Amalina with her dark hair, soft brown eyes, and solid-limbed body. But a shared, twin-like bond between them was there. Pia's lips tightened at the corners, though the knowledge didn't seem to necessarily *displease* her. She looked distantly bemused.

"Cristine," said Amalina, breaking the silence. "May I introduce to you Lady Princess Pia Lampeda from Italy. From *Rome*." Cristine fell to a deep curtsy, spreading her cloak with both hands on either side, and almost touched the dirt with her nose. "Pia, Cristine is my best friend from Korr."

"Milady," said Cristine, humbly.

Pia's arm withdrew from Amalina's. It almost did feel like a snake sliding away. She stared down at Cristine. "Rise. If you're a friend of—um, Amalina—then know you are my friend too."

Cristine stood unsurely, looking to Amalina for guidance. But when her eyes went to Pia, really studying the princess, they traced over her body, taking in the bloodied undergarments and the stained skin; and probably not quite sorting it all into something understandable.

"Thank you, milady," said Cristine.

"But, what are you doing here?" said Amalina. "Why are you—?"

"Well, I came to see you, didn't I? I was bored and I thought it might be fun to visit you—"

"Came by yourself? On your own? At *night*?"

"I didn't mean to be so *late*," said Cristine, putting extra meaning into it. "It wasn't easy getting up here—"

"But how did you? Does your mother know where you are? Your father?"

Cristine shook her head and looked annoyed at having to repeat the conversation from earlier on account of their audience. "Not exactly. Probably they haven't figured it all out yet." She got a clever look that touched her lips. "Now that I'm here though, I can send them a letter and—"

"But you aren't staying," said Amalina definitely, and quickly, bursting at her friend's presumption. Pia's bid to stop her from leaving was bad enough. Cristine, seeing the opportunity to stay, was now about to try to pin her back at the castle—just when she was about to make it out! Her friend's flashing eyes said as much.

But no, thought Amalina suddenly, excited. She tried to still her expression, though her mood flipped again. Amalina now saw Cristine as some kind of godsend. Not only had her friend interrupted whatever was going to happen with Pia, her appearance introduced a superior, worry-free solution for Amalina's choice of route out of Ardeel. Suddenly, Cristine became her best friend in the world. Absolutely.

Feeling elated, but maintaining her stern tone, Amalina said: "You can't be here, my dearest friend. Not even for the night. The castle is already full, and is not mine to give you or anyone permission to stay. The Count has his methods and ways. You wouldn't want to be ... well, we must go. We're leaving anyway," Amalina pointed to the carriage. "I was just leaving, you see. And we can take you back. Yes, your father and mother will be very happy to see you back in their home."

"Back? But, no. I just came—"

"There isn't any arguing about it. You're just lucky we caught you in time, especially where we're going." Amalina turned to Pia, "Maybe you should go back inside, too, Princess. Before uncle returns home. He'd be worried you'd come out so soon and in this way, with so little on. He'd be afraid you would catch your death."

Pia nodded, but with a cool smirk. She'd taken her eyes off Cristine and now would look only at Amalina. Amalina was hers. Nobody else existed. "So you are taking your good friend away, and escorting her back to ...?"

"Excuse us for a moment," said Amalina to Cristine, and turned Pia toward the castle. She leaned in confidentially and whispered so Cristine couldn't hear. "If we're truly friends, Pia, don't tell *him* a thing about who she is. It could go badly. But you understand, she is from Korr, and we were once sworn to each other—sisters in blood—"

"Sisters in blood," repeated Pia.

"And so that is where I have to take her. I must. I always keep my word. Just you tell him, if he ever asks, that I've had a surprise visitor on my way out, you can't recall their name, but they are from Korr, and so we settled on a route. There are now reasons I *must* use the western highway and not the northern one. You are my witness." Amalina explained this new course briefly on their short walk back to the gate.

"*All* the way to Korr?" said Pia.

"It won't be long, I promise." Amalina thought she should touch her friend's shoulder, or take her into a hug, or kiss her on the cheek. Or peck her right on her pouting lips. Something to settle her. But she chose not to. It would feel manipulative and perhaps everyone, Pia, Cristine, even Genadie, even the horses on the carriage, would know it was crass manipulation. "Trust me. Just do me this favor and tell him what Genadie and I are off to do, and we will be back from Korr as fast as we can. And I will see you again, my dear."

"You promise?"

"Yes," said Amalina.

"You promise me, really?"

"Of course. I promise. I swear."

"You swear?"

"Oh, Pia, of course!"

Not if I can help it, Amalina thought guiltily.

. . .

"*All* the way back?" moaned Cristine as they walked to the waiting carriage.

You too? thought Amalina, crossly. It was a fight on all sides to get this plan in motion. Why was it so difficult? she wondered. "Sorry, sister dear. But you should have written me first."

"I did."

"Not that you were coming or I would have warned you off." Amalina motioned to the front of the carriage and the riding bench, all business. "Now let's get up and go."

"Not inside?" asked Cristine, surprised. She jumped to the side of the carriage before Amalina could protest and flung open the small black door with a fresh smile on her face.

Cristine froze. She saw all the important men sitting inside. Their sickening wounds and blood were hidden by their postures, riding coats, and the deep shadows, but their crush together made clear the impossibility of anyone else entering.

"What are you doing?" cried Amalina, taking Cristine's hand away from the door and shutting it. She pushed her forward to the riding box. "Leave them well alone!"

"They're sleeping?" asked Cristine.

Amalina shrugged. "It's full. We ride on top."

"How miserable."

"First thing you must understand," said Amalina. "I am just a lowly servant. That's it. I mean, look at what I'm wearing. I don't get riding privileges. Neither do my friends. Now, up."

"Taking this one with us?" said Genadie as he offered his hand to help Cristine onto the bench. "Oh, a nice, pretty young miss. Out here at night on your own?"

"Yes. And it's on to Korr," Amalina told him. "Non-stop. We have to get her back home. Is that as far away and fast enough for you, Genadie?"

He grunted appreciably. She knew how he felt. *Now* they were on their way.

Cristine paused before ascending to the riding box, and for a last time looked with a touch of longing back at the castle, for the alternate life she was now abandoning. Her eyes narrowed. "Wait. Where did she go?"

Pia, who had been observing them from the gate only a moment ago, was gone.

26

Long Road

The road to Korr and the Ardeelian border was a long one, but the most significant moment of the ride happened right at the start, which would then set the tone for the rest of the trip:

Bundled against the cold on the riding bench, the three travelers a single blanketed mound, Amalina noticed Cristine was still sitting rigidly upright between her and Genadie, her face tense.

"Are you all right?" asked Amalina.

"Besides being spun back round to Korr?" frowned Cristine. "Yes, I'm perfect. Why wouldn't I be?"

"You aren't cold? or tired?"

Cristine turned to Amalina, made a face and pinched her nose; she had noticed Genadie's smell. And while this nervy display was very much what Cristine would do, there was still something awkward and unreal about her.

For a moment, remembering how the Strange Man could alter himself to look like anything or anyone he wished, and assuming the Count could do the same—as all creatures like them could—Amalina suddenly feared he had done just that: the Count had jumped aboard the mission, dressed as her best friend from Korr. What else would explain how a pretty young lady, alone at night outside the castle, would not have been immediately attacked by the Count on his hunt? He might have killed her and then replaced her. But why would he? To act as a spy?

And how could he know Cristine—and know she is my friend? Amalina wondered doubtfully. He claimed to know everyone in Ardeel. But that can't be true. And even if he knew what Amalina's 'sister-in-blood' looked like, he couldn't take on her mannerisms so perfectly. Even if the architect Balbo had gone to him and reported the girl lurking in the forest, he couldn't have told everything that she was, or who she was to Amalina. This girl sitting next to Amalina on the bench, then, *was* Cristine. There had to be another explanation for her odd behavior. So wound tight and uncomfortable. And distant. What could be the reason?

"What?" said Cristine at Amalina's prolonged stare.

"How about something to eat and drink?" suggested Amalina, looking past her to Genadie.

"Already?" howled Genadie. "We've just started out!"

"I'm hungry anyway. How about you, Cristine? I'm sure you are, too."

"Whatever you like," she said without care. But the coldness in her eyes flickered.

Ah, that's it, thought Amalina, as she gladly handed over the large corked horn of wine and a couple strips of dried meat. And sure enough, as Cristine took her sips and chewed into the jerky with a quickening greed, she began to heave and gasp. She even hugged closer to Amalina and shivered after a while.

Her old friend had just been keeping up a pretense of strength and command to mask her weakness and exhaustion. It was almost endearing in spite of the reality of what she'd done.

"But I don't understand," said Amalina, "you came all by yourself?"

Cristine made a ravenous noise.

"By yourself, all the way from Korr?"

"Don't be stupid," she snarled between chews, with renewed strength. "I rode with *them*." She motioned to the carriage they were sitting on.

"The delegation from Germania?" Amalina was stunned. "But you weren't with them when they arrived. And why were you *outside* the castle then?"

"I was only with them as far as Netz village," she explained. She heaved a sigh as if giving in: "Here's how it happened, okay, Amalina? I've seen so many princesses riding through Korr on their way to the Netz Castle. And, well, when these men were trading out horses in Korr, I overheard they were going to the castle there in Netz, too; and knowing that's where you were, I hid with the luggage atop their carriage."

"Cristine!"

"Oh, what's the matter? I can't tell you how *bored* I am there without you! When I saw them, it seemed like my only chance. Aren't you happy I came?"

"But you rode on top of a carriage all the way from Korr—?"

"Oh, no. They spotted me. Only by then they were already on the highway, so I begged for a ride. Told them I needed to get to Netz to see my sister, and they would be too mean to throw me off. They weren't the nicest people about it, but I offered to pay and they let me sit in the carriage. And, well, stupid me, I got off in the village of Netz proper. Because, you see, the village is where I told them I wanted to go. I thought I'd just walk up to the castle from there, you know. After all, it's called the Netz Castle, isn't it? How far away could it be? I really thought it would be an easy enough walk." She shivered. "But, oh, how wrong. How wrong! I've never walked so much. When I realized my mistake, I'd gotten pretty far. But I had to turn back and hire a horse with what little money I had left—for what good that horse was."

"With no food or water for yourself," said Amalina.

"I figured you'd feed me when I reached the castle."

"And not even a light?"

"I didn't know I would *need* one. It was still daylight. And I made good time, all things considered."

"And it's so late in the season, Cristine! A winter storm could have hit and you might have been buried. And then what about the wolves?" Amalina thought of the Count roaming out of the castle again, looking for a victim. Cristine must have the most incredible luck not to have been killed at any point after leaving Netz. "That was so dangerous! Cristine!"

"I see that *now*. But I made it, didn't I? I did take along one of Papa's pistols. Heaven knows if I could figure out how to use it. Oh, I'm so worn out, Amalina. Let's not go on about it."

"But it's too amazing to think!"

"Not so amazing," she whispered to Amalina, leaning closer, as if she might be preparing to sleep. "What's more amazing is I haven't heard any of *them* make a peep yet. And they can't be half as tired as I am. I never saw those geezers so quiet. One or the other was always talking about something. Politics and other boring things … Even in German it was tedious. But one boring thing or another was always being discussed the whole way. You know, some of them had been riding their own horses on the way to the castle … there was room then, inside the compartment, for me to sit comfortably … Too bad now, 'cause I could really use some rest …"

Amalina nodded. She couldn't believe Cristine, normally so perceptive, hadn't caught on that the men in the carriage were dead. She almost wondered if her friend was putting her on. But she wasn't going to add to her distress if she hadn't figured it out. How could she possibly explain it? "That's okay. You're tired, get some rest now."

Cristine peered up at Amalina. "Were you *really* going to leave me outside all night?"

"I didn't!"

"Half the night's gone. I can't believe you. If anything's unbelievable it is the way you treated me. You wouldn't think we were friends at all." She said this, even as she was nuzzling further into Amalina's shoulder. "Wouldn't even let me in the front door, would you? Couldn't have that, *could* you? What kind of friend would do such a thing? But she leaves me outside to freeze. Not a friend at all. More like a snooty princess afraid to let her friends meet her *real* friends; her best friend in the world. Now, I ask you."

Amalina huffed in protest, then turned to Genadie. "You don't mind if we talk, do you?"

"Ladies' voices are like music, Ms. Dalca," he said rather automatically.

She grabbed his side gently, "I mean can we have some privacy? and talk without you listening in?"

"You want me to ride on the roof?" But he didn't wait for her answer. He handed her the reins and climbed up on top of the carriage, taking most of his musty smell with him. "I'll be fine, Ms. Dalca. Let me know when I'm needed."

There was a silence after he'd gone.

. . .

"You know how to drive horses now, Amalina?" said Cristine, snuggling, sounding as if she were ready to drift off.

"Hey, we really *do* need to talk," whispered Amalina crossly, some of her initial indignation returning, "I told you to *write* to the castle not to *come*. I never said you should visit me."

"Not *nowwww*. I'm exhausted. Oh, you can't really be mad to see me, can you? Look, I got tired of writing. I thought, if you're here, why not just come see you where you are."

"But to do something so stupid. It's so dangerous. I told you that. You've no idea how much."

Cristine, her mind still adrift, thought Amalina was still harping about the distance between Korr and the high castle and the dangers of traveling. She petted Amalina's arm reassuringly, "Please, Amalina, I've grown. It's not *so* far away. I just rode their coach and ... well, it's a little walk from the village, but not much, and I did have the horse at first. And it isn't so very dangerous at all, really. Oh, please don't exaggerate as if you know better than me. Just because you've seen the world. I know Ardeel well enough."

Amalina huffed. "I mean the *castle* is dangerous, Cristine. Didn't I warn you about Count Tepsji?"

"Hm? What would *he* do to me?" she laughed. But then she shrugged herself up a little, sensing Amalina's agitation and how serious she was becoming. "He hasn't wronged you yet. Look at you. And so—"

"But that isn't the point. He's a very dangerous man. You don't know everything, and I can't tell you. I've been sworn to secrecy."

"Well, maybe I *do* know something about him," said Cristine coyly. She sat up fully now and eyed Amalina with defiance—or was it jealousy? "I know more than you think I know."

"Says the girl who was riding in the mountains alone," replied Amalina. "You don't know *anything*."

"You've told me a little about him, haven't you?" said Cristine. "So I know *something*. And I've heard things."

"What have you heard?"

"*Things*. But why should I tell you, anyway? You live here. You know it all, right?"

The arguments of a young child, thought Amalina. She could see Cristine's eyes were still innocent enough and searching. She was fishing for information, hoping Amalina would share. And Amalina suddenly felt sorry for her friend. But this wasn't the place for childishness or innocence. "Whatever you've heard, whatever you think you know, it's even worse. Beyond anything I can tell you. You're never coming here again."

Cristine leaned into her: "Why *can't* you tell me, eh?"

"Because if I did you'd be in even greater peril than you already are. It's as simple as that."

"I'm in danger *already*? How? Really, why won't you share with me, Amalina? You're just trying to scare me away, aren't you? It's just as I thought, you don't want me at the castle. You're afraid that I'll embarrass you in front of your new friends."

"No."

"It's the way it's always been: you're the popular one, and now you are hogging it up! You know everything, and you won't even tell me a word. What happened to our oath, eh? What happened to it?" She folded her arms and pouted. At least she hadn't tried to lean over and kiss her eye to Amalina's, as they had done when they were younger, when the blood oath of truth and sorority was still fresh and held some power, when they wanted to reassure each other of it. Amalina might have balked, turned away, given something of their changed circumstance away to Cristine.

"I mean it, Cristine. If I told you just a *little* of what I know, you'd be in deadly trouble and so would I."

"Not if I didn't tell anyone else," Cristine whispered lower. She glanced over her shoulder. "… and nobody found out. Nobody would know."

"Better just to trust me and not to risk the temptation."

"You're saying *I'm* the weak one here? Huh. Let me tell you, I *know* you're the Count's niece. Or you're pretending to be, anyway. *You* are Katarina Tepsji. How is that for a truth? I've figured it out, not that it is so hard to do. But I haven't told anyone about it. I can keep a secret."

"Look," groaned Amalina, "the castle isn't anywhere I'd want to be if I weren't forced to. You understand? I'm leaving as soon as I can. Do you hear me? I'm *trying* to leave it."

"Of course you are, and where to next?" she said with bitter envy. "The Indies, Lady Amalina Dalca? China, Lady Amalina Dalca? The New World, Lady Amalina Dalca?"

"Stop with that," said Amalina. "I'm not Lady Amalina anything. I go where he tells me to go, and I pretend to be who he wants me to be, but—"

"The Count does?" Cristine said with a renewed enthusiasm. "What does he look like? Tell me about *him*." Amalina made a face, so Cristine continued, "You can't convince me it's all that bad for you. It doesn't sound like it. It doesn't *look* like it. To travel? To be a lady of the court? To have romance?"

"Who said anything about romance?"

"Ivanti Vokent!" snapped Cristine. "*Ivanti Ion Vokent!*"

"*Nothing is what it looks like,*" Amalina snapped back, glancing across to make sure Genadie wasn't listening. He seemed to be sliding around on the edge of the slick, lacquered roof. "I don't know why you won't believe me. Look, Cristine, when it is done—and I hope it will be soon—I will tell you everything. I swear. Down to the very last detail, everything."

"Even the romance? *Especially* the romance ..."

"I'm sworn to our oath. I can't wait to tell you everything. I just can't do it *now*."

"Still," said Cristine after a long moment, after looking back to try for a last glimpse of the castle. But it was well gone. All there was was Genadie. "If you don't like it there, you should tell *him* about *me*. Recommend me for your position. I'd just die to do it."

Amalina snorted angrily. "You don't listen! You never listen! I'm trying to tell you!" Then Amalina sighed with exhaustion: "I have all these problems—problems I've caused, but I want to mend them before I can honestly leave for good. And now, even after I've tried to warn you, I have to deal with *this*, too?"

"*This*? You mean *me*?" Cristine sneered. "That's mighty high of you, Amalina. I only want to be with you. But I'm not your responsibility. I'm big enough to look out for myself, thank you very much. I can go anywhere and do whatever I like."

"The fact that you came here despite what I told you means you're trouble."

"Thank you again," said Cristine in a scalding tone. She turned away from Amalina, taking half the blanket.

"Are you done, Ms. Dalca?" rasped Genadie, gently. "Ladies? It's getting rather cold."

"Well, sir, you might as well stop hanging off the side, come up front and warm your hocks," said Cristine, eyeing Amalina, full of resentment. She threw off the blanket entirely. "We are most *definitely* done."

27

The Blood Soaked Curtain

Astinging, throbbing line of fire crossed Attila's neck, just below his jaw. He touched it to make sure the pain was real. He winced in the darkness. *Alive again*, he thought. *Now where am I?*

He opened his eyes. Nothing. He knew he must have fainted for lack of blood. He was weak and it ached to move his limbs. He couldn't sit up. That, paired with the all consuming darkness?

Purgatory, then?

Someone in this purgatory had given him a wool blanket. He clutched its edge, pulled it in tighter and rolled onto his side. It felt like he was laid out on a hard stone floor. Someone had seen to his comfort, anyway. Were there angels in purgatory?

A light appeared.

"Now we'll see if he has survived," said a female voice, passing from outside to inside.

"Think so?" said a man. "Look, he's moved!"

Attila shoved backward and shielded himself with the blanket. Not a female—it was that wrinkled green man, with his high, shrill voice! His tall cutthroat was there too!

Hands pressed and grabbed at Attila, but he spun and the blanket prevented them getting hold.

"Stop it! Stop it!" said the high pitched one. "You'll break the stitches! You're safe!"

Attila sat up now, holding the blanket protectively.

They were not his killers.

The woman held a candle. In the light her face was severe, long, and seemed to have been drafted on an architect's table. Every shape was angular. Geometric. Her hair was tied down so it appeared as if she had a black skull. How unlike when he had woken to Gug Vogoneyevic after his rescue from the river, with her pleasing features and loose blonde hair.

But the same thought ran through his mind as it had back then: *I'm alive. Who is this? Where am I? How did I survive?*

The pain along his jaw throbbed again and brought him back into the moment.

The man joined the woman in the light. He was softer looking and wore a wide-brimmed hat, something like what the western Protestant clergy wore. And while the woman had had no expression whatsoever, the man at her side frowned.

"Let me see," said the woman to Attila, pointing to his neck. "Take care. You don't want to undo those stitches. I don't have much thread left."

"Looks fine," said the man with a melodious, soothing tone. A smile flicked onto his face, meant for her. Her expression did not change, but her eyes seemed to light up from within. Yet they narrowed slightly, too, as if she doubted his assessment. "You've done a good job," he said, "as always."

"You," she pointed at Attila. "Are you cold? Lay down and rest. And for heaven's sake, don't move your head. Not for the next couple days at least. And don't touch it. I'll be bringing some herbs and compounds, and with God's blessing, it won't become infected."

The man started to make a noise, but she cut him off with another look. He said, after a silence, "I-I think we've done enough, missus. Why take risks when we can send the doctor? We *should've* brought the doctor in the first place."

"Aren't you the one who didn't want to touch him? Aren't I the one who wanted to take him back to town?"

"Well, that *is* true," the man admitted, the smile flickering onto his face again. "It wasn't our business. But now that we've done our part ..."

"Not our part," the woman countered, her tone and the anger in her eyes lashing out at him, "God's will!"

"Well, I suppose ..."

"Okay, go and keep an eye out. I'll check the wound once more and then we will be on our way."

The man glanced nervously at Attila.

"He won't hurt me." She asked Attila directly: "Will you? Not if you hope to survive."

With the pain firing at his neck, he wasn't sure if he could trust his voice. He gave a small nod, which hurt him anyway.

"Well, don't pester him," said the man, already starting to back up. It sounded like he was scuffling on sand and stone. "The gentleman looks like he'd like to return to sleep."

When the man had gone away, the woman stared at Attila for a moment. Then she gestured with her hands. She wanted to see his neck again. Attila scooted toward her. He was on a stone floor, all right. Though the gloom prevented him from seeing the walls or the ceiling, by the sound and earthy smell of the place, he presumed he was in a cave, or some large burrow. She was kneeling at the edge of the blanket.

She pointed her thumb over her shoulder after the man: "He wouldn't let me take you back to our home. But he will. He's a good man. Give me time."

Attila nodded.

"God's grace you are alive at all," she said, studying the line of fire, but not pressing it. "You understand, not many people would survive such a wound, or last a night in the woods with all that blood on them and their clothes. The wolves should have gobbled you to bones."

Attila could only nod again.

"You were at the Rock Cup, weren't you? And you spoke of matters—secret things—which upset some people. Got you thrown out into the night. Then someone did this to you, for what you proposed there."

Attila nodded.

"They left your body in the woods. Thought you were dead. Or would be soon enough. They don't know my husband and I like to take long walks, even before dawn sometimes, and we ramble everywhere we are drawn. This morning it was to you."

"Thank you," said Attila.

"Thank God, in his mercy," her voice rose. Her eyes burned but her lips kept straight as a mask. "As will I, sir. Because you have brought to light a secret, a shameful secret of our people. You, brave sir, have called out our blemish without fear and you have demanded it be righted. Is that not true, sir?"

"Yes."

"And what you said at the inn was the truth? About Kyrgil's destruction, what happened there?"

"I have no reason to lie."

"Yes, why lie to get one's throat cut?" she agreed. "Do you know who did this to you?"

Attila did his best to describe them, but he didn't remember much anymore, besides the awful feeling of his own mortality in the moment, their indecent smiles in the darkness, their sadistic laughter. He hadn't heard their names. She shook her head.

"Outsiders. More outsiders. Whether or not they can be brought to justice for what they did—committing murder to silence the truth—they will not prevent the truth from spreading, nor the greater justice to be done." She leaned close to him and put a reassuring hand on his knee. "Let me tell you, I have lived in Korr all my life, and though I am aware of what transpires here and the shameful compact between us and the infernal, many men—those who have recently settled, and almost every woman here—never knew the stain of sin that has carried on for generations. And they would have remained ignorant for their entire lives had you not come to tear aside the blood soaked curtain."

"The women were *never* to know of it," said Attila, to show his surprise that she knew.

"You spoke loud enough for one woman to hear. And that one pushed her husband for the truth, and he confessed. This she told me. I've known of Korr's shame for much longer. My husband hides nothing from me; and certainly nothing as outrageous as that pact, when he first learned of it—though we had to respect the ways of Korr, or risk becoming pariahs. Now, imagine the coincidence: that I should hear of everything that happened at the inn, your speech, your disappearance into the night, and though the lady did not know what happened to you after you left, or why you had gone, we had already found you earlier in the woods, still clinging to life. When we discovered you, my husband tried to convince me it was God's will that you had been put down and we should not interfere. It might have even been the work of our old enemy, which meant you were forbidden. But see how I've mended you back to life. And now, the truth known, you will see to the restoration of our town's pride and our souls. Because you speak the words of justice and goodness."

"H-how long have I been here?" asked Attila, getting the strange sense that with all these events, he'd been here longer than he thought. Not just a few minutes, or hours.

"Not long. But I will get you out. A lowly burrow is no place for a hero like you. My husband will let our home—in the end—be your harbor. He is stubborn when he's afraid, but I will soothe him and change his mind. Now that you are recovering he will have less reason to object."

"I really don't know how to thank you."

"You will get better. And you will lead our good against the forces of evil. If there is any way I can help, I will. Just ask."

Attila brought his finger to his lips. "Can you get me the book I spoke of? The Secret History of Korr? I need to consult it for all its revelations."

She turned to see if her husband was close or coming. "I *will* get this book for you," said the woman. "It'll take some time, but I promise you'll have it. Just as you will have an army of the righteous, in the name of Heaven and God, to do their will and smite down evil."

"Good to hear, but we must be careful," said Attila, pointing to his neck. "Patient and methodical."

"Of course, all in good time. First we will carefully gather our forces. Of those that are pious and trustworthy and are willing to take up the fight."

Attila paused thoughtfully. Then: "What's your name?"

"Sadra."

"Sadra, I've been up and down this country with my message. Few men have listened, even fewer have heeded the call. And I've found no one yet to take up this fight and it see all the way to the end."

"Courage. You haven't been to Korr. Here there may be some who would slit your throat from ear-to-ear, but one who heard you speak in the Rock Cup has already joined the cause. He guards this cave when my husband and I are away. There will be more of us."

She pointed to a basket. "Food and drink, when you need it. Good bye, brave soul."

"Do … do you want to know my name?" asked Attila as she set the candle down.

"Do I need to?" she answered. "It matters not. You're doing the work of heaven; not all angels have names. Now rest."

"Good bye, Sadra," he said, hoping his expression didn't look too indifferent.

28

Korr by Daylight

When the Germanian delegation's carriage finally arrived in Korr, Amalina and Cristine were holding hands and chatting. Not as amiably as they would have once, long ago, as sworn sisters in blood. The dagger of jealousy had cut some connections. But no argument was going to get in the way of their friendship. This Amalina vowed.

Genadie parked the carriage outside of town along the river and removed the harnesses so the horses could have a drink. Some fed from a bag of oats he unpacked from the central compartment containing the bodies. He seemed to be moving with a bit of his old nervous energy, with a grim smile tickling his lips briefly. He was anticipating the work ahead, but also what freedoms lay before him, over the border, after how many years, how many decades spent curtailed by the Count; under his foot.

"Hm," said Cristine with a curious last look at the carriage. She'd said nothing about the oddly quiet, permanently sleeping, men-of-importance inside. No stopping to eat? to relieve themselves? For days silent? And what of the growing smell? Amalina wondered what her friend could be thinking. Could she really not understand they were dead? But Amalina didn't want to raise the subject. Not if the horrifying truth could so easily slip away.

Cristine was talking about something else on their way into town: "While we still have time, before we part again, I would like to know about your new friends. Tell me *everything* about them, please. Don't spare me the details. You can start with the one I met. Princess Lampeda? So strange. I hid when I saw the carriage coming out. I didn't see you at first, and I thought it was the delegation. I was afraid they'd recognize me and think I was up to something again. Then you stopped ... and suddenly your friend was there ... Very strange, as if from nowhere ... and then she disappears again ... So very strange."

Maybe Cristine *was* still perceptive, thought Amalina.

• • •

Amalina and Cristine entered the town on foot, arm in arm, with a jaunty swing of their legs. Cristine was now a more confident girl and high up in the teenage pecking order, she had to be convinced to lower her head and keep herself hidden beneath her cloak's hood. Amalina explained that she shouldn't be seen or recognized by anyone.

From the perspective of Amalina's new worldly eyes, Korr in daylight was still tiny; a bit more alien. The streets were now strangely too narrow. The buildings were old, and while charming in their quaintness they were adamantly rustic. And she'd almost forgotten the sway of the Ardeelian backwardness: it was nearing evening, the sky darkening, and the few people in the streets were hurrying along with superstition nipping at their heels, everyone beginning the shuttering process in anticipation of the evening bell when the village would be sealed tight against the numberless terrors of the night.

Amalina had her own, real fears. She peeked around from under her hood, wary of crossing paths with Sadra, the minister's wife. Every time she had been back to Korr—sneaking into town, wearing a disguise, trying not to be recognized—she had run into the old woman. Sadra would stare at Amalina with her angular grimace, and cry, almost with accusation, "Amalina?" Now Amalina was without a disguise; there would be no mistaking her for anyone else. Amalina watched ahead as best she could, and steered her friend into empty sidestreets and alleys.

"You have to come inside and say hello to mother," insisted Cristine as they neared her home. "Do that, at least. *She* can keep a secret."

"I don't think she'll be happy to see me," said Amalina. "And there's probably going to be an argument waiting for you."

Awakened to the trouble she was heading into, Cristine stiffened. "She won't yell if you're with me. Not *too* bad, anyway. Your pretty face might distract Mama enough she'll forget to be mad at all, and just serve us both some dinner."

"Remember what happened at the tree sculpture, though? I was there, half the town was, and it didn't stop her," Amalina cautioned.

"Isn't the same," sighed Cristine. "Nothing's been damaged like that silly tree. What's the matter, really, when you think about it? I only just left home for a little while. A couple days. A handful. And I left a note, so they could have sent for me if they were really upset."

Amalina's eyebrows went up: "Wait, you told them you were visiting the castle?"

"Shopping the fall market in Netz. I'd heard there were some beautiful new fabrics there and I couldn't wait. They cut good deals at the end of the season, you know. I even borrowed enough money from mother's hidden stash to make it look real. Not that it lasted."

"*And* you took her money?" said Amalina. "Forget an argument, you'll catch a beating."

"I'm too big for her now." Cristine paused to calculate. "Not by Papa, either. He couldn't care *that* much. He'll think it was about time I had some independence—well, here we are. Let's go in and see. Maybe you'll be lucky and no one will be home."

Amalina held back while Cristine pushed on. "It's close to the evening bell. I don't know …"

"It's not like Sadra's waiting for you," Cristine chided. "And it's not like you'll get into trouble if Mama's in. I promise, if it looks like trouble, you can leave."

"Better I'm not seen at all. Nobody should know I'm here, even your mother. I'm supposed to be away."

"Oh, okay then. We'll go straight to my room and you keep your hood down if you like. You'll be someone else if Mama notices. But I'm not letting you go before I have to. Come inside and have some tea and then we can have our proper goodbyes. There's still a half hour yet. There's time, plenty of time. What else are you going to do?"

Amalina allowed herself to be pulled in.

• • •

Growing up, Amalina had never spent much time in Cristine's home. For one thing, she worked five to six days a week, while most Tuesdays and the seventh day were reserved for church. But also, when she did visit Cristine's large, opulent house, it always made her feel slightly uncomfortable. Dragomir could boast of being the most successful baker in town, but his kind of success would never afford a house as large and grand as Cristine's. The wood was the finest oak, the walls were plastered. Portraits and fancy exotic ornaments hung on the walls. On the wealthier east side of town, it looked rich, it smelled rich, it *felt* rich. And with every notable piece in its place in a room, and all of those pieces wildly expensive, the visitor, if they stayed more than a minute, was left feeling sickeningly poor and well out of place; it was like being smothered. And that was the point. Even the hunting rifle mounted over the fireplace, which Amalina remembered and immediately spotted on entering, was the work of a precision craftsman, with a highly polished, engraved wood stock, and intricately etched barrel; something that was meant for reminding guests of the owner's wealth, and would never be removed for protection. This family lived above the Ardeelian mountain standard.

Amalina almost laughed now as she crossed into the living space. She had walked the carpets of some of the richest families in Europe. The discomfort Amalina had experienced before, when a young girl entering Cristine's home, had been washed away by the repeated dazzling exposure to the awe and higher ostentation in the west. Compared to the done-up palaces, Cristine's home felt as humble as the apartments attached to Dragomir's bakery once seemed. Amalina was now nobility entering a common home; if she wanted to take it that way.

. . .

"Well, it's no castle," said Cristine with a sharp look, despite a self-deprecating tone. She must have recognized the critical assessment lighting Amalina's eyes.

"Feels like forever since I've been here," said Amalina, trying to cover. She remembered how she hated the appraising look Katrina Flauna would pour over a place as she walked through it, and was distressed to have done it herself. "I'll bet you don't have half the number of rats we do."

"We don't have *any* rats," said Cristine, disgusted. "Nor mice."

"And your servants are better, of course. At the store it was just Papa and I. And at the Castle it's a whole other story—"

"There's so much more *space* to cover in a castle, which would make it harder to clear vermin out," she said with understanding, but still managing to sound jealous. "Harder than this dinky place."

"Your house is *not* dinky," said Amalina. "But where is everyone?"

"Do I hear voices?" called a heavy baritone. Before they had time to squeal with surprise, a man had stepped into the room behind them, blocking the route to the front door. He placed his hands on his wide hips, and was dressed in a handsome, tight-fitting suit with breeches. His big pink head had one soft roll under the chin and receding tufts of thinning blonde hair on top: the signs of age. But his large, lively, crystal blue eyes somehow made him look younger, slimmer. Coming at them, it looked like he was preparing to deliver a mocking reprimand: "So, *woman*, you're back alread—" but then, "Cristine!" His face erupted into a wide grin of relief, which grew ever wider with delight. "Oh, Cristine! Cristine, Cristine, my little chick!"

He pulled his daughter into his arms and rocked her back and forth. Cristine did not sink into his embrace, but kept her eyes open and looked suspicious. She cut a questioning look to Amalina. She was always embarrassed by his affection.

"Hello, Papa."

Amalina had known Cristine's father as 'Papa', but more so as 'Boss', or *'Papa Szeful'*—*Papa Boss*—because he was Boss Berzweck, the owner of the Berzwecken mining concern and enterprises. Everyone in town called him Boss. Dragomir called him Boss. Even Cristine's mother called him Boss, especially when Cristine was in trouble. *"Just wait until the Boss comes home."* Amalina didn't know what to call him anymore—or really what to say. This once high-stationed man was now, in some sense, below her. So she remained quiet and hoped he wouldn't press her. She tried to pull further back into her hood. Maybe with his daughter in his arms the Boss wouldn't notice her.

"I thought you were going to kill me," said Cristine as she struggled to free herself from his tight hug.

"There'll be time for that later, you naughty girl. When your mother gets home. Did you really go to Netz? I know you didn't. So far away! You were hiding somewhere. With a friend maybe?"

"I have no friends here."

"Or Uncle Jorgu? I think for sure it was Sadra, wasn't it?"

"Why would I hide?"

"But Netz? What a dangerous, stupid thing to do, little one. You aren't a *bad girl*. You've never been. I refuse to believe it, and you'd better not tell your mother, whatever the case." He sighed and after another fond look at Cristine, he finally turned his head toward the stranger, as if noticing her for the first time. "And who is this? You bought a maid from the market, have you?" He knelt to see under the hood. Then he fell back, almost letting his daughter go. Then he stepped forward, eyes wide. "A-Amalina? Amalina Dalca?"

Amalina felt the blush hot on her cheeks. Sweat broke out under her arms and across her back. She didn't want to look up into his eyes. But Amalina couldn't help it now. He was stammering. She gave him a wan smile, and quickly tried to remember Dragomir's cover story. The sick aunt in Germania. What town was it? But then, what had Cristine told him? Had she said anything about France? She felt a new wash of sweat, the cheap dress' fabric matting to her, and hoped he wouldn't begin pressing her with questions.

"Oh, what are you talking about?" cried Cristine, suddenly, breaking out of Papa Szeful's arms and tearing off Amalina's hood. "Amalina?"

"Yes. Yes, Amalina. It's her."

"Papa, this is a gypsy girl. A gypsy! What would Dragomir say if he knew you called his daughter a gypsy? Where are your eyes?"

"But," he looked like he doubted—he refused to believe—he could be losing his mind. He was so sure. "But don't you see the resemblance, daughter? It's remarkable. Look there!"

"She's very nice but she hardly speaks a word. Her family drove me back from Netz so I wouldn't have to wait for the coach. She saw me home, wasn't that very nice, Papa?"

"I would recognize Dragomir's daughter. And if she's not—"

"Papa, please," said Cristine, rolling her eyes with embarrassment. She pushed him back. "Her name's Ebzug. She's a good friend but she isn't Amalina. Believe me. If only she were."

"Well that was nice of her." Papa Szeful wiped his eyes and turned to Amalina again, looking dazed. A titan of local business, a captain's captain, she'd never seen Cristine's father confused or so lost for words. Now he began to right himself from the uncomfortable position with awkward groping gestures: "Where is your family, little Ebzug? Have them come here to my house right away." He consulted the tall clock along the wall. "Well, no … it's too late in the day, I suppose. But come tomorrow morning. Early." He began to pick up steam, his icy eyes trying to warm, to be friendly; to win her confidence. Something he was quite good at. "I can pay you for your trouble, I'm sure whatever my daughter gave you wasn't enough. You will be very well rewarded, your mama and papa. I can't tell you how grateful we are." But then, coming closer, he looked baffled and disbelieving again, and as if he thought he were going crazy, or as if trying to discover some hidden corner of a mask she was wearing. It reminded Amalina of Neku Jonker when she'd posed as his dead wife, the utter confusion. He carried on, dazed, automatically, "I could even provide employment for your brothers and cousins if they wanted it."

"Papa!" shouted Cristine, now pushing Amalina away; around her father and toward the door. "Why do you always have to do that?"

"They helped my daughter; protected her—"

"I know, *I'm* your daughter. But I told you she hardly speaks. And you know gypsies, they don't need one of your jobs. It's why they were free to bring me home right away, at their pleasure. Because they don't sit in one place like you and your people. No anchors. Now just leave her alone. Leave them all alone with your *money* and your talk of it."

"There's no reason to be angry with me," said Papa Szeful, suddenly becoming red and irritable. "I should pay—I must—*You* can take my money, but for them it's not good enough?"

"That isn't what I said! Oh, you're always embarrassing me. Money, money, money. Like everyone's for sale. It's grotesque."

Their old family squabble was brewing. Cristine gave Amalina a quick hug, a wink that her father couldn't see, and then pushed her out the door. "Go on, Ebzug. Say thank you to your folks. Get to their wagons before it's dark, and get away before Papa has you working for him." She was already turning in place to intercept her father when she shut the door on Amalina. From behind the heavy, ornate door, studded with fancy metal points, she could hear, very clearly her friend shout, "*Papa!* What's the matter with you? You always drive away my friends!"

"Friends? *That?* Well if your friends are so great, why don't you just pack up and hop on the caravan! God knows you can teach them a thing or two! If a *tramp* is what you *want* to be."

29

Korr by Night

Walking along the river when the last brilliant bit of sun fell behind the mountain and the whole valley became a grey shadow, and panting with excitement at the nearness of freedom, of escape, just over the border, Amalina wondered if she'd taken the wrong path. Genadie was supposed to wait at the river for her return. But where she thought he had parked the carriage—where she was *sure* he had parked it—there was no carriage at all, no horses, and no Genadie. The church bell sounded. She felt a start of fear, converting her excitement to dread and each toll rang more ominously than the last. It was dark and going to get much darker fast. She had no source of light, and she could not count on the moon just yet. With the wilds on either side of the road made up of tangled bare tree limbs and heavily shadowed evergreens, she felt she was standing on the lip of a sleeping bearded giant. Within this beard roamed his protectors: the bears and the wolves.

Wolves.

Now she knew what was shaking her knees: not just the cold, but the wolves inside the forest, looking for something to eat; wanting to fatten themselves on whatever they could for the winter. For three years running Amalina had been attacked by a wolf pack, led by a monstrous black wolf whom she escaped every time by sheer luck; a wolf who had also managed to miraculously survive the burnings and beatings she'd given him in return. The last time she'd seen him, his head was a deformed mass of hair, teeth, and raw hate, and he'd fallen over the edge of a mountain switchback, one eye pierced by a pistol's loading ramrod, plummeting down the thousand foot chasm. But since she hadn't seen him die on the first two occasions and he'd sprung back at her come the next year, and as she hadn't seen his body after his great fall, he might still be around.

But that had been in Kyrgil, she reminded herself. And that was before the mountain had collapsed and crushed everything around it. If the wolf hadn't died by fall, or by the avalanche of snow and rock that came next, distance would logically say he wasn't roaming around Korr to attack her.

But his wasn't the only wolf-pack in Ardeel. The ones around Korr, the frontier kind, were particularly ferocious, even if they didn't meet the black wolf's terrifying level. And since they could eat a man, a young woman would be easy pickings. And here she was, without protection, and losing her vision in the dwindling twilight.

"Genadie?" she called tentatively, not wanting to be too loud. "Genadie?"

She listened. There was some shifting of branches not far away. It could have been anything. A slip of underbrush. A deer. A wolf. A bear. But not Genadie.

Her mind conjured up Korr's ugly little green-skinned man, saw him peering at her between branches; and she heard his ugly song: "One white leg, fat and fancy. One white arm, that is my doll ..."

Amalina turned on the balls of her feet and hurried back toward Korr. The village would be closed up for the night, of course. But at least there was humanity; and there were street lamps to allow her to see what was coming at her. Maybe even the Count might show, questioning why she'd skewed from his preferred plan to head north through the Borgo, a sudden visit which was both a comforting and unnerving thought.

Imagining the Count, in his black cloak, descending out of the sky like a winged imp, she fell back with a cry when a large shadow flew up before her. She tripped and fell with an outstretched hand. The rocks and cold-hardened stubble of grass skinned her palm.

The shape came for her, larger than life. All she could see was the black shape, trying to swallow her. She screamed.

"Blast," grumbled the giant shape. "You could have been killed!"

The shape stopped as she backed away. In the dull light, she could see a distinct, pumpkin-sized thatch of scraggly hair at its rounded top: this was Gulgas the Hunter. He dropped his musket, which he had pointed at her, and growled some more.

"I could have shot you dead, little girl! Thought you were a wolf! Who is that there, eh?"

Amalina was up. She pulled the hood tight over her head and circled around him, rushing for the town. It was just like Gulgas to be out after sunset. A time he prided as his own, and this was the best season for tracking animals and picking off their thickening bodies.

"Hey, who are you, eh?" Gulgas said, trodding slowly after her. "You think I can't find you if you run away? I'll tell your parents what you were up to. Sneaking out in the middle of the night! Don't you know how dangerous that is? Come back here, you! I said come back!" She didn't, but hurried on. "You're only making it worse! Just slow down, girl, so you don't twist an ankle or break an arm. You little fool. You're lucky I didn't turn you into dead meat."

Amalina recalled how, according to the lie she'd been told long ago, Gulgas had found Lucinda Skeldar's body in the forest, her 'dead meat hanging off the branches'. Well, that had been a lie to cover the story of the

Count having killed the poor girl. But the phrase made Amalina feel slightly ill. Gulgas was a crack shot, she *could* have been killed just now; he could have made it real.

He bellowed behind her: "Your parents are lucky! Hey, now! That boy of yours is lucky, too! You've got him out here, haven't you? You'd better stop and help me find him before I mistake the poor boy for a wolf! No saying you'll be lucky twice. Stop!"

Boy? For one moment Amalina thought he was talking about Genadie. But a boy? She realized he was assuming she was a Korr girl—one of Korr's bad girls—out for a romantic tryst. Why else would a girl be out in the cold forest after dark? There could be no other reason.

Behind her, Gulgas' feet began to pound harder. He breathed heavily and grunted. He had decided to take the challenge and was closing distance between them.

Amalina went up onto the narrow path to the village. In the dim light, the path was a grey-blue strip surrounded by blackness. She couldn't see the village yet, it was still around a mountain bend. If they raced in the forest, she thought, even as big as Gulgas was, he would still have an advantage over her. He knew the terrain and had traveled in it, and at night, for years. On the road, she had a fairly smooth, somewhat straight shot.

On a thought, she dipped her hand into a pocket. She dropped a coin onto the road.

She looked back. The gold coin glimmered even without the moonlight. Gulgas didn't seem to notice. Or he'd noticed but kept coming. The light was a little brighter here and she could make out the heads of the small animal furs that were sewn into his hat and coat. It looked like a ball of woodland creatures had clumped themselves around the hunter.

Amalina dropped another coin. He ignored it. He was getting closer. After he got her he could always turn back and find out what she had dropped.

She turned and threw the next coin hard at him.

Gulgas skidded to a stop.

She threw another coin that smacked him in the middle of the chest. He caught it with a blur of his arm, then looked down into his palm.

"What's this?" he said. When he held it up to his eye he said, with a wheeze of surprise, "Gold?"

"Don't tell anyone," said Amalina, forcing her voice deeper, using an accent that sounded somewhat Greek, somewhat German. "Do you understand?"

He stared at her, his eyes squinting to make her out. How good was his night vision? Probably excellent. Even better than hers.

"Well," he said, tossing back the coin. It landed at her feet. He puffed himself up proudly, "You can keep your money, whoever you are. I don't want it. I've got a decent trade."

"Leave me alone."

"Fair enough. Just you stay out of my workshop: the forest. And from now on you stay in at night like a good girl. Understand what I said?"

Amalina nodded.

He pointed up the road, toward the village. "If you aren't from here … If you haven't a place to go tonight, try the Rock Cup Inn. They'll take you. Gold, girl, will get you their best room. Tell 'em Gulgas sent you."

"And you tell no one," said Amalina. She picked up the coin and threw it back at him. It bounced and rolled into the cold, black grass. "Not *anyone*."

"Whatever you want. How'm I going to explain gold pieces, eh? I ask you that."

Amalina turned.

"On second thought. Don't you tell anyone I let you go," he said. "Or that I told you anything; to go to the Rock Cup or whatever, eh? Fair play. Say nothin'."

She walked back to Korr. Gulgas kept her company, keeping his distance, stopping and starting whenever she tested him. He either wanted to see her safely back to town, or learn where she planned to go.

When she reached the edge of town, she burst into a run and darted down several alleys.

. . .

Jenz Timer and Korr's street sweeper were still lighting lamps. They seemed to be laughing about something and were hugging close to each other for warmth. Timer lifted a bottle to drink then handed it to Street Sweeper, who took a much longer pull off it.

"Did you hear something?" said Jenz.

"Like what?"

"Sh! Sounded like someone walking. Just now. Little steps. Someone's kid? Or maybe someone *sneaking*."

"Sneaking," said Street Sweeper, looking around. "And after all, it's after the bell. It's night."

"I wonder who it is."

"Don't scare me, Jenz. You don't think it could be …"

They both had another drink.

"You know, he killed her right over there, at the other lamp."

"Who?"

"*Him.*"

"I meant *who*? You mean …"

"Limpy Skeldar, of course," said Street Sweeper. "Spread her blood all over the place. What a mess. Was hell to clean up. Almost didn't make it in time."

"Almost didn't make *what* in time?"

"Lay off the bottle," the street sweeper sighed as he swiped the bottle away from Jenz, then laughed and took a long swig. "Almost didn't make it before *sunrise*. Almost had everyone slipping in her blood at the morning bell. But those are our crosses to bear, aren't they?" His head twitched from side to side, turning his ears at the shadows, listening. "Ah, but don't scare me. *He* wouldn't be here, would he? Let's finish off and get ourselves inside; and leave it for the next patrol."

"Leave what?"

"Whoever or whatever's sneaking about."

"Good idea."

When they left, Amalina snuck out of the alley. She went to the bakery door and knocked.

"Who's there?" came Dragomir's voice.

Amalina's heart beat faster. She couldn't tell if she was happy to hear her father or just nervous. Maybe once she was inside and warmed up she would know better. Amalina knocked a little louder and more insistent.

"Is someone knocking? Who's there, eh? Name yourself."

She knocked in the rhythm of a song she used to sing.

"What's going on? Who is out there, eh? Speak up, speak up."

KNOCK-KNOCK-KNOCK!

Amalina could sense her father's frustration as he threw off the wood bolts. It opened quick but stopped hard. He stuck his face into the gap. Then he gargled and moved his mouth up and down, his eyes as round as egg bottoms.

"Amalina!"

He pulled her in quickly, protectively. Then he slammed the door and all the bolts back into place. He hurried her into the back room, as far away from the front door as he could. He picked up a musket and began loading it. It was odd, because he was grinning from ear to ear and kept shooting her with winks.

"Papa, what are you doing?"

"Save the hellos," he said. "No need to talk. Let's just get things in order. I will protect you, no matter what. So glad to see you again, my little dumpling."

"*Dumpling*?" Her father had never called her that before.

"Okay, tell me what's happened. You escaped, have you? Well, that's my Amalina!"

A weak, withered voice came from another room. "Who was it? What's going on?"

"Is that Jenna?" asked Amalina, trying to match the voice to her cousin. What could have happened to make her sound like an old—? "Or, no …"

"Is that Jenna?" said the old voice from the other room.

"Your mother," said Dragomir. Widow Lidsz, he meant. The woman who had *replaced* her mother while Amalina had been away. He went on matter-of-fact: "Jenna's gone. Not sure when she'll be back, Amalina. Or *if* she will. She eloped with the Desclu boy. Fram Desclu, son of Desclu the Tanner. You remember him, don't you?"

"Jenna's married?"

"*Eloped.* Snuck right out your old window when your mother forbid her. Well, I forbid her. But your mother was right. Do you remember Desclu's boy? She could have done better. The matchmaker had her set for Paul, the mayor's brother's son."

"Well," said Amalina, remembering both Fram and Paul, and not knowing what Jenna could hope for in either. It seemed a sad situation for her. Her life was set in a downward course, even having escaped the doom of young 'bad girls' in Korr.

"She said she'll be back. But I'm not counting on it."

"Who are you talking to?" came the Widow's withery call. "Is everything all right?"

"I'm coming," said Dragomir, his face still beaming. "But you'll never guess who has come home to us, my wife."

"At this time of night?" The Widow made a strange noise. "Did she bring *him*? Is Fram here too?"

"Come, Amalina," said Dragomir. "Let's surprise your mother. It will boost her spirits."

Dragomir dragged Amalina by the hand into his bedroom. She was not prepared for the shock.

Widow Lidsz lay naked inside an immense copper pot positioned at the end of the bed. She looked like she had been decorated with slimy black dots at regular intervals over her wrinkly body. Her skin was slightly grey, and she was slumped down in the tub, her eyes closed.

"Look, darling, look who it is!"

Widow Lidsz parted her eyelids with some effort. She was weaker than she sounded. When she saw Amalina, she nodded once and closed her eyes again. "Oh," she said, her lips twitching up and down. "Is that Amalina? Or am I hallucinating?"

"It is Amalina! It is!"

Amalina could not take her eyes off the slimy buttons on the old woman's skin. She'd heard and seen similar sickening black bubbles in books on the plague or in glimpses the several times when a sickness tore through Korr when she was younger. Her father's bedroom didn't have the smell of body excretions and cankerous growths, but Amalina brought her hand up to her mouth protectively just the same.

"Oh, Amalina, that is so good of you to come. But I'm not *that* close to the mortal curtain, am I, Dragomir?"

Dragomir laughed and petted the Widow's arm. "Let's not even think such a thing, my dear. You are quite all right." He gestured to his daughter, then tried to pull her closer to the tub to show her off. "She's come on her own. Well, tell us why you are here, Amalina. You escaped?"

Amalina shook her head. "Is she all right?"

"Dear," he said, turning to the Widow. "I think it's time they come off. Lose any more blood and our daughter will have arrived for your last rites."

Dragomir plucked one of the buttons—a black, bulby leech—off the old woman's skin. The leech was stuck fast and her grey skin pulled out an inch from her body, straightening many folds in the area, before Dragomir could shake it loose with a snap of his powerful wrist. The skin reformed into its corrugations, with a little red puckered oval where the leech had been. Dragomir flicked the leech into a bowl that was one quarter full of the slick, black-red thumbs.

"No, no, it isn't time," said the Widow. Her head came up in protest, but her eyes remained closed. "Please put it back."

"I say she ate more than she should have," Dragomir explained to Amalina as he went fishing in the bowl for the exact leech he'd just removed. "But she convinced the doctor that she picked up an illness from some westerners who visited the shop."

Dragomir stopped looking for the old leech and picked out whichever one his large fingers could pry. Then he set it back in place on the Widow's skin, sealing it there with a gentle tap on its head end. Amalina didn't know what to say, so she stayed quiet, wishing she hadn't come; or that she still had the means of becoming invisible so she could slip out.

"Ten more on," said Widow Lidsz. "You weren't done. I need ten more, or it won't work. I must get the humours out."

"You need to keep some in," said Dragomir, gently. "Here, Amalina, help me get them on your mother or she won't rest."

Amalian swallowed. Now she regretted having skipped the Rock Cup Inn.

"That's a good girl," Dragomir encouraged.

Feeling detached, Amalina saw herself walk to the bowl and reach her hand in. It took a few seconds to lower her hand, and lower it, and lower it. Her fingers tickled the air above the slimy, quivering slugs. When she finally touched one, her skin crawled and she felt as cold as she had in the forest.

She picked the cool, gooey, writhing specimen up quickly, now that she was committed to the act, and hurried it over to her stepmother's naked body.

"Where?"

Dragomir pointed.

Amalina dabbed the leech on, rubbing it this way and that to see how the wrinkles moved; it was like trying to stick a button on a loose set of folds on a drape. The old woman wasn't particularly hot or cold, and she supposed Dragomir's suspicions were right about Widow Lidsz's 'ailment'.

Amalina and her father placed ten more leeches. The Widow must have been counting because she seemed to relax when the tenth went on. Or perhaps she'd fallen into a stupor.

"One more for good luck," he said.

"Oh, no!" moaned Widow Lidsz, but with a smile. "Just ten. That was all. It'll do. Thank you so much, my big dumpling."

Dumpling? thought Amalina. *Ah, I see …*

She wanted to throw up.

• • •

Amalina told Dragomir she was in town on a mission for Count Tepsji. She had decided to wait until the morning, when she was more rested, before she confided more honestly that she was running away; before she tried, once again, to convince him to leave the country with her. It was going to be another battle, as it was the year before when she first tried, and she would need her strength for it. To make it easier, she would tell him that fate had made its interests known: it had given her all the signs that she should escape Ardeel and its monster by providing her the easiest and clearest path to do so. She also had a fat bag of gold coins she would show him, to allay any worry of how they would survive in the years to come. But Dragomir, such a loyal native son to Korr, would still put up a fight; fight her like a dog who won't let go an old bone, even though a new and meatier one was there for the taking. He had put her off pretty harshly last time. But he must see the sense in it now, mustn't he? Half the problem, Amalina thought, was he might be holding on because this town is where his wife— his first wife, her mother—had lived and died and he could never give that up.

But there was a new wife now. Would the Widow make it easier or harder to convince him to leave? The old woman's allergic reaction to westerners was not promising. Maybe her new mother would prefer to head east instead, into Russia, or maybe all the way to China. Unfortunately, those countries were, eventually, all still connected by land to Ardeel.

Escaping from the Count in that direction would not be as permanent. And she wanted to make the separation permanent.

Remembering the Count and his amorous appeals to her, and his tortured arguments for why she should be with him, which made her feel suffocated and trapped, Amalina changed the conversation and asked Dragomir, along a safer line: "Do you think, Papa, is it possible for someone to belong to a family that has never killed someone?"

"What a thing to ask," said Dragomir.

Amalina explained how the Count thought there might be someone on earth who was so innocent, and that every one of their ancestors were so innocent, that not one of them had ever murdered. "All the way down from Adam, I suppose," said Amalina. "Along Abel's side, somehow, or something like that. So that not a single one of them had killed another human being: a *'blood innocent.'*"

"What a thing to believe," said Dragomir again, a little tired now and dumbfounded. "That would be impossible. No."

"What about us? Mother never killed anyone did she?"

"No."

"And you?"

"Almost."

"But you didn't."

"I'm a baker," he explained gently. "But don't put it past me. Now, your grandmother was Saxon. Those people have quite some fight in them. And her father and her uncles were all in wars at some points, as infantry and such. Horrors with the halberd and spear, from what I was told. And my grandfather, who is full-blood Ardeel, he was in some wars; against the Sultan and the Boyars. I know he and some of my uncles made more than a few widows in their days. Not that that's something to be proud of."

"Oh."

"Now your mother's father ... he was a real Saxon killer."

"Was he?"

"I don't want you thinking any less of her for it."

"Why would I?"

"Your mother's grandfather, Decebal, was in the wars against the Germanian invasion, and he killed a good number of them, that's a fact. And so did her father, Blusji was his name; who was maybe responsible for even more. Old Blusji harbored a great hatred of the Saxons, I can tell you that, even after all the fighting was done. He knew my grandfather had taken up with one—Grandmother, you see—and forbid your mother and I from seeing each other. Ever. Almost cracked my skull open on several occasions when I went courting her."

"You never told me that. How did you marry her? Did you elope?"

"Elope? Who'd make Korr's bread? I ask you. No. And he would have done me in for sure if I had. It was your mother's love for me that turned him in the end. And why not? Everyone here in Ardeel is an Ardeelian, depending how you look at it. Yes. Everyone's a mix, and that's all there is to it. We must love everyone."

"So all my grandfathers and great-grandfathers were soldiers? I couldn't be a 'blood innocent' at all. Not like what he was saying."

"You are as innocent as you want to be, my little dumpling."

"You never called me that before," she sighed, not sounding as sour as she wanted. Was everyone a dumpling now?

"Very well," said Dragomir at length. "You're as innocent as you want to be, *my little Amalina.*"

"But I'm definitely not descended from a line of people who have never killed."

"That's asking too much, I think. We all live our own lives. They aren't cold-blooded murderers, anyway. Best to be happy with who you're with and accept their faults. As I said, we must love everyone."

Amalina felt comfortable in her father's arms, and loved hearing about her mother and her ancestors and romantic love. She lay back in her bed, wishing she could drift off to sleep as she had done so many times before as a child. But the thought of leeches and wrinkled skin kept her eyes popping open with a start.

Amalina sighed again, still bothered by the recent event in the copper tub, and whispered, "Papa, how can you *like* that old crone, anyway?"

"You mean—?"

"She has so many wrinkles she looks like a prune, with thick hairs sprouting all over her face."

"Oh, no," said Dragomir, scratching his beard. "Don't say such things. How do you know your mother didn't have wrinkles and hairs sprouting all over *her* face?"

"She was the most beautiful woman in the world."

"You never saw her, Amalina. Not really. You couldn't remember ..."

"You *said* she was the most beautiful woman in the world, Papa."

"And she was. But I never said she didn't have hairs on her face."

"You'd have mentioned if she looked like a prune."

"Well, the widow can't help something like that," he laughed. "Can she?"

"She's older than the mountains."

"She's younger than me."

"She is?" Amalina gasped. "Oh, Papa, that's worse."

"Try not to take it out on her."

"You'd better get back in there and make sure those leeches haven't made off with her."

She suddenly remembered the Count's special rite, where he gave out his gift of power and seeming immortality. Remembered how the Count bled her friends before her eyes. Didn't he have the power to become any creature he wanted? Why not a leech? Wasn't that what he was, essentially? And what would happen if the widow drank the leeches' blood, just as the Count's ladies drank his blood to accept his gift? Would that turn her into one of *them*?

The Widow Lidsz suddenly became a towering leech, with jiggling moles and wiry hairs.

Amalina was dreaming now. Strangely, this nightmare didn't quite bother her. There was only one leech.

30

A Girl in the Forest

Pia Lampeda, with her beautiful, smooth, white skin and lashing tendrils of blood red hair, was now, somehow, Amalina's mother. And she was doing battle with this horse-sized leech: the Widow Leech, who attacked with swipes of her long, white, pin-like fangs. Amalina stuck gold coins onto the Widow Leech's slippery hide; the coins plumping and transforming into golden leeches themselves, to begin draining power. The Widow Leech sucked inward and began to crumple.

Amalina woke knowing that the dream was a warning: that last night she had applied the final leech that had syphoned away her new stepmother's last thimbleful of blood—in other words, killed her. Which, in a way, would make Amalina a murderer, wouldn't it? She felt awful about having been responsible for the woman's death—having hurt someone at all—until she got out of bed and discovered the Widow Lidsz was still alive and eating a melon at the bakery's sideboard.

"Feeling much better," she smiled, sending small sacks of skin—with private gardens of wiry hairs and moles—jostling along her jaw and below her chin. On top of this rough terrain, little red circles of leech prints were dotted on her cheeks, the side of her nose, and forehead below her white cap, appearing the victim of some kind of hideous disease. The Widow Lidsz didn't look very shy about it. She winked cheerfully, as her father would often do. "Thank you, Amalina."

"I only added one or two," said Amalina, defensively. "Where's Papa?"

"At the oven, of course."

"Still? It's a little late for baking. Or have I been sleeping for—?"

"Clearing it out. Nobody's coming for bread today."

Amalina went to the windows. Yes, it's too bright, she thought as she walked toward them. There was a rim of frost on the panes. Looking out the hazy glass, her jaw dropped open.

"I'd say there's more than a foot of it. Maybe two."

The street—and the buildings Amalina could make out—were clapped over with snow. It looked to be a heavy, dense snow fall, with little whirls of fine flakes blowing off it. The wind was still blowing hard, whistling at the rattling glass.

Amalina folded her arms together for warmth and wondered why she hadn't felt a chill yet. She must have been dead asleep all night and her body still hadn't woken up.

Someone buried in a fur coat crossed the street and in a line so deliberate he could only be coming for the shop. Amalina fell back from the window and made sure the bar was still holding the door closed. Then she ran and grabbed the widow's hand. "Come on."

"What's the matter?"

"Someone's coming, let's get out of sight!"

"But a customer!"

"Papa! Papa, customer!" Amalina shouted as she hurried the widow into the rear kitchen area.

"I can handle—" the widow began to say.

"Nobody can know I'm here," she told her father, who stared at her with a surprised look. "Nobody."

"I'm sure nobody's looking for you," said the widow. "And I'll just go—"

There was a loud knock on the door.

"Go answer," she ordered Dragomir. "We'll stay in the kitchen."

"Why should I?" demanded the widow.

Amalina cut a look at the door, to the widow, and then rounded her eyes at her father. *Look at her face!* Her father nodded, wiped his hands on his apron, then leaned over and kissed the widow on the peak of her cap. "Don't want to worry our customers about foreign plagues."

"But I feel perfect now," she protested.

"You know how some people are about these things." He pointed at imaginary spots around his face if she didn't already understand.

"I probably just ate too much," she said. "You were right, I wasn't sick."

The knock came again.

"Get in bed," he said as he went to answer the door. "If it's the doctor, he'll get out the word you're safe."

"Safe!" She appealed to Amalina but got no sympathy.

"Plagues can be hard on our business," Amalina told her stepmother. "You might be surprised. Quick into bed, before they know you've been in our kitchens."

"The world's crazy," she huffed. "If they see me well, they'll know I'm well. If I'm tucked out of sight, I might as well be rotting." But at the sound of the bar being taken off the door, Widow Lidsz scurried through the communicating door to the inner apartments. Amalina noted how, even when hurried, the Widow ambled on stiff legs, like a drunk chicken trying to overcorrect its path.

A ferocious cold whipped in.

"Closed today, Dragomir?" Amalina recognized the voice. It was the deputy sheriff.

"Sorry. The board's up to keep the drifts out."

"Ah, yes." She heard the deputy patting his furs, as her father clunked the bar back into place. "Remarkable storm. Too early in the season for something like this. Nobody was ready. I doubt anyone's stocked up."

"And still, I doubt we'll have a customer besides yourself. Sorry, I've only yesterday's lot, and that isn't much."

Suddenly, to Amalina's surprise, Widow Lidsz was back in the kitchen. She was pointing hard at the oven.

"What?" mouthed Amalina. The widow mouthed something back but she didn't know what it meant. The widow gestured harder. "What?"

"Start. Making. Bread." The widow whispered with a mouth that looked like it was trying to shout, her wattles shivering below her jaw.

"What?"

"Start. Making. Bread. *Now!*"

"Why?"

"If. You. Don't. I. Will." Lidsz wobbled toward the shelf of logs. Amalina warned her off and motioned that she would do it. Lidsz left when she was satisfied Amalina would continue the work.

Amalina didn't know what the point was, but she began prepping the oven. Moving as quiet as a thief, she got the fire going quickly, and started in on the dough starter and ingredients, as she listened to the deputy sheriff go on about the snowstorm and then ask after Widow Lidsz's health. Dragomir said she was doing much better.

"Well now," said the deputy sheriff, getting to his point, "Have you heard from Amalina, Dragomir?"

"The odd letter, now and then. Nothing recent. The naughty girl. But she must be very busy."

"Tending to your aunt, you said? She's been holding on for years."

"Thanks be to heaven. Well, it's a chronic condition, fortunately. She's a nice woman, after all, and I wouldn't want her dying just on my daughter's account. I'm sure Amalina is having a wonderful time and has forgotten all about this place."

"Strange, though. Word is, she's in town."

"What? Where? Who said that?"

"So she hasn't been in to visit you?"

"Impossible," said Dragomir. Amalina heard him walk around the sideboard and she saw his back as he positioned himself just before the doorway to the kitchen. "Who said this?"

"It's not definite, Dragomir. But it's generally around that someone who looks like her—at least—has been in the streets. They heard knocking at your bakery last night."

"Madame Grescu told you, eh? The weather was aching her bones and she spent her insomnia listening for voices at her window again?"

"The night patrol. They saw you letting someone into your home."

Dragomir laughed. "Letting someone in? Letting someone in? Of course they saw me letting someone in." He shrugged. "Who wouldn't open the door to their own wife?"

"Lidsz?"

"I told you she was feeling better, didn't I? Last night, my darling insisted she had forgotten something back in her old house and she had to get it. It was so late, I thought she'd decided to stay there. Maybe she'd met an old friend and they had gotten down to talking. Or maybe I had done something to make her mad, eh? And she wanted to get away!" Dragomir gave another encouraging laugh. "But whatever it was, she came back to me. Knocked on the door and I let her in. If only it were Amalina, I would have been so happy. I would parade her out here for you this very moment. But it was only my sweet little dumpling."

"I can't tell you how happy I am that you are so much more yourself these days, Dragomir. After so many years you wasted as a lonely widower, you'd only gotten back to half what you once were. Along with the drama of your daughter, and then afterward, and her leaving for God knows where, I thought I'd never see the old Dragomir ever again." He sighed with satisfaction. "Married life suits you, my friend. And didn't I tell you she would make a good match?"

There was a strange pause.

"Was there something else, Deputy Sheriff?"

"Well, I was going to say that Gulgas came in this morning. He said there was a young woman out in the forest last night." Amalina clenched her fists and beat the dough batter. *I gave Gulgas four gold coins, the blabbermouth!* "Is there someone back there?"

"Probably just a mouse. I left some ingredients out when I thought I might … Well, just stay there, let me throw the lid on."

Dragomir came into the kitchen, finger up on his lips, shushing her. He saw how far Amalina had gotten with the ingredients, already a large bowl of dough. He flashed a heated, questioning look at her, and brought up his hands helplessly.

Amalina shook her head and pointed at the door. *Not now. Go!*

He made the helpless motion again, shushed her again, returned the smile to his face and went back into the store, closing the door after him.

Amalina set down the bowl and went to listen. How much had Gulgas blabbed?

"A girl in the forest," said Dragomir. "Who was it?"

"He doesn't know. She ran away. He said he'd almost shot her, though. Thought she was a wolf. This was after the bell—and just before the storm, I should say. But *after* the bell, Dragomir. Such a thing."

"Young love," said Dragomir, philosophically.

"People are beginning to forget themselves. I don't know if it is what happened to Kyrgil before their destruction, but we can't let our people forget there are *real* threats in Korr."

"But still," said Dragomir, with a wayward sigh. "Love. You take risks, even in the face of death."

"I said you were back to your old self," the deputy began wryly. "But, my good friend, you and your wife aren't *that* young anymore. Lidsz was out there last night. Here, don't let love turn you two into idiots."

"Oh, no, of course not," he said, clearing his throat. "It's just you can't deny—"

There was a knock at the door.

"Who is that?" said the deputy, as Dragomir pulled the bar. "Looks like Harszu."

"Oh, good day! Good day!" said Harszu. "What a storm, eh? Closed the bakery, Dragomir? Well, how's the wife? Has she recovered? Well, that's good. I heard Amalina's in town, is that true? And have you heard, Gulgas caught a girl in the woods! Snared her in one of his traps! Only way he can catch a girl now, eh? Only figures that the lummox let her get away."

. . .

In an hour, ten men were in the bakery trading gossip like old women. Dragomir's circle of town pillars were there along with some of the lower echelon of tinkerers who wanted to break into the circle. Dragomir kept excusing himself to go into the kitchen on the pretext of warming wine for them. Amalina rounded up as many mugs as she could, and while she waited for the dough to rise, she heated the wine with a sprig of cinnamon and signaled for him to start serving. At any moment she expected someone to sneak back into the kitchen. Or to wander back there with the idea of relieving himself.

She was feeling tired and realized she hadn't worked this hard in a long while, when a cold wind blew in.

"Gulgas!" the chorus shouted.

"Thought you'd all be at the Rock Cup," bellowed Gulgas cheerfully, sounding like he was all smiles. "Who needs bread on a day like this?"

"Have some wine," said Dragomir. "No bread today."

"Heard you caught a boot last night," said someone to Gulgas, with a laugh. Amalina couldn't tell who it was. Their voices were hard to tell apart when they were yelling and laughing. "And the girl got away."

"You can't tell us who it was?" said someone else.

"Don't rightly know. Is Amalina back, Dragomir?"

Amalina couldn't tell if Gulgas said it because he *had* recognized her or he was just trying to switch the subject. Either way, Amalina was beginning to feel trapped in the back room. She wished she hadn't started the dough and began to retreat slowly toward the rear living quarters.

"You think it *was* Amalina?" asked someone new.

"I couldn't say," said Gulgas.

"I heard there were gypsies nearby who've moved in," said someone else. "Was it a gypsy?"

"Who said there are gypsies?" challenged another, as if gypsies in town would upset his day. "Have the gypsies come to Korr again? What will they get up to in this weather? We might be stuck with them for weeks, or months!"

"I didn't see any," said Gulgas.

"Gypsies!"

"They aren't all bad," said Gulgas, bashfully. "They've helped me out of a spot a time or two. And their liquor is harsh but good. They're good people and get a bad rap. I don't like to hear insults spoken about them."

"All right, All right," said another, trying to calm him down.

"You really couldn't tell who it was? Or are you holding out on us?"

"I'd tell you if I knew," said Gulgas. "Just glad I didn't shoot the poor thing. Seen enough dead girls for a lifetime, don't need to add to it by accident."

They all got quiet.

"Sometimes it's necessary," someone muttered, as if needing to give voice to what he thought everyone else was thinking.

"Maybe it was one of them princesses," a new voice broke in, with an upbeat tone to rally them. "Or one of their maids, fell out their carriage and got lost."

"Or maybe she was kicked out."

"Princesses?" said Gulgas.

"Haven't seen our regular coach in a week. But there've been two or three French convoys with that Humphrey, and a German one if I'm right."

"There were just two come through yesterday."

"That's right!"

"Two headed in-country. Both going to Netz, from what I heard."

"And then last evening I saw that small one that ran through here the other day, the one from Germania for sure, the one with government officials in it, running right back in the other direction. Six horses on it, didn't bother to change out. I've never. Sped through just before the bell rang. Now that's the first load I've ever seen *returning* from Netz. I guess Netz is keeping the pretty young women at their leisure, and spitting out the old men like bad nuts."

"That's the way I'd do it."

"Now, Gulgas, do you think it might have been one of them princesses out there? Or a maid?"

"She had an accent," he admitted.

"What kind?"

"They all sound the same to me. Foreign, though. Definitely not from around here."

"Why didn't you tell us before?"

"Just remembered."

"Anything else?"

"Anything else, what?"

"Any detail you are forgetting about this young woman, Gulgas?"

After a pause as large as himself, he said cryptically, to a round of howls: "I think I'd better not."

"Well, gentlemen," said Dragomir over the ruckus, "I'm afraid that was the last drop of winter rations for today. I suggest, before you wake up my recovering wife, you move to the Rock Cup if you wish to continue."

"Come with us, Dragomir."

"No," he demurred. "Seeing how everyone is out on the street despite the storm, I believe I should start baking a quick small batch."

They all moaned, but without more wine, they left willingly, hounding Gulgas for more details.

When Dragomir came to the oven, his cheeks were rosy with wine, but he looked mad. He smacked the counter—though careful to not upset the bowl and the knives.

"You've sided with *her* now?" he said.

"What do you mean?" asked Amalina, confused.

"Why are we making bread today? Have you been gone so long you forgot what a storm like this—but no, *she* spoke to you, and you two ladies have decided to run *my* business for me!"

Widow Lidsz swept into the room, arms outstretched, looking like she wanted to hug Dragomir.

"Now, now, my big dumpling, let's not spoil our morning."

"*My* business! Never forget! It is the Dalca bakery!"

"Just sit down, dumpling, you've had too much to drink. I can do it. Amalina and I can."

"It isn't morning!" shouted Dragomir, leaning against the large central table. "It's nearly afternoon! And see who hasn't come? Customers! I told you no bread today, did I not? I said no. And what do you do, but enlist my own daughter against me."

Amalina looked to Widow Lidsz, and suddenly wondered why she'd felt the need to follow the old woman's orders. She blushed and felt an angry heat rise.

"Yes, yes, you know so much, my big dumpling," said the Widow. "You know how to run a bakery. You make the best bread in all Ardeel. You know when customers are coming. But let me tell you now, my beautiful husband, you don't know what your customers *think*!"

Now he hit the table hard. The bowl leapt. The knives and rollers clanked. "I've been in this business my whole life, woman! You don't think I know my customers?"

"You know them," she said, standing her ground with a warm smile. "Well, of course you do. But I said you don't know how they think. Because you've never been one, my dumpling. But I have, haven't I? Oh, have I!"

"And!" Dragomir hit the table again, though a little less hard, and looking somewhat wary. One eye squinted closed and the other watched his wife. "And you have *never* come here after a sudden storm like this! Maybe midwinter, or if it were a lighter snow. But not—"

"And that's my point, isn't it? Even as a dutiful wife, looking outside on a morning like this, I would think to myself 'I can just stay inside and boil something. The bread can wait for another day.'"

"You're agreeing with me then," growled Dragomir. When she shook her head, he looked to Amalina to see if this made any sense. Amalina was just as confused.

"When we looked out the windows and saw the snow, you said no customers, no bread," said Widow Lidsz. "I said there are customers and so make bread. And you said 'no', just as you want to do right now. But here it is, my dear husband: if your customers do not come to you, then you *go* to your customers. Because they still want your bread. They are huddled by the fire thinking about how to stretch the old loaf they have, and how nice it would be if they had a new one. Now, Dragomir, *there* are your customers. Bake the bread, then deliver it to them."

Dragomir quivered. He leaned heavier on the table. "In this storm? Deliver it to them? Well, I ... well, I ... Amalina, did you know what she was up to?"

"Amalina's a good daughter and does what she thinks is right," declared the widow. "Now, Amalina, does this sound like a good idea to you?"

"The bakery will make some money, anyway," said Amalina, thinking it a strange, but not a mad idea.

"Oh, no. No money," said Lidsz with a confident smile. "They will offer, of course, or they will say they have no money. Either way, you give them the bread as a gift."

"A gift!" shouted Dragomir. He suddenly laughed. "You plan to send me out in the cold to give away my stock?"

"They will be glad to get it, and when they eat it, they will think Dragomir Dalca is the best man in town. And then they will make sure to come by when the store is open, and maybe buy two loaves from time to time. That's what I would have done. Many a storm I had hoped to see you at my door with some bread."

He laughed again. "That's because you loved me."

She nodded. "That's true, my big dumpling. But I was also hungry."

Dragomir tilted his head this way and that, his eyes closed, as he mulled what he'd just heard. "There are many people who are much prouder than you, my love. If I do this, they might think I'm trying to buy their loyalty with a bold stunt. That I'm shameless and not charitable. Or if they take it, they will be resentful for putting a debt in their family's stomachs."

"If on a good day they would come to buy, why would they be resentful of a free loaf now? And they will make up for it later, by buying something extra, which is the money they would have spent the day before if you'd been open. You see? Anyway, they can always refuse if they don't want it. And you can't say it isn't true unless you give it a try." Widow Lidsz nodded, with a smile. "How about this, if you're afraid to lose some money, for every extra loaf not bought in the next month, I'll pay for it."

"Your money is mine already! We'll still be losing money."

"I still have some stashed away, not in our common pot yet."

"You do?" Dragomir gaped at her in shock.

"I'm no fool. Now, what do you say?"

Dragomir looked to Amalina again. "We've given away loaves in the winter plenty of times, I suppose. Just not delivered them. What do you think, little dumpling? A wager sounds like it could be fun."

"It would be fun," said Widow Lidsz, encouragingly. "Little dumpling?"

They were both looking at her, waiting for her answer.

"I think," said Amalina, "the dough is already made and the oven is at temperature. And if they got upset with you for showing up at their door, who are they going to turn to for bread tomorrow? Argus?"

She turned to look at the widow, and the woman's smile still made her want to gag. But there was a warm connection that happened. A lump in her throat, a familial feeling she hadn't experienced in quite a while. Maybe never before. Amalina had her father, but now had a mother, too. She couldn't believe the odd feeling.

"Mom's wager should cover it anyway," said Amalina, past the lump. "Let's do it."

Widow Lidsz chirped happily, "Thank you, Amalina."

Well, thought Amalina in dismay, she's more like a *grandmother*.

"Amalina?" came a stern voice from the store area. "Is Amalina Dalca *here*?"

31

The Back Room Revolutionary

Dragomir stared at the doorway, his hand nervously patted down his beard. He'd forgotten to bar the door. No one had noticed the curl of cold air because they were too close to the oven or were so caught up in the argument. Someone had entered the store, and that person had overheard them talking.

There was no doubt who it must be. Just her voice set off a response within Amalina. Her heart hammered and her body told her to run, as her eyes picked out the door to the attached apartments, the back rooms, the closets, the rear door, even the cabinets, even the oven! Some place to hide. Her limbs demanded she spring for any exit. A more disciplined part—a more mature part, she would like to think—kept her in place. Or was it fear that paralyzed her?

In the shop, the hard-soled shoes clunked across the floor, coming for them. Sadra appeared in the doorway. She was dressed in her black dress, as always, with her only concession to the weather being a small cape and a mannish wide-brimmed hat she might have borrowed from the minister. The outfit was so tight, it showed every corner on her angular figure. Her eyes fastened on Amalina immediately and did not let go.

"Amalina," she said, her face so perfectly set into her mask of inscrutability that there was no inflection, just a very tight word.

"Good day, Sadra," said Dragomir. "If you've come for some bread, there won't be anything fresh until later. I can bring it to you—at your home—if you want. I'll be delivering bread today to my best customers ... later ..."

"Returned have you?" said Sadra, walking slowly into the kitchen, like a mountain lion closing in on its kill. Her eyes were ablaze, even if her face was something hard, chiseled and immovable. She was centering on Amalina. "Returned from Breck ..."

"Uh," said Amalina, nodding slowly.

Widow Lidsz said cheerfully to intercept, "Amalina has just—"

"No," said Sadra, as she stopped before Amalina, leaned over her stiffly from the waist.

"No," said Amalina.

"No," Sadra echoed. One eyebrow lifted, slowly, like a flag of victory. "No, no, no. Never Breck. Never Germania."

"Sadra," said Dragomir softly, "I don't know what you think you know. But …"

"You've lied to me, Dragomir Dalca. Over and again you swore to me Amalina was in some other country, tending to your sickly or dying aunt. And every year," she lifted an accusing finger at Amalina, "it was you who came to town, dressed in some outrageous costume, as if I could not see through it."

"Oh, I don't know about that," said Dragomir.

"I'm sorry," Amalina apologized, not really knowing what she should say, but not wanting to see her father humiliated. Now that the discovery had been made, she felt a little silly. There *had* been a reason for her disguises, but she couldn't think of it at the moment. Not under Sadra's world-flattening gaze.

"We had our reasons," Dragomir began to explain.

"I told him he needn't make those excuses," interrupted Widow Lidsz. "That isn't our way, is it? Truth and honesty are the wings of the soul."

"You've some confessions to make ahead," Sadra told Amalina, lifting a plank-like arm and setting her hand on Amalina's shoulder. It would have seemed friendly, until her fingers dug in. "Many things, I should think, after all this time. To share and unburden yourself."

"She *does* have a mother now, Sadra," said Dragomir. Widow Lidsz shrank back in fear with a hand over her mouth, even before Sadra turned on her.

"Her new mother can have her," said Sadra. "But there *is* a bond between *us*, Amalina and I; built over these many years, since she was a little baby."

"Oh, yes," Dragomir and Widow Lidz agreed.

"I will speak to her and separate this bond of ours." Her voice was oddly lilting. "So, as the young woman she is, she can go where she will. Would you like that Amalina?"

Amalina remembered the time Sadra had stood over her while the old Doctor Alexei poked painfully at her in all the sensitive and private places Sadra told him to.

"I, uh," said Amalina, slightly shaking her head.

"You'll come with me."

"Come with you?" said Dragomir. "She's only arrived."

"When?" shot Sadra. "The coach hasn't been through in a week. Where did she come from? How did she get here? Where has she been hiding, enh?" Sadra then relented. "You two will have Amalina back after she confesses all to our minister. We're looking forward to it, I can tell you. Get dressed now, girl, there is no time to waste."

Sadra had the power to control women twice her age. Amalina had seen it. Never had Amalina felt it until this moment.

"I'm glad you were open today," said Sadra, when they were finally on the way out.

...

As she stamped her feet through the deep, wet snow drifts, Amalina shifted uncomfortably in her clothes. They weren't *her* clothes. The dress and heavy overcloak belonged to Widow Lidsz. Amalina had not wanted to touch them, for fear the cloth might have hairy-mole creating properties. But Dragomir had the idea to put her in them, when he'd convinced Sadra to keep Amalina's return secret. And Amalina alone didn't wonder how long that secret would last, considering Sadra's ability to gossip. Her father would deliver his bread around the village accompanied by Sadra and a heavily bundled 'Widow Lidsz'—Amalina in disguise—until they reached the church. The plan seemed to work, their customers accepting the gift bread with mystified looks, as if they weren't sure if they were being attacked with it, then, confused, charitably offering warm food in return, and Amalina was getting into the performance, hairy moles forgotten, twenty loaves down, basket nearly empty, when they reached the church.

Sadra and Amalina snuck in the side entrance. Sadra locked onto Amalina's wrist as if this was the moment she might try to escape. She was released once inside and the door was closed.

Sadra barred the door.

The church's back room was filled with wooden crates. Like a castle's receiving area after a delivery, which didn't fit with what Amalina had imagined any area of the church would look like. There were no windows, hearth, or candles, so the room, at the moment, was very cold, and it relied on light from an open interior door at its end.

"Where are we?" asked Amalina.

Sadra patted a smaller box. "Sit here. Be quiet."

"Okay."

"I mean, Amalina, you will stay here—right here, and not say one word— until I get back. Leave, and I will have everyone in town looking for you."

"What if I have to pee?"

Sadra stared coldly and then left. Apparently the question didn't rise to the occasion.

Amalina sat listening for noises from the other room, and tried to convince herself not to want to pee, despite having been cinched with the urge since going out into the freezing streets. After a while of tense waiting, she wondered if she would hear the minister praying or something.

Sadra returned. With her was a strange looking man not much larger than Genadie, but different in many ways. He stood straight, almost as stiff as Sadra. His hair was dark and full, and pulled back from his face; a face with a neat white cloth square plastered along his left jaw. His clothes were almost stylish. Impeccable. He had strange eyes that were noticeably round, but cut off in the middle by his eyelids, as if he were about to fall asleep. His features were also slack. Not the anxious little rat Genadie was.

He opened his jacket and put his left hand inside as if to warm it, as he took a moment to study Amalina. "Hello. Your name is Amalina, is it? Amalina Dalca? You're from this village of Korr?"

Amalina nodded.

"And recently you've been living in the castle outside Netz." It was a statement, not a question.

"H-how do you know?"

"Just answer his questions," Sadra ordered.

"But who is he?" she asked, looking at him.

"It's all right," said the man. His face was as oddly expressionless as Sadra's, but without all of Sadra's sharp angles. And his inscrutability wasn't a mask, as hers was, so much as the skin remaining passive, the muscles underneath undisturbed by signals to act. "I will tell you how I know, Amalina Dalca. It is very easy, of course, when you look at it. While you were reported to have traveled to Germania for an extended employment, attending to a sick relative, you were seen by Sadra on several occasions. The first of these, you were in a carriage driven by someone who was rumored to work for Count Tepsji, who lives in the Netz castle. That is simple enough.

"But say Sadra was mistaken," the man went on, the lower half of his dull-lidded eyes staring in a mesmerizing way into Amalina's. "People are capable of being mistaken. But circumstances and evidence are as clear as mileposts. And even if one or two signs are taken or turned, the preponderance of them will determine the true location. A girl in this town told her mother she had seen you in town, and it coincided with the times when Sadra thought she saw you. And more, you had told this girl to send any correspondence to you not through your father, but to post it to a Katarina Tepsji, who resides in the castle outside of Netz."

Amalina forced her face to hold still, but she was ready to curse at the top of her lungs. She just *knew* Cristine would tell someone. She couldn't truly blame her. So what had happened? She'd told her mother who'd then reported the news immediately to Sadra. And why would Cristine not tell her mother? *But*, Amalina remembered sharply, *didn't I keep plenty of her secrets from Papa?* It would only have been fair if she had kept this one …

"Please don't be upset at your young friend," said the man, his dead eyes reading her perfectly. "It is natural for someone to trust a secret to their parent. And her mother shared with Sadra this important information in confidence. Nobody else knows,"—*we've no idea how many other people she's told*, thought Amalina skeptically. But now the man added in a level, reassuring voice, "Nobody else knows besides *us*, and also besides whoever else you might have told." He watched Amalina for her reaction. She didn't. She wasn't trying to deny the truth, but she wasn't ready to give in yet. He seemed unusual and almost clairvoyant. "This girl, your friend, also asserted that you were traveling in France. Perhaps along with the Count's niece?" Amalina did not say. Her silence didn't bother him much, but he paused longer, to let her talk if she wanted.

She didn't. He moved on.

"Also a young man from the village alleged—to your friend—to have seen you in Paris. This would seem to place you not in Germania and more likely in France, during certain periods of time. But I would venture that you traveled throughout the western kingdoms. And not as a servant to a noble, but as the very lady of title herself. The young Lady Tepsji of Ardeel. You are she."

"You conclude a lot," said Amalina thrusting her jaw out, resisting the blush she felt rushing for her cheeks. The sweat, she could not help.

"But not without foundation," he replied without concern. "Maybe I wouldn't know where to start, but the simplest place would be the delegation from Germania that passed through here just a few days ago, headed for Netz, investigating the young Lady Katarina Tepsji; variously Lady, Countess, Lady Princess, or Princess; who had visited their country and made some impression there. Her description is not much different than your own. And while your features are simple enough to be mistaken for many a girl in Ardeel, well … there are few girls who look like you who reside in the castle outside of Netz, travel the various western kingdoms, and happened to begin those travels not long after you yourself, Amalina Dalca, baker's daughter, left this very village to parts unknown; left here after you were perhaps *accosted* by the Count, who resides in that Netz castle …" He shook his head. "No, I'm telling a long story. Simple enough: you were here, you were in Netz, you were in the western kingdoms; then you were in the woods outside of Korr tossing around gold coins," at this a gold coin appeared in the man's hand, "throwing these around just before you arrive back in Korr, and just after the carriage from Germania passes through town again, on its way out. Now, Amalina, while you are dressed before us very much like a servant, as you would have us believe, you bear the remnants of a perfume, and your hair has been recently styled with hot irons, a luxury hardly given to a servant, but seemingly an imperative to young ladies of wealth and power."

Amalina just continued to stare, waiting until it seemed he was done and it was her turn.

"Are you going to be a pest *now*, Amalina Dalca?" said Sadra, her eyes aglow. "Start talking."

"I really don't know what you want me to say."

"It's all right," the man soothed Sadra in a gentle voice. To Amalina, "Never mind what I told you just now. Just tell me what your purpose was in coming to Korr."

"My purpose?"

"Were you aware your young friend, Cristine Berzweck, recently travelled to Netz? She told her mother it was to go to the market, but I can only assume she went to the high castle to hand deliver a letter to you."

Amalina nodded, "We brought her back yesterday."

"You and the delegation?" the man asked. "No. It was the old servant from the castle on the riding bench. And you were in the forest by yourself. Going where? There wasn't a coach yesterday. It had to be the delegation carriage that brought you both. Or you came on foot, in the cold, from Netz? No."

"We came by carriage. The delegation's carriage."

"Then why were you in the forest at night? Why would you be there, when you later ended up at your father's bakery, your home? Why wouldn't you have gone there straightaway after seeing your friend home? Was it to rendezvous with the Count?"

"What!" said Amalina, astonished by the thought.

"Yes," said the man, "What girl from this simple village would trust her life out in the forest at night? Only one who is unafraid of who she might encounter, especially when spurning the protection of a hunter she knows—Gulgas; a lifelong acquaintance—who could keep her safe from the wolves, the mountain lions, the bears, and Ardeel's various natural creatures."

"No," said Amalina, shaking her head. "I wasn't meeting with the Count."

"No, Lady Tepsji?"

"Whatever you think, sir," said Amalina, "it isn't true."

"Then tell me what is true. Tell me everything, starting at the beginning, leaving nothing out. I need to know everything, child, in order to understand the creature." He paused. "Though, for my own selfish reasons, I will be most interested to learn just how you survived the battle on Kyrgil Mountain. That *was* you I saw along the ridge, in the snow, with your friends, just before it began, wasn't it? Before the creatures battled, and it all came down."

• • •

Amalina told the man about her time with the Count. The people, the horrors, the deaths, the attempts to kill him. She couldn't believe she was speaking the words aloud and to someone else. But the more she went on, the harder it was to stop. She wanted to tell him everything, to get it out of her, to release all the worry and the pain. A mental type of escape.

The man nodded throughout, more vigorously at certain points. When she was done he said: "You have led a very eventful life. And you've seen much more than a girl of your age should have seen."

Strangely, Amalina resented the notion. *It's my life*, she thought with a smirk. *Maybe you're right, but it hasn't been* all *bad.*

If it wasn't so bad why are you trying to escape him? Amalina then asked herself. She frowned harder.

"Is something wrong?" he asked.

"Pay attention, Amalina," scolded Sadra.

"No, I was presumptuous," he said. "Either I offended you by reminding you of your hard circumstance, or I unfairly pitied you. The latter, isn't it? Never mind, I should treat you as an equal in these circumstances. You've survived so close to him and for so long. And yet you aren't one of his people."

"As I explained, I have family here that are vulnerable."

"He can threaten you all he likes, it is for their safety and preservation you stay by his side, am I correct? It is to protect them that you do his bidding."

"Do his bidding?" said Amalina, not liking the taste of it.

"To a point," he nodded. "Only to a point. Because you *did* try to end him."

"Yes."

"A dangerous thing to do. And yet you've tried several times."

"I've helped others. And I've seen them fail too many times …"

"You are lucky to be alive. Have you learned anything? How would you kill him now, if you had to?"

"I don't think it can be done alone," she said. "It can't be just one approach, but as many as can be used at once. Kind of the way he doesn't like bees."

"Oh?" this intrigued him. "I suppose because they are too many for him; and they act separately, on their own, from different directions, but operate as a swarm for a unified purpose; toward their one goal. And so like that. Only more so than that. More *is* needed. Many is mandatory."

"Yes. I guess that's right."

"Precisely," nodded the man. "And every weakness of his exploited. That is what is to happen. And when you return to the castle, know that you will now be a crucial part of his downfall."

"When I go back?" she said. "No, I—"

"Where do you think you're going? If you love your family you would not abandon them. It wasn't a *serious* plan you had to leave this country, now was it, Amalina? Not when you come to understand that you—and everyone in Ardeel—will soon be free of this monstrous subjugation.

"Silver is a bane for him," the man continued. "He cannot touch it, he cannot withstand it. It is the reason the metal is forbidden within Ardeel. But, fortunately for us, there is a hidden supply which I have uncovered, and soon it will be used to great advantage. The armies this creature has faced in the past have been helpless against his might because they were defenseless. But as you have observed, he attacks like the animal he is, tearing and biting at his opponent."

"And throwing boulders and shooting cannons, and tearing down mountains."

The man smiled vaguely, as if he were amused at being challenged. "He has to be outside for him to perform those fantastic feats we saw in Kyrgil. In daylight, he could have done none of those things, for it is when the sun is up that he is weakest and vulnerable. Daylight, you see, is another such bane. Exposed to it, he will perish. We both saw what happened when his enemy on that night tried to hide in a suit of armor, and the dawn light penetrated through the cracks."

"That was Vezel," said Amalina.

The man looked surprised. "Who?"

"Vezel. He was disguised as the Count in the armor and the other one was trying to kill him. It's a little confusing, but it was Vezel, and he exploded himself on purpose. " Amalina explained how Vezel's sacrifice was to make the other creature think he'd won against the Count. So the Count could then sneak after him later, when he was off his guard and unaware that the Count was still alive, and assassinate him.

"Vezel," said the man, looking puzzled. "Vezel Umalasju?"

Amalina nodded.

"Not General Zsolt Marosh," the man mumbled to himself.

Amalina hadn't gone into the absolute depths of everything. She'd left Marosh's betrayal and death out of it. She wasn't going to explain, but simply shook her head. "It was Vezel."

The man looked perplexed, but went on: "It was difficult to tell who was who that night. I might have missed some detail, some switch. But no matter. Everything you have said, every new detail you add to it, only bolsters my confidence in our success. The Count cannot expose himself to the light. That is a fact. He cannot tolerate silver. That is a fact. So when he is confronted, suddenly and by surprise, and in the daylight hour, by a countless army clad in silver, fully armed with weapons of silver, he will be meeting a force he cannot touch. And on this occasion, we will avoid the mistake of Commander Kralov and his amateur force, by taking down his castle piece by piece around him, sending the light of day against him and to the lowest depths of his den. He will be fighting an untouchable force bringing enough firepower to make his castle, his shield of stone, disappear almost instantly. He is lost."

• • •

The man, Sadra's revolutionary, confided in his monotone delivery specifics of his plan to defeat Count Tepsji and just where Amalina fit into it. Because Amalina had already seen another creature like the Count, the Strange Man, who was as powerful as he was if not more so, fight the Count and lose—as well, she'd assisted a long string of ordinary men who futilely, pointlessly, met their doom to his bare, infinitely superior hands—and because this man's plan had just enough caution, and foundational difference, to make it sound tempting to try, it was the worst plan she had ever heard.

"But I don't know, sir," said Amalina politely. "What more can I say? As I told you, *my* plan was to escape."

"It isn't anymore," he said, his dead eyes radiating a strange confidence.

"Well ... Well, I ... Still, I don't know what to say," said Amalina. "Where are you getting your armor? or all that silver?"

"By necessity, I'm afraid, only the supreme commander of an operation knows every detail. The soldiers only know their small part. You'll have to take my word on that and know my precaution is also for your protection. However, it is already arranged."

"You're very thorough in your planning," she said. "And it seems a sound plan, at least to someone who hasn't met him."

"I *have* seen him," he reminded her. "I saw them both destroy the mountain. That is why I know the force brought against him must be *precise*."

"But it's all been done before," she said. "Really. Everyone dies."

"My idea has never been tried, girl."

"Not exactly, no. But still ..." She made it look like she was giving it further consideration, though she was only trying to figure how to get out of the room without signing on. "Still, I don't think it will work."

"And still, it's the best plan I have. And it has to be tried, even if all the others have failed."

"I'm very sorry, sir—"

"No need to be sorry. Just promise us both your help."

"H-help you? But, sir, I *am* going to—"

"Yes, I know, Amalina Dalca. You *were* going to escape, but only before you knew that there was an operation in place to defeat this monster. Now you have it. What more can you ask for?"

"But … it's *your* plan—"

"And with your help it will be *our plan*. And with you so perfectly placed at his side, we will have all the more chance of succeeding. You *are* going to help us, aren't you? You must. You couldn't leave this country knowing the trouble you've left behind. Of course you couldn't. No, you wouldn't dare expose your family to what little mercy the creature has. Leave behind everyone you love to his vengeance, girl? No, no. That isn't who you are."

Amalina hesitated, not quite seeing it his way, but also not wanting to disappoint him or Sadra by admitting the truth. She *was* ready to leave Ardeel. Maybe even without her father, if need be. This was her only real chance to escape—and her *family's* chance, if her father did join her. She saw Sadra's eyes had already reignited, now with some kind of wrath, she supposed.

"This revolution will happen, and you're going to help us, Amalina," said Sadra, cutting off the man before he could say anything more. "And before you dare utter another silly word out of that childish head of yours, I'm going to tell you why."

32

The Men of Murder

Two hours later, with night settling on the village, Amalina peeked from under the deep hood of Widow Lidzs' coat. Sadra had told her to keep her head down, her face out of sight as they went to visit the bird keeper. But Amalina was curious to see if the pigeon handler here in Korr resembled the one in Netz. Or could he even be the one person she most dreaded to see: the green man, figgy with wrinkles and odd lines, who regularly fetched the pigeons from the high castle, who she suspected was the orchestrator of the Count's murder service, and who'd assaulted her in the castle hall— *"You're playing with fire"*.

The cage door squeaked open on icy hinges; and then came the protesting warbles and scratches of small feet on frozen wood. He was distracted so Amalina peeked. The man sticking his arms into the birdcage looked nothing remarkable—nothing like the oddly bird-like attendant in Netz, nor the little green wrinkled man. But he was familiar. She had seen this man around the village, she was sure. In church on holy days, it must be. Or entering her bakery from time-to-time with his wife. She noted now there was nothing remarkable about him at all, other than he wore nothing more than a normal cotton shirt and wide stained apron against the sudden winter storm.

Amalina made a small sound when she realized he was looking at her. Sadra smacked down her hood and said, "Take care of yourself *Mrs.* Dalca, or you'll invite back your cold."

"These ones are good," said the bird man, as he caged the selection of birds. "Will fly over a hundred leagues, even in a cold like this. Though don't ever let them go in a storm; they might arrive, they might not."

"I don't think *anyone* would do anything so insensible."

"Many storms in winter," he said, annoyed at Sadra's prickliness. "Crop up fast, as we all see today; I was just giving caution where it's due. Not that it's the normal time of year to be setting up this kind of correspondence, is it? Where are you traveling anyway, Mrs. Smidt, just as winter is hitting the mountains?"

Sadra scolded him with a sharp look as she handed Amalina the small, cooing wood box. "These are presents for a traveling friend. They might not even use one of these birds until the weather improves. In the spring."

"Mrs. Lidsz-Dalca's escaping us then?"

"You need to stop assuming things you don't know, and which aren't your concern. Because you're wrong, it's annoying, and we are getting colder by the minute standing here."

"Yes, Mrs. Smidt! No offence. It's only ... well, you should tell whoever *is* taking these pretties, that if they are going to hold them through the winter, they need to be kept proper. Let them exercise a little from time to time. Feed them; but no more than a small handful every day or they will fatten and never want to leave."

. . .

"Did you get all that, Amalina?" said Sadra as they walked from the coop area.

"I know how they work," said Amalina, who was lugging the rustling box of pigeons against the wind like it was a stubborn bucket of flour. Amalina was thinking how nice it would be to be a real noble lady right about now, with servants to do these kind of chores while she remained comfortably wrapped in furs.

"Filthy things," said Sadra, about the birds.

"I've seen worse. They're highly reliable. And fast."

"You trust them?"

"We have to. Just make sure the bird keeper gets my messages to you straight away when they come in, or it'll all be pointless sending them."

"I'm pleased to see you are taking your role seriously, Amalina Dalca," said Sadra with an appraising look, which ended with a brief, grudging smirk of approval. A rare sight to Amalina. "There aren't too many, you understand. You will use them wisely. And waste none."

"As wise as I can," said Amalina. "He said they're for sending pertinent information. But I don't really know what that means, and I'm worried I will waste one, if not all of them."

"You're a smart girl, Amalina. I trust you will know what he means when the time comes. Something he can make use of and take action on."

This order for inside information against the Count reminded Amalina—terribly so—of Commander Kralov's unconditional command—upon pain of death—that she be his spy and to supply actionable intelligence on the Count and his castle. A demand, repeated and enforced by his lieutenant, the young, brave, handsome Piotr, in order to prove her loyalty to the cause and to aid in his coming battle against the powerful Knight of Ardeel. But what they had wanted to know, it was vague in the most frustrating of ways, almost impossible to fulfill. And she still couldn't help but feel it resulted in the disaster that ended Kralov and Kralov's army—with poor, brave, handsome Piotr in it. How was this any different?

"Most importantly, though," said Sadra, "if nothing more, remember *the map*."

• • •

It was the one item her revolutionary had been explicit on:

"You will draw me a map of the entire castle, with exact footage, the composition of the walls, floors and roof, and an inventory of the contents of every room and a complete list your tenants."

"Tenants?"

"Your friends, of course, and their people. We will see to the protection of all that are innocent, if there are any in his company that can be claimed as such. Only the criminals and the creature will be our target, and the focus of our assault. The rest will be moved out of the way."

"I don't know about the contents of every room. Many doors are locked or are off-limits."

"You will mark that down, and make all attempts to gain knowledge of what is inside."

"And by exact footage, you mean?"

The revolutionary glanced down at Amalina's foot. "Good enough. Pace off each location, toe-to-heel, length and width. Record your findings. I will know what it means."

"If I try, it might look funny and attract attention."

"Only if you aren't careful, or stupid. But you aren't that, are you? You're capable enough. Make a game of it with your friends, and you might get it done twice as fast."

"But the Count—"

"Simple enough to explain, should he wonder," said the revolutionary. "Of course, you are making a map of the castle for all of your friends, to ease their stay. Make as many copies as you like for them, as long as you leave one for me."

"That might work."

"Don't forget to include the castle walls and any cellars and the underworks."

"That might be harder to explain."

"You'll figure it out."

"But a map like that," said Amalina. "It would be much too big for any pigeon to carry."

"Not if you reduce it to 1/50th scale."

"1/50th … scale?"

"And you could break it up into several pieces, thus your flight of birds."

"It would take more than I will be getting, I would need dozens."

"Easy enough, and better for our designs, to prevent loss or anyone from seeing what you are sending. Just send one bird to let me know when you have completed the map, inventory, etc. That is one bird. I will find a way to get the materials from you. Understand, this map, etc., is vital and I am counting on you—we all are—and you will send the bird the moment it is done. The rest of the birds—of which there will be four remaining—will be for other pieces of information that are pertinent, that are crucial to the mission."

This is where the revolutionary, despite his slack expression, gained the empty avaricious air of Commander Kralov. As if there might be some miraculous key ingredient to victory that would magically present itself and guarantee their success, and she would recognize it and get it to him in time.

"Five birds and you are done, you may have your escape. But five birds is the least you can do for our great mission."

. . .

"We should really hurry now," said Amalina, trying to shrug off the ominous feeling brought on by the memory of Kralov's failed assault ... and her culpability there, "the bell will ring soon, I think."

They picked up their pace, but Sadra was never done with an interrogation. She said impatiently: "And when *exactly* are you leaving here, Amalina?"

As they rounded a corner, Amalina glanced up to see if the street ahead was clear. At its far end, two men were crossing through the intersection. Amalina's steps faltered. A chill took hold that sunk to the bone.

Moving slowly, but with some sense of purpose, the two figures appeared as men who were stalked and hounded by Death. The first was slowed by a leg he had to drag, as if Death had one hold on his ankle and was drawing it down, so that he had to lean as far forward as he could to achieve momentum. The second walked with a rearward tilt, as if Death were a sucking wind pulling on him, and only by leveraging his weight was he able to keep from flying away. The first one was as tall, narrow and somber as a gravestone, the other small, wide, and blocky as a tomb.

It was getting dark, with the snow providing ambient upward illumination more than the gloomy sky, so it took Amalina another moment—and with a troubled squint without her glasses—to realize who she was looking at; the short and wide one, with a greenish color to his skin that was wrinkled like a prune; the one who she had been thinking of only a few minutes ago: the pigeon fetcher from Korr with the cart of cages, the high voice, and the nasty rhymes; the ugly little man behind the Count's murder service!

The two men had almost crossed out of sight when they stopped at a lamppost.

Amalina slowed and caught Sadra's woodlike elbow to steer her into a recessed doorway.

"Who is *that*?" whispered Amalina, turning her back to the Men of Death. The two had seemed to be conferring with little gestures about something.

"I don't know," said Sadra, peering into the distance. "I can't say."

"The one with all the wrinkled skin."

Sadra shook her head.

"Are they still there?" said Amalina, not wanting to risk another look.

"No. They've moved on."

"Did you see him? Kind of greenish. Like a moldy toadstool."

"The tall one looked familiar, but I didn't catch them clearly ...Why? Who are they? Or who was that *one*? You know him? What about him?"

Amalina looked up the street. They'd gone all right.

Should she now explain to Sadra those particular details about the Count she'd skipped over in her conversation with Sadra's friend, the revolutionary? As she'd spoken to him, everything had poured out of her in bursts, almost like excited sobs, and he had calmed and guided her with soft, encouraging words toward what he wanted to know. What else had she left out? Omitted because they weren't about the Count, after all, but only a sideshow to him? Marosh's death of course, and Vezel's promotion. She hadn't told him about the Strange Man's gift of the invisibility bone, because it seemed impossible to believe, even with him quite receptive to the impossible, he having seen the battle at Kyrgil. It had seemed just too much to tell. And the ugly green man and the Count's murder service, she'd considered at the time, had nothing to do with what Sadra's back-room revolutionary was really interested in: the Count's full range of powers and weaknesses.

"He's from Korr, I know. And he works for Count Tepsji," she told Sadra. But, in some sense, that wasn't right. More like—impossibly—the Count worked for him. For some reason. Amalina was stammering and fumbling, unable to explain. "Or *him* for him—A-X—"

"Very well," said Sadra, her face hardening as she cut Amalina off. A dark heat filled her eyes. She'd just gotten some new, interesting information, it seemed. "Very well. Are you certain?"

"I—"

"Then let's have a better look."

Sadra bumped past Amalina's shoulder and stamped quickly to the lamppost. She looked to the left, and then to the right, and then to the left again.

"They're gone," said Amalina.

"This information would have been better shared with our friend, Amalina."

"Sorry."

"Too late for that. I can't tell if this is some fanciful bit of your imagination."

"No, I swear …"

"Brought on by your nerves," concluded Sadra. "I want to make sure you understand what I told you, Amalina Dalca. You aren't getting out of this, no matter how scared you think you are. You are working for the good of this world, but also to save your father's life."

"Yes," said Amalina, not able to look into Sadra's eyes. Sadra shook her until she did.

"Listen to me, girl. This town will be made to stand up against that monster. And your father will be stood up with everyone else—"

"He doesn't have to fight."

"He will fight. He is a good and honorable man, and he will do what must be done."

"He's not a violent man," said Amalina. "He's just a baker. Does he have to?"

"So you *didn't* hear me, Amalina."

"I heard you."

"But you didn't listen. By Heaven, all good men of Korr will stand against him on that day. Including Dragomir Dalca. I will make sure he is in the front line, little girl! And should you fail to do your duty, to which you are now sworn, to serve and deliver what is needed, you will be responsible for his death, and the death of every good man in this town. Now, for the second time, do you understand me?"

"I heard you."

"Swear to me that you will do what has been asked of you, faithfully and without fear or falter."

Amalina nodded.

"Swear to Heaven you will do these things that will save your father, preserve your family's good standing, and which the will of all that is righteous in this world now demands of you, regardless the sacrifice. Say it loud."

"I swear," mumbled Amalina.

"Good," said Sadra, her eyes burning. "Very good. I trust you. I hope you satisfy that trust. Five birds is not too much to ask."

Easy for you to ask of me, thought Amalina, sourly.

Sadra continued to stare, trying to read Amalina's thoughts.

"Should we go?" asked Amalina, shifting from the lamppost.

"We'll wait a little longer," said Sadra. "Just a little longer."

"But the bell will ring soon."

"Give them time. Nobody will mind if Sadra and Widow Lidsz are caught out in the streets after curfew. But you've a job to do now, and those evil looking brutes of yours were headed just where we want to go, weren't they?"

. . .

Not long after the bell tolled and the village closed up for the night, Genadie knocked lightly at the bakery's front door. He called out as if wanting to buy some bread, if the baker was willing, even at this prohibited hour.

Amalina nodded to her father.

Dragomir let Genadie in, and his cheeks pulsed red, and his eyebrows crunched down in an angry V above his nose. Genadie did not appear to notice or mind, but shuffled in with a small bow and placating smile.

"You," said Dragomir.

"Mr. Dalca," said Genadie. He spotted Amalina in the back of the store. "*Ms. Dalca*. Come, we are ready."

"You did it by yourself?" asked Amalina.

Genadie nodded. "Oh, yes, I did what I needed to do," he smiled politely, flatteringly to Dragomir, "while I left you to visit with your dear father. Who you've so lovingly described and recounted on numerous occasions at the castle. I thought it only best."

"But I was supposed to help you—"

"It was always going to be difficult. The storm made it much harder, of course. But no matter, no matter." Then he whispered hoarsely from behind his gnarly, cold reddened hand, "At first I thought it might be *you-know-who* working against us, sending this storm, trying to rein us in. But this storm will help with the story perfectly. Make the wreck more believable and the bodies won't be out until spring." Genadie cleared his throat, and he acted like he'd meant to motion for Amalina all along. "Now it is time for us to get on our way."

"You want to leave tonight?" said Dragomir. "Are you sure?"

"Can we?" Amalina asked Genadie.

"Oh, yes, all is ready. I've purchased a covered sleigh. It's best we leave now, with the storm over."

"Papa, I—"

"Leave now," he said. "Go. If you must, you must."

Dragomir hugged his daughter and she hugged him back. They both had that horrible sense, as they had once shared before, when Genadie had first taken her from Korr, that they would never see each other again. Amalina shoved the feeling down and vowed it not to be. To break the moment,

Widow Lidsz threw her arms around them both, and pressed her shriveled, rubbery peach skin against Amalina's wet cheek.

"Send me word," said Dragomir.

Amalina held up the small wood box. "That's what these are for."

He eyed the pigeon box dubiously.

"Maybe some day we will come visit you," said Widow Lidsz, stupidly. *As if thist were a simple visit!* "Or, she can come to us again. As soon as she can."

"Don't let anyone convince you to do something foolish while I'm gone," Amalina warned her father with a whisper.

"Never."

"Don't do anything stupid."

"Your mother will see to that."

Amalina secretly handed him her bag of gold. "And don't spend these, or show them around. Not even to your new wife. But hide them for when it is time."

Once outside and Amalina was certain no neighbors were watching, she climbed into the covered sleigh with bright lamps on its front. Genadie followed, and almost before he'd sat down and pulled the blanket up over their legs, he snapped the whip. "Hyahh, hyahh. Nk! Nk!"

"Genadie," said Amalina, "these horses."

"What about them, Ms. Dalca?"

"These are *your* horses." She stared at the two jet-black haired rear ends and, further on, the swinging heads with the wild eyes. They weren't normal horses, but the kind Genadie would summon with the little flute he used to wear on a string around his neck.

"Well," he said, flicking the reins. "We need their speed. And they are fastest at night."

"But I thought the flute was broken."

Genadie nodded. "It was. I was lucky to have even found the pieces after the mountain fell. It was almost impossible to believe when I found them. As if they were meant to be with me."

"You made a new one then, or—?"

"Oh, no. I fixed it." Amalina thought he was pulling the flute out of his waistline for her to see. But he shook open his little leather bag and fed himself some millet. He crunched loudly, his eyes fixed on the dark, snowy street. As an afterthought he pulled out the old, magical, horse-summoning flute. Where it had been split apart it was tied together with several long, thick hairs, and sealed with a kind of hardened yellow glue. She couldn't tell if the hairs were his.

"You can do that? Mending it works?"

"I think so." He gestured to the horses. "Here they are anyway, these beauties. Came right out when I played. We'll see how well they work, but they seem promising. We'll know how fast they are once we get out onto the highway. Then it's full speed!"

The end of town was coming, and then it would be onto the snow-packed highway, and over that came the border, the frontier, her freedom. She could feel the border ahead like a weird pressure in front of her. Or rather a bar to reach out and grasp. All she had to do was keep going. Keep going, and take it, and she would be free forever. Her and Genadie both.

"Genadie."

"Yes, Ms. Dalca?"

"We, um … I really hate to say this … we're not going …" She looked at him apologetically. "So, um, well … turn around. We aren't escaping. We're going *back* to the high castle."

"Yes, Ms. Dalca."

33

The Follower

A day and a half later, Genadie turned on the sleigh's frozen bench and, through a narrow side-parting in its dark leather roof, sent a quick backward glance. "Someone's following us."

Amalina stirred. Ever since their departure from Korr, heading in the wrong, wrong, wrong direction, she had been curled sulkily into the corner of their riding compartment, not paying attention to the scenery, and now suffering another morning's-long funk of resentment for having her escape once again thwarted, and with a mounting anxiety at returning to the castle, to the Count, to Pia, to Margeta, etc.

But she was trying hard to lift her spirits, convince herself she had instead something to look forward to. Perhaps she had been mistaken all along about the sign she had been given. She hadn't been meant to escape Ardeel, after all. No. She'd been led out of the castle and to Korr to have her true role revealed directly. Amalina had prayed in Margeta's chapel for an answer to what she should do, and her purpose was declared by no less than heaven's own mouthpiece, Sadra: Amalina needed to continue to protect her father any way she could (and, as well, the Widow—her new mother; and in some sense, Cristine and her family, too, and, well ... the whole town of Korr). How so? By returning to the high castle and helping the revolutionary, and finally ridding the world of a monstrous creature! Hadn't Amalina known that all along? But even better, though the revolutionary didn't quite see it, Amalina had her hand on the spigot. She controlled the flow of information vital to his plan, and so she could better time it: the right moment to strike, or to shut it all off to avert its disaster. And now that what she was meant to do was clearly established—and that she was an instrumental piece—her life should become so much easier. Instead of giving into the chaos in the castle, and falling apart at the seams, Amalina had a direction. She could focus. She *would* focus. She would do better this time!

But Amalina's inner spirit lifted only a little at the thought, and it was Genadie's voice that brought her up: "Ms. Dalca. Someone's following again."

Amalina roused slowly and peeked out from her side.

Trailing behind them was a tall, bundled figure on a horse.

"Same as before?" she asked.

Genadie shrugged. "Too far away. But if it is … Well, the first few times could have been coincidence; just another rider on the highway."

"But now?"

Genadie didn't have to answer. The chance of it being a coincidence was cut to almost nothing. They'd left Netz behind, long before dawn, and were on the road to the high castle. There were only a few clusters of farmhouses in the stretch between the two points, and the man's heavy cloak and hat were too ostentatious to be a peasant farmer.

"He's getting closer, isn't he?" said Genadie.

"I think so. You don't happen to have a spyglass on you so we can give him a better look?" But he was gaining ground and she would see him clearly soon enough. Her funk slipped away unnoticed under a flutter of worry. "Who could it be? Not a bandit."

Genadie shrugged, then dug into his bag of millet between them and started grinding away on a handful of seed. The birds in the box between them made hungry noises and tried to peck through the bars at the bits he dropped. He flapped the reins, "Hyahh, Nk! Nk!"

He looked back again as their ragged horses put on speed. When he turned back, he opened the blanket on his lap and adjusted his pistol and his knife. He replaced the blanket and shook his head. "He's coming. He must be familiar with this road and he knows where we are. He's making his play where we'll be out of sight of anyone—from the town or the castle. It's just us … and him."

They were trotting along the portion of road where it doglegged around the mountain and then carried on toward the high castle. On their right, not far in the distance, was the old, burned out, now collapsed and snow-covered farm where Commander Kralov had hid with his doomed forces. To the left was open, swaying land that sloped down gradually to the forest and the river. Before long, racing over the snow-draped, barely-defined road ahead, they would be pinched between the rightward foot of the mountain and the encroaching leftward forest. If they made it through that pinch they would be out onto the long path to the castle where they might be sighted by a telescope on the castle's wall. The rider burst into a gallop. He intended to catch them before the turn.

"What's the matter with these horses?" said Amalina.

"Not much good," he admitted with a crunch on the millet. "It happens sometimes, of course. Could be the flute's been weakened a bit. Or I got them during the late afternoon and not night proper. I don't know. Night's always better." He gave the reins another encouraging flick.

"They're slowing," said Amalina.

"I see." Genadie rubbed his red cheeks to warm them, then opened the blanket again to test his reach for his weapons. "We'll have to meet him, I suppose. See where he is, would you, Ms. Dalca?"

"I'm afraid to," she said as she turned in her seat.

But the powdery gallop could be heard before she peered round. He was so close, at her angle all she saw was the back half of the horse and his drawn back legs and puffs of snow; as the rest was hidden behind the sleigh; because he was charging right up to—

"Olympus!"

Genadie wrenched the reins to the left, steering the sleigh into the rider who was coming alongside. He had both hands on the taut leather straps to keep control. As he came up in the seat his head hit the leather roof, and the sleigh lurched; his knife and pistol clunked off his legs to the floorboard.

A strange whinny sounded; more like a huffing, high-pitched protest. Snow sprayed into the air, then fell away as the rider was driven into a drift. A quick counter-pull on the reins, and Genadie centered the sleigh onto the road. There were some bare patches ahead, where the snow thinned to grey-brown hardened earth. They hadn't greased the sleigh's runners, so they would catch and slow there.

Genadie wrenched the reins again. The sleigh pulled to the right and they dropped off the shallow embankment and veered directly toward the mountain. *No*, thought Amalina, *he's going for the farmhouse*.

During the farm's years of disuse, some neighbors had come along and picked off most of the enormous hills of hay, leaving behind only a few stacks that had moldered and shrunk and hardened into mounds that were high enough to see over, but treacherous to hit at full speed. The horses seemed to have awakened to the coming danger, though they pulled now in a confustion of different directions, and with a wheeze-whinny charged faster. The similarity of sound to these horses' whinnies and the rider's horse's at first didn't register to Amalina, until they took it up again at Genadie's next urging, and they sounded alarmed. Something similar there, in their voices.

Amalina tried to lean out from Genadie's side, fouling his arms. "What are you doing?" He cried in surprise.

The rider had recovered his bearings and was now charging for them. She didn't need to see the horse's eyes, just the way it moved. So mechanical. And with a churning inside of some almost inhuman fire. This rider had the same kind of horse as the ones Genadie would summon with his flute.

"Genadie," said Amalina, about to warn him. But the whole sleigh jumped under her feet.

They'd hit the first mound of hay. Drove straight into it.

The sleigh rocked dangerously from side to side, coming off the runners. The horses pitched into each other. Amalina tried to right herself, to anticipate what would happen next. But the next mound was right in front. With an angry whinny, they were all spinning, tumbling, whirling. Amalina's arms, knees, shins, and head banged off of the interior wood, the pigeon box, and Genadie's hard little body. The action somehow worked her into the reins.

Falling onto its left side, the sleigh came to a lurching, painful stop, with its cloth top shielding them from the mysterious rider out on the road.

"Ugh! Genadie?"

There came a hard knock into the bench above Amalina, followed by a popping sound. As she looked up she saw a small circle of sunlight on the bench, then still higher up, a rough hole in it. A new hole burst open beside the first with a spray of wood slivers. Then came the gunshot's report.

Amalina freed herself from the madly jerking reins, accidently crushing her knee into Genadie's thigh and hip. He moaned too softly, as if she were just pushing the air out of him.

"Genadie, are you all right?" Amalina shoved at him. "Genadie. Genadie!"

Amalina put her eye to one of the small, bright tears in the overturned roof. She could see where the man was, still atop his horse, so many yards away. She couldn't see him perfectly, her eyes being what they were, but by the way he was bent, she assumed he was reloading his weapons.

Amalina fished around below Genadie, pulling up the blanket. She found the pistol.

"Genadie, wake up!" she hissed at him, not wanting to alert the attacker. "Please, he's coming for us."

"Who?" muttered Genadie.

"We have to get out of this sleigh before he fires again."

"Let's just stay down, Ms. Dalca," he mumbled dreamily. "We are under the aegis of Olympus."

"Oh, Genadie, don't be stupid. Wake up!" But now she huddled down, sure their attacker must have reloaded and could fire any second. Or he could be riding up to check on them. All she could hear was the loud protests from their horses struggling to disentangle and right themselves.

"Leave me here, Ms. Dalca. Take a horse. We'll split up."

"The horses are wrapped up with each other."

"Run," he said. "I'll stay. Leave the knife."

"We'll go together."

"No."

"I'm not leaving you to him."

"Ms. Dalca, Olympus protects me. Go to the farmhouse."

"Nobody's there."

A lead ball smacked through the roof and into the wood bench above her head. Then came the report. He was still beside the highway. This happened again, with a pellet knocking off the floorboard, which was now a wall to Amalina's right. It was a wonder they hadn't been hit yet.

Amalina looked out the new hole in the roof and saw the horse amble off the road. Then it stopped. The tall rider atop it stared for some time. Then he leaned over and began to reload.

What a horrible person, thought Amalina. He was just going to keep his distance and fire in at them? How long before he was satisfied they were dead?

She was tempted to call out to him, ask him what he wanted. She covered her mouth with her hand to keep from doing something so foolish.

The sleigh began to pitch and rock. The horses, with their flailing legs, had worked through the snow and were now, with their attempts to free themselves, inadvertently moving them in small forward jolts.

The rider's next shot went into a horse. It managed to sit up and stare angrily at its attacker, as if it knew just where the pellet had come from. The next shot went into the sleigh again.

"Olympus."

Amalina searched Genadie in the cramped space. She opened his heavy coat while he, still half-conscious, smacked his lips, pieces of millet hanging off them. Somehow, and almost immediately, she found what she wanted.

"Go, Amalina," said Genadie, looking tired.

"I'll be back."

"The pistol."

"You have it. If he comes, shoot him."

"The pistol, Ms. Dalca," he insisted, though still half in dream. It looked like he'd parted his eyelids what little way they could just to look—or wink—at her.

But she put the pistol firmly in *his* hands, thumb ready to cock the hammer, finger on the trigger.

"Don't need it," she said. "I'll take the knife."

She didn't have to wait long for the next round of metal balls to hit. As Amalina gave a silent prayer, the roof and bench popped with new hits. But the shots still struck high. Maybe from his vantage a partial mound screened the bottom part of the sleigh.

All she had to do was glance out and see that he had, once again, chosen to reload. *How many bullets and how much powder did he have?* She slipped out of the front of the sleigh, worming herself quickly under the twisted tow shaft and reins, and around its icy front, ducking low below the top runner.

When she was outside and safely on the lee side of the sleigh, she suddenly wished she had taken the pistol. She could easily wait for the man to come closer and then pop out and fire into him when he did. Then, at the foul thought of it—of her missing the shot, or seeing him keel backwards off his horse with blood spraying all over the snow—she shook her head. No, her first idea was best.

She jumped up and hung off the top runner, swinging her weight out, rocking the sleigh. She didn't think it would work the first attempt, but with the effort of the horses still attached, and the generous angle at which the sleigh had come to a stop in the snow, it began to pitch and fall.

Amalina rolled out of the way of the sleigh's hard drop, before the runner could chop down on her. "Hyah, nk!" Amalina shooed at the horses.

But the horses were still a bit tangled. The sleigh budged forward slowly, and only picked up speed after they worked themselves off the hard mound.

Hidden from the man, Amalina ran alongside the sleigh but then at a diverging tangent, aiming for a higher stack of hay further on, or better, to the beginnings of the mountain's forest beyond that. Her knife was in one hand, the other brought the flute to her mouth so she could begin blowing hard into it.

34

The Wolf, Pt. 4

"**I**'m going to kill you, little girl," the man chuckled humorlessly.

Amalina's restrained gasps, and the blood rushing through her ears, muted his voice. But she knew what he'd said. His intent was clear by now. He had rushed after the sleigh when it had taken off, but had changed course when he'd noticed Amalina scrambling for the treeline. He had been so fixated on the sleigh that she'd almost made it into the forest by the time he spun his horse around and came after her. And she had gotten a good distance deeper into the woods before he was forced to abandon his horse and plunge in himself. The heavier drifts of snow stopped at the forest's edge, but there was still enough on the ground and along the mountain slope, littered with leaves, twigs and fallen branches, so that he easily tracked Amalina's wandering path.

Amalina didn't think it would come to this. She had thought somewhere between the sleigh and the mountain forest her efforts on the flute would have brought a horse; and when it did, depending on where the man was in relation to her, she would race him back to Netz, or push on to the castle. For some reason she thought calling a horse with the flute would be easy. She'd already used it once before. Out of the air it had brought her *White Mist*, the veritable recreation of her old horse *White Snow*. White Snow had fallen to the horrific black wolf and his pack; White Mist, his newer incarnation, was almost brought down by those wolves again, led once more by the seemingly indestructible great black wolf; but it had died more certainly in the battle of Kyrgil and the resulting collapse of Kyrgil Mountain. She closed her eyes as she ran and blew and blew into the flute, feeling Genadie's hairs tickling her lips and chin, while trying to form the soundless notes that this tiny fractured-and-repaired instrument would require to bring out a horse. Whatever horse, any horse. It didn't have to be *White-*anything, she thought.

But she'd run on, punching her feet through the snow, trying to stay balanced with one flailing arm, and quickly became breathless. So now she was without a horse, and trying to keep quiet behind a tree trunk and hope, despite her trail, the man would not find her. Hope that he would give up and go away.

"Going to kill you," he chuckled again. "Just wait right there and I'll show you. Run and make this harder than it needs to be, girl? you'll feel the difference. That I promise."

She felt her legs already stiffening in the cold, having run as far and as fast as they could. Could she possibly move now? She was out of energy, out of fight. Even the knife in her hand felt too heavy to lift. She vaguely wondered if Genadie had gotten away. Or if he'd stopped the sleigh, turned, and was making his way to her right now. She *should* have taken the pistol.

The man stood above her suddenly, a few lengths to the right along the mountainside. It was the tall man from Korr, the one who had been with the little wrinkled green man; one of the Men of Death. He dragged his leg along as he moved toward her, rucking up the snow with his slow foot. Up close, his head was long and cylindrical, the mouth stretching around it. He smiled a broken-toothed smile.

"Well, hello," he said. He pointed his pistol at her. She was still out of breath, huffing and puffing. But besides the man's backwards-pulling gait, he appeared in full strength. Relaxed. Excited. "Glad you have some sense in you girl. What is that you have in your hand? Oh." With his free hand he pulled a knife from his belt. It was an exceptionally long blade and curved like a tiger's tooth, a vicious point at the end. "Got one, too. Mine's much bigger, don't you think?"

His smile widened. Amalina frowned.

When he took a step forward, bringing the point up, Amalina said, "Wait."

"What?"

"Why do you want to hurt me?"

"I said I was going to kill you."

"But why? Who are you?"

He took another step, prepared to reach her, to slice at her.

"Hold on," said Amalina, sounding annoyed. "The knife. You promised you would make it fast if I didn't resist."

"Did I?" he chuckled.

"You think this is funny?"

He thought about it. Then he nodded.

"Just use your pistol. Make it quick." Amalina felt sick saying it, but she also meant it.

"Well … I never promised to make it quick. Just that you wouldn't suffer worse. But you're going to have to suffer. That's the way he wants it. The way he likes it."

"Who?"

"The one who sent me," he said, closing toward her again.

Amalina side-stepped, and then backed up from the tree she'd been hiding behind.

He shook his head, disagreeing with her choice, but sneered viciously because that meant he could have his preferred way. It was going to be rough.

There was a movement in the distance. Amalina glanced past him hoping to see Genadie. But it must have been the man's horse. He stopped and turned to see what she was looking at. Nothing.

"You know the way I like it?" asked the man, crunching frozen twigs below his boots, as he took the last several step-drags for her. "Even *he* doesn't know. And the way I figure it, would make him sick if he found out. But you and I are going to know," he chuckled. "It's nice to enjoy myself, once in a while."

There was a loud snap to the right. They spun their heads in surprise.

The horse that trampled the undergrowth and shouldered aside the lower branches was a magnificent charger. It wasn't the man's horse, Amalina saw. It was without a saddle, with golden hair except a white patch between its eyes. There was something familiar to its look, though its eyes were the same strange ones of all horses called out by the flute. Amalina felt the first pulse of surprise and disbelief, even as she began to understand the truth.

White Snow, thought Amalina. She saw the red patches on its haunch, in places where it had once suffered wolf bites.

White Snow, or Mist—or rather, more properly, her favorite charger's *next* incarnation—came to a stop. A full stop, utterly motionless. It watched them. Or, at least, Amalina assumed it was watching her; as much as something that looked like a statue can observe. Was he waiting for instructions?

The man winked at Amalina. "Interesting. I *will* have a witness to my joy, then. Or maybe a helper. Let me just paralyze you and I can have myself a think."

The man fell on Amalina. As they both dropped to the ground, he on top of her, she shouted in protest as he swung his knife down, his other arm scooping over her shoulder to pull her into his blade. She turned at the last moment, flicking her body at the waist, and the knife skidded across her cloak, slicing it, but not stabbing into it. She shot her own knife upward toward his stomach. But their bodies came together hard into a hug as they landed in the snow, and her blade bent back in her hand, the small wristguard dug into her wrist. Then she was crushed against his chest, almost unable to breathe, his large body smothering her, his fingers feeling for her ribs, her bones; vulnerable points on her body to inflict a little pain. His open mouth came down on the bridge of her nose. She felt his teeth clamp onto the skin there, threatening to bite down hard. He was laughing, and she felt the vibrations through her nose, through her skull, down her spine.

Then he lifted his head away and he fell back, his arms going loose in a flailing way. As if death were now really pulling at his leg. Which it was.

"What?" he said, looking back. Then he screamed as he saw the wolf clamped onto his calf. It was dragging him backward, only to allow his brothers and sisters of the pack to jump on him from both sides. The man howled louder, defiantly, as if trying to frighten them. The wolves answered with ravenous, unrelenting growls. They'd just taken their meat, and they weren't giving it back no matter how much noise it made. He tried to grab at Amalina's leg, perhaps to draw her to him, to slide her in front of him like a shield.

Amalina kicked his hand away. Avoiding a revengeful slash, she spun on the ground until she was back up on her feet.

Get to White Snow, she thought. Get on, ride if you can. Get away before he gets loose or the wolves come for you.

The wolves had definitely settled on him. He was larger than she, and wearing a tempting fur over his shoulders that suggested something tasty inside. She was ignored for the moment.

White Snow was gone. A large hole had been opened in the forest debris, a trail White Snow was clearing at a charge. She didn't know why he'd run away. He might have thought she was dead. Or was frightened by the wolves, of course. That would be likely, he having experienced being eaten by them before, and then, on the next go around, nearly eaten by them again.

Amalina took to the scattered trail, finding better footing and an easier path. She wanted to shout after the horse. Command him to return for her, to take her out of the forest. But she didn't know if that would alert the wolves. She kept quiet and scrambled onward, not even daring to breathe. Still feeling too tired to run, she pushed herself beyond endurance to get away.

Suddenly the charger was coming right back at her, whinnying with fright, its weird eyes blanked by fear. It would trample Amalina. She leapt to the side. His powerful shoulder knocked her backward a painful yard. But she landed on her feet and steadied herself, allowing at least a breath.

A very loud and heavy growl, sounding like it had just come dripping out of a bowl of shredded flesh, rose from where White Snow had emerged. Then, in that spot, appeared the monstrous head of the most malign looking beast.

• • •

Amalina fell back, a cry frozen in her throat. She could not believe—could never believe ...

The big block head, broken and malformed by the damage it had sustained, with tears and scars networking through its hair, patches burned away around one yellowed, squirting eye: it was all too impossible. But she recognized who it was; where she'd burned it with a torch, and pummeled its head until it cracked, and where she'd shot it with a pistol, then blinded it with the pistol's ramrod; wounds she'd given it on successive years. And here it was again before her, its one good eye burning with a hatred matched only by the fury of an exploding powder keg, one broken, cracked eye looking like the Eye of Death itself; eyes which could buckle her knees with a glance.

Too exhausted and out of breath, shocked to the last inch of her sanity, Amalina fell to her knees. She kept her face hardened, mouth drawn back into a sneer of angry contempt, to at least look ready for a fight. But to be almost killed by the tall man only to next have to confront the animal that has been her relentless pursuer, her life's greatest menace? Hadn't she endured countless nightmares of being eaten by wolves, her gory fate teased time and again in real life by this one impossible wolf? And now here he was once more, to make it finally happen?

But her grim astonishment was felt only in the first instant: the shock of their meeting.

In the second instant, the black wolf's hatred rose from its eye like a cloud blown by a powerful wind back over its shoulder. The wolf recoiled and winced at the sight of her. It howled and banged its chin on rocks. It turned toward her, then circled away, then looked again, as if not believing. It danced and skipped on the edge of its paws in loops, as if the ground before it had been lit on fire. Astounded. Horrified. It recognized her, too.

Here was the girl that had nearly killed him so many times before. So *many* times before. Now here again? And with a dangerous and clever look to her! He howled angrily, and snarled, and bared his teeth at the nasty little girl.

Then, after another pulse of thought, he was down on his paws, his great misshapen head burrowed into the ground, his burning eye and dead eye staring up at her like he was looking into the sun. Yes, here was the god-like girl that could evade and wound him at will. The child who could disappear, and reappear with weapons of agony and death. He had tried to kill her so many times before, and she had not only survived and slipped away, but had beat him and left him for dead.

He bellowed. Then, with his mouth buried into the ground, he bowed his front shoulders down in a show of absolute capitulation. Or was it admiration? Or fear? Or surrender? Or, could it be the most amazing thing of all: was it the prayer of a convert?

35

The Greatest Change

Amalina and Genadie arrived back at the high castle by late mid-afternoon. While most of the ride after the morning's incident had been conducted in a self-reflective silence—over what they'd just survived, and who it was they had managed to escape—as they closed in on the top of the mountain, the two began to argue over whether they should report the attack.

"He already knows," said Genadie. "Why bother Master with needless details?"

"Bother him? We were almost killed!"

"P-shah!"

"And just what details *does* he know?" said Amalina, from atop her new horse, looking down on him in the sleigh. "That killer was sent by that ugly little man who reclaims the castle's ugly little pigeons. The one who runs the Count's murder service."

"The what?"

"I saw the two of them—this killer and the ugly pigeon-man—talking in Korr near the bakery, just before we left. They must have been keeping watch. And his man came after us."

"Let the dead rest, Ms. Dalca."

"Listen, I didn't survive just to shut up about it. He's going to know what happened and what I think of it!"

"And what then? What can he do about it now?" Genadie petted his grizzled chin with trembling, crooked fingers. "You're worked up about it, that's all. *Let the dead rest.*"

"If he wants to keep me happy, he'll—"

"Keep you happy, Ms. Dalca!" he gaped. "What a thing to say!"

"We could have been half-way to freedom by now. We could have. But *I* turned us around. Now, if we're going to remain on here—a little while longer, anyway—he better do something to keep us happy. We deserve it."

"Us?"

"Yes, *us.*"

"Leave me out of it, Ms. Dalca."

"All right then, me. He's going to make sure *I'm* not under the constant threat of death, every second."

"You're exaggerating a bit, Ms. Dalca," concluded Genadie. "It's not so bad as that."

"Well, even if you aren't going to, I'm going to speak my mind—to him. I will."

"I wish you wouldn't, Ms. Dalca."

. . .

Pia Lampeda was standing outside the gates. If she hadn't changed dress and thrown on an overcoat, it would seem the Roman princess had never left the spot. She greeted the sleigh with a nod and then with a warm, welcoming wave to Amalina. She drew Amalina away, insisting Genadie, or one of the other servants handle the damaged sleigh and settle Amalina's new horse into the barn.

"My uncle will want to speak to me right away," said Amalina as she walked a little faster than Pia in the courtyard, and with purpose, aiming for the Count's study, adding internally: *and I to him.*

"Well, I caught you first," soothed Pia, roping her arm through Amalina's to slow her down. "It's not like he's been waiting for you like I have. And you know it isn't *his* hour of the day, anyway, the busy rascal. Not yet. Let's you and I wait for him together til he wakes. Come."

"I can't imagine how long you were waiting for me, the sunlight doesn't bother you?" asked Amalina when they were back inside the castle, as Pia steered her to her own quarters.

Pia shook her head, her long red hair shifting like limp tentacles, then she touched the back of her hand, which was pink-red in the way such milky-complected skin burns. "It is a little uncomfortable. Nothing I'm not used to, you know. It's all right. Why?"

Amalina wondered how much Pia knew, *really* knew—or fully realized about the Count—about his full nature; the bargain she'd entered into; what she was becoming.

Once in Pia's apartment, Pia threw off her overcoat and helped Amalina out of her jacket next to the fireplace.

"How long were you gone?" asked Pia, slinking her cool arm through Amalina's again to steer her to a couch. They were going to sit; then the princess would lean in and send her limbs around Amalina like a rushing tide to envelope her. Pia's favorite pastime. "It was so long, Katty. It felt like forever."

"Not even a week."

"I thought I'd lost you." said Pia, as they were on the couch and she began the lift of the tide of her body, pressing against Amalina, staring at her. There was something a little lost in those large green eyes.

"I told you I'd be back."

"People say things. Sometimes they say what isn't true. Even when they really meant it, sometimes. Do you know what I mean?"

"Not really."

"You never know what's going to happen. Even when you think you do."

Amalina wondered if Pia was, in another sense, talking about her own transformation; what she had become already, and what she would eventually be. Or if she meant that the Count's promise that Amalina would always be there for her was proving unhappily untrue somehow. But how to ask without putting those thoughts into her head, especially if her statement was something more innocent?

Or maybe she could read Amalina's eyes, and knew she had almost been murdered earlier that day; had come within a knife slash of death.

"How did it go? Everything went well?"

"We did what we were supposed to."

"And you left your friend in your old village?" asked Pia. "Cristine, was it?"

"Yes," sighed Amalina. "She should never have come. I don't know what she was thinking."

"But she was your friend. Your *dearest* friend, right? Why *wouldn't* she want to come to visit you?"

"It's not that simple."

"Oh, I understand," said Pia. "There is the role you are playing here. I get that. And she might not know—or, rather, she wouldn't think you are any different than when you two were little girls. Little Amalina Dalca, the butcher's daughter."

"Baker."

"Yes, *baker*. Sorry. But it's only natural for her to remember you that way. To think of you only in that way and to want to be the friend to the friend she once knew. Until she finds out you aren't the same little friend anymore." Pia brushed back a lock of Amalina's hair. "Did that happen? Did she notice?"

"Notice what?"

"That you aren't the same?"

Amalina settled into the couch, which only brought Pia's body heavier against her. How strange it was, only this morning being crushed into the snowy forest floor by the body of an assassin, intent on killing her, and now to be mushed into a soft couch by someone who clearly loved her. It argued the value of staying alive, to find what's to come next. And to appreciate those who most care about you. But really, wasn't Pia a killer now, too? Amalina tried to shake off that thought. She looked at her friend and took her in as she was, friendly and smiling. Caressing. Pia's hair smelled of a pleasant perfume with a distant note of that musky-herbal scent the Count carried. As much as it should have been predictable, this odor, this small touch of the Count on Pia, it was slightly disappointing. At length, Amalina didn't answer this question about her own transformation into nobility but let it linger, as if she were considering it deeply.

Amalina wanted sleep. Despite her desire to confront the Count at the end of her eventful travel, she had just survived an attempt on her life; had just watched (and heard, which was maybe worse) a man—a bad man, admittedly—be torn to pieces; and she had sobbed herself sick when she'd finally caught up to the sleigh and thought Genadie had been killed (until he'd come round with a gasp). It was a long day, and hard to prop up a smile for this warm creature beside her. Because that *is* what her good friend was now: a creature. Yes, that is, in the end, what she was. She couldn't forget that. One with evil and unquenchable desires, the same as that tall man who'd just come after her. Amalina's weary mind flashed with images of the German delegation torn apart, with Pia in the middle of it all, mercilessly shredding Crutio. Some of it mixed with the tall man getting savaged, his gargling squeals. That wolf was a killer, too. They were all surrounding her.

Pia nudged Amalina awake.

"Oh, was I asleep?"

"Never mind. Tell me more about her, your friend, Cristine. Please. Can we talk about her? Do you mind? She seemed very nice from what I could tell, if a little forward. *Peasanty*." Pia added quickly, "Not in a bad way. Just … you know. Peasanty."

Silence continued. Amalina's eyes began to close heavily.

"Tell me about her," said Pia, shaking her awake.

"Ugh. Now? Why? What's going on?"

"Because it isn't even time for supper so it is no time for you to sleep. And I want to know more about you as the girl from Korr. Who you loved and how you were before all this. I want to know just who you were before you became *my* Katty."

"I'm still the same," mumbled Amalina grouchily, Pia's cool finger spinning a lock of her hair into a curl. She was as relentless, it seemed, as the Count.

"Nobody ever stays the same," said Pia, continuing on with a loving purr, stroking Amalina's hair like a pet dog now. "You've changed since I met you. You've been changing ever since. So I'd like to know the soul you were when you were with Cristine. That would be interesting, yes."

And how ironic, thought Amalina, shifting to get more comfortable, *all this talk about changing, about who was what before when*. As if Pia could point a finger.

Pia massaged Amalina's shoulder here. "Oh, don't be tense. I hope I haven't upset you. I didn't mean anything wrong by asking. Maybe you misunderstand my purpose. You have to understand, Amalina: I'm looking for life. Life is change, you see. And I want to hear about it wherever I can. Especially from you. Because you know how fond I am of you."

This gluey scene lasted forever. Until Pils interrupted to let Amalina know that *other* ladies were asking for her. There were new arrivals.

• • •

Amalina had not only been exhausted from her trip, her escape from death, her desire to confront the Count with what had happened, and her arrival to the ever sticky Pia, but was now dismayed to further depths at finding herself back at a castle after she had thought she'd escaped it forever and, as well, finding that none of the ladies she'd left behind had found a way to escape while she was gone. Of course they wanted to remain there, to capture her uncle's favor. She knew that. But inside, Amalina felt there must be at least one of them who'd grown tired of the petty dramas, too, or the boredom, or sensed the danger, or would simply take her lead as she left. One of them, surely, would have been recalled by a letter from home, or had a dream of such extreme longing or homesickness that convinced them it was time to find an exit. But they were still there, all of them:

Prying Lady Princess Erin Epris; the Sock Personalities of the daredevil Lady Halma Inovala, the timid Lady Jean Hachter-Friecke, and the sensualist Princess Greta La Nevers; The knowledgeable and adventurous Genevieve de Roye; the leggy Power Queen, Lady Anne Brignol; the Woman of Hot Love, Lady Claire Montraine; the True Friend, Lady Elisavet Pattipo; and, of course, as always—the barnacle: Princess Margeta la Brichese.

All of them—placed just where they were as Amalina remembered them.

And then, as Pils had promised, some more ladies, too. Added after she'd left.

"So nice to see you. So happy to meet you again." Amalina held their hands and exchanged kisses-to-cheek. Some kisses were familiar, some warm, others stiff. Amalina accepted the latest batch with a heightening guilt. It was always the same old question she put to herself: How was she succeeding this way, bringing so many women into this cursed castle? They couldn't all have been taken in. Could so many be so desperate for friendship or money that they ignore lies, or rather eat them up without first considering them?

Focus, Amalina, focus, she thought, as she shrugged off the negativity. *You've been given a second chance; a purpose. You're going to do better this time! A map and five birds. That's all you've got to get through.*

"Oh, you came," said Amalina, mentally adding their names and faces, and personalities, to the expanding list of guests. "I'm so glad you made it before winter, before the storm; and before Christmas. I feel bad for your families, but I should be glad that I won't be lonely for the holidays."

"And where is your uncle?" one asked.

"So where is your uncle?" asked another.

"I look forward to meeting Count Tepsji. What a pretty little castle. But I've heard he has many *more* throughout the mountains. Is that true?"

"Is it true that one of his castles was lost to a storm? or a volcano? But something like that couldn't happen here, could it? I hope not. Assure me, Lady Katarina, I've nothing to be afraid of."

Focus!

"I don't know where my uncle is," said Amalina. "But I need to speak to him."

• • •

"There is a certain smell in the castle now," said the Count, privately. He wore a heavy-lidded scowl as he played with his mustache.

Amalina stood before him, as if for instruction. She assumed there was a reason why he'd finally called for her, via Pils, before she could find him out herself. As she waited for him to finish whatever it was he had to say, she felt anxious, because she wanted tell him just what was on *her* mind: she *would* tell him what was on her mind; about the man who'd nearly killed her and Genadie, and how it had to do with the murder service—*his* murder service, tied to the mysterious letters AXP. She would get to the bottom of it all. But first:

"Can you tell what it means, hm, Ms. Dalca? Have you *noticed* how many of your friends are from France? And as you've no doubt marked, they are most interested in *me*, not you. Little delicacy or subtlety there. There must be a downturn in the French economy by just how many have come, and how eager they are. Is there a war on and they need to protect their family fortunes from taxes?"

"I haven't noticed, sir. But, sir, I wanted to tell you something—"

"And so do I, Ms. Dalca," said the Count, growing a wry smile. "I see you are upset. I understand how you might be confused, or jealous, at finding, on every return, my home stocked with more and more ladies who demand my attention more than they seek your company, though they came at *your* invitation."

"*Your* invitation, sir."

"*You* wrote the invitations," he said, almost sounding like he was blaming her for the growing chaos.

"Because you asked me to, sir. I'm just letting you know, sir, I'm not jealous they're here for you instead of me."

"And yet I am sure you must be *disappointed*. Their infidelity. But no matter, I was speaking in another direction. Yes, *yesss* … No, I believe you are not jealous if they've come to my castle just for me, but that they might absorb too much of my time, and, I warrant and I allow, my consideration"—*I, me, I, me, I, me*, as always. He stroked his mustache and drew his eyes up to meet hers with some meaning in them. "These women mean nothing to me, Ms. Dalca. They meet needs; requirements; because no single body can fill every emptiness within a soul." The way he described the soul as being troubled with openings, and Amalina being so fatigued, she couldn't help but picture a bread whose many nooks were stuffed with dark cranberries. Her stomach growled. "However, you are a diamond, Ms. Dalca. You are different from all of them. You are capable, and trustworthy, and dutiful. You ask nothing of me. You keep my interest. I have lived a very long time, as you know, and I have seen and experienced everything a body can. I have reached the pinnacle of science. There is nothing more in that philosophy to be discovered. The only thing fresh for one like me is the blood, and only when I find a new vein, or tributary of a type that I haven't run across. Which means there is very little.

"I believe I have told you before," he continued. "I fear that my mind is stiffening. Like an untreated leather or a drying mortar. As with the great oak, as it grows and grows and it gains its insufferable strength, it looses its flexibility and hardens into iron. In time, if I do not renew my spirit, holed up within this castle, I shall continue to exist, but as what? What will I become without renewal? Shall I be dumb as a statue? As unmoving? Will my thoughts slow to lead?

"Even now, I have begun to lose my hold. I lost many of my natural allies during my battle with that imposter on the mountain. And those who've returned to my lands do not obey as before. They are quiet. Changed. Almost strangers. Some refuse to speak to me. Perhaps it is understandable for what they went through, what I put them through. But, so unlike before. Yes, *changed*."

Amalina thought of the black wolf, three times ready to tear her apart, now bowing to her. This was no doubt one of his 'natural allies', as the high castle's mountain was the wolfpack's natural hunting grounds. But, the black wolf was hers now, not the Count's. She said nothing, but he noticed her look.

"Amalina, I need fresh blood. This explains my harem. But more than that, and here I am forced to repeat myself: I need you."

"Oh? Why, sir?"

"But I have already told you."

"Yet I still don't understand why it *must* be me—"

"Well of course you do. Don't be simple, my little mouse. I am the embodiment of power; some might claim it corruption. You are the perfect representation of purity and innocence; a line of uninterrupted innocence from the beginning of our—your—race, from the time of Eden." He noticed another look. "You have something to say?"

"That isn't true, sir," she said, feeling somewhat embarrassed now that she was admitting it. "I'm not what you think. My grandfathers and great grandfathers were in the war. So on both sides of my family, you see, they were soldiers. They've killed men, of course."

"Perhaps they were cowards and removed themselves before battle?"

"I don't think so. They were known for their ferocity on the field, sir. It's how they achieved rank."

"How do you know this?"

How do you not? wondered Amalina. He was always bragging that he knew everything. This ought to be something he *should* know. "I spoke to my father."

"Naughty girl," said the Count with a proud smile. "That was between you and I. I suppose *that* is why you took the route to Korr? to ask him questions and test your line's purity?"

"I didn't tell him about what you said, sir. I just asked if anyone in our family had ever ... you know."

"Yes, I know."

"So, then, sir, it isn't true, this theory of yours, is it? Not if they killed other men. So I'm not the most innocent creature in the world, as you thought."

"No, I suppose not." He threw back his head and laughed. "Oh, well. *That* isn't it, then. There must be another reason for us to unite. Or maybe none at all."

"You aren't upset, sir?" She was more hoping this information might have at least changed his mind; bucked him off his passionate belief. But maybe he wasn't even really listening to what she had to say. He had his own agenda. The whole purpose of this *tete-a-tete* was to redouble his efforts to draw her close, because he knew, or suspected, just how narrowly he'd come to her slipping out of his cold grasp.

"If it wasn't for you, Amalina, I'd still be babbling in the cellars of my castle," said the Count with a low growl. "I'd be alone with Genadie and pretending my happiest moments were spent with meaningless roués and pointless players like Flauna and Kosche. Not betrothed to someone as meaningful as you."

"Betrothed?" It was out of her mouth before she could stop it. But she'd already known where it was all headed. The relationship committed to. Wife #9. But the cloying romantic expression of it …

"Yes, I see you are troubled with the thought of such a marriage," he rumbled, "mindful of the popular objection to a commoner—the daughter to a baker, such as yourself—marrying into the noble class. But when the rite is performed, we will be as equals … above all others."

"Oh, I see."

"I marry anyone I wish," he said, slightly peevish as she obviously hadn't taken the statement as sweetly as expected. But there was still a tender smile of affection stuck below his mustache. "Don't you think?"

"Sir." She cleared her throat. "The thing I have to tell you is that I was almost killed. Just now. Someone tried to kill me."

"Yes," said the Count, with a slight flicker of confusion.

"You know, sir?"

"What have you to say about it?"

Now Amalina was confused. "Well, sir … What I have to say is, I was almost murdered. He might have killed Genadie, too. But he was after me. If it wasn't for the wolves in the forest, I wouldn't be here talking to you."

"The wolves?" this seemed to interest the Count.

"It's the time of the year they take after anyone," said Amalina. "As you know."

"Where did this happen?"

"Around the mountain. In Netz Valley."

The Count nodded thoughfully. "They attacked him but not you?"

Amalina explained quickly about calling the horse and sneaking away while the man was still the wolves' focus. She said nothing of the black wolf.

"Did you see …?" began the Count, then he hesitated. "I wonder, did you see a wolf with black fur in their pack?"

"I don't know, sir. All I really saw was snow and teeth and then blood. And I heard a lot of growling and him screaming."

"So you didn't see a *black* wolf?"

"Not as I was running away."

The Count nodded, his smile edging downward, flattening. His eyes dulled as his thoughts walked off in a different direction.

"But this man who tried to kill me," said Amalina. "I know him. I mean, I've seen him before. In my village. He's a friend of that ugly little man who handles our pigeons. You know, the one who runs your murder service."

"Murder service? What are you talking about?" said the Count, as though surprised she was aware of such a thing.

"You've told me all about it. Last year. Remember, sir? The man with the birds. He sends you after victims."

"That isn't any of your business, Amalina. Nothing for you to worry about."

"Um, well, isn't it something for me to worry about?"

"How so?"

"They just tried to murder *me*, sir."

"Oh, yes. That. But you see how my mountain forces protected you. They must know your importance to me." He added to himself, "I should—and I shall—reward them."

"Yes, sir. But this man, he said his boss wants me dead, that he was going to torture and kill me."

The Count thought for a moment, then took his finger from his mustache to raise it into the air, his brilliant, toothy smile returning. His basso voice boomed, "Aaaah! I wondered what you were getting at. You fear me! There is a mistrust!"

With a humming graciousness, the Count led Amalina from his divan to his hidden message center: the area beyond the gloating portrait/secret door in his study, past his treasury room stocked with shelf-fulls of bags of gold ingots and where he pressed his own coins, and down below where the massive vault lay. A two-story chamber of shelves and paper, more than double the size of his Great Library. Even after the assault by Commander Kralov and his men, blasting through the place with their bombs, they hadn't wiped out a fraction of the books, contracts, letters, agreements, scrolls, sticks, whatever correspondence with the outside human world which the Count wished to preserve. The vast proof-of-contact and records he seemed to cherish even more than all the gold in the castle. Each town in Ardeel had its own shelf unit, designated by its name painted there. Some towns commanded more than a few shelves, some less.

The Count's route ended at the bottom of the stairs, with a concluding hummed note at his standing desk—at the book sitting atop it. Amalina's heart beat faster when light from her candle flashed off the cover's metal letters: AXP.

"What's this, sir?" she asked innocently, acting as if this were the first time she'd actually laid eyes on this book. Had never touched it.

"I've something to show you," he said with a proud flourish as he slapped the book open on the desk. His movements were precise and his finger fell immediately to a small strip among many that had been pasted onto the book's most recent page.

Amalina was familiar with AXP's book, of course, having seen and pillaged notes from it before. But these were new notes the Count pointed to. She pretended all the same to be surprised by the book itself, its flippy-flappy contents, and leaned over to squint at the smudge on the strip of paper he indicated.

"I suppose you need your glasses, Amalina. But I *will* remind you, the remedy to your blindness waits within my power, which I can share with you; though it *will* stay as your defect until all is ready and the others—"

"Yes, sir. But what do you want me to see here?"

"It is a portrait of you."

"Of me?" A ripple of tension twisted her stomach. Things had gotten worse since she left. "In this book?"

"You spoke of my murder service. Well, here is my commission. For you. With an impeccable portrait so I should not be mistaken who my victim is."

"I don't understand the writing."

He shut the book quickly. "You can see the writing with those earthly eyes of yours?"

"Not really. I mean, I couldn't make out the letters. But what does it say? Why does he want me to die?"

The Count smoothed his cap of black hair while he regarded the book with theatrical contempt, as was his way. "I haven't bothered to learn his prejudices. You shouldn't bother about *any* of it. I only showed you this so you can understand more fully my earnestness, toward you and your safety." He tapped the flickering metal letters AXP. "*This* has been an indispensable instrument for decades now. Every commission I've carried out—whether that offends you or not. You will not speak of this subject again. But know that this is the first commission I have denied." He slapped the book open again. He drew his finger down the column of strips that came after Amalina's portrait. "Look how he protests. Look how enraged he grows at my incompliance." He slammed the book shut again and threw it hard across the room. It crashed into the shelf for Korr, scattering a bloom of papers and scrolls there. "Yet I will not hear his pleas for they offend me so. To ask such a thing, when he knows how valuable you are to me. Had I wished to, had I not cared, you would already be dead, Amalina. But I do not wish to do you harm and I do very much care *not* to." His voice lowered until it sounded like the rumble of a great waterfall. "I care very much for you, Amalina. While I care, I will protect you, and you will never come to harm. This is my proof."

"But," Amalina ventured with a concealed wince, "I did *almost* die, sir. He just sent someone else after me, and I got lucky—"

Wham!

Amalina spun like a top, pirhouetting across the flat stones of her bedroom until she hit the frame of her bed.

That night it was announced that the Count was away on business. Two days later, the gnawed-apart head of the tall man (Amalina recognized him by his hair), and the head of the ugly, green-grey wrinkled man were set on spikes above the gate, facing out to the approach road, lit by the rising sun.

AXP, the murder service, its threat to countless young women and to Amalina's own life, was suddenly over. Lifted.

Pia said to Amalina, sounding a bit jealous: "He confided to me that, for this favor to you, he gave up quite a lot. How flattering it must be."

. . .

It could be readily argued, and Amalina would not disagree when challenged, that the worst disturbance yet in the Palace of Pleasure's short history was more the direct result of her escape from death—from the Man of Death, in the mountains—and her successful return to Count Tepsji; and the continuing glut of Noble Ladies she'd invited to join her.

36

Heavenly Provisions

As Sadra fed Attila some bisquits and wine in the church's back room, he asked: "How did I get here?"

"Heaven provides," was the answer, and she spread her hands open above his meal to demonstrate what else he should be thankful for.

Attila nodded, eyes half-lowered. "I mean more exactly. How did I get to your church? I don't remember."

"I had Gulgas bring you here at night. Nobody saw. He carried you in one of his field-kill bags."

"I'm thankful I don't remember," he said.

"I have a question for you, if you'll allow."

Attila started in on a bisquit and nodded.

"Is there a reason you gave Amalina only five pigeons?" she asked. "We could have done more."

"No," said Attila, between bites. "It was the perfect number."

"Of course. But ... how do you figure?"

"Simple enough," said Attila, holding up a finger, and then raising more along the way. "One bird is for the map. That takes care of one. Allowing for initial mistakes and misadventure, perhaps one or two, if that, four more birds will give us the additional information we need. You see, the Dalca girl was bent on escaping and she may still be, we don't know where her true intention now lies. But she knows she is done with us when she's sent us her five birds. If she quickly rids herself of them, by issuing them rapid-fire—one-two-three-four—and with meaningless drivel, we know she's just trying to speed through her obligations to get it over with. She is not serious and of no further use. She might as well escape, if only to get her out of the way.

"If she sends us nothing, or little to none, it means, either she is in danger, or she is cautious, willing to take her time, and a true ally. And so if she proves serious to our cause, she won't begrudge us if we send her another five to work with, if need be, when the first have run out."

"Or if she sends us nothing," said Sadra, her angular face tightening. "She might only be confused. She seemed unclear of your instructions for 'pertinent information.' And I must admit, if feels confusing to me."

"My vagueness had its purpose."

"Of course. How so?"

"Her confusion, as you put it, will lead to bad information only if she is unserious, or she is stupid. She is not stupid. Which goes back to my first point: is she serious? But, as well, if she is serious and if I were specific with what I want to know—the Count's movements, the number of his forces, threats to our mission, etc.—she might be too focused on those things and either give away her position as a spy by unconsciously leaning toward them, or might overlook other things I might not know were important. In the vagueness of my general instruction, and if she is serious, her instincts will be heightened by both fear and pride that she not fail, and her senses heightened too, as sensitive as a moth's antennae, so that she will seem to the Count on one level of awareness and watchfulness always, unclear to him what she's after, and she can giveaway nothing. She will also be more perceptive of, and discerning of, anything she learns in that castle. Best I keep her in the dark, so that she might shine her own light to us."

"I see. You have some way of thought."

"Indeed. Though, I'll admit, the primary purpose is to gauge how serious she is." Shrugging on the large coat and dropping its hood over his face, he said, "But let's proceed. We've work to do ourselves. Heaven does not labor for those who don't labor for themselves. Let's see what this day brings forth, in answer to us."

"Amen," said Sadra. "But where first? You still haven't told me."

"Yes. One thing at a time."

. . .

"And who have you brought with you today?" asked Dragomir, trying to peek under the deep hood of Sadra's companion. By the clothes it was a man, but it wasn't her husband, the minister. A nervous thought struck him: "A friend in need of some bread, Sadra? Of course I will gladly part with a round to our brothers in bad circumstances. Oh, but I hope our charity loaves haven't given any wrong ideas to the village, or I will be out of business in a month."

"Let's not fear after your profits," said Sadra, sarcastically. "He's not charity, but something much more important. However, you will show us into the kitchen where we can speak privately."

Dragomir looked surprised, but then nodded and led them to the back. Now he wondered if what had caught on in Korr was not free bread but Sadra shepherding mysterious people around the town. He looked at her companion's legs just to make sure it might not be Amalina, ready to spring a surprise.

In the kitchen, Sadra touched the man's arm and he pulled back his hood. He had sleepy looking eyes and a thick bandage on his neck that cocked his head to the side. He didn't look familiar, but Dragomir saw so many faces in a day. No one from the town that he'd ever met, though.

"Dragomir Dalca," said the man, with a stiff bow at the waist. "I'm afraid I cannot identify myself at this time. But I am operating under the direct authority of the governor of Ardeel."

"Straighten up and don't look like that, Dragomir," said Sadra. "He's on our side. Or, rather, we are on his side. For he is on the side of God."

"He said he was from the side of our governor in Tsobl."

"But let us begin," said the man, looking uninterested in the exchange. For a second there was liveliness in his eyes, a flash of quickness: "I am assembling a force from among the most trusted members of this city. Because there are persons who would oppose our mission, this must be a force assembled with the utmost secrecy and only entrusted to those we know are above reproach."

"You have spoken to Daniel, our mayor?" said Dragomir.

"No names will be revealed unless and until it is necessary. Utmost secrecy, do you understand?"

"Do you understand, Dragomir Dalca?" demanded Sadra.

"Only a little. What is this about?"

"Righting an old wrong," said the man, idly scratching at a blob of dried dough on the counter. "Bringing to justice a being of the highest criminal order."

"I'm all for that," said Dragomir. "Who wouldn't be? You two've spoken to the deputy sheriff, Sadra?"

"It isn't that simple," said the man. "As I have said before: there is a counterforce to my mission. One as yet unidentified and of unknown size. Therefore: utmost secrecy."

"This matter will be pursued by the righteous," said Sadra like an ominous Greek chorus.

Dragomir suddenly saw before him the lynch mob that had almost done him in once-upon-a-time during the labor strike. He'd sworn never to be a part of that madness if it ever came to sweep him up in its arms, demanding he join.

"Stop looking like that, Dragomir, and pay attention."

"What is this about, Sadra?"

"A murder," said the man, turning his dead gaze directly on Dragomir. "Some years ago, a man named Neku Jonker was murdered by a vicious criminal."

"Who is that?" said Dragomir.

"Neku Jonker was the attendant of the St. Grigori church's cemetery, the gravedigger. And it was there he fought a valiant battle against someone who had been vandalizing the cemetery for some years, but he could never catch. This criminal made away with the valuables of many of Netz' most worthy citizens, making himself wealthy at their eternal expense. It was during one such plundering of an ancient mausoleum that Neku finally overtook this scandalous monster, only to be killed for his efforts."

"St. Grigori church? In Netz?"

The man nodded slowly, without expression.

"The law there can't handle the matter? I don't understand what—"

"We know who the culprit is, Dragomir Dalca," said the man. "But unfortunately he has power and influence that exceeds the common law."

Dragomir's eyes goggled. He turned to Sadra. "You mean the Cardinal? Is your church finally going to war with Rome? I don't know ... I don't know if I could ..."

Sadra looked stunned.

"At this very moment I cannot reveal who it is," said the man. "Not until we know we have your oath that you will join us in our mission."

"I always want to do what is right and just," assured Dragomir, fidgeting nervously. Was this the kind of silly thing Amalina had warned him against? "But this is Korr, not Netz. Why would you think I would involve myself in something so far away? And on a religious matter—"

"Because it is not a matter of religious schism," said the man. "And your daughter is associated with the criminal. She is helping him on a daily basis."

"My daughter, Amalina?" Dragomir's heart pounded. How did this man know anything about her? What all *did* Sadra know, or had told the stranger already? What had Amalina tried to tell *him* about the Count before she left? "She is away. In Germania."

"She is in Netz," said the man, his eyes unwavering. "Living in the high castle with Count Tepsji."

Dragomir looked to Sadra, feeling his stomach flopping. Her face was as dead as this man's, but her eyes were burning. He appealed to her: "You know, Sadra. She was leaving here for good ... for good ..."

"She is in Netz," said the man. "With Count Tepsji. Do you have something you wish to tell Sadra and I, about this man?"

"Sadra and ..." Dragomir chewed on his beard.

"Be assured, Dragomir Dalca, Sadra and I know everything there is to know about Count Tepsji. All of his crimes. But in order to know our level of common trust, we need to hear it from your lips. Now, as a stranger you may not trust me. But surely you can trust someone you've known and trusted your whole life." The man waved a hand at Sadra. "Someone you trusted your daughter's care to on many occasions."

Dragomir started for the door on the opposite side of the ovens.

"Where do you think you are going, Dragomir?" said Sadra.

"To make sure my dumpling is still in bed."

. . .

Near the end of Dragomir's confession, there was a knock at the bakery door.

"May I answer it?" asked Dragomir, sounding and looking shamed.

"Just so you know," said Attila, "we trust you will not speak a word of our visit with you. Or our purpose within the town, or our very mission."

"No, of course. Never."

"Also, you should know that your daughter has revealed all you've said to Sadra and I. She is as much a part of this endeavor as you are. She has not escaped but returned to him, in the capacity of a rebel."

"I fear for her," said Dragomir. "I thought she was safe. She told me she was leaving—"

"She knows what must be done," said Sadra. "And so do you."

The knock sounded again.

"Yes, I'll do whatever is needed. Of course. How many are there of you so far?"

"Well," said Attila, not looking embarrassed. "Besides your daughter and Sadra? You are my first recruit."

"Do not fear," added Sadra. "Strength, Dragomir. Heaven will provide for us."

Dragomir was dumbstruck, but went off to answer the door.

Sadra held up a finger and whispered. "This might be the beginning of a rush of business. We'll have to leave through the back. Let him think on what we've said. We'll return when we need to."

But Attila held up his own finger and shushed her. He pointed to the store area and cocked his ear.

"… Well, lock the door back up," said a heavy voice. "I believe it is now time for you and I to have a healthy little talk, Dragomir."

"Oh? What's happened?"

"You've said many things about your daughter. About how she has traveled to Germania, no? But there are rumors that she has been seen in town."

"Oh, well, rumors. Didn't you say your daughter told you—?"

"Let's leave Cristine out of this," said the voice. "What she might have told me you can no longer dispute. For I saw her with my own eyes, in my own home: Amalina Dalca! Dragomir, she is living among the foreign princesses and royal ladies up in that little college in Netz."

Attila and Sadra traded what passed for them as looks of astonishment.

"Well …" said Dragomir.

"You are ashamed to admit such a thing to me? to old Boss Berzwecken? Even when you have seen what the Boss' family—my own daughter—has to deal with here when I am accused of having too much money? I should think I am the first person you would come to to commiserate. No? We may be wealthy, but we underlie the people, support them and their needs, and know we must keep to ourselves. Fetch us some drinks and let us talk the truth, for it has been missing between us for a very long time now. Let us bring our families back together. How is life with your new wife? Come, let's talk. Let's talk."

"Stay here," said Dragomir.

He appeared through the door on the way to the wine rack. He looked pale and haggard.

"What do I say?" he asked Attila and Sadra. "What should I say? He knows!"

"Do you trust him?" said Attila.

"Not too much," advised Sadra with a hiss. "Not yet. But I think Heaven has begun to provide for our plans already this day."

"Find out what he knows, and what he doesn't," said Attila. "Just agree to whatever he tells you Amalina told him. We will listen."

Dragomir went back into the store with two bottles of wine, saying: "That naughty Amalina. And just what did she tell you?"

• • •

"From what she's told her father, seems like Cristine knows everything, too," whispered Sadra, as the two men in the other room rose to voluable drunkeness and ranged into other topics while customers would knock, buy a loaf or two and leave. "Not who or what the Count Tepsji is, but he's learned enough. I don't think we have a choice *but* to include him."

"He can be trusted?" said Attila.

"He will be more valuable to this mission—and to us—than a dumb fat baker," she assessed flatly. "Boss Berzwecken is probably the richest man in Ardeel."

"Very good," said Attila, feeling greedy. "We could use resources not tied to the Cardinal's belt."

Sadra agreed with a quick nod. She was still listening intently to the other room.

There was a new knock at the door. This was not the inquiring sort from a tentative patron on a cold winter day. It was loud and confident.

The heavy voice of Boss Berzwecken softened. "By the stars, Dragomir. Look who it is! Answer the door! Answer it now!"

The door opened.

"My lord!" shouted Dragomir. "You get more handsome every time I see you!"

"And about five feet taller," said the Boss. "Or I am shrinking, I swear."

"Hello, gentlemen. Mr. Dalca."

"Are we being invaded?" laughed the Boss. "Look at that terrific uniform. Your father must be very proud."

"Oh, I'm just … This is just my uniform, sir. I travel light."

"Well, I should be going," said the Boss, self-consciously excusing himself. "Much work to do. Armies may quit for the winter, but business never does! You know what I mean, boy? Here, Dragomir, give him some wine and whatever he wants to eat. I'll pay for it. Just bill me later."

"Thank you, sir … *Boss*," said the young man. "Thank you."

Attila nodded his head to the door with a look on his face that asked Sadra, *you know who this person is?*

Sadra nodded back, but was intent on listening to this new conversation. Almost more interested in this one, it seemed than with Boss Berzwecken. Attila leaned forward, too.

"Well, what brings you 'round to Korr, young master Vokent? Are the kingdoms settled into peace at last? Come home to take up your father's trade, like a good boy?"

"I'm afraid not, Mr. Dalca. But … um … I don't know how to say this, sir … I'm here about Amalina. I know what's been happening, and that she is living up in that castle, and she's in danger there …"

"My God," exclaimed Attila under his breath. "We need utmost secrecy and this girl cuts such a wide wake she will sink us before we can start."

"Shh!"

"Don't shh! How can we trust her when she obviously didn't tell us everything? Who all has she spoken to?"

"Pay attention, Mr. Bronk," admonished Sadra. "On this day, Heaven continues to provide for us! First a financier, and now *this*? The Vokent boy is an accomplished military commander, and he knows about Amalina? We have added to ourselves—to our cause—another valuable soldier in less than an hour."

"You think so?" said Attila, a positive flutter in his body dispelling his irritation.

"I think you should be quiet, Mr. Bronk, and we'll hear what he has to say. Then we will march into the next room and introduce ourselves."

"Call me Attila," he said.

PART FOUR
THE BROCADE ARMY

37

Balance Breaker

The winter's peace in the high castle was a strange one. As more ladies braved the treacherous journey into the mountains and to the castle they infused an extra vitality to the already vibrant mix of personalities. And while these newcomers proclaimed—often fervently—their wish to visit Amalina and to have themselves an exotic eastern experience, they stoked embers of already turned jealousies as they sought to stake their own claim on Amalina's uncle, the master of the house. So, within this coterie of ladies, all with a similar sidelong ambition, the smiles on the manic smilers among them hardened, the petty-frowners' frowns deepened, and the joyous parties within the castle amplified to something that resembled a Roman Gala; while the underlying competition led to a general, if embarrassing, self-degradation; and in blew a cold, contemptuous sniping chillier than the winter winds which howled outside their windows. A whole book could be written about it, but lacking space within this account, it would suffice to mention there emerged, in the end, an unusual balance. A delicate, artificially enforced peace, instead of true harmony.

What finally tipped the scales of this balance, sliding their hollow peace into stark horror, would be difficult to pinpoint considering the pile of linked or cross-cutting interests. If nothing more, it could have been, rather than the typical arisocrats within their number—the VandeGardes, the Smeehautes, etc.—it stemmed from the strange procession of unusuals, irregulars, and misfits who appeared so late at the gates.

. . .

Young Lady Jane Ontioc Camper: a friend to Lady Genevieve de Roye, a venturer from the English colonies in America, who could speak pitiably little of the continental languages, but made up for it with her own provincial brashness to dare anything; and who displayed a near pathetic need to establish herself with her European cousins; a desperate neediness which had caused her to accept Amalina's invitation, sent at de Roye's insistence and the Count's curiosity, in order to pursue an unseemly interest in the Count's wealth.

She did not suffer too much from her obvious desperation when debasing herself before her rivals, but used it to energize herself into taking all challenges and engaging in all games and sport and religious activities, sending her voice to the loudest pitch in order to assert her personality and possibly dominate the room. It seemed in Lady Jane Camper's provincial mind that by dominating others there would be no question of her equal station to them. She brought with her a pipe and tobacco.

· · ·

Princess Noka Kunuru Sowa Iwebo: a good-natured daughter to an African king—a true, independent African king, so it was assured to Count Tepsji; one outside the insidious influence of the Ottomans. Whose obsidian-dark skin, long languid body, and impossibly upright posture made her a striking figure among all the snow-pale ladies slouching about in their heavy dresses.

Noka entered *l'entrée grande* with head and shoulders draped in the most pretty white mantilla, a gift from her travels in Spain, having been mistaken there as an Islamic moor—a people who were avid for that kind of clothing. But Noka was no moor. She came from a roving tribe in the deepest sectors of unknown Africa who believed, through their religion, that all the cows in the world had been gifted to them by their benevolent god, Enkai Narok. Her chieftan father had heard rumors of the greater part of the world outside their own stalking grounds, and had sent his eldest daughter to seek out and study these different places and assess the balance of their worldly holdings of cows. A daunting task to someone who had never seen an ocean nor had ever known white people existed. But Noka took to her assignment with extreme interest and an incredible grace.

Jane Camper, and some others who hadn't met Noka in her tour of the courts of France, assumed she was simple and stupid because of her birthplace and her tribal origins. But unless one arrives tethered to an animal trainer's chains, no idiot finds their way into a royal court. Noka and her scouting retinue were keen observers and had picked up French and Spanish upon reaching the coast and made good work of every other language they encountered. Noka was more than smart, she was also quite sweet and charming. Perhaps the finest woman to enter the castle yet.

As if to make up for this, Noka's servants were the ones to display her pride. They did so as diligently as if it were one of their many duties; as if to remind their charge that she was better than anyone else in the lofty European world and she had better not forget it. They referred to their mistress, in French, as *the true Sun King's Daughter*. And sometimes they would pretend they didn't know a Lady was talking about their princess or referring to her unless the Lady also used that name. Noka would always wave at her people as if they were being naughty, and uncivilized, and bow her head to the other Ladies with great humility, and smile and ask for their forgiveness. This happened a lot.

Her man-servant-in-charge, Oroco, called her *'Golden Sun Goddess'* secretly in their own language, and he insisted on grabbing handfuls of flowers from nearby vases and sideboards to throw under the feet of his princess as she walked, even though she admonished him as a blasphemer and reminded him there are only two gods, Enkai and Olapa, and *they* are the sun and the moon. But this princess was so royal in her blood, and so elevated by her own people, that she approached everything with the calm remove of a demi-god.

"Perhaps she *is* of divine origin," said the Count to Amalina, looking as if he'd taken a bite of something delicious. "Noka's skin is as black as her benevolent god, Enkai Narok, and in her placid personality, she matches his renowned elemental grace."

The Count was never above trying to impress Amalina with some esoteric bit of knowledge gleaned from one of their guests, whatever the moment, even if Amalina was trying to get some sleep.

Oh, what do you know about it? Amalina sneered to herself, rolling over in bed and stuffing her pillow into her ear, not wanting his wolfishness to spoil her rest, or her impression of the pretty and pleasant young woman. Everyone, it seemed, was falling in love with Princess Noka Kunuru Sowa Iwebo.

Jane Camper, not happy to find her continental friends taking to Princess Noka as an equal, treated her with cold, cutting remarks meant to reduce her. These were insults to which Noka seemed impervious. The other Ladies refused to translate Camper's darker English insults, but Noka learned soon enough that African people were kept as slaves in the American Colonies—toiling on farms on land that stretched beyond sight, so vast it had yet to be charted—and Camper's family were among those who used such labor. Jane Camper then openly discussed, on a couple occasions, her regret at not having brought a few of her slaves with her on her trip to the continent—having chosen for her travel to be "as indepent ... or, um, as free and cheap as Katarina Tepsji travels"—because if she had taken a slave or two, she felt their display would have provided a "great example" to Noka and her people of what she was talking about; how they should be *used*. Disgusted but unconcerned by the reference to slavery, Noka said she liked the sound of all the American continent's open, fertile plains, and wondered just how far one would need to walk to get to this splendid new land. "And just how many heads of cattle are there, would you say?" she asked Jane Camper, innocently.

Amalina was already throbbing with the story of Elizabeth Tudor, Queen of England, who went to war against the Supreme Emperor of Spain and sunk his powerful Grand Armada with her small but plucky fleets. But Princess Noka Kunuru Sowa Iwebo now confirmed for Amalina, in real life, the idea of female triumph and domination, all the while matching it with a humble, elegant bearing that, like sand on ink, dried into permanence Amalina's fascination with female empowerment.

• • •

Lady Maria di Oscina: who was not Maria di Oscina, after all. Amalina and several of the Ladies who were familiar with L.P. di Oscina were stunned when the young woman who climbed out of the sleigh and then refused to remove her hood for the longest time, until Margeta barked at her for decorum and another impulsive Lady pulled it off, was revealed as Maria's hideous younger sister, Giordina. Giordina began to cry, and begged them all—begged them past her irregularly spaced, stubbly, smelly, blackened-and-pitted teeth—with hands clapped to her prematurely withered cheeks, and wagging her choppy, overgrown eyebrows over her pinched and milky eyes, to allow her this one indulgence undisturbed, let her pretend to be her sister.

'For the di Oscina honor' the Ladies were more than content to keep up the pretense. They also agreed with relief behind her back that the renowned beauty, the real Lady Maria di Oscina, would have been a far more formidable threat to their interests. This substitute 'Maria' could only help their cause by providing a visual contrast.

It was difficult for the Ladies—but more so Amalina and Genadie—to explain to the Count the discrepancy between their reports of Lady Maria's beauty and this one's clear unattractiveness.

To everyone's surprise, the Count flitted around 'Maria' and flattered her as he did with everyone else, as if completely blind to a face that looked to be a viciously hatcheted pole of pale rubber.

• • •

Lady Aria Ecci: the Lady in Amalina's lesson of the salty sea, and of the octopus. The one who had been in the castle the previous year and fled home to Italy after the tragic mountain collapse in Kyrgil, and who now entered the castle as if she were the Count's returning spouse, and smiled light bemusement at the size of the crowd who'd come to celebrate her homecoming. Aria's familiar nature and bawdy cheer allowed her to cut right through the rankings of the other ladies, some of whom had spent longer time with the Count than she had. Just as forward as Princess Greta La Nevers, the two immediately sparred and then hit it off, elevating Aria, Greta, and Margeta as the reigning powers; though it deterred none of the others from vying for the Count's favor.

"Aria," Amalina said to Lady Ecci in a private moment. "I don't understand. You were the first of everyone to leave after … well … after, you know … what happened. You *know* what happened. What *really* happened in Kyrgil. Isn't that why you left?"

"Yes I know what happened," said Aria with a light frown.

"There was a second creature who attacked—"

"Don't bore me, Kat, when I already told you I *know*."

"But … so … why have you come back?"

"Look," sneered Aria, as if she'd been challenged and her good time threatened to be spoiled, "I just needed to see my family one last time and say my farewells. I was always coming back here. You think I was going to be scared off by a mountain slide? Like hell." Then she added mysteriously, but as if she were explaining more clearly: "Margeta sent me a letter, you see."

Camper, Iwebo, di Oscina, Ecci: Introduced like wild sparks within a combustible chamber. Any one of them might have moved the weight.

• • • •

Or the balance might have been tipped because the Count had begun taking more aggressive action with his 'selections'.

He performed the rite on several Ladies, with Amalina assisting him, of course, and timed for when Pia would be out in the night practicing her hunting skills. As before, the rite was a bloody and unsure process, but Amalina had hardened to the point of being able to watch it all the way through, just to make sure that there wasn't a slip-up and a lady pointlessly dead on her conscience.

To those who still didn't know this part of the Count's plans, it was explained that a Lady who was recovering from the rite had 'taken ill'. Their mysterious maladies did not send their rivals scrambling from an epidemic, but caused them to look around in the hope that someone else would get the idea to leave. All stayed put. A true plague, thought Amalina, would have done good business in the castle.

For the few who were aware what the Count was up to, they jealously asked after the lucky lady who had gone before them, acting pleased for her and winking their complicity in keeping up the pretense—in the hopes, of course, that doing so would buy them favor with the Count, and earn them an earlier promotion. Even Pia, who had already undergone the change, took the surprise additions to his ballooning harem in stride. "So is *his* will. *He* is beyond heaven's laws. And even heaven's laws do not forbid a husband taking a new consort; only that he provides for them all. Oh, Katty, at least you and I are still together. Maybe he'll favor you next with this precious gift."

His selections were curious, never obvious, and seemed chosen, as Amalina had accused before, more to provoke one of the other noble ladies than to please himself. His undeniable favorites, heard-hearted and scheming Margeta and the lascivious Aria, were still left untouched, clinging white-knuckled to promises that their turn would soon come, though it never did.

• • •

Or it could have been the time when Genadie was moping about, complaining of how he was forgotten by his Master again; without a real purpose within the Castle and left adrift. Once more he had gained that hard edge of unhappiness and resentment that made her think he was ready to escape (again), if only to put himself out of range of his misery.

Knowing that now, at some point in the future, Sadra's revolutionary intended to march a luckless army against the Count, and knowing that the only way to stop such a calamity was to check the Count first, to somehow remove his threat before they arrive (how?), or failing that, show some proof she'd made strides on the man's map and inventory when the time came— to help aid in all or any of this—Amalina went to Genadie in his cold, drafty little hut and asked if he could repair her invisibility bone the way he had his magical flute. She didn't tell him explicitly what her item was, but he balked anyway and said that he had to think it over, even as she pressed him, explaining to him how important a tool like it would be in their effort to escape. *"To escape, Genadie! Isn't that what we want to do here? Remember?"*

"I thought we'd given up on that," he said.

"It just wasn't the right time," said Amalina, as if he should have known. "There was no way we were going to get through the mountain passes with all that snow."

"Well, what is it?" he asked after a little hesitating sigh, regarding the small fractured bone sitting on her open palm. "What does it do?"

"I bought it from a gypsy. Um, it gives me luck when I hold it. Incredible good luck. It's for *extremely* good luck. I do have the best luck, haven't you noticed?" She was trying hard to sell him on a power it didn't have.

"Oh, yes, that is true. That is very true, Ms. Dalca. You definitely *do* have good luck," he agreed. "You did survive the mountain collapse."

"And that's what broke it," she said. "If it was still working maybe we wouldn't have had a snow storm in Korr and we would have gotten away, like Aklan has. If only I had known it could be fixed. *Can* you fix it?"

"I will try … My, what those brilliant people can't come up with, eh? *Luck.* What will they think of next? Now let me see …"

Genadie helped her after all, on an evening when the Count had left the castle, in some strange rite of Genadie's own devising, with a small boiling cauldron and several lengths of Amalina's hair.

"Here it is," said Genadie, "almost good as new. Give it a try."

Amalina clasped the bone in her hand tightly. "Oh, it does work, I think, Genadie. I feel luckier already."

"Do you, Ms. Dalca?" But his eyes dropped tears as he said this, and his grizzly chin shook under his wriggling lips.

"Oh, no! What's the matter, Genadie?" said Amalina, feeling as if she might cry in sympathy.

"It's a terrible shame what I did tonight," he blubbered, wiping his eyes with his crusty sleeve. "What it means, Ms. Dalca. What it means …"

For him it meant they were beginning the process for real this time; to free themselves of the Count. Again. Finally.

The internal support structure of the Count and his castle was shifting out from underneath him.

Yes, that's what it meant.

Amalina rushed back to her room. *Now to give it a real try,* she thought, *see if his fix worked.*

She clamped the bone lengthwise between her teeth. Her hands and forearms disappeared before her eyes.

It works! It works!

"Well, that *was* very lucky, wasn't it?" she mumbled happily to herself with the bone in her mouth.

We'll see about that, said a critical voice in her head.

. . .

For Amalina, the broken balance was something entirely different and personal. As much as she was making small moves to separate and maneuver away from the creature, and piddle around with building the revolutionary's map and inventory (knowing if she elongated the process enough, she might hold his scheme off), those were little incidents within the framework of her very busy day of seeing to her friends; small actions of sabotage which felt like teeny-tiny splinters suspended within the immense, dense pudding of her daily social obligations; they were essentially meaningless pieces unless they eventually connected, or became something significant on their own.

With the threat of the ugly green man removed—his demand for Amalina's death permanently caught in his wrinkled head, which was stuck atop the gate, frozen and refusing to rot—and with the Count's assurance of her protection from anything or anyone else; and knowing nothing could really be done against the Count to neutralize him (and so to stop the necessity of the revolutionary's coming siege); and that until spring opened the mountain roads the revolutionary couldn't pressure a secluded Amalina to produce information the way Commander Kralov had; nor, alternatively, if things got too bad inside the castle, could Amalina and Genadie just wriggle out and escape; Amalina relaxed into her hosting duties. It was nice to be surrounded by friends again, and she could even pretend they were all holed up in a castle somewhere in a northern city of a western kingdom—perhaps France, since everyone had settled into speaking their most common language, French, exclusively—so somewhere in a modest French castle then, instead of the mountains of her home country. The chime and ring of pretty voices kept the air warm and welcoming to her. Pia's arms circled Amalina at every turn and radiated raw love, so that she didn't resent the frequent kisses, and briefly considered the advantages of accepting the Count's gift—making the irrevocable change—if she could feel so accepted and safe for all time.

"Who do you think is the hairiest one here?" said Greta, spinning up into one of her raucous and unpredictable moods after a playful masked dinner, done in the syle of the Venetian Carnivale, and some wine. "I'll bet I have everyone beat. Look at my little mustache."

"Oh, that's nothing," laughed Aria. "Mine's thicker, I almost have a beard. But look at Margeta's arms. And I've seen her legs. She might just have me beat. Though maybe not."

"That's only because her hair is so black and her skin is so pale," said de Roye. "I'm as hairy as all my brothers, but you wouldn't know it." She pulled up her sleeve to display her arm. "It's blonde, so you can hardly notice. But have a look here, and no tugging. I'm almost as bad as a dog." Now she kicked up her legs to show them off. "No stepping on me, please, though I'm a veritable rug. See? Am I not? Admit it. I'll put money on it."

"Brothers, fathers, uncles," howled Greta with great cheer, yanking at the hip of her skirt, motioning for her maids to come and help her. "I am no man. I am no dog. I am a gorilla! I've got hair right up and all over my ass!"

Clothes were shed and even the maids were carried away in the merriment. An hour later, they were peeing off the battlements.

Such wild abandon.

If Amalina had chosen differently that day, had been of a mind for learning, she could have joined Brignol in the library to read and converse on the merits of an interesting book. She could have sought out a good wager at cards against Montraine or challenged Otterdam at chess or backgammon on one of the Count's fancy sets. Should she have wanted music, or singing, or dancing, or all three, she could have been swept up in the reverie in the great hall. Or appreciated art in the Grand Gallery. Or she could have learned a bit of science from one of the visiting mathematicians, engineers, or architects from Balbo's group, Wanger, Regio, and Balbo, and made her own experiments in the Count's Laboratory. Epris adored cooking and could always be persuaded to try a recipe, or to perfect a sauce in the over-stuffed kitchens. Or Maibrigg Smeehaute would welcome a companion to help compose some literature or a poem. There was always some knitting or sewing to be had to pass a quiet hour—perhaps join Inovala's unending obsession fussing with her seamstress to repair the cartridge pleats at her shoulders, which puffed eccentrically out with such force they would frequently bust stitching or break loose to form unsightly, fingerlike wings above her arms. If not that, she might have practiced the arts of hunting, or horticulture, or simply basked in the presence of the serenely content Noka Iwebo. Or, in the end, failing any of the above, Amalina could have just lay in full repose in front of a warm fire under a blanket with Pia, quietly, and meaninglessly, chatting the time away.

What if we could all be together this way every day? thought Amalina. Laughing and singing and dancing and learning new things and dressing up and having ridiculous contests and games? What if it could be this way *forever*? There were enough personalities under the Count's roof to make eternity seem limitlessly entertaining.

It was a seductive thought. A thought sustained for weeks by Amalina until it seemed inevitable and unavoidable—even with Margeta's loud *tsking* in the corner. *But if Margeta looks down on it so much*, thought Amalina in an idle moment, *what exactly is she waiting around the castle for? Maybe she won't admit it, but even she wants a part of it.*

To be a part of the high castle's brocade army.

And now, Amalina wanted in.

38

The New Recruit

They had been watching the storeroom's outer door for two hours when signs of nerves began to show. Attila glanced at Sadra. She was quietly wringing her hands.

"How much longer before the bell?" he asked.

"I'll go check. I think we still have two hours, though."

"Are you sure he's coming? What did he tell you?"

"Of course he didn't tell me anything. It's his wife I spoke to. She's the only one of them who will. But I know she will make him come."

"His wife," said Attila, looking as if he might suddenly fall asleep. He sagged in place, and began to spread over the crate he was sitting on. "What on earth did you tell her? How much did you give away?"

"She knows nothing but that there is an urgent reason for him to be here tonight. But is there really a good reason to ask him for anything, Attila? Do we really need *him*?"

"He has become the *most* crucial player for our plans. Having heard the Dalca girl's story, I know there can be no more perfect partisan for our cause. If we can win him, with his skills and his self-interest, our victory is assured. Without him, doubt remains."

"There are plenty of others."

"Of lesser ability, and they would need to be paid for. This one will bring his heart … As long as I can speak to him tonight; there *is* an issue of timing."

"If he doesn't come," said Sadra, "I will send a curse up to—"

A shout sounded behind them. The voice was furious.

"Dear God," said Sadra as she leapt for the door on the other side of the store room. "He's here!"

Sadra went through several back rooms until she reached the door leading to the church's high-ceilinged main room. There she paused to open it and to peek into the nave. Attila was close behind her.

"The fool!" she hissed. "I said the back door! And he's drunk as can be!"

Attila could hear the fight clearly:

"All I said was I am glad you've come and you are welcome," said a soft, plaintive voice. This was Sadra's husband, the minister.

"I was told I wouldn't have to see your ugly, lying, Saxon face, Sh-midt!" bellowed the other.

"Who told you that? Listen, get ahold of yourself and stop cursing. You're in God's house."

After cussing loudly into the air, he replied angrily, "Think he heard me that time, Reverend?"

"I understand your pain, brother."

"If you don't shut up, I'll punch you right in the mouth."

"If you would just settle down for a moment and let me—"

"I'll tear this little house apart, bring it down on your head and burn it to ashes. And when you have lost it all, then you will be welcome in *my* house; to show *me* that simpering face and bleat out your easy words of comfort!"

"Well, if you don't want to listen and you don't want our company, you can leave. Before I call the deputy sheriff."

"This was a trap, that's what it was!" the voice was moving back toward the entrance of the church, to the doors. "You think you could trap me, but you'll never! Ever! See if I come again, Reverend. And you can go and tell your twiggy wife she can fuck off!"

"He's leaving," she said to Attila, sounding relieved.

"No," said Attila. "Stop him!"

Attila tried to move past Sadra, but she caught him with a surprisingly strong grip and pulled him back.

"No. Get to the store room."

"We have to stop him before he leaves."

"It's too late," said Sadra, pushing Attila, turning him back, ever further back. "You can't go out *there*."

"We're going to lose him."

"Minister can't see you," said Sadra. "Not yet."

"He doesn't know I'm here?" said Attila, incredulous, but looking half-bored. "After all this time?"

"What did you think? Why else would you be kept to the back rooms? Of course I've been hiding you."

"You said you'd convinced him to accept me here, didn't you?"

"I said I *would* convince him. But as of yet, that hasn't happened. Again, I can't imagine with your intellence you wouldn't wonder, or what you could have thought otherwise—"

"I thought your husband and I were deliberately separated from each other," answered Attila, "so he wouldn't see me and he could freely deny any knowledge I was here, if he were asked, without moral misgiving or a troubled conscience."

"You've a tricky mind," said Sadra, her angular face shifting uncomfortably with some kind of emotion. "But I wouldn't have my husband be a liar in his own house. Better he didn't know at all in the first place."

"You've been keeping me here as some kind of contraband, then?" Attila touched her arms gently, but firmly, and removed them from him. He charged to the back door.

"Where are you going?"

"He can't get away," said Attila over his shoulder. "I have to talk to him."

"He's drunk! You'll be lucky if he doesn't break your neck."

"I'll handle him. I am a man of the law."

"That's worse."

"Which way does he live? What street will he be taking?"

"There's little time before the bell sounds," said Sadra, worried. "You can't. The patrol will catch you."

"It won't take long," he said as he ran out the back door, barely checking for anyone who might be looking. "I'll be back."

Sadra stared at the door for an hour.

. . .

In deference to Heaven and its own natural time, there was no clock within the church. The town's municipal building had the bell tower, and it had rung in the evening a long time ago. Judging by the amount of supper Sadra and her husband had already eaten, and adding to that how long it took to prepare and set it on the table, Sadra guessed it was ten o'clock.

A knock sounded at the front door.

"Who could that be, Mrs. Smidt?" her husband said with a smile but a worried look above it. "Sounds like he has returned to us. But, that couldn't be."

Sadra could only hope he *had* returned, even still drunk, and that it wasn't Attila trying to come in the front door. Or something worse.

"Well, I'll see who is calling," said the minister, standing up.

"No, I can get it. Set down."

"Well, that's nice of you. But if it is him, I had better."

"I can handle him."

"Well, I should really—"

"But you needn't bother—"

"It's really no—"

"I'm already up—"

"But so am I—"

. . .

Two men, Korr's night patrol, bowed with their metal hats off when the minister and Sadra opened the door together.

"Excuse us, Reverend Minister," said the first. "We saw your back door was open. Open it was! We shut it ourselves, but best you should bolt it closed on the inside there before it blows open again."

"Oh," said the Minister. "Yes, thank you. Now, I hope to see you this Sunday, gentlemen."

"Certainly. But these long nights make it rough to rise so early in the morning," said the first.

"Takes a toll on you, Reverend Minister."

"Well, then I hope I should see you Tuesday. Or must I keep my back doors flung open during curfew just for a visit?"

"Oh, ho! *Now, Minister!*"

Sadra's husband let them off gently and shut the door and bolted it.

"I'm sorry," said Sadra. "I must have forgotten to lock it when I threw the offal out this afternoon. That must be it."

"No matter. Kind of them to tell us, anyway. I'll just go—"

"No," said Sadra, using a commanding tone and bustling ahead of him again. "It's my fault, I'll take care of it. One door was enough. Now finish your supper."

"I'm about full," he said.

"Then start cleaning," she said. "Those dirty dishes are *entirely* your fault."

He laughed agreeably behind her as she tore off into the back rooms.

. . .

It was cooler now in the storage area. Had the door really been standing wide open? She'd shut it when Attila had left, she just hadn't locked it. How had it come open?

"Sir? Are you here?" she whispered. "Are you in here, Mr. Bronk?"

At the end of the cramped aisle, the door was open again.

As she walked to it, she pushed a candle into every hiding space, looking behind the boxes and between the stacks of bags. The hair rose on the back of her neck. A creeping feeling, that someone was there who she could not see, made her shudder. Could the monster be back here waiting to punish her? Had he snuck in through the unbolted door on a caprice? or had he caught Attila and extracted a confession that would damn her and her husband?

"Mr. Bronk?"

No answer.

She went on to the door.

As she tried to close it, a hand fell between the opening. She dropped back with a gasp. Attila slipped into the room. He peeked out the door, then shut it.

"Hurry," he said. "Let's get the bolt on."

"I left it unlocked for you," she said. "But it was open—"

"By the time I got here, the patrol was at the door and deciding whether they should go in. They closed it, but it blew open when they went around front. I had to wait to enter until they left for good."

There was a pause after the door was bolted.

"Well?" she asked.

"Thank you," he nodded.

"I meant, you were gone for a long time. I thought you might have been caught and I would have to find you out in the woods again. Dead for good."

He looked surprised at the thought.

"I'm not a ghost," he said matter-of-factly. "Sorry to have put you through the worry. It took longer than I thought."

"But you caught up to him, then? And spoke?"

Attila nodded and sat down on one of the short stacks of grain bags. He looked thoughtful. Then lost himself even deeper in thought.

"And?" she prompted. "How did it go?"

"Better than expected," said Attila. "Better than *you* expected."

"He's with us, then?" she said, looking at his shaking left hand.

"He's going to be," said Attila. He lay back on the bags as if to get comfortable for the night. "Just one more push should do. He's agreed to a short trip. One that will convince him beyond anything I could ever tell him."

"A short trip?"

"Yes. As quick as we can." Attila looked at her. "And now we can test the reliability of one of our founding members. Tomorrow, tell Boss Berzwecken I will need a covered carriage, or a sleigh, with at least two fast and reliable horses for an unexpected trip to Tsobl—I mean, Sobelburg. It will be me alone, and I should have some extra money for incidental traveling expenses." He added as a side note: "As a precaution, so that we are not observed, I've already arranged to meet our potential new recruit outside Korr."

"You're taking him to Tsobl?" she asked.

"Netz. But that's not the Boss' business to know. He just needs to handle our supplies."

39

Danger Returns to Paradise

Winter was seemingly the Count's best season because the nights were almost endless and he was free to roam for hours. But he voiced his frustrations at its limits. The cold, which had the greatest number of people hunkering down inside their homes, and so out of his reach, was not so inhibiting for him as the strengthened winds, which streamed around and over the mountains like God's fingers through his terrestrial locks; and which tossed the Count about by surprise, or sent him toppling into cliff faces, if he wasn't careful on a turn; or it created invisible, impassible walls of pressure that he had to take extra time to work his way around. Equally bothersome was how, except for evergreens, foliage was stripped back to nothing and the ground became a smooth sheen, making it much harder for him to creep and lurk undetected. But still, the Count couldn't have enough nighttime, and to Amalina it seemed that he must even have some control over the natural progress of the day, because before she knew it, the sun would be down as soon as it had risen, and he would be throwing open windows, rejoicing over the beauty of the moon.

Or ... was it not a strange power that sped the sun along, but just that Amalina was enjoying herself and the days flew by naturally?

• • •

Could I ever let myself go all the way? wondered Amalina. *It might be fun. I'm having so much fun now.*

If I did do it, Genadie and Pia would probably turn cartwheels over the moon; they'd be so happy.

And the Count would be so pleased that, as long as I kept all my senses, as long as I'm still myself, I could steer him. Prevent him from hurting anyone else, especially if an army arrived from Korr. I could talk him out of any violence. I'm sure I could. He'd listen to me.

And then I'd just have to reason with Sadra's revolutionary and turn him around. And then everyone would be happy.

But that would only work so long as I was still in full possession of myself. Still myself ... afterward. After the ...

But would I be?

Amalina recalled Pia's mindless attack on the delegation—on her—and it reminded her of the village dog that had suffered the bite of a rabid animal, and how it was transformed into something mindless, hateful, terrifying. But that wasn't exactly the same. She also remembered Jenna's aunt on her father's side, who'd had a fever, and afterward she'd never been the same again, so that they would rarely visit her. The woman had looked like the same person she once was, and she spoke as if she were normal, but it was as if she were someone else entirely, with different memories, and personalities, and tastes. A complete stranger. And so, while Pia seemed to be the same, what was it like inside her head now? Was she truly the same person, with the same values and virtues? How could that be, or were the instincts the rite inspires or awakes so overwhelming?

Amalina imagined the rite being like a cauldron that one entered into, is swallowed by. But when the lid is lifted and one's body reemerges into the world, would one even know who they were before? Could they even *know* it if they were the same?

Tepsji has said many times that the life is in the blood. But if I were to lose all mine, and take his to replace it, what does that make me?

Because there was no urgency to the question, it was barely serious, and because Amalina didn't need to think about it for too long, she didn't.

. . .

One morning, at the sound of the gate's bell—announcing a new arrival, of course—Amalina left her room and went to meet whoever it could be. She tried not to look above the castle's entrance at the icy heads stuck on spikes, but wondered how she would distract her visitor from them. Though she was tired, as it was still early, she found herself actually looking forward to whoever it might be, to add them to the mix.

It was only a resupply delivery from Netz: two large sleighs piled high with boxes and covered with oil cloths, which Pils and the handful of roughs grumbled into the castle. Genadie stared down mournfully and lost-looking from the parapet, still unneeded by the Count. With his ingenious snow-clearing sledge destroyed in the collapse at Kyrgil Mountain, Genadie had become even more useless—to the high castle and to his Master—now that it was filled with servants of every kind, who were bored, equal to any task, and eager to throw their back into it. Amalina waved at the sad figure on the wall, trying to pass to him some of her awakened cheer. He pretended not to notice her, and crunched on his millet furiously with the most disconsolate expression. As the work carried on without him, he eventually turned and hobbled away, clouds of breath steaming around his head.

She watched some of the crates unpacked, to see what goodies they could look forward to. So many racks of wine and massive rounds of cheeses. There were a few wood tubs of imported chocolate which Jane Camper had requested. Barrels of spices. On it went. Amalina was used to the emptiness in the kitchens and the cellars from when she'd first arrived at the castle. Now she doubted there was room enough to fit it all in.

Next came seven bolts of brightly colored silk with cheerful brocade patterns, which the ladies would soon be cooing over, and then fighting over and tearing to shreds to get their better share of it. There would be new or refreshed dresses and corsets for the coming months.

For some reason a couple of the Count's architects had joined the inventory, whispering excitedly to each other. They ran their own tallies on their fingers. Regio seemed to be interested in some small unmarked barrels. Balbo was forward enough to pluck a bottle of wine from the kitchen supply and open it. After slicking down his hair, he winked at Amalina.

Amalina returned to her room and left orders not to be disturbed. She needed rest and had been forcing herself, when she could, to sleep in the daylight hours; a necessary habit for the Count, nearly impossible for Amalina. The attempted readjustment just left her groggy and cranky. But she was getting used to it.

Sleep itself was quite comfortable.

Though Amalina knew she had become more relaxed in her surroundings and to the idea that she might—maybe some day soon—accept living on in the castle, she didn't remark too much about how she'd changed in order to accommodate this idea. Enough time had passed that she'd forgotten, or allowed herself to forget, the administration of her plans to neutralize the Count before the revolutionary army arrived. Only when she considered Genadie pouting off the parapet, did she remember she'd managed to forget one of the plan's elements, one which actually required her constant attention whether she wanted to carry on with her plotting or not. *He claims he's got nothing to do*, she had thought drowsily of Genadie in her forgetfulness, *but he can still look after the birds.*

The birds!

• • •

Amalina shook her head as she ran up the winding stairs to the aviary. How could she have forgotten? The pigeons might all be dead; unless Genadie *had* been feeding them. She could only hope so or they might be feathered skeletons by now. But she had told Genadie she would do it—these were the revolutionary's special secret service birds, after all—and it was her one and only chore these days. There was no reason for Genadie to have checked on the cages.

When Amalina opened the door to the aviary she did not feel the brush of warmth, the bodyheat of hundreds of bats pushing down. She looked up to see if they were still there. Or had they somehow gotten out? But their small bodies rumbled and waved at the disturbance of the door opening, and then they sunk heavy and limp on their legs; small, furry bulbs dangling off the rafters, in what looked like deep hibernation.

They hadn't left. But the room was cold.

The window was open.

Amalina ran to the window and slammed it shut, throwing the bar to brace it against the howling wind. Then she ducked under the bench and threw the covers off the small cages.

Please be alive, she thought, but imagined the grey birds keeled over, hardened into pieces of bird-shaped ice.

The pigeons warbled and burbled, and shuffled eagerly to the bars. They were hungry. Maybe dying of thirst, their water tray iced over, if not fully frozen. Their eyes, always wide and somewhat desperate looking, looked to be scolding her for their neglect.

"Sorry, sorry, sorry," she whispered.

But then she noticed movement further inside the cage. She fell backward, her heart thumping, not ready for the surprise; the skittering sound making her think of a spider. The size of the dark shapes made her think they were as big as her fist.

But they were just more pigeons. Pigeons who'd sought refuge from the cold under the tarp and behind the cages.

Amalina pulled one cage out. Three pigeons shuffled toward her, lethargic but still menacing. Their feathers were uneven and greasy, and they looked as contemptuous and evil as they ever had.

And each one had a small strip of paper wrapped around their leg. Messages from their owner … whose wrinkled head now sat on a spike over the gate.

Or was that not true?

Amalina's eyes narrowed.

These pigeons hadn't been in the aviary when she'd brought up her own birds. The window had been closed tight. Even if they had arrived just before the hideous man's death, or shortly after, they wouldn't have been fed—as they weren't inside the cages where the seed and water were—and they should now be as dead as he. So these ones must have come later, *after* AXP had been killed.

Now she bit her lip, her thoughts heated up.

New messages?

Was AXP not the ugly little man after all, but someone else? Someone who was, to this day, carrying on the infernal correspondence with the Count? A someone still out for her blood?

Had the Count lied to her?

. . .

That night, at the howling of the wolves, which was a sign the Count had left on a hunt, Amalina slipped out of her room, shivering, and with the magical bone gently clamped between her teeth. She hugged close to the chilly stone walls, keeping her glasses wrapped in a silk that she held low to her waist, prepared to drop the small bundle on the ground if anyone should notice something floating along the passage. With all the Ladies and their servants around, Amalina had to be on alert, swinging her head this way and that, listening and watching; the intense dark inside the castle working for and against her. It took her much longer to reach the Count's private study than she had wanted, but once inside, with a torch she'd taken from a wall bracket, she hurried past the open secret door to the message center and down into it. As she passed through the treasury on the way to the stairs, she noted how the shelves didn't seem as packed as they once had with bags of gold ingots. As if the Count had been on a spending spree. But on what? The women were here already. She took the long set of stairs down into the message center, to the standing desk at the bottom.

Amalina would now see if other messages from those nasty birds had been collected. If the Count had mounted more into his book than what he'd shown her the other month.

The metal letters—AXP—flashed at her from the desk top. She opened the book to the last page and saw that the messages ended right where they had before. Nothing new. There were no loose strips sitting on the desk, or inside its narrow drawer below that. So the Count hadn't added to the collection. Maybe he didn't even know the newest pigeons had come.

As if from muscle memory, because she was standing there with the book before her, Amalina plucked out a message strip from one of its first pages. Then she took one from the middle. She avoided the image of Lucinda Skeldar but could not help flipping to the last page again, and stared for a long time at her own portrait, with her glasses perfecting the image for her eyes so she could study its uncanny detail. It really was a picture of Amalina; perhaps a little younger than she was now, with a cheerful smile she hadn't worn in a long time. But it was her. And that meant someone had been watching her, studying her closely, and had taken the time and effort to squeeze their observation onto a little square scrap. And for some reason, that person wanted her dead.

But that person was no longer the little green wrinkled man as she had once supposed. Since his wrinkled head had come off his shoulders and gone up on the spike, the true figure behind the murder service returned; a mystery. Whoever it was, they had sent three more birds with three more messages, which were waiting in the aviary.

Or could there be another explanation for those new birds and the new messages?

She felt something sour in her stomach and doubted.

Amalina picked at the corner of the strip in the book with her portrait. She hesitated. She didn't like the idea of her picture staying there, down in his message center. But still … the Count would notice it missing.

She took a strip from one page back, and made sure to loosen some others around where it had been pasted, to make it look like a message happening to fall from the page was possible, and not unlikely.

She took up the cipher sticks from the desk drawer and blew out a breath. She'd already copied them before: the wood ones and the single metal one. But she'd thrown the page of cipher solutions away when she was traveling the western kingdoms and had felt them irrelevant. There was no need to decode anything if she wasn't going to fight her circumstances, so her thinking went at the time. No need if she was just going to play along to survive. Or find a way to escape. But at that time, she also hadn't been the murder service's intended target.

She had to copy the codes again. To start over. She blew a breath and rubbed her hands together, trying to generate heat.

She took up a sheet of paper from the Count's desk and used his pen with the fancy long plume to transfer the increasingly unusual characters— beginning with just a reordering of letters on the first wood stick cipher, ending with arcane symbols on the final, metal cipher. This, again, took longer than she had hoped. Her hand cramped from cold and fatigue. She wrung her numb paw and shook it. Then she put everything back in its place, praying the Count wouldn't notice any changes; feeling the beginnings of a headache.

On her way back to her room, Amalina found Pils and Anka walking with their heads close together, whispering, with serious looks on their faces. Feeling bold and curious, Amalina snuck up behind them and leaned in close to hear what they were saying.

"*You* should tell her," whispered Anka.

"I don't see why," returned Pils. "She's closer to you. *You* should tell her."

Tell me what? wondered Amalina.

"But you're better at talking to her. I get all clumsy and, anyway, I'd be the first one suspected."

"So then what's the difference? If you'd be the first one suspected anyway, why pull me into it?"

"So I can deny it truthfully, and he will know it's the truth."

"Oh, that just makes me want to tell her all the more, doesn't it?" said Pils, sarcastically. "To be the one who's found out! You go and tell her then."

"You tell her."

It went on like that until it was time to turn down another corridor and she knew they would be up to this nonsense for a while. Who knew what they were talking about? Or who was to be told? She'd got the feeling they were talking about her, but it could be anyone. Amalina slipped away, feeling clever at how stealthy she'd become by sneaking undetected behind them for some length.

Coming up the next hall were a number of Aria Ecci's servants. It was one of the darker corridors and Aria's manservant was in front, holding a torch.

Though Amalina had taken care to fold the cipher page into the smallest packet possible and wrapped it in the silk cloth, and had held it just so as she crept back upstairs, prepared to dash it to the ground if needed—and she did so now, as she met these servants head-on—she'd forgotten one detail.

"My god, what is that?" cried Aria's man servant. But the torch he carried was knocked out of his hands by a sudden surprise blow. "What!"

As the hallway was suddenly lit from below, the torch rolling and sparking on the floor, there was a clatter and a flutter of light and bodies. The shadows of legs and forearms scrambled around the walls and ceiling as a greater confusion set in.

"A bug!" shouted one of them.

"A bug?" said the man servant.

"A bat!" the first cried again.

"A bat?" squeaked one of the maids, and several bodies raced down the hall.

"I'll take care of it, run!" said the first voice again, valiantly, the voice which had cried out both 'bug' and 'bat' as if to encourage the panic.

It was Aklan, and he was giggling as the rest of the servants fled the scene.

Once they were alone, he whispered, "Pretty Princess? I know you're invisible ... but you're still wearing your glasses! *Your glasses!*"

40

I've Got You

"**I** just don't understand it, Aklan," said Amalina, now dressed and wearing a heavy coat with hood up, sitting close to the roaring fireplace. "What are you doing here? *Why* are you here?"

"The rebellion's over," chirped the boy, cheerfully. He sat several feet away from her, nearer the cooler boarded window. "Lucky I found out that we, the Royal Spaarvierlets, retook the crown before I showed myself to my father or mother. They might not have let me go. So now here I am—and once more a prince!"

He clapped his hands together then shook them in the air in triumph.

"I see," said Amalina. *He's escaped his boring life again—now that his true identity has been restored—and returned here … for the fun of it.*

"Oh, but, err," he said blinking at her, wondering at her sudden bemusement at his happiness and good fortune, much less their warm reunion after so long parted. "Well, of course I would never leave you unless it was an emergency, and I would *never* abandon you, not *forever*. I still owe you, don't I?"

"Owe me?"

"You saved me! That is a blood debt a prince would never forget, Pretty Princess! You have my sworn allegiance, to serve and protect you!"

"If you *really* wanted to *help* me," said Amalina with a half-hearted grumble, "you could have stayed home so that I'd have one less person to worry about around here—"

"Ach, but you don't have to worry about *me*, that's my job for *you*. And I can help you much better if I'm right here, eh?"

"I don't see how you can do anything for me, as if you've ever yet—"

"I *will* save you! That's why I'm here! And I *will* help you, whatever way I can. I will!" he insisted. "You'll see!"

He must have spotted her brief smile at his enthusiasm, which toyed at her lips despite her equal frustration and annoyance at him in general.

"But how did you get the bone working again?" He said to change the subject—to switch to a much more important one—and scooted closer, sticking out an open palm for it.

Amalina explained briefly how Genadie had fixed the magic invisibility bone as Aklan twirled the tied-and-glued stick—his eyes narrowed at it in appraisal, mouth open as if he might accidentally stick it in. Then she told him the reason why she'd been using the bone to sneak around the castle.

"Now I have to figure out this code system all over again," she said, pulling up various papers and message strips. "Find out what's really going on, who it is, and why he wants me dead."

"*You dead?*"

"Yes."

"*You*, Pretty Princess*?*"

"AXP's ordered the Count to do it. *He* showed me the note and it's serious. This man, whoever it is, had one of my friends killed before, you know. A girl from my old village." Aklan pouted at the mention of Amalina's village. Korr was a sore point for the boy. He never enjoyed hearing anything that subtracted from Amalina being of true noble blood. "Anyway, the Count said he refused and that he'd put an end to it, made me think he'd killed the man. But if this ... this *villain* is still alive ... I don't know what to think, or what it means. If nothing else, he might send more of his assassins after me if you-know-who won't do it."

"*More* assassins?"

Amalina stated, dryly: "It's been a little exciting since you've been away."

Amalina would set aside the 'excitement' of what Pia had done to the Germanian delegation for another time, if ever. But what happened to her directly, with the tall man in the forest, she quickly recounted to Aklan.

"And the Count did nothing to stop him?"

"At that time of day, how could he do anything about it? No, there's nothing. The problem with him is he didn't put an end *to it all*, the whole service, like he promised. Or, I think that's the case—"

"Blackgaurd," Aklan swore. "I always knew he'd turn on you."

"I don't think he's *turned* on me."

"He did if he pretended to end it just for your benefit, but he really didn't. Maybe he's just waiting for a good reason *to* take this villain's order up again."

"What kind of good reason?" gulped Amalina. She hadn't thought about it that way.

"I don't know. But there's some reason he lied to you. Maybe he only wants a better price."

"No, I don't think it could be that—"

"Why not?"

"Well ... if I can just figure out how to read these secret messages, anyway—"

"Then let's figure out who it is," said Aklan, warming up to a new excitement. "Cut the problem off at the source. We'll take care of him together, Pretty Princess. You and I, both."

Of course she would figure out the messages, she thought. She would crack the code right now, today. With Aklan's confidence added to her own sudden fervor, she felt like she could power right through to its solution.

. . .

"It's not that easy, you see?" muttered Amalina, later, as she held up the strip she'd taken from one of the early pages and shook her fresh cipher sheet. "Look at this. At first, the code was simple enough. Whoever this AXP person is, he used the cipher code A in the beginning. Then, later, he switched to cipher B."

The code sticks had an alphabetic designator on their ends. Each stick had a new variation of letter placement. Aklan was fascinated how, as the sticks progressed toward the final metal one, the lettering of the codes themselves became novel, never-before-seen sets of characters; and intrigued as well at the variety of potential manipulation.

"This one here," she said, switching to a newer note, "came recently. I keep hoping the more difficult the code, the more he might be willing to reveal of himself."

"Well, what does this one say?" said Aklan, coming over and leaning forward to study one of the earlier strips. Just as ugly as the birds themselves, the strips were made of rough pigskin or goatskin, with little coarse hairs still attached to the fringes. She didn't like to even look at one too long, much less touch it.

"Please keep quiet, I'm trying to think."

"Why would he say that?"

"No, no, no. This note here says ... um ... let's see ... 'someone important from Germania is headed to Tsobl'. *I'm* saying, to *you* child, keep quiet."

"But, to be fair, Princess, you were speaking to me first."

"I am, but only so my thoughts aren't stuck in my head. Oh, I've been through this before, and it just doesn't make any sense." She made ink dashes on a loose sheet of paper on her knee, preparing to translate a more difficult message. "And so I need you to stay silent and let me think while I do this."

"Okay. No need to yell when it was you who started it."

"Was I yelling?" said Amalina in a quick, nervous whisper, her eyes looking around at the walls. "Have to be careful about that." She adjusted her glasses and took up the next note. "Now, just keep still and quiet."

"Why'd you invite me in then?" he huffed. "No point if you don't want me here. Ridiculous."

They were about to start bickering, but Amalina stopped. Fighting over nonsense already? It was as if Aklan had never left. How strange it seemed. Once here, once gone, once here again.

But she couldn't have him running loose in the halls. Better to keep him nearby.

"Who said I didn't want your help here, boy? I need you to keep my mind straight. But I just need you to shut your mouth for a minute at least. Please."

"Oh, okay. But, you know, I am pretty great at languages. Any languages."

"You are that," she admitted. And he seemed more eager and full of energy than what she had right now. Maybe two heads might be useful. Or better yet: "Okay, come here, Aklan."

She took up some of the notes from the AXP book. She pointed to the first note before her, one of the recent ones. "Okay, then, let's get to it. Look here. You see this jumble? The later the messages, the more involved the code."

"That's a weird alphabet. Look like hieroglyphs."

"Maybe so, but they aren't. Now pay attention. About halfway through the book, see here, this one is from years ago probably, each word in a message is used with a different key system." She translated as she went, working through each word with a different code stick in sequence; A, then B, then C, etc. "*'She will be in the forest this full moon. Easy enough. Thinks she'll be meeting me. She needs to disappear completely. AXP.'* Poor girl. Anyway ..." Amalina switched back to a newer strip. "But now this latest code doesn't make any sense. All the letters are jumbled. Each and every word—I mean, all the letters in them—is made up of all kinds of characters, from every one of the different code sticks."

"Easy. Each letter is from the next key probably. Still in the pattern."

Amalina shook her head and repositioned her glasses, which had slid down on her heat-damp nose. "Tried that before. But the words are nonsense. Complete nonsense."

"Lemme see." Aklan took a pencil of lead and scratched out the words on a sheet he positioned on his knee. The pencil tore holes in the paper. "Ouch. No, you're right. It doesn't look like it."

After a few minutes, Amalina's mind felt like it was beginning to swim. She blew out a breath and shoved back in her chair.

"It's all yours," she told Aklan, as she stood and motioned to her chair. "Give it a shot. I'll be right back. But don't mess up the papers."

"Back? Where are you going?"

"The privy calls. But I'll also rest my mind a bit and get some fresher air, going to go for a little walk. And while I'm at *that*, I think I'll do some measuring."

"Measuring, Pretty Princess? Measuring what?"

"Why do you you always have to ask questions?"

"But all the same, measuring what?"

"I'm making a map of the castle," she sighed.

"What for, Pretty Princess?"

"For my special friends."

"Special friends?" Aklan's eyed her, and with a sudden, new-found excitment mouthed: *Commander Kralov? The Barbarians?*

"Pray they're better than that. But never you mind. Just get to your work and concentrate on that, while I do mine. And have something good for me when I return."

"Yes, Pretty Princess."

• • •

Amalina listened to make sure nobody was in the corridor. Starting at the far end, she placed her left heel to the wall, and her right heel to her left toe. Then she marched steadily up the hall, as quickly as she could, heel-toe-heel-toe-heel-toe, as she counted off her paces.

This should be easy enough, thought Amalina. While Aklan's puzzling over the code, I can get in some map time, what a help. Heel-toe-heel-toe-heel-toe.

"Ho, ho, ho, ho," boomed the Count, as he entered the hall, his arm locked with one of the noble ladies'. "What have we here? I never know what to expect with my little mouse, or know what she'll be up to next, or where I might find her. You see, you see?"

The noble lady hid her face with a fan as she giggled along with the Count.

Amalina had stopped dead in her tracks, and felt herself blush.

"Sir."

"And what are you up to, my little mouse?"

"Looks like she's measuring the hall," said the Lady.

Amalina blushed harder.

"Is that true, my little mouse? Are you measuring my castle?"

"Yes, sir." At least telling the truth took some of the nervousness away. "That's what I'm doing."

"You see?" said the Lady. But Amalina could not tell who it was from the voice, obscured by the fluttering fan. And with the wig, the gloves, and the heavy housecoat, it could have been Genadie or Durok in a dress for all she knew. The hidden Lady didn't even drop the fan far enough, or shift it to the side, so she could tell if it was 'Maria' with her milky eyes.

"And why would you be measuring my castle, little mouse?" said the Count. He didn't seem amused. More openly suspicious.

"I'm making a map, sir."

"Oh?"

"I thought I'd make a map, sir, so I can give it to our guests and their maids and servants. It's so easy to get lost."

"But there's one already," he said.

"Is there? Can I have it?"

"Maybe later, mouse."

Amalina began her toe-heel walk again.

"I said there is a map," growled Tepsji, though civilly. The Lady giggled. "A proper map."

"I don't need it," she replied, panting lightly as she chugged along. "I want to get this done right away."

"Must this be done right now, Katarina?"

"Yes. I've set my mind on it."

"Excuse me for a moment, my precious bauble, you enchanting creature," said the Count to his anonymous friend behind the fan. "But I won't be able to concentrate with my niece pacing about, creating a commotion all over the castle. Little mouse, come with me now."

The Count brought Amalina down to his private study. From the large trunk, after rooting through the papers in it, he gave her a map of the castle. It was on thick, yellowed vellum.

"You may copy this," he said, with a sigh. "But I trust you will be careful with it. It is old and brittle."

"Thank you, sir."

"It will save you time."

"Sir, you surprised me in the hall. I didn't expect … but may I ask you who that was with you?"

"Does it matter, mouse?"

"Not necessarily," said Amalina. "But I'm curious."

"Yes, always curious. Well, the bauble would rather remain unknown for the moment, the bashful girl. But since you are quick, I will leave you with some hints that should lead you to the right answer. She is not as tall as Lady Iwebo—"

"If it was Noka … Princess Iwebo," said Amalina, "Oroco or one of her servants would have been there."

"No doubt. But I wasn't finished, of course. Not as tall as Lady Brignol, as it now stands, nor as petite as Lady Inovala. Not as fair as Montclaire, nor as plain as di Oscino. Not as severe as Lady Princess la Brichese, nor as open as Lady Princess Ecci. Getting the idea?"

Minus the names mentioned, that still left a lot.

"Lady Fleccevocarre? Maibrigg Smeehaute? Or …" guessed Amalina.

"I've left you some excellent clues already. That should be enough."

"Does she have her own blood in her, or yours?"

He snickered and tugged on his mustache. "Exquisite brain; yours is the snappiest here."

"But … I thought you were out."

"I was. Until I returned."

"Then … shouldn't you be sleeping right now, sir?"

"Shouldn't you?" he countered.

"What time is it?"

The Count pulled out a large, ornate pocket watch.

"It is very late for both of us! But for me, my duties all 'round makes it so hard to find time to rest." He stared dolefully at the watch. It was made of gold, and encrusted with a pattern of diamonds. He saw Amalina looking at it. "A gift from one of your friends. A bribe, but a thoughtful one."

In an instant, his fingers broke it to pieces like it was a cracker. He tossed the debris into a bin next to the desk.

"No, I don't like it either," he said. "Such a noisy thing won't do. And its clamor is so mechanical, unnatural. But anyway, here, have your map and enjoy yourself."

"Yes, sir," she said, taking it.

"But this map for your friends … you do make me wonder, Ms. Dalca."

He stared at her. A stare that went on for an unsettling minute.

"Wonder what, sir?"

"Such a splendid, thoughtful idea." He said, returning to life, but his voice tentative, almost insinuating. "*Why* did you think of it …? *How* did you come up with it before I did? *I* think of everything. Don't I?"

"How's it coming?" Amalina asked Aklan when she arrived back in her room.

The boy's face was flushed and he'd obviously been pulling at his hair. "Not as easy as I thought it would be. But I'm on the verge of success. I can feel it. What do you have there?"

"A map of the castle," said Amalina.

Aklan's jaw dropped. "That fast!"

"No, the Count caught me and gave me this." She set the map on her bed.

"Well, that was easy," he said.

"That was close," she blew out a breath. "I might have blown the whole thing."

"What whole thing?"

"Never you mind."

"Ooh, I can't wait to find out. That was good of him, though. Saved you some time, didn't he? I couldn't imagine how long it would take to map this place."

"Didn't save me time at all," smirked Amalina.

"Why not?"

Amalina studied the map for a moment, then held out the small magic bone for him to see: "Now, besides everything else, I'm going to have to go check this map and see where he's lying. But right now, I'm going to get the measure of that hall if it takes me the rest of the day—er, night—er, day—er, whatever."

She clamped the bone between her teeth and began removing her dress.

. . .

"Get anywhere yet?" said Amalina when she returned, with numbers floating in her head, spitting out the bone and getting back into her clothes.

"No," grunted Aklan in aggravation.

"That's all right, now I've got my blood going and my eyes have had a rest. Let me take a shot at it. I was thinking: maybe he's doing it backwards."

Aklan abandoned his chair for her to sit down. Then he leaned against her shoulder to get a good view. "Away goes our little secret," she said, pocketing the bone. "And on go the glasses."

She reorganized the papers on the desk, blew out a breath and found her sheet of ciphers, which had some scratches of ink by Aklan added to it. She jotted some lines and numbers on a blank sheet, detailing the halls she just walked, to clear her mind.

But after a minute of trying, her 'backwards solution' wasn't it either. "Whoever it is, he's gotten very sharp with it."

Aklan took one of the stiff slips for himself and stared at the squiggles of ink. Stared hard, as if he could will them to bend their shapes and reveal the true language. "Or it's all upside and down …?"

"Maybe it's a new cipher I haven't seen." Amalina rubbed her eyes, tired all over again. What time *was* it? How had she missed the howl of the wolves announcing the Count's return? Or had he never gone out? "Maybe it doesn't really matter, anyway. I know he's still alive, so I'm still in danger. I don't have to be as clever as him with his codes, I just need to be smart enough not to die before … before I'm ready. Better just to get on with my own plans."

This brought Aklan's head up. He crawled over to her knee with a wily grin and whispered, "Eh, Pretty Princess? A plan? What's your plan? You going to tell me now? Does this have to do with your special friends?"

"First, get a note out to Korr," said Amalina. "Let them know someone there in town wants me dead. At least if I die, they can go after him."

"You going to send a coded message to 'em?" said Aklan, looking like he wanted in on it.

That would have been a good idea, thought Amalina. It was a little late now, though. She couldn't very well send a coded message to Sadra and her revolutionary without them knowing how to read it. What could she do? Send a cipher along with it? Or send the cipher first, and then send the message in that code after? But the second option would waste one pigeon right away. And she didn't know if that first note, or any later one, wouldn't be intercepted.

"Wish I would have thought of this sooner," said Amalina. "I was in too much of a hurry at the time, I guess."

"Then how about telling them what you want to say without really saying it?" said Aklan, not losing any of his eagerness. "Who are you sending it to? Maybe there are things only you two know. C'mon, Pretty Princess, it won't be any fun unless we come up with something better than what the killer has."

"This isn't about fun," said Amalina, irritated, spanking him with a look. He may be growing up physically and he'd run half-way home to defend his family, but he was still playing in a fantasy world. And maybe Amalina's strange circumstances only helped reinforce his dream-like thinking. But the Count's suspicious looks and sudden appearances were making her nervous, and those were real enough.

"Of course it's about fun," said Aklan, waving away her scolding look. "What do you want life to be about, Princess? A bunch of boring stuff?"

"I'd settle for boring, I think."

"Nobody wants a boring life."

"I'd take a dead boring life over all this horror and death." She paused. "You wouldn't?"

"Horror and death is all life is!" said Aklan, incredulous, as if Amalina were revealing a glaring misapprehension of reality. "Add boring to it and it isn't worth it. It's better to just make the best of things where you can. You can't tell me you really want to be a baker after being a princess. Who'd want that?"

• • •

Amalina frowned and thought: *How many people are going to beat me up about this?* But maybe she *wasn't* thinking her dilemma all the way through. Maybe being a noble lady *was* more exciting. More preferable. With everyone else pushing her, why shouldn't she question herself? What would her life have been had she remained unaware of—and inexperienced with—this level of comfort, affluence, and style above her own? She'd still be beating dough and hawking loaves to the villagers of Korr. Maybe she would have been eyeing the boys and wondering which one she would marry, or Sadra would have her married off to. Of course, Ivanti Ion Vokent would not have been among them; he'd gone away. She would never have spent time in Vokent's arms, had the Count not torn her out of that life. Would she have wanted that? Which reality would have been preferable?

She put the disagreeable and confusing thoughts of Vokent aside. Left to her former fate, Amalina understood she wouldn't have claimed her own special horse, White Snow, among all the other magical things she'd received over the years. A fairytale life, wasn't it?

There it was again, that warm feeling, pointing her towards the *real* crux of it. She *did* enjoy this life.

. . .

"Let's come up with a code, Princess." *It'll be fun*, his grin told her.

"Nobody would know it but us," Amalina reminded him.

"I'll ride wherever you need and give them the code."

"If you do that you can just hand them the message, no need for a code."

"I'll give them the message *and* the code. That way you can send the birds using it."

"Riding would take too long," said Amalina. "It's winter. I want them to know right now. Let me just send out a first letter, plain and simple. Then we can come up with some cipher of our own that might work."

But suddenly she wasn't sure how strong a need there was to send a message. The revolutionary had said he wanted only useful information. How would he—or Sadra—react when the first letter she sent had nothing to do with the castle or the Count, but only to do with her own troubles?

Who cares? This man's a danger, and it's useful information, anyway, if it frees me from having to worry.

But then again, she considered, better not to waste the few birds given to her on …

As she fretted about this new concern, Aklan was working himself up next to her.

"Yeah, we can turn the letters backwards, and switch the words around," he said, gesturing excitedly, making examples with his hands. "And we can and run all the letters together so they won't know where one starts and the other ends. There's all kinds of things—"

"Wait," said Amalina.

There had been a flash of an idea there; it broke through her fretting. What had Aklan just said? She thought for a moment, wondering what she'd heard, finger on her lips. *Backwards … switch … run … one starts … the other ends …* Then the hooves dug in.

"Wait a minute. What if …?"

Amalina plucked up one of the later notes. She took the pencil from Aklan and began transferring letters to a new sheet of paper, trying not to poke holes. Aklan slipped a book between the paper and her leg and she barely paused as he did so. Her eyes were jumping between the note, the cipher page, and her translation.

"What a mad little system," said Amalina, distractedly in the dying firelight. "Yes, you're quite the clever one, aren't you? But not clever enough. I got you."

"What is it?" said Aklan, trying to see what she was writing.

"The words, the separation between the letters, are nothing. Just meant to throw someone off. To make you think they are words, but really it's just a mash of letters. Or no, look," she said as she ticked the words off with the pencil. "Clever, clever. The number of groupings, the number of words, signifies nothing. It's only the number of sentences that matters. And each letter, starting with the first one, then the second, and so on, is the beginning of a sentence, but each new letter in that sentence doesn't occur until you go through all the other first letters of all the other sentences, regardless of groupings." Aklan looked confused. "Look. There are three stops on the page, so three sentences. And then you apply to the first letter a letter from the A cipher, then keep going along the sentence, using the next code B for the next letter, until you reach the last of the cipher's characters, then you use the A cipher again … No. Wait. The number of words tell you how many words there are in each sentence, and how many letters are in the word. So then you cut across so many letters, for how many sentences there are, but then use the proper cipher as if you are just going across … Yes … Then you break out each sentence from the others. Oh, what a tangle. But it's easy enough. Especially once one sentence runs out, it trails off in x's."

Now *this* will lead to useful information, thought Amalina.

With this method, she translated the note:

> The shipment was assessed at the border. Taxed beyond reason xxxxxx. You need to speak to the Governor about this.
> AXP.

"Boring," said Aklan. "Why have such a confusing secret code just for that?"

Amalina shrugged, it was a note from another time, not about her. Meaningless. She wanted one of the latest messages, one of the ones the newest pigeons had carried to the castle but hadn't been put into the Count's book yet.

Aklan went to get the new notes while she stoked the fire, she felt awake again, her energy pumping. When Aklan returned she hurried through a message at random, who knew which came first and which came last. But they were made of the very same skins as the ones in the book, so they were authentic; from the same man.

"It's working, I'm so glad you're back," she told Aklan as she translated the letters.

"Really?"

"Absolutely. I've got it cracked and I couldn't have done it without you."

> Men are cheap xxxx. Loyal men with the right ideas are not. I don't know what you were thinking but it will cost you as much it cost me to lose those two. But I'm sure you don't mind. Time means nothing to you, that is the disparity between us. AXP.

"What's he talking about?" said Aklan.

Some of the excitement of cracking the code wore off as acid built in her stomach. The man was lamenting the loss of his henchmen. So it was confirmed: AXP *was* someone else besides those two *Men of Death*.

On to the next note. But because Amalina didn't know in what order they had arrived, she realized there might still be something missing until she'd translated them all. She shouldn't start leaping to conclusions.

> Have you written me off? If you think I'm incapable of handling myself, I am about to impress you. I'm going to take care of my end. I look forward to hearing that you have fulfilled your obligations, and that this was all a misunderstanding. AXP.

"Sounds like a love note to me," said Aklan with an extended yawn.

On to the last note. It was the longest and so would take the most time to decipher. When she was done, she said nothing, only stared at it.

> She's been in Korr before, passing your coins around, assessing the tainted water and showing off your silver chain. What can you make out of it but the worst? I warn you for the last time, my oldest and dearest friend, Amalina Dalca intends you harm. Come to reason before it is too late. Kill her. Kill her before she kills <u>you</u>. Kill Amalina now! AXP.

"Dear me, Pretty Princess," said Aklan. "That's not good."

41

The Understanding

After that, Amalina found it difficult not to be nervous around the Count. He hadn't read the warning note she'd deciphered because it had never left the leg of the carrier pigeon—as far as she knew. But how much did he know outside of its warning? And more, she hadn't translated the strips in the book surrounding her portait. Any one of them could have said much the same, or worse. But she let the uncomfortable feeling wash over her freely in his presence now, because he gave her a good excuse to be anxious. He wouldn't suspect her rounded eyes and tense expression as anything more than a natural reaction when he entered her room and announced: "I need your help tonight."

"Help?" said Amalina, her heart beating a little faster. "You mean ... the rite?"

"What else?" he nodded with a lusty grin as he petted one side of his mustache.

"Again? Are you sure? Do you have to do them all now? so quickly?" she asked, hoping to put him off. "Can't you be patient and wait a little?"

"I have lived a very long time, Ms. Dalca. I have already waited for centuries. Allow me to set my own schedule."

"Yes, sir."

"This one will be most interesting, little mouse," purred the Count. "Yes. That colonist is so passionate about racial stratification. Did you notice her humorless reaction to our—only appropriate—regal reception for our African guest, Princess Noka Kunuru Iwebo?"

"You're giving the rite to Miss Jane Camper?" Amalina was surprised. The Count hadn't flitted around Jane Camper much at all. In fact, he had almost seemed to disfavor someone who he had once described disdainfully as a woman who: '... lives across a long, cold sea; on the other side of the world'; was 'a foreigner in every sense of the word'; and is from ' ... a people willfully disconnected from civilization'.

He had decided on *her*?

"Elevate that cold-blooded prude?" he sneered. "Jane Camper doesn't even rise to Margeta's ankles in her harder qualities. She is more base than anything."

"Oh, I thought you said—"

"Princess Noka Kunuru Iwebo." He licked his lips. "What a delight she will be. Have I not said it before? Such a solid body. So deliciously sweet in temperament, but bold in personality."

Really? thought Amalina. *That's what he wants now: sweetness?* Or was it just her extraordinary skin? Or ...?

"It will be interesting to observe Miss Jane Camper's reaction, is what I meant."

"But how will Lady Camper know what's happened to the princess, unless ...?"

"She knows what I am doing here. I've offered her my special gift. Or made it known to her, anyway, you understand ..."

"You just said you didn't like her, why would you make her the offer?" She added at his stern look: "Sir?"

"To gauge her," he grinned slyly. "She's nothing if not reactive, isn't she? *Yesss*, her reaction was quite interesting. And I risked nothing in doing so. It's not as if she can paddle back to her colonies from here if my designs make her unhappy. Wait until she learns of Kunuru's elevation."

This was a game he was playing then, thought Amalina sourly. A private entertainment.

"But ... if you do this and it upsets Miss Camper, she could talk to all the others and tell them everything. She could cause you a lot of problems." She wondered at once, irritably: *And so what? Why am I helping* him?

"I do *wish*," the Count's voice rumbled through her body, "that you'd enjoy this with me, Ms. Dalca."

She made a face.

"There's something else, Ms. Dalca?"

"If I'm going to help you tonight ..." She paused. But she was already nervous, so *why not?*

"Yes?"

"You showed me that book," said Amalina. "Of that man who wanted me dead. AXP."

"Yes."

"What did you do with it?"

"What do you mean, Ms. Dalca?"

"You've taken care of him, haven't you? So what did you do with his book? You don't have any more use for it, do you?"

"I suppose not," he said, tentatively, his mind withdrawing.

"Can I have it?"

"Well, I'm not sure what I did with it."

"You threw it at the shelves, last I saw. Or did you leave it on your desk?"

"Oh, yes."

"Can I have it, sir? Since you won't be needing it."

"Why would you want it?"

"I don't like the thought of it in your little storehouse. I'd rather have it."

The Count became a blur, doors slammed, and suddenly he was standing solidly before her once more, but now with the AXP book in his hand. Or, rather, he was standing facing her, but was across the room, by the fireplace.

"This book?" he asked, his eyebrow arching angularly above his eye.

"Yes, sir."

"And what about it?"

"If you don't need this anymore, which you don't, I will take it."

"Do so, Ms. Dalca."

"Thank you, sir."

He didn't move.

"Sir?"

"You see, I will do you one better. It is worthless. I will destroy it." He quickly tore out the first few pages and threw them in the fire. Before Amalina realized what he was doing, the pages flared bright with colorful sparks in the hearth. He was going to completely destroy the book with all its evidence!

She scrambled forward. "No! Stop! Stop!"

He turned, with a strange smile on his face. He looked heated, manic, but happy or unhappy it was difficult to tell. He had been hurting himself just by doing this. "What, Ms. Dalca?"

"Don't destroy the whole thing. Just give it to me." She tugged the book out of his hands. He offered no resistance and it came out of them like she was pulling it off a shelf. "Please, sir, I know how much you like to keep stuff like this. How much you value your correspondence."

"You do?"

"Even something as evil as this."

"It is merely a way to preserve a record," he said, sounding defensive. "I have so many interractions with the Ardeelian population, sometimes it is hard to keep track. There is no bit of sympathy to it … and as you said, since I will no longer be needing this one …"

She almost laughed at his sorrowful look. He wasn't going to admit how much he really wanted to keep it.

"I'll hold onto it," offered Amalina. "For my peace of mind, sir, it won't be in your storehouse anymore, making me think ill of you. For your peace of mind, it will be with me. Not destroyed. Should you ever like to see it again."

"There is nothing for you to see in it, besides delicate, finely illustrated pictures. You cannot understand the language used."

"That isn't the point, sir. Just to have it out of there, knowing it can never be added to."

"Well, it can't be."

"And better yet, if you don't care for me to handle it, I will have Aklan hide it away somewhere, so even I won't know where it is. But it can be retrieved when needed."

The Count looked relieved, but nodded once slowly while he said, "Now, I have done something for you. You will do something for me."

"Yes, sir. Yes, sir."

"Good." His large eyes flicked up at her. "Er … who did you say you were going to give this insignificant book to?"

"Aklan. My servant, sir. You've seen him plenty of times."

"Yes. *Yessss*. Trustworthy, is he?"

• • • •

"Why did you have to bring me into it?" whispered Aklan later, peering with suspicion at the walls, waiting for the Count to pop his head through. "Now he's going to be thinking about me when I'd rather keep him *not* knowing who I am."

"You'll be all right," said Amalina, looking annoyed as she now paged hungrily, greedily through the AXP book.

"That's easy for you to say."

She went to the fireplace and stared into the fire for any bits she could retrieve.

"He ripped out the whole first section," she said in frustration.

The first section of the book, which wasn't entirely coded. Or coded well. Had he done it on purpose? He could have outright refused her request. He could have thrown the whole thing into the fire right away. But he did not want that book destroyed. Not at all. He was fine with her having it, relished knowing it could be gotten to when he liked or needed it. Still unaware that she knew about the ciphers and the codes, and that she had her own ciphers written out on sheets of paper in her desk. For his purposes he just needed to make sure he didn't leave anything in the book from the earlier, more vulnerable part of the correspondence, anything Amalina could actually read, or use to identify the true culprit. So had he bluffed her then? knowing she would stop him short of destroying it? allowing her a neutered version of the book to keep her satisfied, and pacified? Didn't it look that way?

"Crafty man," muttered Amalina. "Thinks of everything, all right."

There was a knock at the door. Amalina nearly threw the book across the room into Aklan's hands.

"Master is expecting you, milady," announced Pils, from the other side of the door.

• • •

Princess Noka Kunuru Iwebo's body was striking in the bathwater. So incredibly black against the creamy-white, powdered water, it was like darkest midnight swimming within a blinding daylight; swirling together but never mixing, no border between them. Even the Count was unable to keep from whispering to Amalina, in their Ardeelian tongue, "Look, Amalina: the *In-Yang*; the *Taijitu* personified."

Taken by the sight of Noka, his prompting wasn't needed, Amalina couldn't look away.

The princess' eyes were closed and she appeared serene. Her body was a series of round, voluptuous islands rising and shifting out of the milky-white water, looking slick and inviting; to be touched, petted, held onto. The buds of her breasts grew and hardened, limned in gold by the candlelight. Her lips parted in a silent sigh, her throat extended up, muscles under her taut skin moving like graceful waves. Amalina felt a strange stir within that only amplified with the deepening of the rite, and the increasing intensity of the Count's chanting.

The rite seemed faster than before. The Count had been perfecting it, and so now his movements were as assured and smooth as a fish careening in a stream as he circled the splendid white marble tub and his victim; Amalina was really an unnecessary component, though the Count would not have it any other way. He purred his enchantments over Noka, "Now is the time we elevate ourselves. Break free the bonds of your weak, earthly flesh." Even weighted with the Count's heavy accent, Amalina noted, the words sounded much lighter, prettier and refined spoken in French. She felt she just might tell him so later.

"Oui," said Noka Kunuru.

Though Noka was relaxed, there was a flexing of her jaw, a tightening of her facial muscles, as if firmly settling on a course.

"*Ouaiiii*," said the Count.

"*Ouaiiiii*," said Noka.

"Do you know what you are doing?" whispered Amalina.

"Whaaat?" said the princess, dreamily.

"Do you know what is going to happen to you? Do you understand?"

"Power. Great power."

"And what you must do for it?"

Noka's right eyelid parted, she looked sidelong and questioning at Amalina.

"Ms. Dalca," growled the Count in Ardeelian, though in a lilting way, so as not to deviate from the seductive spell he was casting. "I had hoped you might be coming forward *out of curiosity*."

"Do you know the price you must pay, Princess Noka?" whispered Amalina.

"Yes," said Noka. "Of course."

"Ms. Dalca, please."

"How could she know, sir? She's from a whole other part of the world."

"She understands." Here he switched to French, "You know everything—*savez toute*—don't you, *ma chere*?"

"*Sang, mange.*" *Eat the blood.*

"Ms. Dalca," he murmured heavily in their native language, so deep that she felt it through her whole body. "She comes from a tribe that lives by drinking the blood of their livestock. Some eat the flesh of their vanquished enemies. How much do *you* know, Ms. Dalca? Do you know *anything* about your good friend here? Now, please, I think she is a perfect fit for us—for me. That is enough. Don't distract her. Every moment is crucial, and any delay—any needless delay—could cause us enormous trouble. Don't forget your part, little mouse, in the fate of poor Robine ..."

Amalina wanted to hiss at him. She whispered: "I just want to make sure she knows what she's getting into—"

"That is enough. Now ..." He returned to French, shutting Noka's eye with a gentle stroke of his finger, while breathing into her ear, "Now is the end of all tears."

"*Oui.*"

"*Ouaiiiiii.*"

"*Ouaaaiiiiiiii.*" Her thick, sensuous lips pulled back in a decadent smile, her teeth white as bleached bone.

The blood that poured from Princess Kunuru's many wounds looked dark and rich sliding over her skin. But then, not much later, it was like a thinned strawberry sauce as her skin lost its depth of blackness, her body greying as her blood emptied into the water, taking her life with it; it was as if her bold color had been an electic charge, now lost.

42

Dr. Cassette and Ms. Grafo

As one noble lady or another took the Count's offer and accepted his 'gift', there was an outward similarity to how she suddenly "fell ill" and needed to be isolated. In each case, the Lady had "insisted on taking a walk around the castle"—*at night, by herself, unattended.* There was the understandable suspicion of some illicit meeting, but even their closest chambermaid was confined to quarters when she took her fateful walk. Then Anka would arrive an hour or so after the rite was completed, to announce to the Lady's people that their charge had taken ill, and fearing for everyone's health, was removed to a private quarters better suited for recuperation, to be under the supervision of Wanger (of Wanger, Regio, and Balbo), who was a physician and surgeon among his many talents. One servant would be dispatched to their Lady's side, to give her comfort and to verify she was alive, and could report back her condition to the others. This servant would not be allowed close enough to the Lady for them to observe the many wounds on her body, but only to view her through a thin gauzy sheet and speak to her.

Servants could speculate about how their princess might have been troubled by something she had eaten earlier. Or that the poor young woman was dropped by the foul air that wafts up through the privy at certain times of the day. Or that she might have encountered a malevolent spirit on her walk, before or after the rendezvous, and was overcome. But the exact similarities in the various ladies' pre-sickness departures—their insistence on a private midnight walk—which would have been a very suspicious coincidence, did not emerge because the opposing camps were not comparing notes.

During the previous year, the servants were kept isolated and restrained by the intimidating, juggernaut presence of General Marosh and his men. His idea of preserving order, to prevent the many idle attendants from growing bored and then rubbing up against each other to cause trouble, was to scare them into retreat, so that each group huddled around their mistress in the confines of their own apartments, rarely venturing out; as if their one Lady of Title were their only source of warmth on a bitterly cold night. Whether it was by the example set by Margeta's and Pia's remaining servants, who had gone through *the Marosh experience* of the previous year and stuck with it, or instead, that it really was winter and the servants naturally withdrew, the Ladies' entourages, no matter how large, stayed mostly within the orbit of their own Lady's small pen, with little to no fraternization. They bustled about from here to there as servants will, but were like individual icebergs on a busy sea, clattering into each other but never merging. Anka and Pils were their accepted buffers, though the Count's two attendants couldn't speak their foreign languages beyond simple words and phrases, like: "Excuse, but your ladyship was found feeling poorly on the long oriental carpet ..."

Lady Claire Montraine's parents, as a sensible precaution, had secreted into her large entourage a trained doctor and his apprentice: Dr. Cassette and Ms. Grafo. Beyond being vaguely handsome, with his thick, swept-back black hair and discerning eyes, Dr. Cassette was alert and curious and easily bored to distraction. After so many women had fallen ill, even if to a malady which Wanger determined "was not serious" and from which, he vowed, "the lady shall make a full recovery", and even though it did not directly affect his own charge, Claire Montraine, the doctor could not overcome his need to get some answers. Cassette's apprentice, Ms. Grafo, attended.

. . .

"I'm sorry, milady," said Anka to Amalina, who had woken much later in the afternoon than she had wanted, and had just opened the AXP book to begin some serious translating. The book being too difficult to easily slide into the desk drawer to hide, Amalina slammed the cover closed, pushed it to the side, and set her elbow on top of the metal letters. Anka pretended not to notice and continued to look worried.

"What is it, Anka?"

"I really am sorry, but I can't understand a word he is saying. He does seem adamant and I think he wants to talk to your uncle. You know—your uncle, milady. *Your uncle.*"

"Yes, I *know* who my uncle is, Anka. Who is *he*, eh?"

Anka explained he was of Lady Montraine's number. She couldn't tell her anything else.

Amalina said she would meet with the man and then hid the book. She was still exhausted after the previous night's rite, but had so hoped today to take advantage of the opportunity of actually possessing the book, no longer having to sneak down to the message center to rip off a few pieces. She *had the book!* She could read it all, whenever she liked! Somewhere in there she would find out who he, AXP, was!

Now the book went into her standing bureau, beneath a number of shifts and old gowns.

In *l'entrée grande*, Amalina met Montraine's man and he introduced himself, in French, with a bow and a peck to the back of her hand, as Dr. Cassette. He also introduced a cat-like woman as his assistant, Ms. Grafo. Ms. Grafo's face was so round and feline, if it had been covered in a short fur and with whiskers it would have looked natural. She smiled pleasantly and bowed.

"It is like this, Countess," said Dr. Cassette. "I am familiar with diseases and have treated the Montraine family through many illnesses. If it were one lady, I should not be concerned. But this is more than one, no?"

"If you are concerned, Dr. Cassette, if you are concerned at all, we can make arrangements for you and your lady to leave."

"However, it is winter," he said with a slight condescending smile, "and I don't see how that is possible, Countess. But, really—"

"I do want to see to my guests' comfort," said Amalina, quickly. "If Lady Montraine in any way is worried, it will be safe enough to travel down to Netz, where she can wait for better weather to journey home. I don't want her to feel that we are keeping her here. No, not in the slightest. I can write to Mr. Humphrey, he is experienced in winter travel in these mountains, and she can leave Ardeel as fast as humanly possible."

"But, Countess, Countess, please," implored Dr. Cassette with a patient smile. "Be assured, I do not wish to leave here. Neither does my mistress wish to quit you, or your guardian's, warmest company. But my curiosity is piqued by circumstances, and I would like to apply my learning where it can be most helpful. The knowledge possessed by myself and Ms. Grafo, eh? You understand? I would wish my mistress to not know of this request at all. Best to let her sleep."

"I'm sorry, Dr. Cassette," said Amalina. "What is it you want?"

"If I could just examine the stricken ladies. If that would be permitted. Maybe we, Ms. Grafo and I, could assist in their recovery. I do not see the harm in such a thing. Do you? Can you ask your uncle to meet with me, so that I might have his permission?"

• • •

Count Tepsji was found sleeping in his study, but woke instantly and was enlivened by the idea of Dr. Cassette's request. Which thrilled Amalina because she wanted it to happen too; so that she could see where her friends were being stored and how they were coming along in their recoveries. Even Pia was reluctant to say much about them, or even her own process, apparently having been sworn to secrecy. But on top of Amalina's own curiosity about her friends, she realized she might also gain some information that Sadra or the revolutionary might want; and have a more legitimate reason to send out a bird, with an added mention about AXP attached. Seeing the hungry look in the Count's eye though, Amalina regretted asking. When Dr. Cassette's back was turned, she swore she saw the Count's canine tooth sharpen and grow. What was he hoping to happen? That the doctor would discover the truth and need to be killed? Feed him to whichever lady he was examining?

Count Tepsji insisted Dr. Cassette begin his examinations right away, almost refusing the poor doctor to go back to his room to retrieve his medical kitbag. The Count told him he would have to be blind-folded, out of precaution. Black silk sacks were put over his and Ms. Grafo's heads. He then led them by the hand down through his counting house and message chamber and then through the warren of rooms below the castle, many of which Amalina had never seen before. They were small and seemed a little dank for, as Wanger put it, "recuperative purposes".

"All this is quite unnecessary," said Dr. Cassette from within the black sack, politely.

The Count ignored him.

"We seem to be going down," said Dr. Cassette, as if this were a guessing game.

"What did you say?" said the Count, appearing to stifle a giggle.

"We seem to be going down. And down."

"It is a lower area of the castle."

"I would think fresh air would be more to a Lady's liking, and better for their constitution."

"There is a special air in the rocks of these mountains," said the Count. "The castle is built from them. All my guests convalesce much better in the chambers to which I am now taking you."

"I see," said Dr. Cassette. Then he added mirthfully, touching the black hood, "Or rather, I don't see. Yet."

The Count didn't seem to enjoy Dr. Cassette's sense of humor.

. . .

The examinations were conducted back-to-back and were all the same: Dr. Cassette and Ms. Grafo were allowed to view the ladies in the dim candlelight through a sheet of gauze hung over the bed, to ask questions as they liked, and only touch a lady's forehead and whichever arm the lady preferred to lend through the sheet.

The ladies all seemed well on their way to recovery. It was difficult to tell just how pale they were—in a candle's light everyone seemed unhealthily yellow. But their pulses were strong and they spoke from their beds as if they had just been roused from a nap, which was coherent enough. There was no fever, and Dr. Cassette remarked to his assistant that they all seemed to be rather cold to the touch.

The only moment of surprise within the first few examinations was when Dr. Cassette first opened his medical bag and pulled out a small leather case filled with glass vials. The Count's patronizing grin vanished as his eyes pinned one of the bottles.

"Something wrong, uncle?" said Amalina, unable to contain her curiosity. The bottle looked like it held a harmless grey powder, or ashes.

Dr. Cassette turned to the Count looming over him. "Eh?"

"That container carries silver, if I am not mistaken, Doctor." said the Count.

Dr. Cassette had to put his face down close to see the vial, but then nodded. "Silver, yes, sir. You've an excellent eye."

"It is a regulated substance," explained the Count. "It is not allowed within Ardeel and is usually removed by customs agents at the border."

"That's true, Count Tepsji," said Dr. Cassette with a smile, and he winked at the Count in a worldly, man-to-man way. "If they can find it. I snuck it past them."

"I see."

"I assume the law is applied to the general masses and does not affect ones such as yourself and your niece."

"Why would you think that, Dr. Cassette?"

"I thought I once saw your niece wearing some beautiful silver jewelry pieces round her neck and off her ears."

Amalina gulped and felt sweaty.

"But that was not in Ardeel, Doctor," said Amalina, feeling the Count's eyes on her without her looking in his direction. "I borrowed them from a friend."

"Ah!" said Dr. Cassette. He didn't let the subject trouble him and only put away his kit when he was done with the examination. It was something not to bother with, so he seemed to feel, if no one brought it up again.

The final noble lady would be the latest 'stricken'. But when they went to Princess Noka Kunuru Iwebo's room in the lower area, she wasn't there. This surprised even the Count. He frowned at the princess' servant who sat on the bed, waiting patiently in place as if for this moment. The servant nodded to them.

"Sorry, but the princess prefers her first room," said the servant. "Upstairs. Likes it much better there. So she will be staying upstairs, as always."

"Sensible," said Dr. Cassette. Ms. Grafo nodded agreement.

"She is upstairs in the towers, you say?" growled the Count, unhappily.

"No. She's gone to the barn," said the servant. "You just missed her. On her way to get something to eat. Did I say that right?"

"She's walking?" said the Count, astonished.

• • •

Noka Kunuru Iwebo wasn't walking.

Even in the torchlight her skin was grey, ashen. Only her face, left hand, and feet stuck out of holes in the large, bulky bundle of a tapestry that had been wrapped protectively around her body and her wounds. Her eyelids were half-closed, and she trembled as if weak or cold. Two of her servants sat on either side of her in the barn's inner corral, as Oroco chanted over her with one hand on the side of a cow.

The rite stopped when the Count's party entered.

"What is happening here?" rumbled the Count, ominously.

"Hm?" said Noka, her eyes dully turning up. When she saw them she smiled and her eyes closed, like a baby serenely falling asleep. "Ah, *ma Comte*."

Oroco bowed, "The princess is glad you have come to bear witness."

"What is this?" said the Count, as he tried putting his question another way.

Dr. Cassette and Ms. Grafo, grave with concern, moved toward the princess. Two of her warriors stepped out from the corners of the stall and brandished their tribal spears, with their frightening, peculiarly long blades. Cassette and Grafo fell back.

"My Princess is hungry, as you can see," said Oroco, placidy.

"Princess Kunuru should be resting," said the Count.

"My Princess will rest when she wishes," countered Oroco. "Now, she will eat."

"Oh?" The Count smiled and petted his mustache, intrigued. "She has the strength?"

"What does the princess wish to eat?" asked Dr. Cassette, his eyes shooting around the wide stall, but landing again and again on the cow. Oroco patted the cow's neck to reinforce what was about to happen. "I don't understand."

"The princess' people eat cow's blood, Doctor," said Amalina, trying to grasp herself what was going to take place. Last night it was the princess' blood and the Count's blood consumed before her eyes, next it is to be the cow's?

"Very healthy," said Oroco. "Very … *invigorating*. Restores the life, fortifies the soul."

Nobody said anything, the corral became a wooden square of silence and clouds of their breaths in the cold winter's air. Oroco nodded, it was settled. Everyone returned to their respective spots to watch. Except the doctor, his assistant, and the Count, who crept closer in.

Oroco patted the cow significantly now, speaking to it in a chanting rhythm in his own tribal language. Then he took up two long wood sticks with sharp ends. He aimed one into the cow's throat, and hammered its back end with the other. With only a murmur of protest from the cow, the sharp stick popped through the thick hide and then shot back out, followed by an arc of blood, which pattered on the straw at their feet. Amalina was so distracted by the steam that flew off the blood's dark red stream, she didn't notice Oroco switch out his implements to fill a ceremonial wood cup with the blood, until he then brought up the cup toward the princess. The billowing puffs of steam made it appear as if the cup's contents were at a boil. Noka's eyes rose weakly to stare at it.

"Come, Daughter of the Golden Sun," said Oroco, somehow having already stemmed the cut in the cow's neck. "It is ready for you."

Amazingly, Oroco stood there, not bringing the cup to his mistress' mouth, but withholding it, like a challenge to her.

"What is the matter, my Princess?" said Oroco. "Do not let it grow cold." Then he began speaking to her more fluently in their common tongue. Either taunting or reprimanding her.

Princess Noka unwrapped herself from the tapestry, to reveal that she wore a loose black mantilla shawl, which covered all but her face, hands, and feet. She rose slowly, barely keeping her eyes open. The two servants on either side did not move to assist her, but were there, prepared to catch her if she fell. Her legs were wobbly and it looked as if she would topple. Amalina moved forward to help her, but Oroco warned her away with a wave of his hand.

"She can do it, Lady Katarina," said Oroco with a proud, overly broad smile. "Of course she can. She is to be queen one day. She can feed herself like any common woman. She is good. She is well. Come, My Grace. Walk. Walk!"

With Oroco's accompanying nods, Noka staggered and pitched at the cup, lifting her ashen hand to take it. For a second it looked like Oroco was going to take a step backward, to challenge her once more, to test her or prove her strength to everyone in the corral. His eyes were darting at Amalina and the doctor and the assistant and the Count. Especially the Count. His smile hardened, even as the Count's grin grew and a fire of anticipation built in his eyes—not just the reflection of the barn's torches.

Noka took the wood cup from Oroco. She held it and stared at the rich red within it. Then, as Oroco had, her eyes glanced around at her witnesses.

Her body righted just a fraction and she smiled. Then she gently turned the cup toward Amalina. "Would you like a drink, Katty?"

"Um," said Amalina, gulping loudly. "Um, no. No thank you."

Swaying on her feet, she kindly and blindly offered it to her other dinner guests: Dr. Cassette, then Ms. Grafo, who both turned it down, and then, finally to Count Tepsji.

The Count bowed graciously, "Another time, my dear princess. You must see to yourself. We wish you well, and this blood is for you."

Noka bowed her head, her lips curling her smile into something sweeter: appreciation. She closed her eyes and brought the cup to her lips. She took half a sip before she collapsed.

"My God!" shouted Dr. Cassette, as everyone leapt to catch her.

But Dr. Cassette suddenly flew to the side and hit the cow's flank, and Noka's warrior's spears were clattering into the corner of the corral, along with the warriors themselves. The Count alone held Noka's body securely in his arms.

"She did well," said the Count to Oroco, though his mouth was turned down. He was fighting back a fury inside him. "Best not to push her yet."

"I did not push her," argued Oroco, with a fury of his own. "She is great and strong!"

"Of course. But everyone needs to rest, even your Daughter of the Golden Sun. And so she will."

"Upstairs!" demanded Oroco. "As my princess wishes it!"

"I've no objections, Oroco," said the Count in a flat tone. "My lady can lay her head anywhere she wishes."

• • •

As the groups dispersed from the barn, Amalina fought against her usual caution and caught up to Dr. Cassette and Ms. Grafo, who were speaking with one another in a heated way. Dr. Cassette was saying: " ... great and strong? She looked like a newborn calf being rushed to walk!"

"Excuse me, Doctor, Ms. Grafo. I was wondering if you were satisfied with your examinations?"

"Eh?" said Dr. Cassette, startled. "Oh, Countess. Well ... are you asking for your uncle, or for yourself?"

Amalina thought that was a strange question, but said, "Well, for myself I suppose. More for my friends' benefit, and their people."

"I'm sorry that I gave you away to your uncle—about the silver jewelry. I didn't know the ban was as serious as it appears."

"Think nothing of it, but—"

"May I ask something about your uncle? I hope you don't mind." Then he added needlessly, but for some reason a qualification he felt important: "I am a man of the medical discipline."

"Ask me anything."

"Ms. Grafo and I were wondering if your uncle has an unnatural aversion to light." Ms. Grafo didn't nod agreement as she seemed regularly inclined to do, but there was an affirming twinkle in her large, cat-like eyes.

"What do you mean?"

"I don't believe I have seen him outside the castle in the daylight. No, I am—we are both—quite certain we haven't. I would have—well I have; we both have—suspected that he has a sensitivity to the sun. Either it bothers his skin, or his eyes cannot abide the brightness. Perhaps both. We have come across many anecdotes, and have in fact witnessed people with this rare affliction."

"Oh. Really?"

"But now we are confronted with his rather strange obsession of housing the ladies in the lower chambers of his castle. In conditions that are satisfactory, I suppose, but are reminiscent in themselves of dungeon cells. I guess his bed chambers are down there as well?"

"Well, he doesn't bury himself down there," said Amalina, feeling automatically defensive for no good reason. The doctor's eyes were too searching and demanding. Not that there was any immediate danger there. He wasn't suspecting the Count of being a supernatural creature, but accusing the Count of being a type of lunatic.

"I'm sorry if I offended you, Countess," the doctor said quickly, reading her.

"My uncle is unusual but harmless, unless you get on his bad side. I can't say why he is the way he is. He has always been that way since I've known him. I believe he mentioned Dr. Wanger was the one who recommended the removal of the women from our common company to the lower chambers, until everyone's safety can be assured."

"Wanger, yes," said Dr. Cassette, coldly. "Architect or engineer, isn't he?"

"And a surgeon, I was told."

"Very well. Can I speak to him?"

"If I can find him. He's a bit elusive in the castle. Not that that is hard to be, as you know, if one wishes to be. But, um, about the examinations you performed: were you satisfied with our Ladies' conditions?"

Dr. Cassette grimaced. "Besides Princess Kunuru Iwebo, who should be resting, the women in the vaults seem to be doing very well. Maybe that argues for the cellar air theory of ... Architect-Engineer-*Surgeon* Wanger's."

"Would you say they are back to normal, do you think?" Amalina continued on.

"I said they are in superb condition, and can, in our opinion, *return to free society*." Dr. Cassette smiled at his own little joke and Ms. Grafo nodded agreement, with a little smile of her own.

"I meant more personality-wise, though. You spoke to them and asked questions."

"They seemed a little sluggish, some of them. Which would be understandable, under the circumstances. But overall, they were awake and—"

"Did they seem themselves? That's what I meant: did they seem like themselves?"

"I can't really say," he said, looking a little baffled. "I don't really know them—didn't know them much before, did I? They were pleasant enough in our interviews. I can't say otherwise."

"Well, that's good. Thank you, Doctor—and, um, thank you, Ms. Grafo."

"And what did you make of Princess Kunuru's ceremony?"

"Hm?" Amalina's mind flashed to Noka's bloody tiny-death in the Count's marble tub.

"Just now. You knew she was going to do that? You understood that that was her—their—custom?"

"I'd heard of it," said Amalina. "But I've never seen it done."

"You were strong enough to stomach it without much surprise. I would suspect half your guests would have fainted at the sight. Even our Lady Montraine."

"Well ..." said Amalina, suddenly wondering where he was going with this line of thought. Better to not find out and turn it back on him: "And how did you find the ceremony?"

"Intriguing," he said, mulling the question. "Sanitary? Hmmm. Unhealthy? Hmmm. There is something to be said about the richness and vitality of blood; as well as any other mysteries bound up in it."

Ms. Grafo whispered something to him.

"Oh, yes," he said. "We'd add that it felt a little barbaric. But then, when we're the kind of society who hang heads off the battlements, who are we to cast stones?"

They parted company, each side a little unsatisfied with the outcome of the evening, despite how much they had seen and done. Before Amalina could reach the main building, Aklan caught her in the courtyard.

· · ·

"Pretty Princess, another one came," said Aklan, presenting a scrolled skin, fresh off the leg of a greasy pigeon. "Got it as soon as it came in. A big one!"

> Do as you will, my old friend, or do not. It has always been at your discretion. Why you seek to protect one girl in all the world can only be fathomed by yourself, presumably in some higher plan. But one girl in all the world, though not essential, no matter how intricate the scheme, one girl in all the world <u>can</u> cause irreparable harm to any and all our projects through no fault of our own but personal hubris. We understand each other in that, I should hope. Now, if you do not act in my interest in this matter as I require, to eliminate the Dalca chit, and you refuse to rise to your own security, to remove a clear danger to yourself, I trust you will allow me at least to continue to labor on my own behalf without further interference on your part—and without trouble should I succeed. The matter of the loss of my two former associates is forgiven. I understand they were clumsy brutes. My future agents against her will be subtler men. Your friend forever, AXP.

"Ooh, he's getting worse I think, Pretty Princess," commented Aklan. "No, don't like the sound of that at all."

AXP's tone was much softer here than in his several recent notes, thought Amalina as she rubbed her lower lip and analyzed. The expanse of words seemed more carefully chosen. He was being diplomatic. He wasn't at war with the Count and wanted to preserve their friendship. But he was still ready to come for her no matter the cost. And he *was* coming for her. Even now. But at the castle? Would he dare?

Amalina stretched her aching arms. It had taken some time to translate the lengthy message, crossing out all the extra X's within it to get it right. She felt the direct threat of it, and a low burn of fear radiated in her chest. But then she was also burned-out by the day and what she'd learned there; so much so that a comfortable, blanketing numbness settled over her mind and body.

Amalina looked across her desk at the large, shiny metal-lettered book, and remembered what she had been planning to do with it before Dr. Cassette's interruption. Should she return to it? Should she delve further into the messages, decipher them and perhaps discover the true identity of AXP, so she can perhaps find a way to stop him? Or should she finally give in to her fatigue, enter her bed, go to sleep, only to find Lucinda Skeldar waiting for her there, demanding justice?

43

Skeldar

Amalina swore under her breath as she tore a piece of paper into several strips, then did the same crosswise, then threw that confetti into the fire.

"Was it bad, Pretty Princess?" said Aklan who squinted into the fireplace.

"Stop calling me that," said Amalina, shortly.

"As you wish. But you won't say if it was a bad message or not?"

"It was nothing at all. You were right, it's boring, all boring. What a waste."

"Then why keep doing it?"

Amalina lowered her head into her hands and closed her eyes. With a sigh, she thought: *Yes, why keep doing it?*

Why? Because the Count had given her the book. Even if he'd lied about killing AXP—and he really hadn't claimed he'd done *that*, had he? Killed him? She had assumed it. But maybe he felt he was still telling the truth, by simply not honoring the order to kill her, even with his secret master still around. Maybe that's why the ugly pigeons were collecting in the aviary, their notes unclaimed. He was rejecting them. Only in a sense, but still …

Amalina frowned: "There has to be something in this book that will reveal who the person behind the murder service is, and why he wants so many girls dead. Easy enough for me: he wants *me* dead because I'm onto him and he knows it. That *must* be why. But they can't all be threats. Not to him or the Count."

"I don't see how any could be a threat to anyone."

"But anyway," said Amalina. "I can't go to bed. I can barely sleep … Did I tell you I saw the Count kill one of them? the girls?"

"Yes, you've told me, Princess."

"Her name was Lucinda, and she was as harmless as a kitten; a wounded kitten." Amalina closed her eyes again and moaned, "And now every night, when I'm here in the castle, her ghost comes to me in my dreams and begs me to avenge her. And how can I—?"

"What!" Aklan whirled around, excited. "She does? Every night? That's why you're always groaning in your sleep then when you're here?"

"I suppose."

He spun around the room looking into all the darkened corners, very pleased by the novelty and sudden diversion of a ghost. His eyes wide and excited. "Tonight I will wake you, Pretty Princess. When she comes to you, you hold onto her. I will wake you up. And when I do, you will bring her out of your dreams with you."

"Complete nonsense," said Amalina with a smirk. "I've never heard of such a thing."

"But it is true. I've heard stories."

"Anyway, she never reaches me in the dream. And that's beside the point."

"Yes, Pretty Princess," said Aklan, sounding disappointed.

"The point is: how am I supposed to avenge her and settle her spirit when her killer cannot be killed, and the man who ordered her killing is forever a mystery?"

"Just ignore her then." Aklan flopped onto a chair. "Let's think of something else to do."

Amalina folded two more strips from the book—boring, boring messages—and threw them into the fire. They flashed a crazy green color and sent off sparks, as if they had been protected by some magic charm. But then they were gone. Not even carbonized ribbons of skin were left behind.

"There has to be one—at least one—that will give something away. I lived in Korr and I know lots of people. It would be obvious who it is if he wasn't so careful. He simply doesn't reveal enough details."

"But if you could catch her ghost out of your dreams," said Aklan, coming to life again, "you could ask her who he is. Or ... now that I think about it, maybe you could *trick* the Count into telling you by—"

"Aklan, please," said Amalina. "I need real help here and you aren't helping. I mean, for heaven's sake, stop playing like you're in some children's storybook."

"Yes, maybe I could better help by watching for pigeons flying in with new messages to kill you," he snarled sarcastically. "Or secret assassins arriving through the gate."

Amalina didn't know what to say. He wasn't wrong. But then, what he'd said didn't sound too far off from a fantastic story either, which was probably his point.

Aklan threw something at the wall and then left the room with a moody stomp. As soon as he was gone, Amalina felt alone. Very alone. As if the stone walls had taken one step backward in every direction.

"Excuse me, milady," said Anka, peeking her head in. "I thought you should know. Rosczy received visitors earlier and then he left the castle."

"What time is it?" When Anka told her, Amalina exclaimed: "Morning already!"

"Yes, milady."

"But it's Tuesday, isn't it?" said Amalina. "If Father Rosczy left, who is going to run the service today?"

Margeta la Brichese. Margeta had run services whenever there wasn't a personal priest on hand. Which was unfortunate. One of *her* sermons was never something to look forward to. And in its exultingly triumphant way, it always felt slightly sacrilegious.

"One of the visitors will take the service, milady," said Anka over Amalina's thoughts.

"Wait ...visitors?"

Amalina wondered if Aklan had been able to see them when they entered, and get a good look.

"The Cardinal sent them to relieve our priest."

• • •

Rosczy's replacement, accompanied by a robed acolyte, met Amalina in one of the halls leading to the small chapel and waved his hand low at his waist toward her. A discreet gesture. At first she didn't understand what it meant, and she looked at him curiously, with a small bit of apprehension. He didn't look like an assassin from this distance. His head was bent down. With his hair tonsured in the manner of a monasteried priest, his skull looked as if a ringed pumpernickel bread had been dropped onto it. And that image, coupled with the worry that this might be AXP's 'subtle' new man, had distracted her or she would have noticed the man's eyes. In the end, though, it was the shake in his left hand which gave him away.

This was Sadra's revolutionary. His eyes came up briefly to see if his signal had done its work, but then fell back down immediately, and remained, along with the rest of his features, to project an almost universal ennui. He held a crucifix loosely in his hand, as if it were a quill pen he'd forgotten he was holding. And he swung his arms about him as he walked, with an almost mocking performance of the Cardinal.

His gesture, his signal, was meant to warn Amalina not to react to him, to pretend he was another simple priest sent from St. Grigori. She played along, even with a small blush on her cheeks and feeling hot. What was he doing here in the castle?

Sadra's revolutionary performed Tuesday's chapel service and at length, going beyond Roszy's perfunctory renditions—Rosczy seemed always to want to retire as soon as he could from the lectern. The revolutionary hadn't been informed of this, apparently, and took the service to heart, even if his delivery was droning and matter-of-fact, and almost doubting at times. He had all the pious Ladies, and even the non-religious ones who were looking for a distraction, convinced that he was a true man of the cross: quite boring.

After the service, Balbo, who seemed to be the last of the architects regularly hanging around the main parts of the castle, saw something in this new priest as made him fit enough to spar with on ecumenical matters, nodding his large salt-and-pepper-colored beard as they conversed at length, a finger curled pensively over his lip and nodding. He even forgot the Ladies and to slick down his hair.

Then, after taking confession, the priest-in-disguise had a difficult time breaking away from Margeta. But he insisted, after awhile, that he had a private message for Katarina from the Cardinal.

"Where may I speak to you, Lady Tepsji, if you may?" he said, talking around Margeta. "Perhaps my private chamber?"

"Whatever you think is best," said Amalina, looking apologetic to Margeta, and the other Ladies she was going to leave behind.

• • •

When they were in the private chamber and his hooded servant closed the door, the revolutionary said pointedly, "You have something private to confess, Lady Tepsji?"

"I—I don't ..." She wasn't sure what she was supposed to say to him. His expression gave no hints. Was he serious?

"Well, if not, we can observe a private prayer."

"I thought there was a message from the Cardinal for me?"

"Considering the unique traits of your famous family, Lady Tepsji, he thought it wise to keep your true confession away from the others." But as the man said this he pulled out a sheet of paper, and after dabbing a pen in a bottle of ink, began writing quickly. "But I won't push you to do anything uncomfortable, Countess. Come Lazru, attend our good lady. Some wine."

The servant nodded and began pouring wine into two goblets.

Sadra's revolutionary pushed the paper to Amalina.

He'd written:

Is it safe to talk?

Amalina shook her head. He nodded, undisturbed. Or just unreactive. He began writing again, as he said aloud: "Then silent prayer is in order, Lady Tepsji. And quiet contemplation of our place within Heaven's grand design."

Again he placed the paper before Amalina.

Map?

Amalina added next to it:

Incomplete. Sorry.

He added next to that:

I'll take what you have.

Amalina felt sweaty.

Nothing yet on paper. Too dangerous. The calculations are in my head.

The revolutionary nodded again, as if it were expected. He scratched out the interchange and began anew.

You will not react. Notice Lazru.

"Lazru, where is that wine?" he asked the acolyte.

"Here, Father," came the deep, gargled voice.

As Lazru set the cups between Amalina and the revolutionary, she and the acolyte regarded each other in full. And each was as surprised as the other. It took Amalina only a moment longer, as the man called Lazru shook and almost dropped to his knees. His whole body began to tremble, even as his doughy face twisted angrily.

Lazru Skeldar.

Sadra's revolutionary had been a surprise. But Amalina had never expected to see within the Count's high castle Lucinda Skeldar's father. It almost seemed like a dream. She hadn't known him very well, he being an angry recluse and a mean drunk. But all the children had heard the stories and knew the face of the man, and to look out if he was stamping heavily through Korr's streets.

"Oh," said Amalina.

The revolutionary put a warning finger to his lips, even as he started writing again. "Sit down, Lazru, you are making the Lady nervous."

"That's all right," said Amalina.

The revolutionary pointed to a neighboring chair, and Lucinda's father shifted himself laterally onto it. He sat slightly bowed forward, his hands wringing, as if he might come off of it in an instant. He stared at Amalina.

"No need to be kind, milady," said the revolutionary. "Just try to ignore him, and let's redouble our effort to humility and pious thoughts."

I am here for a couple days. You will take me on a tour of the castle, as much of it as I would be allowed to be seen normally, but as thorough as you can. I need to know everything about it.

Amalina nodded. She glanced at Lucinda's father, who looked anxiously at the paper. The revolutionary began to mumble, as if in prayer, as he patted the air in front of Lazru and then started writing again.

He didn't believe your story. He doesn't believe it. But seeing you here will have cleared some of his doubts. You must do the rest, Amalina. Tell him what happened to Lucinda.

"I—" said Amalina, after reading the note, but was interrupted by the revolutionary's waving finger.

"Please, milady." He pointed to his ears and then around at the walls as if she didn't know, or needed reminding, there was a creature that could hear their quiet breaths through four foot thick stone walls, if he chose to. "I know you are young, but that does not excuse you from pursuing good works, and seeking absolution for your family. You understand. Let us focus ourselves on our work." The man tapped the paper and handed her the quill, and then pushed the bottle of ink in her direction.

What am I to say?

The revolutionary's dull mask frowned.

The absolute truth as you know it. But he must see it is your account, unrehearsed, unbidden.

"You mean—?" she asked.

"I mean, keep quiet, Countess. Keep still. Let us ask our creator for forgiveness of all our sins, and those of our forefathers." He pointed at the paper, an eyebrow tilted to show a little irritation.

Amalina wrote:

The Count—

she crossed this off.

I saw Lucinda murdered. It was the creature who did it.

The revolutionary looked at her statement and nodded. He turned the paper on the desk so that Lucinda's father could read it. Lazru's face became a square of teeth and tears amid bunches of whiskers.

The revolutionary wrote:

And that is why you are here, serving Tepsji? As punishment for witnessing this crime?

Amalina read and nodded. The revolutionary tapped the paper. She wrote her answer and it was shown to Lazru.

Now it was Lucinda's father's turn to write; in a heavy, laborman's hand that bent the soft quill almost to snapping.

Are you true? Are you sure?

Amalina read and then nodded.

Lucinda's father tried unsuccessfully not to cry out. He scrapped the paper. "Damn my eyes. I should rip them out!"

"Lazru," said the revolutionary, sternly. "Go sit in the corner. I won't have any more of your outbursts."

"They lied. They lied to me!"

"Lazru. Go. Sit. Down." The revolutionary didn't look troubled, but he did send long looks to the door and at the walls. "The Cardinal did not lie, and neither did I. We were very clear this would be a journey of prayer and contemplation. And if you wish to reform yourself, you will take guidance and example by the good Lady Tepsji here, who is less than half your age. And you will control yourself and observe silence. Do you understand me? Or shall I send you away and have the Cardinal remove you from the protection of St. Grigori?"

Tears were dropping from his red face and he was swinging his torso around in terrible fits of anger, reminding Amalina of Aklan and one of his childish tantrums. But this was something more serious of course. It was pure rage. Forgiveable rage, but rage.

"Perhaps a drink," Amalina suggested, holding out her cup.

"No," said Lucinda's father, suddenly stopping in the middle of the room, his shoulders slumped. "No, thank you, Countess. You are kind, but ... lead us not into temptation."

"Yes," said the revolutionary. "That would be inadvisable. Drink has been this man's crutch for too long. It is why he has sought to mend his ways. I believe, despite his behavior here, he has seen the light. And he knows his true path to righteousness and salvation."

Lucinda's father nodded. Then he unfolded the paper he'd crumpled and took up the quill.

Why?

Lazru splotted ink on the paper when he pointed to his question.

Amalina shook her head. She mouthed, 'I don't know.'

He pounded the table with his enormous hand, his muscled finger pointing again vigorously. And he shouted: "Why, girl? Why? Why!"

The revolutionary shot out his foot, Lucinda's father was suddenly rolling on the floor. The revolutionary was up and standing over the sobbing man.

"That's enough! The Cardinal trusted you were ready, but you have proven us wrong. Shame! It is time you rid yourself of your ghosts. 'Why' is not the question. You know there is no reason for anything on earth but the will of Heaven. It is man's duty to do the righteous work upon this plane of misfortune, regardless of why, and correct the misdeeds of himself and his fellow creatures here. Go, Lazru. Get out! We leave tonight."

Amalina had added a question to Lazru's note:

Why was she out that night?

But the revolutionary seized the paper and threw it into the fire. Lucinda's father stood and patted himself off. His face was still wet and angry, but his eyes had softened. She felt sorry for him, and wondered why this was necessary. What was the point in bringing him to the castle to meet with her?

But there was still the first question Amalina wanted to have answered, and so she began to write again on a new piece of parchment: *Why was Lucinda out—*

The revolutionary shook a finger at her.

"Replace your hood, Lazru," the revolutionary told Lucinda's father. "Prepare the horses and the sleigh. The Cardinal will be disappointed; even more so than I."

The hood nodded.

"You won't stay until tomorrow?" asked Amalina.

"Out of the question now," said the revolutionary. "Lazru, the unworthy, must return."

There was a knock at the door. It opened and Pils stepped in. "His Excellency."

The Count pushed through, sending Pils into the wood of the door.

"Katarina," said the Count. "Are you all right? There were raised voices."

Amalina bowed, the other two took her example. "Uncle ... It was nothing. The priest's servant, he—"

The Count's enormous brown eyes caught flame, the hooded figures before him were mirrored in the twin blazes. "And who is this?"

"A penitent, your majesty," said the revolutionary, calm, his bored expression on. He dared without flinching to place himself between the Count and Lucinda's father. "A wastrel, who the Cardinal had hoped was better than he is, and he thought would be of help in my mission here."

"Your mission?" this interested the Count and he transferred the shared-weight of his stare off Lucinda's father and dropped it fully on the revolutionary.

"Brother Rosczy was needed at the St. Grigori church. I was to cover for him during his absence. This man is my servant now, as your niece explained."

"Of course I knew this. But ... a wastrel?" said the Count, looking round the revolutionary to Lucinda's father again. "Yes, I see what must have happened. Have you lost yourself, or been saved, Lazru? That will be the question. If I am not mistaken, you once had two sons and a daughter. And you are now a long way from home."

Lucinda's father's head dropped, his hands squeezed together.

"He's had a tragic life, yes," said the revolutionary, as if observing an unfortunate chipped plate in the table setting. "But these things happen. He has lost his family and cast off his name, and now belongs to the church."

"And who are you?" said the Count, centering on the revolutionary once more. "I don't recognize you at all."

The revolutionary nodded as a slight bow. "Your excellency, I am Father Jon Farben. Recently relocated from Germania to Tsobl, and then to St. Grigori."

"Jon Farben," said the Count. "I haven't heard of you."

"As I said—"

"Yes. Yesssss. I know. There are many changes these days. The *influx*. I haven't been keeping up as I should. It is almost hard to keep up, but I do."

"Please excuse me and my man. I had no wish to disturb the peace of this castle—*your* castle. I am shamed, my lord."

"As long as my Katarina was not in any danger."

"Far from it. Lazru is a disturbed man, but would never harm an innocent young girl such as your niece. It would be unthinkable."

The Count petted his mustache with muted annoyance. "Your Cardinal is familiar with my peccadillos. I enjoy my peace and privacy, and I guard it jealously, Jon Farben. I do not suffer outbursts, religious or otherwise."

"Yes, your excellency. That is why I am removing myself and my man immediately."

"Very good. I have seen you now, John Farben. I have heard you. I will remember you." It sounded like a threat.

"Yes, your excellency."

"But I hope Father Farben will come again soon," said Amalina, trying to smooth any ideas the Count might have. "He's been my favorite so far. I'll see them out, sir."

The Count nodded and seemed to back out of the room on a set of rollers. "When Princess Margeta finds out what has happened, tell her I won't tolerate any more religious commotion. You make her understand, Amal— Ah, *Katarina*."

. . .

As Lucinda's father hurried to prepare the sleigh. Amalina led the revolutionary on a tour of the castle. She indicated doors and pointed up hallways and told him discreetly what could be found there. It was so much like the other times she'd shown potential revolutionaries through the castle that it felt terribly rehearsed, and Amalina became a little wilted by it. The man's eyes pinned everything with his dull look, calculating something triumphant in his head. But for Amalina, she saw another person preparing their own massacre. It wasn't too hard to picture his corpse sprawled in the courtyard without a head.

After showing Sadra's revolutionary to the upper pigeon coop in order to have him bless some of her pets, and to have him view the messenger pigeons that she would be sending to him when needed—"Five pigeons, still in cages," he commented as if running an inventory, without an expression on his slack face, though his bottom lip seemed to protrude a bit more—and she pointed out the hideous, greasy black ones which she didn't comment on other than to say "I can't imagine where *these* ugly ones come from, some friends of uncle's who aren't very clean" they went down to the courtyard. Amalina was surprised to find the sun was still up, but just about to drop behind the mountain ridge. It seemed like eternal night in the castle sometimes, and on top of that the revolutionary had already been received, read his services, debated, took confessions, and had conducted his interview, it should have been night by now. She said, "Oh, it's afternoon. But you must have arrived very early, which means you must have set out from Netz very, *very* early—"

"I didn't want your service schedule delayed for one minute, Lady Tepsji. Best not to have custom inconvenienced by personal matters."

"But what I mean is, it *is* afternoon, it will take you a while to get back to the village. Well into night."

"It *is* unfortunate I couldn't stay longer," said the revolutionary, observing the sky. "But whether it's the sun or moon as our guide, in our travels Lazru and I should be safe. God protects his allies. I hope." He motioned back at the castle's main building, "I'm afraid your uncle didn't leave us much choice to stay the night."

She took his hands in hers.

"I pray *your servant* will *recover*," she said, the words stilted. But she still wanted to know the point of it all. What was the reason to come and to survey, and more: to bring Lucinda's father and have her confess her truth to him? What was he up to? "I find you so agreeable, Father, you could have stayed here for months, but Lazru's incontinence necessitated your leaving. I don't really understand why *he* was needed at all."

"Milady, to relieve some men of their burdens, they need work. Lazru's vexations were drink, and his refusal to admit the truth. Even now he believes he was lied to by those who love him, though really he's been lying to himself all along. Well, anyway, perhaps this trip has opened his eyes enough to convince him; so that he better sees the light. And he will find the strength in himself to work again. To *work* for us ... and our *greater cause*."

Something clicked and Amalina understood. Lucinda's father had been the village's blacksmith. Its armorer. She felt a pit open in her stomach.

"You ... you aren't going to push him too fast to *return* to his work."

"I think that, despite his behavior, just meeting you today will have inspired him. He will begin again as soon as we reach the St. Grigori. I am confident of this."

"So fast?"

"Well, Lady Tepsji, with the brief life we have there is no time to waste."

How long would it take Lazru to build enough armor for this man's new army? she wondered.

Amalina turned and began to walk along the courtyard, slowly. She pointed to the gate, and said, as low as she could, but still conversationally, "Can you believe, this whole wall was destroyed the other year? Doesn't it look strong? You'd never know something so destructive happened."

"A natural disaster?"

"An army," she said, looking at him meaningfully. "They tried to kill the Count. But that never seems to work. You know, he has so many castles and people are always trying to blow them up. One here, one there. It's no more than a nuisance to us, really."

"So certain a fact must make you feel confident and secure in his protection."

She shook her head and continued, hoping to give out more information but also throw off any eavesdropper: "But when this happens to one of his castles, and this is why I bring it up, he'll get a messenger pigeon from one of his friends. Pretty little birds, not like those ugly ones up in the loft, but much prettier. And they come with a little bell on their legs, jing-jing-jinging—*jing-jing, jing*—like little warning bells, warning him of another fallen castle. Then, while he has to go off to assess the damage and pay for its repair, or have the structure just razed and salvage the parts, I get to have a new pretty pet for a little while, with the cute little bells. *Jing-jing-jing.*"

"Whoever repaired this gate did a splendid job of it," said the revolutionary. "You're right, I'd never have known. By the way, on my way in, I noticed two heads posted above it. Do you know who they were, and their crimes?"

Amalina's eyes goggled for a brief second before she could recover herself, what could she say about them that would be safe for the Count to overhear? And that wasn't what she was trying to tell him, to warn him. "I don't know. I don't know *who* they are. It happens from time-to-time, people who displease my uncle *who get caught.*"

"Caught doing what, I wonder," he said. "By the care taken to dust the snow off them, so that they can be seen clearly, they are not yet forgotten by their judge and executioner, and they must have struck a strong chord against him. Yet I would know their offense, so I can pray for their souls."

"I—" she hesitated. She could tell him one of them was once associated with the greasy pigeons. But how would that help? That the other one had tried to kill her. That the Count had killed them for her. But, really, she couldn't say any of that. Not out loud. And really, that didn't have anything to do with getting through his head what she needed to. "I really can't say. If you wish, I can ask him and send a letter down to St. Grigori. To be honest, I don't like to think of it, and we were talking about something else."

The revolutionary stared at her, thoughts running behind his inscrutable eyes, until he nodded.

"Anyway," she began again, sounding chatty, "whatever it was, Father, as I was saying before, the upstarts, the real, dangeous ones, never get anywhere against my uncle, blowing up his castles like that. It's just a nuisance, if you see what I mean by how well-repaired this old castle is and how he's still alive. But those pretty birds take uncle away for a time, which I tell you can be annoying for us ladies here. Left here all alone, to get up to whatever we'd like; and especially without our little church to occupy our time ... Okay, all right, I suppose sometimes it is a *relief* when he must go and survey the latest damage to another one of his castles, because we *can* get up to whatever we like when he's gone. *Whatever* we *want to do.*" She emphasized that last part with a look, then dismissed it with a wave of her hand. "Oh, perhaps I shouldn't admit *that* to someone like you, if I'm not in confession."

"Fear not," said the revolutionary. "And I take your meaning, Lady Tepsji. God willing, and that Lazru and I make it to Netz safely tonight, I will have the Cardinal send Rosczy straight back to you and your ladies, or someone even better suited to be a steward to your women. By tomorrow at the latest. The church will strive to keep you out of trouble when your lordship isn't around; and until I can return to enjoy your company again."

"Thank you. But I suppose I told you all this about our castle and gave you the tour because it is interesting history ... and I'm afraid you and Lazru will *never* be here again. *Shouldn't* be here again." She spoke with a heavier insistence.

Which he ignored and upped his own determination to have his way: "Don't fear what has happened in the past—the past *is* the past. And be assured, I *will* return."

"However I think it is best not to," said Amalina, her voice rising in pitch, her teeth gritted. *Listen to me*, she was thinking. She continued: "Never mind what I told my uncle inside just now, no matter how we might like you, you've upset him once, and that is enough. Better not to press your luck; think of those heads on the wall you saw. I recommend you send Rosczy, of course, just for his friendship with Margeta, and no one else. But even *he* isn't necessary. Oh, not to hurt your feelings, Father. I will still help you any way I can. But I assure you, I can take care of the ladies, the castle, and my uncle, *all by myself.*"

The revolutionary raised his eyebrow. His look said he was already putting his plan into motion, he did not want her attempting anything he would consider stupid or counterproductive to his cause.

But didn't he still need the map? Amalina mouthed the words: *The Map?*

"Thank you for the tour," he said. "It was good enough to lay my eyes on it, and satisfy my curiosity. But as for you and your lady friends ... *but maybe now more for you* ... Whatever purpose Heaven has given you in this life, and at this point you must know what it is, Heaven stops for no man—or young woman—and it only falls upon your conscience and your soul if you fail to do what is required of you before the hourglass runs out."

"Hourglass, Father?"

"Picture an hourglass, turned over, active, and with its contents draining from the upper chamber."

"Yes?"

"My advice to anyone is: the time is down to its last quarter, with the sand rushing fast."

"Oh, I see."

"Send a note if you change your mind," said Sadra's revolutionary, "or if your uncle does, or if you have something important you think I should know that you're willing to share. Perhaps about those men who lost their heads." He added in a darker tone: "I hope I didn't come here at the wrong time, Lady Tepsji. It seems I might have woken you from a deep and pleasant, and yet an unfortunate and untimely, sleep. I pray I am mistaken."

But he was right, Amalina had been asleep. She was awake now—wakened to the danger. The revolutionary, while she had been daydreaming in the high castle and forgetting about him, had been moving steadily forward with his plan, regardless of her task, and it was now closer than ever to happening. How many did he have in his army? Worse, was her father one of them, as Sadra had promised? How much time was left before the armorer had finished his work and it struck? Surely not before spring. How long was a quarter of an hourglass in the revolutionary's mind? It didn't seem very long at all. It seemed too soon. It seemed immediate.

Amalina's body jangled with alarm. She had to do something to stop him, or to slow him, but she could think of nothing in that moment. She felt so helpless against him that she panicked and hoped the Count would intercept the two on the way back to Netz, just to tear them to pieces out of precaution, stick *their* heads on the wall; or that one of his ladies would kill them for training or sport. It would be so much easier for Amalina—for everyone—if Sadra's man, this dead-eyed agitator, did not continue down a path that would get so many innocent people killed.

But she felt awful hoping the two might be ambushed. To counteract her disturbing and unbidden wish for their deaths, which she pictured in gory detail, Amalina blotted it out by praying they would make it safely through the night. She was ashamed, as well, to realize during this act of contrition that there was a part of her not so immediately concerned about the revolutionary and the inevitable bloody consequences of his plan, but more about how the attack on the castle would upset her life here, now growing so comfortable. It had been an embarrassing, selfish wish brought on by the shock of the revolutionary's unexpected visit; the same kind of shock experienced when she'd discovered that the man behind the murder service was still alive.

Only afterwards, when the revolutionary and Lazru Skeldar were well away, did Amalina think of what she should have done, what she should have said. She felt like a complete fool for not thinking of it at the time, but then ran up to the loft and quickly, and sloppily, jotted a note on a scrap of paper and tied it to the leg of one of her pigeons.

Find AXP in Korr, she had written. Then added, for Lucinda's father's benefit: *C.T. killed Lucinda, but it was this one, AXP, who told him to.*

Oh, it would have been so much better if she had told them while they were here—or had shown it to them in a note. Now she had to rely on the revolutionary receiving it down the road, when he returned to Korr, if he made it that far. Maybe she could find some reason to keep the Count in the castle tonight just to make sure they got away.

It was a perfect device, Amalina thought almost triumphantly about her message. Not just for her sake did she want the revolutionary to get through safely now all the way back to Korr and to read the note, so that Lucinda's father might be distracted from his work by a greater need for revenge against AXP, and thereby prevent or delay the revolutionary's plan. More importantly, the revolutionary might just root out this evil AXP, this man who so wanted Amalina killed; finally put a stop to the entire murder service, bring Lucinda's disquieted soul to rest, and perhaps make it so the Count no longer had to lie to Amalina, which had become such an unspoken discomfort between them. It was a bit of a selfish thing, this note, Amalina knew. But she needed help in solving the mystery of the real killer behind the murder service.

It just has to work, thought Amalina. To end the continued threat to her life and improve matters all around, Sadra's genius revolutionary would be the perfect weapon.

Amalina sent her first pigeon into the darkening sky.

44

The Next Thing She Knew

Once up in the sky, home was definitely—most *definitely*—to the right; just where the sun was going down along the curved line of earth. Home meant food. Home meant warmth. Home meant familiar scents and familiar faces. This thought was a pulling thought, a focusing thought.

In that thought, and then without further thinking, the pigeon flashed its wings and cut a declining course to follow the sinking sun. It wouldn't be long before she was home, maybe even before the darkness made sighting where home was became impossible and she would have to land and settle in for the night. That was a comforting idea, though: to rest on a branch or a sill somewhere, sheltered from the chilling winds. But better to be home. Fly to home. Home was the best, the safest spot to be in all the world.

Few other birds were in the air at this time. The pigeon saw most of them nestling underneath awnings of a house here, and poking out from under the protective arms of a tree there. But those birds were already "home". *Their* home. There'd be plenty of time for rest and to get comfortable when she, too, was within the embrace of her comfortable wood slats and seed bins.

Suddenly, with a shake of her neck, the earth below was magnified, and the pigeon realized she had plunged hundreds of feet. Then there was another shove and a searing pain tore through her shoulders.

Alarms rang through the pigeon's head and she shouted in protest and wheeled in the air to seek—to locate and evade—the threat. What had hit her?

The hawk was smaller than she was, but was looking angry and confident as it spun around the purple-blue sky, circling back to make another run. The pigeon couldn't know how lucky she was the hawk hadn't taken her out in one go, but only glanced its ripping talons through her backfeathers on a poorly timed kill.

The pigeon thought to climb out of reach of her attacker, who was swooping down on her at an impossible speed and likely couldn't correct itself. But with a wincing pain she knew she could not pull up, so she veered down in a zig-zagging line for the treetops.

But the claws nailed into her body and she felt the feathers break out of place, and small muscles snap, and saw the treetops flying at her out of control.

The branches cracked at her head and her body, the padding of snow barely softening the blow, even as the hawk's sharp beak tried to rip at the openings on her shoulder.

The world reeled as she spun and kicked and tried to fight back against this tiny killer, seeing her blood on its beak and hoping to give just as much back. She had to get home after all. She could not allow this monster—

No matter how she twisted her body to get her claws into the hawk, or to bat away its beak with her wings, the hawk's head shot in at her, snipping and scraping pieces of her.

They were on the ground now.

She saw a small house. And several more houses nearby. And she smelled the burning wood and cooking foods that were not unlike the smells around her home. But she was not *there*, and this was not the place. Home was still far away. And this hawk was cutting into her with its razor sharp beak—

The hawk dropped off.

She had given it one good kick. But when she tried to right herself, she heard the squawking and fluttering and knew something else had happened. It was difficult to stand upright, and her wing felt out of joint. She tried to flutter it, to straighten it out, but there was tremendous pain in doing so. The squawking continued. She remembered the hawk and the danger. She flopped to the side.

Only a few feet away, two large birds were dancing in a frenzy of feathers and warbles. Chickens, two hens. Big and brown and furious. They were stamping the hawk into the snow. As soon as one jumped away from the hawk's flashing claws, the other would land right on its head, giving it the same treatment. With their beaks and feet they were pulling large bloody tufts off the hawk. One yanked out its eye.

The pigeon turned in place and flapped her wings, preparing to take off. But the pain in her shoulder flashed. And suddenly she felt tired. Too tired to move. Too cold to move. She felt unwell and sat down in the snow.

The squawking was joined by some strange hoots of humans who had come out of their house to see what the commotion was. They jumped around at the periphery of the fight, shouting and clapping.

For the pigeon, the sky was becoming too dark to see, and she knew she could not find home now. Best just to rest. But she should find a better place to rest. Maybe under that small house that stood on stilts. When she tried to rise, things spun in her head once more, or she was tripping anyway, and fell beak first into the snow.

The next thing she knew, she was very cold and it was somewhere in the middle of the night. She tried to stand, to right herself. She couldn't.

The next thing she knew, she felt a little warmer and the sky was brightening, and she smelled blood in her nostrils.

The next thing she knew, her back was warm and it was late into the day and she was being poked in the side. It was a gentle poke. She tried to stand, but felt frozen into the snow. It felt more comfortable to ignore the poking and go back to sleep. In sleep there wasn't the cold and the pain in her shoulders.

The next thing she knew, she was in human hands. The hold was firm and comforting, like the human in her home. It was saying something that was familiar and reassuring. But this was not home, it couldn't be. It didn't smell right. It didn't feel right.

She was put into a box with straw and some bits of food which she didn't feel like eating. She still couldn't stand. She still wanted to sleep. That is what she did.

. . .

The next thing she knew, she was being held a little too firmly. There was another human there, shouting loudly and grabbing at her with its huge hands. It felt dangerous. The two were squawking at each other just like those hens over the hawk. What had happened to those birds? It felt so long ago.

How many days had she slept?

Groggily the pigeon peered beyond the immediate threat of the humans to get her bearings. They were traveling across the snow, but now were entering one of the houses. It was warm inside and the light was bright. But the humans squawking at each other and how the one clutched tighter onto her small body was very uncomfortable. She would have liked to remain outside and out of their smelly hands.

The next thing the pigeon knew, she was thrown into a puddle of water. But before she could fly out of it, a black lid came clanging down on top. And then she realized how hot the water was. It was making noises and bubbling all around her, and the air seared her lungs. She fluttered upward but struck her beak against a solid black barrier. She began to scream in a panic.

Suddenly the lid was gone. A larger human stuck their head down at the water but then launched backward with a loud yowl. The pigeon saw her chance and flew out of the bubbling hot water and zoomed up to the ceiling and out of the range of all the humans' grasping hands. As they yelled, one tried to push a long stick at her. She evaded it, while fluttering her feathers to get the water out of them, feeling the pain in her shoulders but knowing if she gave into it she would be stuck back down in that water.

A door at the end of the room swung open, and just inside it the largest and hairiest human of them all barked angrily, hands on hips. But the door was open, cold air curling in around its frame, freedom beckoning to the pigeon.

The pigeon hopped off the wood beam and darted expertly through the opening between the human and the doorway.

Then she was up and away again, flying as high as she dared, needing to get away from all that danger, fearing what might be ahead. The sun was dropping down low again. She was bewildered because it seemed it was dawn. She didn't know what time it was, or how much energy she had within her, or even if she could trust her inner bearings which way was which.

But there was something inside that was fully determined: she had to get home. She thought nothing of the little white scroll tied to her leg.

45

Establishing Patterns

While the high castle was still in view, Attila could not help turning round on the cart's seat to look back at it, to see if he could spot the head on its wall. Even after all he'd learned and accomplished with the visit there, his mind was caught and troubled by the head he'd noticed displayed on an iron skewer high up above the gate. The head with fading green skin. The one that must have once been the odious little man in Korr who had almost had Attila killed. Just the odd coloring had caused Attila to recall his face, that terrible moment in the alley. And for the better part of a guess, the savaged head next to that squat green one had belonged to his friend, the one who'd done the cutting. For what reason both had been killed and exposed in such a manner, Attila did not know yet. But it brought out a disagreeable feeling of satisfaction within him. A sickening enjoyment at the reversal of their combined fates—the taste of revenge. He could feel their hands on him, the knife, the momentary burst in his chest of terror and loathing at their smug smiles when his death was at hand; and now they'd gotten it right back. Attila was good enough to realize it was with this sickeningly sweet taste of revenge he meant to ploy into action the man sitting next to him. Now, was that the right thing to do? And was it this forbidden taste secretly driving Attila against the creature? Was it the reward—this buoyant predatory energy—he was after, instead of simply carrying out what was morally right and expected of him as a man sworn to the law? Wouldn't that be wrong? He calmed himself.

The other troublesome aspect to what was brewing in Attila's body, was an almost need to express his supreme exhaltation: that his would-be killers had been punished! Justice was done! Ha, ha! He wished he could scream it out. To turn to Lazru Skeldar and confide to the poor man. But Attila hadn't fully let go of reason, and knew both information and trust are a commodity. And since how the green man's head got removed was still a question, one line of possibility was that the Count had learned that this fellow, his secret agent, had failed to kill an upstart in Korr. And how would he have found out that, but there was someone else close to Attila, on the inside, informing him of the failure? So Attila couldn't trust mentioning the fate of the green man, or what it meant, or even the head on a spike, at all to anyone, not at so vulnerable a point in the operation. He would have to keep it to himself for a while longer, not saying the least bit of anything about it, even to his closest allies, even ones who seemed to share his interest and had protected him so far; even to test them. Not until the release of such information was necessary or useful.

But he knew it would be a challenge to hold back with the knowledge and question of it—and the dismaying delight, which he recognized as a stranger he didn't know had always been there—burning inside him. Luckily he had other things to work with. Better things. More productive things. He calmed himself again.

He still had a mission that was clarifying by the minute. Lazru Skeldar had been positively turned. Next would come the Cardinal, a trickier one, and getting what he needed from him.

* * *

Once Attila had returned to St. Grigori, he soberly asked the Cardinal, who was kneeling before the scores of candles of the side altar, "Do you know where Count Tepsji's properties are?"

The Cardinal motioned with his right hand that he wasn't done with his prayers.

Attila lowered his voice but did not stop: "During excursions into the wilder parts of Ardeel, I made an assessment of his many holdings, his castles, or what remains of them, and his forts and holdouts."

With a reserved look of patience the Cardinal stood, crossed himself, and then gestured for Attila to follow. They walked silently through the church to his private quarters.

"My predecessors left extensive maps of Ardeel and its mountain ranges," said the Cardinal in a rather opaque way, but obviously trying not to fall short of Attila in valuable information. "I have added to those maps where I could with what I've learned through my own sources."

"You'll show them to me," said Attila. "All of them. And I will improve them with my own findings."

"If there are improvements to be made."

"And I trust you're aware of his extensive network of secret informants." Attila tried not to look accusingly at the Cardinal. "You know who they are or how to locate *them*?"

The Cardinal nodded. His lips were pursed shut, and not about to open.

"Some of these operatives communicate with the Count through messenger pigeons," Attila pressed on, recalling the information the Dalca girl had given him, as she'd seemingly tried to warn him off. "Some of these birds are specialized for emergencies; for when one of his properties or castles is under attack. Apparently they have bells on their legs and that is how they can be identified. You will need to seize them immediately. All of them. At our pleasure, we will use them to bother our opponent up in his castle, make him think he is under a constant, ill-timed assault."

"Ruffle his feathers," smiled the Cardinal.

"If there is trouble finding his allies, you might try isolating your search to the people who are spreading certain rumors. It seems the Count has begun a strange campaign to wipe out the memory of the honorable knight and general, Zsolt Marosh, and replace him with a nobody named Vezel Umalasju. A bizzare effort to rewrite history to his liking, I suppose, but will be beneficial to rooting out his agents. I suggest you also look into the national constabulary. As the high constable himself was championing this General Vezel Umalasju to my face, maybe best begin with him."

Attila placed a finger on his own lip, physically preventing it from moving. It would be easy to mention now one such secret agent to the Count, one with green skin who'd been in Korr and had almost killed him, and had had his head stuck on a spike above the Netz castle's gate. It would be interesting to gauge his reaction. He quieted the pressing urge.

"Interesting. If a stranger witnessed this conversation, they would think you are in charge." The Cardinal cocked his head. "But you aren't. Why am *I* to do this?"

"You've the manpower spread through all the cities and towns. And I don't have the time."

"Because you're returning to Korr," he said with open displeasure. "You've found their rough nature to your liking; though I did warn you of the dangers. Returning for what? After all this time, you haven't gained access to their Secret History?"

"I've made good progress in other areas."

"But still no History. Which was your stated purpose for going there."

"I need as much information as I can get."

"I know your fetish for information, and your ways of triangulating and establishing patterns. And still, the pattern begins to emerge that you still haven't seen their book—for whatever you think its worth."

"I haven't."

"They likely recognize your interest in it and are withholding it to keep you captivated, and your money—which is *my* money—flowing." At the mention of flowing he poured a goblet of wine and pushed it toward Attila. "I wonder if I shouldn't keep you here for a little while, out of their hands, to see if the book fever of yours won't break."

"Cardinal," said Attila with the slightest warning tone, eyeing the goblet, recalling the Cardinal's penchant for poisoning those who don't fall into line, "this trip was funded by my own means, so you should not be as put out about it as you seem. And I shouldn't have to feel the need to watch over my shoulder every time we're together."

"I don't know why you do," said the Cardinal, with a vacant, dismissive shrug. "I saved your life. And that is also why I hold the high hand, and why I should be the one giving instruction and not the other way around. Has our adversary given you ideas, so that *you* have taken to rewriting the history of matters?"

"Neither one of us is in the position to dictate to the other—" here the Cardinal shrugged again, but with an added smirk "—however it is *my* plan. Who else would be giving orders then?"

"You are working under my auspices, former low constable, and with my generosity. Barring this most recent trip, I have provided everything you've needed to this day, and am prepared to do so *ad infinitum*—"

"I will need armor," said Attila, cutting him off. "I'm sure many suits can be found among the older nobility who have fallen on harder times. Take them from Tepsji's castles, too, if you can. The caretakers won't miss them. But it must be done quietly, discreetly. Push it as a tithing, maybe. Then you will ready them for transportation to Korr. I trust you have space to store them until I can arrange for the move?"

"I have ample storage. I even have some of the suits of the knights who fell to the Count so long ago. They are in the catacombs and in the mausoleums of St. Grigori's graveyard. Quite a number of them died at his hands, in that armor. But you can have it all, of course, if you imagine you have a use for it."

Attila looked to the Cardinal and wondered if what he'd said was meant as a reminder of the danger of confronting the Count or demoralizing sabotage. But he did not react, other than to take a drink of the wine. "All the better. Bring everything together here, along with the birds and their handlers, and we will have an auspicious spring."

The Cardinal did not look satisfied.

"Is there something else?" asked Attila.

"You've taken up with the invaders' church in Korr," said the Cardinal with a matter-of-fact tone, but a downturn of his lips. The point of mentioning this was to prove he had his own informants all the way to Korr. No surprise. As long as they weren't shared with the Count.

"Yes, I have," said Attila, taking his turn to show he hides nothing. "They are of great assistance."

"Assistance? Do you mean *they* paid for your trip here?"

"No."

"No," nodded the Cardinal. "You understand there is a true Ardeelian church in Korr, at your full disposal. A Roman church."

"Not well attended," answered Attila. "Your man Perdu is no man of the people, like yourself. But the real problem is the minister of the new western church, Minister Smidt has made many converts—almost all of them taken from your church—by his closeness to the people and their needs."

"… And the greater flood of outsiders who are keen to that weak brand," sneered the Cardinal. "But yes, this failure was an oversight by my predecessor. He had a laziness or complacence in our church's station: that we would never lose our flock to the outsiders. But Bishop Perdu, whatever his shortcomings, *is* my man. He is trustworthy and can help you much more easily if you are operating with him, and not with the various outsiders there."

Attila did not try to appear as if considering it, but answered right away: "If I switched allegiances right now I might lose the trust of those with whom I am already established. Especially if I seem to shift loyalty upon my return from meeting with you. It would seem to everyone, even to me, that I'm nothing more than your pawn, at your disposal. Best to let things remain steady for everyone's comfort. When the time is right, I will see about opening them to your man's inclusion."

"Heed me, Attila," grumbled the Cardinal in the same tone he'd used when first trying to warn Attila away from Korr, "it is to your good: Perdu's the only man there who is on your side. He is on your side because I control him. The rest are fickle, unpredictable, and as brutal and stubborn and ignorant and dangerous as wild boars. I see you must know what I mean." He made a slashing motion along his jawline and then pointed to the scar on Attila's neck. "You see, I am observant, too. And I am certain Bishop Perdu didn't put that there."

"I take your point," said Attila, feeling his scar begin to itch. It agitated a pressure inside him. "Oh that reminds me. There are a couple heads mounted to the Count's gate. I think I recognized one of them, I might have seen him in Korr, of all things. Not entirely sure. You wouldn't know anything about who they are, or what happened to them?"

"Mounted on the gate?" The Cardinal shook his head with a look of distaste. "Rosczy hadn't told me. But then it sounds all the more like Korr isn't an easy harbor. Whether you agree or not. Good to have trustworthy friends there, however *unpopular*."

Attila nodded. From the Cardinal's reaction and tone, his continued push toward Father Perdu, he knew nothing on the subject of the green man; he hadn't been informed. The question had been a test for the Cardinal which he'd passed—or so it seemed, but Attila chided himself, anyway. In asking, he'd given into his urges; a dangerous thing. He'd enjoyed that little release, but it would only get worse from there if he continued to indulge them. From now on, he vowed, he'd bury the thoughts entirely, and never say another word about the green man and his chum—the dead heads on the wall; never give into weakness or that tickling impulse. Fix himself tight against it and keep his information close, mind carefully his people, and observe. Because *someone* could not be trusted.

Presently, he said to the Cardinal: "Understood. For my part, I will try to not get myself killed in their company, and also find a way to fold your Bishop Perdu into our efforts. For your part, assuming I succeed, please have everything I've requested ready here upon my return."

"Of course. Shall I say a blessing over this, our honorable work?"

46

AXP
or
Hello Again …

What a complete fool! thought Amalina, beating herself up all over again for the note she'd sent Sadra's revolutionary. *What a complete waist of a bird!* But to be fair, in her haste, with snowflakes on her hands and sprayed across the board where she wrote it, she'd given herself little time to scribble it down. There'd been no time for her to think. Well now, she'd be lucky if it wasn't all a blur of damp ink at the receiving end. And maybe she would be lucky if it turned out illegible, so that any potential spy intercepting the note could not immediately report the information to his master. A spy would probably find more to capitalize on in the message than Sadra's revolutionary would to help:

> Find AXP in Korr. C.T. killed Lucinda, but it was this one,
> AXP, who told him to.

What would the revolutionary make of it? What *could* he make of it? Amalina hoped AXP was someone's initials and not an acronym that would lead to a larger riddle. But by the sophistication of AXP's code, she could only assume it was yet another screen of some kind. All the little slips of paper in the book, regardless of the cipher used for their message, concluded with the big block Roman letters AXP. So it must be some alternate identifier.

Oh well, thought Amalina with a shrug, no point in worrying about the message now. She would have to make sure to put better thought into it next time. For now, she just had to trust the note would get to Sadra. And then the shrewd revolutionary would, if he could, solve whatever puzzle was there.

He'd solve it, that is, if Amalina could not find the solution first! Because what else was there to do in the castle? She saw nothing more demanding of her time, not for weeks at least, until the revolutionary set up his invasion, other than to continue her own investigation into her secret nemesis, AXP.

• • •

Amalina sat at her desk, swept clean of distraction, and leaned back in her chair, concentrating deeply. Her glasses rested on her forehead, her eyes were tired. There would be no reading this time. This time she was going to work inside her mind.

As she ruminated on the letters AXP, they flashed before her. Briefly illuminating something within her memory. Something familiar, but remote. She had seen the letters before. Years ago. Back in Korr, it seemed. It must be. She tried to remember her customers; had they ever signed their names or initials to an order? Had she ever seen anyone's name written down anywhere? She'd witnessed many of their names in the Secret History of the Sheriff of Korr. Wouldn't she have seen the initials there? Or that style of hand for a signature?

She could picture the lettering on those pages of the contract, though only in a haze. She was forcing the letters there.

But she had seen AXP written somewhere else. She was certain. Maybe not too long ago. But long enough to make it feel like ancient history. Initials seen once and she'd not realized they would be important later. Now that those letters' value was realized, it was impossible to recall.

Maybe I'm doing this wrong, she thought.

Turning it to look from a different direction, Amalina considered things anew: AXP was the primary player in the mystery, so it was time to think of this exactly like a mystery: not who AXP was as a specific name, whose matching initials could be tracked down, but who, among the many, could AXP be? Amalina knew this shadowy figure wanted her killed, presumably because she knew too much about the murder service. So she was a threat to him and his enterprise. But he had also had Lucinda Skeldar killed. What reason could someone have for that? Lucinda had been a pathetic young woman with a hobbled leg, who wasn't very popular even among the group of bad girls she was associated with. A sad loner. How could she be a threat to anyone?

Now Amalina sat back further and closed her eyes tight, and returned to the night she'd seen Lucinda die. Something she never did by choice and tried to shake out of her head when the memories came to her unbidden— with images of torn flesh and flowing blood. It was years ago but she could still remember it perfectly when she wanted: Lucinda's uneven gait as she stomped out of an alley, headed toward the fateful intersection ...

Lucinda Skeldar had come from an alley. Had she met someone there? Was she taking a shortcut? She wasn't on her way home; that would have been in the other direction. At the time, by the speed and sureness of her path, Amalina had assumed Lucinda might even be heading out of town.

Amalina remembered the several times she herself was led out of town by Genadie—or other circumstances caused by the Count—sneaking out to a hidden carriage. Was Lucinda's night walk the same kind of rendezvous, perhaps with Genadie in the forest with the Count's carriage awaiting her?

• • •

"Avenge me!" came Lucinda's voice.

As suddenly as the voice sounded, Amalina was in a summer field of barley, and Lucinda's head could be seen in the distance, bobbing toward her.

"Oh, please, I beg of you! Kill my killer, Amalina!"

• • •

Amalina lurched up in her chair. She'd fallen asleep, and the nightmare had come. That was no help. She was wasting time.

Maybe it was better to look at the scene from the reverse end: The afterwards, when Amalina heard on every excited breath that Lucinda had been killed by wolves in the forest, her body discovered by Gulgas on his early morning hunt. It was a lie circulated by everyone in town, even her father, Dragomir. And maintained, most incredibly, by the Street Sweeper and Lygo the Painter, as they and Amalina stood over the spot where Lucinda had been killed, her blood still evident between the hurriedly washed cobblestones.

What of *that*?

Most of the men in Korr had signed the abominable contract permitting the Count to take victims as he saw fit—which allowed everyone else to live peacefully in the mountains without the threat of mass slaughter. But not everyone knew of the Count's murder service for AXP. Presumably only AXP, the Count, and a precious few others were in on it, or else there would be no need for such thorough secrecy in their correspondence. So on the morning after her death, everyone pretending that Lucinda had been killed by the wolves in the forest had only been protecting the Count and preserving their infamous agreement with him; maybe with some of the more innocent people pushing the lie even further than what was originally intended. But there was at least *one* who knew exactly why Lucinda had been selected.

And more: maybe most everyone thought she *had* been killed in the forest, and only AXP and his minions in this malign 'service' knew where she had really died; in the streets of Korr. But if that were true, it would mean Lygo the Painter and the Street Sweeper were deeper in than the others: Lygo had washed the blood off the cobblestones (right outside his home!) before morning; the Street Sweeper had helped him with his lies in covering the Count's tracks.

Could Lygo the Painter be the AXP mastermind? While the killing had taken place right in front of his building, it must have been a coincidence of timing. What reason would he have for killing Lucinda? Then again, the fancy polished metal letters on the AXP book, and the expert penmanship lines of the block letters in the messages, suggested someone with a fine eye for style. And who else could draw such accurate pictures of his intended victims? But Lygo wasn't very bright at all, beyond his genius with paints, which was his true medium; he was rather confused and bumbling and wouldn't be up to conceiving or executing a complex code system. Or was his absent-minded stupidity a put-on, to cover himself? No, he wasn't that cunning. And still, if it was Lygo, how would he have sway over the Count, to get him to agree to such a service?

The Street Sweeper had seemed to be more in charge of the coverup, the way he coached the stammering Lygo through his lies on that morning following Lucinda's death. And the Street Sweeper wasn't just someone who maintained the cleanliness of the streets, he was the one who lit the lamps, and was on the street patrol on nights the patrol was required.

A heavy feeling grew in her stomach. She tried to remember the Street Sweeper's face that morning; whether his expression might have said more than just the awareness of Korr's original sin: their compliance with the Count. Could he have been trying to tidy over his own crime, instead? His face took on a more sinister light. What was his name, then? Were his initials AXP? Could AXP stand for Street Sweeper somehow?

But she couldn't remember his real name. She'd always thought of him, rather childishly she now realized, as 'Street Sweeper', *Mazindstrazi*. The only other name she'd called him was 'Broom Man'. Cristine had dubbed him 'Clean Sweep'. But his name didn't really matter, she couldn't believe he was guilty. Not the Street Sweeper. Not after growing up with his friendly face and helpful lectures.

But, in a turn of thought, he *had* been part of the mob that had almost ransacked her family's store during the baker's strike, and had threatened to string up her father. She could still see his wide open mouth during that mania, his teeth bared. Street Sweeper had a selfish, hateful, vicious side; which made it easy to think poorly of him if she wanted.

But an enactor of heartless assassination? It seemed impossible. And she couldn't imagine him associating with those awful Men of Death, which he would have had to've. Or carrying on a personal relationship—even through letters—with the Count? How would that even begin?

Amalina sat bolt upright again.
Then she ran from the room.

. . .

Amalina stalked along the book cases in the Great Library, scanning and considering the many books on the shelves. Then, in the next second, she ran her eyes down a list of titles (in her own handwriting) listed in the library's catalog, which she held open in her hand. After five circuits of the library and one run-through of the catalog, she realized she needed to do either one or the other: search the cases or scour the catalog. Not both at once.

She needed to calm down. She knew the book would be there. She'd written it into the catalog.

When considering how the Street Sweeper—how anyone—would begin a secret relation with the Count, it had suddenly come to Amalina where she'd first encountered the AXP signature. A manual of some kind; a message trapped in its margins, with a return note from the Count himself. A correspondence! Perhaps their first before they'd moved to the pigeons.

She could picture the letters clearly. Now she only had to find the book amid the thousands of volumes crowding the shelves. She couldn't recall what its cover looked like, so she opened the catalog on her lap, put her finger on the first entry and read down from there. It had to have been one of the early ones. But would she really recognize the title?

"This must be like heaven for you," said a familiar, crystalline voice.

. . .

Amalina hadn't heard anyone enter the library. While it wasn't unthinkable one of the Ladies might wander in, maybe guided by a helpful servant where to find her and had slipped in unannounced, this wasn't one of them.

"Still reading, even with a whole castle at your disposal. I shouldn't be surprised. You never change." Cristine petted the backs of the chairs as she stiffly bounced her way to Amalina, her exaggerated steps like a challenge, or revelling in a small, personal victory. "Though I see you're wearing glasses now. Very cute!"

But then Cristine stood above Amalina, presenting herself for inspection, holding out the wide skirt of a new dress. A pretty, fashionable, western style dress.

"What are you doing here?" said Amalina, astounded. She put aside the catalog but did not reach out. Cristine's off-putting posture and strange expression held her back. "How did you get here? How did you get in?"

There had been no bell for a new arrival. Had there?

"Is it so impossible?" Cristine's cold eyes flashed. "Aren't you happy to see me?"

"Well, of course!" Amalina sat forward and took one of Cristine's hands. It was freezing. She'd just arrived then, after the long sleigh ride from Netz. Yes, and her cheeks were flushed from the cold. She had rushed into the castle, shed her coat and beelined to Amalina. But that still didn't explain how or why she was here. "Of course, my dear, I just wasn't expecting it—"

Then she heard the laugh. The low rumble of a snicker.

There, in the doorway, stood the Count, grin in place, eyes sparkling with amusement.

"Surprise!" he said. "A surprise, just for my little mouse."

"Sir? What's happening?" Amalina couldn't be sure she wasn't dreaming.

"What's happening is I'm here," said Cristine, with a stamp of her foot and throwing her arms open for a hug.

Amalina forced herself off the chair and hugged her cold friend.

"Aren't you surprised, Katarina?" said the Count. With meaningful emphasis on the name he'd used.

"But—"

The Count tapped the air with his hand and held another finger before his lips. "My dear Katarina. I can't say I don't enjoy the expression of shock on your face. It means our little surprise for you worked to perfection."

"But ... how?"

"Simple enough," he said. "When I found your friend here in my forest, where you so heartlessly stowed her, out of sight of our guests, I suppose, out of needless worry of their reaction to an old friend, she explained herself, and her relation to you. And then the game was on, wasn't it?" He grinned and winked at Cristine. "I couldn't have her show up with no proper wardrobe and what she wore—damp and covered with the mud and dust from the road. I sent her back home, promising me to say nothing of our encounter—" Amalina flashed a look at Cristine "—but that I would honor your wish to see your old best friend from Korr, and when the time was right send a card and an envelope, and with a small flag—" here he presented from a pocket in his housecoat, a small colorful silk only a little larger than a handkerchief "—that she should display on her approach to the castle, so that the castle guard, who I had given special instructions to, would not sound the bell, but alert me to Ms. Berzwecken's arrival, and to keep you, my little mouse, unaware. So that we might spring this delightful surprise. Now, admit it, you have been taken!"

"Yes, sir."

"Don't look like that, though," said Cristine, disappointed. "I'm here, as you *wanted*."

"It's just," said Amalina, unable to process the image of both Cristine and the Count within the same view. "I ... I could never have imagined. But thank you uncle, how generous of you. Only, I can barely tell it is my Cristine. Here, let me open the drapes so we can get some real light in here."

As Amalina headed for the immense, double-thick curtains which held back the sunlight behind the two-story set of windows along the far wall, the Count shifted with a start for the door.

"I'll see that Cristine's apartment is made up, while I leave you two to reacquaint yourselves."

He was out the door with a slam before Amalina could sweep open the curtains. They both blinked hard at the blast of sunlight that filled the room.

"I can't believe you did that," said Amalina, rejoining Cristine, as her friend smiled a sharp, naughty smile at her.

"But you are happy, aren't you? I found a way in."

"You didn't tell me you'd met him in the forest! You acted like you didn't even know him."

"That was all part of his plan."

"I can't believe it. We're never supposed to lie to each other. Only the truth between us. Nothing held back."

"Well, a lie for the greater good," said Cristine, eyes radiating her excitement as she took in the immense size of the Great Library. "That's all right."

"I guess it is," said Amalina, struggling to return her smile. "And we'll find a way to fit you in, I'm sure, now that you are here and you have my 'uncle''s blessing."

"Fit me in," she said sourly. "Thanks."

"It's not like that. You know what I mean. But how did you—do your parents know? Or did you run away again?"

"They know."

"They let you come *here*?"

"To visit Katarina Tepsji, niece to a wealthy Count, at her invitation, to the Netz Castle? How could they not?"

"They didn't ask you about ... ? Since when did you know a Lady Katarina Tepsji?"

"All these ladies here aren't your *real* friends, you know," said Cristine, with a slicing lilt. "Why should they get to enjoy your company and not me? That's what I figured, anyway. And you know I get what I want, when I want it bad enough."

Cristine did have a way of working on, and wearing down, her parents; her father, anyway. What must she have said to get this favor? A new, fashionable dress and a trip to the Count's castle? *The Count's castle!* Even her father, the Boss, more indulgent as he was than her mother, must have been reluctant to give in, no matter how sweet or cutting her words. He had to have signed the secret contract with the Knight of Ardeel just like any other man in the village. If he had his suspicions, if he connected 'Count Tepsji' with the 'Knight' of old, he knew what a monster he really was. He must know. Then to send his daughter there?

Amalina leaned forward and whispered cautioningly, "We already talked about this: I'm not Amalina here, they don't know who I really am. So they aren't spending time with *me*, your friend, but—"

"But isn't that just what I said?" said Cristine. "They aren't your real friends. And that means they're eating up your time. I would like some of it for myself. You know I'm quite jealous and I couldn't take the thought anymore."

"But if you are here visiting with me—with *me*—you can never let them know who I really am—"

"I know, I know. Your 'uncle' made it clear enough. And why should I care? And why should *they*? Katarina Tepsji can be familiar with a daughter of a wealthy businessman from her homeland, can't she?" said Cristine. "It's not like my family is *unworthy*. And don't worry, *Lady Katarina*, I can keep any secret you'd like. *Won't that be fun?*"

"Then there's the danger, Cristine," she said, even quieter now. She brought her mouth close to Cristine's ear. "The Count. *He's more dangerous than you know*. Than you could ever *think!*"

Cristine pulled back and held Amalina by the shoulders. She laughed behind a razor-sharp grin. "Thank you, my sister! You *were* going to tell me, weren't you? Not to scare me, but because you care about me so much. Something you would never dare tell anyone you were about share with me … But I already know. I already know *everything* about him."

"About …?"

"About your 'uncle', Count Tepsji. Father told me about him. *Warned* me. Like you were going to do just now. But anyway, I know, my dear. Everything."

"*Everything?*"

Cristine laughed again, and nodded.

Amalina returned to a whisper, to remind her extreme caution was necessary, "And you came here anyway?"

She winked and squeezed Amalina's hand. "I'll tell you what I told Papa Szeful, *Papa the Boss*: 'If my best friend is in that castle—and then to add to *her* more than a dozen *royal* daughters from all over this continent—that castle would seem to be the safest place for me to be in all of Ardeel. Perhaps in all the world.'"

"But it isn't—"

"Pardon, milady—ladies," said Pils, rushing to the window and closing the heavy drapes. The light went out and it seemed the room was completely black for a second. "The Master of the House prefers the drapes closed. And the Master of the House says I should escort Lady Berzwecken to her rooms, they are ready. We will be dining in *l'entrée grande* in a couple hours."

"Oh, of course," said Cristine, bursting over with pure joy. "Lead the way, Pils."

"Yes, milady. Right this way."

"So you *are* staying?" said Amalina, having difficulty believing this was really happening; as if Cristine was just another dream apparition like Lucinda.

"If you'd be kind, my sister, and take your nose out of a book for once, I'd like a tour of the place after I get out of these riding clothes." Her honed smile sharpened more. "Really looking forward to my *official* introductions."

… and Good Bye

"**M**y god, sir, why did you bring her here?" Amalina nearly cried at Tepsji in his private study.

His eyebrows went up, as the corners of his mouth plunged down. Then all his features seemed to quiver. "I'm not suddenly your god now, am I?"

"What?" said Amalina, thrown from her anger. "No."

"Then you won't use that tone with me. And take off those glasses when you don't need them. I loathe them, and you certainly don't need them to see me. And you can at least knock, or say hello, before barging in."

"Yes, sir." She snatched the glasses from her face, trying not to lose whatever intensity she could. "Hello, sir."

"And I didn't appreciate that trick with the curtain, Ms. Dalca. But I suppose it was so you could speak privately to Ms. Berzwecken, so I allowed it."

"Yes, sir. But why did you bring her here, sir?"

"I didn't bring her," he answered. "I allowed her. You know, she is the first person to ask to come to my castle, to stay here, without being requested."

"Besides General Marosh."

"Who?" said the Count with a downward curl at the corner of his mouth. "Don't recognize the name. I don't mean interlopers, anyway."

"But Cristine," said Amalina. "Why her? She's my best friend."

"And so why not? It would seem only natural she should join us."

"From Korr. She's not from the west."

"She couldn't be expected to be, she is your childhood friend."

"She isn't royal blood. How can she fit in?"

"In our limited interactions, I've learned much of this dear friend of yours. Did you know her father is in a trade that brings an income twice that of the Tsobl governership and the entire council combined? And in the practice of his trade, there are points within the year that his company possesses more explosive powder than the occupation army?"

He paused to see if he'd impressed Amalina with his newly gained information. She might have rolled her eyes.

"Now what is power, if not that?" he concluded when she didn't react. "Well, anyway, he is extremely wealthy, and from an ambitious family, and so I felt your friend should fit in nicely. And besides being a fine addition to our various personalities, I wonder if she won't be an excellent draw for all that excess energy you seem to have in your off hours, when not seeing to our guests. With your mysterious special projects." He waited for Amalina to make a comment. "No, you see, I think she will be quite perfect here."

"But it is ..." Amalina shook her head, trying to force out what she wanted to say. "It's dangerous. Here. For her."

"How so? As far as I see it, it isn't dangerous for her in the least. As a matter of fact, your alleging it is somehow unsafe for my new guest has me a little hurt, if not offended."

"How can it not be, sir? Don't you remember what happened here? With the Germanian delegation?" Amalina nodded her head, not wanting to name any names, but to make him understand.

"Ms. Berzwecken's not here to arrest you, is she?"

"It *is* dangerous here, sir, for her," insisted Amalina. "This castle. Its environment; inside and all around it. Absolute peril—"

"Said the one who kept her most cherished friend out in my woods, at night, alone, and without protection. Let me tell you, if I hadn't been curious and stopped to understand what a beautiful young woman was doing, lurking outside my castle, and had she not, at my appearance, uttered the name 'Amalina', thinking I were you, while my night would have concluded more quickly and to my satisfaction, for you and her, it would have been a much different story."

Amalina looked down from his eyes. So it *could* have been worse that night.

"And imagine the story I heard from her pretty lips, eh?" the Count went on. "And you never mentioned her to me, did you? Or this encounter. Or this rendezvous. All these things you kept hidden from me? Why, Ms. Dalca? It is surprising."

"I don't know, sir."

"I don't want to accuse you of having a devious nature. But it becomes increasingly more possible I must come to that unfortunate conclusion. From what Mr. Balbo reported to me after my finding Ms. Berzwecken in the woods. A secret with my Katrina. And what Genadie has told of your adventures in France."

"What Genadie told you?" said Amalina in surprise.

"You think I don't debrief Genadie, as I do you, upon your return?"

Amalina flushed. *That traitor!*

"I am thorough. And I know everything. Have I not impressed that upon you yet? However, I can only blame myself for your condition. You now bear the marks and regrettable reflexes of a compulsive liar. Entirely my fault by enlisting you into my service at such a tender age. Flauna was a professional, and old enough to know herself. I hate to think it might have corrupted my little mouse."

"I'm sorry, sir."

"I believe I've caught you in time. You are my innocent, as always, if you've only become misguided by circumstances. But we must have trust in each other if we are to succeed here. I do trust in you, and am confident that we both shall no longer keep secrets from each other? Do you agree, Ms. Dalca?"

Amalina nodded, still looking at the floor. "Yes, sir. But Cristine ..."

"We weren't speaking of her."

"Does she have to stay here, sir?"

"That decision I leave up to her. She asked to be here. She wants to be here. So 'why not'?"

"Whatever she told you, I never asked her here. And why not? Because what I keep telling you, and I will keep telling you until you listen: the danger."

The count sniffed and pulled a couple times on his mustache, then said gruffly: "Please do not push your fear onto Ms. Berzwecken, Ms. Dalca. I know how you try to impose your beliefs on others—how many countless times have you done so to me? But instead, let her enjoy herself. I believe your misgivings are the product of your lively imagination, your needless fears, and your shock at having her here with you now. I see how you've held yourself back with our guests instead of blossoming. Maybe she is our missing ingredient for you. Yes. *Yesss.* Given time, you will lose these fears for your friend—she is old enough, after all, to make her own decisions— and you'll be glad she came. I dare say, you will thank me for it. Yes. *Oh, yesss.* And now, with your best friend safely in our fold, my little mouse, I can say: the Palace of Pleasures is in full flower."

Amalina had thought she'd return to the Great Library to find the book she'd been looking for. But Cristine had come down from her rooms, and it was time for the grand tour. And by nighttime, Amalina was still so upset, and confused, she went right to bed, expecting that she was so tired that she'd plummet into a deep, dreamless sleep, where not even Lucinda Skeldar could bother her.

• • •

"Why did you bring her here?" asked Pia Lampeda, later that night, suddenly at Amalina's bedside.

Amalina sat bolt upright and clamped the covers to her chin, until she saw who it was. Pia stared down at her, her body a languid form leaning against the bedpost.

"You mean Cristine?" said Amalina. "I didn't."

"Why else would she be here?"

"I didn't ask her to come."

"And it seems she's staying," said Pia with a pout. "She intends to. She's taken a room."

Amalina rubbed her eyes. "I can't refuse her a room if that is what she wants. After all, my uncle has accepted her in, and she's my friend—"

"I know. Your sister in blood." Pia bent her head forward, her fingers seemed to scratch at the post. "But is that what *you* want?"

Amalina paused to think.

"If you asked your uncle to send her away, I'm sure he would. If you told him so, and meant it. But that isn't the question, is it? Do you want her to be here, Kat? Why else would she be here if you hadn't sent for her, or you hadn't given her permission?"

"No! Absolutely not!" insisted Amalina, defensively. "She was invited here by my uncle, of all things. I didn't want her here, so much so I told her not to come. I told her I never wanted her here, ever. She's my best friend, why would I ever want her here? But she came anyway."

"I'm your friend," said Pia, plaintively. "Aren't I?"

"Of course—"

"You sent for me. You invited me."

"Yes," said Amalina, feeling put on the spot. "But that's different."

"How?"

"Everything's different. Cristine wants to be here because I'm here. You didn't come just for me, but to—"

"Yes I did. You're the only reason why I came."

"But I'm not the reason you've stayed on, am I?"

Pia closed her eyes and gave a large sigh.

"I don't understand," said Amalina. "You seemed so interested in Cristine before, always asking about her."

"I was asking about her to find out about you. *She* doesn't need to *be* here."

"Well, it's not just my castle anymore, or my uncle's. It's yours, too. If you want Cristine out, you can—"

"Don't try to make me the villain, Katty," said Pia. "That isn't fair of you. I wouldn't throw her out, unless you wanted me to. But even if you wanted me to, it is your responsibility to do it. You can't just manipulate people into taking care of the inconveniences, and you slide past the uncomfortable spots."

"What are we talking about?" huffed Amalina. She felt like she'd woke in a trap that she didn't understand. First Cristine, now this. "Never mind, I could use some sleep, it's been a long day. I don't know what you're saying."

"Does your Cristine know how dangerous it is here?" said Pia, suggestively.

Amalina couldn't tell if it was concern in Pia's voice, or worse.

"What do you mean?"

"For you, the difference between her and I being here in this castle is really how perilous it is for *her*. Isn't it?"

"I already told you I warned her. And its even more dire for Cristine, because not only is she just like me, in a sense, but she doesn't know half what to look out for, and she's so jealous of me and wanting to be here, she can't be bothered to to listen or to look out. Not for the *real* dangers." At Pia's reaction, a slight flinch, Amalina added: "The dangers ... *with all the other Ladies*, right? and especially Margeta—"

"Margeta, yes," said Pia, almost sarcastically.

"Think of what she did to you, Pia. She sent an assassin."

"Did she? I don't recall. But I'll give you Margeta la Brichese is no one to get on your bad side. Or tangle with. But that is not what I meant, and that is not the danger you warned her of. You meant your uncle." Pia paused for some dramatic effect, as she liked to do. She brought her emerald eyes up to meet Amalina's. "And you meant me."

"You?"

"And the others, now, of course. But you meant me."

"No."

"There's no need to lie," she said, sounding injured.

"Why you?"

"Because of what I can do to her." Again, Pia's fingernails seemed to scratch meaningfully on the bedpost. "Because you're afraid of what I *might* do."

"I never thought that." *Had Pia heard her conversation with the Count?* Amalina felt sweaty. "Why are you doing this? You've never acted like this before, Pia. Really. Come on."

"Don't be so slippery, Katty. You don't know me anymore. Well, you do, and you only think you don't. It's only you just don't understand me. It's all rather my fault, but how could I have known? I didn't understand fully what I was doing, I only meant to ... Well, I leapt before I looked ... and messed it all up between us."

Amalina reached out and took Pia's hand, which was rucking up wood on the bedpost.

"You didn't mess anything up, Pia. Please, don't be—"

Pia slid her hand out of Amalina's and backed away.

"Don't touch me. It hurts me too much."

"Oh."

"My heart," said Pia. "It is still vulnerable, I'm afraid. To you. And so I believe I will withdraw for awhile. Yes. As you like. You won't see me anymore … Maybe never again."

"What? But that's not what I want, Pia. Please."

"It'll give you time with your sister in blood. I see how important that is to you, and I would not seek to interfere. I want you to be happy, always."

"That won't make me happy …you wouldn't be interfering," soothed Amalina. "Please. Please, don't be jealous … if this is what this is. If you just meet Cristine and talk to her I'm sure you'd get along."

"A tradesman's daughter?" sniffed Pia. Then she softened. "Oh, I take that back. I can't believe I said it. Oh, but you know I take everyone as they come. But really, she and I have nothing in common besides you, and she knows only Amalina, not my Katty. Does she know that I'm the one who gave Katty her reading glasses? that I saw that you needed them and had them constructed? No, we aren't the same, the two of us. I'm sure she wouldn't understand me, as much as I wouldn't understand her. And neither of us would put in the effort to understand each other, just the way you haven't done me."

"What do you mean by that?"

"You see? Exactly. Ohhh, but what am I going to do with you this way, my beautiful liar?"

"And what do you mean by *that*?"

"You don't love me. You've never really, if you ever did …"

"Pia, you can't—"

"But never mind," said Pia, withdrawing. "It's all my fault, as I said. Just a big mistake. Maybe someday you will understand me better, or even try But—no, never mind, never mind. I'm just being silly. It's me that didn't understand. Go spend some time with your old best friend. Now that she's here, Katty, best you go on. I will always be in the castle. I just need to figure things out … for me, you see. Pray I make better decisions for myself in the future." At the door, she said: "Um, you know, I'm not the only one who feels she doesn't really belong here. With all the hazards arranged against Cristine, let's hope her stay is short." She bowed her head. "However, it will be interesting to see how long she lasts."

"Pia."

"Good bye."

48

The Rumor Mill

As Sadra and Attila trudged through the snowdrifts in the street, Attila flapped the ends of his cloak distractedly.

"What is it?" asked Sadra.

"What is what?"

"Whenever you do that there is something on your mind."

"Whenever I do what?" he looked at her from deep within the large hood.

"Never mind what, I see you and I *know*. Now tell me."

"You're observant," said Attila, lightly impressed. "I was just thinking it might not be helpful to have both our footprints in the snow side-by-side. They lead from your church to the bakery. The prints leave a record should someone start getting curious. Perhaps I should begin wearing your husband's boots to allay suspicion."

"You're probably the only one in this town that suspicious," said Sadra. "I've never known anyone with such a mind as yours. But if you don't think we should hold our meetings at Dragomir's, I've already offered our church."

"No, it's already set," said Attila. "And to most everyone involved it appears Dragomir began his new enterprise out of his shop. Best to keep it that way. Keep it simple. His bakery is a natural draw for the community, so no one would question a large number of visitors. Anyway, let them think the man in charge is the one they most trust."

"My church is also as natural a draw, as you say, as his bakery. If not more so," objected Sadra.

"Well, the same could be said about one of the inns, or a tavern. But—"

"I am also more trusted than any of them," said Sadra. "More trusted than Dragomir, even. By far. And in the end *you* can't trust any of them— but you know you can trust me."

"In the end, this is a matter of violence," said Attila. "And you are a woman."

In the particular age they lived this was not an insult, and to Sadra sounded sensible. She did not comment further but moved on to another item of concern: "You still haven't told Dragomir that Gulgas and Lazru Skeldar are a part of this project of yours."

"Only when needed. Best to keep various elements separate when we still don't know—"

"Gulgas is probably the most trustworthy of anyone of them. And being a hunter, he is valuable."

"Unfortunately he knows you and your husband found me, and he knows what subject I spoke on at the Rock Cup that night. He knows the reason for my wounds. Until we can be sure who can keep a secret it's best he remain out in the woods. Besides, it would be a bit remarkable to the residents of Korr if this giant were hanging around a bakery all day instead of hunting for his pelts, no? We must be careful."

"You are cautious, indeed," said Sadra. "If I didn't know how brave you are, I would think you somewhat of a coward."

"I am prudent," he said, wondering if she was trying to provoke him. "Each spoke of a wheel does not need to touch—or know—every other part of the wheel, but only move as one when the axle turns them. Dragomir is our town crier and warning bell, and the recruiting officer, and its ostensible head. Boss Berzwecken, who has proven himself by backing my trip to Netz, will be the financier. Ion will serve as the training officer and perhaps our battlefield commander. Lazru the Armorer, our armorer. The rest, when we have sorted them—by their innocence, specialty, and usefulness—become the army. And nobody beyond a key few need know that I alone, and not Dragomir, am the surpreme general of it, or how each of the others shall be tasked."

"Of course Dragomir and Gulgas and Lazru all know the deeper truth of why you are doing this, the true identity of the person you mean to confront," she said, referring to the Count, and respectfully omitting herself.

"Lt. Vokent knows as well," added Attila, also not including her. "They know a bit. But still, not everything. The murderer of Neku Jonker will have to stand for the rest."

"And Amalina knows our real adversary. She is your spy."

"Yes," said Attila. "I hadn't forgotten. Though I think it best not to name our clandestine agent aloud. And I suppose those birds we gave her comprise our communication network. But those two elements know nothing of the rest of the operation, or the identies within it, and shall sensibly remain in the dark. Until I deem it necessary. You see?"

"I'm starting to learn."

Attila seemed satisfied.

"You don't have to answer this," began Sadra, "but I wonder if there are secrets still which you keep from me?"

She waited for him to say something. He did not.

• • •

They arrived at the bakery with hours to spare before the night bell. When the customers became scarce and at some point when the storefront was empty besides Dragomir's cheerful wife, they slipped into the back unnoticed.

Dragomir was talking with several men who had their caps removed and were scratching their heads. Lt. Vokent stood just behind Dragomir with his arms folded, looking martial in his uniform.

"What was that name again?" said one.

"Jonker," said Dragomir with the patience of a children's tutor. "Neku Jonker."

"Strange," said another. "I just heard that name the other day. Was a good man?"

"A very good man," said another.

"A *godly* man," said the third. "Had a beautiful wife, too. That's what they say."

"What happened to him was wrong," said Dragomir, leading them along. "A crime against anyone is worth a noose, but to violate the sacred ground of the dead, and to kill the one who tends to them and protects them ..."

"And before the sounding of Judgement's Trumpet ..." said someone.

"Drawn and quartered," said one.

"Throw him in the fire!" said the second. "You know, I think it has to be one of the students from that School of Darkness I've heard about. Maybe their headmaster put them up to it. Or he did it himself."

"School of Darkness?" said the third man.

"We shall catch the assassin," said Dragomir. "Whoever it is. And we will see he meets his justice."

"Netz Village, you said?" said the first, scratching his head again, sounding unsure. "That's a long way off. They don't have their own—?"

"I marched with General Klauswisz across three kingdoms to put down the Miller's Heresy," said Ion Vokent before this man got too far along. He puffed out his chest.

"In winter you marched, did you?" asked the third skeptically.

"Look at you," scowled Sadra. "Afraid to do Heaven's work when you are called to it? A man is dead who should not be, and by the hands of a villain; one who does not deserve the mercy of the pits of hell for how he mistreated the helpless flesh of our ancestors in that graveyard. Think of what he might have done to *yours*, or to *you*, should you die and be buried there."

"I'll be buried on my farm," said the first. "Not in St. Grigori. Can't see the Cardinal would allow it, or, consecrated ground be damned, that I'd *want* to be set under the foot of the Roman Pope. I wouldn't think you'd like it that way either, Sadra."

"The dead are the dead. The point is a hero of the people must be avenged."

"When did this happen?" asked one.

. . .

A short while later, Boss Berzweck stomped into the store to witness a similar exchange with a new set of patrons, which he observed with a reddening face. The Boss was glad to see them leave, and turned his ire on the company when the door shut.

"Neku Jonker?" said the Boss, with trembling cheeks. "I never heard this name before in my whole life, and for business I travel up and down this country all year long. Suddenly I hear his name from all quarters. I've just received a report from one of my managers in Tsobl on this former non-entity. In another year, I believe he will be promoted into Ardeel's greatest hero!"

Attila nodded contentedly to himself. The governor was at work already spreading the rumors about the tragic murder of Neku Jonker, building the case. Which should make their action against the Count easier.

But the Boss threw his fur hat onto the sideboard in a huff. "What are we playing at here? What is this game? Are we trumpeting the name of this man to the corners of the earth because our cause needs a make-believe hero sewn to it? It first needs an act of outrage? I've been up and down this country, and I know enough of the world to understand what makes a mob tick. We've seen our share of strikes, haven't we, Dragomir? And is that what we're looking for? A mob? One to set after this Count?"

"Um," said Dragomir, glancing for support from Attila and Sadra, which led the Boss' eyes to them. "First we make sure the crime is known by all. Then we announce the culprit."

"And then we have the mob," grumbled Boss Berzweck impatiently. "I get all that. And how long will that take when, after all, we know who the culprit is? I ask you once again, what is this game, and why are we playing it, when we know what we must do and where we must strike? You think that thing up in the mountains won't hear of this and make his own plans; that inhuman monster?"

There was a little gasp between Attila, Sadra, Dragomir, and Ion.

"You think I don't know who we're *really* going after here, Dragomir?" He included everyone in his rage, as he swung his head around to face them down. "He is the Count of Ardeel. The infernal Knight. *That* is our true criminal. And heaven help me if he hears me say it, or should one of his minions, of which there many, should report what I've said—" here he eyed Attila with suspicion "—but he is our enemy, is he not? The contract be torn and burned for all I care! We intend to remove this Tepsji, because he has been the enemy of the people for centuries. Not what he did to some *Neku Junker*."

Still no one spoke. Attila wasn't sure why nobody else did. For his part, he wanted to learn how much more the Boss knew. *Let him talk.*

But Boss Berzweck was already pointing at Attila, singling him out. "This is who has given us this information? *He* told you about this Neku, Dragomir?"

Dragomir nodded.

"How do we know it is true, and not one of the lies famously spread by that architect of amorality, Count Tepsji, and the unscrupulous rogues in his employ?"

"He can be trusted," said Sadra. "I know him and vouch for him; even if his identity necessitates concealment until the right time. You should be satisfied."

"And so it is true?" he barked at Attila, turning on him. "Count Tepsji of Netz and the author of our Secret History's shameful contract are one and the same?"

"No doubt," answered Attila with a dull look.

"Then there's no time to lose. Let's not waste it trying to stoke up a mob. If we are to meet that monster with force, it must be with an army. And not an army of weeds we've plucked from here-and-there out of the farmlands. Damn it all, I own companies. I own men. Miners, who break these mountains to pieces with their brute strength. Hundreds of them. Thousands!"

"It won't be that easy," said Attila.

"Of course not," shouted the Boss. "We're going to need certain metals. Silver. You think I don't know these things? We can hurt him bad if we make a bunch of weapons that can actually wound him."

"Silver," said Attila. "It's not so easy, either. I'm convinced the Count's influence is why there is a ban on the metal in Ardeel."

"I'm sure we can find some in an underground market," said Ion, helpfully. "Or we can order it from abroad in quantity and smuggle it across the border. I know some merchants."

"I have *mines*," snarled the Boss. "You think I can't find silver in the mountains? We'll have more silver than we'd ever need. *Montus et Sylvanum Argenti*. Let's just get to work!"

They were quiet. The Boss took several breaths and then nodded at their unspoken question.

"You're a patient man, Dragomir," said the Boss, softly, graciously, but with a jaw clenched by growing internal tension. "I'm just not one, and I've never been. Somehow, my dear friend, you could keep secret that your little Amalina had gone off to stay in the company of some Count, while knowing it was *him*: the Count of Ardeel! I could never control myself, Dragomir, if my daughter were in his hands, but I would seek to rescue her, even if it meant my life. Not one second would pass that did not witness my fullest effort, to spend my last coin in that cause. And so it shall be. Because—and for this I blame you," he pointed to Attila, "by agreeing to your call for secretiveness—I said nothing of our business. Nor did I speak ill of Count Tepsji, so my daughter should not worry for her friend's safety. And now she has run off from home—against her mother and her father's will—and joined Amalina at his side. Cristine is now, at this very hour, in the Netz Castle. Dragomir, listen to me, we must rescue them immediately!"

• • •

With a calm, heavy-lidded, monotone delivery, Attila talked Boss Berzweck down.

"We need him," Attila told Sadra on their way back to the church. "But not the way he wants. If Mr. Berzweck were to have his say, he would take charge as is his custom. But worse, he would be as rash and as much a danger to our mission as any undisciplined mob."

"He might not like it," said Sadra, "but you calmed him well enough. I think we can trust him not to do anything without asking us first. I'll check in on his wife, just to make sure he isn't talking outside our group. But, you understand, he now suspects that you are the real general here, not Dragomir."

"It was a necessary sacrifice, if that's the case."

She smiled a small angular smile: "To put the Boss in his place—a man who gets whatever he wants when he wants it—it is not something I've ever seen done. It was impressive … Attila."

49

The Experiment

After Pia politely excused herself from the mix, and after a week of mingling in the castle, Cristine had got on well with the rest of the noble ladies; except for, with no surprise, Margeta la Brichese. And when the Count seemed to break from his fascination with his special 'project women'—those he'd given the rite—to favor Cristine with his unctuous flattery, it did nothing to smooth the many wrinkles with Margeta. It also sold, generally, to every other lady, Cristine's place as a contender to be his next chosen. Which was remarkable because of how recently she'd arrived and astounding because of her low birth.

Cristine was enjoying herself, wholly aware of the frustration and bitterness she was causing behind the scenes in the ladies' private chambers. All by just being there. And while Amalina was constantly at her side to act as protection, it was needless. It was as if Amalina's old friend's personality was stretching out with a pleased sigh in every direction, like an over-worked laborer who had fallen into the softest bed on earth. To Cristine's contented mind, these ladies were not the mean and brutal Korr girls, there were no Bossy Bessas to confront. These ambitious Ladies of the Western Kingdoms were connivingly polite or harmlessly profane; they were soft fat. And the Count promoting her made it all the better. Amalina, tired and annoyed, gave up the watch.

It could be argued that Amalina's negligence—and perhaps Cristine, too—was responsible for what happened next.

• • •

"Look at this necklace he gave me," Cristine told Amalina during a moment alone together, when she came to visit Amalina in her room. She ran her thin, white fingers along the necklace's bulky links of gold and gems. The necklace stood up like a collar, with a river of small rubies falling from it. "Isn't it beautiful? It's been in his family for years. I'm not partial to red, but he says it brings out my eyes."

"Are you feeling all right?" said Amalina, unimpressed with the gift, though wondering where it had come from. She'd seen better pieces clamped around necks throughout the western courts; more refined and with better cut stones. More eye-catching were the dark circles under Cristine's eyes, the drooping of her eyelids. The paleness of her lips.

"You couldn't be jealous," said Cristine as if hoping she were.

"I'm not."

"Well don't be." Cristine sat down heavily, still pulling on the necklace, almost making it look like it was uncomfortable; choking her.

"I said I'm not." Amalina tried not to sound annoyed.

"Well then at least acknowledge what I just told you. Don't *you* think it brings out the blue in my eyes?"

"I always thought your eyes more white than blue," said Amalina. "Like ice. But, to be honest, they seem a little grey now. The whites of 'em, too. You look very tired."

"Who isn't? Maybe if you didn't hide yourself away all the time you wouldn't be so fresh either. Why *are* you hiding yourself away from everyone?"

Amalina wanted to lean close to her friend, but something kept her from doing so. The emotional distance growing between them. She dropped her head, and said softly, in confidence, "You know, you don't have to compete with these girls. You do know that, right? I *am* your friend."

"Who's competing? For what?"

"I don't know," said Amalina, not wanting to give away the Count's 'prize' if she didn't know yet—Amalina still hoped she didn't. "But since *I'm* not in the race, I get much more sleep than anyone."

"You're jealous of me." Cristine cut her drowsy eyes at Amalina. "Aren't you jealous, *really*?"

"No. And never mind about me, you can't compete with them all. There are too many. Nobody could keep up. If you haven't noticed, they have enough maids to help them get through the day. Like a bunch of horsetrainers keeping them fed and rested, and out on the field when needed."

"You volunteering for the job, Ama—Katty?" she said, drowsily, yawning, her finger hooked onto the necklace mindlessly, pulling it down.

That's when Amalina saw the dark red mark behind the necklace.

"Cristine!" Amalina shot forward and slipped her own finger through the gold collar, yanking her friend forward. "Cristine, your—!"

Cristine gave her a sly, tired smile, and weakly brushed Amalina's hand away. "No, it's nothing."

"What happened?"

Cristine refused to answer. But the large, rough wound on her neck was obvious, the skin broken and torn in several places. Ugly. And Amalina wondered if it wouldn't become further inflamed or infected with the

Count's gift necklace stuck around it, rubbing against it. But the necklace was there to mask the Count's *real* 'gift', wasn't it? Those wounds ...

But those weren't the wounds from the rite of transformation. It looked like what would have been left of Lucinda Skeldar's neck if she had managed to survive the Count's attack. And though Cristine looked weary and drawn, she didn't have the odd, otherworldly pallor of the Ladies who'd undergone the transition. And if it had been the transition, Cristine would be downstairs, recovering with the others. If the Count had been seeking to replenish his power, she would've been dead. So what was happening here? wondered Amalina. *Was* this the Count's work? Or if not, what else? Could one of the turned Ladies—maybe Pia—have attacked Cristine? and the Count had caught them in time and saved her? and his necklace given to Cristine to hide the embarrassing truth?

"What happened? Did someone do this to you?"

"What are you talking about? It's nothing. Leave me alone. There's no need to go on about it, please. If you want to do something, help me go through my clothes for a dress that matches this beautiful gift from your 'uncle'."

Amalina stared heavily at her friend, who looked so tired, and yet so unconcerned to the point of hinting at some unspoken triumph, whatever that could be. Too confused to demand an answer from Cristine, Amalina was unable to find the words to confront her. Would it have been a sympathetic warning cry? or an accusation made in horror?

• • •

Amalina considered now: was Cristine the only remaining untouched lady who'd suffered such an attack; such a wound? Could there be something greater—or more troubling—happening within the castle? The only way to find out was to corner the Count and ask him; or to search through the ladies for similar gashes and tears, perhaps inexpertly covered up by necklaces, or collars, or ruffs, or neckerchiefs, etc.; or if nothing else, poke around those who'd already been turned for any obvious signs of their guilt in Cristine's maiming.

Amalina entered Aria Ecci's suite. It was lavishly appointed, with furnishings carried from her Venice home and which matched her seductive but overly sensuous nature. The room—and she—naturally attracted the most of the noble ladies on any given day, and because of its lack of windows was a favorite frequent of the Count himself. Amalina found five Ladies lounging around, laid out on narrow, puffy sofas as if the were going to fall asleep. Amalina at first wondered if they had been overtaken by fumes; the heavy scent of incense burning in the fireplace was obnoxious.

"Don't tell me your uncle complained to you, too," Aria snickered to Amalina. She pointed knowingly to her nose. "I'll have the room aired when this is over. But let us enjoy ourselves for an hour or two, if we can. It's the middle of the day, after all. Shouldn't he be sleeping or something? I mean really, I dispatched your Anka to give him warning hours ago."

"He didn't complain to me," said Amalina, walking into the room, trying to cover for her probing glances. "But I was looking for him, actually. He hasn't been here?"

The Ladies shook their heads. She noticed no maids or other servants. They'd been dismissed for some reason. Amalina tried to make a subtle circuit of the room, surveying their bodies for red gashes or punctures.

"What's on your face?" said Aria, her head lifted from her pillow. "Do you have those glasses on? Nose stuck in a book again? You'll wear your eyes out, girl. And where are your twin nuggets: Princess Lampeda and the mineral magnate's daughter?"

"Cristine's sleeping in my bedroom." Now Amalina watched for their reactions, but nobody moved. She thought: *it'd be easier just to check them for scars if they aren't paying attention to me*. Then she finished off-handedly, "She had a late night and needs the rest. Were none of you with her last night?"

"No."

"Not sure where Pia is," said Amalina, sounding somewhat disappointed. She was also still worried Pia had succumbed to an ill-timed craving, or a vengeful spite, or jealousy, and had done the damage to Cristine, and was now lying low to dodge Amalina. Had *she* done it?

"Quit moving around, Kit-Kat, you're going to make us giddy. If you're looking for your uncle, find one of the gatesmen and ask them, they seem to know better than most."

Amalina spun her head, suddenly aware something else was missing from the room. A castle guard was almost always posted at the door, or in the corner of the room. At some point the Count had begun dispersing them through the ladies's quarters, as a claimed added layer of protection. Their true function was to make the impossible task of keeping track of his loves easier, as if he'd broken off pieces of himself and handed them out in armored form.

"We sent them all away," explained Aria. "I ordered them down to the lobby to count out the seconds for two hours so we could have the world to ourselves. Come join us and be intoxicated, Kat. Unless you would prefer the pleasure of *their* company."

"Ew!" exclaimed Greta La Nevers, wrinkling her nose. "You mean one of the *soldiers*?"

"Of course."

This roused Greta even more. "You couldn't be serious."

"Why not?" Aria smiled lasciviously. "There's only one Count to go around, so … So what if the rest of the men among us are on the level of *beasts*? I am not ashamed to admit the depths of my desires. Better we should come clean with our true natures, eh, ladies? Or better still, we should *cherish* our lusts, and respect them for what they are. Because it is all that'll be keeping us company during the long winter ahead."

"But …" Greta still couldn't picture it. "*The sentries?*"

"Huh!" scoffed Aria. "If you think *they*'re bad, I can't tell you what a relief they are compared to the spooky soldiers who were here *before*. Katty, Margeta, and Pia can tell you. Black hoods over their hideously scarred faces."

"No!" cried Greta.

"Yes, *yesss*," grinned Aria. "They burned themselves with acid to prove their loyalty to Count Tepsji. Can you believe it? If you got a look under their hoods, the fools looked like walking corpses. These men now, they are *much* better sights than Marosh's fools." Aria laughed wickedly and licked her lips. "Though they *were* intriguing in their own terrible way. I used to dream they would eat my sex like a fruited bread."

"Aria!"

"Not *Marosh*'s men, Aria," 'Maria' di Oscina corrected. A sheer mustard veil had been self-consciously thrown across her face to obscure it. Her neck, below its folds, appeared untouched. "*Vezel*'s men."

"Marosh was the General," said Aria with a flat voice, irritated.

"No, no. Best forget that name," said di Oscina warningly, her voice rising in agitation, disturbing the peace of the scented air. Some bodies shifted. Amalina observed them for bruises or blood while she had the opening. "That man was a disgrace, according to what I'm told. But you remember, don't you? It's *Vezel*. Vezel Umalasju was our heroic general for the Count."

"Don't lose your brains," said Aria, looking as annoyed as Amalina suddenly felt. The Count's influence—through di Oscina's officious words— was being felt within the room; his insistence on a different history than what had really happened at Kyrgil Castle. It was like a dark current in the air. "Not so quick, 'Maria'. There *was* a Vezel. But wasn't *that* one the *least* interesting of the bunch, Katty? Now, General *Marosh*—"

"Vezel, not Marosh, Aria. Be careful you don't make the mistake again. You know that he insists—"

"So be it, 'Maria'! You weren't here and you wouldn't know. But, for you: Vezel, Vezel, Vezel. Vezel the General. Vezel Umalasju the Conqueror. I didn't like that castrata much but oh, well, if that's the way *he* wants it."

"Why shouldn't you want it that way, too, Aria? Why not, when that's the very truth? Vezel was the general, and he was strong, clever, and *loyal*."

"Yes, loyal …" said Aria without relish. "And still, you wouldn't know anything about it."

"And he still had his *face*, didn't he? I know *that*."

"Yes, he had his face, 'Maria', but nothing else. *Castrata*. Didn't I just say that? Don't you understand?" She rubbed her eyes lazily. "I'd rather have a hooded ravager who can do the job, no matter what's underneath. Take his hood away even, what should I care?"

"That's too much, Aria."

"Not yet, I'm just getting there," said Aria, scooting up on her side and smiling wickedly around the room. "And you should too, if you want to last around here. You better have a strong resolve and be able to do whatever it takes. Not by scraping to his will—to *his* will—but by matching him. How else do you expect to win his affections?"

"Whose?"

"Katty's uncle, of course. Count Tepsji."

"Win his *affections*?" said di Oscina, even more offended than before. "Do you mean? But no … really, he is too old and ugly, why would anyone want to be with him like that?"

"Well, if nothing else, he is a great lover," said Aria. This brought a number of the ladies up from their couches.

"He … makes love to you?" said di Oscina, shocked and appalled by Aria and her candor, her veil dropped off.

"You haven't? I thought with all your fawning and proseletyzing, you must have. Or you *want* to. No?" Now she turned her tigerish grin around to include everyone. "No? Well I have. And he's far better than anyone else. With age comes experience! You should honor your elders, as they say." She sat straight up and gestured with her hands to describe the scene. "He faces you, and surrounds you and fills you." She let her grin take another tour of the tantalized audience. "Not easy to forget, I can tell you. When I got back home last summer, I was reminded right quick how my immature little hometown boys seem to prefer making it in a position where, rather than allowing them to shower my cheek with kisses of passion, they can better watch their roughly chewed thumbnails work their way into my asshole."

This was another of Aria's shocking and somewhat eye-opening education pieces for Amalina, which sent waves of laughter through the older girls, especially Greta.

"That's disgusting and I shouldn't want to know such things," said 'Maria' di Oscina. "How many of you have forsaken not only your honor but your duties to your family? Well, I'm still a virgin!"

"Of course you are," said Aria with a mocking tone. "And with that face, you always will be. By the way, your veil's come off."

"Nobody's perfect," said Greta, somewhat defensively, but Amalina didn't know if that applied to the virgin di Oscino or Greta herself.

"Here, I have an idea for you, 'Maria'," said Aria, jovially. "Speaking of hideousness. I'm sure there must still be some of Marosh's army's—I mean, as you wish, *Vezel's* army's—masks lying around. You could put one of those over your head. Or maybe better, there might still be some of their acid tucked away. Rub it all over your face like they did, to erase what is there. You can always tell people you were beautiful once, before the accident—"

'Maria' di Oscina flew up from the couch and ran out of the room, crying. The others stared, dumbfounded.

"Down goes another," said Aria, with a laugh as she lay back, satisfied at what she'd done.

"Aria!" said Amalina, feeling awful. "She didn't deserve that."

"Of course she did, Kat. She's not my guest, but don't pretend you enjoy her pious scrabbling at your uncle's every utterance, like his word is the scripture." Amalina moved to object, but Aria cut her off. "Yes, yes, I understand, dearest Katty. You love your uncle. I'm sure you do; when he sends you off and funds your travels. But you hate him when he pulls the chain and brings you home. Let's not pretend otherwise. And we, being from *out there*, it is the reverse for us, you see. And we are trapped. We have our duties to our families if nothing else. But let us *not* sacrifice reality for it. That girl will be okay. She'll run off to Margeta and they'll wrack their beads for the night. But that girl didn't belong in this room anyway. Only a few people are born to deserve the richness and the beauty of life."

"If nothing else," echoed Amalina, "you should remember we have to live with her for the rest of the winter, if not longer."

Aria waved her hand as if to send away some bad thought, then grinned naughtily again and stared directly at Amalina. "But speaking of deformity. You knew Vezel better than anyone else here. *Do* you know what they took off his body when he refused the acid? Did you see? Had they cut off his balls? or was it *everything* …?"

Amalina stared at Aria, feeling a fury burning up her chest. Was Aria really now turning on her? trying to embarrass her the way she'd just done Maria? trying to drive her out of the room? in her own castle? Wasn't she, just moments ago, speaking to her as if they were friends and on the same side? And now this?

"Well, I'm sure *she* would never have found out," said Greta La Nevers scoldingly in the awkward pause. "And I never would, either. And I certainly would never brag about such shameful incontinence, like you, Aria. We're not all like *you*; like a common pincushion."

"A common pincushion!" Aria laughed uproariously and clapped her hands. "Now that's the way, Greta! That's it! You've got more balls than

'Maria' and her hero Vezel, combined. See, Amalina? That's what I'm talking about. A woman needs to be herself around here. Whatever she is! Stand up for yourself!"

"Okay," said Amalina, regarding Aria askance. There still seemed to be something on her mind.

"I'll tell you all," said Aria, grouping her friends close again. "Speaking of balls … presently, of the Count's men in this castle, there is one with three balls. And then, there is another who has only one."

"How would you know?"

Aria grinned: "There's a reward—I'll stake a dinner down in Netz, *and* throw a lavish ball to the winner in the spring—for the first one to tell me which one has what." She giggled mischievously. "Feel free to guess. Or … *dare to find out.*"

• • •

"Sir," said Amalina, having tracked the creature down to his laboratory, still feeling a little sick to her stomach at what had happened in Aria's room, but having determined for certain that none of the others had been attacked like Cristine. "Do you know what's happened to Cristine? Did you see?"

"Your friend?" said the Count needlessly, but seeming, after a long pause, to instead make a point out of it. Then he turned to her, and frowned. "*Why, why, why* are you wearing those pebbles of glass before your beautiful eyes? Don't you know they distort your whole face? You are perfection and yet you destroy it with those … manmade abominations?"

"On her neck, sir."

"Hm? Oh. A Tepsji heirloom. Yes."

"She wears it over a wound. Is that why you gave it to her? to help hide the wound?"

"I really didn't give it. She saw that gaudy piece in my treasury and then asked me for it."

Amalina didn't remember seeing any jewelry in the treasury, but she hadn't searched everywhere. And hadn't Princess Lisbet Spaarvierlet once hinted there was *another* treasury, in a lower vault somewhere?

"She isn't looking well, sir. She has a terrible scar on her neck. It almost looks like something might have bit her, or cut her there. I think we need to send her away."

"Away?"

"From the castle. To rest."

"I don't think she would agree to that."

"*You* don't. Well, let's send for a physician, see what he thinks."

"So he can bleed her?" said the Count. "What's the point? I admit, it would save me some time, perhaps. But it would ruin the experiment, wouldn't it?"

"What experiment?'

"Remember when I had worried to you the other month, that all science has been concluded to its greatest reach, and we should have no more advancements to interest me? And you, my little mouse, assured me this must not be true. Well, I am not so small I can't admit when I'm mistaken. And it was you who opened the door to this new corridor for me. This experiment, you can say, little mouse, is your own doing. For you were the one who suggested it."

"Please, sir," said Amalina, shivering, having already pieced together what the Count was getting at, "I was worrying Pia might have ... but you haven't hurt my friend. You wouldn't."

But of course he would, she thought, as he petted his mustache at her with heavy-lidded amusement. It wasn't his nature to admit such a thing unless it would further amuse him somehow. How much more fun was it to play with the ignorant mortal before him? Amalina's cheeks flushed with anger, wanting to cry for Cristine, her old best friend now a victim of some kind. Why had Cristine come to the castle? Why had Amalina allowed her to stay? Between the noble ladies and the Count, there could be only danger ... But, the Count—

"You *did*," said Amalina accusingly. "I know you did it; that's what you mean—"

"I am not doing her harm, Ms. Dalca," he said. "I'm helping her. You told me that this was the kindest way to handle the process—"

"The process! She looks like she's dying!"

"Well, it is all part of the process isn't it? Again, little mouse, you *told* me—you *scolded* me—that this would be the most humane way to—"

"You could feed off of any one of *them*," said Amalina, speaking of the Ladies, feeling strangely ashamed. "I'm sure you would find someone who would let you sustain your power off of them, however you like. But you're doing this to Cristine to spite me, to hurt me, to punish me."

"Amalina, I refuse to repeat myself; you know how I loathe having to say something twice. Now listen to me, I am not *hurting* dear Cristine. And the only way it pertains to you—because, as I have told you before, I would never hurt you—is that I thought this would make you *happy*."

"Oh ..." said Amalina, waking up to the full implication. "You aren't just using Cristine to maintain your power." He shook his head, but with an encouraging smile to try again. "You're trying to give her your ... yours ... little by little."

His eyes flashed and his smile now included his long teeth. "Isn't that wonderful, Amalina? To have so many of your friends enjoying themselves around you, their youth preserved for all time, to be your companions forever?"

"It isn't a favor, really, sir," she concluded, understanding the real import beyond what he was saying, his true purpose. "Because you said it's just an experiment, right?"

She didn't want to complete the thought: Cristine was just an experiment ... *as the others had been.* His aim was to perfect the transformation process into Amalina's preferred method for it, for when the time came to change those who he *really* wanted to elevate. He'd already honed his rite to an exact art, but he knew Amalina considered it too violent, too horrific. She had always advocated for a more humane way, the gradual draining of a convert. So he was trying this new process on Cristine because, if it worked ... he would then, eventually, use it on Amalina.

"I thought science had nothing left to entertain me," growled the Count contentedly. "Isn't it wonderful?"

* * *

"That's it, Pretty Princess," said Aklan grimly after she'd told him what was now happening with Cristine and confessed to him her worries. "Do you know where Genadie put those weapons he hid in the carriage lock box? They aren't there anymore, I've already looked."

"What do you want with those?" asked Amalina with a raised eyebrow from her desk, where she'd been gnawing her anger on a quill pen.

"It's become too dangerous for you here, eh? There's no counting on Genadie, Pils or Anka, or any of your friends for help. No, it'll be me. And if I can't protect you from this AXP, then I can at least ..." here Aklan drew his finger across his neck, then pointed to the floor several times, meaning something very far below the castle.

"What!"

"We know it can be done. And, well, it's only fair I try; you saved my life in France, eh? So now, do you know where that old crumb has put them?"

"I can't imagine. But why those, exactly? There are blades everywhere."

"Because *his* did the job once already," explained Aklan with some dark satisfaction. "And didn't ... " Aklan pointed at the floor again, "Order Genadie to destroy them? And he didn't, but hid them away. Which means they *both* must think there's something to 'em. Something extra."

"Oh," said Amalina, not having thought of it that way. "But all the same, there's no saying they will work twice. Don't try. I order you. Please don't."

To her angst and dismay, Aklan said calmly: "But it's decided."

50

A Man of Action

While Attila was out for a secret stroll in Korr, to get some fresh air and spy on potential recruits, he spotted Sadra in the distance, returning to the church. But her usual quick, insistent gait was slowed and drawn out. She appeared to be reading something, and occupied totally with whatever it was. And then, before entering her church, she folded and placed that something in a hidden pocket of her tight winter coat.

When he met her later inside the church's back rooms, Attila waited for her to tell him she had some bit of news. He waited but she said nothing. And instead, Sadra was quiet and looked uncomfortable. In fact, she watched him with heavy side-glances, or openly glared at him, as if to stare him down. No explanations. He did not ask her about the item, or her curious behavior, but filed this data away. Suspicious.

He did comfort himself that he'd withheld from Sadra the information of his would-be killer's head on a spike at the Count's castle; unsure of the safety in the secret, but better to be cautious. Even with her, apparently.

•••

"When are you going to let everyone know about Lazru Skeldar?" Sadra asked Attila, still later. "They will be wondering how we will have an army equipped with weapons and armor, clad in silver, which is your selling point for this plan."

"The 'selling point', as you call it," said Attila without expression or inflection in his voice, "is the arrest and eradication of a malign criminal—the Assassin of Neku Jonker. Most won't know who exactly this assassin is until the appropriate time arrives to tell them. Once they know who they're fighting, and when they question how we will face the creature and win, that is when they will be presented with the fool-proof method. Until then, it remains a secret."

She nodded. But said now in a delicate voice: "Why must everything remain a secret, Attila? Even this far along. At some point you have to show people you trust them or they will begin to question you and your motives."

"Trust?" said Attila, allowing a small, sardonic smirk. "Yes …"

"Yes, trust."

"Until I am absolutely certain our ranks are pure of his influence, of any duplicitousness, and these men have the strength to resist the strongest of threats and temptation, they will stay separated, with only as much information as needed. But I've said this before."

"You think the Boss won't be asking you these questions? He knows just who we're going after. If you don't have answers—ones good enough to allay his fears and meet his demands for the amount of progress *he* deems reasonable—he might take our group for himself. He *will* take it. Then you will have lost all control."

As if to confirm Sadra's concern, when the inner circle met next in Dragomir's back kitchen, Boss Berzweck beamed as he set a small, somewhat shiny grey ingot onto the bakery's kneading table.

"What is this?" said Dragomir though it was obvious, and he bent over to have a closer look. He reached out but did not touch it. Instead he drew back his hand and wiped his fingers on his apron.

Attila stared down at the ingot with a paralyzed expression. "Yes, Mr. Berzweck, what is *this*?"

"Obvious, no?" said the Boss, somewhat agitated by Attila. "It's that element we need! 95% pure. Shall I name it aloud?"

Silver.

"Where did you get it?"

"My mines, of course, where else? Damn you, I thought you'd be happy. I told you I own these mountains—or what's in them, anyway. I can find silver anywhere if I dig enough, and more than we'll ever need. I have delivered us silver, you stone faced gargoyle!"

"And didn't I tell you not to?" muttered Attila. "This is a formed brick. Which means you had it gathered, refined, alloyed, and poured. Which means you have absolutely violated our rules of secrecy. You have involved men outside our circle in the harvesting and production of this certain illegal material. Word can, and will, circulate. How much have you made already?"

"Dragomir, just who is in charge here?" demanded the Boss.

"How much *have* you made?" said Dragomir, taking Attila's cue.

"Just this," snarled the Boss. "A handful. The same number of men who brought this out for me. And they know nothing of its purpose other than a routine analysis of minerals within our mines. But there are tons more of it and it will all be at the ready when the time comes. So now, you see with your own eyes what I can do." He sneered at Attila, going red in the face. "How about you? Where is your supply?"

"I have it," said Attila, calmly.

"You do? Where did you get it? And tell us how, when it is illegal to possess?"

"All you need to know is that I have it."

"On your word?" howled the Boss. "Who the hell *are* you?"

"I am the man in charge here, under the authority of the governor."

"So you *are* claiming leadership? I thought as much. Well, prove it. Let's see this writ, signed in the governor's own hand. And believe me, I know that man and I will recognize his signature or if it is false. But let's see it."

Attila stared but said nothing.

"He produces no writ," said the Boss, wildly gesturing to the others around the table. "He produces no silver. We talk and talk and talk, and he talks and talks and talks, and he feels free to spend my money and travel all over this country as if it is a winter holiday. Still, nothing is done about our daughters, Dragomir!"

Boss Berzweck slammed his fist on the table. The ingot hopped and knocked around noisily.

"Dragomir?" he asked with a pleading look.

Dragomir turned to Attila, then glanced to Sadra, seeking an answer from them with which he could settle the Boss.

"You know I am making sense here, Dragomir; and you, Vokent lad," said the Boss, appealing to Lt. Vokent. "You both know I am right. I have the material and I have thousands of men at my command who can be our army overnight. Now are we going to keep hanging on to the words of some nobody, or will you listen to me, a dear lifetime friend and a proven man of action?"

"The men at your command are your employees and nothing more," said Attila. "Let's call them mercenaries, because you pay them to be in your service. And should you promise them all the silver in the mountains should they serve you, our enemy will promise them an equal weight in gold, or whatever else they might value. History teems with treacherous mercenary armies turning on the cities that hired them, for nothing more than an enemy's better offer."

"Then tell us *your* plan," said the Boss. "Tell us what we're going to do, how we are going to do it. And then, tell us when it will happen."

"Once we have the number of men needed who meet our standards of loyalty and ability, I will deputize them by law to pursue the murderer of Neku Jonker."

The Boss flipped his hand at Attila: "The murderer of Jonker! A convenient lie, which makes you a liar."

"Our enemy did kill Neku. That is not a lie."

"Then it is just pretext. We all know why we are doing this. It has nothing to do with some meaningless gravedigger."

"However, it is the reason; the legal reason. The sanctioned reason that will keep our necks out of the noose when the king and his council in Sobelburg make inquiries into the action."

"You bore me," said the Boss.

"When we have our forces readied, they will be appropriately outfitted to the task. They will be provided with the weapons and the armor. I anticipate our attack in spring, when we can better hide our movement."

"Hide our movement from whom?" said the Boss.

"From the Count and his allies who are always ready to inform him of threats." Attila swept a quick, half-lidded look across them all, presumably to show his suspicion.

"The faster we move," growled the Boss, looking stunned, "the less chance of him knowing anything. I have mines in the Netz mountains. If I give the word, I can have my men raid that castle without notice. Dragomir, if I simply snap my fingers we could have our daughters back in a week!"

"If you're worried about your daughters," said Attila. "I would suggest you simply send a letter ordering them home. If they are properly obedient, you should be satisfied."

Sadra shot Attila a warning look that said: *Unfair!*

"But that is your personal business, Mr. Berzweck." Attila continued, undeterred. "Our concern is in a successful conclusion to this problem of ours. Which will not happen if we rush into it. The proximity of your mines notwithstanding."

"I doubt dear Cristine has received one letter I've posted," said the Boss, smoldering with rage. "I haven't had so much as a single reply from my willful little daughter. Why should that monster allow her any correspondence which might interfere in the contentment of his lusts? Now, gentlemen, I speak for the last time as your friend. I have the wherewithal and the purpose. If this stranger," here he pointed to Attila, "who we have let into our society cannot prove he is sanctioned by this government, and that he has what is required to destroy the Knight of Ardeel, then I will go forward and do it myself. And you are free to join me. The gargoyle has one week to prove himself."

Boss Berzweck stormed out of the kitchen, slamming the door behind him. Dragomir and Lt. Vokent stared at the door. They avoided looking at Attila.

. . .

"You were right," admitted Attila as he and Sadra snuck back to the church.

"This is Korr, Attila Bronk," she said. "This isn't Tsobl—or Sobelburg, or whatever they want to call it now. We are our own little planet and don't listen to reason as much as we should. Your Neku Jonker gambit might be necessary for the government, and it might work on some of us here. But in the end, we will have to argue with the passion of the truth of what we're *really* setting out to do."

"I will take your counsel from now on, Sadra."

"I feel guilty," she said, a little lower, sounding like she was preparing a confession, "but I was hoping I would be right. And that this would happen with the Boss."

"I only wish you'd better gained my confidence earlier, fool that I am," said Attila. "Rather than having our financier become our rival."

"But that's not what I meant," said Sadra. "We can always win him back to our side. But that he did as he did, and revolted at your delays and is taking control, he proves his good standing ... since, you see, his name is Alexandru." She pulled a folded strip of paper from her jacket. "I received a pigeon message from the castle this morning. From Amalina."

Attila took the small, ragged and wrinkled paper from her and read it with a blank face. This is what Sadra had hid from him earlier. Interesting.

"She rolled it when the ink was too fresh," said Sadra, pointing to the note. "But I think those are supposed to be initials. Begins with an A. Looks like it says AX or AZsomething, P or B. It's all smeared. But Old Boss Berzweck is Alexandru Berzweck. AB, I feared."

"Yes, it could be initials," said Attila, his left arm starting to twitch, making it difficult for him to reread the note. "But we now have a lead to follow, anyway. Some series of letters. 'C.T.' is obvious enough, Count Tepsji, certainly. But as for this other set ... Looks like a P at the end, but it *could* be a B. But you'll note by how the lower bowl of the B is lighter, more smeared, and yet a near reflection of the one above, it's probably a P after all."

"Ah, yes."

"But why not tell me about this earlier? You couldn't trust me?"

"I needed to see the Boss' reaction for myself," said Sadra. "If I told you about Amalina's message, you'd have begun interrogating him immediately and given your suspicions away."

"You should trust me better than that."

"I thought it better if you argue with him, as I knew you would, defending your position as our general, without the distraction of forewarning and mistrust. I didn't know he'd bring out the silver, but he played his part as I'd hoped and proved himself to be true Boss Bezweck, and not a sneaky little spy for our adversary."

"However," said Attila, "there *was* a sneaky little spy in our meeting, hm?"

"I can keep secrets, too," she smiled.

Attila didn't know what to do with her smile. He attempted one himself, but her lips straightened immediately, correcting him. He flattened his.

"In any case," sighed Sadra, covering the slight awkwardness. "With our financier's righteousness all but confirmed, as long as you can bring him back 'round and under your control, you will now have your silver army."

"Good news."

"It is."

Her voice had softened again.

His heart lurched in surprise when he felt her hand join his.

. . .

Along with the unfamiliar throbbing throughout his entire body, there came the lightest echo of a voice from months before: Gug, unclothed, yelling pitiably, demandingly, "Tell me you don't need love too!"

He wouldn't have expected—or even suspected—there would have been a question of it, but her demand—more an *accusation* really, wasn't it?—had also come at the heels of another queer question: "Aren't you human?"

The exhilaration he was feeling now only proved what he'd believed of himself all along, *of course* he was human. *Very much so.* Hadn't almost dying so many times proven it?

But what of it? Hadn't his nanny taught him—shaped him—into a man of great principle, which had then forged him into an instrument of Heaven's Law—and to be such an awesome device, humanity didn't figure.

Being "human", especially at this moment, wasn't the most advantageous thing to be, was it? so his shifting and excited thoughts went. Not when set against an enemy who was the solvent of fragile human kind. Where was the upside to love, then? the reward to base human-ness?

He must be wary! Wasn't everything coming together better than he could have ever hoped? his decision to visit Korr—its cool, calculated thoroughness mocked by the Cardinal—been vindicated beyond any doubt? By coming he'd gained a pool of strong. earnest men from which to draw a formidable force; a true officer to train and lead them; a genius armorer to outfit them; and an independent, filthy-rich financier, one with limitless access to provisions and the needed element to make his hope into reality— who was now cleared as a reliable ally against circumstantial evidence of a traitor in their midst—crucial, helpful evidence for the cause, *gained from the Korrite spy Attila had placed in the enemy's Castle*. All had come into proper alignment this day because of a long route of logical, deliberate steps, however anyone questioned his careful, methodical ways.

Yet, on top of those recent successes, on top of it all, he'd also, on this day, gained the hand of an admirable woman—one of intense rectitude and righteousness; a kindred soul ... who was suddenly—stunningly— connected to his own. A reveal of something greater; a wholeness which had always been.

Not expected this morning, nor even suspected. Almost without reason.

51

The Examination

Amalina punched her pillow, hoping to put it into a shape that would cradle her head and allow her mind to finally get some rest. She wiped away the sweat from her brow, sighed, and closed her eyes.

To Amalina, the thought of losing Cristine was devastating; so much so, the tragedy of it now crowded with the Lucinda nightmare, waking her with a violent jolt. To watch Cristine crumple and whither away in real life, as she did in her tortured dreams, would be difficult to stomach. But worse, her old best friend would emerge from those figurative ashes as a blank-eyed doll, slave to unnatural hungers, altered into just another version of the Count; no longer her friend at all. And Amalina couldn't help but blame herself for it. The Count was in charge of the process, but Cristine would never have been drawn into his malign circle if Amalina hadn't been at the high castle in the first place, acting as a magnet.

To stem the overwhelming guilt, to force herself forward and so to endure this episode—if not mentally vanquish it—the survivor part of Amalina snapped into gear. Outwardly, Amalina got out of bed and sat quietly at her desk to collect her thoughts. Inwardly, she would rigorously test and examine her troubles, see if they were not just in her head.

But it was difficult to focus. Pia's transformation was bad enough, but the Count having gone to work on Cristine was just too much. He was hitting Amalina from both sides now, her closest 'Katarina' friend and her real-life Amalina friend. Never mind also making away with favorites like Noka. It left Amalina feeling surrounded by the Count somehow. And with the continued threat of AXP, and Sadra's revolutionary's coming assault, she didn't know which direction the real threat would emerge.

Never mind threats and danger, thought Amalina. *Concentrate. What are you really worried about? One thing at a time. So … Am I truly losing Cristine?*

The question wasn't different than the one she'd come up with regarding Pia: Were the women the Count changed no longer themselves, but something wholly different? The answer mattered even more now. If Cristine would remain essentially the same soul, only physically stronger, then what was the harm? But if her entire being were to be transplanted by the Count's own … *Pia would argue against that*, remembered Amalina. *She said as much. But let's think about it … and not just for me …*

. . .

Amalina had noted in careful observation that, after recovering from their wounds, all the Count's converts weren't much changed from their old selves when it came to their customs and habits. They were perhaps quieter and introspective at times, and other times resembled animals nervously awaiting a storm, hyper-aware and probing. But aside from Princess Noka, they went out in the sun daily, often for the greater part of the day, and would even retire early at night for sleep. This was the opposite schedule of the Count, and nearly contrary to those unchanged Ladies still pursuing him. Amalina didn't know if the altered ones, by keeping to 'normal' daylight schedules, were testing themselves against the sun, which would one day burn them to dust. Or perhaps they were getting what they might out of their old life while they still could. Amalina had meant to ask Pia or one of the others about it. But then it seemed too intimate a question to ask, despite Amalina having assisted on all the Count's rites, which couldn't be any *more* intrusive.

But, thought Amalina presently, *there is* someone *who offers a remedy to this fundamental question, isn't there?*

"Dr. Cassette, may I borrow you for a moment?" asked Amalina, peeking into Montraine's private quarters while she was off in the library.

"Lady Tepsji?" said Dr. Cassette with a smile, waving Ms. Grafo over. "But of course. I was thinking of asking after you today. Perhaps we are of the same mind now, eh?"

. . .

Dr. Cassette and Ms. Grafo were troubled to learn of Cristine's sudden ailment.

"The same as …?"

"I don't know," said Amalina, truthfully. Who knew how far the Count's process had penetrated? She hurried along the hall, while the doctor and his assistant, with his physician's satchel rattling in hand, tried to keep up. "But she has no real servants to speak of. I am her only friend here. If I could have you take a look and see what you think. Your professional opinion."

"This is where we are headed, Lady Tespji, to appraise Lady Berzweck?"

"Yes. Um, how much *have* you observed of Cristine—um, Lady B?"

"We can't claim much at all. Why?"

"I just wonder when you examine her if you might notice any changes in her, besides physically. Maybe even small changes."

"Yes, these changes again." Dr. Cassette touched his head and winked. "Their minds? How they behave?"

Amalina touched her heart. "Or here. Just anything."

"The intangibles. And is that all we're meant to note in your Lady today?"

"No," said Amalina, definitely. "She seems to have wounds."

"Wounds?"

"It will be obvious."

"This doesn't sound like an illness, then."

"You'll see," promised Amalina, hoping she wasn't pushing this investigation too far; and without the Count's permission.

"At least she is not downstairs like the others," commented Cassette, as they arrived outside Cristine's room, in the upper floors, not far from Lady Camper's suite.

Amalina checked to see they weren't observed, then knocked on the door. Cristine's voice sounded weakly from the other side. Amalina entered, bringing Dr. Cassette and Ms. Grafo with her.

Cristine lay in bed and looked gaunt. Her only color was a red patch running around her neck. When she saw Amalina was not alone, she seized the covers and pulled them to her chin.

"Amalina!" shouted Cristine with what strength as she could muster. "Who are *they*?"

"This is Dr. Cassette and Ms. Grafo. I brought them to look—"

"OUT!"

"But ..."

"OUT! OUT!"

"They just want to look—"

"OUT! OUT! OUT! OUT! OUT!"

With the covers still wrapped around her neck, and a slight grey blush of embarrassment on her colorless cheeks, Cristine rose off the bed, sluggish but enervated. She threw two pillows at them in the doorway, and charged them until they retreated. Cristine slammed closed the door and sounded like she slid down to the floor behind it.

"Cristine, it's all right. They've tended to the others."

"I don't care! How dare you! Go away ..." the last part trailed off like she was running out of energy.

"But they can help."

"I can't believe you, Ama—I mean, Katarina. I can't believe you."

"Just open the door. They can help with the infection."

"There's no infection. Leave me alone."

"If she doesn't want to be seen ..." said the doctor, making a helpless gesture.

"She does," said Amalina. "She's just embarrassed. You saw her neck, didn't you?"

"Leave me alone!" shouted Cristine from the other side of the door. "Stop bothering me! Why do you always do this to me ...? Stop bothering me or I will call your uncle!"

"Is there something wrong?" asked the Count, startling everyone. Amalina knocked her head into the door. "I do wish to keep my Palace of Pleasures without too much noise, and no unneeded upsets to my guests. Oh ... Dr. Cassette, Ms. Grafo ... and my little mouse, Katarina. I would demand to know what you three are doing outside Lady Berzweck's room when she has requested to be left to rest."

"Your niece, Count Tepsji," said Dr. Cassette, unintimidated and looking smitten with curiosity, "has asked us—Ms. Grafo and I—to look after Lady Berzweck. There was a fear that she has fallen ill to the same malady which has affected your other guests."

"A fear. Yes. Now, Katarina ..." He growled through gritted teeth: "Katarina, must you be the constant nagging bee to my Palace's glorious flower? Why do you indulge your fears, instead of celebrating its pageantry?"

"But, Lord Tepsji, it could be something worse," said Dr. Cassette, with a curious expression at his comment, glancing between Amalina and the Count. "I observed a rash of some kind around her neck. Or some wounds."

"You saw this?" asked the Count, suddenly intrigued, one eyebrow lifting high onto his pale forehead, hinged in the middle to an inverted v. "Wounds?"

"Beyond mild blisters, if that's what it was. There was blood, perhaps. She should be looked after, Your Excellency. If it is fresh blood ..."

"Well, if there's something so serious as that, I should like you to see her immediately. Yes, Dr. Cassette, by all means. You must examine Lady Berzweck, and see what is there. Lady Berzweck? Lady Berzweck? I would ask that you allow us to enter so that Dr. Cassette may have a look at you."

"Count Tepsji?" said Cristine, in a dwindling voice.

"Yes. Please allow us to enter your room so that you may be examined."

"I don't think I want to."

"I would ask that you mind me and allow us entrance, Lady Berzweck. We are all friends here and will see to your privacy and safety. Your dear companion, Katarina, my kindly niece, is with us to make sure of it."

"I don't know ..."

"There is nothing to think about but to permit us entrance." The Count smiled at them with amusement at this novel entertainment.

"Are you ... Are you sure?" said Cristine. "Count Tepsji?"

"I am afraid I must insist that this happen, Lady Berzweck. Make yourself decent and we will enter."

There was the sound of a slow, uncoordinated scramble within the room. "Just wait. Just wait. I must make myself decent."

"What is happening here?" said Oroco, wandering up to the gathering, a concerned and curious look on his normally stern face. "I heard shouting."

"It is nothing to bother yourself about," said the Count. "Lady Berzweck is shy, but our Dr. Cassette will be observing her momentarily."

"Lady Berzweck? She has trouble?"

"Ill, I think," said the Count, becoming annoyed.

"Ill? Like the others?" Oroco was also annoyed, for another reason.

"Perhaps, perhaps not, Oroco. Go join your mistress, if you will. This is a private matter."

"But if I may have the good Dr.Cassette join my princess? She asks for him."

"Does she?" said the Count, turning on him fully now. "Why?"

"It can wait," said Oroco, not folding under the Count, but backing away. "Afterward, Count Tepjsi. After he is done here."

The Count turned to the door and knocked. "Lady Berzweck? Are you ready for us?"

"Hold."

"Is everything all right?"

"Just give me a moment to get ordered."

"We've been waiting, Lady Berzweck."

"You may come in, if you insist, milord," said Cristine. "I submit to this intrusion, if that is what you want."

The party made their way through the door and to Cristine's bedside. She had gathered up the covers around her greying face, and she stared out at them helplessly with her blue eyes, frightened. Her face seemed more sharp and pointed over the soft covers.

"There is no need to be scared," said Dr. Cassette.

"No need to be scared," rumbled the Count, in echo, at her. "Let the good doctor examine you."

"Are you really sure?"

"Please," said Dr. Cassette. "Just lay back and rest. And let me see."

Cristine closed her eyes and obeyed. She lay back on the pillow and let go the covers. Dr. Cassette nodded to Amalina, who pulled down the covers slowly to reveal her neck. Amalina made a small noise when she saw the wounds. Dr. Cassette and Ms. Grafo did not react. The Count tempered a smile that ticked below his mustache. His eyes smoothed and lowered their lids, and an almost contented purr could be heard, which was picked up a moment later by Grafo.

Cristine's neck was bleeding again, torn through all around, with horrible gashes and obvious scraping of fingernails up to her chin. Cristine had obscured the marks the Count had given her by replacing them with her own. Dr. Cassette snapped open his bag and took a thick cloth to cover the damage.

"You've scratched your neck, Lady Berzweck?"

Cristine nodded, her eyes now pressed closed.

Dr. Cassette touched her forehead and felt her arms and the top of her chest. He smirked at each spot. Then he shook his head. He turned over Cristine's hands, to reveal blood and pieces of skin on her fingers and stuck under her fingernails. There were also traces of bloody fingerprints on the underside of the covers. Dr. Cassette traded looks with Ms. Grafo.

"Are you not feeling well, Lady Berzweck?"

"I feel … tired. Very tired …"

"You've lost some blood. Which can be healthy, but in moderation. You aren't feverish. Is anything else bothering you? Any aches?"

"No, Doctor."

"Can you tell me why you scratched your neck?"

"It was itchy," said Cristine.

The examination didn't last much longer. Ms. Grafo pulled ointments and herbs out of the medical bag to create a soothing and healing poultice to apply to Cristine's neck—which the Count made a face at, after all this time enjoying how confounded the doctor and his assistant appeared.

"Well?" said the Count, like a cloud hovering over the two. "Are you satisfied?"

"Satisfied with what, Count Tepsji? She will be her old self again if she leaves her neck alone. That much is certain. But why to scratch that deeply when it must be so painful?" Dr. Cassette shook his head, and his assistant shook her head. "I would ask that you not bring her down into your dungeons with the others, in any case."

"My dungeons?" The Count took a beat to understand, but then he laughed. "No, I see no need in that. But they are very nice rooms, Dr. Cassette, I assure you, or I would not prefer them myself."

"You don't like the light?" said Dr. Cassette, sounding off-hand, but eyeing him like a new patient. "The sun bothers you, Count Tepsji?"

"Why do you say that?"

"Your affinity for living underneath the castle, out of the sunlight. You avoid it, it seems."

"I am quite busy with my work during the day, whether the sun is out or not. But it is my work that prevents me, if you will, from partaking in daylight adventures."

"Ah, I see."

"I *do* enjoy the night," the Count went on, his lips pursed, "and I prefer that wonderful time of the day to be my own, free of any work or cares. It is my belief the most pleasurable things in life happen *at night*."

Dr. Cassette accepted this truth with a deep bow of his head.

"But as for where I like to stay within my castle, though at a given hour I can be found anywhere in it, I do *prefer* the moderate temperature in the lower levels. It remains the same the year round. Coldest winter or hottest summer, all the same: comfortably cool. And with a delightful mineral edge to the taste of the air."

"Ah, yes. I see."

"I hope you do," said the Count. He turned to Cristine. "You performed well, Lady Berzweck. I think the doctors here are well satisfied, and you shall make a successful recovery. Just rest. I will see to your comfort. And I'm sure I will find something to relieve your fatigue and lassitude. Consider it a reward for your good behavior."

Cristine did not smile but nodded several times.

"And now you will see to Princess Kunuru Iwebo!" barked Oroco behind them, with a beaming smile.

. . .

Princess Noka Kunuru Iwebo's smile also beamed. But it was more pleasant and cheerful, not insistent like Oroco's. She welcomed her friends into her apartment with a bow and a wave. Her color had mostly returned, and she looked to be steady on her feet as she walked them to the back rooms. The Count cautiously followed her there, wary of any open windows. But the windows were closed and sealed. And soon they were in a room with the cow. The cow had been taken from the barn and given its own space within her quarters. There were little dark dashes—scars—up and down its neck. Its head dipped low. The cow looked as tired as Count Tepsji.

"Thank you for having us, Princess Kunuru Iwebo," said Dr. Cassette with a bow. "It is a pleasure to see you up and about. But what is the reason you have invited us?"

"To see how she has recovered," cheered Oroco. "Look at the Golden Sun Daughter!"

"Stop that, Oroco," snapped Noka with a bashful smile.

"No, my Liege, they must see with their eyes! Do not be ashamed! They must recognize!"

"Leave them alone, Oroco."

"Is that all, milady?" asked the Count. "You do look much improved."

"No, no, no," said Oroco, unsatisfied with their confused expressions. He tossed a bunch of flower petals over Noka, as two attendants tossed some on her legs and feet. "See, see, see."

Noka had been swaddled in an extensive knitted cover that looked like a modified black mantilla blanket. Oroco pulled it off her and gestured for her to spread her arms out as if for review. She was completely naked but for a colorful beaded belt. Amalina was shocked, but Cassette and Grafo remained clinically passive. The Count thrilled to the sight of Noka's beauty.

"No scars," said Oroco, pointing at her neck, her arms, her side, her legs. "No Scars. No scars. No scars."

"No scars, indeed," said Dr. Cassette. "Had she any scars? As Lady Berzweck has?"

"All gone!" said Oroco.

"May I?" asked Dr. Cassette. "May I look?"

Dr. Cassette and Ms. Grafo took Noka's arms and studied them and her neck. Noka observed with a pretty smile as they went about their work.

"You see?" said Oroco. "All gone!"

"You scratched yourself, Lady Oroco? Were you itchy?"

"Itching seems to have been a symptom," said the Count, eyeing Noka.

"The others didn't mention it," said Dr. Cassette. "Besides Lady Berz—"

"For them it wasn't as pronounced as with Lady Berzweck. Just here and there. I'm sure if you asked them again they will recall it for you. Very minor. They have all recovered."

"But none so much as the Golden Sun Daughter!" cheered Oroco. "None so much! Look at her!"

"That is enough," said Noka, still smiling gently. "Let them alone, Oroco. They have seen me. I am not a prize cow."

Oroco fell to the floor, much the way Genadie might before the Count. "Oh, no, no, no, Goddess!"

"I said stop with that," said Noka. "Now, the reason I invited you was to have you see a proper drinking. The last time, I was not feeling up to it. But now that I am mended, you may see how it is done. Oroco!"

Oroco leapt to work at the cow. In no time the two sticks had opened a stream of blood, which he caught in a cup. This time it was the cup made of lead which the Count used in his rites. The Count was overjoyed. There was something white in the cup's bowl that caused the blood to thicken and become rich looking.

"We mix in a little milk," said Noka, over Oroco's chants. "It is good."

Noka picked up her mantilla cover and placed it over her shoulders like a cape. When the cup was ready she stepped forward with two strong strides. There was no doubt that she was incredibly powerful, even with her lithe form. She took the cup from Oroco and brought it to her lips. Then she shook her head, as if she were catching herself being naughty. She held the cup out for the doctor to try. The Count stroked his mustache with an increasing rapidity.

"Yes, of course," said the doctor and accepted the cup with a courtly nod. He took a good swallow of it. "Well, it is warm. And it does have an interesting flavor. As one would expect."

Ms. Grafo passed on the offer with the shake of her head, but the Count accepted the next offering. He drank it, made a slight face and nodded his head to the side—as if to say, *not bad, but I've tasted much better.*

The cup went to Amalina. Amalina stared at it, with the bloody lip prints around the rim and the bubbles on the surface of the drink. She could not imagine. Noka's nose wrinkled as she grinned encouragement and watched Amalina for her reaction. Amalina could not help but glance at the Count, whose large brown eyes had grown twice their size and were ablaze. The way he was stroking his mustache, he might pull the hair right out.

Amalina closed her eyes and drank. Not too much, just a little sip. But somehow it suddenly filled her mouth, and it was as ghastly as she had hoped against. Warm and a bit frothy with the milk, it had the taste of a lost tooth, or a mashed nose. The obnoxious fluid crowded her whole mouth, swam over her tongue. Chemical. Metallic. Unwanted. Amalina winced.

Noka laughed. "Thank you, Katty. That was very brave. So good of you."

"So good," the Count enthused from his corner.

This is not me, this is not me, this is not me, Amalina was thinking.

Oroco replenished the cup and stopped the flow again. Noka held up the cup as if in a toast and then drank heartily. She seemed to shiver. When she was done she handed the cup triumphantly to Oroco. Everyone applauded; out of politeness, or for Noka braving the feat to conclusion, or simply in dumb-founded mechanical compliance to the giddy celebration, while their minds still processed their shock. Amalina's was politeness, but she saw a strange look on Noka's face. Not unlike the one the Count had had after his turn with the cup. No, it was exactly the same look the Count had had. It was as if his face—his lips—were hers; transplanted onto her face.

Oroco noted the smirk, too. "Victory, My Goddess?"

"Stop with that," she chided him, with a little less humor than usual.

"You are not satisfied?"

"It has changed."

"What's that?"

"The flavor has changed."

"It was goat's milk."

"Yes, that must be it."

"But you're good, Princess Kunuru?" asked Amalina in a hopeful voice. "You're feeling better? You look so much healthier. Do you feel stronger?"

Noka nodded with a shy smile, but there was still some dissatisfaction in her expression, which she was trying to hide. It almost looked as if she might cry. She glanced ruefully at the cup.

"But it is working for you," said Amalina. "This cow's blood? She looks exhausted, the poor old girl. We could get you a younger one. We can bring you a whole herd if you like."

"Little mouse, let's let the kind princess choose her own meals," said the Count. "This was only for our benefit. To observe her custom."

"But," said Amalina, taking Noka's hand, speaking meaningfully to her, "You know you can have that—a whole herd of cows—and use it, right? That that is all you'd ever really need to eat."

"I think some vegetables to the diet would be required," said a confused Dr. Cassette. "It can't be cow's blood alone."

"But you know what I mean, though, don't you, Noka? This is all very different, but is very *civilized*."

"Yes, of course," said Noka, looking Amalina in the eye, and then not looking. "Yes … Maybe …"

"What are you talking about, little mouse?" said the Count.

"Nothing. Just being encouraging. And accepting."

"Encouraging and accepting of what?"

"Of her ways."

"Sounds more like pushing her." He sounded irritable. "In a different direction she might not prefer."

"I don't know what you mean."

"I think you do."

Dr. Cassette turned his head sharply between Amalina and the Count, a narrowing look of confusion and curiosity on his face at their strange exchange.

"It's just very civilized, if you think about it, the cow doesn't have to die," said Amalina, trying to cover. "How much livestock do we slaughter every year to feed ourselves?"

"I see. I sssseeee …." The Count tried to shoot her with a reprimanding look, but she saw he was suddenly quivering with nerves. His eyes were bloodshot, and his teeth looked to be twitching behind his lips. His skin was growing dark in patches around his face, threatening to erupt in a dark fur.

Dr. Cassette turned to the Count, blinking, trying to see him clearly in the room's dim light. He wasn't trusting his eyes. Ms. Grafo began to narrow her eyes, too.

"I am famished myself," said the Count loud and abruptly, patting his stomach, becoming overly animated, turning himself into a stretching blur. "I'm afraid this kind of meal is not fortifying to *my* constitution. I will take my leave now. Much work to do tonight. I will perhaps see you tomorrow, Princess Kunuru. It has been educational and, as always, very lovely."

He bowed quickly and left, muttering low to Amalina on his way out, "I need to go *now*."

Amalina let out a sigh of relief. She was afraid he was about to make them all his meal.

Noka cleared her throat and wiped her mouth with the back of her hand. She still had a trace of concern on her face, though more her own expression than the Count's expression now.

"Are you all right, Noka?"

"Yes, Katty," she said softly with a polite smile. "Yes. I guess I don't like goat's milk today. Maybe the goats are different here? Tastes change, anyway. I feel like I will go lie down. Thank you for coming. Dr. Cassette, Ms. Grafo, good night."

The Count and Princess Kunuru had left the room so quickly, the others seemed to be surprised that they were now alone with each other.

"Her recovery is remarkable," said Dr. Cassette to Ms. Grafo. "I hadn't noticed any scars on her last time. But she was covered then and we didn't inspect her. But honestly, I thought she had been near death. Now she is very much at the peak of vitality."

"Would you say she is the same as before?" asked Amalina.

"Eh—what is that, Lady Tepsji?"

"Would you say she is the same person?" repeated Amalina, slightly intimidated by the doctor's look.

"I don't understand what you mean by that, Lady Tepsji. I'm afraid I just don't take your meaning, at all. You said as much before, didn't you? About your friends?" He rounded on her now, as if to give her an exam. Even Ms. Grafo's cat-eyes regarded her more closely, for inspection. "It is a peculiar thing to suggest."

"I'm sorry," said Amalina.

"Nothing to apologize for. I wish I could understand what you are trying to get at. Are you feeling *you* aren't yourself?"

"No, I—"

"I believe the mind also plays a key role in our well being, as much as our various humours. This is an opinion shared by Ms. Grafo and I, as well as a good number of physicians in practice. And if you have developed the belief that people you know are no longer themselves ... Well, I would suggest you look inward, eh? Ask yourself: 'am I myself?'"

"But that's not exactly what I mean."

"Lady Tepsji, you are at an age when many important changes are happening in your life. You may find yourself confused and questioning. This is absolutely natural, let me assure you. Is it not so, Ms Grafo?" Ms. Grafo gave a quick nod, but continued to stare curiously at Amalina, as if Amalina were a specimen to be collected and she was waiting for Cassette to give her the signal. "But as much as we change on the outside, we remain the same on the inside. We are ourselves, whoever we might be."

"So you believe that Noka—um, Princess Kunuru Iwebo, is the same Princess—no changes—who arrived here, and the same one we saw weeks ago, and the same one as now? The very same?"

"Yes. She is the same woman. I like to flatter myself that I can detect nuance. She is the same."

"No," said Oroco. "No."

"What?"

"She *has* changed," growled Oroco.

"How so?"

"She blossoms!"

"Oh, I see. Well, I suppose …"

"No, no, no, no," said Oroco, angrily now. "She has become stronger. She has become a god."

"Of course. If that is what you believe, sir."

"No, no, no, no!" Oroco grabbed the doctor's hand and pulled him along. "Come, come, come, come, come."

Oroco dragged Dr. Cassette to the next room, where Princess Noka was discovered lying on a sofa.

"What is this Oroco?"

"I'm sorry, your highness," the doctor apologized.

"Goddess, Goddess," cried Oroco, "he does not believe."

Oroco pulled the doctor down to Noka's side. He said something to Noka in their language. Noka held out her arm for inspection again.

"She is strong now. Stronger than ten men. Stronger and fiercer than a lion! An elephant! Faster than a jaguar! Feel! Feel! Feel!"

"We're at this again?" said the doctor, in an unfriendly voice to Oroco. "I'm sorry, Princess."

"It's quite all right," said Noka from her reclined position, as if she were sitting in a chair in a theatre observing what her manservant was getting up to on the stage.

"Feel, feel, feel!"

Oroco bent her arm and forced the doctor's hand to touch her. The doctor swatted Oroco's hand away, but then touched Noka's arms gently and squeezed. Oroco said something and Noka made a muscle. Dr. Cassette nodded and soon withdrew his hand.

"She is a goddess!"

"Whatever you like," said Dr. Cassette, looking bored taking his bag from Ms. Grafo.

"Do not insult the goddess!"

"Oroco!" scolded Noka.

"Now listen here," said Dr. Casssette. "I do not intend to insult your princess. She is a fine, lovely woman. But I will not allow you to insult *me*.

Do you hear? Do you understand? Princess Kunuru may be a goddess, I have no idea and no opinion on the subject. But speaking as a doctor, she is just as any other woman on this earth. Just a plain, ordinary woman. Not as strong as ten men. Not as fierce as a lion, nor as mighty as an elephant, nor as fast as a jaguar. A perfectly acceptable, smart, beautiful woman. You'd better learn to accept that." Then he turned to Amalina, who had been frozen in place for the past minute, mouth hanging slightly open. "And she is exactly the same person who entered these gates. Do you understand *that*, Lady Tepsji?"

Dr. Cassette left Oroco and Amalina with a formidable shake of the head, and pegged them with a final glance that told them they were both out of their minds. Ms. Grafo slunk out just behind him, with a more damning smug sniff in their direction.

Amalina went to her room, her fists balled in frustration, with the intention to sleep for the next three days.

. . .

"I found them," whispered Aklan, waking her. His eyes were twinkling mischievously and his cheeks were flushed, making it look like his fluffy blonde hair was set atop a freckled, sly smiling, blue-eyed tomato. "I found them, Pretty Princess!"

She felt a rush of dread as she stared at him from under her pillow. She had gone under it hoping to shut out the light and the world. But the boy …

Aklan, glowing befor her, was too eager, she saw now. She knew what he must mean. *Genadie's weapons!* He'd been looking for them before; searching. She'd forgotten about them … but he hadn't. "Where?"

"Forget it. I just wanted you to know. And I'm going to use them. Use them tonight!"

"No!"

"Oh, yes. I will put them to work and you'll finally be free, Pretty Princess. What do you think of that? I will restore your life. By dawn he will be no more, and you will have a castle and your friends … and the world."

For some reason that sounded frightening.

As he made his way to the door, she scolded him, hissing over and over again, sitting up now. "Don't you dare, you little fool! You're going to get yourself killed and it will all be on my account! I won't have it! I forbid you, I forbid you, I forbid you! Do you hear me?"

"Tonight, you'll see," he promised. "You don't want to be a blood drinker, really."

"I just want to rest, to sleep, and time to think … If you walk out that door," she warned, "If you don't stop and lie down this instant, I will never speak to you again! So … what will it be? Make your choice, boy!"

52

The Power of the Silver Moon

That night, there occurred the worst disturbance in the Palace of Pleasure's short history …

. . .

"My highness," said Oroco, as he bowed before Noka in her room, who was naked and curled into a ball on the sofa. "You are not cold?"

Noka shook her head.

"It grieves me, my highness, to see you this way. This is not who I once knew, the daughter of a king."

"What do you know of anything, Oroco?" said Noka, her voice muffled because her head was still tucked under her arm as it had been hours ago. And it sounded as if she had been, all the while and was still, crying. But that wasn't possible, was it?

"My highness, I understand what troubles you. Because what troubles you falls on my head, like a rain from the sky, to trouble me too."

"Stop with your poetry and leave me alone."

"*Margeta the Witch* convinced some of these pigs that the Count marrying so many women conforms to their early religious laws. Other pigs, I notice, have taken it as a pragmatic concession for what they will gain if they do. But you promised me, you convinced me, that for you, your majesty, it was something more-and-less. This Count Tepsji is but a lion overseeing his pride, whatever their number … but that you, my highness, intended to be like a lioness who strikes out on her own. Owned by nobody if she can help it. A true queen."

"That is what I said, and what shall be," Noka mumbled.

"The Golden Sun Daughter is no more," announced Oroco, sadly. "You were promised the power of the night, of the moon, and we have seen the demonstation of his great power, and heard of it told by your new sister wives. But though you have submitted your body to him, as he demanded, you do not fly. You are not a true queen lioness. You do not ascend to the pantheon of demigods, but are stuck on this … lowly couch."

"I will show you the power I have," warned Noka.

"Yes you will, my highness. For it is arranged that it shall be."

"What nonsense are you talking about, Oroco?"

"I've heard you cursing him in your tears. You know you have been betrayed, because you are not equal to that dog, Tepsji. And how can you ever be, when he has lived for countless years, and has built onto his power like the stones in this castle? You shall always remain behind him, and under him. Behind the other women, too." Oroco made a noise of disgust. "Because they have hunted before you, if some only for animals; they have had more time to water their growing gardens with blood."

"Okay, Oroco," admitted Noka, "So you do understand."

Oroco tutted her with a gesture, his mouth repressing a grim smile.

"Yes, always, my Liege," he said with a bow. "And you will never forget me in my service to you. For I will elevate you faster than the days of this earth would allow."

After this cryptic statement, Oroco took Noka by the hand and, walking backward, bent low at the waist, he led her to the outer chamber of her room.

There in the outer chamber all her retainers were sleeping on their mats. Their spears had been taken away and tied in a corner. In each corner of the room and on either side of a door, Oroco's warriors stood with swords at the ready, a hardened look on their faces.

Oroco swept his hand at the room and her sleeping servants, and whispered: "How many men have these pig-women killed? Not so much as this. How many does it take to reach the power of this Count himself? But you will have it today, my highness. Drink your fill. Stuff yourself beyond measure, until your belly breaks and your skin cries out. So that you can hold your head above those pig-women. With your full power achieved, you can even return to your father and drive out of your lands the enemies of your tribe."

Noka's gaze was solemn and steady. But she also, somehow, looked unsure. And something in her shook, and her eyes seemed to change, revealing a building hunger. "They are giving themselves to Noka?"

"Yes, my highness."

"Willingly?"

"Not all of them know. But most. And they will be glad that, when it is done, they shall be living inside their princess forever. Whatever cowards there are, we brave souls inside you will outnumber and correct their spirits."

"We?"

"Let me spur you on," said Oroco, holding a curved blade to his throat. "You must take us all, every one of your people, without pity. But allow me to be the first step on the path to your rightful place among the stars, Silver Moon Goddess."

• • •

Amalina was suddenly being pulled out of bed.

"What is happening, what is happening, what is happening?" said the man dragging her. She couldn't tell who it was.

"What?"

"Pils, what are you doing?" cried Aklan.

But Pils wouldn't stop whimpering the same question. And now that Amalina was out of her bed, he grabbed her arm and pulled her to the open door. His eyes were large and regarded the doorway and what was beyond with terror.

Aklan tried to break Pils' hold on Amalina. But a scream came from outside and the young prince ran out, pulling his knife.

"No, don't," shouted Pils, trying to tackle Aklan. He disappeared out the door.

Amalina trodded dully after the two, dreading what might be happening in the hall. There were more screams; sad and blood curdling. Had the Count gone insane? or had had some horrid change of heart and was massacring the house? So many voices in torment.

The hallway had trails of blood. Crimson footprints running up the hall. She followed them and their shouts, as they comically looped around this end of the castle as if in a race.

Aklan came charging back at her. "It's the princess! She's gone mad!"

Which one? wondered Amalina. Had Margeta finally decided to whittle down the competition herself? Some of the other Ladies were fragile, but Margeta was the only one vicious enough to resort to open violence. Then Amalina gulped ... or what if it was one of the noble ladies or converts who had turned ...? *Is this Pia?*

She imagined Pia with her ravenous green eyes and bloody mouth tearing apart whoever she could get her hands on. But it could easily be any of the others—who knew what they might do when faced with the hunger?

Who?

One of Noka's servants came screaming around the corner, followed by a second, out of their minds, in full panic flight. Their bodies hurtled past, feet drumming on stone with little control.

"What's happening?" shouted Amalina after them.

But then Dr. Cassette rounded the corner, too, skidding into the wall, then barreling after the servants. When he saw Aklan and Amalina, he scooped them into his arms.

"Countess! Into your room! Lock the door! Barricade it!"

"What's happening?" Amalina demanded again.

But Noka's servants had stopped at another corner in the hall, and now they tripped over each other as they fell back. At the same time, at the end of the hall they'd originally come, one of Noka's warriors appeared, holding his long-bladed spear menacingly, an angry look on his face.

"What's happening!" cried Amalina.

Dr. Cassette shoved Aklan and Amalina aside and put himself between the warrior and the servants.

"Get out of the corridor, Countess," said Dr. Cassette. Then he waved his hands warningly at the warrior walking slowly up the hall at them. He said to the warrior: "Hey! Stay away! Stay away!"

There must have been another warrior, or set of them, coming up the other hallway, from the other direction, in the same steady way, both sets cornering the servants who were scrambling over each other and crying something in their tribal language.

"They, come!" said the warrior, pointing his spear at the servants for Amalina's benefit.

While Noka's servants had been quick studies and were marvelously fluent in a number of languages, Oroco had kept his warriors out of the learning circle. They would be free of the influence of the foreigners and so more easily under his and Noka's control. They knew only a few words.

"Noka Kunuru!" Amalina said to him. "Princess Kunuru! Oroco? Oroco?"

"Oroco's dead," said Dr. Cassette, with measured rage. "Now get out of the way before you get hurt."

The servants huddled in the corner of the hall screamed and leapt over Dr. Cassette, braving the spear of the warrior in front of them. The reason for their new-found courage was Noka, who landed right where they had been, her face, lacy clothes, and body awash in blood. She was laughing madly. But it was her eyes, her burning red eyes that struck fear into everyone, including Cassette. They spoke of a wild, eternal hunger that would not be satisfied; and anyone, everyone, was its prey.

Noka leapt onto the back of the slowest servant, slashing her fingernails at the nape of his neck. The servant dropped to the floor. The faster one shoved past the warrior and darted down the hall and back around the bend.

Dr. Cassette threw Amalina and Aklan into the nearest room and then pounded his entire body into Noka's. It was pandemonium for a second, with three bodies spinning around each other, sprays of blood between them.

Amalina screamed and slammed the door closed, and she and Aklan put their backs to it to brace it closed.

"Did you see her?" panted Aklan. "I should've gotten Genadie's weapons!"

"Lady Tepsji!" said Dr. Cassette on the other side of the door. It sounded like a lamenting cry.

"Dr. Cassette?"

"Come out, it is safe," he said.

Amalina cracked open the door. Cassette was on his hands and knees, his shirt covered in blood, but it didn't appear to be his. He was wiping his right hand on his jacket. Besides him, the hall was empty.

"Oh!" said Amalina, rushing to him.

"Get the women together. Where is the palace guard? Where are they? They need to protect the Ladies. Where is your uncle, Lady Tepsji?"

"Let's get them," said Amalina. She helped the doctor to his feet as Aklan stood guard. But the boy didn't know which way to point his knife, so he pivoted about nervously. "But tell me what's happened—"

"You've seen for yourself, haven't you?" said Dr. Cassette testily. "My god, it is unimaginable, but it is true: Princess Noka—sweet Princess Kunuru Iwebo—has become a bloodthirsty lunatic!"

"Why didn't you try to stop her?"

Dr. Cassette regarded Amalina like the fool he thought she was. She couldn't be someone out to deliberately confound him, after all, but was just a plain dunce. His tone said as much: "*I just did. But you see where it got me. We need the palace guard and your uncle. Now!*"

"Where are you going?"

"To secure my Lady Montraine and then the others. There's no telling what's going to happen next."

"Don't alarm her."

"Go to hell, Lady Tepsji," said Dr. Cassette, coldly. He straightened his shirt. "But first get your fucking palace guard and your fucking uncle here to see to this situation!"

• • •

As Amalina made her way downstairs, cautiously tiptoeing up to and around corners, darting headlong down clear passages and stairways, she would encounter a servant of Noka's here and there, screaming or crying, being pursued by a warrior, the sound of Noka's laughter cracking the air. Amalina dodged her way down to the main floor, and never once saw a castle guard. Servants in *l'entrée grande* peered nervously up the stairwell at her when she arrived. Amalina ordered them to their rooms. "Has anyone seen a guard? Or Durok?" she asked them. "Where is Count Tepsji?"

Anka spoke up as she hurried in another direction: "Left for the evening! Another astronomy outing with the Ladies!"

"Astronomy!" Amalina huffed. "Anka, come back here! Pils! Get up to Cristine's room."

"What!!!" they cried.

"Make sure she's okay. Lock the door, stay with her. Bring something to defend yourself."

"Bring what?" said Pils, turning white.

"Anything, go! I'll get the houseguard. But where are they?"

Amalina didn't head immediately out of the front doors to find a guard. She detoured to Genadie's shack. He was shocked to find Amalina barreling in, sending snow all over his floor.

"Genadie, get the emergency bell!"

"What? What's happened?" croaked Genadie, as he threw off his covers.

"Princess Noka's run amok! She's killing people! We have to get the Count here or we'll all be eaten."

Genadie gulped, but tore through his hovel looking for the bell—the bell specialized to sound emergencies to the Count, wherever he may be in the mountains—eager to do a service for his Master.

"Isn't here, Ms. Dalca! It's gone!"

"Then get your weapons. Bring them out."

"What ... um, what weapons?"

"You know the ones! We need them right now. I don't want to kill her, but if we have to ..."

"Oh, Ms. Dalca!"

"If we can't call your Master, we're going to have to do the job ourselves. You and me! Now let's go! Grab them wherever they are and take them up to Aria's room—that's where most of the ladies will be. If you find any ladies along the way, have them come too. To Aria's room, remember. Take them. Order them. Everyone must stick together."

"Where are you going?" asked Genadie, his mouth hanging open.

"To find out what's happened to the palace guard!"

. . .

Amalina didn't feel the biting wind or the chill of the wet snow sticking to her legs as she fought through the drifts to the front of the courtyard. Along the way she shouted for Durok.

"Up here, Mouse," said Durok. He was looking down at her from the wall. "It's *Captain* Durok."

"Why are you up there—?"

"I'm Captain Durok now. Been promoted, Mouse."

"Good for you, but what are you doing there, for heaven's sake? where are your men? We need them immediately!"

"What's this about?"

"What do you mean, what's it about? It's about everyone inside is in danger. We need help!"

"Princess Kunuru's faction, is it?"

"What's that you have there?" cried Amalina, looking at what he was holding. "Is that Genadie's emergency alarm?"

Durok hugged the bell tight against his chest. "What about it? I've been promoted. It belongs with me."

"Ring it, Durok!" snarled Amalina. "We need the Count here this minute."

"No you don't."

"Yes we do!"

"It's no problem, little mouse. It's all been arranged for."

"What are you talking about?"

"Nothing to fear. The guests are safe. This is an internal matter."

"Ring the bell!"

"Oroco already explained. There may be a bit of a noise, but it's all contained. Strictly Princess Kunuru and her people. There will be no bell. There will be no emergency."

"Nothing's contained, Durok! The princess, her warriors, they are loose and people are dead!"

"I've been instructed," said Captain Durok. "No bell. Do you understand? It's all been arranged. The Master needs his time and concentration tonight, with the others. I'm in charge here."

Amalina swore at him, but then grabbed a hefty and cumbersome number of spears, pikes, and halberds off the weapons rack and left him for the main building.

53

Dawn of the Brocade Army

Part One:
Egalité

Returning to the ladies' apartment floors, the halls and stairs were the same going back up as when Amalina had come down: electrically charged with the frightening cat-and-mouse game being played out between the laughing Princess Noka and her warriors against her terrified, fleeing servants. Amalina, with oversized weapons threatening to spill from her arms at every step, their long shafts knocking clumsily on her knees, kept out of their way and, mercifully, did not see Noka at all. But her heart leapt in her chest at every flick and shadow of the torchlight as she moved along, with the clattering weapons in her hands getting heavier and heavier.

"Noka!" she whispered as loud as she dared. "What are you doing? The others can't know about you! They *shouldn't* know! Noka! Noka!"

Rounding one corner, Jane Camper marched up the corridor with purpose, holding two pistols.

"Where are you going, Jane?" asked Amalina, surprised. "Get in your room!"

"Like hell. One of these bastards tried to hide in my suite. Came barging right in! Then the next thing I know, two more are breaking it down, swords in their hands."

"Come with me then. We're holing up in Aria's room with everyone else."

Just then, one of Noka's servants, looking worn out, stumbled down the hall. But he stopped and doubled back. There was a shout behind Amalina and Jane. From that direction came two warriors.

Jane swung one of her pistols up. The hammer dropped and it hissed and puffed, and then a shot rang out. One of the warriors dropped his long-bladed spear and grabbed at his hip. The other retreated around the corner.

"See what a lady of true Virginia blood can do!" shouted Jane Camper, proudly.

The second warrior reappeared with a pistol in hand, just as the first one recovered and pulled a pistol of his own from his waistband. They both fired in unison, and Jane Camper dropped her guns with a thin spray of blood off her wrists. She looked at her hands as if they had defied her in some unforgiveable way, saying "Ah! Ahhh!"

Amalina supposed Jane had gotten lucky, as there would be little chance anyone could pull off so perfect a harmless wingshot. Jane ran away from the warriors, shouting her dissatisfaction, as they came forward with their spears, trotting after Noka's long disappeared servant. Amalina dropped her weapons to assure them she didn't mean any harm. They moved past her as if she wasn't even there.

• • •

What's to be done? Amalina wondered, as she made her way to Aria's room. Hopefully Genadie had gotten there safely with his creature-killing weapons. But those things wouldn't be of much use, would they? Genadie had used them on the Strange Man when that creature was sleeping and had been made docile and half dead already by a quantity of smoke from a clogged fireplace, well before Genadie's fatal-finisher was sprung. There would be no element of surprise this time. Noka was awake and only getting more ramped-up by the sound of it. She was thrilling at the chase, and building power as she consumed her servants. Again, the image of Pia ripping apart the Germanian delegation flashed through her mind.

Not done yet, the Count's proud voice echoed in Amalina's memory.

Had *he* arranged for this massacre, too? she wondered hotly. He so conveniently out of the way with his other women on an 'astronomy lesson'?

"Countess," said a voice behind her.

Amalina turned with a clattering of the weapons in her arms.

Balbo and one of the castle guard stood at the end of the hall. They'd just come off the stairs. Balbo held two pistols, much like Jane Camper. The guard had a torch and bounced a sword in his other hand nervously. They stared at her, almost unbelieving.

"What is it, Mr. Balbo?"

"What is it?" said Balbo, incredulous, as they came for her, shooting nervous looks all round. "Why … I've come to offer my protection."

"Your protection?"

"The Ladies, *our* Ladies."

"And you're mine," said the guard to Amalina, his beady eyes flashing as bright as the sweat on his brow. "I'm to take you below and into my protection if things get out of hand in the castle. And by the sound of it, time's about ripe—"

"I thought we weren't being protected tonight," snarled Amalina in a scathing tone. "I thought the castle guard were standing down."

"Well, I'm just here to protect *you*, Countess. Special orders."

"Only me?"

"Sorry, Countess. You and you alone." His eyes flashed. "We all have our orders. But if you'll come along now—"

"I'm not going anywhere with you," said Amalina, backing up, leading them further along the hall. They moved slower than Amalina though, as they stepped cautiously under the threat of the screams. She wished she could turn her head to better see where she was going. To watch if Noka suddenly bounded into the hall behind her. "I'm not leaving my guests to fend for themselves."

"Don't you worry your little head, Lady Katarina," said Balbo, trying to sound appropriately condescending, grinding his bearded jaw while attempting to appear confident, despite his goggled eyes and wild tufts of white hair as if he'd just rolled out of bed. "I'll be looking after them."

"All by yourself, Mr. Balbo?" replied Amalina, a little more sarcastically than she meant to. "You think you can manage?"

He seemed to deflate.

"I know it may seem silly to you, Countess," said Balbo, suddenly defensive, swiping at his hair with a pistol to smooth it, his voice fluttery. "I beg you not pass judgement on me just for my looks, milady. I'm not just an engineer, I hold the rank of a colonel in—"

"I don't think it is silly at all, Mr. Balbo!" interrupted Amalina, apologetically; aware that even if the old man did seem meager, and a little pathetic in the crisis, he meant well, anyway. And she might need *everyone* tonight. Any help was worth it. Better to puff him up for the fight. "Sorry if I offended you. I thank you for your bravery and and generous help. You look a lot better armed with those pistols than with a bouquet."

"Oh, well—"

Amalina rounded a corner clumsily.

"And where are your partners, Wanger and Regio? Are they coming to help?"

"Down below," said Balbo. "Safely, I should say. All the actions seems to be up here, Countess. And so if I might advise—"

"You'll be coming with me now, Countess," said the guard, stopping in place as if that would also stop Amalina back-pedaling. When she continued he was forced to follow. "Now, I said—"

"And I say I'm not coming with you," she replied. "Safety in numbers, you're coming with me!" Amalina suddenly reversed course and stomped forward, straight for the guard. "You can protect me just as well anywhere, and I'm not going *anywhere else* until I deliver these!"

"Oof!" She thrust the weapons she was carrying into his arms. The guard struggled to keep them contained. "What's this!"

"You can help me take these to Lady Ecci's room first. Let's go!"

"Oh, ho, now!" But he didn't move. He shook his head, slowly. "No, Countess. Those aren't my orders. You are coming with me, eh?"

Amalina glanced between Balbo and the guard.

"Mr. Balbo?" she appealed to him.

The guard, still holding the torch and his sword, dropped the extra weapons in a loud burst onto the floor. He grimaced at the noise, then at Amalina. "Let's not disobey the Master here," he said, changing his grimace to a tensely polite smile.

"And abandon our guests?" said Amalina. "*My* guests?"

"The guests are taking care of themselves, from the sound of it, Countess. And Mr. Balbo has promised—"

"*You* aren't going to obey *me*?" hissed Amalina at the sweating guard.

"Well ..." he said, unsure. His gritted-tooth smile—or was it his his beady eyes?—didn't seem friendly. "But you aren't going to listen to your uncle, then?"

"He didn't say anything of this protection business to me."

"I'm telling you now."

"All right, I'll do as he wishes," said Amalina, "do you understand? I'll do as he wishes, as soon as *you* do what is right. Pick up those weapons and help me deliver them."

The guard eyed her, his slow mind unable to decide.

Feeling officious and like a real lady of privilege for once, Amalina let her anger ring out. "Seems it's all been left up to *me* to sort things out tonight. Well then I will. Do you understand? I am the only one of rank here. So you, Mr. Balbo, and everyone, you're going to listen, and do as I say." She pointed to the weapons on the floor. "Now pick them up."

"Well ..."

A scream sounded from upstairs.

Amalina hopped over the pile and snatched the torch from the guard's hand as his mouth dropped open.

"Now!" commanded Amalina. "We don't have time to stand here. Get them up and let's go. Move it!"

"Well ..." he said again, his eyes squinted. But he shook his head more firmly now, as if he'd come to a decision, and stooped to begin gathering the weapons.

"Well, nothing, sir! Who is the Countess here? Just drop your sword in with the rest and it will be easier to pick it all up. Do you hear me? Obey."

The guard just gritted his teeth, continued to shake his head, and muttered to himself. " ... I got it ... I got it ..."

"Hurry now," said Amalina, feeling her power. Feeling like she was was almost enjoying it. Maybe it was distracting from the terror of the moment, her voice drowning out the screams. Or maybe it *was* just the exercise of power that thrilled her. She continued: "We haven't time."

"Haven't time she says ..." mumbled the guard.

"No, we haven't time," echoed Amalina.

"... raided the whole armory ..."

"Enough of that jabbering, more effort."

Hugging the weapons, he stood and looked to her for instructions. "Well then, Countess?"

She pointed down the hall. "That way."

"Of course, of course," grumbled the guard with a twist of his neck. "Why not? Only have one job to do ... one simple job ..."

"And you better do it right. You hear me? Better than sleeping in your bunk, waiting for the storm to pass, letting our guests be imperiled—"

The guard wasn't listening. He was shaking his head with a snarl on his face, lost in his own heated thoughts. As the weapons chanked in his arms, threatening to slip free at any step, he ground his teeth and continued to mutter in frustration, " ... that's it, girl ... that's it ... keep talking ... that's all ... that's all ... one simple job ... one girl in all the world ..."

Amalina's hair stood on end.

. . .

Those words: *one girl in all the world.*

Hadn't that been in—?

Suddenly Amalina remembered AXP's last message to the Count—*one girl in all the world is not essential, no matter how intricate the scheme*—and she also recalled how Margeta had once secreted an assassin into the castle.

So, could this guard be ... ?

He *couldn't* be, could he?

. . .

"What's that?" hissed Amalina.

Amalina switched the torch to her other hand and pointed to the guard's back for Balbo's benefit. But even as she stabbed her finger in the guard's direction, the old man's large eyes rounded at her in confusion, and for an explanation. Amalina grabbed one of the pistols from his hands.

"Countess!" exclaimed Balbo.

She leveled the pistol at the guard's back.

"Stop there! You! Stop!"

"What's that?" the guard halted and turned. His eyebrows went up when he saw the pistol in her hand.

"Keep hold of them," she ordered, when it looked like he might set down the bundle.

"What's this?" the guard flicked his eyes at Balbo, then cocked his head, unsure of what was taking place. "Now is not the time for—"

"What did you just say?" she demanded. "Tell me what you just said."

"I … I don't know."

"What's the matter, Countess?" asked Balbo. Pointing his pistol at the guard, too, though looking baffled as to why.

"Who are you?" said Amalina.

"Poul, Countess. No last name. Just Poul. Never knew my parents—"

"I mean *who* are you?"

"What do you mean?"

"He's one of the castle guard, Countess," said Balbo.

The man nodded slowly, pointing his eyes to Balbo. "He's right."

"Okay. Drop it. Drop it all."

The guard set the pile onto the floor as if humoring her, but was wary, again with his tense teeth-gritting smile.

"Something the matter, Countess?" he said. "This isn't the time—"

"Your orders again?"

"Protect you, Countess."

"Orders from who, exactly?"

"Who do you think?"

"Answer me. Was it Captain Durok?"

"As I said. His Excellency. Count Tepsji."

"Is that so?"

The guard nodded.

"What is the matter, Countess?" mumbled Balbo, nervously glancing up and down the hall.

"And what did my uncle say to you, eh?" she asked the guard again. "What were your precise orders? Tell me now. I order you to tell me."

"As I said, to protect you; to see to your safety while he is out of the castle tonight."

"Only me?"

He nodded slowly, his teeth clamped together ferociously.

"The 'one girl in all the world'?" she said, observing his reaction.

"What's that?"

"Mr. Balbo," said Amalina, taking another step back, away from the old man.

"Yes, Countess."

"The Count gave you this order for my protection, too?"

"Me? Oh, no. Not at all. As I said, I was just worried about the princesses ..."

"And that is what brought you up here, Balbo, our Ladies?"

"Yes. Oh, yes."

"Mr. Balbo, how are you in the company of this soldier then?"

"What? Oh, well, Countess, he was asking after ... well ... after you ... or that is ..."

"After me?" said Amalina, now centering her attention on the guard. She said, as if it were unlikely: "He asked *you* about *me*?"

"Yes, that's right."

"For the Countess? Katarina? Or ... *Amalina*?"

"He seemed to know who he was referring to, Countess."

"He mentioned Amalina."

"Um, perhaps. I think so, Countess," said Balbo, not understanding the problem, sweaty and shivering, his eyes darting, his frame quaking at every echoing scream and cackle. He shrugged. "Honestly, I don't remember now. But perhaps this *isn't* the time—"

"It ain't the time, Mr. Balbo," agreed the guard. "It ain't. Now, Countess, why don't you point that gun away and—"

"You'll just stand right there, sir," said Amalina. "And do nothing more until I say so."

"I don't really think you're keen to shoot me, girl," he said, taking half a step toward her, "or have it in you."

"One of us does at least," said Balbo straightening his back, brandishing is own pistol to remind the guard. "If not both. Stay put, as your Mistress says."

The guard fell back a half step with a nod, but eyed Balbo as if sizing him up.

"Thank you, Mr. Balbo."

"Think nothing of it, Countess. But—"

"Mr. Balbo, you've experience with the weapon you are holding? You've used a pistol before?"

"What? Yes. Oh, yes. Many times, Countess. As I was saying, I once served, and am still a ranking officer in—"

"Take another step back, if you will, Mr. Balbo. Away from this man."

"Yes, Countess," he said as he did so.

"And keep your pistol aimed at him."

"Oh? Oh, yes."

"Now what's going on, miss?" asked the guard, his patience at an end. "I don't like any of it. Listen, we need to clear out of this passage before—"

"Mr. Balbo, do you recognize this soldier? Have you seen him before?"

"I can't say I have. But I don't spend much time in their company."

"I don't think he belongs here," said Amalina. "I don't think I've ever seen him before, until this very moment. I don't recognize him at all."

"That wouldn't surprise me one bit, miss," grimaced the guard. "But how is that my fault? I've been serving here at the castle, all this time, all the same. Now—"

"I believe you are an agent."

"A what?"

"You are here in the service of another."

"Another what? I don't know what you're talking about, little girl. Have you lost your senses?"

"Don't be impudent," warned Balbo.

"Mr. Balbo, if you care for my uncle, and for me, and for your life—"

"Oh, of course, of course!"

"—You will keep your pistol trained on this man here—Poul, if that is his real name—and you will take him downstairs with you, in your custody. And should he move in any way that closes the distance between you two, or he and myself, you will shoot him. Do you understand?"

"But I have my orders, Countess," complained the guard.

"And I'm ordering you below. And now Mr. Balbo has his orders, too. To shoot you if you don't obey."

"But ... what's happening here, Countess?" asked Balbo, still befuddled. "I must know."

"Just do as I say, Mr. Balbo. All is well if he remains in your custody. I'll see to the Ladies myself."

"Yes, Countess."

"Leave," said Amalina to the guard, pointing him away from the pile. "Come around and make some distance, if you will."

"You're refusing my protection, Countess?" asked the guard, though circuiting away from her obediently, as if the mouth of her pistol were a cannon. "Don't know if Count Tepsji will forgive me if I don't do my job. You understand what that means for me? what you are doing to me?"

"Worry about that later. The pistols are on you now."

"You'll be all right without my protection, Countess Tepsji?" asked Balbo.

With her eyes and pistol still pointed at the guard, Amalina gathered the pile of weapons back into her arms. She had to strain to keep from looking as if she were straining. As if this were all natural and easy for her.

"The Ladies and I can protect ourselves well enough, don't you worry," she said. "Strength in numbers, as I said. You just worry about yourself, Mr. Balbo, and carry out your orders."

"Y-yes, Countess. Of course." It looked like he wanted to slick down his hair. He twitched his head between his shrugging shoulders. "You'll come with me, sir. Poul, is it?"

"Mr. Balbo," said the guard, "whose side are you on, sir? sensible men, sir, or a girl who has lost her little mind?"

"I said leave off your superior—your Lady—and don't get above yourself."

"If you weren't holding that gun, sir, I'd teach you a lesson."

"However, I am. And the hammer is cocked as you see."

The guard stared daggers at Amalina. "You're doing me wrong with your uncle, miss. That isn't fair."

"AXP will learn to leave me alone," said Amalina. "Tell him so, if you can."

"What? Who?"

"AXP. You heard me."

"I don't know what you're talking about," said the guard. "And I doubt you do, either."

"Maybe not," she allowed. "We'll sort that out later though, won't we? Thank you for your service, Mr. Balbo. It won't be forgotten."

"You're sending a man to his undeserved death, miss," said the guard, his brow awash with sweat, his beady eyes flashing. "Condemned."

Even as she watched them go, Amalina didn't know if she'd just done something right. And as the screams continued to rise around her, she no longer felt like a Lady in Command, but like Amalina Dalca, the little mouse, all over again.

54

Dawn of the Brocade Army

Part Two:
Sororité

In Aria's room, a handful of the Ladies of Title were gathered loosely together, sprinkled in among the larger crush of their servants. Most everyone was terrified, though some of the nobler Ladies looked merely put-off by the awkward circumstance. Standing to the side of them with a lost frown, Genadie seemed as if he were a guest who'd been invited to the wrong party.

"Good evening, Katty," greeted Aria Ecci, as Amalina entered and loosed all the weapons to the floor in front of them. "Oh, you dropped something."

"Here … you can have this." As she caught her breath, Amalina offered Balbo's pistol to Aria. Some of the servants gasped.

Aria pushed the pistol away with the tip of her finger. "I can't imagine what you think I would do with it."

"For protection."

"Those things only fire once," she sneered at it, "don't they?"

"Maybe someone else, then."

One of the male servants held out his hand and Amalina gave it to him. He wandered back into the crowd, acquiring a few admirers.

"Where is everyone else?" Amalina asked Genadie, turning to him. "You couldn't find them?"

"Most have locked themselves in their rooms and didn't want to join us. Princess Margeta la Brichese and Princess Maria di Oscina are holding a midnight service in the chapel."

"I'm here, Pretty Princess," shouted Aklan, waving at the back.

"You haven't passed out *your* weapons?" she asked Genadie. "But you do have them here, right?"

"Lady Tepsji," said Dr. Cassette, coming from nowhere and seizing her hand firmly, ushering her toward a side room. "A word. In private."

"Of course." Amalina put on a game face as she was marched out of the room with everyone watching. No one seemed to be bothered that their host was being led off in such an indelicate manner.

• • •

Dr. Cassette breathed heavily when he closed the door. He bowed to her. "Now, Lady Tepsji, I apologize for how I handled you earlier. But we are going to be honest with each other. No?"

"Of course. What is it?"

"You will tell me what is happening here inside your castle."

"I was asking you earlier, if you remember," said Amalina, feeling defensive again. "Will you tell *me* what happened?"

"All I know is that I had placed Ms. Grafo at Princess Kunuru Iwebo's door, in order to observe—or eavesdrop, if you like—on what might be taking place in her quarters. I was curious after that display with the cow and Oroco's odd behavior. And yours, too, Lady Tepsji. But suddenly we heard a shout. Then several. And it sounded like a struggle. Ms. Grafo and I entered Princess Kunuru Iwebo's suite.

"Oroco was dead on the floor already. And maybe one or two of her servants. And the princess herself was running around the room, chasing after her people, who were screaming and shouting, and being prodded by her warriors to stay within a circle. As soon as we opened the door, they took it as an exit. And then the chase was on.

"Ms. Grafo tried to help one of the servants, who a warrior had gotten hold of. But that warrior put a sword through her. I am afraid she is dead. And that is all that I know. Now, it is your turn, Lady Tepsji, if you please?"

"But I don't know," said Amalina. "I don't. I was there in Noka's chamber with you this evening. Then I went to bed. I woke only to be thrown in the middle of what's occurred."

"She is killing her people, Lady Tepsji," he said matter-of-factly, as if reminding Amalina, but he was energized. "Not by her servants, nor her warriors, but rather *she's* killing them. The warriors are merely collecting for her. She is killing them personally, with her own hands."

"Oh, I see."

"Oroco said she had the power of ten men. Of Lions. Of an elephant. The speed of a Jaguar, wasn't it? I can say it is an exaggeration, but only by a little. She feels as strong as five good men. That is unnatural. I've experienced the incredible strength of madmen, and this is like that in a way but more so. And Oroco spoke of how she had changed. How she was changing physically—not *mentally*, as you'd have it. And when I examined her, she was not insane. She could not have changed—descended into an animal state of madness—so quickly, in so short a time."

Dr. Cassette stopped talking. He watched Amalina expectantly, his eyes ticking back and forth to meet hers. She wasn't sure what to say.

"And so, Lady Tepsji, you were talking—insisting—about changes to your friends. Even Princess Kunuru, when we were in her room. And there was this business of scars. Your friend, the mineral merchant's daughter, Lady Berzweck, with her self-inflicted gouges around her neck. And Oroco claiming that Princess Kunuru had healed from hers." He shifted to get closer to Amalina. He whispered now, confidentially. "And without having to examine you, but just by looking, I can identify a number of old scars that have healed on you. In your hair. On your arms."

Amalina bit her lower lip. The many scars from her tangles with the wolf come back to haunt her. Were they really so visible?

"Now, Lady Tepsji, the scars, the changes: You *know*. Eh? And you will tell me what it all means."

"I ... But it is a matter for you to discuss with your mistress, perhaps. And my uncle."

"Yes? You really won't tell me yourself?"

Amalina shook her head. She couldn't help it. In his eyes. Dr. Cassette was curious, but terrified. She saw Crutio's expression written on his face. She knew if she told him, he would meet Crutio's fate. Erik Kosche's fate. Piotr's Fate. Kralov's fate. If she said nothing, and left the doctor innocent, maybe he would survive. In the silence, he seemed to understand what was waiting for him behind her blank look.

"Are we in danger, Lady Tepsji?"

"I don't think so, but—"

"Is my Lady Montraine in any danger?"

"I believe this is a private matter between Princess Kunuru Iwebo and her people. Really, I believe so. One that has gotten completely out of hand."

"Ms. Grafo is dead."

"I am sorry about that."

"Will you guarantee our safety?"

"I wish I could. But my uncle ... he's the only one who can ... *Really*."

There was a slam and a shout from the other room. Dr. Cassette charged away immediately, almost like he was running away from Amalina.

There came another shout.

. . .

One of Noka's servants had gotten through the door. The Ladies' own attendants formed a ring around him, protecting their charges. They shouted insults at him, and a few kicked at him or braced to push him away. One turned the key in the door, locking it.

"Now now!" yelled Dr. Cassette from outside the circle. "Now now! There is nothing to be alarmed about. This man is on the run and no threat. Isn't that right?"

The servant nodded dumbly as if he couldn't speak the language. He put his fingers to his lips, hoping they would quiet down.

"He's not our enemy," Dr. Cassette continued. His voice was patient but forceful, as if to tamp down the general panic. "We must protect him, as we are agents of goodness and peace. Yes?"

"Thank you," said the servant.

"There appears to have been a civil war that has erupted in Princess Kunuru Iwebo's retinue. A private matter among themselves, and they are at war. But we will offer asylum to any one of them who seeks it, won't we? These are not their lands, and—"

"These aren't *our* lands either," laughed Aria. "Not by far."

"However, our rooms are our rooms. And we can offer refuge, can we not? Lady Ecci?"

"Let Margeta give sanctuary in her chapel," said Greta, more as a joke than out of fear. But fear, made clear by her unstable expression, was what had led her to it.

"Lady Ecci?" Dr. Cassette appealed to her.

"Whatever," said Aria, throwing her hair back over her shoulder. "This is interesting at least. Anyway, do your best."

"But I think we should all help," said Amalina. She picked up a spear from the weapons pile on the floor and handed it to the nearest person. She distributed the rest as she spoke: "We should all be prepared for our defense, just in case."

"Where are your guards? Where is the Count?"

"Well, he's out giving astronomy lessons, and he's taken most of the guard with him to protect them from the wolves."

"Astronomy!" scoffed Aria. "At this hour!"

"Of course, why not? Naturally at this hour! But why wasn't I invited?" whined de Roye.

"But we're here," said Amalina. "And there are enough of us, I think. We can defend ourselves."

"Are you kidding?" shouted Greta.

"I'll help," said Inovala with a cheerful innocence, though she was obviously aware of the danger as she stepped forward and held out a hand to receive a weapon. "I'm sure dear Count Tepsji will return soon. And he will appreciate our effort."

"What effort!" cried her chambermaid, aghast. "Why? What are you talking about, milady? What happens when they come battering down the door? What do you think you're going to do about it?"

Inovala held her halberd unsurely, her arm shaking a little against its weight, then looked to Amalina, "Break down the door? Are they going to …? Would they …?"

"We've wasted enough of our time on this tiresome nonsense," said Montraine, trying to move the others back into the softer parts of the room. "Let's play some cards. Dr. Cassette, thank you, that will be all."

"But if they break down the door …" mumbled Inovala.

"We should ready ourselves," said Amalina.

"Or throw that one out," said another maid, pointing to Noka's servant.

"I've seen battle," announced Aria, with a contemptuous scowl. "Let them come, if that's what they want."

"Yes," said Inovala, straightening her dress as if preparing for battle, she gripped her halberd with two hands now.

"Well, if it's what we're going to do," said Greta, also squaring herself for a fight, motioning for a weapon, "give me—um—*whatever*—too, to fight."

"You'll do no such thing," said her head maid, while others laughed at Inovala's, Aria's, and Greta's bold martial sentiment.

"All I know is I wouldn't let something like *this* happen in my home," one of the Ladies in the back muttered, Amalina couldn't tell which. *Maibrigg Smeehaute? Marie Daume? Elle Fleccevocarre?*

"Are they going to break down the door?" worried a voice from within the entrourage. "But listen! Here they come!"

Feet stamped angrily in the corridor. The room tensed and stared at the door.

There was a solid knock. Everyone traded nervous glances. They held their breaths. The knock came again, insistent.

"Who is it?" asked Amalina.

"Lady Tepsji," said a gruff voice. "Open door."

It was a warrior.

"Is Noka there?" replied Amalina.

"Open door, Lady Tepsji."

"Don't let him in," came a voice from the pack.

Noka's servant went to hide but couldn't find an opening in the surrounding crowd to slip through.

"Let him hide," she whispered.

The warrior at the door began to shout in the tribal language. The servant cowered for a bit under the tirade. But then his posture softened.

"Open the door," said Noka's servant. Calmly, resolutely.

"*Don't!*" cried one of the Ladies' maids. "For all our sakes, don't open that door!"

Dr. Cassette skewered that maid with a look, then glanced to Amalina for an answer.

"You want us to open it?" Amalina asked the servant inside the room, as the warrior continued to berate him from the hall.

"Yes. Go ahead. It's all right. We are ..." He looked around the room at all the fearful white faces staring at him. "We are on the same side. Please." Then he called to the warrior outside. The warrior quieted down. "Please, Lady Tepsji, I will go with them. Open the door."

Cassette unlocked the door and opened it with his chest outthrust, as if to challenge any spear that poked through. Then he opened it all the way.

The group of warriors outside gave Noka's servant a grim stare.

"What's going to happen here?" asked Dr. Cassette.

"I said that will be all, doctor," said Montraine from the card table. "Thank you."

The servant bowed to the warriors, murmured something at them. Then he nodded to Amalina, and Dr. Cassette. "My apologies for the disturbance. It has nothing to do with you fine people, but it is a private affair. We will now go to pacify our princess."

"You don't have to go," said Amalina. "You can stay here. We can protect you all."

The Ladies and their entourages didn't seem to take to Amalina's suggestion. Their expressions dropped. "It's really none of our business, Katty," said one. "You heard him."

"It will be taken care of," Noka's servant comforted Amalina. "It is better we do this thing."

"All right, then. But ... someone should go along to make sure everything is settled. I suppose—"

"Well, she's *your* guest, isn't she, Lady Tepsji?" snarled one of the servants protectively, interrupting Amalina. "It's *your* castle."

"Yes ... my castle," muttered Amalina. "I wasn't asking any of you to come, was I?"

"Do be careful, Katty," said one of the anonymous noble ladies, before her mistress hissed her mouth shut.

There was an awkard silence.

Amalina was handed a pike. It felt top heavy, and as awkward in her hands as the one Inovala was trying to hold upright. Amalina grasped its staff tight, with a short gulp.

"No, Countess," said the servant. "No weapon."

"What?"

"You are our Princess' good friend, as she is yours," he said. "She would never hurt you, you will never come to harm by my mistress' hand."

"But she doesn't seem to be thinking straight ... "

"We will take care of it. You are quite safe."

"Are you sure?"

"To come bearing arms would be disrespectful. An insult to our great Princess Iwebo. Please, Countess."

Amalina nodded and handed back the weapon. She wiped her sweaty hands together.

"Yes, I suppose. She will recognize me as her friend, I'm sure. She must. Yes? All right, then."

And as I'm being devoured, she thought sourly, *I can say it's been proven positively that when you change, you are no longer yourself. At least I'll know that.*

"I'm coming," shouted Aklan, as he bounced forward through the assembly. He now had a pistol and a sword. The sword looked too heavy for him. It tipped his wrist forward as if he were about to drop it, but he was game and didn't seem to mind. "Is it all right if I come along?"

"As you please," said the servant, after the lead warrior nodded with a smirk of contempt. "It is of little matter."

"I suppose it is okay then," said Amalina.

"Do you want *me* to come?" asked Genadie, his eyes blinking rapidly. He had a knife and a pistol—neither of which were his specialty monster killers—tucked in his belt, while he munched nervously on his millet. He took out his pistol. "I'm coming. Of course I am, Ms. D— ... uh, *milady*. We're together, you and I. Always."

"Thank you, Genadie."

"It'll be all right," he said.

"Well, get going," said one of the ruder maids.

55

C'est Finis

As soon as Noka's servant joined the three warriors in the hall, he wiped his eyes, took a tribal spear, squared his shoulders, and put on the same grim mask they all wore. So then there were four warriors in the hall.

They muttered something between each other in their language. Then they marched.

Amalina, Aklan, and Genadie trailed after silently.

Behind them, a voice warned, "Halma, you so much as take a step and by your mother's eyes I'll cut you down myself."

There were some nervous chuckles inside Aria's room at the statement. But certainly none of the brocade army followed into the hall. And with a quick rustle of fabric, they shut the door and began barricading it. Or so it sounded.

Bunch of cowards, thought Amalina, heatedly. *I could never be like that.*

She found it interesting Dr. Cassette had chosen to remain behind in the room with the rest of the craven lot given his forward curiosity from earlier. Amalina reflected darkly that if the other Ladies could be guaranteed to kill Princess Noka without any harm coming to themselves, or receiving the Count's wrath for it, they would have braved their servants and all piled into the hall together, clawing each other to get at the front of the line. But Cassette didn't fit into any of that, with his scientific fervor and boldness. So what had changed his mind, or collapsed his spine so thoroughly? Montraine's orders?

Aklan tried to pull ahead of Amalina, to put himself in front as a barrier. Amalina shooed him back, and Genadie nabbed him further back by the collar. The small group made their way up a couple floors, to Noka's level.

Here there were warm trails of blood, like flattened lengths of red silk against the stone, and bloody foot prints everywhere.

The warriors paused. The servant who'd hid in Aria's room spoke to Amalina:

"Wait." He gestured firmly at the spot, then continued on in a calm, dignified voice, but with a lost smile: "It will be over now. All good, Lady Tepsji. We will make your Count happy and proud; we will take care of everything. Just wait here. Wait right here, *please*. If you will."

"Yes, of course," said Amalina, unsurely. It looked like he was going to cry again, behind the lost smile. "Are you sure? Is everything all right?"

He nodded. Then said something to Noka's warriors.

"Stay here," he told her once more. "You will know when it is over."

The four marched down the corridor with spears tucked upward at their shoulders in a martial way, turned right, and then paraded out of sight.

"Could use another torch," said Aklan after they'd gone and left them in silence. "Can't see very well. What do you think they're going to do? What can they do about her, really?"

"Quiet," said Amalina. But she thought with a frown: *What can* we *do about her?*

Even if she'd taken the heavy pike, it might only have held Noka back for a second.

"Yes, Pretty Princess."

They waited a minute. Then another. Amalina began to wonder just how long she should wait. Or could wait.

"Do you hear that?" asked Aklan.

"What?"

"Sounds like someone is crying."

The hallway was silent to Amalina. At least Noka was no longer laughing her mad laugh. Amalina stepped forward, closer to that dangerous turn in the hall. She heard not a crying sound but more like a wet sound. A dripping sound.

"Milady?"

Pils was peering at her through a half-opened doorway. "Is it over, milady?"

"Get back inside. Wait, how's Cristine?"

"Sleeping like a baby. Anka's watching her. Is it safe to come out?"

"I don't know."

Pils noticed Aklan and Genadie behind her, and he must have concluded they were safe enough. He waved and then, closing the door behind him, he slipped out into the hall. His only defense was a small metal pot he gripped tightly along the rim.

"What are we waiting for, milady?" Pils asked her.

Amalina almost laughed. The fear was tickling her. She shrugged. "I really don't know."

Amalina went and peeked around the corner. It was empty. Empty, all but for the streaks of blood on the floors and walls.

"I guess it's safe."

They traveled this corridor, feeling a build up of tension despite the silence.

On the next turn in the hall, Amalina stepped into a wide pool of blood, with body parts ripped and torn into scraps, the bone and muscle and viscera scattered wildly across the floor, some of it stuck to the walls. At its far end, Noka was hunched over, her eyes red and vicious. The remnants of her four warriors were in large chunks around her, their spears laid down evenly before her, as if they were an offering.

Aklan pushed himself in front of Amalina and held out the point of his sword and the barrel of his pistol and shook them at Noka.

"She's eaten all her people," whispered Pils from the safety of the turn in the hall. "Why?"

There were new screams now. Servants of the noble ladies housed on this floor were coming out, only to discover the true volume of carnage.

Amalina stared at Noka.

Noka's body, which had once looked so elegant and lithe, was bloated and baggy. She must have gained three times her weight, at least. But the savage fire in her eyes disappeared in a blink when she noticed Amalina. She leaned her head back against the wall and, still watching Amalina, smiled a sweet smile—the sweet smile of the young, beautiful, powerful princess who'd once inspired Amalina ... what now felt like years ago.

But is it really the same sweet smile? wondered Amalina, regarding her transformed, terrifyingly altered friend. *Really?*

I would never do that, she thought. *I could never do that. I will never be that.*

"*C'est finis*," sighed Noka.

Epilogue

Interview with the Princess

I

After that difficult night, Count Tepsji's high castle became something hushed and solemn. Everyone spoke in whispers and avoided certain sections. And still, even when the Palace of Pleasures seemed to recover its spirit, one or another would claim they heard *something* just around the corner, and swore they could smell blood in the air wherever they stood.

• • •

Jane Ontioc Camper had been the only one to act immediately, penning a cramped, ten page note from her quarters, with blood spots from her wrists on the page, demanding to be informed when her safety—*"and the lives of the other peace-minded and civilized people"*—could be guaranteed. And she reminded Katarina and her uncle how she had warned them against the savage instincts of *"a certain princess' kind"*, and how, *"like animals, only chains and the use of force can keep them in their rightful place."* They should no longer be allowed their spears, and never a flintlock, she decreed. 'Lady' Camper didn't yet know that they were all gone, to the last person; but for their beloved Princess Noka Kunuru Sowa Iwebo.

"Her skin may be as black as her benevolent god, Enkai Narok," said the Count as he surveyed the cleanup, purring with a kind of admiration, "but she proves as bloody in her fierceness as Enkai's hidden side, his dark side, Enkai Nanyokie, the Red God: the god of anger, vengeance and death."

Amalina was too bedraggled to roll her eyes.

"I'm sorry what's happened to your Palace's flowering, sir," she said, instead. "I tried to help save it tonight."

"What nonsense," mumbled the Count, distracted by the scene. "The ladies and I had our most instructive, pleasurable, and *productive* outing under the stars yet. I would say my Palace of Pleasure's flower is rather on path to its zenith, where it will remain in perfection forever. Like me." He paused to smile down at her. "Of course, it's only waiting for you."

"Oh, yes, perhaps," she lied easily.

"You'll be pleased to know that your best friend has mended herself, and brightened."

"Cristine?"

"Lady Lampeda."

"Oh."

"And we're all waiting for you, as I said."

"Ah, yes. Perhaps … " It didn't sound as good the second time. So to shift away from the subject, Amalina asked: "Sir, this evening, did you order one of the castle guards to protect me?"

"Perhaps," he smiled down at her again, impishly at first. "It *would* be like me to do such a thing. You know how much I care about you."

"But did you?"

"Why do you ask?"

Amalina bit her lip. Did she want to bring up AXP at this point? and directly to him? or was it better just keep mum about what she knew?

"One of them came to me and said you did."

"Then I must have. But *why* do you ask?"

"I just wanted to make sure."

"But *why* do you ask?"

It could go on like that forever.

Meanwhile Genadie swished around through the scene, drenched in gore, moaning pathetically for his Master, and about what his life had been reduced to. "My poor little body, it cannot take much more of this …"

When Amalina found Balbo in *l'entrée grande*, she asked him about the guard who, notably, was no longer with him.

"The man broke free first chance, Countess," reported Balbo, defensively, in a confidential whisper. "Quite desperate. He begged me most pathetically for his life. Said he was a dead man if his Master found he hadn't done his job, so he *had* to get away. Escaped the castle, I'm afraid. Desperate men are known for their speed and strength, which could only explain how he overcame *me* … me with my pistol directly on him. Can you imagine, Countess? I swear it is the absolute truth. I *swear* to you! But please don't tell your uncle about it, or anyone else. Can't imagine how it would effect my standing if word got around and reached him. Oh, what a catastrophe. And to think, I served—and am still—a medalled colonel in—"

"Captain Durok?" said Amalina, after tracking him down on the wall. "Do you have someone in your ranks named Poul?"

Durok hugged the bell protectively still, as if she might take it from him, as if it were directly attached to the Count's belt. "Yes. Why?"

"Do you know if my uncle gave him any special orders earlier this evening, to protect me?"

Durok shrugged after a thought. "I only know what I know. And I only know what he tells me, right? Why do you ask?"

"Never mind."

"Heard he's gone missing from the barracks, Poul has. Know anything about it?"

"Oh … no."

"Why do you bring him up, then?" asked Durok.

But Amalina wandered away into the night, contemplating the meaning of AXP's '*subtler men*' and if she'd just caught one; and trying to forget the horror of everything else.

"You need to get some rest, little mouse."

Aklan, nearby, hissed heatedly to Amalina as she made the long trek back to her room, "The rat's hidden his weapons again! What's he care? At this point you'd think he'd thank me if I killed—"

"Ah well," said Amalina. "There's been enough of that though—killing—hasn't there?"

"Uh … yes, Pretty Princess."

II

Come morning the winds relented and left the air crisp, with a thick, pure snow blanketing the ground: the perfect refuge for anyone wanting to refresh their spirit, and to escape or replace the castle's darkness with the outdoors' bright, immaculate whiteness. There would be no indecorous splashes of red.

"Where are you going?" said Pia, gently hooking her arm through Amalina's. "May I come?"

Amalina was headed out of the open gate, with a heavy winter cloak over her and a bucket in hand. She managed not to drop the bucket, but felt a jolt of energy at the surprise. She looked sidelong at her friend.

"I hope you aren't still mad at me," said Pia.

"Mad at you?" replied Amalina, in a cautious tone. "I was never. You were mad at me. I thought you were going to kill me."

"Never! But you see, you *should* have been mad at me. I was acting so silly, wasn't I? So very silly. So I wouldn't blame you. Well I'd like to come with, if that's all right. If you've forgiven me."

Pia was dressed in a light spring dress with only a large winter hat. Not the least suited for the weather, but Amalina supposed that meant something good for Pia: an improvement to her constitution; an inhuman strengthening and resistance to the elements.

"You can come if you want."

"I do. Thank you."

Is this because Cristine is now on her way to being an equal, so now she's come to butter me up and get on my good side? An uncharitable thought, Amalina knew. Pia had always been innocent and straightforward. Even when angry.

"Is it because of Noka?" said Pia, after Amalina's silence. "Your going out, I mean? You aren't trying to make off, to escape us?"

Amalina shook her head, but wasn't too convincing. She swallowed hard and tried not to feel sick again. "Just a little trip to find some winter berries. The weather is fair today."

"You *heard* what that she did, though, didn't you?" said Pia, looking disturbed, if only for Amalina's sake.

Amalina nodded and tried to appear uninterested in discussing it. She pushed her feet down through the snow with solid crunches and aimed for the forest where the snow wouldn't be as deep. Pia appeared to drift along by her side, not bothering the snow much at all, as if she weighed less than a feather. "Aren't you going to be cold, Pia? I can wait if you want to run and get a jacket."

Her friend's easy hold on her arm kept her moving. "This is good enough for me."

After a few paces more, Amalina asked: "The sun isn't bothering you? Going to bother you?"

Pia shook her head, her expression neutral.

"I can feel *something*," said Pia, leaning her head to the side. "A little ... Well, it *is* a little bright, isn't it? There is a tingle, maybe. I get a little redder now ... and more quickly. I don't know. Nothing as bad as what your uncle describes, obviously."

"I see."

"Thank you for asking."

"I was only wondering ..."

"I know." Pia paused, then let the time pass.

"To be honest, Katty ..." Pia patted the back of her own hand and then said, with a sigh: "What I do feel ...? If you want to know ... I feel ... more like an empty box. A very, very, very empty box. With just a teeny-tiny crumb stuck in the corner; a bit of me that wasn't cleared out. I don't know *what* piece it is, though ... If that's what you wanted to ask, what you're *really* wondering."

"I'm sorry, Pia. That sounds ..."

"Oh, it doesn't bother me. Not really. But I do worry sometimes what is going to fill that space. The way he talks, when I ask him, he doesn't really answer, but I can tell how many little things frighten him—or that isn't the word. How much can hurt him anyway. He is very smart, and very clever, and so very powerful—but then there are his weaknesses, the regrettable vulnerabilities. And never to see the sun again? It seems so very sad. And to outlive your family and anyone you love? How much of this must take up his thoughts?"

Amalina thought of Tepsji's massive message center and knew he was trying to fill something inside himself by holding onto all that ancient correspondence. But she said on a different track, "If he had known his full power and what he could do with it, I suppose he could have performed the rite on his family, too. But he didn't find out what was possible until it was too late. Back when he knew nothing of what ... of what had happened to him ... his transformation ... he just thought he had grown naturally into something greater than any human. That he simply *was* greater. And apart."

"Well, he's right about that," said Pia, with a laugh. "We *are* greater." Her lips tightened. "Greater and lesser, depending on how you look at it. There's no doubt I'm different. The air inside the box that is me begins to feel too much; too empty. When I ate those men's blood ... I don't know how to describe it. You don't mind if I tell you, Kat? May I? I wish to tell someone. To tell *you*. So you understand it."

"You can always tell me everything," said Amalina, strangely feeling closer now to Pia than she ever had. This felt like a normal walk between firm friends. She squeezed the princess's arm.

"When I ate their blood, I felt I joined with the earth. I was as powerful as an elephant, or a river, or a small mountain, because I *was* all of those things. And even though there was still all that emptiness inside me, I was relieved from its suction. The box is still so empty, you know, but the box changed, grew and grew, then shrank and shrank."

"He can transform himself into animals" murmured Amalina. "Into anything. Or into nothing. A vapor. Can you do that?"

"No, no. You know, it might be neat to turn into a cute little puppy, I think. But I don't know if I'd ever *want* to. Maybe in time. There will be a lot of time to get bored, I suppose, and try things. Anything. Even *that*."

The way she was talking, it was almost like she was sharing an experience the way an older sister might—or the way Sadra had performed the same kind of role for Amalina, in place of her mother—describing something Amalina would experience herself someday. Maybe soon.

"I don't think you should blame Noka for what she did," said Pia, returning to a far off subject.

"How can I? I doubt anyone else will, either. The ones who have already ... you know ... like you ... the ones who've already *done* it and *know*—they won't blame her. Which is a relief. I liked Noka. *Like* Noka. And the ones who haven't—"

"Jane blames her," said Pia.

"Jane does, of course. But, you-know-who will convince the rest whatever he likes."

"So then … you've heard Lady Montraine has dismissed Dr. Cassette."

"Has she?"

"The doctor's already left. She ordered him home immediately. He's the one to take the blame for all of it. It's rumored he said some insult or other to Nok-Nok's people, or to Oroco, or to the princess herself, which set them off in an ugly way."

"Ah, I see." Amalina understood that this was the Count's historical persuasion at work, creating a narrative, settling the affair in an acceptable way for his guests. Would Dr. Cassette make it past the border alive with his knowledge and his suspicions of the Count and the women? "It was *His* idea about blaming the doctor, I suppose?"

"But we aren't talking about *Him*," said Pia. "We were talking about Noka, and what really happened."

Amalina nodded, though not really wanting to talk about it. Pia wanted to, for some reason.

"It seems barbaric," said Pia. "But I think her people asked her to do it. Maybe not tear them apart that way, but she probably couldn't help it. She probably thought she was doing what she was supposed to do; was expected to do. Giving in fully to that feeling. And maybe they got scared when it came to it."

Amalina nodded, remembering the limbs scattered like chopped logs across a pond of blood. Their heads had been crushed and torn into sections, mixed among each other. Sharp white shards of bones gleamed in it. She shook her head to get rid of the image.

"I didn't mean to upset you, Katty. I just want you to understand. I'm not like Noka. You saw what I did to Judge Wolcraft and his men, but it was beyond my control at that point. And they were going to hurt you. I thought it was a good excuse. But … please don't think badly of Noka. She's just impatient. She doesn't want to be anything less than what Oroco and her people wanted her to be, what your uncle is now. They think it is her birthright, and they—and I suppose she, as well—couldn't wait for it, and wanted to hurry it along; the process."

"You've spoken to her about it," said Amalina. Pia nodded. "But what about you?"

"I can wait, no one's pressuring me. I don't want to lose the sun, or my family. Or my home. My country." She said after a pause. "Or you."

"That's why I don't understand why you agreed to his proposal. All this sacrifice, and for what? What does he have to offer you, really? To be stuck in these unfamiliar mountains, alone, with him. Forever."

"There are some drawbacks when given the universe," said Pia with a wan smile. "But to *have* the universe. To have *forever*. Again, I can't describe it to you. But wait."

Pia held Amalina back with a wave of her arm. Her attention focused on three small colorful birds, each with a dull red head, a tan wing and a sky blue chest, known as bee-eaters, who were pecking at seeds in the snow at the edge of the forest. She bent low and crept toward them. But crept wasn't exactly it. There was no noise as she moved over the snow, not walking at all it seemed; a cloud blown across the ground. Until she leapt.

The small bird which she aimed for had frozen in place, as if charmed there, while its companions hopped back to a safe distance like they knew what was about to happen. Suddenly Pia's hat was off and toppling away in the breeze, her hair flying in great red waves, blocking the action. Pia had centered on the bird and then was on it, and her body jerked and shook, with an ugly tearing sound.

With a crunch, Pia fell to her knees into the snow. Striped feathers and puffs of white fluff were tumbling onto the ground around her hunched, shaking body, or blowing away. Eventually Pia's body became still. She sat up. Then she stood. Then she turned around.

The lower half of Pia's face was as red as her hair, with bits of feather and tuft stuck on her lips and chin, though she was trying to wipe it away. She glanced at Amalina at first, but then set her gaze fully on her. But with a neutral expression.

"I don't think it quite worked," said Pia.

"Why did you …?"

"Please don't be offended. But it wasn't enough. Let's find another. A finch, mm, yes. Or … could we find a hummingbird so late, do you think?"

"This is what we are doing now?" asked Amalina, somewhat confused and maybe upset. "Hunting birds? Are you hungry?"

"We were just talking about the powers your uncle is giving me."

"You want to turn yourself into a bird?"

Pia shook her head. "I feel a bond, a mental connection between everything in this universe, yes? But I don't exactly understand the words. I think if I do these things to certain animals, if I eat them, their meaning becomes clearer. So imagine that I can find out what birds talk about. All their secrets. Is there a difference between higher and lower birds? Or is it all the same thing? And, if at some point I do get bored enough, think of what it would be like to fly. Just think of it. It might be too scary. But maybe …"

"So *do* you feel different now?" said Amalina.

Pia shook her head, but was staring into the forest with an excited, famished look. "Help me find more. Maybe more …"

"Do you think it will *help*? Really?"

"You don't want to help me, Katty?"

Amalina didn't answer.

"Does this frighten you?" asked Pia, turning to her, realizing. "What I just did?"

Nodding shyly, Amalina said: "I think, a little of everything; yes."

"But there's nothing to be afraid of."

"If the Count can be afraid, so can I."

"That's different, though." Pia shrugged, smiled, and looped her arm through Amalina's again. The hunt for birds was suddenly over, back to hunting berries for Amalina. She guided them further into the forest. "You were something once before, weren't you? A low and humble baker's daughter. *That* you didn't question. Not when you were there. Then you came here and became something else: a charming Lady of Title from the east. Which you also enjoy, no?"

Amalina nodded.

"And now, Katty, won't you join us in this new change? an alteration which you will love even more?"

"Do you love it?" asked Amalina.

"Of course," she replied quickly. "Why wouldn't I? I mean, I don't know everything yet, but ... what choice do I have? It is done."

But I *still have a choice*, thought Amalina. It was a hot and angry thought, full of resentment. Yet, Amalina felt a strange, cool relief at the end of it. She *did* still have a choice, didn't she? What was the point of this excursion now? Amalina had gone out to clear her head and pick berries. What was Pia's purpose in joining? To bribe her, or frighten her?

"But to kill things so easily," said Amalina.

"You shouldn't let what Princess Nok-Nok did upset you too much, Katty."

"Right now I am thinking of the bird you just ate."

"We eat all kinds of birds—chicken, pheasant, goose, squab. So what if this one was a little raw?"

After a quiet hour or so, with no berries yet, Amalina said, in as little an obvious or prying way as she could, "You don't want to be like Noka, you said."

"No," said Pia.

"Nor like the Count."

Pia shook her head.

"But you understand part of the problem for me is that last night, at first, I had no idea who it was running crazy and ... that it *wasn't* you. Because I've seen you ..." Amalina stopped. "You know what he's doing to Cristine?"

"I get the idea, I think."

"Draining her. A little here, a little there. And it could be done like that for another reason. Nobody has to die for this curse—"

"You mean for this *power*?"

"Nobody ever," Amalina continued. "I tried to tell him before he could take a little blood as he needs it. Never killing anyone."

"I see," smiled Pia. "He warned me you'd try to civilize me."

Amalina's eyes widened a little. *Maybe I shouldn't have mentioned it.*

"I can see how difficult it would be for him," said Pia. "What self-control would be required to hold back, to not simply take everything you can; take what is in your power to take. You wouldn't know what I mean unless you felt it. But look at Noka."

"Oh."

Amalina was going to let another hour pass.

"Have you noticed that monstrous wolf following us, Katty? Behind us, over there."

Amalina looked back, saw the black wolf, its battered head bowed low but watching her with interest. She nodded. "I think he likes me."

"Yes, look at him, I do believe he's guarding you ... from me." Pia laughed and squeezed Amalina's arm. "Oh, everyone loves you, don't they? Almost like a curse in itself, I would think." Pia began to sing, then she let the words slide under her breath. When Amalina looked at Pia, the princess pulled aside a thick red lock so she could set both of her green eyes on Amalina, and she purred, "So then civilize me, Katty, I don't mind. I don't want to be like your uncle at all, though I am what I am now, and that's all there is to say. Do it. Civilize me."

AMALINA'S DARK ADVENTURE

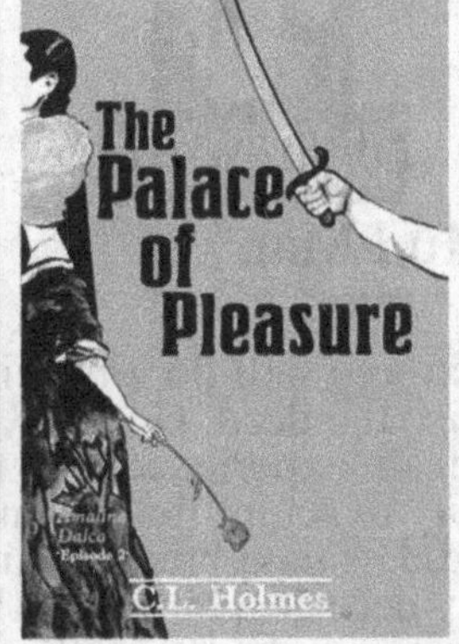

THROUGH IMPOSSIBLE CHALLENGES ...

... AND EVER GREATER DANGERS ...

FOLLOW AMALINA DALCA ...
AS SHE BATTLES HER WAY OUT!

www.badhoundpress.com